SACRIFICE

MARCELLA BALDUCCI WINTON—filled with desires her husband couldn't satisfy, she channels her passions into her writing, her love into her two children. But that isn't enough to stem her sexual longing. . . .

HARRY WINTON—his marriage to Marcella began in poverty. Tempted by Wall Street and a beautiful, forbidden woman, he risks shame and heartbreak for a fortune. He will tear apart his family to punish the woman he married but never understood.

SANTIAGO ROCA—the handsome European who gives Marcella her first true glimpse of the possibilities of love. But he must be her sole possessor, and to have him she must make the one sacrifice she cannot willingly give.

SONIA WINTON—the pawn of warring parents, she lost her innocence while still a little girl, growing up fast—and hard. Her breathtaking beauty marks her for superstardom as a world-famous cover girl and fashion model. But she will endanger her career—and her very life—for a taste of the love she was denied as a child.

MARK WINTON—his mother had made him her sole confidant, creating a bond of affection stronger than all others in their lives. He will test this bond to its breaking point in his all-consuming quest for love.

RAY LEVAR—the sultan of soul music, whose global following would be shocked to learn that his crimes of passion include the ultimate sin. He too has a Winton lover—one who wants to see him lose control, even if it means the destruction of them both.

BOOKS BY HAROLD CARLTON

LABELS

SACRIFICE

SACRIFICE

Harold Carlton

BANTAM BOOKS

New York · Toronto · London · Sydney · Auckland

SACRIFICE
A Bantam Book

PUBLISHING HISTORY
Bantam trade paperback edition published August 1991
Bantam paperback edition / June 1992

ISBN 0-553-29759-7

Published simultaneously in the United States and Canada

Bantam Books are published by Bantam Books, a division of Bantam
Doubleday Dell Publishing Group, Inc. Its trademark, consisting of the
words "Bantam Books" and the portrayal of a rooster, is Registered in U.S.
Patent and Trademark Office and in other countries. Marca Registrada.
Bantam Books, 666 Fifth Avenue, New York, New York 10103.

PRINTED IN THE UNITED STATES OF AMERICA

OPM   0 9 8 7 6 5 4 3 2 1

for

Joan Marquès

ACKNOWLEDGMENTS

For their help, time, patience, or all three, I sincerely thank:

Charlotte Bingham

Jean Csaky

Patricia Curry

J. G. Links

Mary Lutyens

Stanley Orlen

The Honourable Mary Ann Wragg of
Stapleford Arabian Stud, England

My publisher, Linda Grey

My editor, Coleen O'Shea

Barb Burg and Becky Cabaza of Bantam Books

And my agent, Jane Turnbull.

Majorca, Spain, December 1990

The beautiful woman who pushed open the heavy carved doors of the monastery was unlike the usual visitors to the austere retreat. For one thing, she was much better dressed, although her red Chanel outfit was about as alien to the gaunt Majorcan countryside as a spacesuit. For another, most visitors left the place calmed, thoughtful, but this woman's distraught face was streaming with tears. As she stepped out into the bare, stone-flagged courtyard, the late afternoon sun dazzled her. She took a deep shuddering breath, trying to gain control of her feelings, her eyes darting about her as if she were wondering where to go next. The taxi driver waiting for her had parked his car in the shade and was taking a working siesta, a newspaper open on his lap.

She walked quickly past his car, across a garden where neat rows of vegetables grew, and climbed over a low stone wall in which the wind-smoothed stones fitted together without cement. She began to run down the steep slope of the hill, which was big enough to be called a small mountain. She ran without looking where she was going, blinded by tears, stumbling over the tree roots and broken

branches that littered her path. Slipping, she clung to tall
weeds to stay upright, clawed at crusty tree bark as the
ground sharply dipped. Once, she fell headlong, rolling
down the hardened earth until an olive tree stopped her
short. Scrambling to her feet, she continued on downward,
the terrain entirely unsympathetic to her plight, the ground
ungiving, the few grazing goats staring blankly at her as she
passed.

The ditch took her completely by surprise. Camouflaged
by a tall growth of scrub, it lay in wait for her final step on
dry, crumbling dirt. Suddenly there was no ground beneath
her and she hurtled fifteen feet down to a pile of olive
branches that broke her fall.

The fall stunned her. For a few moments she found
herself laughing hysterically. A freak accident such as this
was all she had needed to complete her day. Then she
began to scream for help. When her voice finally gave out,
she crouched, frightened, looking up at the red, dry dirt
walls imprisoning her.

Her clothes were covered with leaves, dirt, and goat
droppings. Brushing herself off, she made an attempt to
climb out of the deep gash in the earth, but her shaky
foothold in the dry dirt gave way before she was one third
of the way up, plunging her back.

This is ridiculous, she thought. She tried to calm the
panic, imagining how she'd tell this story one night around
a cozy Manhattan dinner table, the faces of the guests expressing sympathy for her plight.

"Just like one of your novels!" someone was bound to
comment, and she would make a modest grimace, the
point being that she had survived the nightmare. But right
now the Majorcan countryside was deadly still and the only
sound was the occasional clank of a bell tied around a
grazing sheep's neck. Goats and sheep would be her companions for the night, she realized. Maybe she should have
worn a bell, too. She glanced at her watch. Five-thirty!
How time flies when you're having fun, she thought. When
night fell—quickly as it surely did in winter—who would
think of looking for her here? Who in their right mind
would guess that Marcella Balducci Winton, America's
best-selling author, was stuck in some *this* her punishment for

liking men too much? For needing sex so much? For placing her son before everybody, even before Santiago? She shook her head. First get out of here, she reminded herself, *then* figure out why it happened.

One more try before nightfall, she urged herself. You know you can do it! She studied the olive tree roots at the top of the ditch. If she stepped up, *there*, onto that patch of dried grass, then reached for that gnarled root sticking out above her, surely she could use it to hoist herself up. She pictured herself scrambling out, triumphant, brushing off the leaves and dirt, suffering nothing more than a slightly shaken body and a taxi dash back to the hotel for her suitcase, a fast drive to the airport, the last flight to Madrid. If you visualize something, she told herself, you can make it happen!

She placed her right foot on the patch of grass, leaning her weight forward, concentrating as hard as she had ever concentrated in her life. Okay—she breathed in, looking up—*now*! She straightened, thrust her hands above her to grab at the root, jumped, and caught it! For a few seconds she dangled from the scratchy wood. No one would believe this! she marveled. She made the second huge effort to hoist herself farther up, to pull her body above ground level. Those Olympic champions made it look so simple when they twisted and twirled on their parallel bars, but if you weren't a champion it wasn't that easy. She did just manage to slowly hoist herself up, all her weight on her wrists. It was agonizingly painful and the root began to bend with her weight, but she was going to make it! One further effort and—but there was a crack like a pistol shot as the root snapped, plunging her back to the bottom of the ditch, cracking a pile of broken branches—and a bone in her leg by the feel of it. An intense pain shot through her calf like a giant needle. She cried out, then passed into unconsciousness.

When she next opened her eyes, the navy sky was glittering with stars. Some shone so much brighter than others. Her leg was twisted behind her, swollen and aching. Stiffly bending her arm, she could just read her watch: eleven-forty. How long would it be before someone noticed she had not returned to her hotel? Maybe some early-rising goatherd would be the first to pass by and find her? If not, if she was to be left for dead here among the clanking animals, her son would have to decide whether her autobiography should be published. If it came out, it would be the last of her line of best-sellers. Best-sellers! How meaningless that word sounded here. At this moment, she would gladly exchange all her best-sellers for one flask of hot coffee and a ladder.

She twisted uncomfortably against the sharp branches, resisting an overwhelming desire to bawl like a baby. Don't give in so easily, she scolded herself. Remember your father. Remember your son. Remember your millions of readers. They would all be rooting for you. Crying will do no good at all. But the tears welled up, flowed, and could not be stopped.

Later, when it began to rain, she tried to arrange the olive tree branches into some kind of protective roof over herself and get some sleep. But sleep was impossible. There was nothing to do but reflect on her life. How easy it was to see all her mistakes from this perspective. People ought to fall into ditches more often; the objectivity was staggering!

"Dear God," she found herself praying, clasping her hands as they had not been clasped since childhood. "Dear God, in whom I do not believe. Get me out of this and I swear I'll never look at a man again!" Like all her pacts with the Almighty, she was bound to break this one, because she did not truly believe. And you had to believe in something for it to work. Especially religion.

She found a cigarette in her purse and managed to light it. Never had anything tasted so good. The raindrops fell on her makeshift roof as she smoked thoughtfully. How exactly had she ended up here? How was it that her clairvoyant, always so quick to foretell doom, had not predicted this? Too many traumatic events had happened to her during the last few days. Too much grief to absorb. She had suffered the most tragic event that can happen to a woman: losing a child. She had saved the life—she was certain—of her other one. She had lost, perhaps forever, the only man she'd ever loved. Why had these terrible things happened to her? Had she, somehow, deserved them? And now to be stuck here, shivering, wet, and cold! She shook her head incredulously. It was simply unbelievable to think that just a few days ago she had been preparing to spend the Christmas holidays with her son in New York. Before the chain of nightmarish events had led to this ridiculous situation.

She stubbed out her cigarette on a damp branch. No, she thought. To really understand how she had ended up in a ditch full of goat shit on a freezing mountainside in Majorca, she would need to go much further back than a few days. She would need to go back to why she had become a writer in the first place. Back to before she had even dreamed of becoming one. To when her mother used to wash out her mouth with soap for telling sexy stories to her friends. Back to Little Italy.

BOOK ONE

ONE

Little Italy, 1966

Bloodcurdling screams came from the Balduccis' bathroom window.

"Is somebody torturing a child?" a neighbor cried, poking her head out of a nearby window.

A woman in the street below looked up. "Nobody tortures their children in *this* building!" she told the neighbor indignantly. "It's just Marcella Balducci getting her mouth washed out again. She's been telling her stories! It's a disgrace!"

In the bathroom, Ida Balducci vigorously soaped a washcloth with Dove, holding her daughter's mouth open with the other hand.

"Don't you *dare* bite me!" she warned.

"I'm gonna throw up!" Marcella cried. "I'll be sick to my stomach!" Aldo Balducci leaned against the bathroom door watching, grunting his disapproval.

"Do you have to hold her mouth like an animal?" he asked.

"If she behaves like an animal, she'll be treated like one." Ida panted.

Marcella tried to say that animals did not tell their

friends stories, but her protest was cut off as the soapy cloth was inserted none too gently between her teeth and rubbed over her tongue. She gagged, spitting and struggling.

"This is the only way she'll learn," Ida cried, holding Marcella firmly. "Like a dog whose nose is rubbed in its own mess!"

"Okay, enough now . . ." Aldo removed his wife's arm from around their daughter's neck. "She's learned her lesson." He placed a gentle hand on Marcella's shoulder as she spat into the basin, her whole body trembling. She straightened, her eyes red with angry tears.

"That's the last time you do that to me!" she cried to her mother.

"I hope it *is,* young lady." Ida nodded. "Because if I hear of you telling those filthy stories to your friends once more—I don't know what I'll do, but it'll be a lot worse than washing out your mouth." She folded the towel decisively and hung it over the rail. "A girl of fourteen inventing such stuff! I've told Father Carmello and he wants to see you. Aldo, what did I do to deserve this? Such a lovely girl and such talk!"

Aldo sighed, unable to resist a glance into the mirror at his silver mane of hair and a quick thrust of both hands through it.

"Why don't you blame it on *my* side of the family, eh?" he asked. "My aunt was an opera singer. She had an artist's temperament!"

"Oh, I know all about *her!*" Ida snorted. "She was an opera singer, huh? So how come she never sang in the opera?"

Marcella shot imploring looks at her father as she swilled water around in her mouth and spat out. It would be hours before she lost this soapy taste, and meanwhile her friends were waiting in the ice cream parlor. They had promised to buy her a sundae to make up for this punishment.

Ida sat down heavily on the terry-clothed toilet seat, fanning herself with a newspaper. Marcella ran out of the bathroom.

"*Now* where are you off to?" Ida cried after her.

"You said Father Carmello wanted to see me?" Marcella called back over her shoulder.

Soap will not stop me from telling my stories, she thought as she ran down the stairs of the apartment house. Nothing will—not threats, not a million Hail Marys from Father Carmello!

"Marcella! *Wait!*" her father's voice boomed behind her as she reached the lobby. She leaned against the mailboxes, waiting for him to catch up with her.

"You okay?" he asked, throwing an arm around her. "Your mother doesn't mean to be hard, you know. She just wants you to be a little lady!"

She wriggled from under his arm, too old now to get lost in his big chest.

"She's just jealous!" she told her father.

Aldo frowned. "Jealous of *what*?" he asked.

Marcella tried to find the right words. "Because she knows I love you more than her!" she blurted. She gave him a quick hug, blowing him a kiss. Then she was out of the building and running down the dusty July streets to the ice cream parlor. The girls in the booth screamed when she entered. Marcella nonchalantly sauntered across the shop to their booth, basking in their curious stares.

"Was it real yucky?" Andrea Falucci asked immediately.

"Uh-uh." Marcella shook her head, squeezing into the booth.

"Didja barf?" a girl called Sisi asked.

Marcella just giggled. "I'm getting to like the taste of Dove!" They all laughed.

"What did your mom say?" a redheaded, freckled girl asked.

"Oh, you know how she goes!" Marcella adopted a threatening posture. " 'Your friends can talk as much filth as they like but no daughter of mine, blah, blah, blah!' " She let out a breath. "Boy, I'll kill that little sneak Gina when I see her. Now the whole entire neighborhood knows I tell you sexy stories!"

The waitress was at their table, eyebrows raised at Marcella.

"I'll have a double chocolate fudge, please, Mary," she ordered. "It's on you guys, right?" she asked. Her friends glanced at each other and nodded. "Then give me extra hot chocolate sauce, whipped cream, and nuts!" she quickly added. "You want me to get the taste of soap out of my mouth, don't you?" They nodded reluctantly.

"I have to see Father Carmello," Marcella told them, rolling her eyes, "but I'm not letting him lay that guilt stuff on me. What I tell you is no worse than stories that get published every week! And one day I'm going to write them down and send them to a publisher!"

"Will you still speak to us when you're famous, Marcella?" Sisi asked admiringly.

"Oh sure!" Marcella made a snooty "famous" face and they all laughed, sipping the last noisy dregs of their Cokes and scooping the last drops of melting ice cream from their dishes as Marcella received her sundae.

"My next story will be *about* Father Carmello!" she announced, digging into the dish. "And his secret sex life!" She looked around at their faces. "There'll be this gorgeous girl with huge boobs who wanders into his confessional booth. She has a lot to confess and he can't keep his hands off her!"

The girls gasped. Mixing sex with religion was pretty daring, even for Marcella.

"Aren't you afraid of God striking you down dead for making up stuff like that?" Sisi asked.

Marcella licked chocolate sauce from her spoon. "Not really," she confessed, finally. "At least, not before I write the story and sell it to the movies for ten million dollars!"

"They'd never make a movie about a priest's sex life!" Andrea protested. "Too many Catholics would be against it. It would be sacrilegious! Anyway, someone like Father Carmello would never do sexy stuff like that!"

"He's young enough to. My mom says he's in his twenties!"

"He's real cute!"

Marcella waited until the comments had died down.

"Of course he does stuff," she stated authoritatively. "He's a man, isn't he? Men have to do something; otherwise they wet their beds!"

They all screamed with laughter, staring at Marcella in wonder. How did she know so much about it? Marcella laughed with them, feeling a little sick as she finished the ice cream. She wanted to make up this scandalous new story right then, feasting on their absorbed attention and shocked cries of delight, but too many people could overhear them and she was not quite ready for another mouthwashing.

"*Why* do you tell these stories, Marcella?" Father Carmello asked gently. "What's happened to your faith?"

She could barely see his face through the grille, but she knew it well. It was smooth and round, tanned in summer, with a balding head that got equally tan. He had two wide naive blue eyes that she was glad could not see into hers at moments like these.

"I don't know, Father," she muttered. "Maybe I just like the attention? Mom never really listens. Dad's usually working. The only time anyone pays any attention to me is when I tell my stories."

"And why must they be so preoccupied with sexual matters?" he asked.

Marcella shrugged. "To keep them listening!" she said. "If I told stories about nuns, who would care? So I tell stories about young girls like us who are sex crazy!"

"And *are* you sex crazy?" he asked.

"Not really," she admitted. "I mean, we like looking at boys, but that's about it. . . ."

Who am I kidding? she thought on the way home. Of course I'm sex crazy! The itch had come around her thirteenth birthday, even before that. Touching herself on a hot summer's night. The window open, the net curtain absolutely still because there was no breeze at all. Nothing but a sheet covering her. A sudden hot downpour and that smell of warm rain that would always make her think of sex. Pretending her hand outside the sheet was a man's hand, touching herself through the sheet the way his hand would touch her. A song on the radio with an insistent beat that seemed to urge her on to some sort of climax! Her first! *Why* did she feel so much more adult, so much more knowing, than the other girls? Was it because she was an only child? Was it because of her father? She had always found him exciting. His big handsome face with its leonine head of silver hair. His neatly trimmed moustache. His big body covered with hair that sprouted out of his shirt collar and cuffs. Her dad in his underpants, that mysterious bulge between his legs. It had all been innocent. She was sure it had all been innocent. He had simply loved to touch her, to caress her, his hand stealing up under her blouse to caress her back, her shoulders, her flat breast long before she was formed. As she had approached puberty, she had stopped him, her hand on his wrist. Would they call it child abuse today? She had certainly not felt abused; she had felt loved and treasured, and later in life she would be reduced to jelly by a man's hand touching her in that soft, happy, unconscious way.

She was less enamored of her mother. It was commonly agreed in the neighborhood that Ida had "let herself go." It seemed to Marcella that Italian wives had the choice of starving after marriage or "letting themselves go." The decision centered around pasta, rich sauces, long weekend lunches that dragged on for half the afternoon. It was the old question of glamour girl versus traditional mama. Most husbands wanted both: Ida was definitely in the mama category. Big, efficient, a great cook, and a little jealous of her husband being the more glamorous one. Marcella never saw her parents fight and throw things the way she heard her friends' parents did. Neither did they make up after their arguments with hugs and kisses. She rarely saw them touch, which made sex appear that much more mysterious to her. And most of their disagreements were over her.

"Aldo, you'll turn her head!" Ida cried when her father gave her a compliment.

"Don't give in to her, Aldo, you'll spoil her!" she'd warn, if he offered to buy her something she craved.

Her mother seemed to be on guard between her and the enjoyment of life. Marcella had thought her parents mismatched. Aldo was life affirming; just walking down the street with him was an event. He had the theatrical panache of the true Roman, even though he had never seen Rome. Ida simply looked respectable—it was the best she could do. She made no attempts at fashion, tied her hair back in a bun, left her brows heavy and unplucked. Only on special occasions would she dust powder across her nose and streak her lips with red. Her prominent nose, dark eyes, and determined mouth made up a pleasant face, but Marcella's good looks were from her father.

She had been a late baby, born when Ida was thirty-seven and Aldo forty-five, but instead of feeling cherished by them as a special late gift, she had often felt like a nuisance, an interruption of her parents' middle age. Her father was the one who took her to concerts at Carnegie Hall or in Central Park, instilling a love of music in her. For the park, a picnic meal would be packed by her mother who refused to sit on the ground, even when it was covered by a blanket. On summer evenings, she and her father had spread their worn blanket on the Great Lawn and listened to opera together. By the third act, Marcella usually slept in his lap to the rich sounds of music.

Aldo Balducci worked as a chef at one of the better Little Italy restaurants. Once a month, he cooked for them at home. On that day, Marcella would hover over the wooden chopping boards, watching. Before starting work, he would pluck a hair from her head and slice through it to demonstrate the danger of his sharp knife. The tingle of the snapped hair was the exciting sign that a special day was about to happen. As he worked, singing the barber-shop aria from *The Barber of Seville,* the piles of vegetables and meat were transformed into plates of neat cubes and slices, multicolored and fresh smelling.

The meal was always shared. Friends from the restaurant, card-game buddies, and neighborhood characters were invited, bringing Chianti and turning the apartment into a dive full of talking, laughing, drinking men. A few wives came to keep Ida company. After the meal, they all played cards late into the night. Ida would be vaguely disapproving, but Aldo insisted that at least once a month he must cook for love not money. Marcella was hugged and fussed over and allowed to sip wine from her own tiny glass until it made her sleepy. She would find her way to bed, dizzy and happy, her pillowcase faintly aromatic of the cheap cigar smoke wafting down the passage to her room.

School was a dreary chore, except for English composition class, where she shone, thriving on the praise Miss Woolfe gave her after she read her stories to the class.

"You have the gift of holding the reader," Miss Woolfe told her. Well, she knew that! She held them outside of class too, as she embroidered her stories, making them up as she went along, adding the romance and the sexy bits that kept their interest. Miss Woolfe had no idea of this aspect of her talent.

"I watch the other girls' faces when you read," she told Marcella. "They're spellbound. You *are* going to do something with your gift? Are you thinking of college?"

Marcella doubted that her parents had the money for college for her. Her father sometimes suggested she work as a waitress at his restaurant. He said he could put in a good word for her with the owner—as if it took clout to get a position like that! She knew that would be her fate if she didn't do something, but all she could dream about was getting published. Whenever she was alone in her bedroom, she would begin the enormous task of jotting down the notes, the names, the family histories of the characters she had invented. Legal pads were her raw material, to be organized someday when the threat of work got nearer.

In the meantime, there was Harry Winton. That was the other exciting aspect of school, the part that made her dress carefully in the mornings, sneak the merest smear of makeup on her eyes and lips and arrive early to watch the boys play a show-off game of basketball. Harry Winton was the largest in the sporty set, the biggest boy in the school. Attention from him was some sort of status symbol. And as the most forward girl in the school, she merited attention from the biggest boy. His big moony blue eyes stared at her whenever she was in view. They were physical opposites, Harry the white-skinned, blue-eyed Irish cop's son, and Marcella the volatile, dark-haired, dark-eyed young girl, the Italian's daughter. When he played football for the school, he always looked at her after he'd scored, and she obediently jumped up and down and shrieked. She did not feel pretty because she was not delicate and slim like some of the girls. The rounded shape was a family legacy and she must learn to live with it. Admiration from men was a wonderful reassurance that she was attractive. The problem, as she grew older, was that anyone who expressed interest in her turned her on. The sexual nag had come to stay. When men looked at her, her body started to act up of its own accord, breasts thrusting out, nipples growing erect, a warm moistness down there, *there*—where she had been told it was evil to feel anything! Attention from the male sex left her breathless and unsatisfied and she could not wait to start dating.

At sixteen, she was finally allowed to accept Harry's invitation to a movie. In the theater, her body trembled with anticipation, but on that first date, Harry was very careful to rest his hand respectfully on her shoulder. She tried to push her breast up to his dangling fingers but he remained immobile, eyes on the screen. Later, when he was allowed to use his father's car, he would park around the corner from her home and kiss her neck, her face, her lips, too excited to decide what to kiss next. The car windows would fog as she willed him to be more daring. Sometimes, halfway through their kissing sessions, he would pause for breath, lean back in his seat, and indicate his excitement to her—a long, rounded shape running from his crotch to his stomach. She found the idea that she was responsible for this swelling unbearably exciting. She loved the power she had to get him squirming and uncomfortable just by gazing into his eyes or tickling his palm.

They dated through an entire steamy summer, both painfully aware of the barrier they were tempted to cross. Once, when he showed her how stiff she had made him, she reached out to stroke the outline of his sex through his pants.

"You shouldn't oughta touch it," he muttered huskily, his eyes closed. She moved her hand gently on him and a groan escaped him.

"Why not?" she asked. "You like it, don't you?"

"Yeah," he agreed. "That's the trouble."

"Touch me, Harry," she said, a little amazed at her own daring. She was wearing a miniskirt with short white socks. She parted her legs as Harry's hand stole hesitantly to her thigh. It rested there for a moment, as he kissed her, then moved a little higher, as if idly wandering. It went so furtively, so slowly, as if she would not notice. She almost swooned as his fingers finally came to rest just grazing her panties. She arched her back, pressing herself against his hand. Harry snatched his hand back as if he had burned his fingers.

"Aren't you scared?" he asked.

"What of?" she laughed.

"I don't know," he muttered. "Hell and damnation, I guess. All that stuff they tell you . . ."

Marcella burst out laughing. "I think our bodies were made for us to enjoy." She pulled up her skirt and inserted a finger beneath the edge of her panties, drawing them away from her skin. His watching excited her. She knew she was making his fantasies come true as she pulled down her underwear. Revealing herself to him bathed her body in a delicious glow of shame and excitement. She watched his hand snake toward her almost of its own accord. She offered herself to this hand, invited its touch. Now she could stop imagining, and actually *feel* a man's hand on her. The tips of his fingers reached her, probing so gently she wanted to scream. This clumsy awkward boy was touching her as if he had captured the most fragile butterfly. His fingers fluttered against her sensitive opening, grazing it lightly. She wanted as much of him touching her as she could get—his open palm, the length of his fingers, the strength of his thumb. She shifted her weight from the seat to thrust against him and he pulled back again with a grunt.

"No . . . " she murmured. "Don't stop now!"

"If we keep on . . . something's gonna happen," he said gruffly. She glanced at his lap. She had never seen him straining so uncomfortably against his pants.

"Then take it out," she said, sitting up straight. "Let me see it." He acted reluctant, but she could tell the idea of showing himself to her excited him. When he pulled it out, it looked hard and shiny and red. She grasped him in her fist and his head jerked back with pleasure, his fingers now daring to curve inside her. He suddenly gave an intake of breath and a gasp as the warm semen pulsed out, again and again, over his shorts. He stopped moving and she moaned with frustration, the pressure building up in her, threatening to explode into fireworks. His hand left her and the tingles died away in weak echoes. He mopped up with a wad of tissues, planting his open mouth on hers. She sucked on his tongue until he broke away for air.

"I told you something would happen," he said, falling back in his seat.

"It nearly happened to me, too," she whispered.

The only girl she could talk to about it was Gineeta, an

older girl at school rumored to have had several "affairs." She was darkly beautiful and smoked in an adult way. She and Marcella sometimes met at a nearby coffee shop and discussed boys.

Gineeta was unimpressed at Marcella's news.

"If he was a real man, he'd wait for you to make it before he did!" she said, flicking her cigarette wearily.

"Why?" Marcella asked. Gineeta knew so much more than she did.

"Why?" Gineeta laughed, a rare event. "Because ladies first, that's why."

"The next time his parents go away, I want to go all the way with him," Marcella confided. "You'll cover for me, won't you?"

Gineeta shrugged. "Sure, if that's what you want, but be careful. You know what they say about Irish boys?"

Marcella's eyes widened. "No, what?"

Gineeta stubbed out her cigarette and threw fifty cents on the table.

"Go to bed with them one time, you get a baby."

During the next June, on one of the hottest weekends on record, Harry's parents attended a crime-prevention conference in New Jersey and his sister stayed over with a friend. Harry was to be alone in the apartment all one Sunday. Marcella arranged the alibi with Gineeta and walked over to Harry's home after lunch. Harry opened the door wearing jeans and a tee shirt, looking well scrubbed and rosy pink.

She glanced around as he bolted the door twice behind her. It was a newer apartment block than hers. The decor was the usual: plastic covers over everything, although one large lampshade had escaped imprisonment. Marcella giggled. She walked slowly into the living room, looking at the glass case of china ornaments his mother collected.

"I saw these advertised in a magazine," she said, her nose pressed to the case. They were miniature figurines of characters from the film *The Wizard of Oz.* She had always wondered what sort of people sent away for stuff like this. Now she knew. People like Harry's mother.

"Wanna Coke?" Harry offered. She followed him into the kitchen.

"Don't you have wine or something?" she asked him. "I'm kind of nervous, Harry."

He glanced at her bashfully. "You don't have to do anything you don't want to do, you know," he told her.

She looked affronted. "Backing out?" she asked him.

"No . . ." he said.

He found a bottle of too-sweet red wine and poured them each a glass. She made herself drink it, its warmth unwelcome on this hot day.

He was obviously going to just sit staring at her if she didn't make a move. "Which is your room?" she asked. She walked down the corridor of the apartment, her head starting to buzz from the heavy wine, Harry behind her.

"In there." He gestured, and she walked into his cramped room, sat down on the bed, and looked up at him sexily.

Raising her arms, she asked, "Wanna help me undress?"

He carefully removed every article of her clothing until she was naked. His Adam's apple bobbed each time he swallowed and his breath got louder and louder in the small room. He studied her plump body and she followed his gaze. Her nipples stuck out, erect, and her full breasts hung to one side as she leaned on an elbow, looking up at him questioningly. He stared at her until she slightly parted her legs and saw him sneak a glance there.

She watched the bulge in his jeans as it grew. Hurriedly, he pulled off his clothes, his large white body looking as if the sun never got to it, his erect sex standing straight up before him as he kneeled on the bed, hovering over her. Suddenly he was on her, his lips pressing down on her mouth, his hands full of her breasts, his sex digging at her stomach. She opened her mouth to his tongue, pressed her naked body against his. It felt better than she had ever imagined. When he fixed his lips to one breast and suckled on her, she felt something inside her go wild. He was going too fast, forcing the lower half of his body onto hers, but she wanted so much to experience this that she adjusted to his hurry, opening herself to him, guiding his big excited sex into her, her hands flat on his white chest as she accustomed herself to this wonderful new invasion. She knew she must take him slowly, that she must allow her body to moisten itself with her own desire before letting him inch forward carefully in her. But Harry seemed to lose patience and suddenly pushed himself all the way into her. She screamed with pain but he took no notice, pumping up and down inside her as if he couldn't stop himself. Although it hurt at first, it was also unbearably exciting. She found her body pushing back against his, answering his thrusts, making demands of her own, clutching at him with muscles she had never before used, muscles that urged her to complete this ritual to which her entire young life seemed to have propelled her.

She took his lower lip between her teeth and gently bit on it. He broke away to nuzzle her breasts, to suck on each nipple. The sensations from the nipples connected with what she felt lower down and she was lost in a swoon of sensation, giving herself to the pleasure coming at her from all directions. Big as he was, she wanted even more of him deeper inside, so deep that the two of them would meld and become two halves of the same person. His mouth was bruising hers and she moved her face away, forcing him to lick the side of her neck like a puppy, his body continuing to grind away inside hers until he shouted out his hoarse cry of unbelieving pleasure. He stopped dead, leaving her in a ferment of aroused anticipation, nerve endings tingling, crying out for fulfillment. Frozen, he raised his head and she opened her eyes to watch his expression. Mouth open, eyes tightly shut, his face twisted in pleasure as he came. His pleasure triggered hers and she felt her own pleasure begin. A wave of feeling trembled within her and she pushed back his head with both hands, moving under him, terrified that he might leave her before she had got what she needed from him. Then it came: the wave of pleasure succeeded by another wave, then another, her legs clamping his body to hers, preventing his withdrawal. He was still hard, still panting, as she trembled and fluttered beneath him, her first orgasm with a man inside her, all the fantasies, all the dreams jumbling in her mind and body.

"Love me?" he blurted, hugging her to him as they collapsed.

"I'm crazy about you," she whispered. Then, his head nestled on her shoulder, his hair tickling her chin, they slept on the warm Sunday afternoon, his seed spilling from her, his virile, Irish seed, which, as her friend had warned, would indeed make her pregnant.

TWO

"*Marry* him?" Marcella cried. "But what will I *do* all day?"

"You'll raise your children!" Ida cried. "You'll look after your husband! You'll do what *I* did!"

"I couldn't do what you did!" Marcella shook her head. "You did nothing with your life!"

"I had *you,* didn't I? Are you nothing?"

"I wish you'd never had me! I wish I'd never been born!" Marcella cried, collapsing on her bed in tears, trying to think, but since the positive result of her pregnancy test she had been unable to think clearly. "I was going to be a senior next year!" she wept.

"You should have thought of that before you started fooling around with him," Ida said, shaking her head.

"I wanted to try for a place in college! Miss Woolfe says I can write!" Marcella sobbed.

"Write?" Ida feigned a heart attack. "Weren't those stories what got you into such a hurry to fool around with this boy? *I* married when I was seventeen, *I* didn't get no college!"

Marcella lifted her tear-streaked face. "You didn't have any fun!"

Ida sat down heavily on the bed, reaching out to stroke her daughter's head. Resignedly, as if spelling out something an idiot could understand, she said, "Marcella, marriage is a sacrifice! A sacrifice you make for your children. You think any woman *likes* being a slave to a man who comes home and gulps down his food and ignores her? Ask any woman on this street if she's happy with her husband! They all sacrificed their lives for their children, and that's as it should be!"

Marcella sat up against her mother. "But I didn't choose Harry as my husband," she said. "I just liked going out with him, that's all! He didn't choose *me,* either. He's being forced into it!"

Ida shrugged. "He's doing the only decent thing he can do, Marcella." She got to her feet and left the room.

Marcella lay there, thinking. Sacrifice, what a horrible, loaded word. I don't want to be a human sacrifice for anyone, she decided, least of all my children.

The two sets of parents had a meeting that "the children" were not allowed to attend. There were few secrets in their neighborhood; soon everyone would know that a wedding had been hastily arranged between the Balducci girl and the Wintons' son.

The day after their future had been decided, Marcella went to school early, hoping to find Harry. He was in the playground, kicking a ball around with some boys. She watched him for a moment, trying to believe that she was to be married to this lumbering boy—for the rest of her life. He noticed her, said something to the boys, and left them with a high kick of the ball.

"What's gonna happen?" he muttered as he approached, his round blue eyes looking everywhere but at her.

She glanced sideways at him as he lounged against the brick wall.

"You know, don't you?" she asked. "They think we should marry. How do *you* feel about it?"

He squinted his eyes at some distant point. "I guess I didn't expect to marry this young." He laughed nervously.

"Oh? You think *I* expected to be a mother at seventeen?" she asked. She reached for his hand and he let her hold it for a moment before pulling away.

"*Look* at me, at least, Harry!" she suddenly exploded. "I *am* having your baby!"

It was like acting a scene from a movie. Could this possibly be *her* life? The times she had fantasized some guy asking her to be his wife, she had pictured them in some romantic setting and he had been absolutely crazy about her! And here she was now, in her own dumb schoolyard, almost begging him.

Harry gave a long sigh and looked at her.

"When people marry," Marcella said quietly, "it's usually because they love each other. . . ."

He stared at his feet. "I guess I need a little more time," he said. "To get used to the idea, I mean. I was going to college next year. I was gonna work my way through school and become an accountant."

"I wanted to try for college, too," she reminded him.

"You want to be a writer, right?" He suddenly grinned. "I heard you tell your friends some pretty wild stories."

She made herself smile. "I'll have to forget all about that now, I guess," she said. "But we could still make it fun, Harry. We could be really good parents, too. Not overstrict, like mine."

He nodded, unconvinced. "I guess that's it, then?" he said. He patted her arm and walked back to the group of boys.

"That's it?" she said, under her breath. No "I love you," no nothing? She turned away, tears prickling her eyes. Kids were starting to arrive for school, gathering in groups, discussing homework or tests. And to think these things had once seemed important to her! She had never felt so alone.

"We'll start by saying you got pregnant on the honeymoon," Ida said, bustling around the kitchen that night as they ate dinner.

"They ain't having a honeymoon," Aldo pointed out.

Ida pursed her lips. "So we say the baby came premature. First babies are sometimes late. We'll *still* say it came premature!"

"Look, Ma!" Marcella pushed aside her plate of pasta. "Can we please talk about something else?"

"Sure!" Ida nodded briskly, sitting down. "Certainly! We'll discuss the weather, okay, Miss?"

Marcella beseeched her father with her eyes, but when he looked at her she could see the confusion and disappointment in his eyes.

"My *God*!" She threw down her fork. "I'm not the first girl in Little Italy this has happened to, am I?"

"No. . . ." Her father shook his head. "But you're *our* girl. Every parent wants the very best for his child. We wanted the best for you!" He reached for her hand and squeezed it.

"I know, Dad. . . ." She squeezed his hand back.

"The parents are nice people," Ida said, twirling her spaghetti, "and the important thing is that both families will support you while Harry finishes his accountancy studies. Then Mr. Winton knows this important businessman who owes him a favor. He's promised to find Harry a job when he completes his education. On Wall Street!"

Marcella saw her parents exchange a look that said there was still hope. Hope for prosperity and for grandchildren untainted by this disgrace.

She had always enjoyed the thrill of confessing her sins to Father Carmello and she needed someone to know the truth of what was happening to her. She sought him out in the church the next day after school. He approached her with both hands outstretched, taking hers and pressing them.

"I was hoping you would come," he told her.

"I want to confess," she told him. He heard her out gravely, his hand up to his forehead.

"I don't even *know* Harry that well!" Marcella blurted at the end. "And I don't think I love him!"

"I knew about this, Marcella," Father Carmello admitted in his calm voice. "Mr. and Mrs. Winton have spoken to me. Your families are doing the right thing in supporting this marriage."

"Supporting it?" Marcella echoed. "They're insisting on it!"

"I will marry you," he said. "You will have a legitimate child. And you will come to know and love your husband."

"You *know* that, do you, Father?" she asked sarcastically. "Can you see into the future or something?"

Father Carmello made a tut-tutting noise.

"Oh, Father, can we get out of this closet?" she asked, standing up. "I need some air!"

He smiled and accompanied her to the patch of grass by the side of the church. Marcella leaned back against the church wall.

"I just have this conviction that this is going to ruin my life!" she said.

Father Carmello regarded her sympathetically. "Marcella, you're an intelligent girl; you know that given the circumstances, you don't really have a choice. If you put an effort into this marriage, you'll have a lovely family and . . ." She looked at him, disappointedly.

"Thank you, Father," she said, cutting him off.

She walked home soberly. Is this all that religion could do for her when she was desperate? Tell her she had no choice?

When the school year ended, the only teacher she regretted saying good-bye to was Miss Woolfe.

"Marcella, I hate to see you drop out!" Miss Woolfe looked at her with tired, kind eyes. "Whose stories will we read out in class, now? Can't you wait two more years to marry?"

Marcella suddenly giggled. "Er . . . no!"

"But you'll continue to write?" her teacher asked.

"I'll try to, Miss Woolfe . . ." she said.

Miss Woolfe scribbled her phone number on a scrap of paper. "Take this," she said. "I live in Greenwich Village. If you ever need to find out about further education or anything, please call me, Marcella."

Later, as Marcella and her friends celebrated with a last ice cream sundae, she couldn't help feeling that a part of her life was being taken from her. Her friends chattered excitedly about their summer jobs and she realized that her summer job was marriage.

"Look!" The waiter pulled back the heavy red curtains of Carvelli's second-best banqueting room to show the restaurant's cashier the scene. "Aldo's daughter got married!" The old cashier gazed at the young bride and groom at the head of a table of twenty people.

"They're just children!" she exclaimed.

The waiter shrugged. "Aldo looks happy!" he said.

Aldo Balducci was doing his best to enjoy the evening. You only hosted one marriage if you only had one daughter, and he was determined to enjoy this unique occasion. The blond, ruddy Irish—cousins of Harry's and police-force friends of his father's—perspired in the heat, staring curiously at the table of extroverted Italians to whom some of them were now suddenly related. Aldo had cooked the wedding supper, but he'd had too much wine and his nerves had failed him. The overbaked ziti stood in its smoldering steamer on a side table, daring guests to return for a second helping.

"Such a beautiful ceremony," Ida said, dabbing her eyes, addressing Harry's mother. "Father Carmello gave a wonderful service." Aldo wiped his eyes from time to time when he regarded the grave, beautiful face of his daughter. There was no way he could ignore the sad aspect of today. He shrugged and called for more Asti Spumante, whispering to a waiter, "These Irish know how to drink as well as Italians! Bring another case!" The budget had not stretched to musicians. They made do with the strains of music from the violinist and accordionist in the next room. As a favor to Aldo, they played extra loud.

Marcella wore a short white dress borrowed from a friend of Ida's. She held out her glass for more champagne, hoping she could get a little tipsy, watching Harry, uncomfortable in a new suit.

By the end of the evening there had been several joking comments from the men about Marcella's condition. The wedding party moved to the street, with lots of singing and shouting and even a little dancing. Some of the men offered Harry advice on how to satisfy a woman. This developed into a competition between Irish and Italian to see who could deliver the coarsest gesture, Ida grabbing Aldo's arm as he was about to compete.

Then a straggly line of family escorted them to their new apartment a few blocks away, rented by Harry's father at a special price because a crime had been committed there, the details hushed up for Marcella's sake.

The cheap furnishings had all been chosen by Harry's mother, and Marcella felt strangely lost and temporary in her new home. The first thing Harry did when they closed the front door was to give a tremendous burp.

She glanced at him sharply. "Very romantic!" she said.

"Sorry!" he said, and went to the bedroom.

She carefully hung up her borrowed dress, hurt that he had not embraced or kissed her. In the tiny bathroom with its old pink and black mosaic floor, she rearranged her hair and touched up her face. She slipped into a new robe and joined Harry in the bedroom. He was lying on the bed in a new tee shirt and underpants, so white she imagined his mother had bought them especially for this day.

She sat down on the bed, looking at his inert body. "Aren't you going to wash up?" she asked.

"Too tired." He yawned. "I have school in the morning, remember? I enrolled for this summer course in accounting."

"Oh. Great!" She lay down beside him. Still he did not move. "This is the first time we've been together since . . ." She stopped. Maybe it wasn't too tactful to remind him of the Sunday afternoon a few weeks ago which had led directly to this? "We can do whatever we like now, Harry," she murmured. "We're adults!"

"Yeah, big deal. . . ." He groaned.

A flash of panic rose in her. This would be no good at all unless he was crazy for her! She snuggled up to him, sliding her hands under his tee shirt. She could feel signs of arousal. She could win him over, coax him into a better mood, the way she did with her dad when he was tired and irritable after a long day. She pulled off her robe and let her full breasts dangle near his face. He opened his mouth, taking the tips between his lips, licking them as if they were berries. His first nibbles stirred her desire. She reached inside his underpants, squeezing him in her hand. His breath was hot and moist on her.

"Keep doing that," she sighed.

She turned for him to reach her other breast, pulling down his underpants. He tried to clamber onto her, hot and heavy, his big sex poking between her legs.

"Touch me down there first, Harry," she murmured. "Get me ready for you . . ."

He put his hand down and touched her, roughly.

"Be more gentle." She flinched.

"Will you quit talking all the time?" Harry exploded. He switched off the bedside lamp, then put his hand down under the covers and crudely stuck two fingers into her.

"That *hurt*!" she cried out.

He reared back. "Stop telling me what to do, goddammit! Don't you think I've had other women? Don't you think I know how to do it?"

She blinked back her tears. "Every woman is different, Harry," she whispered. "Sometimes I like to be—"

He twisted his fingers cruelly in her and she felt a part of her heart close off. He was deliberately being hurtful and she could tell the idea excited him. Straddling her, his heavy weight pinning her to the bed, he attempted to push himself into her. She squeezed her legs together, against him.

"I said be gentle!" she cried.

He pressed his mouth down onto hers, his tongue pushing its way through her lips in just the way he was attempting to push into her below. She twisted her head to one side to get her mouth out from beneath his.

"I can't breathe!" she gasped.

"You wanted me excited, didn't you?" he breathed heavily. "Well, I'm excited!"

Her desire vanished. She lay limply on the bed as he stuffed himself into her and, with several excited thrusts, hands clutching at her breasts, reached a noisy climax. He exhaled, his breath pungent with the cigar he had smoked after dinner. She felt her tears run down her cheeks.

"What's the matter?" He touched her face, his voice guilty. "Wasn't it good?"

She bit her lip, saying nothing, sobbing softly. Soon he turned and stretched out on his side of the bed. She heard light snores as he slept. She lay awake, trying to figure out some plan for her life, but there was nothing she could

think of. He was gone when she woke the next morning.
He had not even left a note on the breakfast table, only his
dirty cup and plate.

At first she tried to turn their marriage into a game, playing
house, running the nine blocks to her mother for a recipe,
awaiting Harry's return each night from his accounting
course. It took Harry minutes to eat what she had spent
hours preparing. Then he'd grunt a few replies to her chatter about the day and bury his head in the newspaper. On
hot nights, he stripped to his underwear and worked in the
kitchen, eager to get ahead by studying the next lesson. She
would drift in and out of the kitchen, trying to distract him.
Harry ate and made love in the same way—hurriedly, impatiently, as if eager to get it over with. She tried to explain
to him the Italian concept of sitting around a leisurely meal
and, in bed, the necessity of getting a woman in the right
mood before jumping on top of her. The hardest part was
getting used to living without talking. Her father always
expressed what he felt, sometimes explosively. Harry kept
his feelings inside. His lack of reaction goaded her to flirt
with him, dance around him, sit on his lap or on the table
just to get his attention.

She stretched the housekeeping money. Little things
that she had hardly been aware of before—dry cleaning,
makeup, cleaning supplies—used it up. The first telephone
and electric bills wiped them out. She could wheedle the
odd ten dollars out of her father if she passed by the restaurant, but the parents had agreed it would do the couple
good to learn to economize. By late Saturday night, they
were forced to walk the streets of the Village, looking at
the people eating in the sidewalk cafes.

Harry poked through the kitchen closets to see what she
had bought. "You don't need to buy garbage bags, Marce,"
he told her. "Use the shopping bags the market gives you.
Always buy generic brands, they're cheaper. . . ."

Marcella nodded, seriously. She liked him talking to
her, even though he talked only if he felt he was teaching
her something.

A few weeks of marriage crawled slowly by. Was it her
imagination or was she beginning to show? Her stomach

bulged, but that might have been the ice cream she ate out of boredom in the afternoons.

Sex continued to be unfulfilling; he would not allow her to guide him to the needs of her body. If she tried to show him what she wanted, he became angry, his pride hurt.

"Slow down . . . get me ready for you," she whispered in bed one night.

"You get me too excited, Marce!"

"That's just a cop-out because you can't be bothered!" she cried. When he slept after, she lay awake staring at the pattern the street lamp made on their ceiling, her body refusing to cool down. What could she do? Her mother would be useless—she would just start gabbling about marriage being a sacrifice. Before drifting off into her usual unhappy sleep, she resolved to see Father Carmello.

The next day, she prepared for the visit, making up her face carefully, outlining her dark eyes, smoothing several coats of lipstick on her full lips. After all, she was a married woman now, and she had the right to dress and make up like an adult.

Father Carmello's welcoming smile left his face when Marcella asked to confess.

"What's wrong, Marcella?" he asked gently, in the booth.

"He doesn't make any effort, Father," she began. "If I didn't speak to him when he comes home, he wouldn't say a word to me."

"Is that the problem, Marcella?" he asked. "Lack of conversation?" She looked at his familiar face.

"Can I talk to you about sex, Father?" she asked, hesitantly.

"I am not the proper person to consult, Marcella," he murmured. "You should speak with your doctor or a marriage counsellor. . . ."

"I can't just walk into some stranger's office and tell him I'm not enjoying sex with my husband!" she cried.

Father Carmello shook his head. "Give it time. You've only been married a few weeks, Marcella . . ." he began.

"Yes, but I *know*!" Marcella broke in. "I know it's *never* going to be any good! He doesn't even try to—"

"Marcella!" he cried, interrupting her. "A husband has his needs and you must—"

"What about *my* needs, Father?" she asked. "What do I do about those?"

"Have you tried forgetting your needs for a while, Marcella?" he asked. "Being supremely unselfish?"

She frowned. "Sacrificing myself, you mean?" she asked. "But sex should be the one good thing about my marriage and I don't even have *that*!"

"Then deny your needs, Marcella," Father Carmello advised. "For God. You'll find that—"

"For *God*?" Marcella cried. Before he could reply, she dashed out of the booth and ran from the church. Anger fueling her energy as she walked, her breasts seemed to surge forward, toward the light wind that whirled leaves and dust in little flurries in the corners of school playgrounds and against the stoops. Her nipples brushed against the fabric of her blouse, longing for a man's touch. A gentle touch! She slammed the door behind her when she reached home. She would *never* get what she needed from Harry! The chemistry just wasn't there! It had been the newness, the danger, her own daring that had once been exciting, *not* him!

She took a long shower to calm herself. Then she sat at the kitchen table, brooding over Father Carmello's advice. She saw his well-groomed tanned round head, his sensitive fingers caressing a rosary. He must think *he* was too holy for sex, she thought. Did *he* ever long for a woman the way she longed for a man? Without even thinking about it, she reached for paper and wrote a story about what could have happened if she had tried to seduce the priest. She wrote as an exciting pastime and as a kind of revenge. If he had been a real man, he would have said, "Let me see if *I* can satisfy you, Marcella!" That's what the priest in her story said. She made the account as hot as she could write it, relishing seeing Father Carmello helpless in the throes of sexual passion.

Her story made up in enthusiasm and drive what it lacked in reverence. The priest's body was soon pressed up against the confessional grille. Marcella kicked out the grille in her story, and stuck her hand through to grasp his hot maleness, making him cry out in forbidden pleasure.

She wrote the scene dry mouthed, as breathless as if she were living it. One solid hour of writing put Father Carmello and herself through every sexual variation she could dream up. And when he finally joined her on her side of the booth, he took her standing up, "his knees trembling as she came over and over again, his fingers curved behind her, the warm wetness of them both streaming down their legs."

As she wrote the last pulsing climax, Marcella's left hand snaked into her lap, her fingers pushing their way under the elastic of her damp panties.

By the time she wrote "The End," it was late afternoon and she had two hours in which to prepare dinner. She dragged herself into the bedroom for a little nap. She was drained with emotion, tired out from having discovered, without realizing it, her new career.

She awoke to her face being slapped to the left and right by Harry's large flat palm. She had no idea where she was or what she had done to deserve this. Then the pain seeped into her consciousness and she was suddenly fully awake. Harry gave her a slap which smashed her lower lip against her teeth, filling her mouth with the salty taste of blood. He gave her a final push that sent her sprawling onto the floor.

He brandished the handwritten pages of the yellow pad. "While I work my ass off, you're sitting here getting excited with *this*?"

She rolled away from his feet, wide-eyed, her head ringing from his blows. She glanced at the clock—she had slept solidly for over two hours!

"You had no right to read it!" she cried. She knew the only way to defend herself was to counterattack. "It's private!"

"It was right there on the kitchen table!" he yelled. "And while you're carrying my baby, I have the right to read whatever you write. Did this *happen*?" he shouted. "Is this your diary or what? Do you mean to tell me that Father Carmello, the priest who married us—"

"Of course it's not true!" she cried.

Harry shook his head, sitting down on the bed.

"Somehow, that makes it even worse. . . ." He stared

at her. "Where do you get all this from? Do you think so much about sex?"

"You seem to enjoy it well enough!" she threw back.

She considered running to her parents to show them her bleeding lip. But if she did that, she'd have to explain why he had hit her and her mother would probably agree with him and tell him how *she'd* disciplined her daughter. First you got your mouth washed out, she thought bitterly, then your husband slapped you. It sent a surge of rage through her. She got up from the floor, blotting Kleenex against her mouth.

"If you lay a hand on me again, Harry, I'll kill you!" she promised. "I'm going to be a writer! I can write stories that millions of women will want to read. I *know* I can! And you can't stop me!"

She ran past him, locking herself in the bathroom, amazed at her vow. Was this really how a writer's career began? She had sounded a lot more confident than she felt: she had no idea how to go about becoming a writer.

She stayed in the bathroom bathing her face. When she finally came out, she could see Harry was a little ashamed of losing his temper. She hid the legal pad. That night they had the best sex they had ever had but she was ashamed of herself for responding to him. She lay beside him when it was over, her head accumulating plots for her next stories.

"*Could* I be a writer, Miss Woolfe?" Marcella asked. "Could I really just sit down and *write*? And what would I write about?"

She was sharing a cappuccino with her ex-teacher on the sidewalk of the Café Figaro. She had called Miss Woolfe on an impulse, to discuss writing.

"Write about *three* girls like you," Miss Woolfe suggested. "Each trying to make her marriage work. One could take a job, one might turn to drink or drugs, and one might deceive her husband with a lover. You can insert some very pointed looks at a woman's life today. . . ."

"You always did inspire me!" Marcella squeezed her teacher's hand.

She walked through the dusty streets between the Village and Little Italy, thinking hard.

Being a writer gave her a new power. For a few hours each day she had a sense of importance, controlling the lives of her characters, granting perfect happiness to a few deserving heroines. She used Father Carmello for a story of a tug of war between a priest and a young, unhappily married woman in his parish. She made some photocopies of the story and then went to the local library to look up the addresses of five magazines that published "short fiction." After laboriously addressing five envelopes to five editors and enclosing a note with each story, she felt exhilarated and optimistic: *one* of them would want it, surely? She was able to sail through the next two weeks, imagining the editors jumping on her story, picturing several magazines calling to say they must publish "Confession," by Marcella Balducci Winton.

But she unlocked the mailbox one morning to find three of her large brown envelopes crushed into it. Two of the stories had been returned unread because they were not typed. The third carried a printed note saying it was not what the magazine sought. She lay down on her bed and cried, then reminded herself that there were still two to go. Those came back later in the week, with almost identical notes attached. So much for her writing career. She would never write another story again!

When Harry's parents came for dinner the next weekend, Harry suddenly became a fussy perfectionist, wanting everything to be just right. He hovered behind her as she cooked.

"What about corned beef or something *solid*!" he said, as she prepared pasta. Marcella blew out a breath, flicking flour from her face. "I figured I'd better cook what I know," she said.

Dinner went smoothly, if dully. Harry's mother was a vague, faded woman whose eyes always glanced to her husband for approval. She had decided early on that the only suitable subjects for Marcella and herself to discuss were housework and cooking. Harry's father, a cantankerous ex-cop, enjoyed criticizing the way New York was run, hinting at the secrets of local government figures. He was in his sixties and that year he had taken an early retirement, which made him feel unimportant and bored. After dinner, Harry and his father watched TV as the two women washed dishes.

"What do you do all day while Harry's at school?" Mrs. Winton asked her. "Doesn't it get lonely?"

Marcella thought. She suddenly could not bear to think she might be as dull as Harry's mother. "I'm a writer!" she heard herself say. "I write short stories!"

"Really?" Her mother-in-law turned to her, surprised. "I didn't know! Will they get published?"

Marcella faced her. "I'll send them to every magazine in America until someone likes them!" she declared. "But don't say a word to Harry—I want to surprise him!"

"Of course! How exciting!" Mrs. Winton turned back to the soapsuds, smiling. Marcella continued to dry the dishes, wonderingly. She felt better. She was something other than Harry's wife just waiting for him to come home. She had her own identity. She was a writer!

She borrowed a typewriter from a friend's mother and wrote about a pregnant woman and her dreams for her child during the endless pregnancy. She sent the story out, neatly typed, to half a dozen magazines. This time she must not get her hopes up, she told herself. Sending out dozens of stories was something a professional writer had to do. Even rejects slowly advanced a writer toward her goal.

The only craving she could pinpoint in herself was the old one for sex, which suddenly returned with a vengeance. Since the night after their fight, sex with Harry had once again become hurried and routine. Mid-September exploded with a late-summer heat wave and one afternoon was so hot Marcella sought refuge in the refrigerated section of the largest market, four blocks across town, on the borders of Little Italy. In the New York ethnic mix, many Italian wives bought their food from friendly Puerto Ricans. Marcella wandered into the frozen food section and gazed absently at the meat. Buying a whole chicken would be cheaper, but would mean the oven overheating the kitchen. She glanced up to notice a swarthy assistant watching her, leaning patiently against a doorway to the cooler room as if waiting for her to feel his stare. When he caught her glance, his face broke into a bright, mischievous smile. He had coffee-colored skin with a well-trimmed black moustache and even white teeth. His dark-lashed eyes flashed at her, the pin on his apron reading, "Hi! I'm Angelo! I'm here to help you!"

She smiled at him and moved on, ignoring the jump her stomach gave. Could it be the baby or was it a jump of desire?

He stood by her, tidying the plastic-wrapped packets in the freezer.

"You were thinking about chicken?" He grinned, holding out a packet of chicken breasts. "I like breast very much . . ."

She stared into his cheeky smile, shrugging.

"We have more in the cooler. . . ." He indicated the room behind the freezer with a jerk of his head.

Marcella made a face. "I don't even know if I want to cook chicken tonight. It's so hot . . ."

"Yeah." He winked at her. "I'm hot, too. I'm *very* hot!" He put his hand in his pocket suggestively and she felt a rush of desire sweep her.

"Wanna come inside the cooler?" he asked. "Cool down a little?" He leaned his head a little closer and added, "No one is in there. It will be just you and me . . ."

A leap of excitement, of madness, sounded inside her. She glanced around at the shoppers. Then at his rolled-up, white sleeves, which showed tanned arms and well-kept, clean hands.

"Come." He lightly brushed her arm with a finger.

"I can't," she almost pleaded, softly.

He leaned his head nearer and she could smell his cologne. "Come, beauty," he whispered. "We will have a few minutes of paradise!" He moved behind the freezer, his eyes searching the market efficiently, then stood by the door to the stockroom, nodding encouragingly at her to enter. Dazedly, as if she were someone else, Marcella found herself following.

"Just to cool off for a moment," she murmured as she passed him. It was dark and blessedly cool inside. He nimbly closed the door behind her and bolted it.

"I'm in charge of this section!" He indicated his domain with a proud sweep of his arm. "No one comes in here except me!"

Half pigs dangled from the ceiling, but she hardly

glanced up. She watched him untie the spotless white apron. She was in his arms at once, his smooth lips kissing all over her face before they came to rest full on her mouth. Oh God, this is what she had wanted from Harry, *this* feeling, this *grip*! His warm breath smelled of candymints as his tongue gently pushed its way into her mouth. So smooth, so smooth, making her want more! He unbuttoned her blouse and bent his head down. At first, all he did was to breathe very hotly onto her nipples. When she began to twitch with urgency, he eased off her bra. He stared at her nipples, pointed and hard in the cold room, as sensitive as they had ever been. Then, with a featherlike touch, he brushed his tongue very lightly over them, stirring little rushes of sensation inside her.

"Harder!" she whispered, dizzy. I must be crazy, she thought.

He took one between his teeth and bit softly upon it. She felt herself melting inside. Her crotch was wet and hot, longing for his touch. His hand groped softly up her skirt and when he finally reached between her legs, it was a completely different touch from Harry's, as she had known it would be. This touch was loaded with sex. This touch was one in which she could die from each fingertip. How did he know exactly how to maximize her desire? Pulling down her panties, he brushed his hand over the lips of her sex, just touching, until she pushed against him. As his finger gently entered her, he continued to nuzzle the point of her breast. Oh God, so it was all true! All the suspicions she had nurtured about herself and men! Their desire did magnetize hers! And now she could not stop herself.

The hard outline of his sex pressed against her.

"You want it?" he whispered.

Marcella nodded, unable to speak. He unzipped his jeans, pushing them down to his ankles along with his white Jockeys. Grunting hoarsely, he pressed against her, whispering little bursts of Spanish as he pushed between her thighs, easing her against the wall. She did not take her mouth from under his. The probings and lashings of his tongue in her mouth suggested a whole new art of kissing. She arched her back carefully against the cold wall so that she could receive him at exactly the right angle. She lost her breath awaiting his entry, guiding him inside her, feeling her muscles quiver and welcome him as if he were providing her with a link, a key, to life, to pleasure. His knees bent to match her height. As he slowly straightened, he pushed himself gently all the way up inside her. A long shuddering sigh escaped her. Her pleasure was already about to begin. So soon, so soon, and she wanted it to last forever! She glanced at his face as they moved against each other and saw, from the taut expression, that his pleasure was about to begin, too! And in that next moment, they came together like practiced lovers, their gasps of amazement filling the room as their legs trembled against each other and she pushed back hard against the wall to stay upright. Like waves, the pleasure drenched her and they remained perfectly still, pressed close. She rested unmoving, tasting the last few precious moments as he massaged the back of her head and neck, almost causing her to drift into a relaxed, happy sleep.

He let out a sigh and pulled apart, winking at her. She rearranged her clothing and he replaced his apron, thrusting his fingers through his straight black hair, smiling. She struggled with the large steel bolt on the door.

"I've never done this before," she turned back to tell him breathlessly. He clasped her hand and raised it to his lips, looking up at her with dark, soulful eyes. Then he slowly, deliberately kissed each fingertip. She could only form one thought: why doesn't Harry ever do this to me? She could fall in love with someone who did this to her.

She left quickly, without turning around, her legs wobbly on the walk home, her mood triumphant. She *was* a sensual woman who adored sex and knew how to please a man. She felt anger against Harry. How was it that a supermarket meat packer knew how to please a woman, knew to kiss each finger after giving her such satisfaction? Why did Harry think he could just turn over and sleep?

She prepared dinner very resentfully, hugging the secret of the day to herself, the glow of it echoing in her body. Before Harry returned, she took a shower, washing Angelo's smell from her body.

She awoke in the middle of the night, the stabbing, crippling pains in her stomach making her cry out. It felt as if a giant corkscrew were violating her. She screamed, waking Harry. When he pulled back the covers to look at her jack-knifed body, she saw the blood-soaked sheets and fainted.

In the hospital, they labored quickly and efficiently over her unconscious body. Later, the sister told her that Harry had burst into tears when told the baby was lost.

When she finally regained consciousness, her eyes flickered open. She was in a bed. Not her own, a hospital bed. Harry sat by her side, his eyes closed, his hands clasped on his knee. She saw his face through a blur of medication.

She made herself say his name. "Harry?"

He jumped up and leaned over her. "Are you okay? How do you feel, Marce?"

She pulled a face. "Not so great."

He made a gesture with his hands. "I was so worried. You lost a lot of blood."

"Were you really worried?" she whispered. Her whole body seemed numbed. "What happened to me?"

"You miscarried. We lost our baby, Marce," he said.

She held out her arms to him and he buried his face into the side of her neck. She cried softly.

"I'm so sorry, Harry . . ." she whimpered.

He sat up, looking down at her. "It wasn't your fault," he said.

The words stabbed her, made her start remembering things she did not want to recognize. Not her fault? How she wanted to believe that!

"Could you get me some water?" she asked. "My mouth is dry!" He helped her to sit up in bed and drink. She gasped as she drained the tumbler.

"You better not have any more until the nurse sees you. . . ." He took the glass.

"Thanks," she said. He had a new look in his eyes. Perhaps it took a grief such as this to bring out his feelings.

"I've asked Father Carmello to hold a service for the baby," Harry told her. "It's in four days. Do you think you'll feel well enough to attend?"

She lay back on the pillow. "I'm not sure if I can face it, Harry. Since when did you believe in stuff like that?"

"I wanted to do something," he said. "I was brought up that way."

She was trying to stop her brain from racing forward. What happened now? The baby was the reason they had married. Did that mean she was free? Would he expect to stay married?

"Hold my hand, Harry," she whispered. Right now she needed every bit of comfort she could get. He reached for her hand and took it. She clasped him tightly.

"Hold me!" she begged.

He bent down and took her in his arms. She clung to him. She would never have imagined it could feel this bad. She must have been counting upon this child more than she had admitted to herself.

When her parents visited, Ida bent down to whisper in Marcella's ear.

"We have to be stronger!"

Marcella knew that "we" stood for women. Ida threw a pitying look at Aldo as he wiped a tear from his eyes.

"Oh, Daddy," Marcella said. "I'll be fine!"

He cleared his throat, embarrassed. She only had to exchange a secret look with him to know she had all his sympathy and love.

An infection caused her to stay five more days in the hospital, missing the memorial service the Wintons had arranged.

When she was dismissed from the hospital, she slunk back to their apartment, staying home for days. She felt as guilty as a murderess, hiding away the things she had accumulated for the baby. She tried to stop that supermarket scene from replaying itself over and over in her head. Pregnant women were allowed to make love, she reassured herself. It wasn't as if Angelo had been brutal with her. Nevertheless, it was too much of a coincidence that she had miscarried on the day she had known such pleasure.

On her first visit to her mother, Marcella made herself hold back the tears. In the highly emotional state she was in, she longed to bury her face in Ida's bosom and cry, but Ida had never been that kind of cuddly mother.

"You're depressed, that's only natural," she chattered quickly, leading Marcella through to the kitchen. "I've never seen a man as sad as Harry in that church. He's so relieved you're well."

"But he hasn't touched me since I got back!" Marcella cried. "He acts as if it was my fault I lost the baby!"

"Of course it's not your fault," Ida said, lighting the stove. "Why?" She peered at Marcella. "You didn't do anything to try to get rid of it, did you?"

"Oh, Ma . . ." she sighed, shaking her head at her mother. "What do you think I am?"

Ida poured their coffee. "The doctor said there is nothing wrong. In a few months you'll try again and you'll have a beautiful healthy baby. You'll forget you ever felt like this!"

They sipped the scalding coffee silently for a few minutes.

"Ma?" Marcella replaced her cup in its saucer. "Maybe this was a sign that our marriage wasn't meant to be? We only married because this baby was due. . . ."

"Oh yes? And now I suppose you think you can divorce?" Ida cried. "You're a married woman in God's eyes. What do you think people will say?"

"I'll never love him, Ma," Marcella said.

"*Love?*" Ida laughed with a look that said only too clearly what she thought of love.

Harry enrolled in business college, continuing extra night classes in accounting. Some nights he did not get home until after ten. Marcella wrote story after story, about losing a baby, about marriage, about mothers, about a husband who made his wife feel to blame for a miscarriage. She now had lists of magazines that purported to publish fiction, although none had yet offered to publish her, even for free. She began to regard the returned manuscripts as par for the course, but she never failed to feel excited when she sent off a story, thinking, This one may be the one!

Since the hospital stay, she had not had a tender touch or word from Harry, and at night he stayed rigorously to his side of the bed. It was approaching Christmas and the trees and decorations seemed to mock at her failure to provide a family. The pressure built up in her head until one night, sitting across the kitchen table from him after dinner, she felt the question form itself.

"Do you really want to stay married?" she asked him.

He looked up guiltily, as if she had read his thoughts.

"Do *you*?" he said.

She shook her head. "I asked you first."

He put down his paper, giving a long sigh. "Why ask that now?"

She took a sip of wine. "Because you haven't said one nice thing to me since—" She broke off, holding his gaze.

"You're making me feel like it was all *my* fault," she began again. "Do you realize what it feels like to lose a baby?"

He swallowed, looking down at his plate. "Pretty bad, I guess."

"It's worse than bad," she said. "Your whole body feels as if it's—" She began to cry.

He scraped his chair back from the table and stood near her, his hand touching her shoulder tentatively. She turned toward him and he held her. Oh God, how needy she was! How desperate for some affection! She hated herself for clinging to him as sobs pushed up from the deep place to which she had banished them. Harry held her, confused by all this emotion.

That night in bed she inched nearer his body, thinking how ironic it was that she should have to seduce him all over again. And for what? For a baby, because her life was empty without one. Maybe if her stories had been printed and paid for she would not have this empty gap inside her. With a child she would have someone to pour out her love for, someone who would appreciate her. Her hand touched Harry's.

"Can't you sleep?" he asked. He turned to her and she felt his aroused sex pressing against her. She touched him. "I thought you wouldn't want me for a long time," he said in a husky voice. "Not after—"

She placed her finger on his lips, silencing him. "Just be more gentle and loving with me, Harry," she begged. "We can still have a child. We can still—"

"Oh, Marce!" He clambered on top of her, his heavy body taking her breath away. It wasn't the same if you had to remind a man to be gentle, to be loving.

"Gently," she reminded him as he fumbled with her nightgown. "Very, very gently . . ." she whispered as he felt feverishly all over her and her body began to respond. Could she be so starved that she would now welcome even his clumsy embraces? Or was her mother right about children and sacrifices? Was that really how the human race propagated, through constant sacrifice? Certainly something deep within her now defied reason and only urged her to conceive, to give birth.

She made a pact with God. If He allowed her to conceive again she would be a faithful wife. She would squash the sexual longings that had brought nothing but trouble. She would avoid men's eyes on the street, so that men could not look at her with that expression that both thrilled and scared her, that recognition of something kindred, something wild within her.

When she thought of that market guy, Angelo, now, it was only as a memory for reaching a climax with Harry. Remembering the light way he had brushed her nipples, the exquisite pleasure he had given her, allowed her to reach a climax in spite of Harry's technique. She superimposed her memories over what she was experiencing and sometimes she almost believed she was in Angelo's clean brown arms.

The new year began a new decade: the seventies. In January, she became pregnant again. This child must make up for all she was missing in her life. It would be a boy, she just knew. And even while she carried him in her womb, she loved him with a love she knew must be too much to load onto any child. She pictured the son she would bear, the boy she would love, the child who would bring the joy, the light, back into her life. Even before he was born, she called him the light of her life.

THREE

September 1970

Marcella held her newborn son in her arms, feeling an emotion stronger than any she had felt before. She looked down into his tiny face, the eyes tightly shut against all the fresh sights of the world. She had already made the first sacrifice: her hitherto unblemished body had been ripped by a cesarean incision. It was now more important that *his* body was whole and perfect. She cradled the heavy small head, feeling a swell of joy inside her that threatened to overflow into sobs. This child had felt special even as she had carried him; his birth was simply the first of many events in which she must slowly lose him. She chose the name Mark because it had the first three letters of her name in it: he was part of her.

Harry brought her roses and a gold chain bracelet, absurdly proud at having fathered a son. When his parents visited, they admired their grandson and seemed warmer to her, as if she had proved her worth. Something in her resented Harry's proud smile: she felt he was happy for all the macho reasons men wanted sons, as proof of their virility. When he held Mark, she had to stop herself from reaching out to make a safety net in case Harry dropped him.

She stayed in the hospital for four days, visited by the family and some of her friends from school. The girls were very impressed by the baby and looked at her with awe, making her feel older and strangely apart from them. The idea of telling them sexy stories now seemed ridiculous.

It took months for her body to return to normal, her life and sleeping habits changed. Her determination to breast-feed Mark sometimes tired her.

When they began to make love again, there was a new obstacle to her pleasure; her attention was so fixed upon catching any sound from her sleeping child that she could not lose herself. Harry would have needed to be an extremely skilled, adept lover to coax her toward that wave of pleasure, but he was in his usual hurry, as if to make up for the lost months. He would not allow her to guide him to the subtleties of her body and its reactions. Instead of begging him to slow down, she found she preferred that Harry simply reach his climax as soon as possible. Sex between them could now happen remarkably quickly, and as he slept she wondered how many other wives had followed this route, allowing their marriages to crumble from the bed outward. She comforted herself with the thought that she had her son and he was all that mattered. Any happiness that came into her life would be through Mark. As soon as Harry left for school in the morning, she played classical music on the FM radio at full blast, hoping it would sink into Mark's consciousness and spark a love of music. She wanted him to be an intelligent man and to love the arts.

Mark was nine months old when she attended her old friends' graduation ceremony, the concrete play area of the school festooned with banners on the bright June day. She dressed him in white pants and shirt with a matching baseball cap. Ida came to hold Mark on her lap during the speeches and awards. Marcella wore a burgundy jersey dress that was a little too warm and clung too closely to her new rounded shape.

After the speeches, friends and families of the graduates milled around the yard, posing for photographs and autographing each other's yearbooks. Marcella held Mark in her arms and suddenly collided with a familiar figure.

"Marcella!" It was Miss Woolfe.

Marcella kissed her. "I'm so sorry I've been out of touch. *This* is why!" She indicated Mark. "Mark, say hello to Miss Woolfe!"

Miss Woolfe dutifully chucked Mark under his chin.

"He's adorable. What about your writing?" she asked.

Marcella groaned, heaving Mark into a more comfortable position on her arm.

"All I have to show for it is a collection of rejection slips," she said. "Oh, Miss Woolfe, I'm so depressed about it."

"How many rejections?" Miss Woolfe asked.

"I don't know. Twenty, thirty . . ." Marcella said. "I feel so bad when I get them—so untalented and little. You don't know what it's like!"

"I'm afraid I *do!*" Miss Woolfe told her. "You're not the only writer who gets rejected!"

Marcella's eyes widened. "You too?" she asked.

Miss Woolfe nodded. "I must have over three hundred by now. When *I* get rejections, I use them to make myself give of my best! To write so well they *can't* ignore me!"

Ida suddenly arrived to take Mark to show to another grandmother. Marcella touched Miss Woolfe's arm to move a few steps away from the crowd.

"Even magazines that don't pay reject me!" she told her teacher. "I can't *give* my stuff away!"

"Listen, Marcella," Miss Woolfe said. "You have a writer's ear and eye. You get your emotions across and you have something to say. *That's* what makes a writer! Keep at it. You *will* get published eventually. I know it!"

Marcella looked at her teacher. It had been so long since anyone had spoken to her as if she could achieve anything more than bearing a handsome child. She blinked back her tears.

"You don't know how much your encouragement means to me . . ." she murmured, clutching Miss Woolfe's arm.

"Are you reading good books, Marcella?" her teacher asked.

Marcella laughed. "I guess you'd call them trash! Look, Miss Woolfe—tell me which books I should read. I could kind of educate myself at least."

Miss Woolfe fumbled in her woven shoulder bag and thrust a photocopied list at Marcella.

"Next year's reading list!" she said. "Read one of these each week and in a couple of years you can call yourself pretty well read."

Mark started to cry from somewhere and Marcella's head instinctively turned. Miss Woolfe patted her. "Go find him! I can see he's everything for you! But don't forget to write!"

Marcella impulsively leaned to kiss the older woman's cheek, then ran off to find her son.

As Mark approached his first birthday, his blue eyes stayed that intense color and his thick black hair bespoke his Italian heritage, lushly fringing his eyes, giving him an inquiring, adult gaze. Marcella tore herself away from him for two hours a day, leaving him with his doting grandmother Ida while she marketed. She never shopped at the supermarket where Angelo had made love to her and avoided thinking about sex or noticing men. When she thought about her life and her future, it didn't seem to matter if she were fat or thin, beautiful or unattractive. Harry did that to her. He never discussed their marriage or their relationship; he made her feel uncherished. He put on weight, too, turning into a lumbering, big man with that neglected air of a husband who is not loved. Could she wait five, ten, fifteen years for her son to grow up and talk to her, understand her? She lavished her attention on him, reading him stories, playing him music, hugging him.

"Don't smother the little guy, Marce," Harry would grumble. "Wanna make a mama's boy out of him?"

As Marcella handed her son to his father, she would think, Better a mama's boy than an insensitive slob.

When Harry qualified as an accountant in the fall of 1971, his father contacted the businessman who had always promised to "do something" for his son. He was as good as his word, submitting Harry's name to a prestigious Wall Street brokerage firm of which he was an absentee partner.

Stollman, Weller, Fine and Tellerman was one of the giant firms of the city. Its training program put twenty bright young trainees through a year-long immersion in the business world. After that, they would be graded and selected for certain positions within the firm. It was a competitive program and a big challenge. From what Marcella could see, Harry was not particularly brilliant, but she imagined his trustworthiness and aggressive personality would get him by in this tough, ambitious world.

Harry sat in the firm's canteen on the first coffee break of his first morning, uncomfortable in the scratchy new suit bought the previous Sunday from the "Young Executive" department of a discount warehouse. As he looked around at the new young faces, many of them female, he suddenly realized what he had missed out on by marrying so young: the dating and pursuing of attractive young women.

He began to twist the wedding band on his finger, at first subconsciously, then actually studying it, wondering if he dared remove it each morning on the way to work.

"Forget it!" said a nasal voice next to him. "They've all seen it!" He looked around to see Bernard, a nervous, prematurely balding colleague, who had sat next to him at that morning's briefing.

"Didn't you know wedding rings are the first things girls zero in on when new meat arrives?" Bernard asked him, indicating a table of secretaries opposite them. "But listen, don't worry about it, it doesn't have to harm your chances. Is your wife pretty? Have any children? Where d'you live?"

Harry gulped his coffee, not answering any of these questions.

"I'm an expert on who puts out," Bernard informed him. "Wanna know who puts out here, ask me!"

"Isn't this your first day, too?" Harry asked guardedly.

"Yeah, but I can tell by their eyes," Bernard boasted. He pointed to a skinny brunette secretary at the next table, wearing a name tag. "Her, for example! What you wanna bet?"

Harry read the girl's name tag. Gloria Defries. She smiled at him as he watched her.

Bernard nudged him. "What'd I tell you? Am I right?"

"Cut it out," Harry growled. "You said yourself, I'm a married man."

"Yeah, but *how* married?" Bernard asked. "There's degrees."

When they got up to go, Harry turned around and found her twisted in her seat, awaiting his look. They exchanged the kind of eye contact he had not experienced for a couple of years. At lunchtime, he brushed off his new pal and hung around outside the firm's entrance, hoping that Gloria took a one o'clock lunch. When she emerged, he followed her for one block until she vanished into a coffee shop. Don't get takeout, he prayed. When he entered, he saw her in an empty booth, studying the menu.

She had piled-up dark brown hair and her skinny legs were in sheer black stockings. There was something cheap and available about her. She was still wearing her name tag on her apple-green dress. He stood by the booth.

"May I?" he asked.

She looked up, smiled, and nodded. "Sure."

He slid into the booth opposite her. Soon they were talking easily about the firm.

"I noticed you as soon as you came in," she confessed, peering at him over a bacon, lettuce, and tomato sandwich. "There's something about your walk and the way you hold yourself."

"Yeah?" Harry asked, surprised.

"Mm-hm." She nodded. "Kind of confident. You're gonna need that here. It's strictly dog eat dog. I'm a floater. I go where they need me, and don't think I was too pleased about that, at first. I really resented it at the beginning. I wanted, like, a regular office, a regular boss, you know? But now I wouldn't have it any other way. Now I think I know more about this firm than almost anyone else because I get to see into every department. When I hook up with the right guy—someone really ambitious—watch out, world!" She made an imaginary knockout punch and giggled.

"Why?" he asked, munching his hamburger. "You know the secret code or something?"

Her eyes flickered over him. She was a lot sharper than he thought.

"You ambitious?" she asked.

"I could be. You have to get up and go to work each morning anyway, right?" he asked. "You might as well be ambitious."

She shrugged, dabbing her lips with a paper napkin. "Wall Street is a place where you can make a lot of money. I mean, a *lot!* I've seen guys clean up and get the hell out of there. Get the hell out of the *country!* You're married, right?"

Harry nodded.

"Happily?" she asked.

Harry shrugged. She made a commiserating face, slipped off one shoe under cover of the table, and inserted her stockinged toe under the cuff of his new pants. Keeping her eyes on him, her eyebrows raised, she rubbed the toe up and down his calf. Harry was immediately aroused.

"Wanna tell me about it?" she asked.

He shifted in his seat, glancing down at his lap as he got painfully hard.

"There's not much to tell. She got pregnant and I married her."

"Oh, such a gentleman!" Gloria fluttered her eyes. "Too bad you just had to ruin it by telling me all about it!"

"Well, you asked," he said.

"I guess you did the right thing, at least, huh?" she asked.

"*Was* it the right thing?" Harry asked her meaningfully. He looked deeply in her eyes and she reveled in the attention. She moved her toe slowly up and down.

"What's the matter? Not happy?" she asked him.

Harry gave a great sigh and signaled the waitress.

"Let me put it this way," he said, stirring his coffee. He looked back into her attentive gaze. There was a definite charge between them.

"My wife doesn't understand me," he told her.

Gloria nodded her head up and down several times.

"Another one!" she stated.

Marcella loved the little boy Mark was growing into. She enjoyed taking him to the tiny concrete park down the street and holding him on a swing as he looked around curiously at the other children. In the late afternoons, he took his nap and she wrote her stories.

She wrote about young mothers in Little Italy, wives trapped in loveless marriages. Loveless marriages were her specialty. She wrote of bullying husbands and what happened when their wives suddenly found the courage to stand up to them. She knew she would not have this courage herself until her stories were published, making her officially a writer. Legal pad after legal pad was filled with her thoughts, her imaginings, her fantasies. At first, it was good just to get her thoughts down on paper. But she needed an audience, a reaction. She found her rejection slips and read them again, carefully, trying to find some encouragement in them. If her stories were always out somewhere, she could nurture the dream that she might be discovered at any time. She decided to send out another batch, this time perfecting a covering letter.

The money for the photocopies, envelopes, and postage had to be carefully saved. She economized by not buying flowers, lunching with her mother before leaving Mark with her, and reading only books borrowed from the library. She also needed a new way to handle rejections: she would keep all the brusque little notes, and one day, when she was famous, reveal the names of all the editors who had been too dumb to recognize her talent!

Her mood changed when Harry got home at night. He ate while reading *The Wall Street Journal* and *The New York Times*.

"Do you need to read *both* papers?" she asked one night.

"When you work with money, you can't be too well informed, Marce," he told her.

"Tell me what you did today!" she asked.

He told her about the big money to be made in shares if you acted quickly on the right tip; described, admiringly, the men in his firm who were making over a million dollars a year. He told her how he tried to hang out with the right bunch of guys and of a senior manager who was taking an interest in him and advising him on his career. His eyes

gleamed when he spoke to her about his job, when he mentioned the money that could be made.

"You know, the only time you get at all excited now is
when you're talking about money," she told him. "I'd like
to see you get as excited when Mark says a new word.
Enjoy your son growing up, Harry! Enjoy—"

"Wall Street is an exciting place, Marce," he cut her off.
"You can't work there without money becoming a very important part of your thinking!"

He turned back to his paper when she got up to clear
the dishes. Enjoy Mark growing up, she had said, but she
had wanted to say, "Enjoy *me*! Take *me* out places! Talk to
me about what *I* want, about *my* dreams!" She placed the
dishes in the sink. You couldn't *tell* someone to be interested in you. And what was there about her now to be so
interested in? What was she, other than a drab, overweight
housewife with a son she adored? She scrubbed the plates,
lost in misery, until her other voice reminded her. "You're
a writer, Marcella! The girls at school listened to your stories. Miss Woolfe said you had a gift . . . !"

Yes, and dozens of magazine editors continued to reject
her stories. So what?

So never forget you're a writer! said the voice. Because
that's what's going to save your life! Did everyone have that
little voice within them? she wondered. Or was it just her?

They spent a few evenings with Harry's fellow trainees.
Marcella made an effort to dress up and enjoy these dinners. There would be men there, men whose eyes she
might catch just to reassure herself that she still had what it
took. Why was it that none of the men interested her? She
found them colorless and consumed with ambition. Their
wives were even more ambitious for them than the men
were for themselves. They were condescending when they
heard Marcella lived in Little Italy.

She wrote a story about a dinner of ambitious wives and
the little digs they sneaked into the conversation, the
makes of their cars, the titles of their husbands' jobs, all the
status details she had heard during the dinners. Mark *must*
be above all that pettiness, able to enjoy the finer things in
life, she vowed.

Once a week, she left Mark with her mother and took a subway to Columbus Circle. It was like entering another world at Fifty-seventh Street, walking along it to Fifth Avenue. She browsed in Bergdorf Goodman and Bonwit Teller, defensively at first, thinking, I have as much right as anyone to be here! Later, she learned to smile at the salesladies' offers of help. She loved to touch the beautiful clothes that were so far beyond her means. And, after lingering on all the fashion floors, she would visit a bookstore, usually Doubleday on Fifth Avenue, to drink in the bright, exciting covers of the new novels and biographies, wishing she could afford to buy them.

"Oh, Marcella!" Ida screamed. "You have the handsomest little boy in the neighborhood and now you'll have the prettiest little girl!" she predicted confidently.

It was nearly Christmas, 1971, and she sat on the faded sofa in her mother's living room. How had she allowed herself to become pregnant again? By wanting to provide a brother or sister for Mark? Or by having one of her bad days when she thought of herself not as a writer but as a hopelessly untalented person who just liked to think of herself as one? Perhaps on one of those days she had not bothered to use the birth control foam she always used.

"How excited you must be!" Ida cried. "But what is this?" She peered closer at her daughter. "You act like you don't care. Are you sick?"

"I feel fine, Ma," Marcella said calmly, watching Mark play on the rug of her mother's living room. "I just don't—" she began, then stopped. She suddenly saw her mother's face clearly and objectively. How could she possibly explain this mixture of feelings—of disappointment, pride, and resentment? That was why she'd delayed even telling her mother about the pregnancy. "You're happy because I'm following the approved pattern, Ma," she said finally. "Being *normal,* like everyone else . . ."

Ida made a disapproving grunt. "To you that's a sin, being normal, eh, Marcella?" she asked, shaking her head. "But what's so wrong with a beautiful, loving family? Maybe you *are* normal. Did you ever think of that?"

"God forbid," Marcella said.

This pregnancy was very different from the way she had felt as she carried Mark. Less special. This time she had no picture in her mind of what the child would be like. Despite all the old wives' tales of "carrying high" or dangling a ring from a chain over her belly, she was not at all sure that this would be a sister for Mark. If it was a girl, Harry wanted to call her Sheila. Marcella did not like the name and wanted Sonia, which, to her, suggested a beautiful, classy woman.

Sonia was born in June after ten painful hours of labor. Marcella vowed throughout that this would be her last child. "You forget the pain," her mother kept telling her. But this pain lasted too long to forget. She had finally begged for medication, sinking gratefully into numbness. When she came to and they placed her tiny daughter in her arms, the rush of love surprised her. How could she hold back a welcome for this exquisite creature? The baby was absolutely perfect, beautiful, with none of the raw redness most babies have. Her long, dark eyelashes showed against the smooth rise of her cheeks. As she told her many years later, Sonia was beautiful from birth. Harry fell in love with his daughter at first sight. Sonia was going to be "his," as Mark was "hers."

When she took the baby home, she immediately felt the frustration of the tiny infant's not feeding.

"She refuses my breast!" Marcella cried over the phone to her mother.

"Have you tried formula?" her mother suggested. "Sometimes a baby can prefer that. I'm coming over!"

When Sonia's mouth sucked hungrily from a rubber teat, Marcella bent over, watching. "But *why*?" she asked her mother and Harry. "Why wouldn't she feed from *me*?" she wept.

"Don't get so upset!" Her mother patted her shoulder. "Some babies just don't suckle that well."

It was the first of many times her daughter would find the power to upset her, the very first move of a tug-of-war between mother and child.

When she introduced Mark to his new sister he reached

for the baby's hand and kissed it. He showed no jealousy, no resentment.

"That's very nice, darling," Marcella told him. "I want you to look after her. Be her big brother. Be her best friend!"

Mark nodded seriously, peering over the crib at his sister's pretty face.

At her parents' home one Sunday, when Sonia was five months old and evidently thriving on formula, Marcella showed her father how Mark reacted to the music she played him from the FM channel. At two, he showed an excitement and sensitivity to the rhythm and music, waving his hands and jumping in time with it.

"That's from his great-aunt, I tell you!" Aldo said approvingly. "What a voice she had. She never did achieve her ambition to sing at La Scala. Maybe Mark will be a musician? Promise me if he is, he will use the name of Balducci?"

"How *can* he, Dad?" Marcella smiled fondly at her father. "His name is Winton. But I promise you if I ever get one of my stories published, I'll sign it 'Marcella Balducci Winton.' "

"What sort of stories?" Ida called over doubtfully, and Harry looked across at her, holding Sonia on his lap.

"Show your mother that story you wrote about the priest who married us, Marce," he suggested. "She'd love that!"

"You wrote a story about Father Carmello?" Ida asked. "Let me read it, Marcella!"

Marcella shot Harry an angry look. "He was just kidding, Ma," she said.

"No!" Harry insisted, laughing. "You should have read the things that priest got up to, Ida!"

"You don't mean—Marcella, you didn't—" Ida came to stand over Marcella, holding a stack of dishes. "A woman with two children writing such things?"

Marcella gave a weary sigh.

"Listen, everybody!" she announced, looking from her mother to Harry. "I *am* going to be a writer if it takes my entire life to get something published! And sometimes it will be romantic or sexy—why not? Do you *see* what's getting into print these days?"

"I don't want to know!" Ida waved aside a decade of modern literature. "The world's going crazy. Ever since these hippies, there's too much sex!"

Emboldened by her vow to her mother and Harry, she wrote a new story about a sex-starved wife visiting a supermarket and falling for the man at the meat counter, basing it almost entirely on the incident between herself and Angelo, piling on all the sensual details she could remember of their encounter. The climate of the early 1970s had allowed fiction to become as outspoken as it had ever been. This time, she sent the story to *Cosmopolitan,* figuring that its readers would appreciate the earthiness and humor of her tale.

The mail arrived long after Harry had left for work, and on Saturdays, she made a point of running out for it while Harry took his shower. The envelope from *Cosmopolitan* appeared a month later. She gave a cry of disappointment on finding her story inside, the pages looking untouched and unread. She had grown to hate the printed rejection of her writing that always began "The Editors regret . . . ," without the tiniest piece of encouragement.

"Well, was I getting *warm*?" Marcella cried out aloud to her empty kitchen. "Have I gotten any better? Is what I write just *crap*?"

The rejection slip didn't answer. It just sneered its regret that the story did not quite meet the magazine's needs.

April 1973

It was spring and there was a certain jauntiness to Harry's walk. He had a lunch date with Gloria to celebrate his second promotion in eighteen months at the firm. He became a different person as he walked the three long blocks to the subway each morning. Leaving behind the doubts, the frustrations, the silence of a man who did not communicate, he took on the confident air of a man heading for a place where he knew what he was doing. And if he played his cards right, Gloria was going to help him make a million dollars!

Sometimes, if he could not face the stuffy subway car, he hailed a cab; the couple of dollars' worth of indulgence gave him an air of success that could last through the whole day. By the time he sat opposite Gloria in the Wall Street Brasserie, her favorite place, he felt like a polished sophisticate.

His rise at the firm had been heady, but he had deliberately been very low-key about it at home because he had not wanted to share the triumph with Marcella. The triumph was his and Gloria's. His intuitive sense of the market and his quick grasp of figures had not hurt. But what had rocketed him from the trainee program into assistant managership of the money market division was Gloria. And what made it especially meaningful were Gloria's eyes always on him, urging him on.

Now their meetings were a carefully kept secret; no one in the firm could know of their relationship, of the source of his information. Gloria had been extremely helpful, letting him know which director's door to knock on just before a vacancy came up in a department. Her "floater" status, giving her entry to many departments, meant that she often heard about dismissals, resignations, and transfers before anyone else. She understood corporation life and had perfected her "dumb secretary" act, dressing in sexy clothing to create an image that nobody felt they had to fear. She was just Gloria, as familiar in the office as a water cooler, and about as threatening. As she had said on their first meeting, all she needed was the right ambitious guy with whom to share her knowledge. She passed on her understanding of office politics to Harry.

"When a young, ambitious guy comes into his boss's office and starts asking for things," she had told him, "the boss kind of admires it. The guy may be asking for too much too soon, but if he keeps coming to ask for more, he's the kind of guy the boss wants working for him. Thick-skinned, get it? Not afraid."

"That's good, because I've never been afraid of anything in my life!" he had boasted to her.

"That's *unreal*!" she had marveled, her greatest compliment, giving him that look that always made him want to be even better for her.

"You know why?" he had asked her. "Because four years ago, I thought I was all washed up. When I had to get married, I did the right thing, but I was dead. Now I'm alive again, Gloria! I had no idea working on Wall Street would be like this!"

And now he was assistant manager of a whole fucking department!

"Make sure you ask for me when you need a secretary." Gloria smiled. "But not *too* often!"

They toasted each other in champagne across the white table.

"It's fantastic to have your support," he told her over lunch. "If you weren't here, I would never have made it."

She stroked his knee under the tablecloth. "That's what I figured." She giggled. "That you needed me."

"Oh, I need you, all right," Harry said.

"Doesn't *she* support you?" she asked.

Harry met her questioning eyes, shrugging. "She's a whole other ball game to you, Gloria. She could care less about my career. She's all wrapped up in the kids and her writing. Money isn't too important to her—"

"As long as you're bringing it home?" Gloria finished for him. She smiled. "Oh boy, I know that type so well! They look down their noses at you, but they know how to spend money the same as everyone else. What does she think about you becoming assistant manager, huh?"

His pale blue eyes gazed honestly into hers. "I haven't told her about it yet, Gloria. I wanted *us* to celebrate it first!"

She raised her glass of champagne again. "So let's celebrate!" She drained her glass, studying him.

"You wanna get yourself some better threads, Harry," she advised. "It's like you've been wearing that suit every day since we met. If you start looking a little better turned out than anyone else, they'll pick you, without even knowing why. I wanna see you in more tailored suits, better fabrics. Lighter weight, maybe, so you don't seem so stiff. The mood on Wall Street is a little more relaxed now, Harry." She giggled. "More Giorgio Armani!"

"Yeah, do me a favor with that Giorgio Armani!" He laughed. "You seen what his suits *cost*?"

"They're an investment," Gloria assured him. "And you're earning more—spend a little on yourself!"

"If I dress better, don't you think she'll notice?" he asked.

Gloria raised her eyes. "When a woman doesn't love a man, you think she notices if he's wearing Saint Laurie or Brooks Brothers? I've seen those wives taking their husbands' suits into the dry cleaners, holding them at arm's length, like they stink or something!"

"Okay . . ." He felt for her hand under the white linen cloth. "I'll let you talk me into some late-night shopping. . . ."

She wrinkled her nose at him. "I see you in pale gray . . ." she said, squinting her eyes. "Kind of *dove*! You'd look real distinguished!"

He leaned across the table. "You gonna give me a kiss on this day?"

She glanced around them. "Don't let success go to your head. All we need is for some fink to spot us and tell—"

He kissed her before she could finish. "I don't get it." He leaned back in his chair. "When I met you, every guy in the department was panting to get in the sack with you—why *me*?"

"This is more creative!" She squeezed his hand under the table. "There's something very sexy about being the woman behind the man. You were like, *raw*! I like molding you!"

"I'm like putty in your hands, huh?" he chuckled.

She nodded. "You *need* me!"

He laughed. "That's funny. If you told Marcella I was a guy who needed her, she'd never believe it. You must bring out something special in me, Gloria."

"That's what I *mean*!" she whispered in her baby voice. She lowered her eyes and gently prodded his chest. "I'm creative, see? If I can guide you into the right position, you can *really* start to use the stuff I know. The *things* I hear. You'd be surprised what people say in front of me. I've been around so long, they don't even *see* me! Oh, I figured out a long time ago I was better off to stay right where I am and wait until I met the right guy. We're going places, Harry!"

On the way out, in the discreet vestibule, they exchanged another kiss. They had still done nothing more than kiss at lunchtime. Now and then, she slithered her stockinged foot up his pants leg, and he still got hard when she played with his hand. He desired her, but it was an unspoken agreement between them that they would wait a little longer. He wanted her, but it had not yet exploded into that kind of passion between them—it was still the controlled, shared passion of his climb in the firm.

The next week they shopped for a new suit. Gloria held out for that special shade of gray. She said it set off his coloring. No one had ever mentioned his coloring before; no one had ever taken this kind of interest in him. He made love to Marcella one night imagining it was Gloria lying beneath him. He knew it wouldn't be long before that fantasy came true.

Marcella's favorite writer was Amy Jagger, a lively redhead who often appeared on talk shows with sex experts, assuring unhappy wives that the answers to their problems were to be found in her latest novel. Her greatest success, *Zippers,* had sold five million copies a few years ago, heralding the sexually free seventies. It had been about a lusty female, also named Amy, who devoted her entire waking life and even part of her sleeping life to the pursuit and enjoyment of sexual pleasure.

Her theme—that women should be more daring—had titillated women all over America. When the book appeared in Marcella's supermarket, she had slipped it in the cart beside her groceries and spent two afternoons devouring it. The sex scenes coincided so with her own fantasies that she had experienced an orgasm with Harry that night, due entirely to Amy Jagger's writing and not to any improvement in Harry's technique. Since then, Marcella had read all Jagger's other books. If what Amy Jagger wrote about other women fiercely desiring men was true, it certainly made Marcella feel less alone.

When Sonia was three, Marcella enrolled both children in a local nursery school and herself into a writing course at an adult education center in Greenwich Village. She told Harry she was learning to type and take shorthand, carrying her portable typewriter to class each week.

Her new writing teacher was a plain, plump lady named Nancy Warner. She was in her fifties and had a constant giggle that was almost hysterical. She soon adopted Marcella as a teacher's pet. For the class, Marcella cut the sexual passages out of her stories, too embarrassed to read them aloud. The other students' work was so dull that it was hardly a compliment to be singled out from their thinly disguised family histories, memories of boring childhoods, and, in one painful case, bad science fiction written by the sole male, a blushing computer programmer.

Marcella usually shared the coffee break with Nancy, talking of writing.

"Amy *Jagger*?" Nancy sputtered when Marcella named her favorite author on one such break. "That isn't literature, Marcella," she said. "It's more like . . . soap opera."

"*Zippers* sold over five million copies!" Marcella pointed out. "She must have something!"

"Maybe that's why I don't like her," Nancy groaned. "I've been hawking *my* novel around to publishers for years. Of course, I've had some *very* complimentary turndowns."

"What's it about?" Marcella asked.

"Oh, a woman dedicated to literature who is forced to look after her invalid mother," Nancy said. "It ends with the mother dying, liberating her daughter at the age of fifty!"

"Sounds really interesting," Marcella said, thinking she now knew the whole story of Nancy's life. She walked alongside Nancy back to the classroom. "I think I know what women want to read," she said. "They like to feel their thoughts are shared by other women. That they're not alone. It's how I feel when I read Amy Jagger and that's why I love her. If I ever write a novel, I'd make it full of the longings and needs I have in *me*!"

"If you write it, I promise to give you an honest critique!" Nancy promised.

"Some magazines now use four or five short stories per

issue," Nancy told them that evening. "Let's see if we can break into that market!" She loved to use professional-sounding words and phrases like "market" and "selling manuscripts," as if they were all published authors. "We'll write a story with a particular magazine in mind. We'll submit our manuscripts and see if anyone bites! Marcella!" she called over to her. "*Yours* should be *Cosmo!*"

She walked home excitedly that night, mapping out a story based on something that had recently happened to her in Bonwit's. An attractive man had asked her advice on which purse to buy his wife. He had flirted a little as the sales-clerk wrapped the purse and Marcella had lingered for a few moments, teasing herself as well as him, before coolly saying good-bye. What if she *had* responded to his obvious interest? In her story she could discover the adventure that in real life she had denied herself. What if he had called his wife to say he'd be in town late and she had done the same with Harry? In her story, the couple booked a hotel room, signed in as husband and wife, drank a couple of cocktails and took an elevator up for two hours of passion. Her readers would see and feel every detail—the sensuous coolness of the bed's satin coverlet, the man's hairy chest against the woman, the new, welcome hands exploring her body. She wrote so the reader would actually feel she was eavesdropping inches away from the lovers twisting on the hotel sheets. Her body grew moist and wanting as she wrote *and* lived the scene. At one point, she went to the bathroom, lifted her blouse and regarded her erect nipples. Get back to the typewriter and pour the sex into the story, she told herself.

"*Marcella!*" Nancy Warner cried a week later, turning crimson as she handed back the story to Marcella in the school's canteen.

"I'm returning this to you privately, because, well, *really*!" Her embarrassment was contagious and Marcella felt her own cheeks burning. She had told herself that Nancy's opinion didn't matter; now she found she was counting on her praise.

"Should I just tear it up?" she asked Nancy.

Nancy's eyes opened wide. "You'll do no such thing!" she cried. Lowering her voice, she murmured: "It's incredibly sexy! I'm almost sorry I read it! Makes me realize what I'm missing!"

Marcella burst out laughing. "Sex isn't always that good," she consoled her.

"No, of course not!" Nancy agreed brusquely. "Fantasy, isn't it? But very effective, Marcella. Really quite shocking. All those shiny, pink cocks!" She blushed scarlet again at her own daring.

"There was only *one*!" Marcella protested.

"Yes, but referred to so *often*!" Nancy cried. She fanned herself with the story. "It happened to *you*, didn't it?" she almost begged, her eyes searching Marcella's. "It *must* have, it was so *real*! *Are* there really men like that? Men who take all that trouble to satisfy a woman?"

Marcella laughed. "Nancy, we're a *fiction*-writing class, aren't we?"

"Then you're much better than I thought!" Nancy said. "*Cosmo* should *grab* it! It's exactly their market!"

"You think so?" Marcella breathed. "My husband will kill me if it gets published!"

"That would count as justifiable homicide," Nancy said. "Unless your male character is based on him?" She peered at Marcella, frowning. But Marcella just smiled mysteriously.

They all sent in their stories the following week and she let Mark kiss her envelope for luck.

Harry had been promoted at work and had bought himself a new suit. Marcella thought it was not quite his style and was puzzled that he had not asked her to shop with him. When she listened to his work talk after dinner, it all sounded so competitive; even the terms he used—"a killing," "sharks," "carving up the competition"—were aggressive and violent. Harry took them to Central Park on weekends so the children could get some fresh air. It was late fall and Mark loved to sail his boat on the small lake near Fifth Avenue. Marcella enjoyed watching him play with his sister, so patient and protective, wanting to teach her his superior knowledge of the world.

Later, Harry would play ball with Mark, sometimes hurling the ball quite hard at him. Mark tried bravely to enjoy it, but Marcella could tell he did not like playing with his father.

One afternoon, Harry caught the side of Mark's face with the ball and Mark burst into tears, running to her.

"Be a little gentler with him!" Marcella cried.

"I'm trying to make a man out of him," Harry explained. "Men aren't gentle!" He looked on impatiently as she comforted Mark.

"Being considerate doesn't make you any less of a man, Harry," she told him. "He's only a kid, for God's sake."

"Go play with Daddy," she said lightly, giving Mark a little push toward his father. Men aren't gentle! That was so typical of Harry! If he couldn't be gentle with her in bed, how could she expect him to be gentle with his own son?

Sonia sat threading beads, very intent on getting her necklace just right. She had become a serious little girl, her great beauty somehow endowing her with magic. Harry called her his little princess, and she did indeed comport herself like one, as if allowing them to pay homage to her. Marcella made special efforts to be attentive to her, slightly guilty at having loved Mark for the one and a half years before Sonia existed. There was a deeper bond between herself and Mark, she had to admit. When Harry called Sonia "my little princess, my little girl," Mark always looked to her to say, "And Mark is Mommy's little boy."

The telephone call came on a November morning when Sonia was sick with a virus and Marcella was scrubbing the bathroom floor. She tore off one rubber glove as she ran to the phone, trying to pull off the other one as she cradled the receiver against her ear.

"Marcella Winton? Shirley Reager, Ellen Farrell's assistant," the voice said. "Miss Farrell likes your story very much and wants to use it for July's *Cosmo*. Do you have an agent? You didn't list one."

"I—no—well, I wasn't—" Marcella stammered.

"Is this your first published story? You didn't enclose credits."

"I haven't—well, of course, I've—" Marcella searched furiously for the right words as the excitement mixed with the strange unreality of hearing what she had dreamed of hearing for so long.

"Oh. Ellen will speak to you now. . . ."

Waiting, Marcella managed to snap off the tight rubber glove. She flung it to the floor, only to hear Sonia begin to cry. Torn between the fiction editor of *Cosmopolitan* and her child, Marcella raced to Sonia's room to pick up her daughter, running back to the phone holding her. Ellen Farrell was talking away, very softly, and Marcella had to press the receiver close to her ear.

". . . crying out for editing, of course," the breathy voice said, "and the ending needs tightening—you don't have to go so much into her guilt and remorse. 'In Town Late' doesn't work as a title—it sounds like a 1940s radio show. How about 'Sex Cocktails,' since they meet over drinks?"

"Oh *no*!" Marcella cried. "I don't like that at *all*!"

"We pay five hundred dollars for first authors," Ellen continued over Marcella's protest. "I'll send you a copy of the manuscript with my editing suggestions. You'll agree on most points I'm sure and—"

Sonia began to wail again.

"My little girl is home sick today," Marcella apologized. "Can I call you back?"

"No need!" Ellen said briskly. "I'll messenger your manuscript to you and we'll need it back here as soon as possible. Talk to you then. Oh, Marcella? We can buy more if you have other stories of this quality."

"I'll . . . check my files!" Marcella managed to blurt out. A brusque click ended contact with the glamorous world of publishing.

Her head was whirling. Five hundred dollars! The first money she had ever earned! A fiction editor talking to her as if she were a real author! Which, as of now, she *was*! She poured apple juice for Sonia. She could not wait to tell Nancy. Harry needn't know. He would think she had based her story on something that had happened to her and he would be more or less right!

When the manuscript arrived by messenger a month later, it looked like an exam paper marked by a viciously critical professor. Nearly every sentence had been attacked, with words like "Why?" and "How?" questioning every detail of her story.

"She must *really* know her market!" Nancy said, studying it over celebratory wine spritzers at a Village bar after class. Marcella had told Harry that the members of her typing class would be going out for pizza.

Harry sniffed suspiciously when she got home that night.

"We had a few drinks," Marcella quickly said before he could comment. He looked at her. "I said you could take a typing class. Not go out drinking with a bunch of hens."

Today she could not accept the put-down.

"Listen." She swung around to him. "I *don't* need your permission to do things."

"Just don't do them on my money!" Harry cut in. He stood to face her and she felt the suppressed rage between them like an electric current.

He made her so mad she longed to tell him her news.

"Is *that* it?" she asked, instead. "*Money?* Well, I could get a job and earn my own, you know. I type pretty well now."

He turned away. "The kids need a full-time mother. *That's* your job right now!"

She had to bite her lip to keep from bursting out that she was on the way to becoming a famous writer who'd make more money than he ever dreamed of.

"It's Mommy's story!" she cried, pulling Mark into her bedroom so that Sonia wouldn't see. The advance copy of July's *Cosmopolitan* arrived at the end of March, something she had looked forward to during the long, cold winter. "Don't say anything to Daddy," she warned Mark, opening the envelope. "It's our secret!" She flipped through the pages until she found her story, the double-paged start splashed with a color illustration of the heroine in a phone booth, anxiously dialing her husband while a rainstorm raged outside. Her name was in heavy block type under her new title, "Happy Hour." It looked so professional, and her writing seemed so important set in real type. Mark watched her as she read it through.

"Are you happy, Mommy?" he asked.

"As happy as I've ever been in my life," she said, hugging him as tears ran down her cheeks.

"Then why are you crying?" he asked.

"I don't know!" she laughed.

She bought a dozen copies of the magazine when it hit the newsstands in July, hiding them in her closet. Now that she was a published writer, her fellow students in the writing class stared at her in awe. Even the science-fiction buff approached her to ask whether she had double- or triple-spaced her manuscript.

Nancy cashed the check for her. With ten fresh fifty-dollar bills in her purse, Marcella taxied to Bergdorf Goodman, going directly to the children's department to buy some clothing for the children. She would tell Harry her mother had found it wholesale, downtown. For herself, she bought some long-needed plain black pumps that she could wear with everything. Then she found a Pucci dress, marked down, in exactly the pinks and blues she loved. Three decadently expensive bars of French soap for herself, her mother, and Nancy, and, in a nearby Doubleday, some new paperbacks and the latest Amy Jagger novel—the first hardback book she had bought. In the taxi to her mother's to pick up the children, she counted ninety dollars left.

That evening, she turned the thick white pages of Amy Jagger's new novel, *Abandoned,* behind a magazine so that Harry would not ask why she'd spent twelve dollars on a book. The back cover showed the author in white fox, staring insolently into the lens, a mischievous smile on her face. "Amy Jagger *is Abandoned*!" the ads had screamed all over town. How wonderful to have that kind of fame! And right at that moment, the name of Marcella Balducci

Winton was printed in heavy black type on hundreds of thousands of copies of *Cosmopolitan*. When *she* was emblazoned all over the cover of her first novel, she would casually walk Harry into a bookstore and show him. The expression on his face would be worth everything!

FOUR

July 1978

Marcella had three more stories published in *Cosmopolitan* over the next two years, each time getting five hundred dollars. Her secret savings account was making interest for her, and her secret file contained mail from readers telling her how much they enjoyed her writing.

But although the fiction editor had promised they'd lunch together one day, it had never happened, and Marcella had not been swept away into the glamorous world of publishing. Her biggest fan was still Nancy Warner, and she continued to attend the writing class.

Over their occasional lunches together, Nancy encouraged her to begin a novel.

"I'm trying, I'm trying!" Marcella assured her. "But it's so difficult. Maybe an entire book-length plot is beyond me, Nancy. Sometimes, I just sit with my head in my hands!"

"That's a good start!" Nancy nodded.

"Yes, but meanwhile I have housework and shopping and cooking for four to do!" Marcella groaned. "I can only work until four-thirty before I have to collect the children . . ."

And serve dinner to Harry, get Sonia ready for bed, and brush her thick dark hair as Sonia stared gravely at her in the mirror. Sometimes her daughter seemed like a beautiful stranger to her, saving all her questions and hugs and kisses for her father. Mark was the only one who seemed to know how she felt. They were mysteriously in tune with each other and she spoke to him as if he were an adult, capable of understanding everything. She had wheedled tuition fees for piano lessons from her father, promising him that Mark would continue the "Balducci tradition" of which he was so proud, and for which Mark was showing astonishing aptitude.

Her novel progressed from rough outline to first chapter. It was semiautobiographical, of course. Manuella, her main character, started off as a woman forced into a loveless marriage to a bully. There the resemblance ended. Through some strange process, Manuella developed her own traits and her own life. She was the daughter of Spanish immigrants, her fiery temperament allowing her to get away with much more than Marcella would attempt. Manuella was crazy about men from the very first chapter. In the cold room of a supermarket, with a handsome man who could have been Angelo's twin brother, Manuella was tenderly placed across a meat table and brought to a rousing climax. Marcella returned to the scene each day to add another detail, layering the audacious things her lover did until he became the ultimate fantasy stud.

The first chapter took an entire month of her precious afternoons. That meant a book might take two years! Before investing all that time, she needed a professional opinion. This was too important for Nancy to advise on. In her closet, a familiar face seemed to wink at her from the back cover of a book. Amy Jagger! She picked up the book and stared at the mischievous laughing eyes. All she could say was no, or not reply at all. Marcella stood to lose only the cost of a stamp.

She spent hours composing her letter to Amy Jagger. This cry for help to her dearest source of inspiration had to be just right.

"*Dear Ms. Jagger,*" her final draft read. (She had read that the much-divorced Amy preferred "Ms.")

You probably receive a dozen letters like this each day, but this is the first time I've written to an author— forgive me if I'm unequal to the task. Firstly, I want to thank you for the pleasure your writing has given me. Each time I finish one of your books, and I've read them all, I feel I am not alone, that there are other women out there like me. I think like you. I feel like you. Your books have really kept me going. When you write about men, I agree with what you say. The parts of a man's body your heroines say they like are the same parts that I like. The smooth side of the ribs you describe is a place my husband does not like to be touched. He pushes my hand away. I guess you can imagine the kind of marriage I have. Everything on his terms. My writing is the only part of my life that is really mine—that's why it is so precious to me. If it wasn't for our two beautiful children, I guess I would leave him.

I could not write this to anyone but you because I feel you would understand. Your humanity comes through in your books. You sound like you love men but you also respect and like women. I am trying to write a novel for other women. I think they will appreciate my book, although I cannot compare myself to you. The only work I've had published is some short stories in Cosmopolitan *magazine. I don't have the guts, discipline, or* time *to write an entire novel without getting some encouragement. If that encouragement came from you, it would be the most wonderful, important thing that ever happened in my life. Will you read the enclosed chapter? It's all I've written of my novel so far. Please tell me if I have any hope of becoming a novelist. Be honest, I can take it! And I'll appreciate your help for the rest of my life. With sincere thanks,*

Marcella B. Winton

She mailed the letter to Amy Jagger care of her publisher, Volumes, Inc. Then she tried to forget about it because just writing it had helped.

The letter arrived two weeks later, "Amy Jagger" expensively engraved in navy raised type on the gray envelope. Marcella sat down on the sofa and ripped open the envelope. She hesitated before unfolding the heavy paper, imagining the worst—a printed announcement stating Ms. Jagger did not enter into personal correspondence. But as she unfolded the letter, she saw at once it was neither printed nor a brush-off. She read it through twice, each time her heart beating faster.

"*Dear Mrs. Winton,*" Amy had written.

> *Oh, to hell with it, I'm going to call you Marcella because I feel as if we're old friends. In answer to your first comment, yes, I do get a dozen letters a day from readers, but not many of them as warm and sweet as yours. And definitely none enclosing writing as interesting. In answer to your second question, yes, you have talent! Damn it, I'm jealous of your talent, Marcella! Who taught you to write like that? I have a hunch you are self-taught, am I right? You have one of the sexiest imaginations and ways of writing about sex I've ever encountered. And I'm talking Henry Miller, John Updike, Erica Jong, myself! In the part where they're in the supermarket, I could smell the guy's cologne, feel the sawdust under my soles on that cold-room floor, see those awful whole pigs hanging from the ceiling! Wow! What kind of woman are you? You write almost nothing about yourself! Dump that husband of yours one day and let's eat, drink, laugh, and talk! In the meantime, I'm acting as unofficial agent and passing on your chapter to my Volumes editor, Scott MacEvoy. I'll probably regret it for the rest of my life, or maybe if he sounds interested, I'll turn official agent and reap my ten percent? You didn't enclose your home number, so here's mine. Call me and let's make a date to discuss your writing career—and you! Love, Amy.*

"*Mark!*" Marcella screamed.

He ran into the living room. "She's written to me,

Mark!" she cried, waving the letter at him. "The lady on the book has written!"

He stared up at her. "Is it good?" he asked.

"She wants to meet me!" Marcella cried, hugging him. "Oh, *Mark!*"

"Lunch! Lunch! *Lunch!*" Amy Jagger cried when Marcella finally found the courage to call her the following week. "Somewhere very ritzy! On me, of course! I've never discovered anyone before and I intend to make the most of it. I may even wear a hat! Do you have any more chapters to bring with you?"

Marcella hesitated. "I only wrote that one. You see, it's my first novel and—"

"But *not* the last!" Amy prophesied. "Le Cirque?" she suggested. "One-thirty Wednesday? We'll make a grand entrance! Get used to the best places, Marcella! Nothing's gonna stop you now!"

Marcella hung up, giddy. Everything sounded so easy! Lunch at Le Cirque! Nothing was going to stop her? She could think of a dozen things that might. The days until Wednesday seemed stretched out, full of little traps that slowed her down. She had to sidestep the traps adroitly; when a fellow mother could not fetch Marcella's children from school, she enlisted the help of another.

"I'm planning a little surprise for my husband," she lied.

By Tuesday night, her head was whirling with plans—the conversation she would have with Amy, the way she would present her life so that it did not seem too hopeless. When Harry arrived home that night, he was very excited. Some men on his floor had made a killing on the stock market that day.

"They used inside info," he told her. "And you know what they walked off with?" He got a can of beer from the fridge. "Half a million bucks!"

"Are they allowed to do that?" she asked.

"Allowed?" he repeated, and laughed. "Everyone does it, Marce. . . ." He straddled a kitchen chair, taking a swig of beer.

"What about the days when they *lose* half a million?" she asked him. "Do they brag about that?"

He shook his head. "They don't risk losing half a million. These guys act on information. Someone owes someone a favor, so they make a quick telephone call advising them to buy shares in a firm that's about to be taken over or about to release great sales figures or something. It doesn't harm anyone and it makes everybody happy."

"Don't they ever get caught?" she asked.

He shrugged, finishing off his beer in one long gulp. "Now and then the police do a sweep and pick up a few jerks to make an example of. They get some poor sap who doesn't have enough favors due . . ."

"Well, don't *you* ever do it, Harry," she said. "Let your colleagues and their greedy little wives lie awake at night wondering if they'll get caught."

"Oh Marce." He sighed, looking at her. "You still think small."

"I think *safe*," she corrected him. "Your money wouldn't be much use to you in jail, would it?"

He made a mock repentant face, getting another beer from the fridge.

"Listen," he said, turning to her as he ripped off the top. "I have all the advantages at the office. They're the perks. They *expect* us to use them, and it'd be just plain dumb *not* to!"

She continued to prepare dinner, only half listening. He was in the mood for a discussion, and she had other things to think about.

If Amy Jagger was right about her writing talent, she was about to be swept into a fabulous new world. Publishers, editors, and bookstore owners would court her with happy lights in their eyes. She could finally acknowledge that little spark within her that had always told her she was different. She could hardly get to sleep that night.

Next morning, she walked the four blocks to the children's new public school, checked for the third time with her neighbor about picking them up and taking them back to play with their friends, and then ran home for a soak in the tub. A new pink lipstick was carefully applied along with extra makeup for her eyes; the Pucci dress slithered over her body, slightly slimmer since the crash diet she'd begun the day of receiving Amy Jagger's letter. She checked herself in the mirror: face, hose, dress. The modest, neat apartment was very quiet at twelve-thirty. She gave it a long, careful look before leaving, as if she were departing on a long voyage. She had a sudden premonition that after this lunch nothing would ever be the same.

"Miss Jagger's guest? Of course! Welcome to Le Cirque!" The maitre d' beckoned with a smile on his face, and Marcella's worried expression relaxed into a smile too. She had sat so carefully on the subway so as not to crease her Pucci. She had envisioned a receiving line of flunkeys at Le Cirque, looking down their noses as she climbed steep, slippery flights of steps. She had seen herself tripping at the very top or finding her dress had worked its way up her buttocks. But there were no steps, and she was being welcomed as if she belonged here. She checked her appearance in a large mirror as she passed and thanked God that this was one of those days when she looked good. Her long chestnut hair flowed behind her as she followed the maitre d', her figure still pleasingly rounded, the bosom and derriere proclaiming her a real woman for the men who liked real women. Evidently, there were plenty lunching that day, intrigued enough to glance up from their lunching companions to stare at her. In this humming, chic restaurant, they were more used to anorexic society ladies. People here were different; glossy, careless, arrogant, they toyed with their food, pretending to keep their eye on their partners while still roaming the room.

In the center of the restaurant, the maitre d' came to a sudden halt, having evidently reached the border of his territory. He beckoned to a waiter, handing her over to this lesser mortal, bidding Marcella, "Enjoy your lunch!"

She followed her new guide, looking around her. Everyone was chattering, laughing, watching, and flirting. Marcella felt a thrill run through her: this world was already inspiring her. The more she saw of it, the more she would spill out her feelings. She wanted to amaze these cool, slightly bored people whose idea of suffering was to get a bad table at Le Cirque.

"Here she is, Miss Jagger!" the waiter delivered her up, past a flower arrangement more luxurious and exotic than any she had ever seen, to a table where a tiny redheaded woman sat.

"This is Marcella?" a throaty voice gasped, and Amy Jagger jumped to her feet and ran around the table, arms outstretched. *"Darling!"* she cried.

She was smaller, finer, and older than in the Scavullo photographs on her covers. She hugged Marcella tightly for several seconds, clouds of perfume overcoming Marcella, as well as the surprising strength of this skinny body. Finally, Amy thrust her at arm's length to look her up and down.

"Absolutely gorgeous!" she cried. She peered at Marcella's hair. "Is that your own color? Your skin is pure Renoir! C'mon, darling, get your butt into a chair, I want to hear all about you!"

Blushing, feeling almost unfairly beautiful, Marcella slipped into the chair held by a patient waiter.

Amy sat too, leaning her chin on her fists, devouring Marcella with her emerald eyes. Those eyes were all one saw at first; only later, when Marcella tore her gaze from their mischievous greenness, did she notice the fine, crinkly laugh lines around them. Amy's ivory skin was the type that never tanned, the light dusting of freckles adding a homespun, little-girl touch at odds with the extreme sophistication. The frizzy, fiery red hair was too red to be natural and the slim body boasted a waist that a man's hands could easily span and probably often did.

"Food!" Amy cried, handing her a menu. Marcella couldn't have felt less like eating. Over the huge menu, she continued to study her new mentor. Amy wore a burgundy suede jacket, curving to her body, her feet exquisitely shod in matching pumps. Her hands sported blood-red, perfect nails. A fuzzy white angora sweater framed her face in a cloudy, luxurious haze. Her refined appearance made the hoarse voice with its hint of Brooklyn even more unexpected. Amy Jagger had long since shed her inhibitions—if there had ever been any.

The waiter filled Marcella's tulip-shaped goblet with champagne.

"To my new friend!" Amy proposed. They clinked crystal and Marcella sipped.

"Mmm . . ." The bubbles expired dryly down her

throat. "Is this French?" she asked, and Amy nodded. "The first *real* champagne I've ever tasted!" Marcella admitted, draining her glass thirstily.

Amy studied her as the waiter refilled their glasses.

"Yeah, it's a lot of fun getting used to the good stuff," she said approvingly. "*I* started out in life very modestly, Marcella. My father was lucky if there was beer in the fridge, forget Moët et Chandon! But I knew I had a brain! And I knew I had a pussy! They've been fighting it out together ever since!" She gave a little high-pitched scream and Marcella burst out laughing, too.

"Grilled salmon!" Amy cried to the waiter.

"I'll have the same," Marcella agreed with relief.

"This is such a treat for me," Amy told Marcella, touching her hand, as the waiter scurried off. "I love to meet new people!"

Marcella glanced at the third place setting. "Who is this for?" she asked.

"Scott MacEvoy, my editor, talked his way into this lunch," Amy said. "But I said *only* for dessert!"

"And why is he coming, Amy?" Marcella asked.

Amy raised her eyebrows. "Any man who read that first chapter would be curious to meet you! Scott can't wait to settle our bet!"

"Which bet?"

Amy giggled. "On what you'd look like, Marcella! I said you'd be pretty and he said you wrote sexy to compensate for your homeliness. So he owes me twenty-five bucks before we even begin to talk about the book!"

"What did he think of my writing?" Marcella asked hesitantly.

"We . . . ell . . ." Amy drawled. "If his reaction was anything at all like mine, he'll walk in with the biggest hard-on Le Cirque has ever seen!"

Amy's language and the champagne made Marcella giggle. Soon she found herself telling Amy all about herself. Amy was a wonderful listener, her green eyes opening as if she had never heard such fascinating things. Marcella vowed to use that technique—it made the speaker feel so good. By the time their food arrived, she felt as sophisticated as her new friend.

"So you're unsatisfied with your husband." Amy nodded. "*I* write my best when I'm horny, too."

Marcella smiled. "It goes way past feeling horny, Amy. This is like a great empty gap in me forever crying out for attention. When a man gives me that look, I've had it! *I* want *him* as much as he wants *me*! That's why it's better if I just stay home and write."

"*Why* is it better?" Amy cried, slicing into her fish. "You think that husband of yours isn't screwing every girl in sight?"

"Well . . ." She tried to eat her delicious salmon but she had no appetite. "Harry's marital demands are pretty much every night. If he was fooling around, I don't think—"

"Forget it!" Amy cut in. "My second husband fooled around like crazy and *he* still touched base every night! Of course"—she leaned her head nearer Marcella's—"I *loved* having my base touched!"

They had finished the champagne, and Amy signaled for another bottle. By now, Marcella felt she had been cut adrift from all anchors to reality and was floating several feet above the carpeted floor.

"Amy, I don't know if I've been blessed or cursed, but I seem to have a greater sensuality than other women I know," she blurted out. "I'm scared to even let it out! If I wasn't with Harry, I'd run wild probably! I seem to *feel* things more than other people do . . ."

"Absolutely." Amy nodded as if this were perfectly normal. "And hundreds of thousands of women will cheerfully pay three ninety-five to vicariously experience those feelings! As a writer, you will be paid to go through the mill for women who can't find the energy or time to do it!"

Their plates were swept away and the waiter proffered dessert menus.

Amy leaned toward Marcella. "Let's talk business before Scott gets here. I want to act as your agent, Marcella."

Marcella faltered. "I'm not too sure what an agent does," she said.

Amy ordered coffee for them. "I would negotiate with the publisher for the price of the book," she told Marcella. "That means getting you an advance payment on your royalties. I'd inspect your contract with a magnifying glass, reading all the fine print. Haggle over royalties on the New Zealand and Hebrew editions. Stuff like that!"

Marcella nodded. "But why would you do all that for me?"

"Because I've been an unpaid agent for years!" Amy explained. "Unpublished writers are always sending me manuscripts which—if they're any good—I've passed on to agents or editors. You know how jealous writers are? If we were rivals, I'd want to scratch your eyes out! This way, we get to stay friends *and* I get ten percent!"

"It's okay with me!" Marcella agreed. "I'd be honored to have you as an agent."

She suddenly looked up to see a tall, bearded man standing by their table. He was in his late thirties and his trim dark beard was several shades darker than his blond hair. He stared at Marcella with piercing hazel eyes. He wore a navy suit with a bright pink silk knit tie. Very deliberately, he took out his wallet and extracted a twenty and a five.

"You win," he said, handing them to Amy.

Marcella burst out laughing, feeling her cheeks flush.

"Scott, meet Marcella Balducci Winton, my discovery and client!" Amy said. Scott leaned over Marcella's hand and kissed it.

"I've never done that before," he confessed. "But you're the type of lady who demands to have her hand kissed!"

"What about *me*, Scott?" Amy wailed. "What do *I* demand to have kissed?"

"Your ass," Scott said grimly, sitting down. "Excuse me, Marcella, but Amy likes her colleagues Rabelaisian!"

Marcella smiled, a little embarrassed because he was so good-looking. Why couldn't Amy's editor have been a dour, intellectual professor type with thick rimless spectacles? Scott glowed with health and gleamed with good grooming, and his all-American, clean-cut features were perfectly offset by the raffish beard. His amused, sexy gaze returned to her as Amy chattered.

"Marcella's agreed to my acting as her agent, Scott!" Amy told him proudly.

"Really?" He frowned. "Since when are *you* in the agenting racket?"

Amy placed a protective arm around Marcella. "Since half an hour ago!" she said.

The waiter distributed dessert menus and Scott peered into his.

"I *only* want the chocolate mousse if it's hazardous to your health," Amy told the waiter. "Share it with me, Marcella?"

"Fresh fruit salad," Scott ordered. "And a *large* espresso. I see I'm going to need all my wits about me!"

Amy lit a cigarette.

"It may have escaped your notice, Scott," she told him, "now that you're editor in chief, but I've been my own agent for years! There's nothing about the book business I don't know," she boasted.

"That's what I'm afraid of," Scott muttered.

Amy poured him champagne and he held his glass to Marcella's.

"To your new career as a writer," he proposed. "And to yours as an agent!" he said to Amy. He was giving Marcella the look that undid her. The wine hit her hard and suddenly. When Scott's knee nudged hers, she did not move away. Warmth from his body spread to her.

"Are you set up to be an agent?" Scott asked Amy.

"I have Volumes panting for her, don't I?" Amy baited him. "What else do I need?"

Scott made a few noisy pants and Marcella found even those exciting.

"I'm not even sure there *is* a whole novel," she told them. "I've written a chapter, but that doesn't mean I'll be able to finish it. . . ."

"Ve agents haff *vays* of making you finish it!" Amy said.

"And we pay your royalties in advance, so you're duty-bound to finish it!" Scott said.

The chocolate mousse arrived in time to give her a little sugary energy and to allow Amy to mime a very convincing orgasm from the tiny spoonful she tried.

After dessert, Amy sprang up, marching Marcella off to the ladies' lounge. "Whaddya think?" she asked out of the corner of her mouth as they entered the mirrored quietness. "Sexy, no? For an editor?"

"Too good to be true," Marcella groaned.

"Mm-hm." Amy stared into the mirror. "And one of the

conditions of my being agent is that I'll want to know exactly what happens between you two!"

Marcella watched her fluffing her hair.

"What do you expect to happen?" she asked.

Amy winked. "If I know Scott, he'll invite you back to his office for a meeting after this," she said. "I only hope he has a sofa by now."

Marcella felt an excited jump in her stomach. "But—" She faltered, "I won't know how to handle someone like him! Come with us, Amy, please!"

Amy gave her a withering look. "Don't you want a close, chummy relationship with your editor, darling?" she asked.

"I don't know!" Marcella said. "*Do* I?"

Amy helped open the door. "It's absolutely essential," she said brusquely.

At three-thirty Scott invited her back to his office, as predicted. "*Without* Amy," he said firmly.

Marcella excused herself, heart pounding, to call her neighbor and make sure the children could stay with her until six-thirty.

Amy ran off after kisses and promises to get together very soon, hissing, "I'll call you tomorrow!" in Marcella's ear.

Chattering nervously, she walked alongside Scott to the Sixth Avenue block where Volumes occupied ten floors.

"I don't think I want a contract or an advance payment." She laughed. "I'm frightened it will stop me from writing. I know it's silly, but—"

His hand lightly touched her elbow to guide her into the building. The elevator was empty and he turned to her as the doors closed, giving her such a wondering, frank look of inquiry that she felt her pulse quicken. He glanced down at the front of his pants.

"See what you're doing to me?" he asked. She kept her eyes on his, saying nothing, fighting all her impulses.

"Hitchcock said the best woman of all was high-bred and elegant, but behaved like a whore in bed," he said. "Do you agree?"

"Whores in bed only spread their legs, don't they?" She tried to laugh. "They're only earning their living."

"What would *your* heroine do if a man wanted her?" he asked.

"She wouldn't spread her legs until the last possible moment," she told him. "She'd make the man *beg* for it!"

"Is that what you like?" He leaned his head closer. "Men to beg you?"

She shook her head. "Not me. My heroine."

Her body was starting to tremble, to burn, then turn icy in a matter of seconds. The elevator stopped, the doors opened, and Scott guided her through a maze of cubicles and offices. She eyed his broad shoulders as he strode ahead, then ushered her through a door with his name on it.

"I'm in a meeting!" he instructed the secretary in the outer office.

He closed the door of his office behind her, locking it and leaning back. The large room was gray carpeted. As Amy had warned, there was no sofa, but there were lots of plants, a huge desk, and a couple of large flower arrangements. The windows framed the tops of neighboring skyscrapers.

"Is that what you call it?" Marcella queried. "A meeting?"

Scott approached her. The Pucci dress was clinging to her warm body and all she wanted was for him to remove it, to lose herself in that feeling her whole body cried out for.

"When a man and a woman meet, it's a meeting, isn't it?" he asked, his voice low.

She tried to smile cynically but he had already placed his hand gently between her legs and a low moan escaped her. She wanted sex too much to be able to smile.

Even if she had wanted to turn back now, her body would not have allowed her to. After the glamorous lunch, she wanted the rest of this day's soaring ride, and the champagne proved a willing assistant. She wanted his naked body, clean, wide, sweet smelling, over her. Wanted that well-trimmed, bearded chin between her legs, his tongue flicking out to touch her where she now ached to be touched.

His eyes tried to read her thoughts as he watched her like a man with a wild animal. She could not stand the suspense and sank to the floor, kneeling before him, ridiculously vulnerable. He knelt, too, leaning toward her. She opened her mouth to his. His hand slithered up her silk dress. Nothing was as important as this first touch. She moved her knees apart so that her sex was available to him and he slipped his fingers beneath the silk panties to hesitantly touch the very core of her being. Her breath came in short gasps now, accompanying the pleasure. She stood for him to pull her dress carefully over her head. When he removed her bra and panties, he knelt before her and studied her body. Her breasts awaited his mouth, their nipples almost painfully erect and sensitive. He buried his face between them, pressing their points against his closed eyelids. He took off his clothes and she removed her earrings, watch, and ring. She wanted nothing to touch her naked body but his.

Each time she had sex with a new man she found out new things about herself. Now she realized she enjoyed being looked at when she was naked, enjoyed watching his obvious reaction to her curves as his sex slowly moved into its straining, stiff erection. Lying down on the floor, on his back, he whispered: "Lower yourself very gently onto me, so that your tits touch me first . . ."

His instructions, and his language, caused a new leap of desire within her. She spread-eagled herself above him and slowly lowered herself so that the tips of her breasts just hovered over his chest, trying to match up their nipples, shivering as his hair tickled her. His sex stabbed between her legs and she took it in her hand, ready for him to enter her, make her feel what she had missed feeling for so long. She guided him into her body, welcoming him, relishing the wonder of a man becoming part of her gently, exactly as she wanted it, slowly, carefully, her breath held as they joined. Scott remained motionless inside her for a few moments, groaning. When he gently rolled atop her without leaving her body, she *wanted* the deep plunges he began to take into her, again and again, his chest grazing her, her back arched over his strong arm. He made each plunge release another sob of pleasure inside her, and she silently urged him to increase the pressure, to crush her with his desire. She pushed back at him, crying out, as he led her to the very pinnacle of wanting, and she hovered, her mouth soundlessly open, eyes tightly shut, as she felt she was about to be gorgeously, generously satiated. Seconds later, they climaxed together, her body unbelievingly accepting this intense wave of pleasure, his bearded face rubbing her cheek and almost hurting as her heartbeat raced to accompany the sensations that wracked her, leaving her trembling with pleasure.

Slowly, the thick pile of the rug against her brought her back to reality. She gazed at his handsome face, his eyes closed as he relished the last moments of their loving. Could she fall in love with a man like this? She looked down at his hands. Of course, he was wearing a wedding band—but so was she!

She knew she would be unable to find a cab, that when she found one, the journey home would run into heavy traffic and red lights all the way. That Harry, far from arriving home conveniently late that night, would leave work early for the first time. She was right on all counts.

"Where the hell have *you* been?" Harry cried, when she got home. The neighbor had finally delivered the children at seven and they, sensing Harry's anger, had burst into tears on finding only him at home. Her mind worked fast as she kicked off her shoes, gathered the children in her arms, soothing them.

"I was uptown and I suddenly felt dizzy on the train," she told him. "I thought I'd faint, so I got off. Then I couldn't face getting back on a hot train again, so I had to wait ages to find a taxi . . ." It was the truth, she *had* been dizzy. From sex!

"Why are you so dolled up?" Harry asked. "When did you buy that dress?"

"Today!" she lied, taking the children into their room. "Do you like it?" she called back gaily over her shoulder. Two professional people had told her she would be successful, rich, acclaimed. A handsome man had made glorious love to her and satisfied her body utterly and completely. She no longer needed to be frightened of Harry.

"Why didn't you get the children ready for bed?" she asked, as he followed her into their room, watching. "Sonia, at least! You know what she's like when she's—"

"I've had a helluva day!" Harry turned away angrily. "There was a crisis in the silver market and we lost a lot of money. I don't know how to handle these kids when they start screaming. We thought you'd been in an accident or something. . . ." he said gruffly.

"Start dinner for us, will you?" she called out casually, undressing Sonia. "The oven needs turning on, that's all . . ." At least she had thought ahead enough to prepare something to simply warm up.

Mark looked accusingly at her as she pulled on Sonia's pajamas.

"We thought you were going to leave us!" he suddenly blurted out.

"Now why would you think that?" she asked him, placing Sonia, half asleep, in bed and turning to him. He sat, legs dangling, on a chest of drawers, his eyes sparkling from all the shed tears. "You're going to be eight soon, darling, and I want you to act like a big boy."

He held on to her as she hugged him, twisting his feet around her back as she carried him into the kitchen. "How could you possibly think I'd leave any of you?" she whispered into his hair as they walked. "Especially *you*!" She hugged him again. It was exactly with such special words that she bound him to her.

"I like the colors of your dress," he told her as they entered the kitchen where Harry sat glowering.

"Yes?" She set Mark down. "Daddy doesn't seem to care for it . . ."

She bent to the oven. "Oh Harry, that's *much* too high!" Make him feel in the wrong, she thought. Don't give him a chance to attack.

After dinner, she managed to lock herself in the bathroom, her tiny haven of privacy.

She took a warm bath, soaking the passion from her body, reliving that incredible afternoon. It had been like being on the moon. And she had to hug it all to herself, to say nothing at all about it to Harry.

Next morning, as she returned from taking the children to school, the phone rang.

"Was he good?" Amy's voice crackled across Manhattan. "Or did he behave himself? Did he talk about a contract? Were any figures mentioned?"

Marcella took a deep breath. This must be the price for

joining a sophisticated segment of society—intimate questions, what her mother would call plain nosiness.

"He made a little pass," she lied to Amy. "I told you there's no room in my life for an affair, didn't I? I got into enough trouble for having lunch!"

"A jealous husband, too?" Amy groaned. "Oh, I can't bear it. I want you to be my new friend. I want to play Pygmalion and see you get all the goodies due to you. It'll be such fun to watch someone like you go through the same things I did: I can enjoy it all again vicariously. Scott was very impressed, so whip that outline into shape and let's get some money out of him while he's hot for you. Give yourself a deadline of a month! And call me if you need someone to talk over the plot with!"

"I'll do my best," Marcella promised. "And thank you, Amy, for the most wonderful lunch of my life!"

"Oh, there will be lots of those, darling!" Amy rang off.

Scott called her later to ask when they'd be seeing each other.

"You're married," she said.

"So?" he asked. "Isn't everybody?"

"Yes, well, I don't fool around . . ." she said idiotically.

"Really?" Scott laughed. "You could have fooled me."

"So you liked it?" she couldn't resist asking.

"What do you think?" he asked hoarsely. "An editor's life isn't usually quite so uninhibited. Usually we just edit."

"That's the problem, Scott," she said. "*I'm* not uninhibited. That was the champagne. Two bottles!"

"Too bad," he said. "But we will be seeing each other, Marcella? Amy tells me you'll have an outline for me within a month. We'll talk before then, I hope?"

When she hung up, she decided to invite her parents for her own secret celebration dinner that weekend. She would make lasagna the way her father liked it, would drink lots of Chianti, and maybe afterward, through the blur, Harry could douse some of the fire that now raged in her body.

Saturday's dinner was festive. Even Harry seemed in a good mood and they laughed and drank and ate the way the Balduccis had done on Saturday nights at Aldo's dinners.

As usual, Ida jumped up the moment the dessert was over to wash the dishes, even though Marcella begged her to leave them for her to do. But housework was the only thing Ida knew how to give. After cuddling her grandchildren and tucking them in bed, it was her way of saying, "This is what we women do best. . . ." A part of Marcella always rebelled against it.

Aldo was getting Harry to explain what "futures" were, and Marcella was listening, having always wanted to understand the mysteries of pork belly and orange juice futures.

Ida impatiently grabbed an armful of dishes.

"Wait, Ma." She patted her mother's hand. "I'd just like to hear this." She was always amazed at how Harry came alive when the subject was money or his work. Had she made him feel so inadequate as a man that the only way he could feel important was through money?

Ida began a series of treks out to the kitchen, each time taking on a bigger load. Finally, Marcella rose to help her.

"There's a female liberation movement, you know," she half joked by the sink. "Women don't always do the dishes while the men talk. Sometimes, the men even *help*!"

Ida shook her head. "Always wanting to be different, Marcella, huh?" she said, sending a torrent of hot soapy water over a pan.

Marcella shook her head and took her old place at her mother's left, drying dishes. She longed to tell someone of her triumphant week, but she knew Ida would not approve. Her father would be proud of her if he knew, and when they rejoined "the men," she crouched beside him and gave him a hug.

"Great dinner," he complimented her.

Before they left, Harry took Ida to see the sleeping children.

Her father approached her. "You have two beautiful children. And Harry's a good man," he told her, slipping her a twenty-dollar bill. "Here, buy them something. . . ."

"Thank you, Dad." She kissed him. "Mark's doing really well with his piano lessons."

Aldo nodded. "We have music in our blood."

She gazed at him, her eyes brimming, longing to tell him that her life was about to change, in ways even she didn't know yet. That she would be rocking the boat, making waves, doing all the things she had been brainwashed not to do.

"Two angels," Ida said, returning, arranging a shawl around her even on this warm night.

Marcella poured out the last of the wine and swallowed it. It was too sweet, not nearly as magical as that French champagne she and Amy had managed to get through last week. Last *week*? It seemed like several lifetimes ago!

Harry offered to walk her parents home, but they insisted they would be all right.

"Then call me when you get home," Marcella said. She closed the door on them with a small sigh and then put away the dishes.

In the bathroom, she looked at her naked body in the mirror. Stay in shape, she reminded herself. Stay trim. She examined her breasts, trying to see them as Scott had seen them for the first time, wondering how sexy they had looked.

Harry was lying on their bed in his underwear, waiting. He no longer even tried to get her into a romantic mood. His body, clad in underwear, lying outside of the bed-clothes, simply meant they would be having sex. She went along with it because he could be unpleasant if she refused. It was simpler to do it. She dabbed perfume on her neck, breasts, and arms. She would remember Scott and the excitement they had sparked off in each other, the instructions he had given her on how to lower her naked body to his. She began by trying to lie atop Harry that way, but he soon reversed their positions, crushing her with his weight. She tried to keep her fantasy going. Scott's trim, tanned body. The feel of his beard against her. The way he had touched her hesitantly at first and how she had opened herself to him. . . . Harry pulled down his underpants and, as usual, he entered her before she was ready, hurting. She tried to accommodate him, moving gently against him. He was panting in her face, grunting noisily, when the phone next to the bed rang shrilly, startling them. She realized it had been a long time since her parents had left; they had taken over an hour to call. She reached out for the receiver.

"Okay?" she asked.

A stranger's voice informed her he worked for the

nearby hospital and that her parents had just been brought into the emergency room. She sat up, pushing Harry off her.

"Why? What's wrong with them?" she cried.

"They've been involved in an accident . . ." the man said.

"Oh my God! How serious is it?" she asked.

"You'd better come right over!"

A car, driven by a drunk driver who was now dead, had swerved and mounted the sidewalk, crushing her parents against a wall. Her father was brain-dead, they told her. She watched her mother, hooked up to tubes and bottles, fighting for her life, unconscious. She held Harry's hand tightly, paralyzed, unable to cry. At three in the morning, she signed permission for the doctors to turn off her father's life-support. One word only sounded in her like a cry on some empty cold night: never, *never*! It cried out inside her, over and over again, tearing her brain with its insistence, searing her soul forever! Through her numbness she could feel only one conviction: that this was another punishment for her sins.

FIVE

November 1978

She was only dimly aware of attending her father's funeral, so deep was the pain. The confusing part was everyone being so nice to her, not realizing that she was to blame. She concentrated on her children's clothing; it suddenly seemed enormously important that they be immaculate, as if only then would their appearance be a mark of respect to her father. Through the long walk to the cemetery, during the service and the reception, she could not look at the children without the thought that their grandfather would never see them growing up, playing the piano, or dancing, carrying on what he had half jokingly called "the Balducci tradition."

When it was over, she left the children with Harry and rushed back to the hospital to be at her mother's side. Ida had not yet been told of her husband's death and slept through most of the day. Marcella got home late that night, exhausted. She found Harry sitting in the kitchen.

"The kids are asleep." He looked up at her.

"Did you eat?" she asked. He shook his head. She heated some soup for them. He caught at her hand as she put out some crackers.

"I liked him a lot better than my own father, Marce," he told her.

"I know," she nodded, serving the soup. "He liked you, too. He felt you were the son he never had."

She spooned the soup to her mouth, not tasting it. Now and then they caught each other's eyes, but she was unable to put into words all her confused thoughts. Later, she just wanted to stare at the television, thinking of nothing.

In bed that night, she thought: this is why marriages fail —one partner not communicating with the other. Sometimes it's me, sometimes Harry. There is just never a time we *both* feel the same, when we *both* want to share something—a thought, a touch. Harry turned out the light and, perhaps out of respect for her grief, kept to his side of the bed. She wanted to tell him that this was when she needed to be held in his arms, protected, have him reassure her that now *he* would look out for her, now *he* would be her father. She was unable to do so. How she hated marriage! How it had failed her. She cried herself silently to sleep, the hurt like a steel ball in her belly.

The only positive action she could make was to spend as much time as possible at the hospital with her mother as she recovered. For the first week, she fielded her mother's anxious questions about Aldo, saying, "*You* get better, first. Then we'll talk about Daddy." "But can't I see him? How bad is he hurt?" Ida cried. Finally Marcella had to lie and say he was fighting for his life. When the doctors decided her mother was ready to learn the truth, Harry offered to break it to her, but Marcella felt it was her duty. That afternoon, she took her mother's hand.

"Ma, I've got some very sad news about Dad for you," she began. "Are you ready for it?"

Ida stared at the tears running down Marcella's face, her grip tightening on her daughter's hand.

"He's dead, huh?" she asked. Marcella nodded. Ida nodded her head several times, as if trying to convince herself. Then they cried together.

"I wasn't as good to him as I should have been," Ida sobbed, turning her face away. "I could never forgive him . . ."

"For what, Ma?" Marcella asked her gently.

But Ida shook her head, her lips tightly pressed together.

"Some other woman, probably. What else could it be?" Amy guessed. Four months after the accident, she sat opposite Marcella in the salmon-pink coffee shop of the hospital, absurdly glamorous in bright green suede, an obvious attempt, like the pink coffee shop, to be cheerful. She touched Marcella's arm. "Darling, I know it's hell to lose a parent, but you seem to be taking this so badly. Were you *so* close to him?"

Marcella nodded. "Pretty close. He was a loving father, a sweet man." She accepted the cigarette Amy offered, lighting it. "That's not what's tearing me apart, Amy."

"What *is*?" Amy asked.

Marcella regarded her friend. Amy had proved surprisingly supportive, keeping her company through the long vigils as Ida underwent three separate leg operations, a comforting reminder of the lush uptown life that now seemed so out of reach.

"She is improving, isn't she?" Amy prompted.

"So the doctors say." Marcella nodded.

"Doctors!" Amy sniffed, gazing around them. "Remind me to avoid this place if I ever get sick. No one here looks anything *like* Richard Chamberlain! I guess there's nothing I can tell Scott?" she tried. "About the book?"

Marcella shrugged. "He sent such gorgeous flowers. I wrote him a thank-you card. I haven't written one word of the outline," she confessed. "Has he said anything about me?"

"Apart from the usual inquiries, no. *Why?*" Amy leaned forward urgently. "*Did* something happen between you two?"

Marcella took a long draw on her cigarette.

"Are you going to tell me, Marcella?" Amy cried.

Marcella shrugged, glancing at her. "Why not?" she said, finally. "It's as if it all happened to someone else, anyway. We made love. After lunch that day. In his office."

"My God!" Amy cried. "Any good?"

"*Yes!*" Marcella turned urgently to her. "*Yes,* don't you understand? It was *wonderful*! God, Amy, I hadn't had sex like that in *years*! He's not even my type, but he wanted *me,* and that alone was enough to—"

"I know." Amy nodded. "So what's the problem? You didn't fall in love with the guy?"

Marcella clutched Amy's hand and stared at her. "Will you think I'm bananas if I tell you something? Something I honestly believe?"

"Of course not!" Amy said indignantly.

"Then *swear*!" Marcella insisted. "Swear you won't!"

Amy shook her head unbelievingly. "Okay! I swear I won't think you're bananas! What *is* this?"

Marcella stared into the dregs of her coffee.

"The first time I cheated on Harry I felt I was punished for it," she said in a low voice. "By losing my baby. Scott was the second time I cheated and I lost my father. Maybe it's nothing but guilt, but if anything happened to my children, I'd—"

"*Marcella!*" Amy put her arm around her. "Don't talk yourself into this divine retribution crap! Am I friends with Billy Graham or with a sensual, earthy female who writes the sexiest scenes I've ever—"

"*Wrote!*" Marcella cut her off. "I'm not sure I can do it anymore."

"Why?" Amy's eyes blazed. "Scared you'll be struck down by lightning? *Really!*" She thrust Marcella away, glaring. "You don't need God to punish you, Marcella! You do a great job of punishing yourself!"

"But *why* do I do it?" Marcella pleaded. "I *do* think women deserve sexual equality, freedom, and all that!"

"It must be your Catholic upbringing, darling," Amy said. "Don't be so hard on yourself! *I* believe in you, whatever happens!"

Marcella reached for Amy's hand and pressed it. "Thank you, Amy," she said. She fumbled for a tissue and dabbed her eyes. "I *have* to survive all this, and I *will* write my book, somehow! I'll find the strength when my mother gets out of this place and I don't have to keep running to and fro."

Amy passed her a Chanel compact and Marcella powdered her nose.

"Mmm, this smells so rich! Of a different life!" she sighed.

"You could have the same life!" Amy told her. "Just write the book! Christ, if God zapped everyone who cheated on their mates, I wouldn't know a soul and we'd have a near-zero population by now. A drunk driver killed your father, Marcella. It's as simple and tragic as that."

Ida was discharged from the hospital a few weeks later. She moved in with Marcella and Harry, obliging the children to share a room. Ida could walk very stiffly using crutches and she had the use of a wheelchair. Going to the market with her took up most of Marcella's morning, but it was Ida's one outing of the day, a chance to see her neighborhood friends, and Marcella never failed to take her.

After a few weeks, they moved Ida's belongings from her old home and gave away Aldo Balducci's clothing to the poor men of the neighborhood. The spare room that Marcella had hoped to turn into a study one day for her writing was now her mother's. Marcella didn't complain. She felt so guilty that she was happy to pay off this spiritual debt if it would ensure a safe passage for her children.

With both children at public school, Ida's claims on her time and attention were the new obstacles to her writing. Dazed on painkillers and television, her mother was an unsettling presence, and Marcella overcompensated by pampering her. Soon, she felt almost as if she had never left her parents' home, sitting at Ida's side most of the day, cooking for Harry at night.

Over the next year, she tried to get her mind back to the world of her novel, rediscovering her characters as if they were old neglected friends. She would finish her house-work early, set out her typewriter on the kitchen table, sip a small espresso and attack the keyboard with that burst of caffeine energy. Then Ida would get her chair stuck in the narrow hallway or need to be walked into the bathroom. In the mornings, Ida's TV droned a continuous babble of soap opera or the excited squeals of game shows. The only quiet place to think in was the church, and Marcella sometimes sought sanctuary there, sitting quietly in the darkened hush, nodding at Father Carmello, who knew she came to be alone and respected this.

Now more than ever, Mark was the light at the end of her day. Where Sonia was cool and self-absorbed, Mark seemed to know how she was feeling and would stare into her eyes, touch her hand, give her strangely adult support. Harry had bought an old upright piano for him to practice on at home. He attacked it the moment he came home from school. At five o'clock, the dinner ready to cook, she would take a warm bath and wrap herself in a robe and lie on Mark's bed. He would run into the room and hug her so tightly she would have to pull him off her in order to breathe. He would play Debussy, Bach, and the simpler Chopin nocturnes for her. Each day she would thank him for the "concert" with a hug and a whisper in his ear that he was the light of her life, now more than ever.

Mark hated her to go out at night, and the problem of leaving him had built up until he would cry helplessly when she and Harry went to a movie or had dinner with Harry's colleagues. There would be a leave-taking drama, with Harry waiting impatient and tight-lipped as she pulled Mark off her. He was nine now and she knew such behavior was not normal. She did not tell Harry that on some occasions Mark had vomited with nerves. She knew, too, that it was her fault, as Harry never stopped reminding her.

"I'm scared I love Mark too much for his own good," she confessed to Amy at one of their monthly lunches at a glassed-in, heated sidewalk café on Columbus Avenue on a cold April day.

"*Can* one love a child too much?" Amy asked. "Remember, I've never had one."

Marcella twisted some pasta on her fork, looking up at Amy.

"Motherhood means letting your child touch wet paint to learn it's wet," she told her. "Burning himself to learn the stove is hot. Sitting there and watching him fall on his nose, bleed, cry . . ." She shook her head. "I can't let Mark fall on his nose—I'm there to catch him *before* he hits the ground! I've built up such a close, protective relationship with him—now he can hardly bear to let me out of his sight. . . ."

Amy leaned back against the mink-lined coat she had thrown over her chair. "You make me glad I'm not a mother," she sighed. "I don't suppose you're doing any writing?" she asked Marcella as the waiter brought coffee.

Marcella shook her head, lighting a cigarette. "I like to make sure Mother is all right. I keep looking in on her, chatting: could *you* write if your mother was around?"

Amy laughed. "Just knowing she's in Miami waiting for early-bird special dinnertime to roll around makes me nervous."

The waiter placed two pastry forks by the rich wedge of cake. Amy took a forkful and closed her eyes.

"Mmm . . ." She leaned forward excitedly, lowering her voice. "This incredible club has opened just down the street from me," she told Marcella. "It's called Members— very simple, very private, and *very* expensive. It has everything! Pool, gym, restaurant, bar, disco, and movie theater. You could spend the entire day there!"

"And *do* you?" Marcella asked.

Amy shrugged. "I started going there to take a very gentle workout in the gym. I went to the little movie theater a couple of times before I caught on to what was going on down there. . . ."

"And what *was* going on?" Marcella frowned.

"A guy's knee brushing up against mine, a hand touching my leg—" Amy pulled a face. "Stuff like that. Not creepy raincoated guys—these are nice-looking, expensive guys—fellow *members*! The next time I felt a knee brush up against mine, I didn't flinch away, and I suddenly found a hand in my lap!"

"*Amy!*" Marcella cried. "I don't believe this!"

"It started to move . . . " Amy continued, fixing Marcella with her green-eyed stare. "And you know something? I found it an incredible turn-on! This guy I didn't know from Adam, sitting next to me, giving me this silent manual stimulation that was the most skillful, exciting . . ."

"Amy!" Marcella cut in. "This is worse than any of your novels!"

Amy's eyes widened innocently. "Then I won't go

on . . ." she said, turning her attention to the chocolate cake. "I'm shocking you."

Marcella bit her lip. "You've gone this far, you might as well tell me what happened!" she said.

Amy smiled. "I was getting so much pleasure that I thought it was unfair not to give some back, so I put *my* hand in *his* lap! It was like being back at school or in the backseat of a car. We exchanged . . . shall we call it 'caresses?' And he left before I caught his name, or his face."

Marcella shook her head wonderingly. "You just let a complete stranger touch you up in a movie theater?"

Amy pursed her mouth. "Don't make it sound tacky!" she said. "It's all rather luxurious. It's a *very* expensive club, remember. They keep out the riffraff. The seats are covered in deep-pile velvet. There's the odd Havana cigar and plenty of delicious cologne wafting around. And the management provides lots of nooks and crannies where people can . . . well, get to know each other. It's very *exciting,* Marcella! I've been back several times."

They finished their cake in silence.

"I could never, *never* do that!" Marcella marveled.

Amy smiled. "Sure you could," she said. "If you were horny enough. I'll give you a membership, Marcella. Just in case."

When they left the restaurant, Amy clutched her coat around her, her hand high in the air for a cab.

"I'm heading for Members!" she giggled. "Telling you about it has given me the urge!" As a cab pulled up, she put her mouth to Marcella's ear. "Enough self-punishment, darling," she pleaded. "You're beautiful, you have talent, you've paid your dues. *Please,* Marcella, I care about you and it's tearing me up to see you looking like this. Call me, okay?"

Marcella looked after her fluttering hand as the cab sped off to some unimaginable world of mysterious sex. She was soon in the muggy warmth of the subway car, hating the tired reflection that leered at her from the lurching car window opposite.

It was all guilt, of course, self-punishment, as Amy so rightly said. Wouldn't that terrible accident have happened anyway, even if she had resisted Scott? What if that drunk driver got drunk every Saturday night and it was sheer bad luck that her parents were walking on the street that night? You had something special, she told herself. Don't lose it! It's so easy to lose it and be as drab as everyone else.

She vowed there and then, on the grubby train, that she would finish her book if it took a superhuman effort.

When she turned the corner of her street she saw Mark's head in the window, watching out for her. She waved. He had stayed with his grandmother while Harry had taken Sonia to a Saturday ballet matinee. Only his daughter had the power to get Harry to the ballet—he would do anything for her.

She brewed coffee for her mother and herself, listening to Mark's chatter about a concert he had just seen on Channel 13. Amy, glamorous and successful as she was, had no beautiful children and was not close to her mother. She bent down to hug Mark and Ida at that thought. Her new resolution went through her mind. It wasn't the money: she must be recognized for what she was—a writer —even if it was simply to give Mark a mother to be truly proud of.

That summer, Gloria allowed Harry to make love to her and showed him how to make money. Using her contacts in other brokerage houses, exchanging information, favors, and tips, she introduced him to the little secret network of people scratching each other's backs on Wall Street.

Their first windfall was fifty thousand dollars, which they split, Gloria insisting he join her in putting down a year's rent of twelve thousand on a Greenwich Village studio apartment in a high-rise, furnished with one king-size futon—"All we'll need!" she had giggled.

"And this is just the start, Harry," she promised, lying in his arms one hot July afternoon.

He glanced at his watch and she gave a sigh of exasperation.

"Scared you'll be late?" she asked. "What'll she do— put you over her knee and spank you?"

"I said I'd pick up Sonia from her dance class." He gave her a stern look. "It's a couple of blocks away."

Gloria looked suitably chastened. If there was one thing she had learned about being with Harry it was never to look anything less than reverent when he mentioned Sonia. She lit a cigarette and Harry moved away, his arm behind his head, studying the bare bulb that hung from the white ceiling.

"What does our landlord think of the way we furnished this place?" he laughed.

"He thinks we're two poor newlyweds, saving up for a Castro convertible!" Gloria giggled. She turned onto her stomach, resting her chin on Harry's chest. He watched the cheap way she smoked, so different from the classy way Marcella blew out smoke. He was very aware of the difference between the two women and told himself he needed to keep them both. He could, too, if he was careful. One for moments like this and one to be a good mother to his children.

"You like making money with me, huh?" Gloria teased, playing with his ear.

"What guy wouldn't?" Harry smiled lazily. He had never realized that making money could be so sexy. Making love with Gloria had been one of the great experiences of his life. He had relished this new power to make a woman cry out with pleasure. To make her look at him with such want in her eyes that he felt inspired to do all he could to please her. And somehow she kept him on the edge of his pleasure for minutes on end, forcing him to delay his climax, as if she were capable of imparting staying power so they could enjoy their intense pleasure together.

"It's the chemistry," she breathed in his ear. "The sheer sexual chemistry between us, Harry. Why did you have to marry her? Why?"

"Yeah, well, I was green . . ." he marveled, half to himself. "I was at the age when kids still listened to their parents. The revolution didn't reach Little Italy. And now it's too late."

"Why?" Gloria cried.

Harry groaned. "Hey, gimme a break, okay?" he asked. "For once, can we have a relaxing time without the third degree afterward?"

"Well, I just want to know why you can't get away from her," Gloria said sulkily. "She looks down her nose at you and she's training your kids to do the same!"

"Not my daughter!" Harry growled.

"She's destroying your potential, Harry!" Gloria cried.

"No one's destroying anything of mine," he said. "Did I ever tell you I was available? At least, not until my daughter is fully grown up. That could be ten, twelve years. I don't want my kid to feel abandoned and I can't afford to run two houses. It would be another story if I was a co-director, pulling down a six-figure salary. . . ."

"Is that what it would take?" she snorted, stubbing out her cigarette in the cheap Azuma ashtray she'd bought. She traced a line down his chest with her long-nailed finger. "Just dumb stupid money?"

"Yeah, if it's so dumb and stupid, how come *you* were so excited about haulin' in fifty grand?" he asked her.

"Because we were doing it *together*. Don't you understand?" she cried. "*That* was what was exciting! And I'll do it plenty more times with you, but not if you spend it on keeping your marriage together. Remember what I told you the first day we met? All I need is one ambitious man . . . ?"

"Maybe I'm not ambitious enough?" Harry shrugged.

She tried to tickle him. "Oh yes you are!" she said. "You *know* you are!"

He shook his head. "How d'you know all this stuff, anyway, Gloria?"

She sat up straight on the mattress, leaning her naked back against the cool wall.

"I'm real sharp and I have an uncanny memory," she told him. "This guy in market analysis really liked me. He showed me stuff he never shoulda showed me. Once someone shows me something, I remember it."

"What sorta stuff?" Harry asked.

Gloria shrugged. "Just access to computers and how to listen in on phone calls and how to pick up on stuff floating around the office," she listed. "People get excited on the phone sometimes and they don't realize who's listening. If you're expecting it, one little word can tip you off to something real important."

"And I'm the first guy you pulled into your act?" Harry asked.

"No." She eyed him. "I made a little money before you, Harry, with other guys."

"Yeah?" He raised his eyebrows. "What happened to them? They all in jail now?"

"Uh-uh. . . ." She shook her head. "They got scared and chickened out. They're all in other firms, now."

"What were they so scared of?" he asked her. "You said there was no risk."

"Oh, *please!*" She stood and looked for her underwear, pulling it on briskly. "There's a risk when you cross the street or take a plane trip, right?" She pulled a cotton sweater over her head. He watched the way her braless breasts became snugly outlined inside it. "The good thing about risks is that they can pay off. If we go carefully, we could pull in . . . oh—" She glanced over at him. "Just how much do you need in your back pocket to feel you could leave that wife of yours?"

"I'd want custody of my daughter," he pointed out.

"You know you'd never get that!" Gloria made a face. She pulled out a little mirror from her purse and applied some lipstick. "The mother nearly always gets the children. Unless you had some real fancy lawyer, maybe. Or if you took the children and just disappeared."

"Disappeared? To where?" he asked. He groaned as he got to his feet and collected his clothes from where he had thrown them on the floor.

"I don't know . . ." She wriggled her shoes on. "South America, Hawaii?"

"Let's make the money first, then we'll talk." He tried to make it sound like a joke, but he meant it.

She walked over to him as he sat on the low mattress, bending to prod his chest.

"How much, Harry?" she asked him. "What are we going for next?"

Harry looked up from lacing his shoes. "How about two million?" he said. "We'll split it right down the middle?"

Marcella's fierce resolution to write had to last her through the four toughest years of her life. She made herself available to her children and she nursed her mother. They came first. Then her novel. Then Harry. Her mother's addiction to painkillers made her increasingly difficult to handle but Marcella never complained. Nursing her mother was the least she could do, she felt; it helped lay to rest the nagging guilt that tried to tell her she was responsible for her mother's condition. Meanwhile, Harry rose and rose at his firm. Perhaps his failure to please her as a woman blinded *her* to his capabilities, but his bosses had discovered a streak of intuition for dealing with money futures that resulted in promotion after promotion. It was difficult to adjust to this new successful image of Harry each time she visited him and found him ensconced in his own office, with his own secretary, a skinny girl called Gloria who stared impudently at Marcella and the children. It crossed her mind that Gloria might well be "the other woman," which would explain Harry's late nights at the office and the fact that his sexual demands on her had decreased to almost zero. She was not jealous. Their marriage had reached the point where she welcomed the possibility that he found sex elsewhere. They had a kind of unspoken agreement that they were staying together for the children, anyway.

Harry often urged her to find a bigger apartment in a better neighborhood. Each time she had looked at new apartment buildings and weighed the pros and cons for moving, she had decided against. Her mother's small daily pleasures came through being familiar with the streets and stores around her. There were always neighbors and friends to keep her company when Marcella went out; they would be hard to replace in a new neighborhood. She used the extra money Harry gave her to refurbish the apartment and pay for extra visits by a nurse who bathed and massaged Ida. This had given her extra hours in which to write; somehow she had made the time she needed each afternoon, delving deep into herself for the energy and love the book demanded.

She intended the title of her book, *In the Name of Love,* to illustrate all the deeds done in love's name, good or bad. She adored her main character, Manuella, who had accidentally killed her violent husband as he raped her. At her trial, she falls in love with the prosecuting attorney, a distinguished, gray-templed type, and thus has a double motive for proving her innocence. His sympathetic summing-up helps get Manuella's sentence suspended, and he falls in love with her. Marcella had waited for the right mood in which to write their prison and courtroom love scenes, and the final consummation of their love when Manuella is released was the most erotic, meaningful writing she had yet produced. For that scene, she had summoned up all the women who would be reading her words, cramming her very soul into the pages, expressing all the longing and desire she had in her heart.

July 1984

And now the book was finished and she could hardly wait for a reaction from Amy! She brushed aside the anticlimax that most writers feel when ending a novel and losing their best friends, the characters. On her way to the local copy shop for photocopies, she mentally composed a casual note to attach to Scott's manuscript. Six *years* since she had met him! Six years since she had last experienced exciting sex!

Scott had called her to say hello now and then, but it was Amy who had truly supported her through this time; Amy who had lunched and encouraged her, who had acted as fairy godmother. And it was Amy who had made her a "lifelong member" of Members, her sexy club, even though Marcella had never used the lasered silver card.

Unable to find the right words for her note to Scott, she called Amy for guidance.

"*No* note!" Amy commanded imperiously. "I'll send my driver for *both* manuscripts and *I'll* read it *before* Scott! *Then* I'll send it to him. Oh my God, I can't believe you've *finished* it, Marcella! I'll cancel all engagements this weekend and devote myself to reading it!"

That weekend passed unbearably slowly for Marcella. She wandered around the apartment on Saturday afternoon while the children were at the movies with Harry, feeling strangely bereft without the book on the kitchen table to work on and polish. She made endless cups of coffee, cleared out the bedroom closets, noting all the expensive new clothing, some of it custom made, that Harry had sneaked in without showing to her. Separate lives, she thought. A good title for a new book, but too sad. Why did he feel guilty about buying new clothes for himself? He earned the money and he deserved to spend it. He was generous to her and the children. Sonia was now a tall twelve-year-old devoted to her ballet class. And Mark, handsomer than ever at fourteen, now got private lessons on the piano at home and was quite a musical prodigy.

A little wine got her through Saturday night, helped by cooking an intricate dinner as a distraction. By Sunday afternoon she was jumpy and nervous. How long would it take Amy to finish the goddamn book? If she had really loved it, surely she would have stayed up all Saturday night? She made Harry take the children to the park, then paced the apartment wondering whether to call Amy.

At five-thirty, Amy's call came.

"Marcella, it's absolutely marvelous!" she cried excitedly, and Marcella felt as if a ten-ton weight had been removed from her head. She sank down into an armchair, her eyes closed.

"Did you really like it? What took you so long?" she gasped.

"I wanted to read it at a decent pace, not skip through like I usually do," Amy told her, "and I truly love it! It's not just sexy, although it's that, too. It has heart and soul and I love the characters. Would *I* love to meet that lawyer! Harrison Ford for him, no? And who for Manuella? Joan Collins?"

"She's too old—what about Michelle Pfeiffer?"

"Too blond! Well, there's time for all that. . . ."

"What did you think of the scene when they finally made love?" Marcella asked.

Amy screamed. "*Ooh!* I had to read it under a cold shower!" she cried. "Now, I'm not saying another word until Scott reads it. Let's make a date for lunch at Le Cirque a week from tomorrow. We'll drink champagne until it runs out of our ears! On Volumes, of course! And bring that husband of yours; it's time we met, for God's sake. He's going to find out you're a writer, so you may as well break it to him over a good meal."

"He'll never agree to a Monday," Marcella said. "He's scared he'll miss something in the market if he goes to the john! Can it possibly be a Saturday, Amy?"

"An editor in chief lunching his author and her agent on a *Saturday*?" Amy cried. "That will *really* test my clout!"

Scott could not attend a Saturday lunch in town before

September, but he promised to read the book on his next weekend in the Hamptons.

Marcella did not find the courage to break the news of the lunch to Harry until the Friday before, as he turned on the television for that evening's news.

"We've been invited out for lunch tomorrow at Le Cirque, Harry," she said casually. "I've made a new friend, Amy Jagger. She's quite a well-known writer. She gave a lecture at a writing class I went to once and—"

Harry had risen. "When did you take a writing class?" he asked.

"It was a typing and shorthand course, remember?" she lied furiously. "But when the teacher didn't show up, they put us in with the writing class and we got to hear their lectures. Amy was one of the speakers and we've kept in touch . . ." She saw the suspicion in his eyes.

"I've written a novel," she continued quickly. "She wants to be my agent and sell it for me. Her editor wants to meet me. And *you!*"

"What do *I* have to do with it?" he asked, frowning.

Marcella laughed. "I just thought you should be there to pick me up if he offers to publish the book," she joked. "I've found a neighbor to sit with Ida and the children. Please come!"

"Where are you eating?"

"Le Cirque," she told him.

Harry whistled. "Do you know how much that joint charges for lunch?"

She shrugged. "I'm sure Volumes can afford it. They've sold millions of Amy's books."

"Is this your sex stuff again?" he asked her.

"Oh, it has a little of everything in it," she said. "Sex, murder, the whole bit. . . ."

"I guess I have to wear a tie?" he said. He went back to reading his paper and she exulted. It hadn't been so difficult. Maybe in his funny way, he'd even be quite proud of her? She called Amy while Harry was in the shower, warning her to remind Scott to act as if tomorrow were their first meeting.

The following Saturday, Le Cirque was half-empty. They arrived early, Harry blundering into the maitre d' and growling, "I don't know whose name our table's in—you seem to have plenty, anyway. . . ."

"Scott MacEvoy," Marcella said quickly.

They were shown to a good table and offered a cocktail. Harry's presence somehow withdrew all the style from the occasion. He seemed uncomfortable in his expensive clothes, as though they belonged to another man. She had chosen a cranberry wool dress that was a little tight for her —would Scott even notice her weight? She felt self-conscious and was furious at herself for reacting this way after handling lunch here so well the first time. If anything, she was more beautiful now, her full figure still well proportioned, her auburn hair more stylish, gently waved, a new depth to her eyes.

Harry whistled at the prices on the menu.

"Please don't do that," she asked.

"This could be the first eighteen-dollar hamburger I've eaten," he said. "Either they're very interested in your book or this is a very expensive turndown. What's the book about, anyway?"

"It's basically a murder trial," she told him. "This woman kills her husband and—"

"What is it?" he broke in. "Wish fulfillment?"

She hushed him as Amy entered the restaurant with Scott. She was in black pants with an oversized red blazer and her trademark white angora turtleneck. Scott held her arm and Amy did a good job of pretending to introduce them for the first time.

"A great pleasure to meet you, Mrs. Winton." Scott hammed it up, holding her eyes for a brief flickering moment.

"Please call me Marcella," she said, dropping her eyes.

"And this must be *Mr.* Winton?" Amy turned with a flourish to Harry.

"Harry," he muttered.

Scott scarcely looked older than at their last meeting. It wasn't fair, Marcella thought. He was as handsome as she remembered. *This* was a man who knew how to wear expensive clothes, she thought, noting the navy Armani suit and the delicious forest green tie and light blue shirt. Harry looked five years out of date in his conservative pinstripe.

"We're very excited about your wife, Harry," Scott told him after they'd ordered. Marcella watched Harry become cold and gruff. He was not crazy about strange men telling him how wonderful his wife was.

Scott was completely at ease as the champagne was poured, telling jokes, giving attention to both women, including Harry in all the trade talk.

Amy laughed and flirted with Harry as if she found him irresistibly sexy, pressing his hand whenever he uttered a monosyllable. She did not get very far. From time to time, either Scott or Amy managed to nudge or pinch Marcella's knee. With each sip of wine, Marcella tried to shrug off the brooding atmosphere that Harry created.

She felt as if the three of them were acting some silly scene that Harry could never be part of. Amy was in her element, twittering and giggling, drinking champagne, exclaiming over the food, serving Harry tidbits off her fork. Harry ate at his usual speed.

Dessert arrived and espresso was ceremoniously poured. Scott sat up straight: it was time to talk business.

"I've read *In the Name of Love,* Marcella," Scott began, his eyes darting from her face to Amy's to Harry's, and then back to hers. *"Twice*—just to make sure I wasn't fooling myself or had eaten a particularly good meal before the first reading!" They all laughed. "Marcella Balducci Winton," he nodded formally, "you have a gift for narrative. It's the most exciting and commercial manuscript I've read since . . . well, since Amy Jagger's *Zippers*!"

Amy gave a little squeak. Marcella felt a warm glow of pleasure spreading inside her.

"And if I tell you that big, tough Scott MacEvoy cried at the ending," Scott continued, "well, we can imagine what it will do to a normal, non-hardboiled reader!" He shrugged. "A ten-Kleenex book!"

"Scott!" Amy cried, leaning to put her hands around his throat and pretending to strangle him. "If you don't say what Volumes is offering, I'll pee in my pants!"

Scott laughed. "Ms. Amy Jagger wants me to put my

money where my mouth is and I don't blame her." He reached into his breast pocket.

Marcella closed her eyes. The moment became stretched out like a photograph melting in a fire. It didn't matter how much they offered, the main thing was that they were acknowledging her talent for writing. It almost made all those painful rejections worth it! Because all the time, I *knew*! she thought. I knew I had this special gift inside me! She opened her eyes as Scott withdrew a long piece of paper from his pocket.

"This is probably the best way of communicating our excitement over *In the Name of Love*," he said, turning over a check.

Amy leaped to her feet to peer over Scott's shoulder and let out a yell that made everyone in the restaurant turn to stare. Marcella tried to focus on the check. It appeared to be covered in number threes.

"This represents the first third of our advance," Scott said.

"Three hundred and thirty-three thousand *bucks*?" Amy cried. "In other words, a million dollars for the book? A million *dollars,* Marcella!"

Marcella's heart skipped a whole beat. For a moment, she felt as if she were going to lose consciousness. When she next looked at the check, Harry was holding it in both hands, studying it.

"Marcella! Scott! Oh God! Harry!" Amy cried each name, hugged them in turn, ran around their table like a clockwork toy and finally fell back into her chair exhausted. "Scott!" she gasped, "I am *not* going to give you a hard time! We *accept*! God, I should have become an agent years ago, I'm so *good* at it! A million for her *first* novel!"

"Why is it made out to Amy?" Harry suddenly asked.

"Harry!" Marcella cried, embarrassed.

"That's all right," Amy soothed her, turning to Harry. "As your wife's agent, I take my percentage and pass on the rest to her."

"Am I dreaming?" Marcella laughed. "Should I pinch myself, Amy?"

"Why waste time pinching?" Amy cried. "You could be shopping!" She held up her glass. "To *you,* darling! To selling ten million copies of *In the Name of Love*!"

She was touching her glass to Marcella's when Harry suddenly cried, *"No!"* He was on his feet, staring at them all.

Amy giggled. "What is it, Harry?" she cried. "Didn't you think your wife could ever bring home this kind of bacon?"

Harry made an unintelligible mumble and snatched the check out of Marcella's hand. He tore it into confetti, scattering the pieces in an ashtray.

"That check was made out to *me!*" Amy cried. "You had no right to do that!"

Scott got to his feet, leaning across the table.

"Are you out of your mind?" he asked Harry. "That check wasn't your property! It'll cause a great deal of inconvenience to get it reissued. We—"

"Don't bother because she won't take it," Harry told him. "I know the kind of stuff she writes. Why do you think she didn't let me see it?" His contemptuous look swept the three of them. "It's filth, isn't it? That's what you three are getting so excited about! She's always written about it! She likes to wallow in it!"

"No!" Marcella cried, stopping him. "You haven't read it, you don't *know*! Oh, you'd ruin everything for me if you could! But there's *nothing* you can do to stop this, Harry! It's *my* book!"

Harry threw his bunched-up napkin to the table, turned, and walked out.

There was a stunned silence in the restaurant. The fellow lunchers who had ignored their food to witness this scene stared at Marcella. Then, slowly, waiters appeared to clear away the dessert plates and refill the tiny espresso cups.

"Well . . ." Scott breathed. "If *that* wasn't a scene from *In the Name of Love*! Never let an author tell you her work isn't autobiographical!"

"Shut up, Scott, and get her a brandy!" Amy murmured, putting an arm around Marcella. "She's trembling. I don't think I've *ever*—"

"Excuse me," Marcella whispered. She stood up and ran to the exit, out onto the street. She spotted Harry half a block down Madison Avenue.

"Harry!" she called, running after him. *"Wait!"*

She caught up with him on the corner of Sixty-third Street and Madison.

"Don't just run away!" She pulled him around to face her. "This is important! Our lives will never be the same after today! Can't we try to enjoy it together? For the children's sake?"

Harry smiled grimly. "You think the children will be proud of their mother writing a dirty book?" he asked. "Sonia's just at the age now when—"

"It is not *dirty,* Harry!" she cried. "You can read it. It has sex and love in it, but it's not—"

"For them to hand out *that* kind of money?" he sneered. "It's got to be one long fuck from beginning to end!"

"No!" She stared into his angry eyes and suddenly realized she was no longer frightened of him. Is that what money did for you? she wondered, feeling an exhilarating rush of independence.

"You're running away from my earning a million dollars!" she told him. *"That's* what you can't stand!"

He shook his head, bringing his face nearer hers.

"Everyone who reads it will think it's about us—you and me," he said. "And if it's *not* about us, they'll wonder how come you know so much about what sex is like with different men!"

She shook her head with a bitter laugh. "I have to imagine all that, Harry!" she cried. "I've been living without it for so long because you never took the trouble to find out what *I* wanted! *You* made me a writer, because I damn well had to imagine what I never got!"

His eyes flickered away from hers and his mouth turned down in a grim kind of a grin she'd never seen before.

"That's your opinion," he growled. "There are other women out there who don't share it."

"Great!" she cried. "So go and find one of them!"

"I did!" he exulted.

She turned to go but he grasped her arm, making her wait. "You've always tried to make me feel you were too good for me, too intelligent for a dumb son of an Irish cop," he said. "But tell me what you had to feel so superior about? Your dad cooked spaghetti! Does that make him any better than—"

"Don't you *dare* say a word against my father!" she said

through clenched teeth. "I stuck it out with you because of the children! I've done my duty—"

"Yeah—and you always made me feel that's what it was —duty!"

"My parents made me marry you, remember?" she demanded.

"Yes, I remember!" he said bitterly. "My parents did the same thing. And I've never stopped regretting it!"

"Neither have I!" she cried, her tears overflowing.

Harry's face looked as if she'd struck him. He raised his arm as if to strike her. She flinched and then he let her go and walked on. She stood there for one moment, biting her lip and feeling the hot tears turn cold on her face.

Amy was twisted around in her chair, scanning the restaurant's entrance, when Marcella reappeared.

"Oh you poor darling!" Amy ran over to her, guiding her back to their table. "You're in shock! I thought we'd never see you again! Drink some brandy, quick!"

Marcella stumbled into her chair and sipped at the balloon of amber liquid Scott proffered.

"What did he say?" Amy finally asked.

"He hates my writing, always has." Marcella spoke quietly as the liquor spread its warmth through her. "He once read a story I'd written and beat me up. Naturally, I've kept my writing hidden ever since."

"Oh, great!" Amy gulped her drink. "Battered wife makes million bucks! Think the *Enquirer* would run it, Scott?"

Scott hushed her, putting his arm around Marcella. "That guy is dangerous. I'd say he was a little disturbed," he said.

"Forgive him for ruining our lovely lunch," Marcella apologized. "He just isn't used to this kind of thing."

Scott squeezed her. "Don't make excuses for him. Find a good divorce lawyer, move out, make up, whatever, because we'll be promoting *you*! You'll be doing interviews on TV and radio, signings in bookstores—the whole bit. You're going to need all your energy!"

Marcella stared at him. She could not think further ahead than that night and her confrontation with Harry when she got home.

"Listen, kids," Amy said. "It's crazy to sit around here

drinking at these prices, even with Volumes paying. I have perfectly good booze at home."

Scott signed the bill and Amy repaired her makeup. Marcella felt drained. She wanted to celebrate her good fortune with her children and her mother.

Out on the street, Scott kissed them both good-bye. "We'll issue a new check next week," he promised Marcella. "Congratulations! You should be a very happy lady!"

She walked quietly alongside Amy down Madison to Fifty-ninth and across to Central Park South. In the mirrored luxury of Amy's apartment, she relaxed on the apricot velvet sofa as Amy poured two generous brandies.

"To Marcella Balducci, bachelor-girl! Life without Harry!" Amy proposed.

Marcella stared at her. "What do you mean?" she asked.

Amy tucked in her chin and frowned at her. "You wouldn't stay with him after *that* little performance? Tearing up our check as if he were your keeper?"

Marcella sipped her drink. "He's always had that Irish temper. He'll come around once I explain to him that we—"

"Explain to *me,* first!" Amy put her hand on Marcella's arm. "Why would a beautiful woman with a million dollars even *dream* of staying with a man who—" She broke off, shaking her head. "If it happened in one of my novels, Scott would edit it out!"

"We lost a child together, Amy," Marcella tried to explain. "That's an experience so awful it pulls two people together. I've never lived alone before and the thought of trying to do it at this moment in my life—"

"But you wouldn't *be* alone!" Amy cried. "Tonight you'd sleep here. Tomorrow we have a shrewd little brunch at a place in SoHo where a lot of writers hang out. I can't *wait* to see *their* little faces when I announce your million bucks! Monday morning we get a new check from Scott, put down the payment on a one-bedroom co-op in this very building, and you're off!"

Marcella smiled. "You left out two children and a semi-invalid mother, Amy!" she reminded her.

"Okay," Amy shrugged. "So you put down a payment

on a *three*-bedroom apartment! There's one going on the
fifth floor!"

Marcella shook her head. "I'm not ready for that many
changes in one weekend. Harry and I said some very cruel
things to each other today. Maybe *I* haven't been totally
fair to *him,* either. . . ."

Amy groaned. "You're playing the bird who can't fly out
of its gilded cage, Marcella. From what I saw today, your
marriage stinks! Face it! You'll leave him sooner or later,
so why not sooner?"

Why not sooner? The words echoed in her head as she
dashed into Bergdorf's later to buy some gifts for everyone. She had borrowed a hundred dollars from Amy and
she quickly blew it on a silk tie for Harry as a peace offering, soap for her mother, and candy for the kids. Then she
treated herself to a cab home. Harry would have cooled
down by now, she thought, glancing at her watch. Tonight
they could discuss their marriage and decide together
whether it could be salvaged for the children's sake. They
could discuss where to look for a new apartment and how
to invest the money. She would allow him to feel he was
advising her. She was willing to go without the sexual satisfaction to keep some peace and order in her life.

She looked down at the gifts she had bought, in their
pretty wrappings. Having some money to spend would
gloss over the next few years. Then she could think again.

The apartment was very quiet as she let herself in.
There were no sounds of Mark practicing the piano or
Sonia dancing around as there usually were in the early
evening.

"Marcella!" her mother's voice called. "Is that you?"

She walked quickly to her mother's room and opened
the door.

"Where has everyone gone?" her mother asked. "I was
supposed to take my pills at four-thirty and no one brought
me a drink."

She leaned over her mother to plump up her back cushion.

"Did Harry take them out?" she asked.

"They all kissed me good-bye a long time ago," Ida

grunted. "Such banging around and noise! It sounded as if the whole house was being turned upside down. He dressed them up very nicely. Where were they going?"

"I've no idea—" Marcella began, and then a warning alarm sounded deep within her. She left her mother and ran down the narrow passage that led to the children's room, dropping the gifts she had bought them. A sudden sickening sensation in the pit of her stomach made her feel as if she were in a falling elevator. Even before she opened their door, she had a premonition of what she would see. Their closets were wide open, emptied of clothing. The odd toy or sock on the bed and floor announced the haste of their departure. She bent down to pick up a raggedy teddy bear that Sonia still slept with. In her room, an envelope rested on her pillow, her name scrawled on it.

Don't try to find us. I'll take good care of them. Better than you did. Harry.

She stared at the note. For a few moments its meaning did not get through to her; then its message slowly percolated from her brain down to her guts. Her mother was calling out her name as a black dizziness engulfed her.

BOOK TWO

BOOK TWO

SIX

Mark had never hated his father this much. Usually he managed to ignore him, but now he knew beyond all doubt that his father was a liar and he would never trust him again. He exchanged a look with Sonia as the car hurtled down the freeway. He hadn't even known his father *had* a car. It was probably rented, he decided. And the way his father had thrown all their clothes into suitcases, not even bothering to fold them the way he had seen his mother folding their clothes—the impatient, rushed manner in which Harry had hustled them—had told him that something was very wrong. Mom could not possibly know about this. Or she had died. He was not sure which. He only knew that he must not give in to his overwhelming desire to cry or throw up because Dad would laugh at him and things would get even worse. If Mom was dead . . . he cursed himself for not having rehearsed this part so he could have been ready for it. Lying in bed at night, thinking how much he loved her, he had often made himself imagine her funeral, and tears had rolled down his cheeks as he saw himself bereft of the most important person in his life. He had wanted to be ready for it in case it actually happened. Now he was furious with himself for not having foreseen *how* the dreadful news would be broken to him, for not realizing that his father would be the bearer. He should have been prepared for exactly this kind of nightmarish afternoon—being whisked away in a new car, with no explanations, to a destination he could not even imagine.

He shot a furtive look at his father's reflected eyes in the driving mirror and felt a jolt of loathing and dread.

"Where are we going, Dad?" he heard himself ask without meaning to.

"Mark, if you ask me that one more time . . ." Harry warned. "I told you: you'll see when you get there!"

"Are we almost there, Daddy?" Sonia asked.

"Almost, princess."

Mark could not understand why his sister was taking it all so quietly. She leaned on her chin, staring out of the window. She noticed him watching her and told him, "I've counted eight white cars!" Mark shrugged. She didn't understand that something terrible was happening. She had never cried when their mother left them. Only he had done that, and it was something of which he was bitterly ashamed. He resolved to keep his voice firm as he tried a different question, the question he had been holding back for the last hour.

"Will Mom be there?"

It was more a hopeful thought than a question, and a few moments passed as he waited for an answer. Maybe his father was thinking about telling them the truth. Finally Mark asked, "Is Mom all right?"

"Is Mom alive?" Sonia laughed, pressing against him, looking at him mischievously.

"Shut up!" Mark pushed at her, pushing away the fear that tugged at his heart. "You don't know anything!"

"Keep quiet back there!" Harry shouted. "Mark! Don't hit your sister! Shut up, both of you!"

It seemed to him they had driven for hours, his brain turning as fast as the wheels, trying to figure out all the things now liable to happen to him, wondering why life had suddenly changed at three-thirty that Saturday afternoon. Why his mother, who had looked so pretty as she had gone

out with his father for lunch, hadn't returned with him.
Why?

By the time they pulled up in the drive of a house on a
street of similar houses, it was almost dark and Sonia was
sleeping soundly. She did not wake even when Harry
scooped her off the backseat into his arms.

"Where are we?" Mark asked, his voice sounding loud
and high in the quiet street.

"This is your new home," Harry said.

He hated his new home, if it really was that. And he
hated the lady who opened the door and held out her arms
to him, as if she knew him, saying "Hi!" She wore too
much makeup and seemed very nervous.

"This has to be Mark!" she cried, hugging him. He
stood stiffly in her embrace.

"You know Gloria, don't you?" his father turned to ask.
"You met her at my office."

"Hi, Mark!" Gloria tried again. She smiled, but somehow Mark knew she was just pretending to be nice. Underneath, she was like his father.

"And this must be the princess!" she cooed, looking
into Harry's arms full of Sonia. "And I must be the queen
'cause I'm her new mommy!" she giggled.

"Don't say that, Gloria!" Harry snapped. "You'll con-
fuse them!"

"That's okay! I'm confused, too!" she answered.

Mark frowned; could an adult be confused?

"Are you coming in?" Gloria held the door wide open
and they stepped into a new-smelling house, its brightly
colored floors covered in new-carpet fluff. The walls were
painted white or yellow.

"Give Mark something to eat, I'll take Sonia up to bed,"
his father said. The new lady guided Mark into a kitchen,
also brand-new. There were sandwiches set out on a large
cardboard plate and some plastic glasses and a carton of
milk. She handed him a paper plate.

"You want milk?" she asked. "I have some chocolate
syrup if you like that."

Mark nodded. He knew he'd get on better with her if he
pretended to like her. Grown-ups like her, who spoke to
children as if they were babies, always liked you better if
you liked them.

He watched her pour the syrup. She gave him a straw for the chocolate milk. He was so hungry and thirsty that for a while he forgot his fears and ate. When he had finished the sandwich, he looked up and found her staring at him. He stared back.

"You're not a bit like your dad," she said. Most people would call her pretty, he thought. But not him. He had the most beautiful mother in the world, and anything else was just a poor, cheap substitute.

"Remember me, now?" she asked. "You met me a couple of times when you visited your dad's office? I work with him!"

"You're his secretary!" he said. "But what—" He broke off, confused. He didn't know how to ask her what she was doing there and why they were in her house. Instead, he continued, "—what happened to my mother?"

"Nothing's happened to her, honey." She handed him a paper napkin to wipe his mouth and he automatically dabbed his lips, still staring at her.

"Your daddy thought you'd be better off here, that's all!" she told him.

"Better off?" he repeated, frowning.

"Yeah, you know . . ." she said, nodding. "More comfortable."

His eyes flashed at her. "I'll never be comfortable *here*!" he told her. "I want to go home!"

"Well, you'll have to figure that out with your dad," she said crossly.

To his great embarrassment, he felt two huge tears rolling down his cheeks, quickly followed by two others. And once a few tears had got started, he couldn't seem to stop. To add to his distress, he felt his lower lip turn down in his grief. He knew, from sometimes glancing in the mirror when crying, that he looked ridiculous.

"Aw now, honey . . ." She tentatively touched him. "Give this a chance, huh? You might grow to like it here! You're gonna be real happy!"

This absurd prediction proved to Mark that they were not speaking the same language and made him cry even more.

"I *thought* a man who could tear up a third of a million bucks had to be a *teensy* bit bananas!" Amy said. "I mean, I know a mad glint in an eye when I see one, and when I met Harry . . ."

Marcella didn't answer. One of the advantages of having Amy for a friend was that Amy could do all the reacting when Marcella was too weary to react for herself.

It was early Monday morning and she had not slept for two days. She had never before been kept awake by anger, but now her rage against Harry and a constant sick worry for the children ensured sleeplessness. Slumped on a chair in Amy's kitchen, she watched Amy prepare coffee.

"Just leave it to me, will you, Marcella?" Amy handed her a mug. "I have connections and my connections have connections. Today is a regular working day. Watch me go into action!" She reached for the phone.

She was a miracle, Marcella had to admit. By noon she had spoken to the best detectives from the best agencies, the best attorney specializing in child-abduction cases, and the most helpful police staff. She put down the phone, gasping for water, giving Marcella a baleful stare over the glass.

"Well!" she panted, swallowing, "*I've* learned something, anyway! Believe it or not, Harry has *not* committed a crime! Since you're both still married, in the eyes of the law you both have custody of your children."

Marcella stared at her. "You mean I just have to sit here and lose my children?" She began to cry, and Amy stood to put an arm around her.

"Let it go, darling!" She hugged her. "Cry your little heart out! Of *course* you don't have to just sit here and take it. We'll hire a private detective, for a start. And I've nagged the police department to send someone around here to explain. He'll be here in an hour."

Marcella took a shower and tried to pull herself together. Amy insisted on her taking half a Valium before the police officer arrived. She dialed her own number and spoke to her mother, who was being taken care of by a twenty-four-hour nurse Amy had installed, insisting that Marcella stay in her apartment. Ida seemed perfectly satisfied with the explanation that Harry had taken the children on a surprise visit to an aunt in Canada. Marcella pretended that she had just joined them and was calling from Canada.

"Do you like your nurse?" she asked Ida.

"Oh, she's lovely!" Ida said. "She's teaching me to play cards."

Marcella put the phone down. "I feel like Alice in Wonderland," she told Amy. "Everything is so *weird*!"

She felt even odder when the police officer arrived and sat gingerly in the living room, his tall, blond looks and big hands oddly reminiscent of Harry.

He explained gently, apologetically, why Harry could not be arrested.

"The only thing you can do is start a court action trying to get sole custody over the children," he told her.

"How long would that take?" she asked.

He shrugged. "I don't know exactly, but it could drag out over several months . . ." He stopped, seeing her face. "Listen, ma'am, do you mind if I give you a little advice? I've seen a lot of these cases . . ."

She leaned forward. "Please!" she urged.

"We often find that these family disagreements arrange themselves within a few days," he told her. "The father grabs the kids and storms out in a rage, but a day or two later, he sees the situation more clearly and . . . well, ma'am, I don't know about your children, but kids aren't always easy to handle. He may have had enough when they start getting demanding, know what I mean?"

She tried to smile. "I hope you're right. It's just so . . . tough to sit here and wait, feeling so helpless!"

He nodded. "But sometimes that's the coolest thing you can do. If he's crossing state lines, each county's laws are different. *You* say he abducted them, *he* says he's taking them on vacation. Just sit tight; I guarantee you he'll contact you!"

"Well, that's a start!" Amy tried to cheer her when the officer left. She pushed a sandwich at Marcella. "You must eat something, Marcella. There's nothing but black coffee sloshing about inside you." She took a bite of her sandwich. "You'll have them back within the week, and then you slap Harry Winton with the biggest goddamn alimony suit Manhattan has ever seen!"

Marcella lit another cigarette and let Amy chatter on,

enumerating all the things she would do to Harry if they ever crossed paths again, listing all the places she would kick him, "including right in the balls!"

By Monday evening, Marcella was too exhausted not to sleep. They had interviewed and hired a private detective to see whether he could discover Harry's whereabouts. The idea of her husband and children being hunted down like criminals disturbed her terribly and made her imagine violent car chases, gun-toting gangsters, and the frightened faces of Mark and Sonia. When the phone by her bed rang, she incorporated it into her nightmare for several seconds before reaching out for it.

It was the detective, reporting on his first day's findings.

"Did you know your husband had resigned from his job two weeks ago?" he asked her.

No, she hadn't known. Harry had been leaving the house at the usual time each morning. She hung up and fell asleep.

The phone rang again, twenty minutes later.

"Did you know your husband had made a large sum of money in the market some months ago? A *lot* of money, according to some colleagues."

No, she hadn't known.

"Did you know your husband was keeping company with a secretary called Gloria Defries?"

"*Listen!*" Marcella exploded at the third call, sitting up in bed. "Obviously my husband was leading a whole secret life that I knew nothing about. I don't *care* about that! I just want my children back!"

"Mrs. Winton," the detective said in patient tones, "these details will lead us to your children. Perhaps your husband planned to share a new life with his secretary?"

"*No!*" By now she was shouting. "No! *No!*"

"My God, what *is* it?" Amy raced into her room just as Marcella hung up.

Marcella reached for a cigarette and repeated the news.

Amy shot her a knowing look. "His *secretary*? What a cliché! So you weren't the only one leading a secret life?"

Marcella swung her legs out of bed and sat on the edge.

"I didn't really believe he worked out twice a week, Amy," she said. "But I was so wrapped up in finishing this book, I didn't even care. Oh, Amy! He beat me to it, that's all! Who's to say *I* wouldn't have grabbed the kids and walked out on *him*? I'd have done it more gently, that's all, with visiting rights and explanations. It's a terrible thing to do to kids who don't really understand what's happening. If only I knew what they were going through. If only I could be there, reassuring them that everything will be all right."

"Marcella?" Harry's familiar voice sounded so close that she jumped. It was five days since they had left, and she was back in her own apartment.

"Where *are* you, you bastard?" she cried. "Where are my children?"

"I can't do anything with your son," Harry complained. "He's impossible! He hasn't stopped crying for his mommy since we—"

"Put him on!" she demanded.

Mark was stammering when he came on the line.

"Darling?" Marcella asked, tears running down her cheeks. "Are you all right? There hasn't been one second when I wasn't thinking hard of you and Sonia. We'll be together soon, Mark, I promise you. Is Sonia all right?"

She heard his deep, shuddering breath. "She's okay," he said. "She likes it here. I want to come home."

"I miss you so much, my darling," she told him. "I'm going to ask Daddy to send you both back to me. Tell your sister I love her, and remember what you are to me!"

"What?" he asked.

"You're the light of my life, darling. Now be brave, for your sister and your father."

When Harry came back on the line, she wiped her tears.

"Do you realize the damage you've done?" she asked him. "It's probably irreparable!"

"I didn't want my children brought up by you!" he said.

"Oh?" She felt the hard ball of helpless rage inside her. "You think your slut of a secretary will do a better job?" she asked. "I'll get a court order and fight you if it takes every cent of my money. They're my children, Harry, and I want them back! Right *now*!"

There was a pause.

"Sonia wants to stay with us," he said. "I can't handle the boy. You've ruined that kid, Marcella. I've been too busy to see what you've done to him. He won't be a man, that's for sure."

"Whatever he becomes, it will be a better person than you," she said. "Someone who considers people's feelings—"

"I'm willing to make a deal with you, Marce," he cut in.

"You're in too much trouble to make deals!" she cried. "You're going to have to keep running from state to state! Just send the children back to me before you ruin their lives, too!"

"No . . ." he said. She waited. "You can have your son, but I get to keep my daughter. Now that's fair, Marcella."

"Are you insane?" she yelled. "I want them *both*! Here with me, where they belong!"

"You think a court order is going to be plain sailing for you?" He laughed. "When a judge sees the kind of stuff *you* write? I have enough money to buy a better attorney than yours!"

"They're brother and sister, Harry," she pleaded. "You can't split them up. Sonia's just a child!"

"She wants to stay with me," he said firmly. "Now I'm not giving you a choice. Mark will be at the information desk at Penn Station this afternoon at five-thirty. That's *it*!"

"I won't agree to separating them, Harry! I—"

But the click was final, the line dead.

At Penn Station that afternoon, as the first wave of commuters returning home flooded the space, Marcella spotted Mark at the information desk. She held out her arms and he saw her and ran toward her. He gave a great leap into her arms. He would not let go until Amy pulled them apart.

Amy invited them home for tea. At her apartment, they fell on the couch and listened as Mark breathlessly described his last five days, how he had refused to eat and how his father had become more and more impatient with him.

"I even thought of running away in the middle of the night, but I didn't have much money on me, and I didn't like leaving Sonia with him. But I left her with him, anyway . . ." he said, sadly. Marcella did not let go of his hand, and Amy fed him cookies and milk that he ate with the other.

"And did Sonia really want to stay with Daddy?" Marcella finally asked.

He nodded seriously. "She *liked* Gloria! I couldn't stand her."

Amy glanced at Marcella's face. "She didn't know what she was saying," she said quickly. "Having a new mommy is a novelty for a few days—she'll want to come home, I'm sure."

"Could a child be that cruel?" Marcella wondered aloud. "My own daughter?" It hurt because it made her examine her own feelings for Sonia. She loved her, but her enormous relief that Mark was back demonstrated very clearly that there was only one firstborn in any mother's life. While she brooded, Amy showed Mark around her apartment. Like Marcella, he loved luxury and bright colors, and he appreciated the happy atmosphere Amy had created.

At home that night, he begged to be allowed to sleep in Marcella's bed. After all the trauma he had been through, Marcella saw no harm in letting him. Tomorrow Mark would speak to the detective, although he had little idea of where Harry's house was, and Harry had seemed to be planning to move on anyway. That night, she slept with her arms around her son, reveling in the relief of his safety, kissing the back of his neck and wondering if she would ever have both her children with her again.

The next week brought a continuous flow of news from the detective and a visit from two plainclothes officers she had not met before.

"I thought the police refused to get involved with cases like this," she said, showing them into her apartment.

"Ma'am?" The balding, overweight one frowned.

"Which case were you referring to?" his partner questioned.

"My daughter, of course . . ." she said, uncertainly. "My husband abducted my children last week and I'm starting a court action to—" She hesitated because she could see they had no idea what she was talking about. "You *are* here about my husband, aren't you?" she asked.

They nodded. "Your husband's firm has started an investigation into that particular day's trading when a few people in your husband's office got lucky," the first officer explained. "I say 'got lucky' because there is a slight chance that luck came into it, but more probably they used privileged information. Your husband is not the only person who has left the company since that day. There was Gloria Defries, his secretary, and two other men who left the country as well. They're all being sought. Your husband is not on the run because he wants custody of your daughter."

"How serious is it?" Marcella sat down, suddenly.

The officer shrugged. "Anything from a big fine to several years in jail."

"Great!" She nodded. "So now Sonia gets a jailbird father when you catch up with him."

She saw them out, asking them to keep her informed. She was glad she had kept on the nurse for Ida during this crisis, but now there was no time to enjoy having Mark back with her. Volumes announced her record-breaking advance payment, and the news was splashed in the papers, Marcella's novel described as "a sweeping, romantic, feminist saga!"

The major talk-show talent coordinators agreed to schedule interviews with Marcella on the publication of her book. This gave her a nine-month breathing space. Scott was calling her several times a day, asking her to come in to meet the Volumes staff and publisher and discuss the editing of her book. Amy nagged at her to make an offer for the apartment in her building that Marcella had looked at and liked. If she moved, it would mean enrolling Mark in a nearby school, one which would encourage his talent for the piano. The Jacinthe Music Academy, an East Side high school which emphasized intensive extracurricular music studies, seemed the best choice, if they would agree to accept Mark two weeks after the term's start.

Marcella finally summoned up reserves of strength and made some decisions. She submitted an offer for the apartment four floors beneath Amy's, keeping the day nurse to look after Ida in a self-contained part of the apartment. At the bank where she and Harry had maintained a joint account, she met the manager and worked out a mortgage, giving Volumes as a reference. The apartment was expensive, but her new accountant said mortgage payments would be tax deductible, with one room counting as working space. When she handed in the edited novel, she would receive another third of a million dollars, so she would have enough to live on.

They made the move uptown as soon as the Jacinthe Academy accepted Mark. Ida and her nurse sat in the backseat of Amy's Rolls, with Marcella following in a taxi piled with suitcases and bags. After, Amy whisked Marcella off to Bloomingdale's for furniture, crystal, linens, and china, airily mentioning the parties Marcella would be giving, the entertaining an author was more or less obliged to do. By the time she got home, she found her mother utterly confused, clinging to her new nurse, eyes furtively darting about the apartment as if she were trespassing and the new place was not really her home.

That night, as she and Mark unpacked cartons, they kept stopping to peer out at Central Park. It seemed hardly believable that it could be right outside their window.

She hesitated when he came to the door of her bedroom that night.

"You must get used to your new room, Mark," she told him. "You're too old to be sleeping with your mommy!"

"Please!" he pleaded, his blue eyes pained. "I have such terrible nightmares!"

Had Harry done this to him? she wondered that night, her arm around his waist as he slept. His body near hers was wonderfully comforting, but he slept fitfully, waking her when his nightmares made him cling to her as if someone were pulling them apart.

The detective reported that Harry had been spotted in a motel near Pittsburgh, that a girl answering Sonia's description, but called Sonia Aster, had been entered into a Massachusetts school as a temporary student. There were several false leads. Each time, before a state court order could be issued the pair had disappeared. Harry was becoming adept at dodging, but Marcella vowed to chase him across the country via court orders if she had to. She was sick with anguish for her daughter. Sonia had never been a very dedicated student; this would play havoc with her grades.

More details of Harry's financial dealings came to light as officials of his company decided to press charges. Gloria Defries was found living in the New Jersey house and taken in for questioning. The police officer who had visited Marcella called her to tell her that Gloria was turning state's witness in exchange for not being prosecuted.

"But why? She was living with my husband," Marcella said.

"Evidently they had a fight the day your son was returned to you," the officer told her. "She said that your husband was abusive to her and that he went off with your daughter, dumping her."

Each ring of the phone scared her now. Her daughter was being dragged around the country by an angry, aggressive man.

She was swept into her new life so fast it seemed as if the Little Italy life had belonged to someone else. She adored waking up knowing she was on Central Park South, in the middle of Manhattan, the smell of the horse-drawn carriages outside the Plaza just faint enough to be appealing. She called all her old friends with her new address and number, urging them to drop in to see her, but she could hear from their voices that they felt she had moved to some level way beyond them. Some had read the newspaper stories about the million-dollar payment and sounded awed. Only Nancy Warner seemed genuinely happy for her, rushing over to look at the new apartment and rhapsodizing over the view.

"You'll *really* be able to write here!" she approved.

The Jacinthe Music Academy was impressed with Mark, and he settled quickly into his new school. Marcella walked him there some mornings, stopping off on the way back for cappuccino and muffins from a French bakery, taking them up to Amy, who was still in bed at ten, looking absurdly fragile in a lacy nightgown. Sometimes Marcella caught a man slipping out of the apartment just as she got there.

"*Where* do you find them?" she asked Amy, sitting down on her bed one Friday morning, handing her the cup of coffee. It was her fifth week in her new home. "They're always so handsome!"

Amy sniffed the cinnamon appreciatively. "Come to Members with me one night and you'll see!" She laughed.

"No, thanks." Marcella sipped at her coffee. "Funny, at one time I would have found the idea so exciting, Amy! Now, sex is about the furthest thing from my mind!"

"You're still in shock," Amy sympathized. "There's plenty of time to find your feet. But you *must* let Scott show you off to the bigwigs at Volumes. He expects you on Monday at ten. He knows about Harry and Sonia and he's been very understanding, but they're investing a million bucks in you. The least you can do is make an appearance and dazzle the pants off 'em!"

Marcella pulled a face. "I don't feel too dazzling these days," she sighed.

"It's part of being a writer, today, darling," Amy said, sipping her coffee. "*Anyone* can write a book, Marcella. It's what you do after it that separates the girls from the women. You think Judy Krantz or Danielle Steel just sit back and *hope* their books sell? You have to get out there and *push*! Make a stink over the cover if you don't like it. *Beg* for more advertising money! Travel out to the sticks to talk on obscure radio shows. Sign books in the Poughkeepsie branch of Barnes and Noble—until you're known!"

Marcella groaned.

"Appear on Johnny Carson," Amy continued. "Phil Donahue, Oprah! Answering with the title of your book, *whatever* question they ask you! 'Alligators? Funny you should mention those, Johnny, because in my book *In the Name of Love,* I blah, blah, blah! I—' See?" She stopped for breath, eyebrows raised high at Marcella. "You bring the subject back to your book, whatever they say. That's an art, Marcella, and you have to learn it."

"Do you really think I'll get on the Johnny Carson show?" she asked Amy.

"If he hasn't just interviewed Vidal or Mailer, why not?" Amy shrugged. "It's all timing and luck. And it *must* coincide with the week your book hits the stores or the viewers won't be able to find it, and that's death."

On Monday morning, Marcella modeled her new navy linen Italian suit for Amy as she waited for the driver Amy was providing as a boost to her morale.

"A million bucks!" Amy whistled as Marcella twirled.

"That's almost what it cost!" Marcella told her, laughing.

"Yes, but look what the jacket *does* for you," Amy said. The reflection in the hall mirror *did* show a longer, leaner Marcella. The buzzer sounded and Amy grabbed the house phone.

"She'll be right down," she told the driver. *"Now!"* Amy pressed the elevator button in the hall and brushed a hair from Marcella's shoulder. "Walk in there with your head held high. They thought enough of your book to pay a million bucks—more than they've paid any other first novelist."

As the Rolls drove her toward Volumes' offices, she smoothed the new skirt across her thighs and glanced down at her elegant feet in their three-hundred-dollar Manolo Blahniks. If only Sonia were found, everything would be so perfect, she thought. Why did life never allow you to have everything right at the same time?

Scott awaited her on the thirtieth floor. He kissed both her cheeks in the chic Manhattan tradition copied from France. She was surprised at how easy it was to be businesslike with him.

"I have a new office now . . ." he said, leading her to it.

Good, she thought. She had not relished the thought of seeing the place where they had made love so passionately six years ago. He led her into a corner suite that contained several elaborate arrangements of flowers. Behind his desk, shelves of recent best-sellers glinted, as if challenging her to match them.

"Any news of your daughter?" he asked gently.

She knew this was just politeness, but she appreciated the gesture.

"No . . . nothing," she said, facing him.

"I'm sorry," he said, offering her a cigarette. "It must be hell." He lit her cigarette. "I know you're probably not in the mood for this, but we are terribly excited about the book! Everyone wants to meet you. Most of them have read the manuscript, but I want to talk about editing and promotion plans for it. By the way, you're looking extremely beautiful, Marcella."

"Thank you, Scott," she murmured. Surprisingly, she felt absolutely nothing for him. Would that urge that used to seize her—that terrible, exciting urge, ever return? Or had it been a temporary madness, brought on by the frustration of being married to Harry?

"First we'll meet the publisher, Sydney Burroughs," Scott was saying. "Then a few department heads—foreign rights, publicity, art, and sales. There's a mock-up of the cover . . ."

"Already?" she asked. "I can't wait to see it!"

"No author ever likes her cover, you know," he warned. "Or very rarely. And your title's very long. You wouldn't like to change it, would you? 'In the Name of Love' takes up a lot of space. You could shorten it to 'Name of Love,' for example."

"That doesn't have the same meaning," she said, firmly.

" 'Name of Love'?" he cocked his head, trying it out. "*I* think it's snappy. Think about it."

Marcella shook her head. "I like my title," she said.

"And your name, Marcella . . ." Scott began.

"What's wrong with *that*?" She exhaled some smoke.

"Do you really need all three names? Couldn't you be just Marcella Winton?"

"*Scott!*" She leaned over to stub out her cigarette in his ashtray. "I made my father a promise that somehow I'd carry on his name. This is the only way I can do it!"

"Okay, okay." He jumped up, taking her arm. "I just thought I'd put in a word for the art department. They're very big on large type!"

They made the rounds of the editorial floors, and Scott introduced her to various editors, male and female, and their bright young assistants. Everyone had a compliment for Marcella, a wish of good luck for the book, and what seemed like a genuine enthusiasm. She was soon lost in the maze of warrenlike corridors and tiny cubicles where editors held their cramped meetings. Stacks of books, posters of previous successes, charts of works-in-progress, and shelves of manuscripts displayed the large amounts of work

Volumes editors were expected to do. The names of these smiling, professional faces went in and out of her memory as Scott introduced her. She vowed to bring a notebook next time.

Sydney Burroughs, an imposing man with a full head of white hair, was at the door of his large office when they arrived. He took Marcella's hand to kiss it.

"Our great white hope for 1985!" he greeted Marcella. "We're very excited about the book, and I see you're as pretty as Scott led me to believe!"

They sat in the corner section of his room, arranged like a lounge with sofas and table. As publisher, Burroughs was entitled to four large displays of flowers, she counted.

"I guess you read that everyone out there is hopping mad at us for paying you so much?" Sydney Burroughs gestured at the view across the skyscrapers outside. "They're scared every author will expect a million dollars for his book now!" He laughed. "But we've already got *over* a million dollars' worth of goodwill and publicity. Our British subsidiary has paid a quarter million dollars for the British rights. And a hundred housewives have sent us their secret novels."

"Oh *no*!" Scott groaned. "We'll need to hire more readers . . ."

Burroughs nodded. "But we'll also get the hottest novels from the hottest agents all year, because they'll *all* be looking for that million dollars!"

A secretary entered with coffee.

"Of course, we won't be paying a million dollars for many novels, Marcella," Burroughs assured her, as coffee was served. "Not everyone has your ability to sweep away the reader with that kind of forceful narrative. And *you* have great promotional value. She'll be on all the major talk shows, won't she, Scott?"

Scott nodded. "The modest little housewife who made a million with her very first novel. Every woman in the country will identify with her. They'll want to know why the book made so much money—is it sexy? Is it dirty? Does it make you cry? We'll groom Marcella to give all the right answers. She has a good start—her agent is Amy Jagger."

"You couldn't have a better master," Burroughs approved. "Or should I say 'mistress'? Of promotion, I mean."

"Scavullo will do her back-cover portrait," Scott told them. "Glamorous but not intimidating. Marcella should be accessible—to her readers."

Burroughs smiled at Marcella, replacing his coffee cup. "It sounds as if you're on the way to becoming a brand-name author, my dear." He stood up, to show them their interview was at an end. Holding out his hand, he said, "Glad to have you aboard."

After Burroughs, she met the foreign rights director, a glamorous brunette named Jaqui Nelson, who assured Marcella that rights to *In the Name of Love* would be snapped up by many countries in Europe and anywhere else where books were read. Scott took her into the publicity office next, where a couple of assistants cooed and fussed over her. Then the entire art department met her in a studio where a mock-up cover of the book awaited inspection. As she was introduced to the art director and his assistants, Marcella caught a glimpse of the cover. A woman's profile, nose buried in a bouquet held by a man's hand, filled the rectangle. The title, *In the Name of Love,* was splashed across the top, in curling, purple letters. Her shortened name, "Marcella Winton," occupied the bottom right-hand corner.

"Here's our author!" Scott announced. "Our Jackie Susann, Judy Krantz and Danielle Steel rolled up into one!"

Marcella smiled modestly; she was getting used to the outrageous claims Scott was making for her. She received some curious, appreciative glances from the young men, some interested looks from the women. They all turned back to the cover.

"My name, Scott . . ." she prompted.

"Oh, yes." Scott nodded. "I'm afraid you're going to have to squeeze in one more name down there, fellers," he told them. Someone groaned. He turned to Marcella. "What d'you think?" he asked.

They all looked at her and she knew she would have to be tactful. She had visualized a sexy cover; naked limbs or a bronzed couple embracing.

"It's interesting," she said, carefully. "Different . . . I

had thought you'd do something a little . . . I don't know
. . . sexier?"

The art director glanced at her. "Everyone's doing sexy
covers next season, so we thought *we'd* go for romance.
We're not entirely satisfied with it—it still needs some
work . . ."

After art, they moved on to one of Volumes' legal advi-
sors, a bright, bespectacled blond named Janey Bridgewa-
ter, who asked Marcella if there was anything potentially
libelous in her novel.

"For example, is any character based on a living person?" she asked.

"Only me!" Marcella glanced across at Scott and
laughed. "And I promise not to sue."

A few quick chats with the salespeople, who sat
hunched over computer screens in their sales center, and
then they headed back to Scott's office, where she collapsed on his sofa.

"You'll have to give me a list," she asked Scott. "I just
can't take in all those names at once."

"Good people, huh?" Scott said. He leaned over with a
light for her cigarette. "Now let's talk editing. There's a lot
of work that needs doing."

"What kind of work?" Marcella asked him.

"Well." He went back to his desk and sat down behind
it. "First I'd like you to do a little work on this!" he said.
He seemed to be holding something in his lap and she
strained to see what it was.

"What?" she asked, peering over the desk.

"Come see . . ." he urged her.

She frowned, getting to her feet and walking over to his
desk. Scott had unzipped his pants and was playing with
himself. He was rigid at the thought of what they were
about to do. Her eyes widened.

"Why don't you take off your panties and just come sit
on my lap?" he urged huskily. "I've locked the door; we
won't be disturbed!"

"I don't *believe* this!" Marcella cried. She felt ridiculously shocked, like some naive little girl. Perhaps it was
because sex could not have been further from her mind at
that moment. She walked back to the sofa and sat down,

facing him. "I can't believe you'd be so crude, Scott," she said.

"That's funny—you didn't think it was crude the last time we had a meeting," he pointed out. "That was quite a session."

"I'm a different person now," she said.

"What made you different?" he asked. "Having money?"

"No," she said sharply. "Having my kids kidnapped!"

"But you have the boy back," he said. "And you *are* the sexiest writer I've ever edited."

"Don't be so damned patronizing, Scott." She stubbed out her cigarette. "We're working on this book together, so please let's stay businesslike. I'm under a lot of pressure and the last thing I need is to be chased around a desk by you."

"Okay! Fine!" he said, zipping himself up. She could see his male pride was hurt. He grabbed the manuscript. "Let's get down to the holes in your story!"

"Which holes?" Marcella asked.

Scott squinted at her through the smoke. "We need to identify a lot more with Manuella. Understand *why* she allows her husband to abuse her for years—"

"She's frightened of him," Marcella cut in. "She's devoted to her children and—"

"And it's slow starting," Scott continued. "Let's cut out her childhood and get straight into the story. Let's build up the character of the attorney and see him away from the law courts, know *him* a little better. The law process has to be explained—legal accuracies, Marcella! Explain *how* this woman who kills her husband gets off scot-free because of her articulate attorney . . ."

"Scott . . . wait!" she stopped him. "Aren't you overdoing this a little? You've just taken me around the offices meeting about fifty people who all said they *love* the book, including the publisher!"

"They're aware it's going to be edited," he said.

"*Is* this editing?" she asked him. "Or is it taking out your hurt pride on my book?"

Scott shook his head. "I'd be saying the same things if we had just sweated through a hot and steamy session, Marcella."

"It sounds like you want me to write a different book!" She sighed. "I'm not even sure I *can* get back into the mood of that book again. I've lived it for so many years— it's over now for me."

Scott gave a deadly little smile. "I guess for a million dollars you can talk yourself back into it, huh?"

Marcella flushed.

"The million dollars was your idea, not mine," she said quietly. "I'd have been happy with one tenth of that."

Scott's eyes widened, then he burst out laughing. "Well, you're an original, Marcella, I'll give you that! Never let Sydney Burroughs hear what you said. Or Amy!"

She felt like a wrung-out rag as Amy's Rolls took her home. Scott had promised—or threatened?—to go through her manuscript page by page, marking the parts he felt needed "tightening up," making notes on the characters. *Her* characters! She went straight up to see Amy, fuming.

"How can he know what *my* characters think and do?" she exploded.

"Because he's an editor." Amy made a commiserating face as she plonked a bottle of champagne in an ice bucket. "Listen, my poor darling, no one just *gives* you a million bucks just like that. They make you sweat blood for it. Sure they like the book, but they figure you can make it just that bit better. So you do a little polishing."

Marcella sat hunched over on the sofa, her chin in her hands.

"It'll lose all its freshness!" she complained.

Amy popped the champagne cork and poured them both wine. "Rewriting is what makes us pros, Marcella. If it starts to go stale on you, go back to your very first draft when it was all new and fresh: snip out sentences and Scotch-tape them into your rewrite. That's how we old hacks do it! Cheers!"

They clinked glasses and drank some champagne. "It'll be a success," Amy assured her. "Don't worry! It *has* to be! How was Scott?"

Marcella glanced ruefully at her. "He made a really

crude pass," she told her. "Right out of one of *your* novels!"

"Oh my heavens . . . !" Amy trilled. "What a big, pumped-up thing it must be. I'm talking about Scott's ego! *How* did you handle it?"

"I was offended," Marcella told her. "I couldn't have been less in the mood."

"Too bad . . ." Amy sighed, sipping her champagne. "You two could have had the best editor-author relationship in the business."

After the manuscript of the novel was returned to her— and hardly a page had escaped Scott's critical scrawls— Marcella became so involved in her rewrite that she managed to stop thinking of her missing daughter for a few hours each day. Harry was still finding places where state laws allowed him to stay during the time-consuming process of applying for warrants and he hired lawyers who obstructed Marcella with counterclaims. Getting Sonia back was going to take a long time, although Amy's lawyer was working for her now and had filed a writ of habeas corpus before a New York judge. Marcella tried to resign herself to missing a chunk of Sonia's childhood, the important part as she changed from child to young woman, the part where a daughter most needed her mother. It was the time when she had hoped she and Sonia would draw closer, and she bitterly resented Harry for stealing it from her.

Mark continued to sleep in her bed most nights, claiming that it was the only way he could get a good night's rest. She knew it was wrong to continue this habit, but with her fingers in his soft hair and the warmth of his body near hers, it was some consolation for the loss of Sonia.

When Mark got home from school in the late afternoon, she put her work to one side and spent time with him and her mother. The nurse left at seven, and she or Mark would serve Ida her light supper in bed. Ida never asked about Sonia or Harry. The move to new surroundings had disoriented her, making her vague and forgetful. It was, Marcella regretfully realized, the start of senility.

Her greatest relaxation was still hearing Mark practice on the beautiful new baby grand she had bought him. Lying outstretched on the sofa, the leafy greenness of Central Park filling the windows, she would listen to Mark play Debussy and Chopin. She pictured Sonia growing up, playing with new friends, hopefully out in the open somewhere. She wondered if Sonia would ever be able to find out their new address or phone number and surprise them with a call.

Volumes refined the dust jacket for *In the Name of Love.* The woman's nose was still buried in a bouquet held by a man's hand, but now her hair was sleeker, her makeup heavier. The man's wrist showed expensive gold cuffs; the woman wore discreet diamonds at her throat and ears. Marcella saw no resemblance to her fiery heroine and gritty attorney, but Volumes' salespeople swore it got the message of the book across. Amy swooned over the cover, claiming it would be *"the* beach book" for next year. Marcella finished the rewrite in two months. The book would be rushed through for publication in July.

The second part of her advance was paid: money was disappearing at an alarming rate—Ida's nurse was expensive and so was Mark's school. She paid off some of her mortgage and let Amy guide her to hairstylists and makeup experts for "makeovers" that completely changed her. She was becoming a sophisticated, polished lady. Worry about Sonia and the family had cut her appetite; no longer did she devour plates of pasta. Her face, more defined because of her weight loss, now boasted flattering hollows below her cheekbones.

Amy's makeover of Marcella's social life was less successful. All the rewriting and worry had taken its toll on her energy, and she was constantly tired. Her natural instinct was to stay home, see Nancy Warner for an occasional dinner, or catch a movie with Mark. She did not feel up to dazzling the literary set as Amy expected her to do. Amy's little dinners for twelve to which Marcella was invited terrified her. She was not nearly sure enough of herself to enjoy conversing with heavyweights like Norman Mailer or Tom Wolfe or any of the other names that tended to pop up at Amy's glittering table. Amy always introduced her as "the writer who made a million dollars with her first book!" or "the writer whose earnings I'm retiring on!" Someone would ask, "What does it feel like?" Marcella would croak out, "Great!" and the evening would go downhill from then on, her fellow guests reducing her to an awed silence. Amy entertained everyone with outrageous stories, pouring champagne nonstop and serving up delicious food, none of which she prepared herself. She was expert at "improving" food with sprinkles of fresh coriander or dollops of sour cream and caviar. She was a generous, witty, sparkling hostess and she exhausted Marcella, who had no wish to compete. The beautiful crystal and china Amy had insisted she buy stayed in their wrappings.

When not entertaining at home, Amy was out.

"Members is still the hottest place," she told Marcella. "You *do* still have your membership card, don't you? When are you going to give us the honor of appearing there?"

Marcella had passed the building a hundred times, never feeling any desire to enter.

"*I* couldn't live without it." Amy vowed. "Come with me the next time I go, Marcella; it'll change your life!"

"Do you still visit that movie theater?" Marcella asked. "The one where they do disgusting things?"

Amy laughed. "I finally kicked *that* habit. But some of my best friends were hooked. It *was* almost perfect, sex with no strings! Very tempting, Marcella!"

When the first proofs for the book were back at the printers, Marcella suddenly had nothing much to do. She was marking time, waiting for publication. Under these conditions, she agreed to visit Members for the first time on a cold March evening.

Gossip columns had dubbed Members "*the* place for the '80s," its mood "tapping into the consciousness of the decade!" Sex seemed to be going undercover, to be replaced by health. This trend was being mirrored by more joggers and less attendance at nightclubs. Members simply created what Tom Wolfe called "the perfect environment for the Me Decade!" The gym, pool, sauna, and squash courts were booked ahead for weeks. It was said you could get an excellent massage and workout. The restaurant, bar, and nightclub easily accommodated the overflow, and members felt a self-approving glow simply from drinking a Perrier in these surroundings. At ten, Marcella and Amy arrived in the Rolls. Members took up one whole block on Ninth Avenue at Fifty-seventh Street. The building had once been an enormous movie theater, and clever architects had retained the art deco exterior. The details were highlighted with neon in unusual colors—cream, pale pistachio, lavender. No name appeared on the building, which was painted matte black, adding to its mysterious quality. It was designed to be exclusive and anonymous, the lasered membership card sliding into a slot to spring open the door. A nightly straggle of would-be guests huddled outside the door, watching arrivals, hoping that if they caught the right eyes, they might be invited in as someone's guest. Inside, moody blackness reigned, with rows of tiny bulbs outlining doors, elevators, and escalators in a chic, high-tech-sauvage decor of pipes, Grecian pillars, weird antiques, and stuffed animals. Ceilings sparkled or reflected, and the floors were black and slippery, giving the impression of being carved from black marble.

They looked in at the dark bar with its fake old-master paintings, overstuffed couches covered in black-and-white gingham, and a lady harpist plucking soothing medleys. Amy ushered her into an elevator, whisking them down to the basement.

"I want you to see the movie club," she winked. "Just in case." They stepped out of the elevator. There was a mock candy counter that dispensed free cartons of popcorn. It was utterly silent as Marcella glanced down the mirrored dark corridor that led into the theater.

"Uncomplicated, anonymous, pure sex," Amy murmured in her ear. "The most exciting kind in the world."

The miniature marquee listed an "Alfred Hitchcock Season" and detailed the week's showings. A burst of muffled background music reached them from inside. Suddenly Marcella's heart began to pound with an odd mixture of longing and dread. She tried to imagine Amy, a multimillionairess, a beautiful successful woman, entering a place like this, sliding down in her seat and parting her legs to let a stranger grope her. The lewdness of it made her shiver.

"I'd scream if a strange hand touched me," she murmured, leading Amy back to the elevator. Amy smiled secretively. "It's like caviar," she said, "an acquired taste!"

Marcella glanced at their reflections in the elevator mirror as it purred to the top floor's restaurant. Amy must have something stunted within her to enjoy that kind of sex. Worse, she must have recognized the same quality in Marcella even to suggest it. But the idea lodged in her mind. All evening, as they ate, drank, and watched the dancing in the disco, she thought of that silent, dark theater in the basement and imagined what must be going on down there. One day perhaps, she promised herself. If I'm ever brave or desperate enough . . .

SEVEN

"You think *I'm* crazy?" Sonia would ask of the people around her, later, when she was famous and successful. "You should have seen my childhood!" Well, of course it hadn't really been a childhood. More like a hard-edged video called "On the Lam with Dad." "On the Road." "On the Run." Whatever.

The twelve-year-old child had not fully understood what was going on then. She had only known she was now sharing life with her daddy. That life, one Saturday afternoon, had changed from its usual predictable pattern to something fast and dangerous.

It had started out as fairy-tale wonderful. From the moment Daddy had asked, "Do you want to stay with me or go back to Mommy with Mark?" she had realized what had been wrong with her life up to then: she had never had enough of him to herself. Now she would no longer need to feel left out when Mark and Mommy shared their private talks and jokes and looks; she had *him*! But from the first terrifying night Mark left, from that dreadful moment when she had seen her sweet loving daddy get so mad that he had pushed Gloria to the floor and kicked her, she had realized her daddy had two sides to him and life with him was going to be exciting and scary because he might one day show that other side to her. She had never seen Daddy so mad before, his face absolutely frightening as he bundled all their clothes into their suitcases for the second time that week, hustled her into the car, and with Gloria's yells still echoing behind them, driven off fast into the night. Since then, they hadn't stopped. And those screams, of a woman hurt by her daddy, continued to echo in her nightmares as she slept fitfully, rocked on the backseat.

"Why were you so mad at her?" she asked when they stopped at a coffee shop the next morning and he bent, grimfaced, over a map.

He looked up and she got a little thrill because he talked to her like an adult. "People think they own you because they help you make a little money," he said. "Well, nobody owns *me!*"

She had nodded, pretending to understand and agree.

And so they ran. From town to town, she did not always understand why they were running until Daddy turned it into a game. "Running away," the game was called. From Mommy. From the police. It was a grown-up version of hide-and-seek, using the entire country instead of a few rooms in an apartment. If they were found, Daddy told her, she would have to return to New York without him and would not see him for a long, long time. She couldn't bear the thought of that, so she never complained about the constant traveling, hardly blinked an eye when she got home from yet another new school to find their bags packed and Daddy giving her that look, telling her: "We're on the road again, princess!"

They lived in six, eight, ten different places before she lost count, until Daddy's finger on the map showed just how far they had come from New York. It was like living in a constant crisis, but her child's mind adapted immediately. She loved the idea of escaping from whomever was looking for them, of fooling them. But there were many things she did not understand. The different new mommies, for instance. Why did they start off so friendly with Daddy and end up fighting with him? Why was there a different mommy every few days, even when they stayed awhile in the same town? Why did they slip into bed with Daddy only when they thought she was asleep? She had heard a lot of things by pretending to be asleep. She knew, for example, that Daddy had found a lot of money because sometimes, when he thought she was sleeping, he counted it. Great piles of hundred-dollar bills that filled almost a whole suitcase!

Once they had given a lady a lift in their car, but she had said something that made Daddy mad and he had stopped the car in the middle of a long, hot road and just tipped the lady's suitcase out of the car and made her get out, too. The lady had screamed at him as he pushed her out of the car, slammed the door, and drove off. Sonia had glanced at her dad's tight profile and finally asked, in a very small voice, "Are you just leaving her there?"

He had said, very angrily, "Damn right I am!"

That night, in the motel, she had her first nightmare about Daddy throwing *her* out of the car in the middle of a freeway and woke up sobbing, clinging damply to him, too terrified to put into words the images and fears that had haunted her. She loved him and she was afraid of him at the same time. She had to treat him carefully because if he ever got the slightest bit mad at her for some little thing, she felt the panic bubble up inside her that would not be stilled until he called her his princess and assured her he would never leave her. She only had him, there was no one else to turn to, to talk to, to advise her: Daddy was everything.

There were other weird things in this new life that she had to grow used to. Like her clothes. Mommy would never have let her wear a pair of socks two days in a row, and she had developed into a fastidious, well-groomed little girl. Now, when she sniffed at her clothes, they smelled back at her, the jeans often showing traces of dried food— patches of spilled catsup from endless cheeseburgers, mustard dripped from hot dogs. When they ventured into more elegant restaurants to vary their diet, she felt everyone was staring at her messy clothes.

Sometimes she had a tummy ache. Sometimes Daddy took all their clothes to a washing machine, leaving her naked in bed at night, the motel room door locked until his return. Her clothes would come back streaked with other colors, creased, never pressed flat like Mommy had done. Her tee-shirts shrank in the hot water Daddy used and a bare midriff became her uniform.

As several new mommies came and went in the weeks after Gloria, she began to realize that these women were not mommies at all. They were simply friends of Daddy's, women who were nice to him and cuddled up to him in bed because he was lonely. Sometimes they made funny sighing noises and moved around a lot in the bed with him; and Sonia, if she were in the same room, closed her eyes tightly and stuck her fingers in her ears. Once or twice, she heard him telling a lady that he liked her a lot but that they had to move on because Sonia's mommy was looking for her. That taught her that even when a man liked a lady a lot, he was forced to leave her. Often, she would return from her new school and find him drinking from a bottle of strong-smelling stuff, telling her he was alone. She would get that feeling of wanting to stop him from ever being sad again, a feeling inside her that felt as if it would explode. She would touch his hand or hug him until he felt better. It always worked. After a while, he would get up and say, "Okay, princess! Looks like it's just you and me!" Then he would talk to her because there was no one else to talk to, and her big violet eyes would lap up his words, adoring his confiding in her. She was only twelve but she had played the part of a woman since Mark had left them: she was responsible for her daddy.

They finally reached a town that, as he pointed out on the map, was in the very center of the country.

"They'll never think of looking for us here," he told her. After that, he grew a beard and didn't even look like her daddy anymore. They rented a small house that reminded her of movies she had seen on television, a house that stood all on its own in a yard with a white fence around it. She was enrolled in the local school, where the other kids mocked her stuck-up airs and were mean to her. But when they saw she could be just as mean back, they finally accepted her. She was just starting to make new friends when Daddy said it was time to move on again.

Sometimes Daddy met a nice new lady who had other children. They were once invited into a lady's house for a few nights and a great fuss was made of Sonia. She suddenly had a new brother and sister, both around her age, and the lady ironed her clothes beautifully like her real mommy had done, brushing her hair and braiding it. Sonia cried when they left because she suddenly missed her own mommy. She was very wary of the next lady to make a fuss of her and told her, "You're only being nice to me so my daddy will like you!"

The lady had slapped her for that, hard, and said, "What a nasty mind you have!" but Sonia knew she was right. She became used to being an object of curiosity. Everyone at school stared at her, no matter how she tried to look like them and blend in. Being stared at became her natural state.

"You know why they stare at you, princess?" Daddy asked her when she complained.

She nodded gravely. "I guess so."

"It's because you're the most beautiful girl in the world and everyone else is jealous!"

She would make a horrible face and he would laugh. She loved the achievement of cheering him up.

"You think *I'm* crazy?" Sonia would ask much later. "You should have seen my childhood!"

On Sundays they went to church and she watched Daddy on his knees praying so sincerely. After, local women would gather around and praise him for being such a devoted father. He told them her mother was dead and she didn't dare contradict him.

"Why?" she asked, afterward.

"We can never tell anyone that we ran away from New York," he warned her. "It's a secret!"

She liked sharing this important secret with him, along with all the others—the money, the many mommies, the way he had kicked Gloria, the way he could become another frightening scary person if he chose.

One night, he woke her up to watch a movie on television. The movie was called *National Velvet* and he said the little girl in it looked like her. She thought so too—they could have been sisters. She wanted to go back to sleep but the story gripped her. She identified so much with the girl riding the horse that from then on she knew she would never be happy until she had a horse of her own.

It had begun as a game, their life on the road, but she got tired of playing the same game. She began to nag Daddy about a horse until he promised her she could learn to ride when they settled down. When would that be? she wondered. It felt as if they had been traveling for years, had led twenty different lives, met hundreds of people, made dozens of false starts, but it had only been six months. She was sick of smelly, creased clothes and eating in coffee shops. When she complained to Dad, he would say, "But we're *winning*, princess!" Her mom still hadn't caught up with them, they had crossed the entire country, and they were free!

They ended up in California, in a small coastal town that was horse crazy. It was by a large racetrack that enjoyed a long season from April to October. They arrived in late September, renting a small furnished clapboard house by the sea. Harry enrolled her at a local private school where she once again expected to be stared at or teased, but the kids here were from rich families and had seen too many other kids come and go to be impressed or curious.

All she wanted now was to learn to ride, to have her own horse, to groom it and love it and be like that little girl in the movie. Dad wouldn't let her take riding lessons at first, in case they had to move on quickly. But after a few weeks, she felt him relax. It was such a slow, sleepy town that it was impossible to believe anything bad could happen to you here. People seemed to mind their own business, and no curious waitress or schoolteacher ever asked Dad what he was doing all alone with his little girl, or where her mommy was.

Dad stayed home alone all day, hunched over newspapers and figuring out long columns of numbers. He woke up very early each morning to call New York because it was three hours ahead of their time. That made her feel even more cut off from their former life, as if they lived on another planet where even the time was different. When she asked him who he called each morning, he said it was a friend who did business for him but charged a lot of money for doing it. "Bleeding me!" was the way her dad put it. He told her it might be better if they changed their name from

Winton to Ashton, and she obediently practiced her new signature, Sonia Ashton, on her schoolbooks.

She liked getting a new name because she could invent a new Sonia to go with it. This girl could hide the old Sonia, provide a refuge for her. She learned to camouflage her startling beauty, the beauty that worked so well with grown-ups but seemed to cause resentment among kids her own age. If she dressed in the ripped jeans and worn tee-shirts that were now the uniform of every California child, unruly hair curtaining her purple gaze, mouth contorted by bubble gum chewed in a tough manner, she would not be so stared at, so exclaimed over. The new tough Sonia only had a father. The old Sonia had a mother and a brother who either thought her dead or who hated her for having run away from them.

She lay awake in bed each night thinking about her new life. She still got that old panicky feeling in her stomach when she came home from school each afternoon, expecting to see their suitcases packed. She had to survive this split in her life, in her thinking, this split that told her to put on her tough face as she left the house each morning for school, pulling on a baseball cap sideways over tangled hair that no mother bothered to brush, twisting her jaw into a cool scowl. She had tremendous, secret power within her because she could go from this character to becoming Dad's beautiful princess simply by scraping back her hair and relaxing her jaw. Without actually defining it to herself, she was these two Sonias and she had different names and two different signatures to prove it.

She made a new friend at school, Gemma, who shared her passion for horses, inviting her to watch her classes at the Laurie Cass Riding Academy. The riding school was a few blocks' walk from where Sonia lived. After the lesson, one of the stable hands, a black boy named Eddie with a smiling round face, let them help him groom and feed the horses. Gemma's mother, a tall, faded blond lady, would collect them and sometimes take them for a frozen yogurt at a nearby outdoor stand. Sonia called Gemma's mother Mrs. Hailey. She was divorced—that was probably why she looked so sad, Sonia thought. Mrs. Hailey sometimes reached out her hand to sweep back Sonia's hair.

"If you held your head up, you could be a model, Sonia," she said. "You could make a lot of money."

Sonia laughed. Grown-ups could be so silly. A lot of passersby had told her or her dad that she could be one of those grinning girls in the magazines or on television commercials. It was just about the last thing she wanted to be.

"Dad would never let me," she told Mrs. Hailey.

She watched so many of Gemma's lessons that she felt she already knew how to ride. In her dreams, her legs gripped the back of a horse as they rode for miles along a beach. In her dreams, the horse was half human and read her thoughts and spoke back to her. There was something familiar and loving about the horse and Sonia dearly loved him back, waking each morning with the heartbreak of losing an old, dear friend.

She adored the owner of the riding academy, Laurie Cass, and told her father about her.

"She's real pretty and she's strict, but nice, and she loves horses as much as Gemma and I do . . ." she said.

Laurie Cass was an outdoorsy type with red hair and white skin, and one afternoon she hoisted Sonia onto the saddle before her, on the back of her favorite mare, Red. They rode fast, Laurie holding tightly on to her, Sonia's legs dangling over the sides of the horse, forced to find the rhythm and bounce up and down to it with Laurie.

The wind swept into her face and it seemed to her that no one had ever moved this fast across the ground, the hooves hitting the earth with such weight, such speed. When she got off, she was dizzy with pleasure and she thought that ride had been the dearest, most generous thing an adult had ever done for her.

"Thank you so much, Laurie!" She hung on to Red's reins, her face glowing as she looked up. "I ask my dad every day if I can have riding lessons. He's got to give in soon!"

Laurie laughed. "Don't overdo the nagging, honey— you know what men are like!"

But persistent nagging did finally get her the riding lessons she craved, *and* the jodhpurs and the hat and everything else Gemma had and that she had so coveted. She begged her father to watch the lessons. It got him out of the house, away from being hunched over the newspapers and phone, and soon he was talking and laughing and listening to Laurie the way everyone else did, and he seemed to like her as much as Sonia did. When he suddenly shaved off his beard, Laurie said how young her father looked.

Laurie Cass was Sonia's ideal of what a woman should be—beautiful and sporty at the same time. There was nothing tough about her, but she could be strict and she would yell at someone if they disobeyed her instructions. She had dead straight auburn hair that swung against her cheeks as she rode. Her face had freckled white skin and her pale blue eyes sparkled. She always wore navy mascara that caught the light and made her glamorous.

"I'd look like an albino without this." She laughed when Sonia caught her applying it using a small mirror in the stables. Sonia promised herself that one day she would wear navy mascara too. She had adoringly asked Laurie her age and Laurie had laughed and said, "Ninety!" Grown-ups were funny about age, scared of seeming too old, yet Sonia couldn't wait to be older. She guessed Laurie was around thirty.

"Why aren't you married?" she asked Laurie as they groomed Red. Part of her course included grooming and it was her favorite part.

"Oh, I was, honey." Laurie did not look up from the broad brush strokes she was applying to Red's back. "To a very beautiful man. He was killed in Vietnam."

Because she was embarrassed about the death part, Sonia asked, "How can a man be beautiful, Laurie?"

Laurie smiled to herself. "See this horse?" she asked Sonia. "Isn't *she* beautiful? That's how a man can be beautiful. And *he* loved horses, too. We would have run this place together, that was our dream. His life insurance started this off. He would have been pleased about that."

Sonia begged her father to give a barbecue in their backyard one Sunday afternoon. She wanted to repay all the kindnesses Gemma's mom had shown her and also to invite Laurie. He agreed, and they bought hot dogs and steaks. Sonia noticed that her father spent a lot of time talking with Laurie and that Laurie looked prettier than usual, with more makeup on than she wore at the stables and, for the first time, a dress—a white, silky one that blew in the breeze.

Soon Laurie Cass began visiting them often, sharing dinner some nights, cooking more barbecues just for the three of them. And early one Saturday morning, Laurie Cass was in a white toweling robe belonging to her father, standing in the kitchen brewing coffee and scrambling eggs for their breakfast. She looked up, smiling, as Sonia hesitated on the threshold of the kitchen.

"Guess I stayed pretty late last night!" she said by way of explanation.

Her father joined them, fully dressed, saying "Morning!" gruffly, winking at Sonia, as if a breakfast guest was nothing unusual.

Sonia suddenly ran out of the kitchen to her room, slamming the door of her bedroom. She stood by her bed, frowning, as different reactions raced around her brain. She felt furious, but she did not know at what. She kicked the bed, hard, a couple of times, to get rid of that feeling. Then she felt terribly happy that Laurie was now going to be one of the family and rejoined them for breakfast, determined to be as adult as they were.

"They're *lovers*!" she couldn't wait to tell Gemma later that morning, when Harry and Laurie had gone out.

"Only if they slept in the same bed!" Gemma insisted. "And if they did, she's pregnant!"

Sonia shook her head. "The bed was made when I looked in his room after breakfast and Dad *never* makes it till the night. *She* must have made it!"

Gemma's eyes widened. "Your dad will marry Laurie and she'll be your stepmother! You'll get to ride Red as much as you want—*neat*!"

Sonia thought. They were sitting on the front porch of the house, sipping chocolate milk.

"He can't marry her," she told Gemma, remembering he was still married.

"Why not?" Gemma asked. "Laurie's a widow. And your dad's a widower!"

Sonia regarded her friend. "He just wouldn't, that's all," she said.

Not long after that, her father called her into his study while Laurie was at the stables.

"What would you say to Laurie moving in with us?" he asked, smiling.

What would she *say*? It was wonderful, a dream come true! Gemma could be as jealous as she liked! She would have Laurie all the time, more of an elder sister than a mother.

"Have you told Laurie anything?" her father asked. "About the family and all?"

"Of course not, Dad!" Sonia cried resentfully. "I never say anything to anyone, not even Gemma!"

"Good. . . ." He leaned on the desk. "If Laurie asks you, say your mother's dead. *And* your brother."

Sonia frowned. "Why?"

"Because if Laurie knew I was married, maybe she wouldn't bother with me," he said, embarrassed. "She's a very decent woman and I—"

"But you would *like* to marry her?" Sonia asked him.

He nodded, holding out his hands for hers. "Sure I would, but I'd have to divorce your mother first. Then your mother would get you back and I'd lose you. You don't want me to lose you, do you, princess?"

She ran behind the desk to hug him, shaking her head.

"So if I married Laurie, I'd have to lose you, and I'm never going to let *you* go, princess, *never*!" he promised.

She held on to him tightly, thinking this was the happiest moment in her life.

Early in the new year, they moved to a larger house, closer to the stables, and Laurie moved in with them. Maybe her father and Laurie were not exactly married but they were as good as. Laurie said she didn't give a damn what people thought. That was another thing Sonia loved about her. She decided to adopt the same attitude and not give a damn either. This new family, this new life-style, was as near as her new life had come so far to being normal. Only when she thought back on it, much later, did she see the unreality of it, highlighted as it had been by that perpetual hard-edged California sun, red-orange by five o'clock, making everything seem like a Hollywood movie anyway.

She remembered then the constant fear she had lived with, that feeling that her new life could suddenly, nervously, end at any moment, as quickly and as oddly as it had begun.

June 1985

"Heeeeeeeeere's *Johnny*!" Ed McMahon cried, and the audience screamed, cheered, and whooped just as it had when Marcella had watched the show at eleven-thirty in New York during all those early years of her marriage. She glanced at the monitor in the hospitality room of NBC-TV in Burbank, California, shivering from the air-conditioning and from fear. They had flown out the night before, staying at the Beverly Hilton.

The publication date for *In the Name of Love* was officially the next day, but the book had already been shipped to stores around the country. The enormous shipments reflected the "buzz" that Volumes had successfully spread about the book, their provocative advertising campaign alerting both the public and the book trade to expect something special.

The press had been eager to interview the "million-dollar author," portraying Marcella as a thrilled housewife who had been lucky enough to sell her first book for a seven-figure sum. Although she had pointed out to each journalist how long it had taken her to launch her career and how many rejections of her stories she had received, they always made her success sound easy. Now, even if the book fell flat on its face, there had been enough noise made to boost Volumes' recognition factor and Marcella Winton's name.

Marcella clenched her jaw to keep her teeth from chattering with fear.

"I've never been so scared in my life!" she confessed.

Amy glanced at her. "How can you be? I gave you an industrial-strength tranquilizer that could knock out a *bull*! We've gone over this a hundred times. You look terrific. You know what to say. *Relax!* In an hour it will all be over and we'll go get smashed at Spago. What do you say?"

Marcella stared at her. "I say I'm gonna throw up!"

Amy patted her hand. "No, you won't."

They watched a well-known star with a well-known "abuse problem" cluck past with secretary, hairstylist, and makeup man in attendance. Marcella had already gotten her brief handshake from Johnny Carson in orange makeup just before he went on.

"Some people have called *In the Name of Love* a dirty book!" she rehearsed in her mind. "I happen to think it's romantic. Sexy books have always been written: I thought, 'Why don't *I* write one?' What's wrong with men and women making love, Johnny?"

Suddenly everything she had planned to say sounded utterly stupid and banal.

"I'll never be able to say any of the lines you've pounded into me," she burst out to Amy. "Tell them I'm sick." She stared helplessly at her friend. "I can't go on. . . ."

"Marcella . . . darling . . ." Amy placed her arm around Marcella's quivering shoulders. "Remember when you were fourteen and your mother washed your mouth out with soap for telling sexy stories? You told me you wanted to kill her, right? Well, I want you to use that anger to give you the energy to go out there and explain to everyone why you *love* writing these stories now! Be the wonderful Marcella I was so delighted to discover at Le Cirque all those years ago. Tomorrow women are going to walk into those bookstores, see your book, and say, 'Oh *yes*! I saw her on the Johnny Carson show last night. . . .' *You're* going to make them want to buy the book. So go out there and *sell* it!"

"Maybe if I had a drink?" Marcella moaned through clenched teeth.

"Not after that tranquilizer, Marcella." Amy shook her head. "We want you *alive* for Johnny. *Flirt* with him! The audience loves that. Say outrageous things so he can go into his embarrassed 'aw, shucks' routine. That's what *I* do with him. Stand up to him."

"Will you shut up, Amy?" Marcella growled.

She watched, speechless with fear, as the guest before her, a male singer with a comeback hit, prepared to go on.

A production assistant approached. "Marcella?" She smiled, listening to something in her earphone. "Watch me, okay? As they applaud him, we'll go to commercials and then I'll give you the sign. You come to the side of the stage and wait for your introduction. When they start playing the music, I'll give you another sign and that's when you walk out."

"And if I throw up?" Marcella asked.

The assistant winked at Amy. "We'll edit it out of the tape," she assured Marcella, and walked away. Marcella swallowed hard and watched the monitor. She tried not to imagine her own face appearing on it, as that made her even more nervous. She reached for Amy's hand and held tightly on to it, like a little kid.

Her dress was emerald green, a discreet diamond clip borrowed from Amy at the neck. Her auburn hair had been pinned up by the Beverly Hilton hairstylist, her makeup somewhat muted by the NBC makeup room, so that she would not come across as too glamorous.

"You are supposed to be the average American housewife," Amy reminded her. "But that doesn't mean you can't be sexy, too," she hissed, adjusting Marcella's neckline to show a little more cleavage.

A passing technician stared at them and Amy giggled.

"He thinks we're two dykes!" she said.

The singer was only halfway through his song and Marcella was trying to take some deep breaths, but suddenly she was unable to breathe in very deeply. Time was moving faster than she wanted it to. She was just aware of the applause and Amy's last encouraging little push when the assistant's hand signaled her and suddenly the moment had come. She was now standing behind the curtain, listening to Johnny Carson introducing a new author. He was talking about *her*!

"As you know, we always try to keep you abreast of all the latest literary trends"—(audience laughter)—"so tonight we're talking to a lady who has never been on the show before. She's just sold her very first book for a million dollars, so she must be doing something right. Let's find out what it is. Please welcome Marcella Balducci Winton!"

Although they had never heard of her, there was a burst of applause. The orchestra struck up "Some Enchanted Evening," and feeling utterly ridiculous, Marcella made herself smile and walk out into the light. The atmosphere was stiflingly hot, the music and applause deafening. She blacked out and went through the rest of her appearance unconscious.

"*Why* is your book worth a million dollars?" had been the first question. She had explained that that was what Volumes estimated it could earn.

"I haven't had time to read it," Johnny had apologized, "but I flipped through it and it seemed to give off a little steam . . ."

"It sure did!" Ed had boomed.

Johnny gave his famous quizzical expression. "Kind of spicy?" he asked.

Ed laughed his famous laugh. "Well, I'd say so! Kinda!"

"Okay." Johnny got serious. "Let's not beat around the bush here. Let's get right to the point. Is this a dirty book, Marcella?"

She laughed. "Some people think so. But I've never thought sex was dirty. The book is uninhibited. It's romantic. There's a lot of passion!" She broke off, as Johnny mugged various funny expressions at the audience. And so it went, through a dozen gags, questions, and replies until suddenly Johnny was saying: "We wish you the very best of luck," holding up the book. "*In the Name of Love!* Everyone, go out and make Marcella Balducci a multimillionaire! Ed says it's hot! And thank you very much for coming on the show!"

A burst of applause and she was shaking hands with Johnny, and Ed was holding on to her other arm so that she could not leave the set until the commercials began.

She was unceremoniously helped from the chair as a makeup girl rushed to dab at Johnny's forehead. Marcella hovered at the edge of the set for a moment, watching her host sip water, trying to catch his eyes so that she could thank him or perhaps flirt with him, but all was high-powered professionalism here at the very pinnacle of fame and success. She suddenly understood how hard everyone worked to keep their hard-won positions; romance did not get a look-in.

She rushed into Amy's arms in the hospitality room. "I am never, *never* going to go through that again, I don't care how many books it sells!" she vowed. "I am *not* a performer!" she exploded, collapsing on a chair.

"You have Phil Donahue and Oprah Winfrey next week and you are going to win new fans on *both* shows!" Amy said firmly. "You will also appear on *any* small-town TV show that wants you, and *every* pokey radio station that shows the slightest interest!"

"Okay, but now I *don't* want to go to Spago," Marcella groaned. "I just want to go home."

They watched the show in their hotel bedroom when it aired that night, Marcella flat out on the bed, basking in the relief of her ordeal being over but hating the sight of herself and the sound of her voice. Amy plucked at grapes from the fruit hamper sent by Volumes. Mark called after he had seen the show in New York.

"You looked beautiful, Mom! I'm so proud of you!" he told her. The only other compliments came from Scott, when she returned to New York the next day, and her dry cleaner, to whom she took the emerald dress, imagining it soaked with nervous sweat.

When she walked back to her apartment, one of the doormen brandished her book. "My wife saw you on Carson," he told Marcella gruffly. "Can you put 'To Alma,' please? Was Johnny Carson a nice guy, Mrs. Winton?"

"Absolutely charming," she assured him, wondering if any guest ever got to know Mr. Carson.

Her mother's nurse assured her that they had both watched the show, the nurse staying over while Marcella was away.

"Did she recognize me?" Marcella asked, holding her mother's hand.

"I think she fell asleep, actually, Mrs. Winton," the nurse said. "But *I* saw you, and you were great!"

"Thank you!" Marcella kissed her mother's cheek, catching the nurse's eye. There was a kind of understanding between the nurse and herself not to admit that Ida recognized no one these days and hardly spoke. It made Marcella so sad that she could not face it.

There were messages on her answering machine from various heads of Volumes' departments: the publicist, the salespeople, and Scott asking if she could be at his office at six that evening. She assumed it was another press interview and dressed in one of her glamorous outfits, arriving promptly at six.

When Scott saw her, he slapped his forehead.

"Oh, I should have told you to wear scruffy clothes!" he said. "We're going to the warehouse."

"Which warehouse?" she asked.

"You'll see," Scott said mysteriously.

He drove her in his car to Queens, talking about the book and its promotion all the way.

"Our salespeople have done a terrific job," he told her. "There are cutouts, posters, and displays wherever Volumes' books are sold. We got the bookstores to feature you, Marcella, and we're very pleased with how you came across on Carson. It'll sell a lot of books. That modest little housewife act is brilliant."

"What if I told you it wasn't an act at all?" She twisted to look at him. "Maybe I'm not a housewife, but I still cannot believe all this is happening to me."

"Believe it!" he said. "We're shipping out a hell of a lot of books."

"What happens if they don't all sell?"

"Oh, you'll see 'em a few months later in the bargain bookstores, marked down to one ninety-five." Scott laughed. "And if you look up, you'll see me on the window ledge outside Volumes, wondering when to jump."

They finally reached a large neon sign proclaiming VOLUMES amidst some gray industrial buildings. Scott pulled up outside a long, low warehouse surrounded by railings and rang the bell. A security guard let them in. There were several outbuildings and the guard stopped outside one, handing Scott a bunch of keys. Scott crouched, as the guard left them, and unlocked a huge bolt. He pushed back a sliding steel door, revealing stacks upon stacks of cartons, each with a stenciled sign of NAME/LOVE on it. He managed to pull out a carton from one of the piles and rip it open with his hands. Twenty-four bright new copies of her novel fell out. As Marcella exclaimed in delight, he fumbled in his pocket for a small camera to take some shots of her.

"Just thought you'd like to see what a quarter of a million books look like!" He laughed. "The other quarter million are in the stores. If they sell, these follow them!"

"Oh, Scott!" She hugged him impulsively. "Thank you so much for bringing me here. I wouldn't have missed it."

She immediately regretted her action. Scott hugged her

back urgently, his grip pulling her close to him, his mouth suddenly covering hers. He kissed her and as his tongue broke through her lips, she backed off, surprised.

"Scott," she said. "If I'm not careful, you'll make love to me over a couple of cartons of my own book!"

"Would that be such a bad idea?" he murmured, holding her. "That guard won't be back until I buzz him."

She shook her head, kneeling to pile her books neatly. "You never give up, do you?"

He knelt, facing her, his hands on her wrists. "You used to be a very passionate sexy woman, Marcella. Don't tell me you didn't enjoy that first time together. I *know* you did!"

"Yes, I did." She took her hands from beneath his. "But things are different now. I don't like to mix business with pleasure."

"That first time wasn't business?" he asked.

She stood, brushing down her dress.

"I don't want to be one of the women you fool around with, Scott," she told him. "I'm looking for something much more than that."

"What are you doing for sex in the meantime?" he asked.

She smiled at him. "I put it all into my writing. That's why it's so sexy."

He shook his head, grinning. "What can I say? I guess as your editor, I can hardly complain. I'm here if you need me, okay?"

"Right." She nodded brusquely. "Now what do we do with all these books? You pretty much destroyed the carton!"

"Why don't you sign them personally for all the guys who work here?" Scott suggested. "They'd really appreciate that. We'll get the guard to tell us their names."

They carried a dozen books to the car and she sat with the door open, inscribing the books. Why had she not simply let Scott make love to her? she wondered. Was sex now so far down on her list of priorities that she was able to get through life without it, like Nancy Warner? Oh God, she hoped not.

On the drive back to town, Scott handed her a couple of magazines.

"Seen the trades?" he asked. "Not bad, considering . . ."

She turned to the pages marked in red. *Publishers Weekly* and the *Kirkus Service* had given her grudgingly good notices. "*In the Name of Love* is not nearly as bad as you'd expect," Marcella read out. She turned to Scott. "That's a *good* review?"

He laughed. "Coming from that guy, it's practically a rave!"

"Marcella Balducci Winton has a definite gift for stirring the heart and making the reader turn pages," she went on. "She could be a big-stakes novelist in the Krantz-Steel tradition. . . . We await her follow-up with great interest."

She shuddered. "This book is hardly out and they're putting on the pressure for a follow-up."

Next week, Marcella dutifully appeared on *Oprah Winfrey* and on a panel of writers including Amy, for a Phil Donahue show called "Whither Sex?"

"And now, we just have to sit back and see whether the thing sells!" Amy said.

Calls from Scott every few days advised her of its nationwide progress. The reorders from chain stores would be the first clue to its sales.

"It's *got* to be on the list by next week or the week after!" Amy called to say. "I'm more excited about it than if it were my own book!"

"The list" was *The New York Times* Book Review bestsellers list, which came out with the Sunday *Times.* Volumes had already taken a double-page advertisement to announce the book's publication. Now they awaited the news that Marcella's was among the fifteen best-selling books in the country.

"New York and Los Angeles are one thing, but we need all the states in between to become a true best-seller," Amy warned her. "They have to love you in Des Moines, too, honey!"

Marcella was too nervous and excited to do anything. She cleared her desk twice. Cleaned the apartment. Visited with her mother a dozen times a day. Cooked intricate dishes for herself and Mark. Writing was out of the question. And finally the news came one Thursday morning when the *Times* Book Review was printed that *In the Name of Love* had entered the list at number fourteen. Flowers arrived from Volumes and from Amy. Marcella sent flowers to Amy. Mark sent flowers to his mother. Champagne was toasted to the book's climb. Now the question was, How high would it climb? The following week it reached number eleven. Then nine. Then eight. By the end of August, the book had made it to number four.

"Let's see . . ." Amy ticked off the top three immovable books of that summer. "We have a spy novel, a historical saga, and a well-hyped piece of shit called *Hollywood Brats* by some ex-movie star. I don't think you could have done much better, Marcella. You are one of the big summer books!"

EIGHT

Just before her thirteenth birthday, Sonia's body began changing. A little later than usual, according to Laurie, who was wonderfully reassuring and helped Sonia buy a bra, gently explaining what was happening to her.

"There might be a day or two each month when you won't feel like riding," Laurie told her.

After her shower, Sonia would stare at herself in the bathroom mirror, noting each change. Girls at school giggled constantly about boys and sex. Sonia felt more grown-up than them because she was allowed to watch a mare foal. Eddie, the black boy who worked in the stables, had been there, too.

"A man can be as beautiful as a horse," Laurie had said. She had seen the head, then the body, hang out of the mare, get shaken and wriggled until it finally dropped, all shiny, to the ground, and then get licked clean as it stumbled on its shaky legs.

When she began to become a woman, so young, so early, her body stretched long and willowy, as tall as her father's, two small high breasts budding in her faded tee-shirt, hidden in the bra Laurie had bought her.

"You aren't even going through an awkward phase!" Laurie marveled. "No spots, no fat, and no antisocial fits, I hope!"

Slowly, carefully, she learned to apply makeup, not enough to upset her father, as she was very aware that he did not like the fact that she was growing up so quickly. If he noticed that she'd borrowed Laurie's lipstick or mascara for a special dinner, he made her wipe it off, as if he had become the barrier between her childhood and her adulthood. He noticed everything she did, wore, or said, as if he were studying her under a microscope.

For a while, in no hurry to forsake her tomboy activities, she followed his rules. No makeup, no heels, silly stuff like that which she didn't even care about. She playacted being a child for him. It was pretty easy—if you just ignored what was happening to your body. She liked her boobs staying small—they did not get in the way of riding. She and Gemma often giggled at the mature ladies with huge boobs bouncing up and down as their horses cantered.

She turned thirteen in June. Now the process of maturing was not something she could stop. With makeup and heels and adult clothing, she could look seventeen or eighteen. It almost frightened her to see how gorgeous she could become simply by piling up her hair and outlining her lips and eyes with makeup. She and Gemma tried it out one night when she slept over at Gemma's house and Mrs. Hailey was out. They dressed up in Mrs. Hailey's clothes, using her makeup. They went out at eight o'clock to a nearby singles bar, all painted and made-up, pinching each other to keep from exploding into giggles. They were just about to be served the tequila sunrises they had ordered when the bartender took a closer look and demanded IDs. The pair of them had taken to their precarious heels and run from the bar, screaming with laughter all the way home. There they had ripped off their clothes and washed off their makeup to become little girls again. They sat there, staring solemnly at each other, giggling now and then. For Sonia it had been an exciting taste of adulthood; the way those men had seriously looked at her as she had walked into the bar had given her an impression of the power she would possess as a woman.

Dad got more interested in the riding academy, and after dinner he and Laurie would discuss it for hours. Sonia listened to their talks on how to enlarge it, how to put more money into new stables, taking on more pupils, buying more horses, making it more profitable. When they discussed horse breeding, Laurie's eyes lit up. She said it was what she had always dreamed of doing, but was too expensive for her to try alone. She spoke of Arabian horses and thoroughbreds, steeds worth over a million dollars. A million dollars for one horse! Sonia reported the sum to Gemma and they both longed to see a horse that was worth a million, to see how it was groomed, how it moved, what made it worth that much.

Dad started to visit the stables. Then he invested in them. They were still called the Laurie Cass Riding Academy, but now he was there every afternoon in Laurie's office. He supervised the building of new stables, told Laurie to order new horses, wrote new advertisements to recruit pupils. They took on more riding instructors, too, to accommodate the growth.

"Your dad must have a lot of money!" Gemma marveled. Sonia said nothing. Some time ago, Dad had called her into the den and shown her several large pillows on the couch there. He unzipped one and showed her the white cover inside, which he unzipped too. Nestling between two slices of foam rubber were rolls and rolls of hundred-dollar bills.

"If anything ever happens to me," he told her, "you grab this!"

She eyed the money anxiously. "Why don't you keep it in a bank?" she asked.

"This is better than any bank," he told her. "This is your education, your security. This way they don't know what we've got."

She sometimes unzipped the cushion and felt inside to make sure the money was still there.

She heard lots of whispers and rumors about sex and knew roughly what men and women did together. Gemma provided more details. "He sticks his thing in her and they make a baby!" she told her. "Can you imagine how that feels?"

"Does it hurt?" Sonia asked.

"Yes!" Gemma said. "The woman screams, it hurts so much. And they can only do it if they're married."

Her father and Laurie were not married so maybe they did not do it, Sonia thought. Maybe they just cuddled up together the way she used to do with him when they had shared beds.

The only boy she was close to was Eddie. He was several years older than her and had been discovered by Laurie riding at Del Mar racetrack, down the coast. He was Laurie's favorite employee and certainly the most trusted. He had a friendly manner and a nice round face with a chunky, compact body. He was always doing special things for Sonia, handing her the wide bristled brush for grooming Red the moment she appeared. Gemma said he must be in love with her, but Sonia ignored that. She did not even think of Eddie like that. He was her friend, a kind of friend-animal-man, halfway between the horses and herself. When he stripped to the waist to throw buckets of water over the horses, his shiny black back matched the wet shiny coat of the black mare. She liked to hang around the stables helping Eddie, talking about horses and riders, breathing in that heavenly smell of horses and hay.

Her father told her not to hang around Eddie so much.

"Why not?" Sonia asked. She was starting to tire of the long list of things her father said not to do.

"When someone works for you, it's better not to get too close," he said. "Eddie is an employee. It's not good for your reputation when—"

"What's a reputation?" she interrupted.

"It's what people think of you," he explained.

"But I don't *care* what people think of me!" she assured him. "Neither does Laurie! She often says so!"

"Look, don't give me a hard time, Sonia," he suddenly growled. "I'm your father and what I say goes. At least until you're earning your own living."

Sonia's lips trembled. She couldn't stand it when he called her by her name because she knew he didn't love her then. It brought back all the old fears that he would walk out on her.

She ran to find Laurie, watching her preparing dinner in the kitchen for a moment, then bursting into tears.

"Why, what *is* it, honey?" Laurie dropped the vegetables she was peeling and took Sonia in her arms.

"Dad said I mustn't hang around Eddie," Sonia sobbed. "Eddie's my friend and I—"

"Oh, honey, don't get so upset!" Laurie soothed her, finding a handkerchief and wiping Sonia's cheeks. "Let me explain something about fathers and their daughters, Sonia. You've been your daddy's little girl all your life and now he sees you growing up, right? Maybe he feels he's about to start losing you and he's a little jealous of any boy you like?"

"Gemma says Eddie's in love with me," Sonia sniffed. "Is he, Laurie?"

"I think he loves you like a brother would love you," Laurie said.

"I *have* a—" Sonia began, then stopped. "I had a brother," she said.

"I know, baby," Laurie said, her mouth muffled in Sonia's hair. "Your daddy told me all about it. I'm so sorry . . ." Laurie's arms tightened around her and Sonia felt such a fake. She returned the handkerchief to Laurie and broke away.

"Do you really love my dad, Laurie?" she asked.

"I love you both," Laurie answered easily. "How else could I put up with you two?"

"And does Dad really love you?" Sonia persisted.

"Why don't you ask him?" Laurie smiled. "No!" She shook her head. "On second thought, *don't*! Men hate talking about love!"

Sonia did not pursue the subject. She instinctively knew that Laurie must be right. Men hated talking about love, she had said. Laurie was always saying things that pulled her up short and made her think. A man could be as beautiful as a horse. Laurie had said that, too.

That summer, Harry drove them down the coast for a vacation. They stayed in a beautiful old village called La Jolla, with the best views of the ocean she had ever seen. Each day they watched the racing at Del Mar racetrack. Guided by Laurie, Dad bet on the horses and won a lot of money. He laughed and hugged her and Laurie. In the town later, he told them to choose anything they wanted. Sonia dearly wanted a complete makeup kit that came in a transparent vinyl bag, but she sensed he would not approve and she didn't want the day spoiled with an argument. She settled for a portable stereo set with headphones and tapes of Kiss, Earth Wind and Fire, and Stevie Wonder.

While on vacation, they went to look at houses in a quiet rural area called Rancho Santa Fe. One home cost nearly a million dollars.

"What do you think?" Dad asked them.

She exchanged looks with Laurie. It was the most beautiful place Sonia had ever seen, with acres of grounds, two barns divided into stables, a tennis court, and a pool. It was like something out of a magazine. Small orchards of fruit trees surrounded the house. The village was just a few, sleepy well-kept streets. The real estate agent told them it was the place Hollywood stars came to for restful weekends. When Harry suddenly said he would buy it for them, she joined hands with Laurie and they jumped up and down, whooping with laughter and excitement.

They moved into their new home the following spring. Once they were settled in, Sonia would sometimes catch her father's eye and they would exchange happy, knowing looks. They had won! It had taken all fall and winter for the alterations to be done. Sonia was due to start a new school nearby, private and exclusive, with great emphasis placed on sports and riding. She wanted to take extra dance and acting classes, and Laurie promised to drive her into San Diego for those. Dad was going to breed a special horse just for her, out of Red.

Laurie was keeping on the old stables, commuting every two weeks to keep an eye on it. She was bringing the best horses to the Rancho Santa Fe house, and Eddie was coming to look after them.

Sonia celebrated her fourteenth birthday a month after their move. Gemma and her mother drove down for the occasion, at which Red was led from the stables by Laurie, a huge white satin ribbon tied in a bow around her neck.

"She's *yours,* Sonia!" Laurie announced, and everyone clapped and cheered and sang "Happy Birthday" as Sonia hugged her father and Laurie, thanking them. She threw her arms around her favorite horse and hugged her, too.

"I just can't believe she's mine!" she kept saying all that day. "My life is perfect now!"

At fourteen, she was very beautiful. Her body was long, lithe, athletic, and trim. Her breasts remained small. Her hips were boyish. Her voice was changing: drama lessons kept it breathy and low, disturbingly adult and sexy. In her dance and acting classes, she was by far the most talented. Now for the first time her beauty was an asset, not something to hide. She spent evenings in front of her bathroom mirror, finding different ways to fix her hair. Clothes were suddenly of great interest to her. It appeared to Sonia that her entire little world revolved around her, and she liked it that way.

"Don't you have to be Arab to breed Arabian horses?" she asked Laurie.

Laurie laughed. "No, just rich! Although these two brothers are Egyptian. I met them up at that horse auction last month and we got talking. They bought the very best—must be loaded. We could use just one morning of their stallion! When Red comes into season she could be the mother!"

"Oh, Laurie! I'll *die!*" Sonia cried. "My darling Red—a mommy!"

"I thought I'd invite them down," Laurie said. "Be real hospitable and friendly, and see if *they'll* be a little more cooperative. You know, maybe lower their price? It costs a fortune to get a horse like that for one morning. We'd have to pay transport, insurance, vet, all that stuff."

They had been living at Rancho Santa Fe only ten weeks when the Fazeen brothers accepted Laurie's invitation to see the ranch.

Sonia could not imagine what they would look like.

"This is just a friendly visit," Laurie told her. "They're

sizing us up. Seeing if we deserve to pay for their stallion's time!"

"What are their names?" Sonia asked.

"Fazeen," Laurie said. "Ashid and Gamal Fazeen. Ashid is the younger one. He's real cute. Pour on all the charm, Sonia . . ."

She frowned at Laurie and then caught her father's eye. He never got mad at Laurie, but she knew he did not like that comment.

"My princess doesn't have to put herself out to charm two Egyptian horse breeders," he said, chucking Sonia under the chin. "She's charming to everyone, aren't you, baby?"

Sonia made one of her horrible, cross-eyed faces and they all laughed.

She made up very carefully the morning of the brothers' visit, glad that the April weather was warm and sunny. She wanted her makeup to be very flattering and yet natural. She followed the lines of her eyelids with a dark gray pencil, then coated the lashes with the lightest touch of navy mascara. She only dared use Cherry Chapstick on her lips, but she touched her eyelids with lavender shadow and wore a lavender tracksuit that brought out the purple of her eyes and complemented the light tan of her skin.

Half hidden behind her bedroom curtain, she watched the brothers' Porsche purr slowly up the front drive. When Harry walked out to greet them, she crept downstairs and hid behind Laurie, waiting for them to enter the house. At the front door, Ashid stood just behind his brother. As Sonia craned her neck to see him, their eyes met. His dark gleaming eyes mesmerized her and she simply stared. She had vaguely imagined men in robes and headdresses, but Ashid was like no man she had ever seen. Around twenty-five, tall, tawny, glossy, with huge, sleepy black eyes rimmed with almost feminine long thick lashes and a moustache outlining a sensual mouth. A bright pink tongue flicked out nervously every couple of minutes to lick his lips. His straight black hair was oiled and brushed flat, sleek to his head. He wore an outfit she had never seen in California—a beautifully cut, light-gray suit, fresh white shirt, and tie. His polished loafers shone in the sunlight. Sonia hardly glanced at his older brother, Gamal, who was much fatter, with a drooping walrus moustache and a round face with weary eyes. Gamal's hair was receding and he kept mopping his forehead with a white handkerchief.

"This is our daughter, Sonia," Laurie introduced her. They had decided it would be simpler to pretend to be a family.

Sonia gave Ashid her most dazzling smile as they shook hands. His eyelids drooped almost flirtatiously, then assumed a sheepish, shy look as he glanced back at her. She shook hands with Gamal. Laurie served coffee and muffins and they chatted for a while, sitting in the den. Sonia couldn't keep her eyes off Ashid. He tried to escape her stare, looking at the others as he followed their conversation, but his eyes kept returning to hers, disturbed, confused, as if wondering how old she was or whether they would find a way to share a moment alone. It was the first time she had found herself attracted to a man and she cursed the fact that she was only fourteen. She would be nothing more than a child to him.

They toured the grounds, inspecting the stables, all remaining very quiet as Gamal gave one intent glance at the horses, which Eddie and his team had burnished to a gloss. They sat around the pool on wicker chairs after, discussing the brothers' operations. Harry was particularly interested in how a prize stallion was loaned out for breeding, what it cost, how the horse was insured and transported.

"It is very expensive, Mr. Ashton," Gamal murmured with a throwaway gesture. "*Very* expensive!" as though Harry could not possibly afford it. It was obvious, from the weary way he answered Harry's questions, that he was unimpressed by the size or the quality of the stables.

Sonia felt a fierce rush of defensive anger. They had all worked so hard to make the stables look good.

Languidly, Gamal accepted a glass of Perrier and one of the dainty sandwiches that Laurie had decided was suitable Egyptian fare. Sonia continued to hold Ashid's eyes in her purple gaze. If she projected enough emotion through her eyes, she thought, as she had been taught in drama school, perhaps *she* could persuade Ashid to convince his brother to supply the stallion.

She wandered over to refill Ashid's Coke and hand him a dish of nuts, allowing their fingers to touch. It wasn't her imagination: there was a definite jolt of electricity between them. Dad and Laurie were so intent on impressing Gamal that they noticed nothing. But if Ashid could have blushed, he would have been blushing by now. His olive-skinned face, with its heavy shadow of beard, looked hot. His eyes darted furiously around, coming back to settle on Sonia for one confused moment, then took off in all directions again. She felt a surge of triumph.

Suddenly, Laurie looked over at them. Playfully, she asked, "And what about Ashid? What do *you* think about all this?"

Ashid waved a modest hand.

"Oh, I leave all the business to Gamal!" He laughed. "I am merely training to become an attorney!"

Sonia seized her chance, grabbing Ashid's hand and pulling him to his feet."

"C'mon, I'll show you around," she said, before her father could object.

When they were out of sight of her father, she dropped Ashid's hand. It was hot and clammy. He shot her a sidelong glance as they crossed the orange orchard.

"How old *are* you?" he suddenly asked.

She laughed out loud. "I *knew* that's what you were wondering!" she told him. She struck a pose. *"Guess!"*

He stopped walking and faced her.

"It is always difficult to tell with American girls. . . ." he frowned. She loved the way his handsome face studied her, as if she were an important problem to be solved.

"Either you are very young and trying to seem older," he concluded, "or . . ." his black eyes sparkled, "you are fairly old and trying to seem younger!"

Sonia gave a peal of laughter. At that moment, in the shadow of the orange trees, she looked so fresh, so tantalizingly on the borderline between child and adult, that to Ashid she was quite irresistible.

"Okay. Sixteen?" he guessed.

She pursed her lips, cocking her head. "Not bad. Fourteen!"

"Oh. . . ." He shook his head solemnly at her. *"Much* too young!"

"Much too young for you?" She pouted.

"Much too young to be such a shameless little flirt!" He laughed. "You shall have to be my little sister."

They resumed their walk and reached the tennis court. She stopped at the net and stuck her fingers through it, turning to him.

"Your brother isn't very impressed by our horses, is he?" she asked.

"Probably not," Ashid agreed, to her disappointment. "But Gamal is almost never impressed. *He* has the best, he thinks!"

She took his arm and hung from it.

"The horse my father wants to breed from is mine, Ashid." She looked up at him. "Can't you use your influence? I'd *die* to see my horse's foal! I'm crazy about horses. . . ."

"I don't *have* much influence, I'm afraid," Ashid said very seriously. "I am simply Gamal's younger brother."

"Promise you'll try?" she urged. "It would mean so much to my Dad and—I'd get a chance to see you again!"

"I would like that," he said, looking down at their two hands together. Her hand looked very white in his large, bronzed one. She moved closer to him, her cool fingers moving in his palm until that sheepish look came over his face again.

"You're so handsome," she whispered.

"Yes?" He tore his eyes away from their hands to search her face and she saw, to her thrilled delight, that he was nakedly looking for some clue to her sincerity. He swallowed and she watched his Adam's apple move against his shirt collar.

Lightly, he said, "And you speak like this with all the men who come to do business with your father?"

She dropped his hand, lowering her eyes. "You're the first man I've ever spoken to on my own. . . ." She put on a hurt face and turned away.

"Sonia! Wait!" He took a big step and caught at her hand. Then he brought it to his lips and kissed it. His dark eyes gazed wonderingly into hers. "I think you must be the most beautiful girl I have ever seen!"

She smiled into his eyes. "Thank you, kind sir," she said.

She had heard someone say that in a movie and had saved it up for just such a moment.

"I'll talk to Gamal on the way home," Ashid promised. "But I warn you, he rarely listens to me!"

"Thank you," she whispered. "Thank you so much, Ashid." She put her hands on his arms and tiptoed to kiss him. His lips were so much softer than she'd imagined. As they kissed, lightly, she noticed his eyes close as if he were giving in to some forbidden bliss.

The brothers left twenty minutes later, refusing Laurie's offer of lunch. Sonia exchanged one last meaningful look with Ashid as their car moved down the long drive.

"Whew!" Harry put an arm around Laurie and one around Sonia as they walked back toward the house. "A hundred thousand bucks for one morning of a stallion's time!" He whistled. "That's the business to be in, huh? He only needs to lend that horse out once a month to bring in a million bucks a year!"

"Maybe the horse isn't always in the mood?" Laurie giggled.

Ashid sat silently alongside his brother in the Porsche on their long drive home. As they neared the Santa Barbara exit, he glanced at his impassive brother.

"You will lend them the stallion, Gamal," he said quietly.

Gamal snorted. "Will I? But I have turned down dozens of breeders who don't meet my qualifications. I must be careful with this bloodline. I cannot allow just anyone to—"

"Gamal," Ashid said quietly, *"I* am asking."

"Oh yes?" Gamal chuckled. "And who are you?"

"The youngest son of our father," Ashid reminded him.

"And you liked the youngest daughter of *that* father!" Gamal said triumphantly. "Am I not right?"

Ashid said nothing and after a few minutes Gamal gave a resigned sigh. "It is never good to do things against our will to please a family member," he said sadly.

In the Name of Love stayed on the best-seller list through the fall, getting very near the half-million sales they had aimed for. Somehow, this success made Marcella miss Sonia more than ever.

"If only Sonia was with us," she sighed to Mark as they walked by the Central Park lake where he and Sonia had played as children. Her detective had lost Harry's trail. Reluctantly, Marcella dispensed with his services. It had been over a year since Harry had left, and the leads had gone cold. The police felt Harry had run to earth somewhere in California. He must have changed his name and his appearance, they felt, and would now be almost impossible to find.

Now in his second year at the Jacinthe Music Academy, Mark was regularly chosen to play at school concerts. Marcella would sit rigid with nerves and pride when Mark played, applauding loudly at the end, wanting to tell everyone around her that this was her son. His teachers were very pleased with his progress. It was as if she had wished a perfect son into existence and he was following all her dreams for him.

If he kept up his excellent grades for the next four years, he would be eligible to audition for a scholarship at the Bologna Music Institute in Italy, under the personal tutelage of Franco Gianni. Gianni took on only three pupils a year, and the top students from the world's schools were encouraged to apply. He kept students for two years, grooming them, rehearsing them, and finally releasing them with his own stamp of musical style and greatness. Many of Gianni's ex-pupils were now concert musicians with their own followings, record contracts, and recitals, their careers assured. Marcella had often heard her father talk of the concert he had heard Gianni play at Carnegie Hall. To have Mark study under the famous Italian had started off as a dream, but as Mark did better and better at Jacinthe, it became a real possibility. She talked about it with Mark and his teachers, and soon it became their shared aim.

In the Name of Love left the best-seller list, after several months, and the fuss slowly died down. A new book was making its presence felt in Marcella's imagination. She wanted to put into a novel some of the feelings she harbored about her daughter having been taken from her. And losing a husband she didn't love was another complicated mixture of feelings that she needed to sort out on paper.

She followed the beauty routines with Amy through the fall, getting pampered at Elizabeth Arden each Monday, eating out at expensive "in" restaurants, and people-watching. Amy gave a series of "ladies' lunches" where all were encouraged to let their hair down, but usually they all ended up watching Amy let hers down. She still invited Marcella to her Saturday night "literary" dinners. And through it all, the new story started to tell itself to her.

It would be about a woman who had lost her family, as Marcella had, but through a tragedy, a fire, which she felt had possibly been her fault. How would this woman cope? How would she find another man? Marcella made the woman so sympathetic, so vulnerable, that the reader would long to know what was going to happen to her. She would be thirty-five, sensual, and terrified at suddenly being single again, liking men and sensitive to the hurts and pressures. When she finally meets a loving man, she hesitates and has to come to terms with herself before accepting him. *Second Husband* was the title she chose.

She outlined the plot to Amy over lunch in her own apartment. To her dismay, Amy seemed unimpressed.

"It's a tad heavy, isn't it?" she asked after listening politely. "Remember, your readers need to be taken out of themselves after a hard day with their kids or at work. They want lifting *up,* Marcella, not being brought down. Now, *my* next book is about this woman who finds out she's multiorgasmic. But *only* if she's on the move—in a car, a ship, a train. So she signs up for this world cruise and—"

"Amy!" Marcella cried. "I'm writing this because I'm *living* what my character is going through. I'm writing it because I *have* to. That urgency will communicate itself to the reader . . ."

Amy raised her eyebrows. "Well, you know that any book you come up with I'll tell Scott is better than *Zippers.*

That's what agents are for. But *I* think the follow-up to your first book should be a swooningly romantic story that women can curl up with alongside a box of chocolates and *devour*! Don't aim too high; stay accessible!"

Marcella shook her head. "Have you forgotten that *I* was one of your devoted readers, Amy? We're not dummies! Any woman who plunks down her money for a book *is* choosing to buy something for her *mind*, no?"

Amy lit a cigarette and regarded her thoughtfully.

"What would you say your next three books are worth, Marcella?" she asked her.

Marcella laughed. "I don't have three books in mind. Just the outline of this one."

"That doesn't matter." Amy waved her cigarette impatiently. "You're bound to write three more books, so we may as well offer them to Volumes as a package. Five million for the three, say?"

"Amy!" Marcella gasped. "That's crazy! And what would I do with five million dollars?"

"Give *me* ten percent for a start," Amy said. "Then the IRS gets *its* share. I wouldn't worry about how to spend the rest, darling!"

She was back to her working schedule: rising around noon, after writing deep into the night. She would go through the mail, which Mark brought up before he left for school, then shower, visit her mother, and have some fresh orange juice and espresso. At about one, a burst of creative energy would course through her, aided by the espresso. This was the wonderful moment when her story took over and poured out of her.

She never got used to the expensive word processor that she had allowed Amy to talk her into and that stood in the corner of her office. She preferred to pound out the words on the same portable typewriter on which she had bashed out *In the Name of Love* in Little Italy. Each day she could hardly wait to start writing to find out what was going to happen to her brave, resilient heroine. As she wrote about her character's sexual urges, she found her own starting up in sympathy. How would this woman cope? How would *she* cope? She could not hide away from sex for the rest of her life. She sometimes saw attractive men at Amy's gatherings, but they were always married. Should she overcome her natural aversion to having an affair with a married man? For the moment, she poured her passion into her novel.

Through the winter her creativity flowed. She felt she had mastered some tough foe—sex and how to live without it. She still had the Members card in her wallet and had even fantasized about visiting the movie theater. But that had been on the rare nights when she had not stayed at her typewriter until three a.m., before tottering into bed to fall immediately asleep.

Mark still slept with her sometimes. He would have bursts of being independent and grown-up, when he would sleep alone. Then work pressure at school would make him edgy and he would say he needed to sleep in her bed. Apart from this, he was adult for his fifteen years: she confided in him as though he were her equal. However much she tried to hold back, they were so much more than mother and son. They seemed to know each other's thoughts.

In bed, he now wore pajamas and she smiled at the careful way he buttoned and tied them. He was as tall as she was, his voice had broken a year ago, and down had appeared on his upper lip; soon he would need to shave. He was devastatingly handsome, with none of the awkwardness of adolescence, and sometimes her heart ached for the little boy she'd lost. Recently, in bed together, they had embraced and she had found that his little boy's body had changed into a man's. She was aware that she was now sharing her bed with an adult male, and for that reason she tried to discourage the habit. She would lecture him on how childish it was. But in the small hours of the morning he would clamber into her bed and snuggle up as if it were perfectly natural, and she would be too sleepy to argue. They had not had a natural family life; he had never really known his father; maybe he truly needed this nurturing.

Amy was always urging her to travel more, to visit Europe, but something kept her in New York. Her mother, her son, perhaps herself. Recently, she had felt a longing to visit Italy, and one evening she went to Mark's room to ask him if he would like a ten-day vacation during his Easter break for a look at their heritage.

With no secrets from each other, they never locked their doors. When she opened his door that evening, Mark did not hear her enter. He was very engrossed in what he was doing to himself before his closet mirror. His shirt was open, his pants lowered, and she watched his face, strained in ecstasy, for several seconds before she realized what was happening. His eyes were tightly closed, and the expression on his face was pure lust, even if it was lust for himself. It was impossible to see this without in some way echoing his feelings. Paralyzed, her eyes widened and a powerful throb of sexual desire made itself felt within her. Desire, not for her son, but for sex itself. She quickly shut the door, her entire body aflame, her face burning. She lit a cigarette and walked blindly into another room, that old familiar feeling stealing over her. Oh God, and she thought she had learned how to deal with it. *Wrong!* She was as randy as she had been on those hot summer nights in Little Italy, lying in bed, pretending her hand outside the sheet belonged to a man.

She went to the windows in the living room, staring out, taking a long drag on her cigarette. Where to go? It was eight-thirty and fully dark outside. One of the first warm spring weeks of the year. The sap rising, she thought. Tiny buds of new leaves on the Central Park trees. Many opposing forces coursed through her. Only one thing seemed very clear: she could not remain in this apartment right now, waiting for Mark to be through and come in and talk to her as if she had not experienced his sexuality in that one shocking moment.

She grabbed a coat and took the elevator down to the street. The terrible thing was that she knew where she was heading and did not really want to go there. But where else could she go? she asked herself as she walked. She examined the men she passed. This wasn't Little Italy. There were no blue-collar workers whistling at women here. The well-dressed men she saw were oblivious to her as they hailed taxis or walked briskly to appointments. The feeling was suffusing her brain and her body. Was this how an alcoholic feels after not touching a drop for years? The first touch of a man would completely undo her, she knew.

So go home, she told herself, go back to your apartment and do some writing or take a long warm soak in the tub. Try pouring this feeling, too strong to reason with, into your book. But her feet were taking her toward Ninth Avenue. Research, she told herself, desperately searching for a justification. Firsthand observation of a New York phenomenon. A true writer would find it essential viewing. And that's all *I'm* going to do, she assured herself, *watch*! But the moment she came within the vicinity of Ninth, her legs began to tremble as if they would give way.

I'll only do it if I have the card in my purse, she tried. If she did not have the card with her, it would be God telling her she must not try this dangerous new pastime. If she didn't have the card, she would go straight home.

She unsnapped her purse in the shelter of a store's doorway and found the card. She was honor-bound to enter now. But if a man lays one finger on me, she promised, I'll run. Another voice inside her laughed and said, "Liar!"

The big black building housing Members loomed before her. The usual hopeful little crowd waited in front of it, begging for invitations. The high membership fee keeps out the riffraff, Amy had said.

She fumbled her card into the slot, catching a glimpse of the envious faces in the crowd watching. The door sprung open and she was inside the cool, dark interior, the tiny light bulbs outlining the escalators and elevators. It was a little early for much action.

"Welcome to Members," the uniformed man just inside the door greeted her. She turned away from him, walking over the black, slippery floor to the escalator that carried her down to the basement. As she sank beneath ground level, her heart beat furiously and she felt as if she might pass out at any moment. At the same time, her consciousness seemed heightened, so aroused that she felt she was moving onto another plane of life, a more intense, more real plane. It was as if a part of her knew she had to do this, to be this. To be *what*? she asked herself as the escalator deposited her at the end of its descent. To be a woman who needs casual sex, she answered herself. To be a woman who will go with any man who wants her. The very idea took her breath away. She had to lean against the black wall for a moment. How had she ever believed she had sex under control? It had simply been waiting, crouched inside her for just such an evening to release all her untamed instincts. She paused at the mock box office. CARY GRANT SEASON, the marquee announced. She could hear on-screen voices urgently discussing some plan, then a burst of dramatic music: the tantalizing sounds of a movie one cannot see. Once again, no one was around.

Her feet moved her slowly along the passage into the theater. It seemed harmless enough inside. About fifteen rows of luxuriously upholstered seats, such as one would see in any small theater. The screen was quite small and high. I'll only watch, she promised herself. One or two shapes of men were standing at the back, as if waiting for the exact moment of the film at which they had come in. Then she made out the seated silhouettes. A woman sat with her legs on each side of a man who knelt on the floor before her. Marcella moved slowly down the center aisle, peering across the rows. A man glanced up interestedly at her and she quickly moved on. You don't have to do anything you don't want to do, she assured herself. You don't even need to stay here. You could leave right now and return to the warm safety, the decency, of your home. Your home where your son is playing with himself! She moved into a row of empty seats, holding on to the backs of the row in front, accustoming her eyes to the darkness. Some of the men who turned to regard her were quite presentable. One or two seemed handsome. I must be crazy, she thought, sitting down. I must be totally out of my mind.

NINE

California, Spring 1986

The entire studfarm buzzed with excitement on the morning of the mating. Sonia woke at seven to steal down to the stables. She found Eddie feeding the mare. Red whinnied and neighed, restless, knowing something was to happen that day.

"Don't fret, baby," Sonia whispered into the velvety ear. "You're going to have a new boyfriend! A wonderful romance with a handsome Arabian stud!"

She watched Eddie carefully wind a thick white bandage around the tail.

"What the hell is *that* for?" she asked him.

Eddie gave an embarrassed laugh. "So we can . . . you know, jerk her tail out of the way."

She frowned at him. "Out of the way of what?"

Eddie sighed and went back to winding. "Sonia . . ." he said, "don't you know how little horses are made? Want me to explain to you?" He grinned up at her and she made an irritated face.

"Out of the way of the stallion's . . . you know, *thing*!" he said.

"Oh!" She glanced away from his grinning face. "How

gross!" She sat down on a crate. "Is she okay, Eddie? Is she in heat?"

He chuckled. "Oh sure, she's in heat all right." He shook his head. "But I still think this is a hell of a lot of trouble to go to just to get two horses together. They must think their stallion is mighty precious."

"It's worth a million dollars!" she reminded him proudly. "But couldn't we have sent Red up to *them*?"

"Uh-uh." He shook his head, tying a neat bow under the horse's tail. "She'd have got homesick and gone out of season up there. Now listen, Princess Sonia. Both your daddy and Laurie said they don't want you hangin' round watching this. It can get kinda hairy."

"Two horses fuckin'?" She snatched his packet of cigarettes and withdrew one. "How hairy can it get?"

"Cut that out!" He flicked the cigarette from her hand. "A stable fire is all we need today."

She sighed. "And what's all this for?" She indicated a padded wall set up beside Red's stall.

"It's a kicking stall. It protects the mare if the stud goes, you know, like a little crazy," he said.

"Why would it go crazy?" she asked, facing him, hands on her hips.

"From passion!" Eddie said. "Oh, go ask Laurie to explain it all to you."

"I don't need to," she said. "I'm going to watch it all. I'll hide inside here and peer out through the slats."

"Your dad said to stay in the house," Eddie said. "If he finds you in here, it'll be *my* ass!"

She touched Eddie's arm as he neatly wound the bandage tape onto the roll, tidying up. "Let me stay, *please,* Eddie!" she begged. "I'll be very quiet. No one has to know. . . ."

"*I'll* know!" Laurie said, walking into the stable. She wore a man's shirt over jeans and boots and looked very businesslike.

"How is she today, Eddie?" she asked. "A little jumpy? That's my girl. . . ." She patted Red's forehead. "Sonia, baby, just one little visit and then you get out and stay out, okay? I mean it, honey."

A surge of anger flowed over Sonia's features. *"Why?"*

she cried, glaring at Laurie. "You can't tell me what to do! You're not my mother. . . ."

Laurie gazed at her coolly. "Your dad and I agreed this wasn't something you had to see right now. One day, but not right now. And please don't choose today to become a rebellious teenager. I don't think I can take it!"

She walked out, calling over her shoulder: "I'll give you ten minutes, young lady!"

"Young lady!" Sonia echoed disgustedly. She pulled a face at Eddie.

"You shouldn't oughta talk back to her like that," he said. "She's a fine lady!"

Sonia shrugged. "Well, she shouldn't treat me like a child. She's not even married to my father: they're only lovers."

Eddie burst out laughing. "You can be the darnedest little brat sometimes, Sonia, I swear!"

She giggled, too. "Eddie, have you seen many matings?" she asked.

"Sure," he nodded.

"What do horses do? Do they kiss?"

His eyes sparkled at her. "More like little love bites. Nips."

"Show me!"

He snapped his teeth at her. *"Whow!"* he chomped. "Like that."

She wondered how it would feel if Eddie kissed her. Would his full lips be as soft as the Egyptian's? Would he put his tongue in her, the way Gemma told her grown-ups did?

From the shy little glances he sometimes gave her, she knew Eddie would like to touch her body. She stretched herself, patting her tight jeans and pulling down her white crew-neck sweater.

"Here!" He held out some sugar cubes in the palm of his hand. "Feed these to the other horses and quit being such a nuisance."

She glanced around. "I could crouch right here," she told him. "Behind this stall."

"Oh yeah?" Eddie said. "And what if your father finds you here?"

"But he *won't*!" she cried. "I *promise*, Eddie. And you could crouch over me. You know you'd like that!"

She stared at him suggestively.

He shook his head. "Well, if you ain't the—" He broke off. Then he gave her the look that made Gemma say he was in love with her. It was so easy, Sonia thought, surprised. You could get boys, men even, to do anything for you if you kept hinting, kept promising. Like today, for example. She was sure that the stallion was only being lent out because of her. Because of the way she had flirted with Ashid the first time he came.

"It won't be a pretty thing to watch, I warn you," Eddie said.

"I can handle it," she promised him. She gave him a wink and ran off back to the house.

Up in her room, she made up as carefully as she had the first time the brothers had visited, three months ago. This time, she was leaning out of her window at nine o'clock when the small caravan of horse van, Porsche, and Mercedes rolled in through the front gate and climbed up the drive. She ran down to her father's office.

He was on the phone and he covered the mouthpiece as she bent to kiss him, crying, "They're here!"

". . . maximum insurance," he was saying. "I'll leave it in your hands. Thanks."

As he replaced the phone, his big worried face creased into a smile. "Okay, now keep out of the way, princess. If it goes well, I'll call you down for a drink, but don't go near the stables while the mating's taking place. I don't want my little girl to see stuff like that."

"Oh Dad . . ." She acted very disappointed. "I'm not a little girl anymore!"

She ran into the drive to greet the brothers, making sure she took Gamal's hand first, to keep Ashid waiting. When she faced him, he was as handsome as ever, his smiling face aglow, his burnished skin copper brown.

"Good luck!" she wished him, holding his hand.

"Thank you, but it is the horses who need the luck!" He smiled. She watched as the magnificent steed who was worth so much was ceremoniously led from the van that had transported him. He shook his head, giving a proud neigh. He was led by his trainer to the paddock to stretch his legs.

Laurie had set up a table alongside the stables with trays of sandwiches and flasks of coffee on it. The third car disgorged a vet, an insurance man, and an extra stable hand from the Fazeen brothers' stables.

Sonia poured some coffee for Ashid. "I'm not allowed to watch," she told him, sadly.

"I should think not!" he said, pretending to be shocked. She handed him the coffee and he kept his hand over hers on the cup. His broad shoulders filled out a gray sweater. "It is not a sight for innocent young ladies," he laughed.

"I'm not innocent!" she said.

"In my country, a girl is not even allowed to take a walk in public without a chaperone," he told her.

"Can't you be *my* chaperon, Ashid?" she teased. "Listen . . ." she said, bending her head nearer him. "I know I have *you* to thank for this."

Ashid made a noncommittal face.

"I do, don't I?" she persisted.

He shot her a flustered look as Harry came over to greet him.

"Hi, Ashid, how are you? Did you try a sandwich?"

Sonia knew she would have to act fast while everyone was watching the stallion canter gracefully around the exercise ring, putting on a performance. Laurie took Polaroids of the horses. Sonia left Ashid talking to her father and slipped into the stable just as Eddie was tying fabric covers over Red's feet.

"In case she kicks," he told her. Sonia went to lie on a pile of straw in the shadows, giving Eddie a meaningful look. She could peer through a slat at the scene outside like a privileged spectator in some strange theater.

There was a long time to wait before anything interesting happened. As she had guessed, Laurie and her dad completely forgot about her. She watched their deep conversations with the vet and with the insurance man. God, she thought, what a fuss about two horses! But if it resulted in the perfect horse for her, it would be well worth it. Two stable hands fed the stallion carrots and sugar for energy. The horse submitted to a huge thermometer shoved up it;

another one was stuck into Red. There was more conferring and talking until it was finally time for Eddie to lead out Red.

She padded out in her stockinged hooves like a nervous bride. When she saw the stallion she gave a series of whinnies. Sonia's eyes widened. They rolled one of the padded stands near to Red and soon she began to call out for a partner, her head twisting from side to side. Two men led the stallion up behind her. The horse wore a bridle.

Sonia watched the horse sniff at the mare and take a series of little nips along her mane—love bites Eddie had called them. Red's bandaged tail added a weird note and she saw a man tweak it aside to inspect the horse, calling out, "She's okay!" As she heard this, a sudden weight descended on her, almost making her cry out. Eddie was on top of her, his mouth near her ear as he watched through the same slit as she did.

"If you make the slightest sound, we're both goners," he whispered, his warm breath tickling her. "Your dad just asked me where you were and I said in the house. Don't let me down, now. . . ." His weight pressed down uncomfortably.

"Give me room to breathe!" she gasped. He adjusted his body. They were only a few yards from the mating. The horses were in full view, with the spectators, including Harry, Laurie, the Fazeens, and their attendants, watching from the sides. As they watched, the mare suddenly lifted her tail and ejected a strong stream of urine; the two men standing behind her shifted their feet to escape the downpour.

Sonia muffled a giggle. "Great time to take a leak!" she whispered.

"It means she's ready," Eddie told her.

The stallion was led gently to his place. Sonia watched as the penis grew to an engorged length of eighteen inches.

"Christ!" Sonia whispered.

Eddie grunted, his breath hot on her neck.

She tried to twist around to look in his eyes. "Do men's things get that big?" she asked.

He muffled a laugh.

Saliva began to drip in gobs from the stallion's mouth as

the man holding him restrained him. He started to buck and rear.

Another man held Red's tail to one side, saying, "She's winking, now! She's winking!"

"What's 'winking'?" Sonia whispered.

"It's when her—you know, her hole opens and closes," Eddie said. "It means she wants him inside her. . . ." Eddie pressed a little closer and it occurred to Sonia that he was excited, too. Excited at the horses doing this and at lying on her.

The stallion was directly behind the mare. Suddenly, he roared and reared up, walking toward her on his hind legs. The enlarged penis stuck up straight before him. There were excited cries from the watchers.

"Okay, they're ready! They're ready now! Gently!"

"Okay, I have her!"

The hands were throwing directions at each other, sensitive to the horses' sudden movements. Sonia's eyes widened as she watched. She could feel Eddie fidgeting behind her, rubbing himself against her.

"Cut it out, Eddie!" she muttered, pushing at him.

The stallion lunged at Red and mounted her, clasping her around the middle with his forelegs. He held on by biting her neck along the mane, hanging on by his teeth. The man standing by the mare guided the penis toward the opening.

"He'll hurt her! Oh God, he'll *hurt* her!" Sonia cried.

"Will you keep quiet?" Eddie hissed, placing his hand over her mouth. "She's *fine*. She's having the time of her life!"

A strong odor came off the two horses and Sonia could see a fine steam from their bodies wafting into the air. The stallion gleamed with sweat as it pushed itself deep into Red, grunting at the back of its throat. Sonia stared unbelievingly at the animals. She felt she was witnessing something startling, new, yet something she had always known about, even before the dirty jokes and wild rumors at school. It was as if she were watching the reenactment of a myth that had been buried in her subconscious, a dream she'd once had but had forgotten until this moment. Things would get faster and faster and would end in some kind of dramatic explosion, she guessed. Two living things, moving so fast, one inside the other, must surely be working toward a finale, a climax. As she watched, Eddie's breath in her ear, warm and moist, she felt his hands gently touching her, exploring her body. He suddenly slipped his hands up under her sweater and cupped her small breasts in his hands. Sonia lay statue still, cold as ice, too shocked to make any sound. When she felt him unzip his jeans and lay the hot length of his aroused sex on her thigh, she found her voice.

"What the fuck do you think you're doing?" she cried, through clenched teeth.

"I thought this was part of our deal?" he whispered back.

His weight numbed her. A piece of straw was sticking into her cheek. He unzipped her jeans and peeled them down so that she felt his hot body against her. The stallion labored on in the mare, quivering, the flanks moving so fast they seemed out of control. Red's head was trembling from the thrusts but she seemed calm and quiet, just letting this happen. Everyone stayed silent, watching. The stallion's eyes were rolling in its head, signaling its approaching release, and Eddie was gasping in her ear, moving his sex carefully in the center crease of her buttocks, pushing against her. His sex felt so hot. And his seed, as it expelled over her, was hot too. She held her breath, unable to believe this was happening to her. Eddie was panting now, in short gasps, as the last tremors pulsed through his body. The man holding the stallion's reins signaled the two others to join him. The tendons and veins in the stallion's neck swelled and seemed about to burst. The horse's entire body was lathered in white foam, the same white as the foam that spilled from his lips chewing at the bit.

Eddie wiped her and pulled her jeans back up, adjusting his clothing.

"I'm sorry. I didn't mean to—" he stammered behind her.

"I'll get you fired for this!" she muttered, watching the horses.

The stallion shuddered and jerked now, obviously beyond its own control, beside itself with the impending release.

A man touched the base of the penis and nodded to the onlookers.

"I'd say he's just about ready!" he shouted.

The horse let out a great roar of something that could have been pain or pleasure or anger. He jerked his huge head back in what seemed to be a desperate effort to obtain freedom, to enjoy its ecstasy, to gain one last great independent moment of pleasure that would be his alone. Sonia understood everything the horse was aiming for and willed it to have that moment it strove for: it now meant everything to her, too. But suddenly, just as it was about to be achieved, the stallion gave a snort and, blood bubbling from its mouth, collapsed. Laurie screamed as the powerful head snapped, slack, to one side, inert over the mare, the huge tongue lolling out of the mouth as if its tethers had detached. A final shudder rippled the entire body and it slid off the mare and slumped on the ground, resisting all the men's efforts to rouse it. A hand threw a bucket of water over the head, but there was no reaction. Gamal cried out some furious Egyptian curses, and ran to stand over his prized possession, wringing his hands in grief. Red whinnied pitifully, twisting her head to look behind her at the fallen horse.

"It's *dead*!" Eddie whispered. "It just dropped dead!"

"*No!*" Sonia screamed, forgetting she was supposed to be hidden. Sobs welled up in her chest, forcing themselves out. Suddenly, they burst loudly from her. It was just too much to have witnessed. She felt Eddie's weight lift itself from her and she cried her heart out, facedown in the straw. As she cried, another hand grabbed her from behind, forcing her to sit up and whirling her furiously around, and she received a series of sharp slaps about her face. She opened her eyes to see her father's face staring at her, twisted in fury.

"Didn't I tell you to stay in the house?" he shouted. "Didn't I say you were not to watch this?"

It was his temper, the temper she had always dreaded, and it was finally directed at *her*! Yet she knew it was the horse's dying that had made him so angry, and she had simply gotten in the way.

Everyone had followed Harry into the stables to watch this new turn of events.

"Mr. Winton!" Gamal called from the doorway. "The horse is dead!"

Out of the corner of her eye, Sonia saw Ashid's face stretched with anguish and grief for her. Her father's eyes were wide open, glaring as if he were crazy.

"You're not old enough to watch!" he shouted.

Sonia pulled away from him and lay on the straw. Blood mixed with saliva in her mouth and she retched and spat. She could sense they were all watching her, that she was providing a little light relief from the horses.

"My horse is dead, Mr. Winton!" Gamal repeated.

"Sonia, honey." Laurie pushed past Harry to get to her. She put her arm around Sonia and helped her to her feet, wiping her face with a handkerchief.

"Leave me *alone*!" Sonia screamed, pushing her away. "I'm not a baby! I don't need *any* of you!" She glared at her father through streaming, reddened eyes.

"I'm sorry!" he said. "I'm so sorry, princess. I didn't mean to—" He held out his hand to her and she took it and quickly bit it. He yelped with pain as she wiped her mouth. She eyed him coldly, brushing down her jeans. "I'll *never* forgive you for this," she told him. "*Never!* I swear!"

She pushed past them all, past Laurie, past Eddie. As she ran to the house, she heard Gamal say for the third time, "The horse is dead, Mr. Winton!" and she saw her father suddenly turn on him to ask, "*So?* Whose fault is that?" The kneeling vet said, "It was an embolism. It can happen at any time, like a heart attack. Very unfortunate!" and Harry responded, "We're covered for it, aren't we? It's not an act of God?"

They would drag the million-dollar stallion onto a pickup, she guessed. Now it would be worth only a few dollars as horsemeat. She felt sick to her stomach. Red would run joyfully to the meadow and prance around, not understanding any of this. She slammed her bedroom door shut and threw herself on her bed, sobbing.

"This is a matter for the police!" she heard Gamal shouting as she fell into an exhausted sleep.

When she came to, everything was quiet, and she realized that a soft knocking at her door had awakened her. She had been sobbing as she dreamed. She had lost some innocence. Now she was an adult. Eddie had made a kind of

love to her. The horse had died just before achieving its
ecstasy. These two weird events had happened to her on
the same day, at the same moment almost, and she wondered if they were somehow connected. Her father had
humiliated her in front of everyone, and that was the worst
part of all. She tried to sort out her thoughts as the soft
knocking sounded again. Perhaps her dad wanted to apologize to her? She called out, "Come in," but did not change
her position, facedown on the bed.

She felt the bed give as someone sat carefully beside
her. If it was Dad, she would make it plenty tough for him.

"Sonia?" said a deep voice.

It was Ashid! She kept her face buried in the pillow.

"They are making such a commotion downstairs, I
thought I would find out how you are . . ." he said softly.
His hand hesitantly touched her shoulder.

Damn! she thought. He would choose this moment to
visit her. She must have cried all her makeup off. She
turned slowly to face him, running a finger under each eye
to smooth out any streaked mascara. His handsome face
was twisted with concern for her.

"You are all right, Sonia?" he asked. "I am so very
sorry. I would have killed your father, but you're his daughter and he has the right to treat you however he likes."

"You think so?" she sniffed, reaching for a tissue. "*I*
don't. I'll never forgive him for this! In front of you and
your brother. What must you think of us?" She blew her
nose and wiped her eyes.

"I think your father did not want you to see such a
scene." He pressed her hand. "And now he is going to owe
my brother a great deal of money. . . ."

"But it wasn't his fault the horse died!" she cried. She
threw herself into his arms and he hugged her slim little
body tenderly to him. He pressed his lips against the side of
her neck in soft kisses. To her surprise, she liked being held
by him. A feeling of excitement, of blood running hotly
through her, made her want to pull him down onto her.
She clung to his strong torso for several long moments. She
broke away, her tear-stained face beseeching him.

"Don't make him pay! It wasn't his fault!"

Ashid carefully moved a strand of hair from her eyes.
"It will be complicated; the insurance covered every possi-

bility but that. . . ." He shrugged. "My brother says not enough safety precautions were taken."

"You can persuade him, Ashid!" she pleaded. "He listens to you."

Ashid made a wry face. "Yes, he listened to me when I asked him to bring the horse here—"

She hugged him. "You *did* ask him? For me?"

He dropped his eyes shyly, looking down at her hand in his. "Yes," he admitted. "For you. I must be very stupid, no? But now I cannot ask any more favors. I am just along for the ride, as you would say."

She stared at him. "Where is everybody?"

"They are all by the stables. Gamal feels this is a matter for the police. Your father is trying to settle it between them. . . ."

"Is the . . . dead horse still there?"

"They have sent for a service to dispose of it," he said. "Gamal has every right to be sad, Sonia. He did this for me and look how he has been repaid. Oh Sonia, how I regret everything that has happened!"

She jumped off the bed and grabbed a sweater to tie around her waist. Peering into her dressing-table mirror, she checked her makeup, applying more lipstick. She swung around and grabbed Ashid's hand.

"Can we go for a drive?" she asked him.

He looked at her with his big serious black eyes. "A drive to where?"

"Anywhere!" She shrugged. She pulled him out of her room. "I've just got to get out of here!"

They ran from the house like two schoolchildren playing hookey, and Sonia made straight for his Porsche. He got in beside her and reversed very fast down the long driveway. Out on the street, he headed toward the ocean.

She buckled her seat belt and turned to watch him drive. His spicy strong cologne filled the car.

"Let's just drive until we reach the end of the world!" Sonia cried.

Ashid laughed. "Okay!"

He swerved as an oncoming car nearly swiped them, sounding its horn with a long zigzag wail.

"Will you please stop driving like a maniac?" she asked him. "You're scaring me. There's no hurry!"

"This is my normal speed!" He laughed again.

He drove through forests and past golf courses. Past a very elegant shopping center of natural redwood buildings. Alongside a college campus deserted for the day. Finally, as they came within sight of a blue band of ocean, he pulled the car to a halt. They were in an empty recreational area with picnic tables and barbecues, and there was no one in sight.

"Why *here*?" she asked, frowning.

He pulled her to him and kissed her, his eyes tightly closed. His tongue explored her mouth, and she watched curiously as a line of white showed under his lids, like a man in a delirious trance. She broke away from him, her hand on the door handle.

"Let's take a walk!" she said. She tried the door, but it was locked.

He pulled her back to him, harder this time, burying his mouth in her neck, her hair.

"Sonia . . ." he groaned. "Sonia! I haven't stopped thinking about you since we met. What spell have you cast on me? Oh, darling."

She sat up straight in her seat, watching him warily. He took one of her hands in his big hand and caressed it, then suddenly pressed a lever that made their seat backs collapse, leaving them lying flat on their backs. He snuggled over to her, his hand on her thigh. She was a little excited, but also frightened; he was so much bigger than her.

"Will you please put my seat back up?" she asked, struggling to sit up straight.

"Why?" he asked. "It is not nice like this?" His breathing turned to gasps and his eyes closed again as he put his hands on her, spreading them open over her breasts.

"No . . ." she said. It was too much in one day to have two men pawing over her. *"Don't!"*

His hand stole up under her sweater, gently into her bra and he held her nipple between his fingers, squeezing it. She held her breath. She felt the nipple grow hard and a curious shame descended on her. If she just let him go ahead and do what he wanted, she would emerge an adult from today. Ashid pushed up her sweater and fastened his mouth onto first one nipple, then the other, sucking gently on them. It was not unpleasant but she thought it terribly silly. Tentatively, she ran her hand over his thick neck. He groaned.

"Oh Sonia, you have such a beautiful body," he told her, rubbing his face over it, "like a young boy's. . . ." She frowned: some compliment! She hoped things would stop right there, but he unzipped his pants and pulled them down over his knees, his shorts entwined in them. His erect sex surged toward her, stiff and swollen. She moved to the very edge of the flat leather seat.

"No . . ." she murmured.

He reached over to her hips with both hands and unzipped her jeans, tugging them down, dragging her panties off so that she was naked to him.

"No! I don't want to!" she cried.

He ate up her body with his eyes, then pushed his face down between her legs. She felt his tongue poking at her, attempting to get into her. She squeezed her limbs together against this strange intrusion. He tugged at her jeans, trying to get them down further, feverishly licking her thighs and her knees. When her shoes fell off and she was finally naked on the cold black leather, her mind went blank; she no longer knew what to think. She simply hadn't thought this far ahead. All she could do was to tell him, over and over again, "I don't want to do this, Ashid," hoping he would finally get the message.

He pulled off his clothes and flung them on the backseat. His naked, bronzed body hovered over hers, his aroused sex digging into her stomach, his tongue flicking her throat. She realized that he was going to do what the stallion had done to Red that morning, impale her on this thing that stuck out so tremblingly before him. He was lying upon her now, pushing her knees apart, reaching down to guide himself between her legs. She almost laughed at the impossibility of it.

"You think you're going to stick *that* in me?" she cried out. "No *way*!" But he managed to get the tip of it inside her and now he was pushing, as if expecting the rest to follow.

"It's too big!" she screamed. "Ashid, I *can't*! You're *hurting* me!" And suddenly she remembered the girls at school giggling as Gemma told them, "He sticks it in the woman and that's how they make a baby . . . but *only* if they're married!" She was suddenly terrified. He was pushing it up into her and she was much too young to have a baby, and that's exactly what the horses had been trying to produce this morning!

"Stop! *Please!*" she screamed.

"Don't stop me now, Sonia," he groaned in her ear. "I can't stop myself. I *must* have you! I *must!*"

Her hands fluttered around the car for something to hold on to, something with which to steel herself against this invasion. They found the looped leather straps that hung from the sides of the car's interior for passengers to hold. Ashid pushed her wrists through the loops then quickly buckled them to tabs on the car roof, handcuffing her. She tried to pull out, but the leather edges cut sharply into her wrists. In panic, she kicked her legs, smashing one foot against the window, and he held her feet down with one hand, searching for something in the door pocket. Finally, he pulled her scarf from around her neck and deftly tied it around one ankle, attaching the other end to the brake pedal. From the glove compartment, he took a length of elasticized cord that he fastened to her other ankle, tying it to the door handle on his side. His panting was now the only sound in the car. She was spread-eagled now, completely helpless. As he leered over her body, touching her sex, the tips of her breasts, a shame that was almost invigorating swept her. Then her eyes opened wide in fear as he positioned himself over her and started the whole pushing entry all over again. He grunted and pushed and she felt him slowly enter. There was a moment of pain and she knew that something had broken and she was no longer a virgin. It can happen when you're horse riding, she remembered Laurie telling her, and of course she would tell everyone that's what had happened. Ashid moved away and moved back, letting himself slide up and down in her, and soon she felt herself moist down there, where he was in her. The moistness helped to ease the pain, which was slowly turning to a kind of pleasure. Ashid was no longer panting, but making little yelps in her ears. His eyes were more rolled up than ever, and his eyelids were fluttering. She could see he had no control over what he was doing, that his body was more or less acting for him, and all she could pray for was that he wouldn't suddenly drop dead, as the horse had done that morning. The worst thing of all was that each time he pushed into her, she felt new sensations happening to her down there, felt like pushing back at him, meeting him halfway, to add to the pleasure. He suckled at her breasts as he moved and she fought the shameful pleasure this produced. He covered her lips with his lips, sucking them inside his mouth, then using his incredibly strong tongue to probe her mouth, and she felt the first wave of something intense and delicious break over her. She moaned, furious with herself, and he answered with his own muffled groan, moving even faster inside her. He was slipping in and out of her so fast now that she was sore. When did this end? That strange, fresh new pleasure swept over her again and again, fainter each time, until she knew she could not take it anymore.

"Please!" she cried out. *"Please!"*

Ashid gave a mighty roar and his body jerked spasmodically, as if he were being given jolts of electric current. In the driving mirror, she could see his muscular, bronze buttocks quiver, then stay still as his whole body went limp on her. Don't die on me! she prayed. They lay very still, his weight paralyzing, then numbing her. The pleasure gave faint echoes inside her and she felt him shrivel and slip out of her, leaving her strangely relaxed, triumphant, yet horribly ashamed of everything that had happened.

In a dead voice she ordered, "Take me home."

He untied her and she quietly pulled on her clothes. He dressed quickly and started the car. They drove back to the stables in complete silence, Sonia staring unseeingly out of the window.

He pulled into the drive of the house, leaning across her to open the car door. She flinched.

"My dad'll kill you!" she told him.

"Go now!" he said, not looking at her. He gave her a rough shove and she fell out of the car onto the gravel.

She looked up at his stolid face. "You *animal*!" she screamed. "I swear to God my dad'll tear you apart!"

Ashid shot her one agonized look and then reached out to pull the door closed. She scrambled to her feet as he started up the engine and screeched forward, backward, reversing his way out of the grounds. She watched him drive off and then dragged herself up the gravel drive toward the house.

The house was strangely silent. She stood in the downstairs hall and yelled, *"Dad? Laurie?"* a sob breaking out of her constricted throat.

Laurie appeared at the top of the stairs, looking down at her, a strange new expression on her face.

"Where in God's name have *you* been?" she cried. "We've been looking everywhere for you! Come up here and help me—you won't believe what's happened!" Her voice was harsh and unfriendly.

"Ashid took me in his car, Laurie." Sonia suddenly found herself sobbing. Laurie had turned away, calling back over her shoulder.

"We'll have to get out of here pretty fast now. They'll want to talk to you, too, but—"

Sonia made herself grasp the handrail and pull herself up the stairs. At the top, her legs gave way beneath her and she collapsed on the rug.

"Where's *Dad*?" she cried.

Laurie came back, her arms full of clothing. "What's the matter with you?" She stared at Sonia. "Didn't you know what was happening all along? He's *gone*! Your precious daddy's gone! The police took him! The game's up, Sonia. It's all *over*!"

"What game? I don't understand." Sonia felt a freezing fear mounting inside her. Had the world chosen today to go completely crazy?

"Okay!" Laurie crouched down next to her. "I'll spell it out if you're gonna play dumb. That crazy Egyptian was so broken up over his horse dying that he called the police and made a complaint against Harry. They looked up your father and found out he was a wanted man! Do you understand *that,* little miss princess? Your father's a *crook*! A *criminal*! This house, these stables, everything I ever worked for, will be taken by the state, that's for sure! They've been looking for you two for two years, as you very well know, so stop sitting there looking like little miss innocent!"

"No!" Sonia shook her head, dazed. She held up her hands as if defending herself from an attack. "No, Laurie,"

she said in a child's voice. "We were running away from my mom! She wanted custody of me!"

"Bullshit!" Laurie cried. "You're not that dumb! Where did you think all your father's money came from—Father Christmas? He and his pals got over three million out of their little swindles. Your father is nothing more than a lousy thief! And I *loved* him!"

"Where is he now?" Sonia whispered.

"I *told* you!" Laurie sighed. "They arrested him. He'll never raise the bail. And I'm *not* selling off my old stables to raise the money. I'm just thanking God I held on to them, or where would I be now?" She pulled Sonia to her feet. "Now help me pack. We'd better get the hell out of here before they come back with some judge's order to grab everything. Eddie's putting the horses in vans and we'll drive them back to my place tonight. If you want to ride with Eddie, you can—"

The pillow! Suddenly she thought of the pillow. This pillow is your security, princess, he had said. If anything happens to me—Sonia broke away and raced downstairs.

"Where the hell are you going now?" Laurie cried.

If the pillow was not there, she would be dependent on Laurie—a changed Laurie who obviously blamed them for lying to her. Her brain was whirling as she ran to the sofa. The pillow was there all right, thrown casually under some others. She unzipped it and quickly felt inside. The notes were still there, wads of them. She ran out of the house, holding the pillow. She found Eddie in the stables, throwing saddles and riding equipment into a box.

She forced herself to meet his eyes.

"Where's Red?" she asked him.

"Did you hear the news?" he asked.

"Where *is* she?" she asked again, urgently.

"In the meadow. Laurie's looking for you!"

She grabbed her saddle from the box and ran toward the meadow. Already her legs felt weightless and her mind was not in her head but floating alongside it, outside, watching her, telling her what she had to do.

Red was running in glorious freedom around the track, cantering for the sheer joy of it. She ran up to the fence when she saw Sonia. Sonia hung over the fencing, stroking Red's smooth forehead.

"My baby, my sweet thing," she cooed. She climbed over the fence and strapped the saddle on Red. Red stood still as she put on the bridle, giving a little snort from time to time. "It's just you and me now, baby," Sonia whispered into the pointed ears, smoothing them with her fingers. Ignoring the soreness she still felt, she hoisted herself lightly into the saddle and guided Red out of the meadow.

"Laurie says we have to be outta here by eight!" Eddie was shouting from outside the stables as she rode by. Sonia flicked the reins, and Red cantered down the driveway.

"Sonia!" Eddie called after her. "Don't ride her *now*! I could use your help!"

She crouched down to feel at one with the horse, close to its back. Its movement was a wonderful relief, a kind of freedom. It was something that humans could never understand, but *she* understood it. She needed it.

"Good-bye, Eddie!" Sonia called out because she knew she would not be seeing him again. He looked across the drive at her strangely as she guided Red toward the house.

As she trotted past the house, Laurie leaned out of an upstairs window, as Sonia had known she would, as if she had dreamed all this before in an unfinished dream.

Where are you *going*? she heard the words in her head.

"Where are you *going*?" Laurie cried. "Come help me pack! These are *your* things too, you know!"

They had reached the road outside the house, and Red hesitated.

"Come on, baby," Sonia urged. She stuck the pillow up her sweater and hunched over the reins. "Take me away. Just take me away!"

And Red broke into a slow trot, then a canter, then a gallop. Past the neat lawns and estates, past the grandiose mansions, the ranches, past a gas station, until they met the freeway. She guided Red along a parallel lane that cyclists used, picking up speed, watched by astonished, grinning motorists. Red would take her somewhere! In her dream, they would have risen way up into the sky, flying over cities, but this was real life and she had to settle for the freeway. She wanted to gallop as fast as she could: away from the uncertain childhood, the lying, the illusions. When we stop, she found herself thinking to the horse, I'll tether you. When we reach sanctuary. She should be frantic, she knew, but as she rode, she felt a deep inner peace descend on her, even though she had a feeling those police car sirens she could hear in the distance were coming after her.

My poor baby, she thought as she leaned against the breeze, her cheek against Red's mane. We've both been well and truly fucked today! She glanced at the hills to her left, showing a lavender haze of smog or smoke, the sea to her right glinting turquoise, gray, and navy as the sun reflected off it. When we reach sanctuary, she thought again, liking the peaceful sound of that word. Red was enjoying the escape, too, easily stretching her body and her legs as she galloped. And what if they never reached a fucking sanctuary?

She left her childhood behind as Red galloped at the side of the freeway, parallel to the railway lines, to the sea. Don't let me down, baby, she thought, holding the reins. Don't *you* let me down, too.

They reached La Jolla half an hour later, Red dripping with sweat, and Sonia no longer the two Sonias she had been. She was now a new Sonia, but she didn't have any idea who that Sonia might be. It was a Sonia who wouldn't trust any man, that was for sure, a Sonia who would know how to use men.

A Highway Patrol car and two officers accompanied her as she rode into town. She clutched the pillow under her arm, suddenly feeling very calm, able to handle anything. She would play a child now, assuming her most dazzling smile as she gracefully slipped down off the horse. They were by a little green park overlooking the sea at the back of the main hotel. The sun was turning its eight o'clock orange, lighting the scene with an unreal Technicolor.

"Thank heavens you're here!" she cried to the officers, turning on all her charm. "This horse staged a runaway! I couldn't control her. It's been a big day for her and she just went crazy, I guess. . . ."

"You're lucky to be alive, miss," one of the officers said, eyeing the drenched animal. "What happened? It got tired out?"

"I guess so. . . ." Sonia took the reins in her hands. "I'll just tether her to these railings for a moment and call my stables. They'll send a van for her. . . ."

"Which stables is it from? What's the address?" The

taller one spoke up. "You caused quite a commotion on the highway. . . ."

She turned tear-filled eyes on the man. "But it wasn't my *fault*!" she cried. "The horse just ran away with me—what could I do? I've been trying to stop it for half an hour! You said yourself, I nearly got killed. . . ."

The officers exchanged glances. "Well," the tall man faltered. "You can't just tie it to the railings here."

"Why not?" she pleaded. "She's too tired to do anything and I have to call my stables."

The first man nodded to the taller man. "Okay, make that call. Then we'll pass by again in twenty minutes. If that horse is still here, we'll be forced to do something. . . ."

A bunch of kids who had been playing with a ball gathered around the horse, staring at it and Sonia. She spoke to the oldest boy.

"Keep an eye on her for me, will you?" she asked him. "I have to make a telephone call."

She found a phone box outside the public restrooms and made a collect call.

"Where are you, Sonia? Are you all right?" Laurie sounded anxious, almost like the old Laurie again. "You *are* coming with us, aren't you, honey?" she asked.

Sonia hesitated, holding on to the phone. Laurie's voice was so concerned and caring that for a moment she was tempted to forget this new plan and go back. Stay with Laurie and grow up with her.

"I just want you to know that Red is tied to the railings at La Jolla beach," Sonia said flatly. "Send Eddie with the van. She won't be able to get home on her own."

"But what are you doing in La Jolla?" Laurie cried.

"Good-bye, Laurie," Sonia said. "I'm sorry about this, 'cause I really loved you."

She hung up quickly. On the street, the last Saturday afternoon shoppers were idly glancing into windows or deciding where to eat. Poor Red was whinnying and shuddering, needing food and water. The officers were hanging about uncomfortably, knowing they should be doing something. Sonia returned to them. "Someone will be here in twenty minutes," she promised them.

As soon as they had driven off, she turned to the boy

she had spoken to and said, "Can you get her a bucket of water from somewhere?"

He shrugged. "I'll try."

When he went off to look, she spoke to a tall tomboyish girl. "Look after her for a moment, will you?" she asked her. "I gotta use the bathroom." The girl proudly held the reins and Sonia leaned toward Red.

"Thank you, baby," she whispered in her ear. "Thank you and take care now, okay? You know I love you more than anyone in the whole world now, don't you? I'm gonna miss you so much. Oh, so much, baby . . ." One more stroke of the velvety ears, one more caress between the eyes on that broad, silky brow. Red's eyes seemed to know. Sonia hung on to the mare's neck for a moment, tears running down her face. The tomboy girl stared at her. She tore herself away. Red was making little whinnies as Sonia took those first steps, as if the horse knew that this was good-bye. There was no room for a horse in her life now, even if it was one she loved with all her heart. Sonia did not look back.

Weightless, walking on air, Sonia crossed the small park. She found the public restrooms and disappeared into the women's room, holding the pillow. Sitting on the seat in a locked stall, she unzipped the cover and extracted just one hundred-dollar bill. She tidied herself, splashing cold water on her hot face.

Then she made for the main street. As she walked, she tried to tell herself that this was not really her, that this was the new Sonia, the fearless Sonia. People were staring at her and she felt her thoughts fly out of control. People were always staring at her; Daddy had said they were just jealous of her beauty. He hadn't even said good-bye to her. She bumped into an elderly woman who looked angrily at her at first, then, concerned, asked, "Are you all right, dear?" Sonia wandered on without replying.

In a luggage store, she bought a small leather carryall and put the pillow inside. Outside on the street, she looked down at her feet and couldn't decide which direction to take. She felt a flash of panic. Wandering past a bookstore, she caught sight of something in the window, walked by, then stopped. Something made her go back. She looked carefully into the window again. A huge display of a paperback called *In the Name of Love* had a large black-and-white portrait of a beautiful woman at its center. Sonia stared into the familiar, hurt eyes of this woman, reading her name. Marcella Balducci Winton.

She let her forehead push against the cool glass as her lips soundlessly mouthed the word: *Mother.* The eyes were so understanding, so sad. The tears finally pushed their way out, coursing down Sonia's cheeks.

"Mom!" She fell onto her knees on the hard sidewalk. "Oh God, *Mom!*"

The elderly woman she had bumped into had been watching her from a distance. She hurried over to Sonia's side, crouching down next to her, her arm around her shoulder.

"Now, now, honey," she soothed. "Don't you cry. We'll find your mother. . . ."

TEN

In the darkness of the theater, Marcella watched Cary Grant light a woman's cigarette. The movie theater was alive with rustlings and murmurs.

"*Everyone* goes," Amy had told her. "Wall Street brokers, sports jocks, newscasters, Mafia types, tourists . . ."

Marcella peered at the silhouettes in the dark, trying to discover whom she was sitting near. Could something like this possibly work if she adjusted her mind and her expectations? It was just as well that it was pitch-black because she was sure her face was bright red with embarrassment. There was a deep feeling of shame in her, but, curiously, this shameful feeling only added to the excitement. The first man to approach and touch her must have thought she was ill, so violently did she shiver when he placed his hand gently on her thigh.

"You okay?" he whispered, glancing at her in the reflected light from the screen.

She nodded, her throat so dry she was unable to speak. She was going to let him. She had made up her mind that the first man would do. Her neighbor was dark with regular features and a clean cologne smell. She placed her fingers on the back of the wrist that lay so casually on her thigh, feeling the hairs on it, feeling its thickness and strength. She tried to swallow, the noise she made sounding deafening to her. Unbelievably, she already felt moist between the legs from the very idea of what she was doing. Awaiting his first intimate touch, her legs apart, she held her breath as his hand moved almost imperceptibly toward her lap. She wanted him to be stealthy, furtive. Each time the screen lit with an outdoor shot, she glanced sideways. He was in his forties, she guessed, with neatly combed hair. Her first. And as furtive as she could wish for. He remained facing the screen as his hand slid, very gently and silkily, beneath her skirt. When the tips of his careful fingers reached her, she felt her entire body shudder, a moan involuntarily escaping her. She leaned back in her seat, giving herself up to his strong, confident hand. She could see the people sitting together all over the theater. They were all there for the same thing. His hand placed itself square upon her sex, touching through her sheer panties. When she allowed him to drag those down, raising herself from the velvet seat to wriggle out of them, he placed his palm flat on her naked sex. She gave a sharp intake of breath. He began gently massaging the lips, the crevice, passing his forefinger firmly over and over the enlarged bud. She had never felt anything so wonderful. Pure sex, Amy had said, and she was right. But how could she be sitting there, letting some man she didn't know do this to her? And how could it seem perfectly natural, not strange at all? She closed her eyes, giving herself up to the sheer enjoyment of physical pleasure. The pleasure existed of itself, there were no mental associations, no guesses as to what would become of their relationship: there *was* no relationship. It was simply his hand and her groin existing in the now, in the pleasurable *now*. His fingers curved under her and into her and she hardly dared breathe. He seemed to know just how far to go. She accommodated him, shifting slightly to the edge of her seat. When he took her right hand and placed it on the outline of his erection, she almost panicked. How much would she be expected to do? She played with him. Pure sex, Amy had said. Safe and pure. It's the only way to avoid all risks. Of course, thinking of it in this way, as medicinal, as socially considerate, helped justify it. One could also say that this was more honest, less time-consuming, less game playing, than—

"Aah . . ." Marcella moaned softly. How was it that he seemed to know exactly how she liked to be touched, how much pressure she needed to keep her hovering over her pleasure like this, until she began to feel the wave building up inside her. Awkwardly, she pulled down his zipper and reached into his pants. Not because she really wanted to, but because she felt obliged to return this pleasure he was giving her. She held the stiff shape through his cotton briefs. He was clean, immaculately groomed, his body giving off a stronger aroma of cologne as he became more excited. He bent toward her to nuzzle one nipple through her blouse and she unbuttoned it and freed a breast from her bra. His warm moist mouth seized an erect tip, suckling, sending tingles down into her. She freed his sex and held him in her hand, gently caressing. Warm stuff spilled from her as his fingers worked inside her, wriggling, never easing up the pressure on her bud with his other hand, his mouth glued to her breast.

The pleasure was coming from everywhere now, from his fingers, from his mouth, from his other hand. Her mind could no longer separate the pleasure points as she slumped in her seat, engulfed in a blur of sex, everything in her brain screaming that this was wrong, everything in her body affirming it to be right. She glanced up at the screen, not even registering the images that flickered across her gaze, giving herself a respite from the relentless prod of pleasure that threatened to burst into glorious orgasm very soon. And then she started to come. Oh God, how she was going to come! Silently, of course, holding back the sighs and moans she longed to make, the waves breaking over and over her, her eyes tightly shut against such intense pleasure. A woman is made to feel this, she thought; I have denied it to myself for too long. It drenched her, at the final wave, thoroughly pleasuring every nerve ending. And before she could turn to thank the man he had suddenly, lithely, left her in the dark almost sobbing with relief. It *couldn't* be that easy, that wonderful!

She adjusted her clothes, smoothed out her skirt, knowing then that she would return and return, just as Amy had. It would be her shameful secret that she would reveal to no one, because no one would understand, not even Amy. For Amy, it was just another way to get kicks, but for Marcella, it was an amazing affirmation of her body's possibilities for pleasure, a fulfilling, mysterious experience. No one could be allowed to share in this triumph, this way of beating the odds. The odds against a woman in Manhattan achieving sexual happiness. She did not need Amy's approving smile; she wanted to keep this secret all to herself. She stumbled out of the club a different person. What had happened in there had altered everything she thought she knew about herself.

"Boobs!" Sonia told the distinguished surgeon in his La Jolla office as she undid her white robe. "Big, luscious, sexy *boobs!"* She opened the robe and displayed her naked body.

"Not too big, I hope," he said, eyeing her body professionally, then, with a slight leer, unprofessionally.

"Why not?" She touched herself provocatively, smiling at him. He was fat and bald and around fifty and he stared at her through powerful bifocals. He was the fourth plastic surgeon she had seen; the other three had all turned her down.

"Because they would be out of proportion to your body." He leaned over the desk and gently touched her breasts with his pale doctor's hands. He sat back, indicating that she could close her robe. "You're a very beautiful young lady," he told her. "What makes you think you need surgery?"

"I'm a model." Sonia assumed her sincere, open-eyed look. "I want as much work as I can get, and they want models with boobs now. Where will the scar be? Will I see it?"

"Only some lucky fellow standing beneath you might," he said, smiling, "if you were naked. If he lifted your breasts."

"So they'll hang down over it?" she asked.

"Silicone implants don't hang," he corrected her. "My scars heal ninety percent invisibly. Do you really want that much silicone?"

Sonia nodded. "As much as it takes."

"And you are—?" he asked, his hand poised to fill out a form. "How old, Miss Winton?"

"Eighteen," she said. "I have ID." A guy from the hotel where she was staying had faked one for her. She handed it to the doctor. He glanced at it.

"You're a little young to be getting a major cosmetic implant," he said. "Couldn't it wait a year or two? What do your parents think?"

"I'm an orphan," she said. "While you're doing it, I'd like a smaller nose. Can you do them both at the same time?"

"And what do you imagine is wrong with your nose?" He frowned. "It looks perfect to me."

"In real life, maybe," she sighed patiently, "but for photographs, the smaller your nose, the better. I'd just like it real *tiny*! I don't care what it costs. My parents left me a lot of money. So whaddya think? Can you do both things at the same time?"

He glanced up irritably at her, closing the file he had been preparing, screwing the top onto his Mont Blanc pen. "I'm afraid I could do neither," he told her. "I'm not a nose man and I don't believe you're eighteen, ID or no ID. I'd place you at around fifteen. I'm not in the habit of even interviewing young girls without a parent or guardian present."

Sonia pursed her lips, giving him a flash of her violet eyes.

"What does it matter how old I am as long as I can pay for it?" she asked, standing. "I have cash! There's no law against it, is there?"

He shrugged, pushing her file aside. "I'd have to get my attorney to check on whether it's actually illegal, but I have my own personal rule not to operate on minors unless it's vital. Now go away and forget about an operation and come back in five years' time if you really want it then. You're still a child!"

She threw open her robe. "Really? Is this a child's body?"

He glanced at her. "You'll have to find someone much less reputable than I if you insist on this self-mutilation. I very much hope you don't find anyone to do what you want. Your body has not finished growing. There could be all kinds of complications."

"Oh *shit!*" Sonia stalked out of his office into the changing room. So far her age had been her greatest obstacle. She threw on her clothes and stalked out of the offices into the street, into the waiting cab.

She stared at the ocean as they sped past La Jolla Shores. She had been able to talk the old lady who had wanted to help her find her mother into checking her into the best hotel in La Jolla, La Residencia. Because she had no credit card, she had been asked to pay in advance. That had been two weeks ago, and since then the staff of the hotel had listened sympathetically to her story of being a rich orphan treating herself to a vacation after a terrible car accident had killed both parents. The fifty-dollar tips she had lavished on maids and waiters had ensured her popularity, and when too many eyebrows had been raised at her seemingly endless supply of cash, she had bought traveler's checks.

The most helpful person so far had been the straight-looking guy who dressed like a bank manager and was in charge of the hotel's accounts department. From the moment Sonia had paid him with a fat wad of notes, he had been fascinated by her, offering to help her out with a fake ID card when she had confided in him. His reward was to be a dinner date with her, but she kept putting him off. He was too serious, too smitten, and she feared a repetition of the events the Egyptian had put her through in the car three Saturdays ago. That now seemed like three years ago in her fast-changing life. She was still not sure how she felt about that. One part of her was outraged, scared, and hurt, and the other part, the more grown-up, daring Sonia, was starting to feel that under the right circumstances, those weird things he had done to her would have been exciting. There would be plenty of time to explore all that when she had completed her makeover.

At fourteen, she was living a make-believe adult life that amazed and delighted her. She had been forced to grow up quickly in these last few weeks. She knew it was an act, a veneer; that she was simply aping the way she thought adults behaved, but it was a very good veneer, polished by drama lessons, honed by her will to survive this exciting

new runaway life. She still looked juvenile when she
scraped off the makeup and unpinned her hair, but so far
no one had seen her like that and no one had called her
bluff. All she needed was to convince some doctor that she
was old enough for surgery. Right now, it was back to the
hotel to thumb through the Yellow Pages again.

That afternoon, she called more doctors and hospitals,
and an office called the Californian Beauty Hospitalization
Referral Plan.

She eventually found a Doctor Kaplan, who asked for
fifteen thousand dollars cash in advance. Sonia thought
that was a lot, but she was tired of looking and paid up. He
also made her sign what seemed like a dozen forms waiving
indemnity if anything went wrong.

"Why?" she giggled. "So I can't sue you if I come out
looking like the hunchback of Notre Dame?"

"You won't be a hunchback!" he promised. "It's just a
formality." He looked at her weirdly, she thought, but she
had no choice but to trust him. It was better than remaining a child forever.

She stayed in a private clinic the night before her operations, fussed over by Korean nurses, watching her slim
body in the mirror as they carefully shaved her armpits.
Like a young boy, the Egyptian had said. No one would
ever say *that* to her again, she promised herself.

After the gruelling double operation on her nose and
breasts, she came to feeling as sore and ill as if she had
been run over by a truck. They kept her in bed for two
weeks before removing the bandages. She was bruised and
red, but she adored her new spherical breasts. Doctor Kaplan had given her enough silicone to make them ripe, luscious. Her nipples were painfully swollen, and her tiny, tip-
tilted, square-ended nose made her eyes look slightly
crossed, but it was definitely a new Sonia who stared back
at her from the mirror, a new Sonia to match the new
person she had become.

She returned to La Residencia and healed surprisingly
quickly in the following weeks, helped by huge doses of
vitamin C that she swallowed in handfuls. She made daily
visits to the clinic for supervision, sunbathed very carefully,

and ate a balanced diet. She wondered whether she should try to contact Laurie, but when she remembered the look on Laurie's face as she had screamed at her, she decided not to.

On several occasions she picked up the phone to call the police to find out where her father was being held, but each time she thought better of it. They might claim the money, and this would restrict her plans. She was lonely at times, but she liked this new life. It was better to stay incognito until she was a professional model, something she now realized she had been destined to become. After all, people had always been telling her how beautiful she was: now she would use that beauty.

Slowly, she accumulated a wardrobe of clinging clothes in silk, linen, and cashmere, all showing off her new figure. She loved hitting the boutiques in the mornings, before too many people were around, trying on clothes and preening before the admiring salesgirls. In the evenings, she studied issues of *Vogue* and *Bazaar,* experimenting with her hair and makeup, strolling the seafront. Men spoke to her as she passed through bars or ate in elegant restaurants. Many men tried to pick her up. Jerks, she thought. One guy said he was a photographer and would do free shots for her portfolio if she gave him free modeling time. She asked him lots of questions about modeling and photography, but did not show up for their date.

Each morning, she bought *The New York Times* from a dispenser near the seafront, flipping through the pages as she ate breakfast back at the hotel, until one day, next to the book review, she found what she was looking for: an advertisement, placed by Volumes and Doubleday, announcing that Marcella Balducci Winton, author of the phenomenally successful *In the Name of Love,* would be signing copies of the new paperback edition at Doubleday's Fifth Avenue store on Friday afternoon. It was Wednesday. That morning, Sonia bought a first-class ticket to New York from the hotel's travel shop.

"Round trip?" the clerk asked.

"Uh-uh." She looked through the plate-glass window at the blue Pacific outside. "I'm not coming back."

She told the man who worked in accounts to make up her bill. He persuaded her to have dinner with him, since it was her last night. But first she needed one more favor. She asked him to call the Plaza Hotel in New York and make a reservation for her, pretending to be a fond uncle giving a trip to a niece. He charged three nights of a suite to his credit card and Sonia repaid him in crisp hundred-dollar bills. He was so respectful and awestruck that she decided to get all dressed up for this last night of the Californian Sonia.

That evening, in the restaurant on the hotel's top floor, she ordered the most expensive dish on the menu—lobster thermidor, and French champagne at one hundred and fifty dollars a bottle just to see what it tasted like. It wasn't so hot, she thought. They made small talk through dinner and he touched her knee a couple of times. She found him dull, but it was fascinating to see the power she could wield over an adult. After dinner, he suggested they watch television in her room. She agreed, letting him into her suite and disappearing into the bathroom.

She ran the water ice-cold in the basin, giggling, soaking a hand towel in the sink and squeezing out the excess water, twisting the towel into a mean whip. When she opened the door, he was relaxing in an armchair with his jacket off. His eyes widened in surprise as she came at him, flicking the towel with all her force. She caught him on the cheek, leaving a cruel welt there, then on the forehead, and she was aiming for his eyes when he grabbed his jacket and ran out of the room. He scuttled down the corridor to the elevator, looking back fearfully at her. Sonia closed the door and leaned back on it and laughed and laughed. If this was a new game, it was hilarious! She'd never starve with men like that around! She spent the rest of the evening packing her new clothes, peering at her new breasts in the bathroom mirror, lifting them gently to see the red lines, which the doctor had promised would disappear in a few more weeks. She slept soundly on her last night in California.

Marcella slipped into a seat in the back row of the theater. It was her tenth visit in as many weeks. If she had heard of any other woman returning so often to a place like this, she would have condemned her as a slut. But oh, how attentive, how gentle, her lovers in the dark had been. With their strong confident hands, they were absolute masters at bringing a woman to orgasm. The most intensely pleasurable peaks she had ever experienced had come about in this dark haven. At first she had been so grateful for each caress, so surprised by the gentleness she had received. How tender everyone was at six-thirty, the hour the businessmen stopped in on their way home. How warmly they stroked her, put their arms around her, did everything but kiss her lips, something she was too frightened to allow. She was as grateful to them as they were to her, for showing her how simple it was, how uncomplicated. For always being there when she needed them. And each time, upon leaving, she told herself that she was insane to do this, promising herself it was the last time.

She felt the possible danger at each visit. What if a man carried a knife? What if she sat next to a psychopath? She continually promised herself that if anything even remotely disagreeable happened, she would forget about this place. But so far it had remained a fairy tale, a fantasyland, a place of pleasure.

She placed her arm casually over the seat next to hers, a sign language she had picked up. A man would approach, sit a seat or two away, look over at her. When she did not like someone's look or the mood he projected—and it was amazing how accurately her sexual radar worked—she would withdraw her arm and ignore him. But now, as a serious, dark-haired, shy-seeming man approached, she knew he would do. She extended her arm encouragingly. Soon his warm hand tentatively touched hers. She liked the gentleness of his touch. It followed a pattern. It was always good. He moved discreetly to occupy the seat next to hers. Soon his hand was in her lap, massaging her. Just a hand, just five fingers, just a touch, but she could have swooned from this feeling. He was unsure, investigating, a little timid, so she extended her body toward him, urging him on. His hand gently cupped her breast. She knew by now to wear no bra. He held a nipple between two fingers. He moved his other hand on her. Marcella leaned way back in her seat. She had come to know these seats very well, knew just how far she had to slither her legs under the seat in front to allow her head to rest back on the edge of the velvet, to lie almost horizontal, giving herself up to that male hand, the touch that brought such fulfillment. He began to work on her in earnest, her orgasm his aim. A sound made her turn her head to see a swarthy, good-looking younger man hovering behind her seat, watching them. He smiled at her. Many men liked to watch a woman being pleasured, but she did not encourage it. This man seemed sexy and nice. She inclined her head. The man next to her leaned over and buried his face in her lap, licking broad tongue strokes of pleasure over her. She wondered what Emily Post would have said about greeting a man while another man was lapping between one's legs. The new man suddenly dived under her seat. His head appeared between her legs and suddenly two men were lapping at her. Her head jerked back at the pleasure. Giving herself over to it, she watched them divide up the territory, one licking the insides of her thighs, the other, as if intoxicated by the perfume with which she had splashed herself, sniffing, rubbing his nose appreciatively in her, like a cat with catnip.

The two worked well together, the first seeming not to resent his partner. They were like conscientious doctors laboring over a patient, artisans lovingly shaping their crafts, old lovers who knew exactly how to please. Gently, sweetly, they hoisted her legs, hooking her ankles over the seat in front, her skirt gathered until it rested in folds on her stomach. Exposed to them, she allowed the two men to run their tongues over her most sensitive area, to rub chins and noses in her bush, to play with her lips, to touch her crevice with their wondering fingertips. She saw their tongues sometimes brush, saw their utter engrossment in her and her pleasure. Her nipples stiffened as hands reached up to unbutton the front of her blouse and take a breast in each hand. A roar of pleasure sounded in her, surging quietly through her. Two men working to please her! God, she had never experienced this! Spread-eagled over the red velvet seats, she was living a dream, a fantasy! She began to come. She fought to keep silent. God, multi-orgasmic, she came again and again, over and over, groaning softly, her groans unnoticed among all the others in the theater. This must be the last time I do this, she promised, hovering in ecstasy, the pleasure suffusing her. The men slid into the seats on either side of her. Reaching out, she felt their cocks. One withdrew his sex, inviting her to hold it. She slid her hand along the thick shaft and he took her hand, spat in it, and replaced it on him. The lubrication made him moan and he came, spurting in the air. The other man came too, and for a moment they looked like some three-headed deity, a six-armed Indian god engaging in some Kama Sutra ritual.

The men tidied themselves, gave her affectionate pats, leaned to brush her cheek with their lips. Soon she was alone again. For a few minutes she hovered between consciousness and a kind of dream. But men strolling the aisle peered interestedly at her state of disarray and she had to button her blouse, pull down her skirt, make herself stand tremblingly, and leave.

What kind of woman would do this? she asked herself. *You.* She left the club by a fire exit, walking down a frighteningly dark alley to avoid being seen: she doubted that any of the Members moviegoers were her readers or knew her face, but it was better to be sure. Crossing Ninth Avenue, she walked east on Fifty-seventh Street, her body still throbbing from the pleasure she had received.

She peered along the street when she reached Broadway, waiting for the one great extravagance of her life to appear. She had hated feeling like Amy's poor relative, borrowing her car only when it was free. When her novel had reached its seventh printing, she bought herself a Rolls-Royce, choosing a luscious navy for it and hiring Donald, a dignified black driver. Now perhaps she could begin to lead the life she had dreamed of. She did not need a Southampton mansion and swimming pool. Just her comfortable apartment on Central Park South and this gorgeous car, this willing driver, taking her anywhere she wanted to go. And right now, she just wanted to go home.

The car appeared on the prearranged corner. She always had Donald drop her off and pick her up some blocks from Members, so her entrances and exits would be as inconspicuous as possible. Although Members had a gym and a restaurant and various other meeting places, she felt sure that everyone would know she was going to the movie theater. Wearily, she climbed into the backseat, and Donald arranged a cashmere throw over her lap. She could not meet his eyes, as if he knew her secret, as if he could smell the sex on her. He drove her home and she bade him good night, telling him she'd need the car at ten the next morning.

One of the doormen rode up in the elevator with her, saying good night at her floor. Finally, she was home in her beloved cocoon of an apartment. She took a warm bath and, later, played back her telephone messages while staring out her workroom window at Central Park, midnight green below. The messages were all business; somehow, she had created a life for herself that centered around her books.

Before she climbed into the clean white bed, she knelt on the rug, forehead leaning against her joined hands, elbows resting on the bed. Forgive me, she prayed. She was not sure who she was asking to do this.

The young man sleeping in her bed was so quiet, so still, that anyone else might almost have believed him to be dead. But she knew his ways, knew he was apt to suddenly give a tremendous start, then turn, groaning out something before sinking back into that deep, deep slumber she so envied. She slipped into bed beside her son, not touching him, glancing across at his perfect profile, the slightly smiling lips. She lay on her back, eyes open. If it was so wrong, and she knew it was wrong, why did she feel so good? If it feels good, do it! Isn't that what they used to say? If it feels good, why feel guilty? Why fear that this strange, wonderful addiction was robbing her of something—something really valuable? Dear God, she prayed again. In whom I do not believe. Forgive me. I am horrified at myself. Soon she slept.

"Yummy!" Amy piled goat cheese high onto a wedge of French baguette. They were lunching at Ultimo, a new Italian place on upper Broadway, on one of the first hot summer days. "Remember that movie theater I showed you in Members?" she asked Marcella. "A gal I know got completely hooked. I mean, had to go every night for weeks! I liked it fine for a few times, but . . ." She raised her eyebrows.

"How could someone get hooked on a place like that?"

Marcella asked, trying to keep her voice casual. She sipped at her strong black coffee.

"Maybe it reminds some girls of the first furtive sex they ever had?" Amy suggested, dabbing at her mouth. "You know, women of my age group who grew up before the so-called revolution. We fumbled in the dark a lot. They say your first times leave an indelible impression. Mine were *always* on backseats! Perhaps that's why I have a thing for taxis and limos?" She giggled.

Marcella's mind raced. Was she about to get addicted? The sweet sexy solace of her encounters was already an important part of her life. Did the darkness and the groping harken back to nearly forgotten memories of her father stroking her, Harry touching her, the darkness of the confessional booth and Father Carmello hearing her out, scolding her gently for her transgressions?

"Someday I'm going to write about that place," Amy vowed. She began to peel a ripe fig. "If anyone could believe it . . ."

"Yes . . ." Marcella nodded. "It is a little hard to believe."

Amy looked up at her sharply. "And what are *you* doing for sex?" she asked suddenly. "You're getting it, I can tell. There's a certain look on a woman's face when she's starved of it—kind of pinched. You don't have that pinched look, Marcella. . . ."

Marcella lit a cigarette, avoiding Amy's scrutiny.

"I plead the Fifth Amendment." She laughed, taking a long drag of smoke and exhaling it.

"Holding out on me, eh?" Amy tried to joke. Marcella could see she was slightly annoyed. Too bad, she thought. She's my agent and friend, not my father confessor.

She had been there again last night, early in the evening. After, she had walked slowly back up Ninth Avenue, looking for Donald and the car on Fifty-seventh Street, her legs wobbly with pleasure. And at home, after her shower, she had stretched out on her bed and Mark had tapped on her door.

"Would you like some music?" he had asked.

"I'd love some, darling," she had said.

He had gone to the living room, leaving her door ajar, and soon the beautiful clear notes of Debussy had sounded and she had closed her eyes and blessed her life. Had she found the answer? The Debussy floated on the air, and for that moment, she had never felt so happy.

"So what about tomorrow?" Amy's voice broke in on her thoughts. "Do you have your outfit and everything?"

"Tomorrow! Yes!" Marcella stubbed out her cigarette. "A noon signing at Doubleday's. The cream linen suit, I thought."

"Absolutely!" Amy approved. "And take the Rolls, even though it's only a few blocks away. Those paperback readers expect a little glamour for their four bucks!"

"Only purchasers of the Volumes paperback by Marcella Balducci Winton will be allowed into the signing area," warned a hand-lettered sign at Doubleday the next day, announcing a personal appearance of the author of *In the Name of Love*—"the million-dollar, million-seller novel."

Scott was there to guide her through the milling crowd of women to the table laden with hundreds of copies of her book and a giant flower arrangement. A water carafe stood next to the flowers, as if Marcella were expected to speak.

A snaking line of women doubled back and forth inside the red velvet rope, patiently clutching their copies of the book. As Marcella entered the store, the crowd jostled to get nearer. It was the first time she had publicly tasted her fame and it was curiously frightening, as if these people wanted even more of her than the self she had revealed in her book. She sat at the table and the crowd surged forward, thrusting books.

"Hysteria!" Scott cried happily. "We'll be number one within two weeks!"

Marcella began signing. The books were pushed at her, different perfumes assaulting her nose, names shyly given for her to inscribe.

"To Judy, please."

"For Joan."

"Could you put 'To my best friend Renée'?"

And there were many too shy to ask for anything, for whom she thankfully signed her name only. The store became strangely quiet except for the cash register ringing up further sales of her book. A hundred women passed through.

"Oh, Mrs. Winton, I loved your book!" a fiftyish woman with Lucille Ball lips gushed. "This copy is for my mother!"

"Good luck to you, my dear." An older lady winked.

"Manuella is *me*!" a girl whispered.

Marcella tried to keep cool. My readers, she thought. She said a few words to each one.

"How's the new book coming along?" Scott murmured during a quiet spell. She glanced up at him.

"I'm nearly through the first rough draft," she told him.

"Good. Great," he said. "We want you on a schedule. One every eighteen months."

Another hundred readers, some men this time. She was signing names she had never heard of before. African, Chinese, invented names. Inscriptions to husbands, to daughters, to sisters and best friends. She tried to take a moment to digest each compliment, to study each face, to remember what they said about crying at the ending or identifying with her heroine. All these comments would keep her company and give her courage to finish the next book.

After an hour, Scott announced: "We'll take a short break!"

He poured some water for her and she shook her right hand free of the cramp that had seized it, glancing gratefully up at Scott.

"Thanks for being here!" she told him.

He smiled. "Line of duty, ma'am."

The manager suggested she sign an extra hundred copies "for the store," and she promised to do that.

When she returned to signing she could see the line snaking out of the front door and down the street. She longed to be back in her apartment, away from all these curious stares that seemed to be eating her up.

"For Anna, please."

"Can you write 'To my darling Patricia'?"

"For Susan Weston, my greatest fan."

"For Sonia, please!"

The name struck Marcella with a pang.

"Oh!" She started to look up. "I have a daughter called
—" She stopped. She was staring into a pair of violet eyes whose expression dared her to recognize them. The tall

young woman stood poised over her, holding an open book.

"*Sonia?*" Marcella cried. She stood up suddenly, the carafe crashing to the floor, a nearby reader crying out as the water splashed her.

The girl, taller than she was, seemed different, was no longer her little child but a fully developed, stunning young woman. And she had the strangest expression on her face. Pure bravado, as if daring Marcella to want her back. Marcella threw her arms around her.

"Oh Sonia! *Sonia!* How we've looked for you!"

She forgot the crowd watching, and for a moment it was a fairy tale come true, the beautiful young daughter reunited with her loving mother.

Scott said, "So *this* is Sonia!" admiringly, and the watching women applauded, not knowing what they were applauding.

"Everybody!" Marcella suddenly announced, her eyes pouring with tears, one arm around Sonia's shoulder. "My daughter, Sonia, who I haven't seen for two years! She's come back!"

They exclaimed and applauded again, as if she had written a new dramatic scene for her next book. But this was no book, this was *real*, this was her *life*! She hugged Sonia to her again, trying to feel what she knew she should be feeling—the return of a daughter. But nothing, not the smell, not the feel of this young woman in her arms, not her face, her expression, felt in the least familiar. This beautiful young woman who called her "mother" was a total stranger.

Sonia stood a little stiffly in her mother's embrace, then suddenly wriggled out of it.

"This is very touching, Mother dear," she said, "but let's not get too gushy. Finish signing your books. I'll wait." She strode off to the art books. Marcella watched her casually leafing through a volume, trying to still the strange hurt inside her.

"Scott?" she murmured, reaching for the next book. "If you expect me to do another hour here, you'd better send out for a triple Scotch!"

"Mark, this is your sister!" Marcella announced that afternoon.

Mark let drop the book he was holding and jumped to his feet, gazing at his sister in astonishment.

"Sonia!" he cried. He rushed to embrace her and she proffered her cheek for him to kiss. Then he stared at her, mystified. "I'd never have recognized you! *Never!* You've changed your nose, haven't you?"

"I *knew* there was something different!" Marcella said, reaching for Sonia's face.

Sonia gave a shout of laughter and ran to the other side of the room. "Broke it, falling off my horse!" she said. "A surgeon had to reset it and everything. I said, 'While you're about it, give me a Kimberly Evans nose!' You know who *she* is, don't you? She's the Estée Lauder model."

They said nothing, watching her as she glanced around the apartment, stepped out onto the small balcony, and peered at the street below.

"Well!" She turned to face them. "I'm back!" She said it almost as a challenge. "So this is where we live now!"

Marcella stared at her, trying not to label the emotions that fought inside her. This was not at all how she had imagined their reunion.

"Now tell me where you got that body?" she asked Sonia. "No one in our family had a body like that!"

Sonia glanced down at her body proudly. She was wearing a clinging thin black sweater and straight black pants. Marcella noticed that every accessory—the earrings, the shoes—was of the highest quality and very chic. "This body took hours and hours of sweat to achieve," Sonia told them. "Dance class, exercise, and riding! *That's* my secret. I had my own horse. God, I'm going to miss her!" She pulled her sweater down tight over her torso, glancing at Marcella and Mark as if flirting with them. Then she did a leap into the air and plonked herself down on the living room floor.

"You'll find lots of exciting things to do here, darling!" Marcella pulled her to her feet. "Come say hello to Grandma. Let's see if she remembers you. . . ."

"Oh God, does *she* live here, too?" Sonia groaned.

Marcella stared at her, guiding her to the corridor. "Of course she does! She has a nurse and her own bathroom and she's completely self-contained. She'll be so surprised!" Her mother's door was opened by the nurse.

"Oh, how lovely!" the nurse cried, turning to Ida. "You have visitors!"

Ida did not look up.

"Mom?" Marcella knelt down by Ida's side, kissing her. "We have a wonderful surprise for you, darling! Sonia's back."

Marcella looked behind her for Sonia, who hung back fearfully, clutching Mark and hiding behind him, peeping over his shoulder as if she were terrified, as if Ida were a dangerous lunatic.

"Come and kiss her, Sonia!" Marcella urged. Stepping gingerly forward, Sonia bent down and gave Ida a quick peck on her cheek.

Ida stared at her.

"She's been living with her father for two years!" Marcella cried. "Now she's here with us! Isn't it wonderful?"

Ida turned back to the television screen.

Sonia burst out laughing. "She doesn't even know who I am!" she cried.

"No! Don't say that!" Marcella put her hand protectively on her mother's shoulder. "She's a little forgetful sometimes. *Help* her remember you!"

Sonia made a face, crouching down to her grandmother's level.

"Hi, Gram, remember *me*?" She stood upright again, watching her. Ida suddenly put out a hand and attempted to push Sonia away.

"You see?" Sonia made for the door. "She doesn't even want me here." She gave a dazzling smile at the nurse. Marcella followed her out of the room. In the corridor, Sonia's hand was over her mouth, muffling her giggles.

"Spend a little time with her, Sonia," Marcella begged. "You too, Mark. Maybe we can help her to remember things, if we try."

In the living room, she put her arm around each child. "We're a family again!" she said. "I can't wait for Amy to meet you, Sonia. Amy Jagger is my agent and a great writer. She lives right here in this building. There's so much to catch up on. When I heard your father had been arrested, I wondered if I would hear from you. I was hoping—"

Sonia shook her head. "We're not a family again, Mother," she said. "Not until Daddy's free."

Marcella lit a cigarette and sat down on the sofa. Sonia sat on the rug in front of her.

"You know I'm divorcing your father, don't you, Sonia?" she asked.

Sonia stared at her coolly. "I figured. What do you need him for when your book's selling like that, huh?"

Marcella shot a glance at Mark. "Get us something to drink, Mark, will you, darling?"

"Sure." He headed for the kitchen.

She looked back to Sonia. "Is that why you think I married your father?" she asked her.

Sonia shrugged. "Plenty of women marry because they can't make their own bread. I want to earn my own living as soon as I can!"

"That's fine," Marcella smiled, "if you can do it."

"Oh, I can do it all right," Sonia said. "Guys are always stopping me on the street to say, 'You could be a model!' Now I'm going to follow up on it."

"You have plenty of time for that, darling," Marcella said, stubbing out her cigarette. "First you need a decent education. What sort of grades have you been getting?"

They discussed Sonia's schooling, her horse riding, her dancing lessons. Marcella knew instinctively that to discuss Harry would be skating on thin ice.

In the evening, they all went to a nearby French brasserie and continued to catch up on the last two years. Sonia's last two years, that is, because she did not seem particularly interested in theirs. Marcella watched her two children interestedly as they attempted to pick up their relationship.

"You cannot imagine how many different places we lived in," Sonia told them. "Dad was so paranoid! All that *driving*! Finally we settled in California, and once I had my horse to ride, I didn't care where I was! It was kinda fun, I guess! I miss my friend Gemma!"

"And your father was living with someone at the time of his arrest?" Marcella asked carefully.

"Yeah. Laurie. I miss *her,* too," Sonia said, then shrugged. "I guess I'm better off with my real mother."

"I hope so, darling." Marcella attempted again to hug her, again getting no response.

"Where's she gonna sleep?" Mark asked when they got home and Sonia collapsed on the sofa, falling asleep immediately. "She can have my bed."

Marcella drew a light quilt over Sonia. "And where do you think you'd sleep?" She threw him a look.

"With you!" he said.

She turned out the lights in the living room. Mark followed her to her bedroom. "I don't think she should see us sleeping together, Mark," she told him. "You're sixteen and it's time we stopped. Sonia could use a normal family life right now. And an elder brother to look up to. She's had a crazy life for the last two years, so let's try to make it up to her. Remember, she's only a child."

"Yeah, fourteen going on forty!" Mark laughed. "She's the most precocious kid *I've* ever met!"

"Mark?" She kissed his forehead. "Be patient with her. For me."

She could not get to sleep that night. She tossed on the hot sheets and thought about how Sonia could fit back into their lives. In her head she redecorated her small dressing room, turning it into a writing room so she could give her office to Sonia. At four o'clock, her head whirling, she switched on her lamp to make some sketches of the new rooms. Mark appeared at her door.

"I have a recital tomorrow. If I don't get some sleep, I'll screw up!" he pleaded. He climbed into bed with her and she switched off the light. They both fell asleep almost immediately.

They were awakened by Sonia's hoots of laughter the next morning at eight. She stood over them as they slept, laughing.

"My God, what a pair!" she cried.

Mark opened one eye and grunted, turning over.

"Do you still breast-feed him?" Sonia asked her mother.

Marcella sat up in bed, annoyed. "I need another hour of sleep, Sonia. Mark thought you might want his bed if you woke in the middle of the night. Now close the door, please. In this house, we knock before we enter someone's bedroom."

"Yeah!" Sonia stuck her hands in her jeans as she turned away. "I bet you do!"

Marcella heard the front door slam as Sonia left the apartment. She was too angry to get back to sleep. She sat up, shaking Mark awake.

"See what you've done?" she asked. "I knew I shouldn't have let you sleep here! It's extremely important that Sonia feels loved and welcomed back here, not shut out!"

He gave her a sleepy look as he headed for the bathroom.

After Mark had brought up the mail and left for school, she decided to make a quick trip to Bloomingdale's to buy Sonia some new clothes. Hopefully, they would help her forget this morning's scene.

She was not sure what a fourteen-year-old would wear these days, but she found armfuls of warm-up suits, pants, a blazer, and several blouses and sweaters, all in Sonia's favorite shades of lavender and purple. She took a taxi home with the bulging shopping bags, laying out the clothing on the living room sofa as a surprise.

Sonia returned just before lunch, with the doorman staggering under two heavy suitcases. Marcella helped her drag them into Mark's room and made some room for her things in his closet. Sonia unlocked her Louis Vuitton cases, revealing piles of expensive French and Italian clothing. Most of it was adult, slinky, suitable for a femme fatale.

"I went on a shopping spree for you this morning, darling. . . ." She took Sonia to show her the stuff on the sofa. After the contents of the suitcases, this looked like children's wear. "I hope you like what I chose. Kids in New York have to be dressed for the streets. You'll find you get less bothered if you dress really casually here."

Sonia bent to touch the clothing lightly, a trying-not-to-laugh look on her face.

"I'm sorry, Mother dear, but I never heard of any of

these designers," she dismissed them. "Anyway, this is *not* my look!"

"I thought you were crazy about purple?" Marcella asked, disappointed.

"When I was *ten*!" Sonia laughed. "Black is my color now. Can't you see?" She indicated the black clinging jeans and ribbed cotton tee-shirt.

"Oh." Marcella felt a stab of hurt. "I'm sorry. Let's have a sandwich and go back and exchange them."

Going out onto the street with her daughter was an event. Sonia's tightly clad body attracted double takes and whistles from construction workers and stares from men they passed on the street. The provocative way Sonia walked, breasts forward, long loping strides, mouth half open, made her look as if she were posing for a photograph. At Bloomingdale's, she managed to find one very expensive, tight black dress that cost more than all the returned clothing combined. She held the filmy garment against her body, purring. "*This* is what I want!" She strutted before the mirror, holding it. "This is *hot*!"

Marcella glanced around at the other customers staring at Sonia's performance.

"When would you possibly wear *that*?" she asked.

"Plenty of places!" Sonia shrugged. "Hanging out . . ."

Marcella sighed. "See if you can find something more suitable, darling. Younger."

Sonia shot her a weary look, hanging the dress back on its rack. "Forget it! I'll come in and get it myself some other time." She sulked all the way home in the taxi.

They got through that summer lounging at Amy's Southampton house most of the weekends, splashing in the pool, watching the visiting male authors ogle Sonia's bikini-clad body. Amy was bewitched by Sonia.

"She's more beautiful and outrageous than any of my heroines!" she declared, seating Sonia next to the oldest, randiest men she knew at her Saturday dinners, enjoying the drama.

In September, Marcella enrolled Sonia at a private

school where French was the main language spoken and there was a concentration on the arts. Sonia demanded singing, dancing, and exercise classes, signing up with various schools in the midtown and Broadway area. Once her term had started, she was always out. Her alibis were work, courses, classes, and an occasional audition. Some mornings she was so tired that she would still be asleep when the housecleaner arrived at eleven. On weekends she either disappeared or ate nonstop in the kitchen, as though nothing could assuage her hunger. She disrupted their little household like a boulder dropped into a calm pool. At night, she cried out in her sleep, but insisted that nothing was wrong when Marcella rushed to her side. The purple eyes that could be so beautiful when she wanted something seemed to harden when she looked at her mother. There were no intimate little moments between them. Marcella's dream of having a daughter to do things with, shop together, walk with in the park, evaporated each time this lovely, cold stranger entered the room.

"And my protective brother act is not working," Mark confided. Obviously Sonia had suffered disturbing injuries. When her anger erupted, it was terrifying. A chance remark from Mark could prompt her nails to fly in his face. She would apologize to him later, saying, "I just felt like hurting you."

After not speaking to him for days, she would suddenly enter his room and chat, telling him about some school friend's father she was in love with. "He'd leave his wife for me tomorrow if I was older," she'd tell him.

"You're insane, you know that?" he'd say.

She would smile. "At least *I* don't sleep with my mommy! That's what *I* call insane! You know, sometimes I cut school to look for modeling work. The fashion business is crawling with cute guys like you, Mark. They're all crazy about me—they love my face, my boobs, my hair, all that, but they're like brothers to me. I know a lot of cute guys who'd like to meet you. What'd you say, Mark? Come with me, sometime, I'll introduce you. . . ."

She would lope out of his room, smiling secretly to herself, leaving him strangely dissatisfied, as though she had seen into some part of him he had never admitted to, not even to himself.

When a letter arrived for her via Harry's attorney, Sonia stared at the envelope suspiciously.

"How did he know I was here?" she demanded.

Marcella, in the kitchen brewing coffee, turned to look at her. "You were an officially listed missing person, darling. Naturally, everyone was informed when you showed up, including the police and your father's attorney."

She could see the conflicting emotions in Sonia's eyes as she played with the envelope. "Darling," Marcella reached out to touch her shoulder, "don't be so touchy about everything!"

Sonia shrugged and went off to school.

At dinner that night, Marcella asked, "And how is Daddy?"

"Christ!" Sonia threw down her fork. "The way you say his *name*! Like he's public enemy number one! Why did you marry him if you hated him?"

Marcella sipped her wine, forcing herself not to look at Mark. She knew their exchanged glances only infuriated Sonia.

"Sonia," she said carefully. "I know you think you're very grown-up now, but don't forget I'm still your mother and I don't want you to talk to me like that—ever! I don't hate your father, and remember, he walked out on me! Taking *you* with him! Now he's been arrested on serious charges and he faces a sentence of up to fifteen years in jail. He's being held on bail of half a million dollars, which he's been unable to raise. That's all *I* know; maybe you know more?"

Sonia stared into the last drops of Coke she was swirling around her glass and raised her violet eyes to her mother's. "Couldn't *you* pay his bail?" she asked.

Marcella held her gaze. "No," she said simply.

Sonia played with an empty cigarette packet. "And the ranch, the stables, my horse?"

"I don't know about all that, but I imagine it's all held by the state to pay the trial costs," Marcella told her.

"And you're lucky *you're* not in jail, too," Mark told her. "As an accessory!"

"You shut the fuck up!" Sonia yelled at him. "I'm not afraid of going to jail!"

"Sonia!" Marcella cried. "Where did you learn that kind of talk?"

Sonia stood up. "From your books, I guess." She glanced at Mark and giggled. "Can I have Donald and the car to visit Dad on Sunday?"

"I'm afraid Donald doesn't work on Sundays. You can take a cab," Marcella offered.

Sonia shook her head. "It would only be fun to visit a jail in a Rolls. Like *Breakfast at Tiffany's.*"

"If you write your father, you can give him this phone number and he can call you here," Marcella offered.

"Thanks," Sonia called over her shoulder as she left the room. "That's *real* generous of you, Mother dear."

Marcella looked around for a fresh pack of cigarettes, and Mark came to sit next to her.

"It's the age," he reassured her. "Your hormones get into an uproar and you want to hit out at somebody. Anybody!"

Marcella smiled at him, shaking her head. "No . . ." she told him. "She has a kind of talent for twisting whatever I say to her, making it sound bad."

Sonia locked her bedroom door and sat on the bed, shaking out the money she had hidden in a new quilted makeup bag. God, it had gone fast! Some clothes—the best, naturally—a few dozen meals and drinks—at the most expensive places in town. A few weeks in the top hotels, an operation or two, and all that was left was a little over a hundred thousand. *Not* enough for poor Dad's bail. She had big plans for making this money work for her anyway. The best makeup, the best haircut, the best portfolio; in other words, the best fucking package that any model had going for her in the entire country! She scribbled a note to her father, giving him her phone number, saying how much she missed him.

Harry called three weeks later, when Sonia was home between school and dance class, bolting down a doughnut and milk, about to change into leotards.

"Princess?" His voice was gruff, already a stranger's voice. "What happened to you? I called the house all that Saturday and couldn't get you. Laurie said you'd run away. They found Red in La Jolla. I was worried sick about you."

"Oh *Daddy*!" She instantly became his little girl again. "I was so scared! Laurie was screaming at me and—I came back here because I didn't know where else to go!"

"Now, don't you worry, princess," he told her. "I'll be out of here before you know it, I promise you. The important thing I have to ask you is this—did you take that pillow? That pillow with the money in it?"

"Oh *God*!" She could act this part very well; she was ready for it. "Christ, I forgot all about it!"

"Well, Laurie says it's gone, and she wouldn't lie to me. You wouldn't either, would you, princess?" he asked. "You see, that money could get me out of here. It would pay for bail and—" He sighed wearily, as if his last hope had been dashed. "I told you so often about that money, how could you have forgotten it?" he asked.

"Maybe if you hadn't slapped me so hard in front of everyone, I'd have remembered," she whispered.

"I'm sorry I raised my hand to you, princess." Harry's voice was low. "I've thought of it a hundred times when they lock me in here at six o'clock at night."

Sonia glanced at the clock on her radio. "Is that why you called, Dad?" she asked. "To find out about the money?"

"Of course not," he said. "You're still my princess, aren't you? I wanted to hear what happened to you and how you are. Where were you when they took me away? We looked everywhere—"

"Ashid took me for a drive. I guess he wanted to cheer me up after that morning. . . ."

"Yeah, well . . ." Harry sighed.

"Why'd you do it, Dad?" she asked. "Why'd you steal all that money?"

"I didn't steal, Sonia," he said firmly. "It's a legitimate way of making money that doesn't harm anyone. Rich, important men do it all the time, only they don't get caught. I merely used my special knowledge to—"

"Insider knowledge?" she asked.

"Well, yes, that's what they call it. But it doesn't hurt anyone. It doesn't make me a thief or a killer or"—he made a disgusted sound—"like some of these other animals I'm locked up here with."

Sonia smiled grimly. "Yeah. I'm sorry, Dad. I have to go to dance class now."

"Wait a minute—don't you want to know where I am?" he cried. "Aren't you coming to visit me? God damn it, Sonia, don't you care what's happened to me?"

She swallowed, saying nothing.

"Princess?" he asked.

"Did *you* care what was happening to *me* that Saturday?" she whispered. "I got back and you were gone—just when I really needed you. Don't you care what that Egyptian basket case did to me?"

"What? What's that, Sonia?" Harry cried. "If that guy laid one finger on you, I'll—"

"He laid more than a finger on me. . . ." She began to cry. "He strung me up in his car like a plucked chicken and he *fucked* me! He fucked me so hard I was sore for *days* after!"

"Don't use those *words*, Sonia!" Harry shouted. "Did you go to the police?"

"Are you kidding?" She wiped her eyes. "You think they'd be on *my* side?"

"Sonia, I—"

"I gotta go now, Dad," she cut him off. "I'll try to visit." She replaced the phone and sat there staring at it for a moment before gathering up her stuff and leaving for dance class.

Sonia hurried to her dance class, a half-eaten doughnut in one hand, swerving between walkers, dodging traffic, running to beat a light. It was October and the city still smelled of the entire hot summer. She walked fast yet carefully because the cartilage-fine filament of silicone inserted in her nose, the stuff that made her flaring nostrils so photogenic, was extremely fragile. One knock could cause its collapse, and her doctor had warned her that reconstruction would be expensive and painful. She kept her head down. The nose had not been completely successful. Perhaps the surgeon had not walked around his work, as a sculptor is supposed to do, viewing it from all angles. The squared-off, delicate tip seemed natural from the front, but from the side it had that slightly blank look of most nose jobs. Men still stared at her. All that riding, exercise, and dance class had given her body the nubile look of a young colt. Walking, she exuded grace and energy. Her teasing leotards, high rounded buttocks, slightly muscular calves, and thrusting, unbelievable breasts were mocking invitations. Invitations that her haughty expression denied. Her busy, moving figure defied men's lust, kept her tantalizingly out of reach. On cold days, she cinched a coat tightly around her tiny waist to accentuate her long legs, which, hugged by dark tights, looked as if they had been dipped into soft, black paint.

"It's getting so that the only guys I feel safe around are fags!" she joked to the honey blond sitting next to her at a model agency call-in one afternoon after school. The girl stared at her.

"You don't need to worry, dear," she told her. "Just tell them you're jailbait. How old *are* you, anyway? Eleven or something?"

Sonia smiled vaguely. "What's the difference if I'm ten or twenty, if I'm right for the job?"

She visited the best photographers, spinning each a different story. To most she confided, touchingly, that she was saving up money to spring her dad. It presented her in a perfect light, as a caring, deserving sweetheart and as the innocent daughter of a criminal, spreading a glamorous aura of the underworld about her. They weren't listening to what she said, anyway. They were squinting at her cheekbones, imagining how that nose, which in real life seemed to be lacking something, would rectify itself beautifully on film. Her youth intrigued everyone. Her dirty language was a turn-on. They couldn't wait to photograph her. She soon had a fabulous portfolio. Photography added years to her age. She photographed twenty, but with a glow of youth that hardworking twenty-year-olds had already lost. She had plenty of that dewy freshness of skin so sought after by cosmetics companies, and photographers were crazy for her full bust that made clothes look so new, so sexy, after years of flat-chested models. Nobody saw her without makeup or knew her real age.

"No one has looked like you since the late fifties!" a fashion photographer told her rapturously. Her violet eyes, black hair, and full breasts made people think of Elizabeth Taylor, "but a stretched-out *fashion* Liz Taylor!" she heard an excited stylist hiss into a phone.

Soon every agency in town was interested in representing her, but only Idols, a small, exclusive firm that handled just a few top models and actresses, agreed to Sonia's condition that she work only weekends.

"Some afternoons if it's *really* necessary," Sonia conceded. "But I have to reserve *some* time for school!"

"I wouldn't even bother with the little people, darling," the head of Idols, Carmen Frantzen, a tall, controlled German ex-model, told her, twisting Sonia's face in her hand to catch the light. "With those cheekbones and eyes, I'd showcase you! I'd go direct to *Vogue, Elle, Bazaar*—the top, top *cream*. In a year or two, Lauder, Lancôme, and Caresse will be begging me for you!"

Not even to Carmen, whose professional, protective clucking she liked a lot, would she confess her real age, in case it might cause problems. She had to sign a contract allowing Idols to represent her, to collect fees on her behalf, and to take twenty percent of her earnings, knowing it was invalid, assuring Carmen she was eighteen.

She began her career by fitting in jobs on weekends or at night after school, missing dance or exercise classes. But sometimes bookings came along that were too important to turn down and she would miss whole days of school. Her absences became too glaring not to be noticed at school and she was called into the principal's office in the second month.

"Is there some medical condition I should know about, dear?" the dignified white-haired lady, whom everyone called "Mademoiselle," asked.

Sonia giggled. "Not that *I* know of, Mademoiselle."

"Then suppose you tell me, Sonia, or do I have to call your mother?"

Sonia leaned forward earnestly. "I'm doing part-time modeling work, Mademoiselle. I'm trying to save up enough money to pay my dad's bail. He's in prison awaiting trial and I *know* he didn't do anything wrong! Nothing that would hurt anybody. I get modeling work to save up money for him so he can be free. Please don't tell my mother, Mademoiselle! They're divorcing and she'd be mad at me. . . ."

Mademoiselle looked down at her hands with their colorless nails. "I see," she said.

Later, she called in the assistant principal, Madame de la Hay.

"I'm not sure we want that kind of girl in this school," she told her. "She could be a disturbing influence on the other girls."

When Marcella got back from book signings in Boston, Miami, Denver, and Washington, D.C., there was a message from Mademoiselle suggesting a meeting to talk over Sonia's poor attendance. At the meeting, Marcella promised that Sonia would improve.

"Where do you think she goes?" Amy asked her. "You're letting that sexy little time-bomb run all over New York? God knows what she gets up to."

"She says she wants to be a model. . . ." Marcella sighed. "Listen, Amy, I can't think about my new book, promote my old book, *and* keep track of Sonia's whereabouts. She's too fast—it's as if she has more senses than we have."

Amy hugged her quickly. "Let *me* talk to her. There's so much tension between you two—maybe you need an intermediary."

She stuck a note on Sonia's bedroom door: "Come up and see your Aunt Amy. Sunday, 'High Tea,' 4 p.m."

"Your mother and I are good friends, Sonia," Amy told her the following Sunday, handing her a cup of coffee and some cookies. "I hate to see anything upsetting her. . . ."

"Distracting her from writing another book, you mean?" Sonia asked mockingly.

Amy ignored that. "Why don't you two get along?" she asked.

Sonia sat bolt upright on the sofa, her eyes innocently wide. "I thought we were getting along just fine!" Sonia said. "I didn't *choose* to come back here, you know. I got home one Saturday night and found I'd been slung out of my home, my dad arrested—the works!"

Amy regarded her, trying to feel sympathetic. "Darling, you're so beautiful, why don't you drop this tough veneer? You're at an age when life looks a lot more complicated than it really is. Take things a little easier! You're so young, you have so much time ahead of you."

Sonia shook her head vehemently. "I'll be fifteen next birthday. In this business, the younger you are, the better. Brooke Shields was modeling adult clothes at twelve!"

Amy replaced her cup. "What do you think the *real* problem is between your mother and you? It's not just school and career, is it?"

Sonia leaned forward eagerly. "No! She doesn't like me working to make money for my dad, Amy," she confided. "They never really loved each other, I guess. I'm trying to save up his bail money so he can get out of jail. I have to make half a million dollars! *That's* why I cut school every time there's a well-paid job."

"Uh-uh." Amy shook her head. "I don't buy that one at all. Your mother tells me you haven't even visited your father. . . ."

"Because the only day I don't have classes is Sunday and we don't have the car that day. Lend me your car, Amy," Sonia cried, putting her hand on Amy's knee. "Lend me your car. Costa could drive me! Oh, please!"

The following Sunday, Sonia sat in the front seat of Amy's Rolls, alongside Costa, Amy's driver, as it sped down the New Jersey Turnpike. She was nervously excited at the prospect of seeing her father. She had felt pretty bad since their telephone conversation, almost guilty. As if one of the old Sonias still living inside her needed her father. His approval or his love or something, she figured, glancing out of the window. At least this was doing it in style!

It was six months since they had seen each other, and

she wanted him to be impressed with her new image. She wore the usual clinging black tights, with a black cashmere sweater tossed lightly around her neck against the gray October day. She had lightly outlined her eyes in dark gray, with purple shadow on the lids. Her lips were bright pink. She had pushed a pair of tinted shades up onto her forehead, and her hair was pulled back tightly into a ponytail.

"I'm not sure how long I'll be," she told the driver when they pulled up at an anonymous-looking building that announced itself as the Joseph P. Haynes Correctional Institute, in the far reaches of New Jersey.

She joined the group of people, mostly mothers with children, waiting outside the main gates of the building, pulling her shades over her eyes, tying a purple scarf around her head. At three o'clock exactly, they were allowed inside and, after passing through a metal detector, into the visitors' room. When the inmates shuffled in, she spotted her father with a gasp of surprise. He had aged so much, not only in his physical appearance but in the defeated way he walked. He had a stoop she had never seen before. She whipped off her glasses and scarf so he would recognize her, yet his gaze swept the crowd twice before she held up a hand and they connected.

He gave a wry smile and indicated a table they could use.

"Princess!" he said when she reached him and kissed his cheek. "But what happened to you?" he asked, taking a good look at her face.

"I've grown a little, Dad," she giggled, hollowing her body to absorb the bust, smiling shyly at him.

He squinted at her. "Did you do something to your nose, Sonia? It looks different. Have you been fooling around with the perfectly good body you were given?"

"Oh Dad, really!" She laughed. "Let's talk about you. Are you getting a trial soon?"

He stared closer at her face. "Tell me what you've done to yourself, first, and explain why!"

She shrugged, searched in her purse for some gum.

"Oh, big deal!" She offered him some gum. "I had my nose done. You knew I wanted to be a model, didn't you? I'm getting work, Dad, I'm saving up money to help you get out of this place!"

"What about that?" He indicated her bust with a jerk of his head. "Are you padding yourself, Sonia?"

She glanced down at the tight sweater outlining the perfect spheres. "I had a little help from a cosmetic surgeon. *Everybody* does it, Dad!"

He frowned, staring at her strangely, and she felt a small stir of fear as if he were about to strike her.

"Let's face it, I was pretty small on top," she said, fumbling in her bag again, this time for photographs to show him.

"But my God, Sonia, you're only a child!"

"Nearly fifteen now, Dad. I'm a big girl! See these photos?"

He did not look at them. His hands were on her arm and she looked down at them and saw how rough they looked, the nails bitten.

"Those kinds of operations are expensive," he said. "Who paid for them? Your mother?"

"Listen—" She brushed aside his questions. "When I get you out of here I wanna live with you and Laurie again. I don't really fit in with Mom and Mark. We could go back to California, to Laurie's place maybe? Or upstate New York? Anywhere where I could ride would be okay. . . ."

Harry's eyes did not leave her face. She watched as his love for her left him, as his expression darkened and died.

"No!" she cried, putting her hands up to his wide shoulders and gently shaking him. "You still believe in me, don't you? I'm still your princess?"

Harry shook his head wonderingly. "You *did* find the money, didn't you? You had it all the time I've been here?"

"What do you mean?" she said.

"You paid to distort yourself. To turn yourself into—" He broke off, his desperate stare sucking her in. It mattered so much to him; he stared so penetratingly into her that she knew he could read her mind.

"You weren't there," she said tonelessly. "That day I really needed you!" She stared at her hands. "That guy *raped* me! I got back home and he kicked me out of the car like a sack of garbage. I was hysterical! I needed you so badly then, to make it all right. And you weren't *there*, Dad!"

He flinched as if she'd struck him. "Sonia, I—"

"So I grabbed the money," she cut him off. "I did all this to myself so I could have a fantastic career, and it's *working*! See these?" She spread out her photographs, but he did not move his eyes from hers.

"I was stuck in jail," he began slowly. "And you were fooling around with your face and body? You're doomed now. As far as I'm concerned, you're not even my daughter!"

She tried to press the photographs into his hand. "Don't say that, Dad!" she laughed. "Lighten up! Don't be so paranoid! I'm saving all the money I earn for *you*! You'll be outta here soon and we'll—"

"It's too late!" He gave an impatient grunt, standing up. "My trial comes up in a couple of months, and to judge from the incompetent lawyer they've given me, I'll be stuck here for years. Now get out of my sight. I don't care if I never see you again!"

Her photographs fluttered to the floor as he pushed past her, walking through the groups of visitors with his old man's defeated walk. Sonia stared after him, her mouth open. A nearby table of Chinese people watched her curiously and she turned to them, giving a little shrug.

"Guess he's a little grouchy today," she told them. "It must be this creepy place!"

One of the women giggled and crouched down beside Sonia to gather up the photographs and hand them back to her.

"Are these of *you*?" she asked, glancing at them. "Oh, you are so beautiful!"

"Thank you!" Sonia said, giving her a dazzling smile. She took out her compact and used the mirror to apply more lipstick with a shaky hand. Then she pulled her shades down over her eyes and tied the scarf over her head. She walked slowly out of the detention center into the street. By the time she found the car, something had broken in her, something hurt so badly she didn't even know how to experience it. She stood still for a moment, frowning. It was as if the Sonia she had so carefully created in California had been whipped away, peeled painfully off, leaving a raw child beneath, and this child was utterly vulnerable.

Costa held open the door to the front seat, grinning

mockingly at her as if he were just playing the role of driver. She shot an annoyed glance at him. He was around thirty, with slitty eyes and pockmarked cheeks, dark hair cut almost army short, and a stocky boastful little body. He wore his chauffeur's cap tilted.

She slithered into the front seat and Costa started the car. The new Sonia could still be salvaged, developed, made sexier than ever. She gathered her new image about her as if it were a coat ripped into shreds that she must save at all costs. She still had plenty going for her, she reassured herself. If enough men liked her, it would wipe out her father's disgust, which had cut through her like a knife. The new Sonia could conquer this pain, get her revenge.

Later, they got stuck in heavy traffic inching toward Manhattan. Staring straight ahead of her through the window, she let her hand move closer to the gray-panted thigh beside her. She gave Costa a sidelong glance and placed her hand over his crotch. God, he was cool! He didn't say a word, just smirked and continued to drive.

She moved her hand in his lap.

"Aren't you a little young for this?" he asked, glancing down.

She squeezed. "Get hard!" she said.

"Is that an order?" he asked.

She nodded, unzipping him, and soon his erection stuck up straight before him and she was stroking it. Her strokes speeded up, but he shook his head.

"Uh-uh," he said, stepping on the brake. "That can be dangerous. Why don't I just pull over?"

He stopped the car in a small park by the side of the freeway and she clambered into the backseat, pulling off her panty hose. Her miniskirt was cut way above her knees. She handed him the panty hose as she stuck one wrist through the passenger loop hanging at the window. He got into the back of the car.

"Tie my foot to the other loop!" she breathed.

Using the hose, he obeyed. She was stretched across the width of the car. Spread-eagled, she awaited him.

"Now, fuck me as hard as you can!" she cried. "Fuck me as though you were raping me!"

"Hey, what kind of a flake *are* you?" he asked her.

He made a goofy face when she didn't answer. Unzipping his tight pants, he glanced to each side of the car. No one around. He shrugged. His sex was still hard and soon he was pumping it into her and she felt bruised and battered but wonderfully alive. "Harder!" she yelled at him. *"Harder!"* Her voice wobbled with his thrusts. "Don't you understand, you fucker, I want it to *hurt*!" And soon the pain of her whole strained aching body revived her, focused her, blotted out the other, far greater pain.

"Oh . . . *yes!*" she screamed. She was starting to get that feeling she had felt only once before, with the Egyptian. When it swept her, it mingled deliciously with the pain, with her contempt of the driver, with the sheer pointlessness of doing this. She would forget her dad, forget this dumb driver with his big Greek dick, forget every fucking man who ever looked at her. From now on, she understood what she wanted from men and what she was prepared to give. Everything, and yet nothing! Her body, and her contempt. When he was finished, he untied her and she lay panting on the backseat, exhausted yet strangely triumphant as Costa sped her back to Manhattan.

ELEVEN

"**M**arcella?"

Harry's voice in her ear sent a shock through her, as if she were being pulled back into their old life together. She shrugged off the ridiculous thought.

"Hello, Harry." She tried to sound brisk. "I guess you want to speak with Sonia. She isn't here right now."

"I wanted to speak with *you*, Marce," he said.

No one had used that stupid name since Harry. She was not "Marce" and never had been. His call had interrupted a difficult scene she was writing. She sighed, pushing back her chair from her desk, lighting a cigarette. She took a deep drag.

"What can you possibly think we have to say to each other?" she asked.

"We could start by discussing why you're letting Sonia dress like some whore," he said.

"*Letting* her?" She laughed bitterly. "You think I have any influence? When you kidnap a child of twelve, you can't complain about the outcome."

"I didn't kidnap her, Marce," he said. "She chose to stay with me."

Marcella waited. "What do you want?" she asked.

"I need your help," he said.

"And what makes you think I'd help you now?"

"Because I'm still the father of our children. Because I think you're a good person who doesn't kick someone when he's down. I just fired my lawyer, Marcella."

"So?"

"So I need a lawyer. That guy was working for the state and all he could do was talk about plea bargaining or ratting on my colleagues. I won't do that."

"That's very noble," she said. "But that does imply there's something to rat about?"

"Marce," he asked hoarsely. "Don't make it harder on me. I'm asking if you'll pay for a good lawyer. Think of it as a loan that I'll repay as soon as I can. I have a good chance to get off lightly with a bright guy. I'd also like you to attend my trial in February and bring the children. It would look a lot better for me if they see a family behind me. Will you think about it at least?"

"You're insane," she sighed, stubbing out a cigarette, thinking. Where was the anger that should be bursting up inside her at his request? She found nothing but sadness and a deep regret.

"Why should I put myself out for a man who harmed my children?" she asked him. "They both bear the scars of what you did. Give me a good reason to help you."

"A good reason?" Harry repeated. "I go over and over in my head at night looking for good reasons for everything I've done. I guess we never should have married in the first place, Marce. . . ."

"I figured that out for myself a long time ago, Harry!" She gave a hard laugh.

"You know what they say about forgiving?" he asked her. "To forgive is divine, right? I just thought maybe you'd like to be the good one. I'm sorry."

She took a faltering breath. Helping Harry would not be entirely for him. "If I did anything for you now, it would be for Sonia," she told him. "She has quite a chip on her shoulder and I'd like to smooth it out. Maybe if she knew I was helping you, she'd be less hostile."

"Whoever you do it for, I'll be eternally grateful," Harry said.

"I don't want your gratitude, Harry," she said, hanging up.

She spoke to the children that night after dinner. Sonia bit her lip, saying nothing, an obstinate expression on her face. Mark was the first to speak.

"I don't want to go to his trial," he said. "I honestly feel I don't owe Dad anything."

"Thanks a lot!" Sonia said. She turned to look at Marcella. "Why are you doing this? To make yourself look good?"

Marcella shook her head. "Why are you so cynical? You think I need this kind of publicity? Being known as the wife of a criminal? I'm going to use every contact I have to make sure there won't *be* any publicity. And I'll attend the hearings with you only if you dress decently. Nothing outrageous. The whole point is to back up your father."

"But *why* are you suddenly helping him?" Sonia demanded.

"Because he asked me to." Marcella sighed. "And because I want you to see I don't hate him. I'm trying to forgive him for taking you away from me for two years. Maybe this can be part of a decent ending to that awful time when we were split apart."

Sonia looked away, unconvinced. Mark touched her arm. "Give Mom a break, will you, Sonia?" he said. "She doesn't have to help the jerk at all. He got *himself* into this mess."

"You shut up!" Sonia cried, pushing his hand away. "Don't talk about him like that!"

He laughed. "I guess *you* love Dad with all your heart?" he asked.

"Damned right I do!" She got up from the table and looked down at them. "And you know something? I'm the only one who does." She had not been able to stop thinking about her father since seeing him so cowed, so broken, in prison. She had tried to keep hating him, but his rejection of her had hurt too much. She had had to admit to herself that he was the one person in the world whose approval she needed.

"Sure, I can find you a lawyer," Amy agreed the next morning when Marcella went up to see her. "One of the best. If you're sure you want to do this."

"I'm sure." Marcella nodded. She watched Amy flip through her Rolodex.

"You realize this will cost an arm and a leg?" Amy asked, glancing up. "Turning the other cheek is an expensive pastime in Manhattan!"

Marcella nodded. "This way I'll feel I did all I could for him. He sounded pretty pathetic, having to ask my help."

Amy threw her a dubious glance as she dialed a number.

"You're too much, Marcella," she warned. "One of these days, all your repressed aggression is going to come bouncing back on you. Overnight, you'll turn into a bitch!" She winked. "I *hope!*"

A few phone calls later, she triumphantly scribbled a name and number on her memo pad.

"A twenty-five-grand retainer!" She whistled. "Before he even lifts a pencil! Paul Stopler!" She brandished the pad at Marcella. "Got Bobbie Chasen's husband off on fraud charges last year. . . ." She pulled an impressed face.

Marcella spoke to Paul Stopler and it was agreed that he would call Harry. In her apartment that afternoon, she also called Scott to ask him to help her avoid publicity at the trial.

"It's a little outside my beat, Marcella," Scott confessed. "We're not dealing with book reviewers here. These will be hard-boiled crime reporters. If they smell a juicy headline, they'll pick up on it. Be prepared. But don't worry—it won't harm your sales. Any publicity is good!"

"Even a criminal trial?" Marcella questioned.

"Sympathy backlash," Scott assured her. "Works wonders!"

Unable to concentrate on writing, Marcella used her free time to lunch with Nancy Warner, check royalty statements with Amy, visit with her mother. She tried to explain the trial to Ida, but Ida was incapable of grasping the idea.

"The man I was married to?" Marcella tried. "Harry! Remember?" The little Filipino nurse looked on, nodding and smiling, as if willing Ida to remember.

"She really doesn't know who I am anymore, does she,

Peggy?" Marcella suddenly asked her. They both watched Ida turn her gaze back to the television screen.

The nurse smiled sadly. "Oh, she forget, Mrs. Winton. She forget the words for many things, you know."

"She doesn't seem to enjoy anything now," Marcella said.

"She like to play cards," the nurse said. "But not a real game. Just pretend."

Marcella stayed for an hour playing a nonsensical game of laying out cards on a table, her mother concentrating hard on gathering them up. She left, promising Peggy, "I'll come back and do this more often with her," as if the nurse were somehow judging her.

Any hope that she would be overlooked by the press evaporated on the first morning of Harry's trial in February, held in a New Jersey court because the company was registered there. Sonia and she dressed sedately, Marcella in a navy dress and matching coat, Sonia in a slim purple skirt and white blouse under a quilted black skiing coat. Reporters begged for quotes and cameras buzzed excitedly as Paul Stopler led them through the crowd into the courtroom.

"How's Dad doing?" Sonia whispered to him.

"He's very pleased you're here," the lawyer told them. "It can only help."

When Harry finally appeared in court, Marcella was shocked. She had not seen him for nearly three years and she was not prepared for the great change in him. He seemed many years older. When he smiled at her, she tried to smile back. He gave a wink to Sonia, and Marcella felt Sonia's hand reach for hers and hold it tightly.

Several of Harry's former colleagues were called as witnesses, and Marcella got a good look at Gloria Defries when she testified for the state. Was *this* Harry's taste? she wondered. This cocky young woman who seemed to be doing a parody of a gangster's moll? She recognized some of the men from the dinners she had attended with Harry. Their wives in the courtroom stared curiously at Marcella.

The newspapers had fun with the headlines: NOVEL SCHEME NETS WRITER'S HUSBAND MILLIONS, and variations on the theme. Photographs of Marcella were usually cap-tioned "Estranged wife, million-dollar authoress Marcella Balducci Winton." As Scott had predicted, the sales of her book were boosted by this publicity, and *In the Name of Love* was soon back at number one on the paperback best-sellers list.

By the time the trial ended, Marcella wanted to retire to her little writing room, never to be stared at again.

Even with an expensive attorney, Harry's luck failed. He was used as an example to discourage the new wave of insider-trading breaking out on Wall Street.

"We have to show people like yourself that they cannot get away with this kind of crime," the judge summed up when Harry was found guilty. "Because it *is* a crime, even though it appears to involve nothing more than a couple of casual telephone calls."

The courtroom gasped when a ten-year sentence was handed down. Harry's face blanched, and Sonia sobbed as Marcella put an arm around her. They pushed through the crowd to get out of the court.

At the car, Sonia suddenly decided she wanted to say good-bye to her father. She slipped back to find him, and Marcella sat in the car, smoking. When Sonia returned, her face was tearstained and she looked as vulnerable as Marcella had ever seen her. The overweening bravado and the sophisticated pose had vanished. This, at last, was a fifteen-year-old girl. Donald opened the door for Sonia and she gave a sob and threw herself onto Marcella's lap.

They drove through the empty streets toward the freeway, and for a few minutes, with Sonia in her arms, Marcella experienced what it felt like to have a young daughter who needed her. In spite of the circumstances, it felt wonderful. Her heart soared; perhaps now they could become a real mother and daughter? She tried not to listen to the voice that told her it was all an illusion, brought on by that week's drama.

"Thank you for trying to help him," Sonia murmured from her lap.

Marcella hugged her, saying nothing. The moment was too precious to spoil. It was like holding a cat on her lap, feeling the body strain to be free. And sure enough, a few minutes later, Sonia sat up, blew her nose, applied some makeup, and moved across the seat to the other window.

Marcella felt her daughter's mind shift gear, cut off the closeness. Embarrassed at having revealed her vulnerability, Sonia stared silently out at the traffic.

They celebrated Sonia's fifteenth birthday at the Four Seasons, the wrong choice, as Marcella realized the moment they walked into the room. The businessmen dining together were riveted by Sonia's appearance. Sulky, refusing to dress up, bored, she managed to ruin the occasion by ordering the most expensive items on the menu and then playing with her meal for two minutes before rushing off "to make a phone call." Her face was starting to appear in magazines. Editors had called it "a face for the nineties."

A month after her birthday, Mademoiselle decided Sonia's presence at her exclusive school was not an asset. She called Marcella to ask her to remove Sonia.

"We'll refund the balance of the fee, of course," she purred in her expensively quiet voice.

"What has she done?" Marcella leaned back in her chair.

"I don't know how to describe it," the principal began. "She's hardly ever in attendance, for a start. But when she is here, little work gets done. She seems to create an atmosphere, a mood, that somehow ruins everyone's concentration."

I know that mood, Marcella thought. It ruins *my* concentration, too.

"She's such a lovely girl," the principal was saying. "I wish we could be of more help to you, but perhaps this is not the right school for Sonia. She's so advanced for her age. We do feel that those lingerie advertisements she's doing are not correct."

Marcella sighed. "She *can* stay until the end of the semester? It's not worth enrolling her into a new school just for June. . . ."

The principal agreed. "Very well, Mrs. Winton."

"Who said you could do lingerie ads?" Marcella asked Sonia when she arrived home that evening.

Sonia grinned, throwing herself onto the sofa, her feet up on the coffee table.

"Everyone wants to undress me," she said, smirking. "It pays well and it gets me noticed."

Marcella walked over to her. "But you're much too young for that kind of work. And don't the men you work with bother you?"

"Are you *kidding*?" Sonia snorted. "They all suck cock."

"Sonia!" Marcella cried. "What kind of language is that?"

Sonia laughed. "You should see your face! You use the same words in your books."

Marcella shook her head. "In literature, you can—"

"Literature?" Sonia echoed. "You think what *you* write is literature? Oh, Mother, you should see the misfits, the dregs of society, who drool over your books in the subway. They're practically illiterate!"

Marcella tried to control her anger. "Well, they manage to write me beautiful, literate letters about how much they enjoy my book," she said. "But we were talking about you now. The principal of your school called me today—she wants you to leave. *Now* what do I do with you, Sonia?"

Sonia blew out an exasperated breath, her feet up on the coffee table. "Check me into some other creepy rich kids' school, I guess," she said, giving a dazzling smile.

"That's not a very positive attitude," Marcella said.

Sonia rolled her eyes. "I could be *very* positive if you'd let me live my own life! Let me move out and find an apartment. I'd pay my own rent. I'd be out of your hair, earning good money . . ."

"And your schooling?" Marcella asked.

Sonia shrugged. "School and I just don't mix. So why not cut our losses? I could be launching a big-time career *now,* while I'm *young*!"

Marcella gently pushed Sonia's feet off the coffee table, sitting down on the couch next to her.

"You'll still be young in three years' time, darling," she said, touching Sonia's arm. "I remember what it's like to be fifteen, believe me! I was as impatient as you for all the adult things. Be patient for a few more years. It's so much more rewarding to be educated, so that when people talk to you they see you're intelligent, knowledgeable, not just beautiful. . . ."

Sonia scowled. "But I'm not asking you for anything!" she said tightly.

"You'll leave when the year ends in June," Marcella told her firmly. "And in September you'll start at another school. You *must* make an effort to study then. If not for me, then for your father. He'd be so proud of you if you got somewhere on your brains, not just your looks."

Sonia made a face and left the room.

"You must come out with another book within two years of the first, or readers will forget who you are, Marcella!" Amy told her at one of their morning meetings in Amy's apartment.

"I know. . . ." Marcella looked at her friend helplessly. "I just have a lot of other things distracting me at the moment. Sonia is a problem. I don't know how to handle her. And my mother gets worse each week. I don't think she knows who I am anymore. I really don't know how much longer I can keep her at home, Amy."

Amy held out her arms to Marcella. "Oh, you poor love!" she cried. "Do you want me to help you start looking at homes for her?"

"I can't do that, yet." Marcella shuddered. "That's so final and so sad."

"You'll have to do it one day, darling," Amy said gently. "If the woman doesn't know you, how will she notice the difference?"

Marcella looked at her friend.

"*I'll* notice the difference, Amy," she told her.

She stared at herself in the elevator mirror as she went down to her apartment. She was only thirty-five, but she could see the beginnings of a distinctly matronly look. There were new little lines around her eyes. The pressures of her family and the new book together were just too much. She longed to run out to Members right then, just to get away from everything. A quick fix of sex would give her the fresh viewpoint on her life that she needed. It was becoming an all-purpose palliative, an antidote to just about any malaise. And sometimes it was simply a place in

which to think, the way the church in Little Italy had been
—a darkened, hushed retreat in the middle of the noisy
city.

But she resisted the temptation to go out, and instead
put in two hours of work on her novel. At lunchtime, she
visited her mother, watching the nurse patiently feed her
soup as Ida stared at the television.

"Let me." Marcella motioned to the nurse for the
spoon. "Why don't you take off a half hour, Peggy? It's
such a nice day."

The nurse left and Marcella fed her mother the soup.
When she had finished feeding her, she put her arm about
her mother. Ida opened her mouth for more soup and
Marcella showed her the empty bowl.

"Look! All gone!" It was the way she had fed the children, she realized. She leaned against her mother's shoulder, imagining she could smell the fragrance of baking in
Ida's clothes, recalling the plates of cookies and cakes her
mother had produced in Little Italy. On an impulse, Marcella went to her bedroom and returned with their old photograph album, opening it on Ida's lap.

"That's Daddy," she pointed out. "Your husband, Aldo.
See how handsome he was? And this is me, when I was a
baby. . . ."

Her mother's eyes followed Marcella's finger at first, but
then she tried to push the book off her lap.

"You're about to become a publishing phenomenon, Marcella!" Scott's voice shouted joyfully through the phone the
following Tuesday. "I have next Sunday's *Times* with me—
you're still on the paperback list, after fifty-three weeks!
The trial helped, of course. We're reprinting yet again,
Marcella—the seventeenth printing!"

Now that *In the Name of Love* was such a success, interviewers were clamoring to speak to its author. Through
Amy, the requests flooded in from *People* magazine, *New
York* magazine, and *Cosmopolitan*. She was asked for comments for articles, invited to edit a problems page, and
requested for discussion panels and for judging short-story
contests. She turned down most requests. When *People* did
their feature on "a day in the life of a millionaire novelist,"

she was photographed watering plants on the balcony of her apartment, lunching with Amy at Le Cirque, and walking in the street with Mark and Sonia as if they were one big happy family.

"If I thought this smug lady had any resemblance to me, I'd kill myself," Marcella said, poring over an advance copy of the layout with Amy. She particularly hated a shot showing her, elegantly suited, sitting at a word processor. The caption read: "Marcella puts in a twelve-hour day. At eight-thirty, she was revising the previous day's writing!"

"It was noon! You can see by my puffy eyes that I'd just gotten up. . . ." Marcella laughed. "I told them I write in a warm-up suit, but they didn't want that!"

"Of course not." Amy peered at the spread. "Readers want you larger than life, glamorous! Moving in a totally different world from theirs. Then they can praise you for being so down-to-earth and unpretentious!"

She had always been a night owl, and now she delighted in writing into the small hours, while Manhattan slept. She would collapse in her big wide bed at four or five in the morning and sleep until noon if there were no appointments. Mark still brought up her mail before he left for school. The heartfelt letters that arrived from readers made her feel she had hundreds of friends. She always wrote back, remembering how much Amy's letter had meant to her. These letters provided the energy that propelled her to the typewriter each day.

Sonia was enrolled in a private school purporting to specialize in difficult students. Marcella finished the first draft of *Second Husband* by early spring the next year, certain she had written a much better book than her first. She had so much more to say now that she had been through losing and finding Sonia, watching Mark grow into a man, becoming responsible for her mother. It added up to feeling more intensely about her life and wanting to share those new feelings. This second novel was crucial; it would make or break her as a big-name novelist.

In April, Amy read it, over a weekend. On Monday morning at ten, Marcella nervously took the elevator up to Amy's apartment.

"Breakfast?" Amy ushered her into the sunny, glassed-in terrace and sat her down on mounds of yellow cushions topping the wicker chairs.

"Just orange juice and coffee, Amy, please," Marcella requested. "And for God's sake don't torture me. You hate it, right?"

"I don't hate it," Amy said, calmly pouring juice for Marcella and coffee for them both. She sat down and regarded Marcella, buttering a croissant. "Second books are the big test of a writer. We all know that," she began. "Critics love to say the second book doesn't live up to the 'promise' of the first, even though they said your first stank!"

Marcella sipped her juice. "Just tell me if you like it," she said.

"Listen," Amy spread her hands. "It's very good. It's fine. It's not as exciting and breathless as *In the Name of Love,* but we'll never admit that! A lot of women will identify with your heroine trying to build a new life for herself. *I'd* have given her a few dozen more orgasms, but that's *me*! Scott may pressure you to lighten it up a bit . . ."

"Does he have to see it yet?" Marcella asked. "It's only a first draft—there's a lot more work to be done on it."

Amy reached down and heaved the manuscript up onto the table. "I know, darling, but I *would* like him to see this, just so he knows there *is* a book! You'd be amazed how many writers and editors haggle over books that don't exist. *This*"—she weighed the stack of pages in one hand—"will make him think he's getting something for the five million bucks I'm asking for your next three!"

"What did he say to that?" Marcella sipped some coffee.

"He's speechless, of course." Amy laughed. "We'll haggle a little. If you don't ask, you don't get! Sales of *In the Name of Love* are nudging three million, for God's sake. That's *incredible* for a first novel! Harry's trial and your two gorgeous children don't exactly hurt your image, either. You've caught the fancy of the press and the public. But tell me something, Marcella . . ." She leaned forward anxiously. "Are you really as vulnerable as this main character? It makes you sound a little sad and lonely. Aren't you having fun?"

"I'm not the character, Amy. She isn't me," Marcella said.

Amy made an impatient noise. "Come on, Marcella, you know we always put ourselves into our main characters!"

Marcella lit a cigarette and drew on it.

"Okay. Well, fun isn't exactly the word I'd use to sum up my life at the moment." She smiled thoughtfully.

"You could use a man to complete the picture?" Amy asked. "Well, you can't say I don't encourage you, darling." She raised her eyebrows. "I invite you to every single dinner or brunch I give, don't I? Not out of pity, but because you are an asset to any dinner table. I always have plenty of men at my gatherings, but you never *linger* with anyone. For a sexy lady, you can sure seem aloof!"

Marcella exhaled some smoke. "I guess I'd prefer to seem aloof than like those lady barracudas who crowd an attractive man. They're so fierce! You forget I'm just a little girl from Little Italy, Amy. I had no real education. I fake it a lot. When you sit me next to illustrious writers, I clam up. I'm terrified they'll find me out! They're all married, anyway."

"So what?" Amy asked.

"If I bother to get involved with someone, I'd like to think there could be *some* kind of future with the guy," Marcella said.

"An incurable romantic!" Amy laughed.

"Look, if I run into an attractive, kind, sexy, successful man in his forties or fifties, I won't ignore him, okay?" Marcella promised. "But you know how rare those men are in Manhattan. If they exist, they're ogling twenty-five-year-olds!"

"So *you* ogle twenty-five-year-olds!" Amy cried.

When she left Amy to return to her apartment later, she went straight to her bedroom. She threw open her closet doors and looked at the gorgeous negligees and lacy robes she had bought for a life she never lived. She hadn't dared confess to Amy that Members provided all the sex she needed, but none of the love.

The summons to see Scott came after he had read the manuscript the following week. She dressed carefully for their meeting, angry at herself for feeling nervous.

"Relax, Marcella!" Scott said as soon as he saw her face. "I like it!" He motioned for her to sit alongside him on the couch in his office. "Coffee? Perrier? *Me?*" he offered.

She laughed. "No, thanks, Scott." She lit a cigarette and waited.

"It's more serious than your first." He tapped the manuscript. "Better written, no?" he asked.

She nodded. "I hope so."

"Just don't improve yourself out of the mass market, Marcella," he warned. "We have dozens of brilliant writers on our lists who don't sell three million books like yours did."

"I want to improve as a writer with each book," she told him, leaning forward. "And I'll take my readers with me. The women who read my books aren't stupid. They're ready to go on to more serious themes."

He studied her. "Don't be so sure you know your readers, Marcella. Volumes does a very thorough job of targeting an audience."

"I agree, but a book doesn't go on selling for a year, like mine has, if there aren't a lot of women urging their friends to buy it," she said. "Word of mouth has kept this book going, Scott. I have the letters to prove it."

"What kind of writer do you want to be, Marcella?" he asked. "Who do you want to be like?"

"Not like anyone, Scott!" She stubbed out her cigarette and looked him full in the eyes. "I want to be unique."

"Okay." He nodded. "Unique. We won't compare you with Amy or with Danielle Steel or Judith Krantz. You want to carve out your own territory? Do you think women enjoy reading about a woman getting older, fearful that she won't find a man, awkward on her first dates with one?"

"Why not?" Marcella asked. "Everything that happens in life is possible material for a book, *if* you write about it well. Bringing up children, becoming responsible for your parents. Just growing older is a huge experience, Scott!"

"Yes!" he groaned. "A depressing one! Your readers want to be *distracted* from the aging process, Marcella!"

"I've had dozens of intelligent letters from women. I

think they can handle some of the tough facts of life!" she told him.

"Maybe for one book," he allowed, "but if you want a string of successes, the way Amy has had, you have to think ahead. Why don't you let *me* plan the themes for your books, map out the characters? All you'd have to do is write."

"Couldn't you use a computer for that?" she asked.

"I *could,* but it wouldn't be a quarter as sexy as you, Marcella!"

"Oh Scott . . ." She shook her head, laughing. "Is this the annual pass?"

"Well, you always sit as far away from me as you can get," he complained. "Was I such a lousy lay?"

"No, you were very good," she smiled. "As I remember!"

"Well, as *I* remember, you were damned fabulous!" Scott said. "But my glamorous superstar writer and I only got *one* lousy chance!"

Marcella looked across at him and took a deep breath.

"Scott, considering I've sold three million books for Volumes, I think I deserve better treatment than this. We're discussing my new book, not our sex lives. . . ."

"They could be intertwined, Marcella!" He moved closer to her, a hand on her bare arm. "Listen, I could make you *bigger* than Danielle Steel with your next three books! Let's form a new kind of team. We can have sexy, satisfying sessions in here and come up with super-best-sellers, Marcella. We'd be unbeatable!"

She stood up. "You never take me seriously, and if there's one thing I need from a man it's to be taken seriously! Does that answer all your questions?"

He looked at her seriously. "Yes," he said.

There was an awkward silence between them. "Where do we go from here?" she asked.

Scott sat at his desk, picked up a pen, and doodled on a pad. "If you're this serious about your writing, I'll try to accommodate you. Maybe you *can* establish a new kind of thinking best-seller for a new kind of reader. But you'll need a much catchier, sexier title than 'Second Husband.' "

She replaced the empty glass, thinking. "You could be right about that. I'll try to think up some alternative titles."

It had been a disturbing meeting, but she felt she had established some important points. She was not going to let Scott walk all over her. Writing was hard enough without all this other bullshit, she thought. How different the world of publishing was from the way she and Nancy Warner had pictured it during those years when they had fought to be published. Everyone wanted to think they had a hand in her book, but it went out with *her* name on the cover, and she would fight for every word!

The new title came to her on the way home. "The Greatest Love of All," because when her heroine fell in love for the second time, that is what she believed her love to be.

"I *love* it!" Scott enthused over the phone when she called to tell him her idea. "It would be nice if your novels always had the word 'love' in the title, Marcella. It could be your signature trademark!"

"Let's see," Marcella said tactfully. She didn't want her titles to *always* have anything! Each novel would be different and she wanted her readers to be surprised by each one. Her heroine of thirty-five searching for a second husband was pure fiction; she herself had just about given up on the idea of finding a partner. The men Amy continued to seat her next to at her dinners did nothing for her. It was a cynical, Manhattan fact that, if not married or homosexual, they invariably had some overwhelming defect that had kept them single—unattractive looks, a hair transplant that hadn't taken, a grouchy disposition, or a nervous tic. The charming, handsome ones often turned out to be penniless fortune hunters.

Her anonymous encounters in Members' theater continued, as exciting and erotic as ever, yet with a new, disturbing tendency. She forgot—almost upon leaving—the faces of the men who had pleasured her. She had become physically dependent on her visits, hating herself for breaking her promise each week to make it "the last time." She had demoted sex to about the level of a good backscratch, and she knew she would pay for it somehow. Yet the dark theater still represented a kind of reservoir of love into which she could dip when she needed reassurance that she was desirable, sensual, female.

Spring Sundays demanded long walks in Central Park. With Mark, she watched the roller-disco and the skating, window-shopped on Columbus Avenue, and browsed in the antique fairs that sprung up in deserted school playgrounds. Sonia left them each Sunday at noon, saying she was going to visit her father. He had been moved to a minimum-security jail in New Jersey, and Sonia told them she took the train to get there. Marcella and Mark would try one of the new Columbus Avenue restaurants for brunch, getting home at five or six to read the papers, Marcella marking the book reviews for books that caught her interest. Later, Mark might meet friends for a concert or practice the piano.

He was practicing when the phone rang at eight one Sunday evening, and Marcella glanced questioningly at him as he took the call. Sonia was still out. She often went straight from visiting her father to meeting friends. Marcella worried, but she felt that being more strict might only worsen the already tense atmosphere between them.

"Hello?" Mark said, then mouthed "Sonia" at her.

"Can *she* hear?" Sonia's voice rasped through the wire. She always made Mark feel like a conspirator in one of her plots.

"Of course!" Mark said, smiling.

"Listen, Mark. Make up any story you want," Sonia said breathlessly. "Say I'm stuck without money at Grand Central or say I fainted in the street, but get your ass over to—got a pencil?—sixty East Seventy-first, *pronto*!" She giggled. "Slip the doorman ten bucks and tell him you're a friend of Gerry Manston. Got it? Ask for Penthouse B. He'll show you up—he's used to it. Come fast—I'm in *trouble*!"

"Okay," Mark said. He hung up, turning to Marcella. "She's stuck at Grand Central without money. Wants me to rescue her. . . ." Only Sonia could make him lie to his mother.

Marcella breathed out a sigh of relief. "There's some money in the kitchen, darling."

Mark took three ten-dollar bills and found a taxi in the street. At the address on East Seventy-first Street, the doorman pocketed ten dollars with a wink and took him up to Penthouse B, unlocking the door from a huge bunch of keys.

Sonia's voice cried out, "In *here*!"

He closed the front door and followed her voice down a wide corridor hung with Robert Mapplethorpe photographs. He opened a glass door to the main room. Sonia was lying in the center of the room on the floor, naked, strapped into some kind of leather harness, ankles manacled to wrists. The telephone lay off the hook near her face.

Mark stared at her, surprise freezing him.

"Recognize this room?" Sonia asked him.

He tore his eyes away from her body to glance at their surroundings. The room was white, the parquet flooring covered in kilims, the walls boasting paintings by Picasso, Rouault, and Hockney.

"No . . ." he shook his head dazedly. "Should I?"

"It was in last month's *House & Garden*," Sonia crowed. "Gerry Manston, art collector. He hid all the bondage stuff and hung a huge fern from that hook. Six fucking pages! He'd better make the most of it because he won't be featured again after I'm through with this place! Now get me out of this!"

Mark threw a jacket over her nakedness, vaguely taking in the long limbs, the patch of dark hair between her legs, the spherical breasts that stayed aloft even while she was lolling on the floor.

"It took two hours to push the receiver off the hook with my tongue!" she boasted. "Then I had to press out the number! My tongue aches! You'll never undo this thing— get a knife from the kitchen."

As if in some weird dream, Mark walked into the kitchen, all immaculate stainless steel, and found a sharp bread knife hanging from a rack of knives. He crouched next to his sister to study the intricate straps and knots that bound her.

"I don't get it—what *is* this?" he asked.

Sonia groaned. "Don't talk, just get me out of this thing!" she cried.

Carefully, he sawed through two thick leather straps. Once her hands were free, she helped him unravel the expertly tied knots, gasping as they flew open, rubbing her ankles and wrists. She stared in fascinated horror at the angry red welts.

"Will you just *look* at what this guy *did* to me!" she said wonderingly. "Oh, *Mark*!" She suddenly threw herself into his arms. "I've never been so damn scared in my *life*! I thought he was going to kill me!"

He held her as she trembled in his arms. In spite of his horror and disgust, he felt protective of her, sorry for her. She cried as she clung to him, a high-pitched sound whining in her throat, so unlike the Sonia he thought he knew. In a rare moment of softness between them, he stroked her long dark hair out of her face.

"It's all right now," he whispered. "It's okay."

"What if I hadn't got to the phone?" She shivered. "What if he'd stayed away for days and just let me starve to death?"

Mark sat up, frowning. "Who the hell is this guy, anyway?" he asked. "And why are you fooling around with crazy people like him?"

Sonia broke away from him and got to her feet, stretching her aching body.

"I *told* you! Oooh!" She arched her back. "Gerry Manston, art collector. He's been trying to get me up here for months. I suddenly thought, What the hell? and came!"

She looked around for her jeans and pulled them on. "He's a big fat drug-dealing city pig swilling money on Wall Street. Thinks he's an art collector because one or two art dealers pay for their coke with canvases!" She pulled on a soft black sweater and thrust her hands through her hair. "The point is, I *know* him! I *trusted* him! It wasn't supposed to go this far. He knows I'm a model, for Christ's sake! I know his wife, his friends, everything! But watch me get even! Watch me ruin this guy's life!"

Mark shook his head. "Why don't we just forget the revenge for the moment and get the hell out of here before he comes back?"

"Why? What's the hurry?" Sonia giggled, looking around her. "He thinks he'll get back here and find me all strung up just like he left me. I wanna give him a little surprise!" She grabbed a bottle of ink from the art deco desk, and before Mark could stop her, she hurled it at one of the white walls. Navy rivulets ran down the wall, splashing cushions and rugs.

"Now he can tell everyone he has an original Sonia Winton mural!" she laughed, running into the kitchen. Mark looked around the room, feeling nauseous.

"Sonia!" he called out. "Let's just go now, okay?"

She came back with a tray holding bottles of ketchup, mustard, vinegar, and wine. Arms outstretched, holding a couple of bottles in each hand, she did a mad whirling spin, faster and faster, letting the bottles fly from her hands. The bottles flew around the room, into mirrors and paintings, cracking and splintering, filling the room with the smell of alcohol and food.

"Sonia!" He tried to catch hold of her, but she ducked and ran to a white canvas sofa, crouching on top of it. "My God, you're—"

She lowered her jeans, giggling, and urinated.

"What the hell did you do *that* for?" he asked.

She pulled up her jeans. "I just wanted him to have a little memento of me," she laughed. She dipped her finger in a pool of ketchup and wrote FUCK YOU in large letters on a wall. Mark grabbed her arm.

"The doorman's seen us, for God's sake. We could get into a lot of trouble for this!"

"Think so?" She wriggled out of his grip, hunting around the room. She found her purse and picked up a video camera from a shelf. "This ape couldn't possibly press charges after what he's done to me! I'm only sixteen, remember? I could put him in jail tomorrow! He took a whole fucking video of me!" She ejected a cassette from the camera and stuffed it in her purse, letting the camera smash to the floor. Suddenly, she glanced at her watch. "Oh, I promised to do a fashion show in SoHo!" she cried. "I was supposed to be rehearsing in this fag's loft a half hour ago. Go down and hold me a taxi, Mark. I can just make it! Got any money?"

She pocketed his twenty dollars and he stared helplessly around at the chaos she had created. When he looked back at her she was primping her hair in the mirror. He shook his head and went downstairs. He found a cab and when

Sonia ran out of the apartment house, waving good-bye to the doorman, she was as fresh as a daisy.

She slid into the taxi and slammed the door.

"Wanna go home?" she asked Mark. He nodded. Sonia gave the driver both addresses. Mark glanced at her as they drove down Park Avenue.

"Is this really how you want to live, Sonia?" he asked.

She frowned, fumbling in her purse to find a cigarette. "What's wrong with it?" she asked, lighting it.

"So you don't visit Dad?" he said.

She laughed. "Dad doesn't want to see me. Thinks I'm a slut. He passes judgment on me even from jail!"

Mark felt a sick weight in his stomach. He glanced out of the window miserably. Manhattan looked different, weird, and, he had to admit, somehow more glamorous this Sunday night.

"This'll do!" he told the driver when they got to Fifty-ninth Street. He got out and stood holding the door handle, not wanting to let her go. As her older brother, he had some kind of responsibility to tell her something, to warn her. She had made him feel protective. It was a heady new emotion.

"Sonia, I don't feel good about this," he faltered.

She reached for the door handle, slamming the door shut impatiently.

"Listen," she told him through the open window. "I honestly don't give a shit!"

"But how can you possibly model tonight?" he asked.

"Makeup!" she grinned. "It covers everything!"

"But—" He broke off, his throat dry. He suddenly felt, absurdly, like crying. "You're so beautiful!" he said, lamely.

She stared at him with wide eyes. "What the fuck does *that* have to do with anything?" she laughed. The car sped off.

"It *does*!" Mark shouted after it. "You should value yourself more!" Her proud head, upright in the back window, gave an imperceptible shrug. Her long flowing hair, those violet eyes, he thought, looking after her. How many women would give anything to look like her? He walked toward home. Her behavior went against all the rules that kept life in place, that controlled luck and fate. Something inside him both disapproved of and yearned for the freedom, the adventure, that she sped toward.

During that summer Marcella corrected the final proofs of *The Greatest Love of All,* which Volumes was rushing out for publication before Christmas. She did some of her work at Amy's Southampton house. Mark and Sonia came out to visit on weekends. They found a nearby stables where Sonia could ride, and for a few weeks Marcella enjoyed seeing Sonia's face without that sulky look on it. Laughing and riding in the open air, mounted with the assurance and poise of a practiced rider on the best horse the stables could provide, Sonia glowed and became a different person. She helped Amy and Marcella prepare the salads and fresh pasta and fruit they existed on that summer. Amy adopted Mark and Sonia as walking companions for moonlit walks by the seashore so easily reached from her house.

Marcella hung back a little one night, as Mark and Sonia strolled in front. "It's so wonderful seeing her like this," she told Amy. "A healthy, happy sixteen-year-old child!"

Amy pursed her lips. "An exquisitely beautiful, unbelievably sexy little time bomb," she corrected.

"In town, maybe," Marcella agreed. "But do you see her face when she's on a horse, Amy? How beautiful she looks then? *This* is the child she was supposed to be!"

When they returned to New York in September, Marcella chose a new school for Sonia, one with a reputation for handling students with learning difficulties.

In late September, Marcella flew to London to launch the British paperback edition of *In the Name of Love.* Her English publisher provided warm, friendly company, along with a bubbly young publicity girl who shepherded her to book signings at Harrods and Hatchard's and accompanied her to the mandatory television appearances. Terry Wogan, the British version of Johnny Carson, held up her book and assured viewers it was a sexy read. Michael Aspel, a charming rival talk-show host, talked more seriously with her on his Saturday night show about how to write a best-seller. Newspaper and magazine interviews helped to push the book straight to number one in its first week of release. Marcella was dined nightly by the directors of the British publishing house. Their wives came too, just in case the glamorous American authoress was on a manhunt, but looking at the pink-cheeked, balding, polite middle-aged men, Marcella wanted to assure their wives that there was no possible danger. The atmosphere of London, she couldn't help feeling, was against matters sexual. There was just time to visit some men's stores in Jermyn Street for shirts and ties for Mark and perfume for Sonia and Amy before taking the Concorde home.

The Greatest Love of All was launched with another well-orchestrated blitz of publicity at the end of October. Volumes was distributing its usual displays, and the press-kits included a new color photograph of Marcella in a small gift frame.

When the book tour began, she embarked alone, met by publicity people and Volumes' representatives in the key book-buying cities. Everywhere, she repeated the same stories, smiled at the same questions, ran for the limo with her neatly packed suitcase to drive to the next television or radio station. It was ten days of utter madness, and she hated every moment. The lonely dinners in the "theme restaurants" of the hotels she stayed in. The walks to stretch her legs in some godforsaken downtown district. The interviewers who hadn't read her book and asked questions about it as if they had. She had to be charming to everyone: the object was to get good publicity for the book, so it was Amy she complained to, at night, from her anonymous hotel rooms. Amy had been through it all before and knew the right words with which to soothe Marcella.

When it was all over, Marcella collapsed back in New York, staying in bed around the clock for one entire day.

The book burst onto the best-seller list at number six. There was a celebration with champagne toasts and speeches at dinner in Amy's apartment. Marcella made sure that Amy invited Nancy Warner, who was openly adoring of all the writers she met and unexpectedly amusing when she held the table enthralled with accounts of her writing classes.

As the book climbed to number two, she had to agree with Amy that a best-seller gave you a feeling that nothing else approached. Knowing that hundreds of thousands of people were buying and reading her work was the most rewarding lift. She had signed a new four-million-dollar contract with Volumes for the next three books. Not quite as much as Amy had hoped for, but still a lot more, Marcella felt secretly, than she deserved.

Sex had been absent from her life during the months when her book was in production, and the London trip had distracted her from her usual needs. But her body would suddenly remember how much it needed sex and there would be a spurt of visits to that familiar dark place where whispered requests and tentative hands plunged her into the world of men, a whole variety of men. She might spend time with a seasoned, worldly fifty-year-old or a fresh-faced young athletic type. He might be American, European, Argentinian, or Japanese, but he was always well behaved, considerate, tender. Perhaps it was all an illusion, but she felt as if she experienced whole affairs condensed into thirty minutes. A man's arms made her feel cherished, needed; the fact that she would never see him again added a certain poignancy. There was no time for the harsh realities of life to intrude or spoil anything. She had established a whole new philosophy of judging a man by his touch. The only thing that puzzled her was the question of whether this was harmful.

Some days after her return from London, a good-looking man in his thirties, trim and fit, twisted his body in his seat so he could watch as first she, then he, achieved satisfaction. He wanted to continue to touch her, but she pushed him away, unable to take any more pleasure.

He offered her a drink at the bar, as many men did. She refused, as usual. She had sectioned off the social part of her life from this—it must never intrude. If she discovered what this man did, how he lived, whether there was any possibility of a relationship beyond these red velvet seats, her life would be in chaos. Fantasy must be treated as such, and that was why this was so good. That was why it worked. It was completely outside the normal rules of life and therefore exciting.

She kissed his smooth cheek good-bye, leaving the theater the moment her composure was restored. That afternoon, she knew she was untidy, her lipstick surely smudged, her eyes bleary from pleasure. She pulled on dark glasses before leaving, which meant she had to feel her way along the black, shiny passage illuminated by the lines of tiny white bulbs. She was never able to leave this place without fearing she would see someone she knew. It was unlikely that any of the men here read her books, but what if she met someone from Volumes, like Scott or a publicity or sales director? As she nervously ran a hand through her hair, a figure stepped out of the darkness and gripped her arm.

"And people say *I'm* crazy!" Sonia's voice said.

Marcella whirled about. The grinning, triumphant face of her daughter leered at her. For a moment, Marcella panicked and tried to pull away. She had a crazy notion of ducking back into the dark theater and staying there until Sonia went away. But Sonia's grip was too strong. She hung on to Marcella's arm, staring at her.

A dozen expressions flitted over Marcella's face before she finally found a smile, her mind racing.

"Are you a Paul Newman fan, too?" she asked her daughter.

Sonia shook her head mockingly. "Oh, you'll have to do a lot better than *that,* Mother dear," she said. "You *must* know the reputation this place has! It is *not* for catching up with old movies, even the classics. . . ." She glanced at the poster announcing a Tennessee Williams season. "I guess *Cat on a Hot Tin Roof* counts as a classic, huh?" She kept her finger on the call button of the elevator. "So *this* is where you go," she said. "I was so curious to see where my dear, righteous, romantic goody-goody of a mother disappeared to so often in the afternoon when she should be home working. It was rather exciting to grab a cab and say, 'Follow that Rolls!' You looked so guilty when Donald let you off a few blocks away. One thing you must learn, Mother: Be *brazen*! *Then* you can get away with anything!" She pressed the button again. "Now let's get the hell out of here before someone sees *me* and tells everyone *I* come here!"

The elevator finally arrived and the doors slid open. They stepped into its mirrored darkness.

She has no proof, Marcella assured herself, trembling. Except for the look on my face she has no proof. On the ground floor, they headed for the exit, Sonia still holding Marcella's arm as if frightened she'd escape. The brightness of Fifty-seventh Street was like an exploding flashbulb.

"I don't suppose Donald waits for you here?" Sonia asked, hustling her quickly along, heading east, lifting her dark glasses to peer at her mother's face.

"He's at Seventh Avenue," Marcella murmured.

"Oh, Mother . . . " Sonia groaned, still walking fast. "See, there is this big difference between us. I do things, I hang out places, that your wildest fantasies wouldn't feature. People call me crazy but I honestly don't give a shit because *no* one's opinion matters to me! But I'm up-front about it. What you see with me is what you get. I don't hide behind some goody-goody fake face, pretending to—"

"*Stop* it!" Marcella cried, finally wresting her elbow out of Sonia's grip. "I don't know what you think you've discovered other than that I sometimes see an afternoon movie, but—"

"We'll talk to Markie-boy about it," Sonia cut her off, propelling her forward again. "Let's see how *he* takes to the idea of his precious mother catching up on classic movies in the afternoons at Members—the swingers' club— coming out looking all hot and messy . . ."

"You are *not* to mention this to Mark!" Marcella cried. "You can think whatever *you* like, but keep him out of it."

Sonia gave a laugh. "We'll talk about it when we find the car," she shrugged.

The Rolls was waiting at the corner of Fifty-seventh and Seventh, Donald greeting Sonia as he opened the door for them. They climbed in the backseat, Sonia firmly pushing the glass partition shut. As the car drove east, she faced Marcella, speaking in a low, confident murmur.

"Now I'll tell you what's going to happen," she said. "I've found an apartment I like in the east sixties. One bedroom. Very expensive, but I'm getting so much work I can afford it. I don't need one penny from you! Just your signature on the lease because I'm under-age. I'll move out next week."

Marcella found a cigarette and lit it shakily.

"Why are you in such a hurry to move out?" she asked Sonia. "You think you can blackmail me to—"

"Coming back was a mistake," Sonia shrugged. "But I didn't know where else to go. I'd forgotten what you and Mark were like together—you turn my stomach!"

"Couldn't you believe how glad we were to have you back with us again?" Marcella asked. "Can't you believe that Mark and I love you?"

Sonia shrugged in an annoyed way. *"Please!"* she shuddered. "Spare me the saccharine!"

"I thought we'd finally be a family," Marcella told her.

"A *family*?" Sonia repeated. "Seeing you two exchanging looks, sitting at dreary dinners while you and Mark discuss his music! You don't understand *me*! What *I* want! What *I'm* going to achieve! I'll be *ten* times as famous as Mark. You watch! *If* I can get away from you two!"

Marcella watched her, staring at the manic light in her eyes.

"How did you *get* like this, Sonia?" she asked her softly. "So tough, so bitter, and only sixteen! What happened to you during those two years? What did your father *do* to you?"

Sonia almost snarled at her. "He didn't do anything to me—he was a *wonderful* father!" she cried. "I was his princess, you know, and that's how he treated me. When he gets out of jail, we're going to live together again. In California! I'll have made lots of money by then; we'll have horses and I'll—" She shook her head, suddenly unable to speak, her eyes filled with tears.

She's only a child! Marcella found herself thinking. And in spite of all that had happened she wanted to hold her and tell her everything would be all right. She put her hand on Sonia's arm.

"What's *wrong*, Sonia? Tell me. Maybe I can help?" she tried.

Sonia closed her eyes, leaning her head back against the white leather seat. When she opened her eyes, the purple irises were flooded with tears, fragmented like a kaleidoscope into shards of red and blue. She stared helplessly at Marcella.

"Just let me go. Just let me lead my own life. I'll be fine. I'm not asking for anything from you."

She moved out the following weekend, three days after Marcella had signed the lease on the apartment.

Marcella watched her load shopping bags spilling with clothes into the Rolls, helped by Donald and Mark.

"It's funny," she murmured to Amy, standing in the foyer with her. "She so nearly let me get close. Last week . . . something happened that seemed to tear down the barrier between us."

"And now she's moving out?" Amy asked. "So much for closeness! But she's just a kid, for God's sake, Marcella. How can you let her do this?"

Marcella shook her head, watching Mark heave a small television set onto the backseat. "You don't know, Amy," she said. "You just don't know. She's no kid. I'm not sure what she is, but she has the hunger of someone determined to make it. She's in this ferocious *hurry*!"

"Lucky she's so beautiful," Amy said. "She'd be a rather scary character without the looks. . . ."

Donald heaved the last shopping bag into the trunk. Sonia kissed Mark and slipped into the front seat beside Donald.

"Sure you don't want us to come over with you and settle you in?" Amy called.

Sonia shook her head. "There are two makeup artists hanging drapes as we speak!" she called. "And I didn't even *want* drapes! Bye, Mark! Bye, Amy! Bye, Mother dear! Thanks for having me! And don't forget to forward any mail!"

In their apartment, Mark threw his arms around Marcella. "It's just the two of us now." He hugged her. "And that's how I like it!"

As much as she loved his arms clinging to her, she wriggled out of their clasp and faced him.

"And you're my next problem!" she told him.

He grinned at her as if she were teasing.

"I mean it, Mark!" she said as he thrust out his lower lip

in a mock pout. "Sometimes I think we're too close, you and I. According to Sonia, *we* drove her out! What will you do when I meet someone one day? Someone I might want to marry? How would we ever lead a normal life?"

"Normal?" Mark gave a wild giggle. "Our lives could never be normal. Sonia's appearing half naked in every subway and bus ad in town. Dad's in jail! Your books are everywhere, and I'm going to be a famous pianist!"

He ran to the piano and, standing, began to play a crazy honky-tonk jazz tune as she laughed. She had to admit he had a point. "Normal" had not applied to their lives since the moment Scott had dangled that check before her at Le Cirque.

Ida's nurse left at eight o'clock and Marcella would then check on her mother every twenty minutes as she prepared dinner for herself and Mark. If they ate out, she paid the nurse to stay on for two extra hours. One evening, she found Ida fiddling with the back of the television set while it was still switched on. Using a knife, she had managed to remove two screws.

"She'll burn down the entire building if you don't watch out," Amy warned when she heard about it. "She really should be in a good home, Marcella. For her own sake."

For her own sake. In her own interests. When it came to the time to decide between their own or their parents' lives, people trotted out these justifying thoughts. Marcella hated the phrases, thought them hypocritical.

"I don't know whether I'm waiting for a terrible accident to happen or what," she sighed to Mark. "She might have electrocuted herself. If I put her in a home, it's so terribly final! She'll die there, and I can't bear to think of my own mother dying among strangers."

The problem kept her awake at night. One night, after she had finally drifted off to sleep, she was awakened by a burning smell. She got up quickly and grabbed her robe. She found her mother's room empty. She made her way back to the kitchen where light showed under the closed door. Pushing open the door, she found her mother, fully dressed, standing by the stove, stirring a pot of bubbling thick liquid.

"Mother!" She ran to Ida's side and switched off the gas, peering into the pot where a thick paste gave off a disgusting odor. She glanced at the ingredients that Ida had left on the counter—ketchup, grape jelly, peanut butter, mayonnaise, and milk.

Ida pushed her away irritably and continued to stir.

"Are you hungry, darling?" Marcella asked her. She collapsed on a kitchen chair, watching her mother, tears spilling from her eyes.

The next day, Donald drove Marcella to Connecticut to look at several nursing homes. She took her mother with her the day after that to see the best ones, hoping Ida might indicate which she preferred. But Ida gazed blankly into the well-kept gardens and determinedly cheerful rooms and showed no reaction. Marcella chose the most expensive and the prettiest, just outside New Haven.

The next week, the home's consulting doctor examined Ida thoroughly. "You know she has Alzheimer's disease?" he asked afterward, as Marcella studied the brain scan. "These show large areas of damaged brain cells," he told her, pointing. "Her cognitive functions are very limited at this point, I'm afraid."

She handed back the scans, glancing at her mother.

"Yes, I know," she admitted. "I've tried to put off dealing with it for as long as possible."

"Is she incontinent?" he asked her.

Marcella swallowed. "Sometimes. I have a private nurse for her."

"It's good that you've decided to enter her into care now, Mrs. Winton," he said. "If you had let her get much worse at home, fewer places would have wanted to accept her." Thanking the doctor, Marcella walked Ida around the gardens, pointing out the other old people sitting in chairs on the lawns, tended by nurses moving in slow motion to match their charges.

"You'll love it here," she told her, guiding Ida's shuffling steps. "You'll make lots of new friends and Mark and I will come visit you each week, I promise."

She carefully unpacked the case of clothes Donald brought up to the second-floor room.

"Don't visit her for the first two weeks," the doctor advised. "Give her time to adjust."

"Will you give her tranquilizers?" Marcella asked fearfully.

"Only if she seems anxious." He touched Ida's shoulder. "I don't think we'll have any problems, will we, Mrs. Balducci?"

Marcella knelt by her mother's chair before leaving.

"Good-bye, darling," Marcella said, kissing her cheek. Ida stared at her and suddenly, irritably pushed her away. She was thankful that her mother did that. It helped her accept the cruel fact that her mother no longer knew her. She stumbled down the corridor, turning back once to see that Ida was not even looking after her.

On the drive home, Marcella wept. The two weeks of enforced separation would wipe out any traces of her mother's memory that might remain.

"Now it really *is* just us two," she told Mark that night.

He took her in his arms and held her. "Was it awful?" he asked.

She broke down and sobbed in her son's embrace.

"I'll never do that to you," he promised. "Never!"

She looked at him pleadingly. "Don't say that; it makes it worse! Do you think I *wanted* to put her in a home? I did it because I was afraid she would hurt herself if she didn't have twenty-four-hour supervision."

She called the home every day to check on Ida's condition. When she and Mark began to visit her, she seemed none the worse for living under these new conditions. They sat in the garden and talked to her and patted her hand, a one-sided conversation that Marcella could only hope was a source of comfort to her.

Mark and she were an exclusive club of two, dining out, walking in the park, going to movies. On weekends, Donald drove them down to the Village or SoHo so they could browse and stroll among the crowds. She had her mother's room redecorated and made it her new office.

Sonia was becoming the darling of the photographers. Her cover picture on *Vogue,* tongue saucily stuck out, a fashion hot topic, launched her as *the* face. Soon her violet gaze was staring from newsstands every month and from posters at bus stops. Marcella tried calling Sonia from time to time, but there was only an answering machine to talk to; Sonia never called back.

Mark was eighteen, on the threshold of manhood, so startlingly handsome that Marcella feared for him. She knew that no man that good-looking would be allowed to lead a balanced life. She worried that his looks would overshadow his musical brilliance. For the moment, though, he appeared to be leading the life of a model student. Hardworking and serious, he was the center of a circle of young musicians who attended concerts together and enjoyed picnics in the park and outings upstate. They went to Carnegie Hall and Lincoln Center concerts, and Mark would invite the group home after for coffee. He told Marcella, laughing gently, of girls at school who had developed crushes on him. He seemed slightly sorry for them, had tactfully discouraged them by saying his work came first. She tried very hard not to be curious about his private life.

"I'm a late developer," he told her mysteriously. He had all the confidence of someone who knows he is attractive, but none of the vanity. She sometimes worried that Mark showed no great interest in girls, but estimating the sexuality of one's own child was impossible to do, she decided.

The person he spoke of most often was a teacher who had recently been appointed to the Jacinthe faculty, a musician called Cole Ferrer who had inaugurated a hotly debated new course on jazz, swing, boogie, and syncopation. The school's administration had decided that such a class would help students become more rounded, and most students had taken readily to it.

"They're saying that no classical pianist can be truly versatile without knowing at least some jazz," Mark told Marcella, swiveling on the piano stool and playing a few bars of boogie. "Boogie really strengthens your left hand. . . ."

Marcella stared at his hands on the keys.

"I can see that, but you won't play *too* much of it, will you, Mark?" she asked him. "It sounds wrong, somehow, coming from you."

"Ferrer is pretty vicious to students who don't take it seriously; *that's* why I practice!" Mark laughed. "The guy's a sadist. He's totally unlike the other teachers—the way he dresses, the way he talks to us . . ."

When Mark's friends came back to the apartment, Marcella heard them discussing their new teacher in awed tones. One day Mark confessed that Cole Ferrer had actually made him cry when he had played a Gershwin piece particularly badly.

She read an article about Ferrer in the next week's Sunday *Times*. His position at Jacinthe had been called into question when he began appearing in a late-night engagement at the Carlyle Lounge. He was playing and singing the Gershwin and Cole Porter repertoire he excelled at. Suavely, he shrugged off the criticism, saying, "I'm a performer. I play anywhere they pay me!"

The better-heeled students ventured uptown and paid the twenty-five-dollar cover charge to hear their teacher play on Friday nights. During his six-week stint at the lounge, Cole Ferrer built up quite a cult following.

At Monday morning classes he stared at Mark with his hypnotic black eyes. He also told the few fellow teachers in whom he confided that he had never coached a more talented pupil. More than one teacher wondered whether it was Mark's talent that impressed him so, or his looks. Certainly, Mark had had nothing complimentary to say about his teacher, describing him as "ice-cold" or "arrogant."

Marcella was surprised, therefore, when, just before Christmas, Mark told her he had invited Cole Ferrer, along with some fellow pupils, back to the apartment after a Chopin concert at Carnegie Hall.

The Greatest Love of All had been on the best-seller list for many weeks; now, as Christmas gift books began to fill the windows, it was beginning to slide. Amy was starting to throw questions at Marcella, urging her to start a new book. She had not yet found a theme and used any excuse to stay out of her study.

"We'll give a party!" she suggested to Mark. "Cole Ferrer *is* quite a celebrity, isn't he?"

She usually enjoyed the young people Mark invited home, especially the girls who threw such adoring looks at her son, confirming her own high opinion of him.

"Tell me *why* you're inviting him, Mark?" she asked. "I thought he was disliked at the school."

Mark winked at her. "Public relations. I thought if he met you he might be a little less hard on me! You don't mind my using you, do you, Mom? Look as glamorous as you can!"

Thinking that Mark must be matchmaking, she decided to humor him and go all out to charm this man, buttering him up so that he'd give Mark good grades and a peaceful classroom life.

She ordered several trays of tiny pastries from the French bakery on Columbus she loved, decorating the living room with towering arrangements of lilies, roses, and orchids. Dozens of candles flickered around the room as she dressed and made up as carefully as she could on the night of the concert. She was ready for their guests when the downstairs buzzer sounded at ten forty-five.

The matchmaking idea disappeared the moment Marcella laid eyes on Cole Ferrer. Very rarely did she dislike someone on sight, but she found the smile freezing on her face as Mark ushered in the tall, dark man.

"Mother—Cole Ferrer, my most terrifying instructor!" Mark presented him. "He's also a big fan of yours!"

She raised her eyebrows as Ferrer took her hand and pressed it to his lips. The photograph of him had not prepared her for his height, about six feet three inches, and his commanding presence. He had a long face with sleepy eyelids and eyes so dark you could hardly see their expression. Sleeked-back black hair. A lean, languid body framed in a long overcoat worn over his shoulders like an opera cape. He was from another decade, perhaps another century.

"I'm delighted to meet you," he murmured. "I've read your books."

His lips were disdainful and hung a little slack when he was not curling them. Marcella shuddered as they brushed the back of her hand, feeling as if she had touched the skin of a lizard.

"My books are usually read by women!" Marcella said.

He laughed easily. "Absolutely, and what good taste they have!" he agreed. "My mother read *In the Name of Love,* then somehow it found its way to my bedside table. I started and I couldn't put it down. What a gift for narrative you have! It made me rush out to buy *The Greatest Love of All,* which I liked even more. Are you working on a third?"

"I'm trying to." She withdrew her hand, a little confused. She sensed a man this fastidious did not give out many compliments and she distrusted his attempts to ingratiate himself. She greeted Mark's other friends, most of whom she knew. She glanced in a mirror on her way to the kitchen, regretting having dressed up so. She had made herself much too glamorous for a little get-together over hot chocolate and cookies.

She carried a tray of pastries into the living room, and Cole immediately seized it from her. "Where would you like these?" he asked.

"On the piano will do," she nodded. "If you don't think that's sacrilege?"

His eyes twinkled as he turned to face her. He gave her a thorough going-over from her coiffure to the tips of her shoes, weighing up each item and grading it according to taste. His eyes then swept the room, doing the same thing to the furnishings.

"I see you collect?" He raised his eyebrows. "May I look?"

"Of course." She made a gesture. "I'll get you some hot chocolate. Or would you rather a drink?"

"Hot chocolate sounds perfect!"

She kept an eye on him as she waited for Mark to pour hot chocolate from an antique Dutch china pot she had bought recently. She watched Cole wander around the room, acquainting himself with her books, her furniture, her small collection of Victorian glass and porcelain.

She took him his chocolate, interrupting his examination of a shelf of English knickknacks she had bought too quickly in a London antique market. He was probably going to tell her they were fake, she thought, as he turned to her.

"Mark's told me how close you are." He accepted the cup with a nod, sitting next to her on a sofa, a little apart from the young people. "I empathize of course. My own mother is my dearest friend and I can't imagine living with anyone else now, although many people think it odd. She spoils me rotten, of course. As you do Mark, I'm sure!"

"I don't think I spoil him." Marcella frowned, lighting a cigarette. "Anything I can do to make life easier gives him more time and energy to study."

"And he's a genius, as you know," Cole added matter-of-factly, "and geniuses have their own rules."

Marcella's heart jumped and she felt a smile spreading over her face.

"Do you really think so?" she asked.

"I wouldn't be so hard on him if I didn't," Cole said. "Hasn't he told you what a bastard I am? He shows the most amazing aptitude for jazz. Unexpected in one so classically trained."

"But it *is* just to help his classical studies?" Marcella asked. "He'd never give up his intention to become a concert pianist? To get the Gianni scholarship?"

Cole glanced at her, surprised. "Surely you discuss all that with him?" He raised an eyebrow. "Mmm . . ." He sipped his chocolate like a cat sipping cream. "This is delicious!" He dabbed his mouth with a napkin. "Did you add a touch of nutmeg? Mrs. Winton . . ." He replaced the cup carefully, turning to her. "I once taught a boy who played Bach like an angel. He could have become the greatest organist in the world. *He* amazed me by turning out to be lead singer for Control—the rock group? They're still churning out hit albums, and he's a multimillionaire."

Marcella leaned toward him urgently. "Mark never needs to neglect his music to make money! I have all the money he needs!"

"Quite," Cole nodded. "But young people like to make their own money these days, haven't you noticed? And Mark has to do what Mark wants to do. I've learned through my considerable teaching experience that you can lead a musician to the music stand but you can't make him play. . . ."

He finished his chocolate as she stared at him, disturbed, his words floating ominously on the air.

Mark approached them to ask, "How about playing for your supper, Mr. Ferrer? My mother's never heard you. . . ."

Cole Ferrer stood, brushing crumbs from his lap.

"Outside school, it's Cole," he corrected Mark. The pastries were removed from the piano and the lid opened. There was a hush as Cole sat down. Smoothly, he rippled out some chords.

"What a lovely tone!" he complimented them. Mark squeezed his mother's hand as Cole began to play. He played Gershwin as Marcella had never heard it before. He played it with the delicacy and respect due to Debussy or Chopin. He had arranged some of the tunes himself and brought out subtleties in the melodies that changed Marcella's attitude toward the music. She had always thought of Gershwin as lushly romantic, nostalgic music for movies or for summoning up a lost era over cocktails. Ferrer played the well-known pieces with such freshness that Marcella could not help admiring him. She watched Mark watching him. Was Mark about to hero-worship this man? she wondered. Mark had missed out on a loving caring father, but surely no one qualified less as a father figure than Cole Ferrer.

She circulated among Mark's friends when the performance was over.

"Please eat all these pastries," she begged. "I won't be able to sleep tonight if I know they're in the house!" She longed for them all to leave so she could voice her fears to Mark and have him soothe her.

Much later, as Mark's friends were finally leaving, Cole Ferrer took her hand and told her sincerely, "Mother will be beside herself when I tell her I met you! We're both longing for your next book!"

She waited with Mark at the elevator to see everyone out. As the elevator doors slid closed, Mark turned eagerly to her. "Well? What did you think of him?"

His intense blue eyes scanned her face for approval as he led her back to the living room, his arm in hers.

"You've done quite an about-face!" she marveled. "He used to terrify you!"

"I learned to use humor!" Mark grinned. "He has such a warped sense of humor, and he likes it when you stand up to him!" He poured himself a glass of wine and added some ice. "And I needed a kick in the pants—musically! I was becoming a bit of a snob. You heard how marvelous Gershwin can be if it's played with the right musical sensibility."

"He's a very interesting man." Marcella turned her head to light a cigarette so Mark would not see her eyes. Each always knew when the other was lying. "Extremely cultivated. Is he English? I thought there was an accent."

"He taught in London for three years," Mark said. "He caught the accent!"

"He certainly thinks highly of your playing, Mark," she told him.

"God, if I could play like *him*!" Mark said, clearing some plates from a side table. "We'll go to the Carlyle one night to hear him!"

She followed him into the kitchen, holding full ashtrays.

"You won't play too much of that stuff, will you, darling?" she asked. He went back to the living room for more plates and she followed.

"I don't know!" Mark stacked some plates, then threw himself onto a sofa and stretched, kicking off his shoes. "Jazz and blues and ragtime practically *is* a classical repertoire now. You know what Hans Dichter sang as an encore at his recital tonight? 'Summertime'!"

"It's not a classical repertoire to Franco Gianni," she reminded him.

"Is that what you're worried about?" Mark sat up and gave her that heart-stopping smile that only he could give. Jumping to his feet, he ran over to kiss her cheek. "Mother, you *know* how hard I've been working toward this scholarship! Of *course*, Chopin comes first! Even *without* the lyrics!"

They visited the Carlyle with Amy the next Friday night. The room was packed, the audience hushed as if frightened to miss the echo of one of Cole's notes. Marcella was forced to admit that he was a superb pianist and singer. She smiled as Mark applauded with his hands high above his head after each song. If it was hero worship, it was surely harmless, she thought.

He joined their table after his set, along with some record company types who were trying to lure him away from his present label. Marcella and Amy found the men absolutely fascinating, with their chunky gold jewelry and hip speech.

Cole apologized when they finally left. "Sorry about the Las Vegas types, but they provide the rent for Mother and I. I have to be careful. I'm not about to become the nineteen-eighties answer to Liberace! I'm terribly allergic to candelabra!"

Marcella and Amy couldn't help laughing at his world-weary tones. Mark hung on every word.

"Just a phase they go through," Amy consoled Marcella on their trip to the ladies' lounge. "Or so I've heard."

When she got home that night, Marcella lay awake with a new idea for a book. The atmosphere in the hotel lounge that night and the strange relation between classical and popular music had triggered off something in her imagination. Cole had provided her with a new, original character to work on. He was larger than life, dramatic! If she improved his physical appearance considerably, making him attractive, macho, virile, and gave him a beautiful young female pupil who was desperately in love with him . . . made him a cruel, handsome, demanding music teacher . . . she could have fun with a Svengali type of passion between pupil and teacher. Switching on her bedside lamp, she began to make notes. She could use all she had learned about the music world from Mark, making the romantic story span two decades and the concert halls of Europe and America. The stormy balance of power between pupil and teacher would change as the pupil became world-famous. She had the title immediately: "Music of Love." Scott would love it because it had the word "love" in the title, and her readers would love the sheer entertainment, as she swept them into a story they'd be unable to put down until the last page.

She had not realized how much she would miss her mother's presence, nor how many times she had stopped writing to visit her, share a cup of coffee with the nurse, make sure everything was all right. Now she was completely alone all day, able to work from noon through to evening, stopping only for a sandwich at her desk. The solitude made the work pour out. Mark read some chapters and advised her on the musical parts. By working long days, often seven days a week, she found she had written the entire novel in an astonishing four and a half months.

"What are you, a fucking novel-machine?" Amy gasped when presented with the manuscript at the end of April. "*I* seem to take longer and longer to write a book. Of course my new one, *Between My Legs,* does need an awful lot of research!"

Marcella laughed. "This was a fluke," she said modestly. "See how you like it before you start patting me on the back."

"It's another hit, Marcella!" Amy sang out over the phone, a few days later. "So we must celebrate! It's time you had a vacation and I'm just the person to introduce you to Europe."

"*Where* in Europe?" Marcella asked doubtfully.

"Majorca!" Amy cried. "The almond trees will be in blossom in May. Piney air and turquoise, crystal sea! You will not be able to resist. Oh, Marcella, come up tonight at eight—I'll give you a preview!"

A map of Spain was pinned to the dining room wall when Marcella arrived at Amy's apartment that evening. The Mediterranean island of Majorca was outlined in purple felt-tip.

Amy sat Marcella down with a bottle of icy champagne and plates of delicious things to nibble on, then stood by the map holding a silver toasting fork.

"Our objective!" she announced, pronging Palma, the capital. She swept the fork across the Mediterranean to Spain's mainland. "After our flight to Barcelona, we take a thirty-minute flight across the sea. Majorca is *the* original magical mystery isle—one of the best-kept secrets in Europe! From Americans, that is; the Europeans know *all* about it!"

Marcella sipped her wine, relaxing against the heap of cushions Amy had piled behind her. Outside, Central Park was at its darkest green, the towers lined up at its perimeters sparkling with lights.

"And *why* is it so special?" Marcella smiled. "I know you're dying to tell me!"

Amy shrugged and took a swallow of wine, gesticulating in a throwaway gesture with the toasting fork. "Okay . . ." she admitted, "so the most gorgeous men in the world are located in Spain and on its isles: is that a crime? We stay at a very proper hotel, the Son Vida, high on a hill above Palma. In the evenings, we creep down to the action. If we're lucky enough to meet real Majorcans, they'll show us the nontourist parts of the island and you'll think you're in Eden, I swear! I was there years ago—I don't know why I didn't stay."

Marcella closed her eyes, leaning back. "It sounds like heaven!" she said.

BOOK THREE

BOOK THREE

TWELVE

They flew into Palma as the sun blazed gold on a late afternoon in May. From the plane, Marcella noticed the intense aquamarine and prussian blue of the sea. As soon as they stepped out of the aircraft they caught the smell of pines baking in the sun mixed with the briny smell of the sea.

An immaculate car from the hotel awaited, their names chalked on a blackboard held by the driver.

"Winton and Jagger?" Amy read, climbing in. "We sound like a goddamn law firm."

Their car climbed slowly around a hill that was almost a mountain, toward the luxury hotel nestled among acres and acres of pine trees. Down in the city, the cathedral glowed golden in the sun. When they got out of the car to take in the view and breathe the pure air, Marcella stretched her arms in joy.

"Two weeks of nothing but this will be perfect for me!" she laughed.

"It's a fairy tale, isn't it?" Amy agreed. She ran through the terrace of tables and chairs, waltzing across the outdoor dance floor, Marcella following her. They stopped at the low wall that gave onto a perfect view of the coastline below.

To one side the sea lay far beneath them, glittering and clear, the hotel so high above the city that the noise from below came through as a veiled hum, sifted through thousands of pines before it reached the ears of Son Vida's guests. They leaned over the balustrade looking at the view, and Marcella's eyes sparkled as she turned to Amy.

"I love it," she said.

After checking into their rooms, they met for a drink on the terrace. The guests were magnificently arrogant: rich families, some Arabs, older couples, and a few discreet, polite Britishers. Marcella had explored the luxurious hotel before Amy came down, watching an elegant, thin, tall ugly woman staring into the hotel's jewelry store in a little street of shops in the basement. The woman wore a couture dress —Ungaro or Lacroix—in a big colorful print with monstrous puffed sleeves. The covetous expression on her face as she stared at the jewelry in the closed store made Marcella shiver. Then Amy's heels clicking across the tiled floor made her turn around.

"They're having a flamenco show on the terrace tonight," Amy told her. "Wanna stay home?"

Marcella nodded excitedly.

They chose the outdoor buffet for dinner, returning again and again to the fiery grill where huge fresh shrimp were tossed and turned by white-hatted chefs. Between them, they consumed a bottle of fruity Spanish wine.

"No unattached males!" Marcella said, looking around at the British, French, and Italian couples.

"Of course not." Amy didn't even bother to follow her gaze. "They're awaiting us down there!" She indicated the lights of Palma, far down below. The night was navy, the stars amazingly white.

The flamenco began at eleven, as most of the guests sat down to eat. It began with a female dancer seated upright on a chair, very still as the spotlight picked out her fitted ruffled dress, as clean and white as a swan. Slowly, she arched her body, stretched it, and got to her feet. Marcella was mesmerized by her confidence, her presence. When the dancer's feet began to move, she performed a surprised mime, as if astonished at what they were doing. Her face retained its haughty expression as her feet seemed to act independently. Like me, Marcella thought, watching her. The top half of my body not knowing what the bottom half is doing, pretending not to be responsible. Members' movie theater flashed into her mind and she tried to count the dozens of men who had touched her. Then the male dancer joined the woman and they went through the stylized, witty, sexual ritual of a man being seduced by a woman, a woman teasing a man, both knowing exactly what they were doing.

"The Spanish *know,* don't they?" Amy whispered.

Marcella and Amy went to bed after one, when the dancing had ended, both of them exhausted by the travel, deliciously tired, breathing in the fresh piney air.

At eleven the next morning, Marcella was at the pool, the sun hot on her back, when Amy came out and threw a tee-shirt over her.

"Don't get too tan, Marcella," she said. "You want to look pale and interesting for tonight, don't you? How will they know you're fresh if you're as tan as everyone else?"

Before lunch, she led Marcella to her room. "I've got something for you," she said, beckoning. "A little presentation I want to make in honor of our first day here." She delved into the suitcase on the floor of her dressing room, coming up with a gray lizard-covered case crammed with glass jars and bottles. "From me." She handed it to Marcella. "Made by a very exclusive and very fucked Hungarian princess in Paris, exclusively for that part of your body which I pray you regain the use of tonight!"

The beautifully packaged emollients, creams, and lotions were made with essential oils and other natural ingredients for cleaning, purifying, and strengthening the vaginal area.

"She only lets the top whores and society ladies of Europe subscribe to these little chaps. . . ." Amy dripped a pearl of lotion onto the back of Marcella's hand and rubbed it in. "I've used so much, she's started to give me a wholesale discount."

"And does it really work?" Marcella asked, sniffing her hand.

"Ask him tomorrow," Amy said.

They set out for the town at four. It had been five years since Amy's last visit and she needed recommendations and tips about the current hot places.

"Hairdressers know everything!" she said.

The taxi took fifteen minutes to whisk them down to the center of town: long narrow warrens of lanes, packed with stores, and a tree-lined central boulevard containing a fountain and a huge newsstand. The windows of the stores were filled with leather goods and chunky gold jewelry. In the most elegant street, Jaime III, they ordered coffee and the local sugar-powdered *ensaimadas,* at an outdoor terrace. As they began their explorations, they found themselves standing before a smart hairdressing salon, staring into the window at a giant photograph of the queen of Spain.

"If it's good enough for her, it's good enough for me!" Amy decided promptly, walking in.

Minutes later, Marcella met her first Latin Lover when, after her shampoo, she was allocated Roman. He greeted her with a polite nod and listened as she described her usual, flowing style. If she had tried to imagine the stereotypical Latin, she could not have done better than Roman. His brilliantined black hair and proud profile suggested a nineteen-forties matinee idol. The only thing that detracted from the dignity of his bearing was his height; he was short but powerfully stocky. He pressed his body close to Marcella as he combed and dried her hair, his fingertips just grazing the skin behind her ears. Each time she thought he might be flirting with her, she would glance at his very stern expression and put the idea out of her head.

Amy, a few feet away in the next chair, was being tended by a woman.

"What d'you think, Amy?" Marcella called over softly. "He doesn't speak much English."

Amy frowned, studying him. "It's hard to tell with hairdressers. Could be bicoastal?"

"Pliss!" Roman suddenly said, turning her head back to face the front.

Amy giggled.

Roman gave no reaction but continued to caress Marcella's neck, sending hungry shivers through her. At the end of his meticulous styling, she found he had given her a perfect Mary Tyler Moore look, circa 1970.

"Do you believe this?" she whispered to Amy, showing off her bouffant locks. "The minute I get back to the hotel, I'll wash it out!"

"And *I* look like a cross between a drowned rat and Florence Henderson's *older* sister!" Amy complained, studying her red spikes. "Okay . . ." she handed her stylist a generous tip. "You speak *some* Spanish, don't you, Marcella? Ask Rudolph Valentino where two women can go in the evenings these days?"

In her halting Spanish, liberally sprinkled with Italian, Marcella questioned the stern Roman. He gave her a frown and disappeared, returning two minutes later with a small piece of white paper. On it, he had written "Omar."

"Club," he shrugged. "But not to go before midnight!"

They paid their bills and she just had time to notice that his eyes, the color of amber, gleamed wickedly beneath incredibly long lashes, before he took the five-hundred-peseta tip she handed him, made a stiff bow, almost clicked his heels, and showed them out.

"Let me see!" On the street, Amy grabbed the slip of paper and read the name. "He didn't even put the address. I guess every taxi driver in town knows it. . . ." She looked at Marcella and shrugged. "It's worth a try, huh?"

It was twelve-thirty when the two women stepped through the mirrored doors of Omar, off the Plaza Gomilla area where Palma's nightlife happened. Omar was evidently supposed to be Russian in theme, with posters and stills from the movie *Doctor Zhivago* supplying the decor against scarlet walls and red velvet seating.

"It is *definitely* a little seedy!" Amy approved, looking around.

Roman was hovering just inside, and he greeted Marcella as if they were old friends. He gave a quick, hurt look at Marcella's hair, which, thanks to shampoo and plenty of mousse, she had managed to coax back to current fashion. He had a friend with him, a kind of look-alike of himself, also smallish, stocky, powerfully built, proud, and dark.

"This must be for me!" Amy said, smiling.

Roman introduced them very formally, inclining his head toward Amy to catch her name. The place was smoky, crowded, and hot. Women sat alone at tables, nursing their drinks. The room was encircled by a long, winding bar at which restless, prowling men sometimes stopped for a drink. It was very obviously Majorca's version of a singles bar.

"Classy, huh?" Amy winked at Marcella. She smiled at Marcella's worried expression. "Oh come on, darling, let's enjoy it! After all, we'd never go anywhere like this in New York!"

"Wouldn't we?" Marcella said.

"If you're referring to Members, I'll have you know a membership there costs more than anyone here earns in—"

She was still talking when Roman's friend pulled her onto the dance floor. A dance band pounded out a nonstop medley of popular tunes. Proudly placing a firm arm around her, Roman piloted Marcella onto the dance floor. Instantly, she was transported back in time to some macho, Spanish movie, a melodrama where men were men and women were hopelessly smitten and did as they were bid. Roman gave himself to the beat. Marcella watched him, amazed. She had never seen a man hold his head, his body, this proudly, this puffed up with pride. It was so absurd it was almost touching. The fact that he was about an inch smaller than her aroused something in her. He broke away to turn a complete circle like a wound-up doll. She tried to keep pace with him, using a mixture of samba, rhumba, and cha-cha-cha.

They danced every dance until the band suddenly stopped and, downing their instruments, headed for the bar. Rock records blared over a muffled sound system and the floor was quickly deserted. As Roman guided her to a table, she realized she had never been this thirsty in her life. She downed the rum and Coke the moment it was served, letting the ice cubes melt in her mouth. Roman attempted some halting conversation in English and between that and her Spanish-Italian they managed to establish that he was from Andalusia and had twelve brothers and sisters. Soon the noise around them made them give up. Marcella wore a short black dress, and her shoulders, despite Amy's sun ban, were golden, thanks to a half hour on her balcony after lunch. She had anointed herself with the Hungarian princess's lotions after her shower that evening, feeling foolish. Now, catching Roman's gleaming eye, she knew the emollients would be doing their job that very night. He placed his hand gently on her upper arm and she felt his heat. His long-lashed eyes glanced sideways at her, appraisingly. He had damped his hair and combed it straight back so that it gleamed and made him look more like an old-time movie idol than ever. She was not sure if this disguise was deliberate, like the hip young kids in New York dressing out of the forties, or entirely unawares. He leaned forward suddenly and pressed his full, molded lips on hers. They kissed and she felt his tongue ready to spring into action. He opened his eyes and indicated the door with raised eyebrows and a jerk of his head. "What about my friend?" she asked. Roman shrugged. The cheap rum had gone to her head and it was pounding a sensual beat of its own. She found Amy on the dance floor and yelled over the music that they were leaving. "See you tomorrow!" Amy winked. The street was deliciously cool after the club. This was the trashy, tourist part of town and they walked past several hamburger and pizza joints and a mock-German beer hall before they reached Roman's small black car.

He gave her one lust-filled glance before driving to his apartment in the middle of town, a couple of blocks from the hairdressing salon. It was a straight-to-bed seduction with no flirtation, only a slight step above Members' theater sex. They were both naked, embracing, within minutes of entering his dark, sparsely furnished apartment. His clean tanned body smelled of the sun as he earnestly licked her face like a puppy, inserting the tip of his tongue in her ear and making her shiver. Then he crouched at the foot of the bed and deliberately held her feet to kiss each toe, slowly moving his mouth up each leg, burying his face in her, finally, to flick her most sensitive part with his tongue, striking the bud, groaning and growling with desire as he did so. How much better it was on a bed! she thought. She even liked his slightly rough urgency when he grabbed her ankles and swung her around to sit up on the edge of the bed while he sat on the floor with his face twisting from side to side in her lap, inflaming her so that she grabbed him under the arms and pulled him up onto her. He turned onto his back, urging her to lie upon him. He hooked his hands under her arms and with immense strength held her weight aloft as he arranged his brown body beneath hers, lowering her gently down so that their bodies touched at every point. She felt the roughness of his thick thighs, the satin smoothness of his ribs, the sex continually flexing under her belly, the quick thrusts of his tongue in her mouth. Then he reversed their positions again, lying full-length upon her. How wonderful it felt to have a man on her who did not crush her with his weight! Her eyes closed as he fingered her nipples, making them hard, cupping his hand under her to just graze her opening with his fingers. The more he did to her, the more excited he became, suddenly moving so fast, touching, licking, biting in so many different places, that she had the impression of several men surrounding her, violating her.

When he confidently entered her, smoothly and firmly, with his thick, hard sex, she opened her eyes and saw his black hair had shaken loose to hang, unruly, in his face. His lips pursed as he slid softly up into her, his mouth petulantly demanding hers. When he was fully inside her, he allowed their mouths to meet, his tongue entering her mouth and thrashing about inside it, mimicking the action down below. His relentless, oiled movement had a mechanical, untiring quality about it that brought her incredibly quickly toward a chasm of pleasure. She sobbed as the feeling swept her. When she glanced at him, his face was contorted, almost angry, his eyes glaring at her. He opened his mouth, his eyes rolled back, and he roared aloud. She felt his shudders of pleasure inside her, and the feeling took equal hold of her, surrounded her, forcing her sweet long dive into a swoon of sexual release. They froze for one wonderful moment. Then moved a little, moaning as their pleasure completed itself, wringing the last delicious sensations from their joined bodies.

Roman fell asleep almost immediately and was soon snoring. Marcella managed to move him off her, but his arms still clung to her, like a spoilt little boy. She glanced around the bare room, unable to stop herself from imagining the nice little touches she could bring to it. A length of good fabric at the windows, a couple of decent armchairs. She imagined a very intense sexual relationship without much talking. How would she tell people that her lover was a hairdresser? she wondered. Well, it was a good, honest job and he probably made a decent living. She drifted off to sleep in his arms.

She awoke with a pounding headache, harsh sunlight glaring in her eyes. She shifted, touching him. He was slumped on his face like a dead man. They were both naked, without even a sheet covering them. The room was airless, hot, the windows tightly shut.

She leaned over him. His lower lip jutted petulantly even in sleep and the long black lashes gave his sensual face a touch of childish innocence. She had to admit he was gorgeous. A photograph of his profile as it looked right now could easily be used to sell cologne, she thought.

The bathroom was dark, even with the tiny yellow bulb switched on. She rinsed her mouth and bathed her face, noting all the things a single man forgot to have in his home—nice towels, a bathmat to stand on. Would he let her go shopping for things to add a little color and warmth? She imagined herself flying back and forth from New York, bringing supplies from Macy's and Bloomingdale's to make his life more comfortable. Sometimes he would come to New York for a week or two. When sex was this good between two people, they could find a way to be together.

She crept back to the bedroom, trying to open a window to let in some air. It was stuck but finally gave with a loud crack that woke him. Roman scrambled to a sitting position very quickly, glaring at her as if she were an intruder. She smiled and gave him a little wave.

"*Buenos días,* Roman!" she trilled. He snorted and turned over. As welcome fresh air poured into the room, she clambered onto the bed and snuggled next to him.

There was stale tobacco smoke in his hair and he had sour breath. She drifted off to sleep again. When they awoke an hour later, he climbed on top of her, half asleep. He was less gentle this time, but brought her again to a quick, efficient climax, his possessive enjoyment of her body a kind of stimulant.

He went to the bathroom, noisily locking the door, and she heard the shower running. When he finally emerged, his hair was gleaming wet and combed straight back. He strode purposefully to the kitchen to make a pot of strong coffee, setting out a can of crackers and a slab of butter on a saucer, with all the solemnity of an old British butler. She took a robe from the bathroom to breakfast in. Roman wore pajama pants. He poured hot milk into her coffee before she could stop him. The milk smelt scorched. It was eleven-thirty. Roman hadn't said a word. The coffee was bitter but she forced herself to drink it. He moodily sipped his, dipping buttered crackers in it. He lit a cigarette and stood to wash the dishes, waving away her offer of help. She stood behind him for a moment, about to caress the square tanned shoulders, but somehow feeling that this would not be the right thing to do. She decided that she had better leave.

She dressed in her clothes from the night before, redid her makeup, and found her sunglasses in her purse. When she went to the kitchen, he was thoughtfully drying the dishes between puffs on his cigarette. A wave of irritation passed over her. Could she have been so wrong?

"Adiós," she tried.

He turned. *"Adiós,"* he agreed.

At the front door she hesitated. Was she being silly?

"Are we going to see each other again or what?" she asked him.

He mimed speaking into a phone. "Telephone," he said. "At the salon."

She smiled. "Would you like to have dinner tonight?"

"I am busy," he shook his head impatiently. "You call me!"

"I have a better idea," she said, taking the card of the salon he handed her. On the back she wrote her name, her room number, and the name of her hotel, handing it back to him. "You call *me.*"

She leaned to kiss his lips. She could have sworn they had had a special sexual chemistry together. She glanced back at the undecorated apartment. Maybe it would have to survive without her touch.

She stepped out into the hallway for the elevator and pressed the call button. As she turned back to say good-bye, she heard the door slam and the bolts slide to, noisily.

"And *adiós* to you, too," she said, surprised. As she rode down in the elevator, she tried to feel cool, triumphant. She'd got what she wanted, hadn't she? But outside, on the hot, deserted Sunday street, with all its stores shuttered, she felt angry and humiliated. She felt he might be watching her from his balcony window and she tried to walk jauntily under the heavy midday sun, as though she often promenaded in a black cocktail dress down an empty Majorcan street at noon.

"You expected him to fall in love with you, maybe?" Amy laughed. They were sitting by the hotel pool later that day in the shade of a large orange umbrella, sipping fresh grapefruit juice.

Marcella pulled a wry face. "I don't know what I expected," she said. "Perhaps just a little more than I got."

"Well, you got a lot more than most Manhattan women got last night!" Amy pointed out.

Marcella put her glass down. "I'd have liked it if he had wanted to see me again, *that's* all!" she said.

Amy stared at her. "The only serious question you should be asking is whether you need him to do your hair again." She giggled.

Marcella shook her head. "Only if nineteen-sixties bouffants really come back!" she muttered.

"That's the girl!" Amy approved. "Don't ever forget your sense of humor. You came here to enjoy yourself, not to get hung up over some hairdresser! The men here are better if you keep them to one night. Now, let me tell you about Juan. . . ."

After five more nights and five more men, Marcella's memories began to blur. Why was she doing this? she asked herself. Why was she reducing herself to this ridiculous level?

One very young, remarkably handsome boy had sat next to her in a late-night bar, miming fainting with desire for her. His act had turned her on. He had dragged her back to his stuffy little apartment almost next door, as if he lay in wait for women like a spider in a web. He had stripped naked and jumped into the grubby bed, sitting up to watch her do the same. Later, she cursed herself for being so submissive. Of course if you stripped naked for a man an hour after meeting him, you couldn't exactly expect a whole lot of respect!

Another man she met had been several inches shorter than she, bearded, not handsome but with the most compellingly sweet touch. There was a vibration about him that seemed overwhelmingly sexy to her. They had driven for what felt like hours to the other side of the island. In his bedroom, he had dragged a large wardrobe halfway across the room so that it would reflect their bodies in its mirrored door as they made love. He had sneaked little glances into the mirror as if he were watching a porno film. Amy nearly fell off her chair at breakfast the next morning when Marcella told her about it.

"Are *you* going to use that in a book or can I?" she begged.

What Marcella had not dared tell her was that she had pressed the hotel's phone number onto the little bearded man, practically begging him to call her. When he did not call the next day, she had actually been very upset. What was wrong with her? She was behaving like an adolescent! Was it because, apart from Harry, she had never dated? Could she not handle the simplest relationship? This was, she reminded herself, only a more comfortable version of sex at Members, substituting a bed for a tip-up velvet seat.

On her sixth day, Marcella played hookey from Amy and the posh hotel to explore the twisting, cobbled lanes of Palma's old city district. Here, in the shadow of the enormous cathedral, were real people and real faces, not just sunburnt tourists. Down here, people looked at her, smiled, reacted. She walked happily, appreciating the European smells of strong tobacco, drains, coffee, sunny hot walls, and dank alleyways swarming with stray cats. Women took children home from school. Old men sat reading newspapers spread on café tables. A mixture of languages —Spanish, German, English, French—swirled around her. At least this trip had given her an idea for a book, a story about two women on a man-hunting vacation. One would thoroughly enjoy it (Amy), while the other would be made miserable by sleeping around (herself). She would disguise her two women, of course, changing their careers. They would be two secretaries who had saved up for two years for this trip. She could give ironical but sexy accounts of the affairs, based on all the men she had met. The sober character would come to realize that she needed a man not simply for sex but to do things with, to talk to. Oh, how she longed for a man to talk to, to eat dinner with, to discuss, to stroll with, to be civilized with, to share life's simplest pleasures.

She imagined how this vacation could be with someone she loved by her side, sharing her discoveries on a morning like this, looking with her into the store windows at the strange mixtures of merchandise. She would have liked to point out the little shop that sold nothing but soap and ladies' underwear, as if they somehow went together. The housewares store that displayed packets of cleaning materials and scrubbing brushes in a clean bare window, enough space around each object to give it the importance of a precious jewel. She wanted to nudge someone over the stores kept in darkness, a dusty yellow bulb switched on only if someone ventured in.

She bought some colored tee-shirts for Mark because buying him something brought her closer to him for a few moments. She prodded, like an aching tooth, her failure with Sonia, their estrangement, vowing to try harder with her when she got back to New York. Could she possibly speak frankly to her about *why* she was going to Members, get her to understand the urges that even Marcella herself did not fully comprehend?

And then, as she walked down a street lit by slanting rays of sun, she decided she would not sleep with any more men on this trip. No more strange beds. The few hours of intimacy only made her feel worse later. She felt much better after this decision, as if she had moved up to a new, serene level. Let Amy get up to anything she liked, *she* would stay at the hotel in the evenings and catch up on the books she had brought with her or make notes on the new novel she had in her head. She would write about love instead of stupidly searching for it. Writing was so much easier than living, anyway.

She had reached the end of a narrow street. She looked up and saw a balcony above her, laden with potted plants, the tops of the tallest palms just catching the sun. A parrot squawked from its cage. Strings of washing were draped across the street like a painted backdrop for an operetta. She made notes on these details in her diary, so she could refer to them when she wrote the story. Behind everything, the cathedral's honey-colored walls loomed high, glowing in the sun. She felt a sudden desire to go into the cathedral and light candles for her father, here in Majorca, where he had never been.

The walk up an old cobbled street was steep, and a grandiose flight of steps led to the massive wood-framed entrance. Dozens of angels had been carved in deep relief into the doors. Inside, Marcella could see nothing for a moment, dazzled by walking from bright sunlight into a dark interior. She walked carefully toward the glow of lit candles at a wrought-iron stand halfway down the side of the cathedral. Gleaming patches of deep red, royal blue, and yellow, made by the sun streaming through the massive round stained-glass windows, splashed across the flagstone floor.

Slowly, she registered the forms of black-dressed women, scarves over their heads, kneeling or sitting on the worn wooden pews, their heads bowed, lips moving.

Candles were twenty-five pesetas and she bought two, depositing the coins in a wooden box. She lit them from the other candles, sticking them into metal holders. For you, Dad, she thought. Are you watching me? It was a wonderfully comforting thought at that moment to believe he was with her. But if she wanted the comfort of that belief, she also had to believe he had been watching her nights as well as the days. She thought of New York as if she had turned a telescope onto Manhattan and could see, reflected as a tiny image, her own figure approaching Ninth Avenue in search of gratification. From this distance, she could not understand why she had ever set foot in Members. Both that and her previous nights in Majorca suddenly appeared unbelievably grubby and unworthy of her.

Reviewing her last five evenings in merciless detail, she saw her supplicating body, her hope that each man might simply be nice or considerate to her, give her some confirmation of her worth. She saw, clearly, what a stupid way she had chosen to find that. What she needed involved so much more than sex. It was her own image of herself as a person, a woman offering love and needing it returned. *Needing it returned!* How could she ever have imagined it would be returned under these conditions? And why had she been so needy? Her father had loved her. Her son loved her. She did not need to panic and grab for anything that passed her way.

She sat in the calm, majestic cathedral for some minutes, feeling a new strength flooding her. She had come to a new chapter in her life: how she welcomed it! She remained in the semidarkness for a while, letting her mind flow free, enjoying the new calm of her thoughts. Then, quieted and refreshed, she got to her feet, making for the big carved doors through which she had entered.

A man was sitting some rows behind her. Nights at Members had sharpened her sight in the dark and this man was exceptional, whether in a theater or a church. He was very good-looking and had a serious sweet face with intense eyes that were watching her as she approached. She walked slowly up the aisle, trying not to stare back. Had she not just vowed very solemnly to stop meeting men? Nevertheless, he *was* very good-looking, about forty, with the sensuous full lips and carved, dramatic features that always caught her eye. She tore her gaze away, passing him, forbidding herself to turn to see if he was looking after her. A church was not the place for a pickup, even a spiritual one. Outside, the glare of the sun dizzied her. Fumbling for dark glasses, she sat down on one of the benches by the side of the entrance. Would he follow her? Could a woman leaving a cathedral, having vowed very sincerely to stop looking for a man, find one on her way out?

He appeared in the doorway and she watched him blink in the sunlight as she had. As he glanced about him, their eyes met. They stared at each other familiarly, as if they had known one another at some other time. He looked

Italian, perhaps Spanish, with big black sad eyes. He had the perfect grooming of a well-to-do European, pressed gray slacks, clean black leather loafers. They looked at each other with wondering, inquiring looks, holding each other's gaze for as long as a man and a woman can without talking or laughing. She could not make the first move: it would go against everything she had promised herself in the cathedral. They did not even smile. His lips parted slightly and he frowned. Marcella stood, waiting a few moments. Then they turned their backs on each other and walked off in opposite directions.

Damn it! she cursed as she walked, her new serene mood ruined. She was as upset as if she had lost a lover of long standing. This had been *exactly* the man she'd pictured when she had first agreed to visit Europe and imagined, as she always did, falling in love. That serious, handsome face was a guarantee that an affair would last. A man like that did not slam a door and bolt it before you got into the elevator!

She walked on, thoughtfully. In a way, it was reassuring just to know that such a man did exist, a man too polite and too serious to speak to a woman on the street, especially if they had both just left a cathedral. After walking down two streets, she turned, just in case he had decided to follow her, but there was no sign of him. She found the post office and got on line to buy stamps for postcards. Then she visited a perfume store and bought a gift for Nancy Warner. In the tree-lined *avenida* called Es Borne, she decided to have some coffee. It was nearly one: the stores would close soon for the three-hour siesta.

She chose the most old-fashioned café, which still boasted its original art nouveau windows and lamps, the old waiters elegant in white jackets. At a shady table, she ordered *café con leche*.

"Dear Mark," she wrote on a postcard. "It is so beautiful here that—"

Someone sat down at the next table. Without looking up, she was aware of who it was. His presence seemed to spread a warmth across to her. She looked up and once again found herself gazing into dark eyes so familiar it felt absolutely natural to smile into them and say, "Hello."

"Hello. You are English?" he asked softly, with an accent.

"No. American," she said.

"I do not believe!" he said.

"Italian-American?" she tried.

"Ah! Yes. This is possible," he allowed. He stood. "May I please invite you?" he asked, deftly removing her check from beneath a tiny saucer.

"Thank you," she said.

He sat down at her table. Up close, he was extremely handsome, with a tanned, beautifully sculpted face. It was the soulful expression in his dark eyes that made him special, plus the long sweeping lashes that veiled his gaze, giving him a shy look. His presence was confident and reassuring. He ordered coffee from the hovering waiter. She knew, before she glanced down at his hands, what they would be like: slender, brown fingers with short strong nails. Wide, capable palms. Familiar hands. His lips were full, and his white teeth protruded slightly, in a charming way. In America, they would have been corrected in his teens. Here, they had been left natural, and each time he smiled, he tried to keep his lips together, not succeeding, making his smile shy.

"How well do you know Majorca?" he asked her. "Are you just holidaying here?"

"Yes. For the first time. And you?"

"I live here some of the year, and I visit often. I sell paintings to people who wish to buy them. I am not good at selling to people who do not wish to buy, so I don't make a lot of money at it!"

"You speak very good English."

"I see many American movies!"

His coffee was served and he emptied a packet of sugar into it, stirring it slowly and looking at her.

"You will forgive me that I could not think you were American," he asked. "I always think of Americans as blond with blue eyes, and you look so Mediterranean."

"I do feel at home here," she told him. "My father was Italian; maybe that's why."

"You have seen the island?" he asked.

She nodded. "It's so beautiful. I'm staying at the Son Vida. The view is fabulous!"

"But—" he frowned. "Of course you have seen the other places? Valldemossa? Deya?"

"No," Marcella said. "Just Palma. Today I was doing a little exploring on my own in the cathedral area. . . ."

"You will let me show you my island?" He leaned forward earnestly. "It is the most beautiful, enchanted place. One of our old songs calls it the *'isla misteriosa.'* It is full of surprises. I would be very sad to think that someone like you had visited and left without seeing it well."

She looked into his serious eyes. He was different from any other man she'd met. The funny thing was that it did not really matter what they said. There was some odd undercurrent that had nothing to do with their conversation.

"My name is Santiago Roca." He held out his hand and she gave hers into his warm clasp. "My family and friends call me Santi."

"Santi," she almost whispered.

He let go of her hand, smiling. "And your name?" he asked.

"I'm sorry. Marcella Winton."

"Winton is Italian?"

"It's my married name. I call myself Marcella Balducci Winton."

He nodded. "In Spain we keep our three names, too. I am really Santiago Roca Grimalt."

He said it with such pride that she could not help smiling.

"Marcella . . ." he said her name slowly, caressing it with his soft accent, rolling the "r." "So you are married?"

"Divorced," she said.

"I am divorced also." He smiled sadly. "A long time ago."

"You said you lived here some of the year?" she asked. "Where are you during the other part?"

"In Barcelona," he said. "I come here on my business and also to see to my house. My mother is Majorcan. Her sister left me her house. My father is from Barcelona, so I have both sides in me."

"*Both* sides?" She frowned.

"Majorcan and Spanish!"

"I thought Majorca *was* Spanish?"

"No, they are very different." His eyes opened wide. "Of course, officially Majorca *is* Spanish, but the people, the customs . . ." He made a defeated gesture. "I shall have to show you. It is easier than to talk! I—" He stopped, frowning. "When I saw you before, in the cathedral . . . then outside the cathedral, I—" He grazed the sleeve of her dress with the tips of his fingers, shaking his head. "Please forgive me," he begged. "I have never done such a thing before. I have a horror of those men who sit down beside beautiful women in cafés and try to—" He stopped. "I had to talk to you because . . ." He broke off again, lifting his eyes to hers. "I felt we must know each other. That we *have* known each other, even before today."

"In some other life?" Marcella prompted, laughing.

He nodded, a smile replacing his serious frown, with the most devastating effect. "You believe in—" he pursed his lips, searching his memory. "Shirley MacLaine?"

"I'm starting to." She laughed. "Because you seem very familiar to me, too. But anyway, here we are, and we've introduced ourselves. I'm a writer. I write novels. I live in New York and I—"

"Marcella!" He cut her off, looking almost wounded. She had never seen that expression on a man's face before, half wonder, half sadness. "Maybe you will think me crazy to say so, but I feel we will be together for the rest of our lives. You may laugh, but I just wanted to say it to you now."

She did laugh, but it caught in her throat. Her heart turned upside down, but she reminded herself of her vow in the cathedral that morning, and she quickly turned the moment into a joke.

"Absolutely!" she cried. She would go along with the game. "And not just *this* life but the one after, when we come back as cats or fish!"

He peered at her a little worriedly, as if she had not come up to his expectations.

"Even outside the cathedral," he continued, "when I had no courage to speak to you, I left and I was, how do you say, beating myself?" he said.

" 'Kicking myself,' " she corrected.

"Yes!" he nodded. "How I was kicking myself for not

speaking. I thought 'This is a small island. I will see her again. If fate wishes it. . . .' "

"That's the way *I* think," she admitted. Fate! Yes, it was nice to believe that, but she had also promised to take charge of her own life now.

"And so now . . ." Santi looked at her happily and let his words trail away. He took a sip of coffee. "Now, there is nothing more to be said," he finished.

He let a silence rest over them and it was a relaxing, tranquil one, not the usual awkward silence between two strangers. She glanced sideways at his profile. He was either insane or the most romantic man she had ever met. What would Amy say? She could hear her voice: "You and your romances, Marcella! I give it three days!"

"I'm here with a friend," Marcella suddenly said. She glanced at her watch. "I promised to be back for lunch."

He was so beautiful, so nice, she wanted to get away and think about him. It wasn't possible that he was real—that would be too much on this strange morning.

"Of course!" He stood politely as she gathered her shopping bags. "But you will let me show you the island?"

"I—" She stuffed her postcards in her purse and glanced at the street to see if there was a taxi. "I'd love it, of course, but—"

"Tonight?" he asked. "I could come for you at eight. There would still be time to see Valldemossa before dark!"

She paused, flustered. Then she said, "Fine! Thank you. But you must not mind my friend," she warned. "She is very curious and she'll ask you many questions!"

He laughed, putting some money on the table. Then he hailed a taxi for her.

"I do not mind questions. I have a lot to ask you, too, Marcella!" He helped her into the taxi and closed the door.

"Thank you for the coffee," she said, through the window.

"Please!" He made a dismissive gesture. He told the driver, "Hotel Son Vida, *por favor*!" and waved as she rode away.

She twisted to look back through the window as the cab sped off, to make sure she had not dreamed him up.

〰〰〰

"Am I glad to see *you*!" Amy exploded when Marcella found her in the terrace buffet, piling her plate with salad. "I've just arranged the most exciting double date for us tonight. Green-eyed Spaniards! Longest eyelashes you ever saw and *great* bodies! They're picking us up at nine. What is this, *crab*?" She thrust a plate into Marcella's hands.

"What's with *you*? You look different."

Marcella held the plate, staring at her. She could see the sexual desperation on Amy's face. The reason you slept or had sex with man after man, stranger upon stranger, was because you never made *one* satisfying, good relation with *one* man! How could something so simple have taken so many years to sink in? she wondered. She let Amy pile salad onto her platter, following as she led the way to a table overlooking the bay of Palma below. Amy was wearing hot pink matador pants, and her big dark glasses slid down her nose as she swiveled in her seat to stare at Marcella.

"I've never seen you like this!" she said. "What happened?"

Marcella laughed, tucking a napkin across her lap as the waiter served wine.

"First thing this morning, I went into the cathedral, which is glorious!" she said.

Amy frowned, lifting a forkful of salad to her mouth.

"Then I prayed, Amy," Marcella told her.

Amy's fork froze. "I had no idea," she said, looking at her.

"Usually I'm not very religious," Marcella assured her. "But today I needed help."

"I thought you were having a marvelous time!" Amy cried. "Why didn't you knock on my door for a Valium?"

Marcella touched her hand. "Please don't take this personally, Amy," she said. "I suddenly realized how much I've hated what I've been doing here. Not just here, in New York too. I'm so glad I went into that cathedral. I lit a candle for my father and I took a good hard look at my life and I prayed."

"From the look on your face, no prayer was ever answered so quickly," Amy said, dazed. "What happened? Did you see your book in a store window?"

Marcella burst out laughing. She gave Amy a calm account of how she had met Santi. Amy heard her out, staring at her with a blank, amazed look. When Marcella stopped, she reached over for her plate.

"You're not going to eat one bite of that salad, are you?" she asked. She exchanged their plates and continued to eat.

"You don't believe me, do you?" Marcella cried. "And yet your novels are full of women meeting delightful men!"

"That's fiction!" Amy stated firmly. "Remember how hurt you were by that dumb little hairdresser? I don't like seeing you go to pieces over each casual fling. Hold on to your heart, Marcella. This one sounds too good to be true!"

"If he wants to show me some of the beautiful sights of this island, what can I lose?" Marcella asked.

"I just told you," Amy said grimly. "Your heart!"

After lunch, Marcella went to her room. Don't fall for him even before your first date, she scolded herself. Yet, just remembering the way he had looked into her eyes, she knew she could trust him. The feeling was safe and loving, insistent. She had imagined it, written about it, but never lived it before today. That feeling when you've met someone and have all day to look forward to seeing him. When it is still unknown and fresh and mysterious and something inside you knows it will be special. If she could only get down onto paper *exactly* how this felt, but life was already surpassing her talents; writing these feelings down would not do them justice. For the first time, for today at least, living was *better* than writing!

THIRTEEN

At two minutes to eight, Santi drove up to the hotel in a small orange car. Marcella was standing near the reception desk, watching. She saw him pull carefully to a stop and then glance in the rearview mirror to smooth down his hair, which had been dampened and combed back, making his dark eyes seem even larger. As he got out of the car, Marcella ran back to where Amy was sitting in the lounge on an overstuffed couch, before a bottle of champagne on ice.

"I've never been so terrified in my life," she confessed to Amy, taking a gulp of champagne. "You won't forget the code word?" They had established that if Amy mentioned Coca-Cola, it would mean she thought Santi was "the real thing."

"Do you think he'll see us?" she asked Amy, leaning forward for a view of the front revolving door.

"Relax!" Amy laughed. "He'll find you!"

Santi entered the lobby and Marcella stood and waved at his tall, hesitating figure. He wore a blazer over gray pants and an immaculate white shirt open at the neck. She was wearing a cool green linen suit with low-heeled suede sling-backs. She hurried over to him, and he took her hand and kissed it. Then she led him back to Amy.

"This is my very good friend Amy Jagger," she introduced him. "And this is my very *new* friend, Santi Roca," she told Amy.

"Any relation to Almond?" Amy gagged.

Santi brushed her hand with his lips. "I'm sorry?" he asked.

Amy patted him. "Don't mind me. I'm full of jokes!"

"I have read some of them," he informed her. "In a book of yours called *Zippers*. It was very interesting, very funny, and very well written."

Amy's eyes widened. "I knew it had been translated into Spanish, but I had no idea anyone had actually read it," she said. She looked across at Marcella. "Let's order some Coca-Cola," she suggested.

"We have champagne!" Marcella said, then stopped and smiled, taking Santi's arm, exchanging looks with Amy.

"Have you read Marcella's book, Santi?" Amy asked.

"I still have that pleasure to come," he said.

Amy's mouth hesitated over a wisecrack and Marcella caught her eye, willing her not to make it. They all sat down on the couch, and Amy poured them each a glass of champagne.

"So let's drink to all that tonight holds!" Amy proposed, holding her glass high. She eyed Marcella over the rim of her glass, rolling her eyes as if words failed her.

They bade Amy good-bye. Santi's car was modest, but he kept it so clean and strapped the safety belt so carefully over her shoulder that she felt she was about to be swept away on a magical trip.

As they descended the curving roads sloping down from the hotel, Santi told her, "We go to Valldemossa. Chopin stayed there for a winter in 1887. Unfortunately he picked a very bad winter and his tuberculosis became worse. George Sand was his lover and lived with him. In spite of his sickness he managed to write some of his finest pieces there."

"My son studies the piano," she said. "He'll be thrilled when I tell him about this."

"You have other children?" Santi asked.

"Sonia, who is seventeen, and Mark is eighteen."

"They live with you?" he asked.

She hesitated. "Yes," she said, feeling it would be too difficult to explain why Sonia had moved out.

They drove across some flat countryside, through fields of olive trees, before starting a winding ascent of another hill, almost a small mountain. It was eight-fifteen and the sunlight had become rosy gold. It shone through smoke from an occasional bonfire of dead branches, illuminating the landscape with a lavender, misty haze.

"We approach Valldemossa," Santi announced as they rounded a curve and the village came into view, high above them. From this angle and in this light, it appeared to be suspended in the sky.

"My God!" Marcella gasped. "I had no *idea*!"

The streets of old, beautifully preserved houses and churches were in wedding-cake layers, the tallest buildings boasting spires or bell towers, decoratively pointing to the sky. Small cypresses punctuated the buildings with their cigarlike shapes, and the houses were made from the same pink-colored rock as the mountains surrounding them. They all boasted the same worn, pink-tiled roofs.

The dusk was still a mauve mist when Santi parked the car by a monastery and they walked through the cloisters into the fragrant rose gardens where Chopin had once walked. A few solitary tourists lingered, but it felt as if they had the place to themselves. By the garden's boundary wall, they looked down at the valley beneath them, the aroma of bonfire smoke mingling with the perfume of roses and pines. Marcella breathed in deeply, closing her eyes. I never want to forget this scent, she told herself. Or this moment. She opened her eyes and found herself looking directly into Santi's gaze as he leaned next to her.

"It's the most beautiful scenery I've ever seen," she murmured. "And how delicious it smells! I would never have seen this if you hadn't brought me here. Thank you!"

His smile showed her how proud of his island he was. They walked around the sleepy little village as the sun went down and groups of people pulled chairs outside their homes to sit in the street and catch the cool evening air.

"Most visitors to Majorca believe it is all hotels, restaurants, and discotheques," he said. "In the nineteen-sixties, a tourist boom *did* spoil large parts of the coast, but we saved half of the island for ourselves and that is the half I will show you!"

The streets were cobbled, steep, and quite slippery from the years of wear. When she slipped in her new shoes, Santi's hand was there to gently guide her. Her elbow in his hand felt his warmth, a quiet, steady glow so different from the hands of the other men she had met.

As it got dark, he steered her toward a little old-fashioned bar paneled in wood, with round marble-topped tables and newspapers for customers to read.

"Have you tried our liqueur Palo?" he asked her as they sat. "You can find it only in Majorca. It is a strange drink. Visitors either like it very much or hate it. If you hate it, *I* shall drink it!" he assured her. When the drinks arrived, he held his much larger glass against hers.

"Why does yours have ice and lemon?" she asked.

"Because there are two ways to drink Palo. You should try both."

She sipped from her tiny glass. The liquid was thick, dark red, fiery and sweet. It spread a warm glow through her stomach.

"Mmm, I like it," she said. "It's very strong, though."

He offered his glass, politely untouched. "Now try mine!"

"I prefer yours!" she admitted. "It's less sweet and less thick."

Santi beamed. "That is the true Majorcan way," he nodded, pleased, and Marcella felt as if she had passed a test. He returned Marcella's drink to the waiter with instructions to improve it.

She leaned on the table, regarding his grave, handsome face. She could watch for hours the way his expressions changed with all the naiveté and earnestness of a child, yet with an adult's seriousness.

"Why are you so pleased when I like Majorcan things?" she asked him.

"I think I am more Majorcan than Spanish," he admitted, smiling. "Maybe because my mother was Majorcan and we spent a lot of time here during my youth—the entire summer, the Easter holiday, Christmas and New Year. It came to represent magic for me."

"And what makes Majorcans so different from the Spanish?" she asked.

He made a face. "That is difficult to explain without sounding conceited and superior," he prefaced. He frowned, playing with the red liquid in his glass, turning it this way and that. "We are an island people. I think we are calmer, quieter, and more controlled than the Spanish. We have always been more liberal, a little in advance. The Majorcan attitude to life is very tolerant and very discreet."

"Yes," she said. "I've noticed how nice Majorcans are. The waiters in my hotel always—"

"They are not Majorcans!" Santi said quickly. "I am sure that I am the first Majorcan you have met!"

She frowned. "How do you know?"

"Because the tourist industry is mostly staffed by Spanish from the mainland," he said. "The Majorcans are not so visible. You may see them in their stores, perhaps. But most are professionals and work in the banks or offices, or as doctors or lawyers. Families sold their land when the boom began thirty years ago. But they always kept back a house and an orchard for themselves, and they live quietly there."

It was after ten by the time they started driving toward Palma.

"You are hungry?" he asked her.

"Not at all."

Back in town, he pulled up in a quiet residential street. He ushered her through the entrance of a small modern building, across a white-marbled lobby. In the elevator he stood close but did not touch her. They got out on the top floor.

"I have two homes here," he explained, unlocking a door. "My house in Deya has been closed for the winter. I want you to see that, but during the daytime. This is where I stay when I come on business."

Their footsteps echoed on white tiles as they walked in. She glanced around curiously. She had had an image of Santi's apartment being like the three other shabby places she had slept in that week, perhaps a little cleaner. But as he switched on the lights, she gave a cry of surprise. It displayed a taste and bespoke an upbringing that answered the last remaining wariness in her. This was a person she could learn from, improve with. She swallowed the sudden lump in her throat as Santi pulled up the white blinds and opened doors onto a balcony, switching on the outside lamp to illuminate some cane chairs and tables. They walked out onto the balcony and looked at the view over Palma. In the distance, at the edge of a black sea, the cathedral was brightly floodlit, its spires white against the dark sky.

"To think we met in that tiny building this morning," Marcella said, pointing at it.

Santi disappeared into the kitchen and she heard the chink of glasses and bottles. He returned with a tray of olives, nuts, and a chilled bottle of wine. She looked back into the room as he uncorked the bottle. It was simple and unpretentious. The color came from the huge abstract paintings hung or leaning against the walls. Most were bold abstracts, although there was a freestyle landscape here and there, and one beautiful large canvas of a palm blowing in the wind, painted in vivid purples and blacks.

A long couch, a couple of armchairs, a glass coffee table, and two reading lamps completed the somewhat ascetic room. A quirky collection of small sculptures, shells, polished stones, and fossils filled a set of shelves on a wall. A facing bookshelf was heavy with art books and novels.

She indicated the paintings. "Are these the artists you deal with?" she asked.

"Most of them, yes. You like them?"

She looked carefully at each painting as he poured wine. They walked back into the room, holding their glasses.

"I like them all!" she laughed. "You have good taste. Why did you choose to work with art?"

Santi smiled. "It was art or religion—which would you have chosen?" He laughed. "I decided art was *more* religious, *more* spiritual than the church!"

She stared at him. "Were you seriously thinking of entering the church?"

He nodded. "When I was growing up, it was considered quite a smart thing to have a priest in the family. My father worked for the local government in Barcelona. I think my mother imagined me as a bishop, but I wanted to be an artist. There was no money for art studies, so I made myself believe the church was right for me. Just as I was about to register as a novice, my aunt died and left all her land to me, her only nephew. I sold it off, keeping just the house in Deyá. And suddenly I could afford to study art at the university."

"Wonderful!" Marcella clapped her hands.

Santi nodded. "Then, after all my studies, I realized that I was *not* an artist after all. I wanted to stay near the world of art, so I set up a gallery."

"Where?" she asked. "Barcelona?"

He took a sip of wine, nodding. "The most unfashionable part," he laughed, "but it is light and spacious. It has been hard work establishing it, but for me, art is still better than religion. And there is nothing so thrilling as to find good new artists and getting them established."

"How do you do that?" she asked.

"Oh, if I believe in an artist, I can be quite persuasive," he smiled. "We have yuppies in Spain now, you know? They are starting to collect art. Here, I visit hotels, banks, restaurants—any place that might need some paintings. I exhibit at the Madrid art fair, too."

He sat down next to her on the sofa, taking her hand. "I want to hear about *your* life!" he said.

She lay back against the cushion, holding his hand. "Oh God, Santi—how to sum *that* up? Sometimes I feel I'm living one of my own novels. . . ." But she told him. About her marriage. About Harry and the children. About the struggle to find time to write her first novel and the incredible moment when she was offered a contract. She did not mention the million dollars, not wanting to scare him. He listened attentively to her, pressing her hand as she made a point, making an agonized face when she told him how Harry had taken the children. She had never spoken so easily to a man. Conversation with men across Amy's dinner table had felt more like squaring off, making the right moves. She tried to describe to Santi the difference between American men and Europeans. Then they discussed the advantages of living in New York or Barcelona or Majorca, almost as if they had decided they would be living together.

"Marcella," he said, bringing her fingers up to touch his lips. "I cannot imagine you in Majorca before today.

Where did you go? What did you do? Last night, for example?"

He leaned forward eagerly and she frowned, pretending to try to remember. Last night, she and Amy had returned to Omar.

"I, oh—" she stammered. "Oh, what the hell, Santi, I might as well tell you. We went to a club called Omar's. Do you know it?"

He smiled, puzzled. "Isn't it a place where men go to pick up women?"

She nodded. "Amy wanted to go there, so I—" She stopped, looking him straight in the eyes. "*I* wanted to go," she said.

His eyes bore into hers. "Why would *you* go to such a place?" he asked.

"Maybe I thought I'd meet you there," she said simply.

He laughed. "But I have never been in there! I would more likely be in Palma Cathedral!"

"So religion still means a lot to you?" she questioned.

He shrugged. "I am like most people: when I am unhappy, I ask God to help me!"

She laughed aloud. "Sounds like me! So what were you unhappy about today?"

He became very grave. "What were *you* unhappy about today?" he asked her. "Why were you at Omar's last night and the next morning in a cathedral?"

She made a face. "Probably because I had such a bad time at Omar's!" she laughed. She saw from his expression that this wasn't the moment to kid around. "Okay," she said. "I'll tell you if you tell me first."

He poured some more wine and took a sip of his.

"I am not frightened of being alone, Marcella . . ." he began. "I have good friends. I am like a father to some of my young artists. I can enjoy reading and listening to music—"

She nodded. "I can, too, but I'm so tired of doing things alone!"

"These last few years," he went on, "when I come to Majorca it is usually in the spring and summer . . ." He broke off, looking up at her. "I was wondering whether I would ever allow myself to fall in love again." His voice was quiet and serious. "My divorce hurt me very much. I was very much in love with my wife. She was a beautiful person, inside *and* out. Like I can see *you* are!"

"Santi!" she protested.

"No! I *feel* these things." He touched his heart. *"Here."* He made a throwaway gesture. "My divorce was several years ago. Time to forget, no?"

She nodded and he took her face lovingly in his hands.

"Why were you looking for a man last night?" he demanded. "A beautiful, intelligent woman like you—"

"Don't say that!" she cut him off. "Just this morning, I suddenly realized I've been living my life all wrong. I was trying to figure it all out in the cathedral when I saw you. I felt so ashamed—"

"No!" He put his arm around her. "Do not feel ashamed! We are together now and you never need to feel ashamed or desperate or lonely again. It doesn't matter how we met—maybe God helped us? I was too proud to go to bars or discotheques—that is not my style. Besides, we have a saying in Spanish that you cannot look for love, love finds *you!*" He moved nearer and kissed her gently. She closed her eyes tightly against his soft touch, against the tears that suddenly threatened to overwhelm her. She wanted to stay enfolded in his arms forever, but she found herself violently trembling, her teeth chattering as if she had a fever.

"It's all right," Santi whispered, calming her. "We have found each other, Marcella. . . ."

He held her until the trembling stopped and she had swallowed the tears and what seemed like a volcano of grief about to surge up in her.

"It is very late," Santi said, standing up. "Your friend will be worried." He reached for her hand, helping her to her feet. She watched him dazedly as he closed the balcony doors and picked up his car keys.

"You want to take me back to my hotel?" she asked stupidly. It hadn't occurred to her that they would do anything but go into his bedroom and make love. Her body had been ready for it and she felt almost disappointed. He drove her to the hotel in silence. She already felt sick with anxiety that he would not call her tomorrow, like all the other men she had so far met here. If he didn't, she vowed, he would be the last man she would consider attempting a relationship with. She would rely on casual sex and forget the fact that men and women usually shared their lives.

"I come for you at ten o'clock tomorrow," he said, breaking in on her thoughts. "I have a lot to show you. Please be ready!"

"Yes," she said. "I'll be ready."

When they stopped he got out of the car to see her up the steps of the hotel. There, he kissed her lingeringly on her mouth. He had soft, sensitive lips and kissing him so chastely was a new and different experience for her. She wanted to feel his tongue in her mouth, but he wasn't in a hurry like all her previous men. Just imagining how he would take his time when they finally, wonderfully made love made her feel weak. Even thinking of sex with him felt a little wrong, it was all so veiled with romantic love, and yet the sex appeal was there strongly, behind everything. He broke away from her, looking into her eyes with his smoldering dark gaze.

"Pack a bag with overnight things," he said. "Just in case we stay in Deya. I am hoping you'll fall in love with it, as I have. . . ."

"Thank you for showing me that magic village, Santi," she said. "I've had one of the most beautiful evenings of my life."

That was quite true. In her room she undressed automatically, getting into the tee-shirt she slept in, although she knew she would not sleep. There had been no light under the door of Amy's room, and Marcella hung a DO NOT DISTURB sign on her door, just in case Amy took it into her head to knock on her door at four o'clock to hear how the evening had gone. It was the kind of thing Amy would do, and she suddenly realized she didn't want to hear any of Amy's cynical, mocking advice about men or sex or love. All this was happening to her because of Amy, because of Amy's faith in her, so she tried not to blame her for the negative aspects of her new life. Nevertheless, today she had outgrown Amy, and she now saw Amy's life-style as something she had no wish to emulate. She turned out the light, resting on her back in bed. Her mind did not stop whirling until dawn came up over the mountains and the city and she sank into an unconsciousness full of the mystery and adventure of her future.

Santi called her at nine, waking her from this deep sleep.

"I just wanted to make sure you would be awake," he said.

She yawned sleepily. "I'm glad you called. I'll start getting ready. . . ." To avoid Amy's questioning gaze, she ordered coffee from room service. She smiled to herself, imagining all that Amy would say of a man who had not pulled her into bed on their first night. Then, packing an overnight bag, she slipped a note under Amy's door telling her she might be away for a couple of nights.

Santi drew up in front of the hotel at ten, looking as if he had come fresh from the shower. He leapt from the car to embrace her, and she knew she had not exaggerated all that had happened last night: he *was* the one! The one she had always hoped to meet.

"You would like to see my house?" he asked her. "We go to Deya?"

"Yes!" She hugged him. "Yes, please!"

Deya was perched spectacularly on a mountain, with other mountains towering even higher behind it. The village was ancient, the only hotel an elegant old farmhouse converted into a deluxe inn. There were no high rises, no billboards, no neon; the village had been very carefully preserved, and it was easy to believe one had stepped back in time two or three hundred years but for the modern faces of German and English tourists.

"My mother was born here," Santi explained. "It was a quiet place before some English writers and artists discovered it in the nineteen-forties. They turned it into an artists' colony and it became quite elegant. Like your Greenwich Village! Now my house is valuable, but I would never sell it."

To reach the house, they took a curving road that climbed high around the back of the village so they could look down on the faded tiled roofs. In the midday sun, the scent of orange blossom was strong, mingling deliciously with that of the pines. The house stood in its own gardens leafy with trees.

"Figs, almonds, oranges, lemons, and clementines!" Santi pointed out proudly. A rusty old bell rang as Santi pushed open the gate and beckoned her through. He unlocked the door and shivered. In spite of its being a warm day, the interior was icy. Santi rushed to throw open the shutters, letting in the warm air, rubbing his hands together.

"These thick stone walls keep out the heat," he explained. "I shall light a fire."

She looked around, enchanted. There was a damp smell that she found unbearably reminiscent of her childhood—an aunt's apartment in Brooklyn. The rooms were whitewashed and the floors were the original stone flagging. Dressers and wooden chests inlaid with marquetry hugged the walls; huge mirrors thickly framed in mahogany were hung at an angle to the wall, their silvery aged surfaces reflecting the floors. It was the country effect that hundreds of American decorators aimed for, Marcella thought, smiling, but that only loved family pieces and time can achieve.

Santi pulled her into the different rooms like an excited boy.

"Look at this kitchen!" He took her hand and led her in. "This is the original stove, no gas. Just wood to be laid underneath and lit. What would they say to that in America, Marcella?"

"They'd love it," she said.

It was his elegant taste that made the house so beautiful, she realized, for the few modern sofas and armchairs had been carefully chosen so as not to clash, covered in neutral fabrics so that they were almost invisible, letting the old furniture and wooden beams stand out in contrast. He grabbed a bottle of olive oil from the kitchen and dragged her out a side door into the garden. At the first fig tree, he stopped, pouring a little oil into his hand.

"This is what we do to make the figs grow fat," he told her, massaging the oil into the green, unripe fruit. "Here." He held out the bottle. "You do it, too!"

She poured some oil into her palm and massaged a fig, feeling slightly ridiculous and giggling.

"You must do them *all*!" he urged, laughing.

She gave up after another five, and he handed her a towel to wipe her hands. Then he took her on a tour of the garden, pointing out each tree. There was a delightful overgrown pond, almost a swimming pool, with a huge tree next to it, around which a rough wooden table had been built. White wrought-iron chairs were scattered about, and a decorative old lamppost had been erected to cast its light over evening meals.

"Santi! Santi!" a high little voice called, and Marcella looked around to see who had found them.

"Oh, it is my neighbor," Santi explained, running into the road where a tiny, bent old lady with a face as wrinkled as a walnut stood waving. He beckoned to Marcella to join them and introduced her. The old lady took Marcella's hand, gripping it hard, studying her curiously. Then she broke into a toothless grin and said something very quickly to Santi in Spanish, cackling after it like a kind little witch.

"She's known me all my life," Santi explained.

The woman babbled another fast torrent of Spanish, indicating Marcella, and Santi laughed and went red. He put his arm around Marcella protectively, leading her back into the house.

"What did she say?" Marcella asked.

"She said we looked as if we belonged together," he told her. He glanced sideways at her and frowned.

She clasped him to her. "*I* think we do, too," she said.

The fire Santi built was of dry olive-tree branches and pine cones, and it soon warmed up the living room. He switched on electric heaters in the other rooms. She breathed in the aroma of the smoldering twigs, helping Santi to toss pine cones into the flames.

"You would like to spend the night here?" he asked her, raising his eyebrows.

It was said so innocently that she knew they would have separate rooms if she requested them. But she wouldn't request them. They would belong together tonight. Tonight Santi would make love to her and she would know for sure what she already knew: that they were destined to be together.

"I'd like to spend the night here," she nodded, smiling.

He was building the fire and he looked back at her. "It is a very simple life here, Marcella," he said, as if warning her.

"Yes," she agreed. "Simple and beautiful."

He took her to the sleepy little village, even smaller than Valldemossa. It had only one main street, containing a few stores and two art galleries. They lunched at the typical restaurant where old ladies and very young boys brought them bowls of a thick bread and vegetable broth.

"It is *Sopas mallorquinas*—poor people's soup," Santi explained, watching her eat. "Its ingredients are cheap, but I think it is one of the most delicious dishes in the world, and if you have a little money, you can break an egg into it!" He laughed. "Now it has become once again chic to eat it!"

The peasant food seemed to trigger off ancestral longings in Marcella for the Italian food of her family. Santi grinned as he watched her attempt to finish the enormous bowlful. Dessert was a piece of fresh white cheese covered in mountain honey, followed by a tiny cup of strong black coffee. She sat back, watching his face as they talked. They had so much to tell each other, stories of their childhoods, of their first marriages, of their friends and parents.

In the afternoon they drove further down the coast to a very grand mansion built by an Austrian duke one hundred and fifty years ago, looking out over a beautiful, unspoilt stretch of coastline and deep blue sea. There was a small domed "folly" of white marble in the garden, which they stood under for a moment before exploring the elegant estate.

"You like to cook?" he asked, as they drove back toward Deya in the early evening.

She turned to him. "Sure!" she said. "What should we cook? I'm great at pasta!"

"How about chicken?" he asked.

"Without gas?" she laughed. "What'll we do, barbecue it?"

"Of course!" he said. "I shall buy a chicken in Deya and some potatoes to bake. And some wine. You will like that?"

She held his eyes before he turned back to the road. "I will like it," she said.

By nine o'clock, Santi was building a fire on a blackened patch of earth near the house, spreading chicken pieces rubbed with garlic, salt, and oil over a grill he placed on top of the flames. Marcella rinsed a lettuce and peeled an avocado and produced a salad as near to her usual one as she could get. The lamp was switched on and two cushions were placed on the iron chairs. The wine was placed in the freezer compartment of the refrigerator, a bottle of champagne next to it. Dessert was to be a bowl of bright red cherries.

After dinner, they sipped apple schnapps, gazing at the embers of the fire, the smoldering smell of charcoal mingling with the aroma of orange blossoms, which intensified at night, like jasmine.

"We will stay here tonight?" Santi looked across questioningly. She almost laughed because he had no idea how to flirt. She glanced at her watch.

"Well, it *is* after one," she told him. "And you did ask me the same question this afternoon. And I said yes then!"

"You are already laughing at me?" he asked mournfully. He looked at her with so much love in his eyes that she stood to lean over him, kissing his mouth.

"Never, my darling." She gave him a meaningful look, then went inside the house and turned down the bed he had made up that afternoon. She undressed, dabbing perfume on her body, lying down in the slightly damp bed, waiting for him. This was the wedding night she had always pictured for herself, albeit in a different setting! She could hear Santi as he stamped out the embers in the garden and closed the shutters.

He entered the bedroom and sat down on the bed, looking at her with such a sweet gaze that her tears began almost at once. He removed his clothes and slipped into bed beside her. When he took her in his arms, their bodies simply melted together. Nothing about his body seemed strange to her, as if they had made love many times before. Now she could finally experience what sex and love together were like.

"I've searched for you all my life, Marcella," he whispered.

"And if I had written a description of the perfect man for me, he would not have been as wonderful as you," she told him.

Moonlight flowing through the shutters illuminated his eyes. So this was how it happened, she thought. Just as you gave up, just as you renounced men and sex and love, you met a man like Santi. Sex was not something urgent, to be grabbed at hungrily; she would have been content to re-

main in his arms like this all night. Each time she looked
into his glistening eyes, each time she took his head between her hands like a blind person memorizing the sculp-
tured feel of him, her eyes overflowed. He was holding her
as if she were the most desirable, precious woman in the
world, as if he had been awarded some unhoped-for prize.
She had needed just one man like him to make her feel
valuable.

They made love as if they had been born on opposite
sides of the world to be joined at this moment. Her drawn-
out, suspended pleasure was such as she had never known
before, almost too intense to be enjoyed, needing to be
distilled by time, by this new love, by her coming to terms
with finding him.

All the emotions she had kept inside her over the past
years seemed to surge up, demanding to be released. She
remembered how as a child she had cut her knee at school
and how brave she had been all day until her father had
arrived. One look at his loving face and she had burst into
tears. And that was how she now felt with Santi as she wept
with relief.

"You'll never let me go?" she heard herself sob, clinging
to him.

His warm hand stroked her back. "We will not let each
other go," his deep voice promised.

She sobbed in his arms for a long time, until he asked
her, "But tell me, Marcella my darling, *why* are you crying?" making her laugh and shake her head. "I don't
know!" she admitted.

He lay under her tears for an hour. Finally, she cried
herself out and slept.

She woke throughout the night to the wonderful feeling
of Santi holding her from behind, his lips pressed against
the back of her neck, his warm breath on her shoulders.
Each time, she thought, *I've found him!* enjoying that surge
of happiness. She turned sleepily to embrace him, inhaling
the smell of sun from their bodies. She had found a man
with enough tenderness to caress her for hours, his touch
sweetly reminiscent of the way her father had caressed her
as a child.

In the morning, she awoke refreshed and light, as if an
enormous weight had been lifted from her. She could hear

cocks crowing and dogs barking. Santi slept soundly. She pulled on a robe and wandered into the garden wet with dew, her mind alive with thoughts of their future, of how she would fit into his life or he into hers. A new life had offered itself to her and, yes, she could see herself living in this peaceful setting, wandering down each day to the village for bread, tomatoes, and eggs, writing her next book, which would be set in Majorca, about a thirty-five-year-old woman meeting a man like Santi and falling in love with him and his island.

As she breathed in the morning air from the mountains, she noticed the bent old lady in the next garden examining her trees and plants, followed by several curious cats. The woman looked up and waved to Marcella, flashing her a toothless grin and returning to her rounds.

At eight, Marcella prepared coffee for Santi and took it to him in bed, watching him sleep for a few moments before gently awakening him.

"Stay with me here, forever," he said immediately. "I love you."

"Oh, I *could,* darling." She set the breakfast tray to one side and cuddled up to him. "But forever is a long time. . . ."

"Maybe." He kissed her. "But for us, forever begins tonight." He gently kissed her face and neck, and she closed her eyes tightly against the tears that threatened again. Forever begins tonight! Only a man who did not speak perfect English would dream of saying something so beautiful, she thought. She knew, even as he uttered the words, that it would have to be the title of her next book and that it would be her most romantic book ever! Her last restraint, her last wariness, fell away from her. So it really does exist, she marveled, this world I thought I had invented! Now I'm actually living it! She clung to him as he undid her robe, and for the first time in her life, as she turned toward him, she knew she was not giving just her body to a man, but her self.

Santi was a marvelous guide. They made one trip back to the hotel for more clothing, Marcella assuring Amy she was in safe hands, and then, during the next three days, he brought the island to vivid life for her.

He showed her the toylike electric railway that wound its way through the mountains, from Palma to the bustling port of Sóller on the other side of the island. At Pollensa they climbed the dreamlike staircase of three hundred and sixty-five steps—one for each day of the year—and scaled the cliffs overlooking the dark blue sea at Formentor.

He rarely touched her in public, but as they stood alone in Formentor, at the top of a rough-hewn cliff on this desolate, beautiful corner of the island, he placed his arm around her. Everywhere they went, orange blossoms scented the air and the olive and almond trees seemed to watch them approvingly. She would say, "I'm not used to being this happy. I keep thinking I'll wake up!"

They returned to Deya for three more nights. She wondered if she would be able to extend her trip. Santi had some business to do in Palma, and she used that as an excuse to return to the hotel and see Amy. He dropped her at the Son Vida, agreeing to meet her for lunch at two-thirty in the Palma café where they had first met.

There was a message in her pigeonhole from Mark, asking her to call him in New York. A pang of guilt sounded in her: for the first time since his birth, she had not thought about her son. She wondered if he would be very disappointed if she decided to stay on another week. She waited until two o'clock to place the call, so it would be eight a.m. in New York. That would make her a little late for lunch with Santi. Reality was already calling her back.

Amy was sitting rather forlornly at the pool, reduced to flirting with a sixty-five-year-old Brazilian sporting a diamond pinky ring. He spoke little English and Amy was having trouble communicating.

"I thought we made a pact—no pinky rings?" Marcella said, sneaking up behind her.

"Marcella!" Amy jumped to her feet and hugged her. "God, I've missed you! Ramón Ramirez, this is my dear friend Marcella Winton. Has it all been wonderful? To die from?" she asked, her eyes wide with curiosity.

"I was having a great time, until this!" She held out the telephone message.

Amy glanced at it. "Probably just wants to know where his clean socks are," she said.

It took forever for two o'clock to come. Marcella filled the two hours describing Deya and how they had massaged the green figs with olive oil and the little old bent lady down the road and the damp bed. Amy listened with her special glassy-eyed expression, as if Marcella were describing life on the moon.

"Did he take you to good restaurants? Nightclubs?" she prompted.

Marcella shook her head. "We just enjoyed his home and some very modest little restaurants that serve Majorcan food. Very pleasant and simple . . ."

Amy shrugged. "He's quite a find," she finally said. She continued to stare expectantly at Marcella, an unspoken question on her face. Marcella tried not to laugh. She knew Amy was longing to know about sex but could not quite bring herself to ask right out. If she had asked, Marcella would not have said much. She had loved being held by Santi, being kissed by him, making love with him. But after that first wonderful time when it had almost been too good to enjoy, some kind of barrier had been erected—by *her*—cutting off the ultimate pleasure, keeping it dangling, cruelly, out of reach. She excused herself from Amy's inquisitive look to go to her room and pack a new overnight bag. She was much too scared of what was happening to begin to express to Amy her fear that by using Members for uninvolved sex she might have destroyed some ability in herself to enjoy sex accompanied by love.

She stood on her balcony staring down at the bay of Palma, so blue and clear in the midday sunlight. With the sun blazing down on her like this, her fears seemed grotesque and ridiculous.

At two, the hotel operator put through her call to New York.

"Mom?" Mark's voice crackled excitedly through the line. "I hope I'm not disturbing your trip. Having fun?"

"It's paradise, Mark!" she cried. "I can't wait for you to see it! We visited a monastery where Chopin composed some of his music. His piano is still there and you can actually feel his presence!"

"Wow! I'd love to be there with you both. Give my love to Amy."

"I will. Are you all right, darling?" she asked. "Why did you call? Just to say hello?"

"No, I wanted to tell you my news," he said. "You're not going to love it, but try to be happy for me. I'm taking over from Cole at the Carlyle next week! Cole arranged an audition and they liked me! It will only be for a couple of weeks, while he takes his mother to Palm Springs. I didn't want you to think I snuck off behind your back to do it, because . . ."

"No, that's wonderful, Mark. It's incredible." Perhaps if she were understanding about this he would give her some understanding for Santi. Then she wondered why she felt she had to justify Santi.

"I open three days after you get back!" Mark was saying. "Sonia's promised to bring some of the fashion crowd, and I thought you and Amy could dredge up a few literary types. You know, to applaud and yell 'Bravo!' and 'Encore!' "

"Of course!" she cried, her heart sinking as she realized she would not be able to prolong her stay. "I'll get Amy to call Norman Mailer right now! Are you very excited, darling?"

"I'm *paralyzed*!" he laughed. "Maybe this will help me with my stage fright?"

"I can't picture you in white tie and tails, crooning Gershwin, Mark, but I wouldn't miss it for the world," she assured him.

She hung up after they had said good-bye, feeling oddly guilty.

She relished the last few days with Santi with an even keener edge of pleasure. They hardly mentioned the future, but if they did it was as if they would one day be sharing a life. He had agreed to shuffle his commitments so he could visit New York in three weeks' time. They would play it by ear. She vaguely imagined spending the summer in Deya, writing a new book, Santi returning to New York with her in the fall, then zigzagging between Europe and New York the way she imagined many people did.

They stayed in his town apartment for the last two nights. She watched him as he walked out onto his balcony each morning to water his plants or inspect a new leaf, then coming back in to prepare coffee for them, or to run downstairs to the bakery for fresh *ensaimadas.* Everything he did had a touch of grace to it. She watched him as she would a dancer or a cat, for the pleasure of his movements. She loved the way he ducked under a cold running tap when he got hot, then shook his head like a dog, sleeking back his raven-black hair with his fingers, making her laugh as he resembled Rudolph Valentino for a few minutes while his hair dried.

She browsed through his large collection of record albums, rejoicing when she found one that she had bought as a teenager, too. He also had Balinese, Japanese, and Indian music. The stacks of novels showed his taste for serious European writers whose names she did not know. And staying with him, she marveled at his calm, unhurried pace, whether preparing the table for lunch or dressing to go out.

"The Spanish sense of time," she said, and laughed.

"No," he corrected her gently. "It's the Majorcan sense of *calma.* They also call this the *'isla de la calma'!"*

If an American had been as proud of his country, she would have found it quaintly old-fashioned, even irritating, but in Santi this pride seemed natural and beautiful to her. When he invited some Majorcan friends to meet her one evening, serving drinks on the balcony, she understood better. They were reserved, dignified, rather formal people whose grandparents had left them land that they had sold years ago, each holding on to one little house in the mountains or by the sea, called a *finca.* Each one had a *finca* in the family, for relaxing in at weekends or during the hot summer months. Most of Santi's Majorcan friends were fellow gallery owners or artists, with a sprinkling of professional types like bankers and doctors. She liked their reserve and discretion, but she especially liked the way they accepted her so readily, speaking in their broken English or trying to understand her Spanish-Italian. She was Santi's friend, and if Santi had chosen her, it was obviously all right with them. She felt very proud by his side, helping to serve drinks, feeling like part of a couple.

Their last day together came so soon it took her by surprise. Sitting on his balcony, eating breakfast, he asked her what she would like to do.

"Let's say good-bye to Deya," she suggested. "I'd like to photograph you in the garden of the house and have lunch at the little restaurant in town, check up on the figs' progress, see the bent old lady . . ."

He laughed, happy that she loved Deya too. "All right. Give me a couple of hours in town, and we go at noon."

It was a perfect day and they drove up into the mountains under a cloudless sky. He took her on a little detour beyond Deya to point out a forbidding monastery on a hill a couple of miles outside the town.

"They take guests—people who wish to make a retreat," he told her, pointing up at it. "That is where I shall go if you leave me."

She looked up at it curiously, not sure if he was joking. "Don't bother to make a reservation," she laughed, kissing him. "I have no intention of leaving you!"

They passed another magical day, Santi clearing up the garden while she stuffed dead leaves and branches into plastic bags to be left outside for the garbage collection. They bade a formal good-bye to the little kind old witch next door. They drove back to Palma, and that night, Marcella began to feel emotions she had not felt before. They took her by surprise, these intimations of how much she would miss him, of how emotionally dependent she had become so quickly, on a man she had known for just over one week.

"It's as if you've always been part of my life," she murmured, lying in his arms that night. "I felt that way when I first saw you outside the cathedral, Santi. As if we were related somehow, as if you were in my family!"

"I feel the same," his deep voice agreed.

"I don't know how I'll get through the next three weeks without you," she told him. "We'll speak every day?"

"Maybe just one minute each night," he allowed. "It is very expensive to call America. . . ."

She wanted to say she would call him for an hour each morning and each night, but she had been careful about not forcing her wealth upon him. She realized how proud he was, and she was already planning how to play down the chauffeured Rolls and Central Park South apartment.

On this last night in Palma, his embrace was so loving, so warmly secure, that sex was somehow beside the point.

She could feel Santi was trying hard to pleasure her, almost exhausting her body with his attentions.

"I'm sorry, my darling," she finally had to whisper. "I love you too much and I'm too sad about leaving. I suddenly don't care about sex."

He achieved his pleasure when she urged him to, panting softly in her face, kissing her gratefully.

"You *will* be satisfied with me, Marcella," he promised her later. "My body knows it. We feel so right together. Sex between us has not even begun yet—the real sex! Someone as sensitive as you needs time to get used to a man."

"Yes," she murmured, stroking his head as he fell asleep. If only you knew how much time I usually need, she thought. A whole two minutes to get used to a stranger. She tried to picture Members' theater, inwardly exulting at never having to go there again. She refused to worry about sex between them; she knew it would be all right. She calmed herself by listening to his heartbeat. When he arrived in New York next month she would be ready for him, her body starved for sex. They would simply melt together again as they had that first time before she had erected this ridiculous barrier, this defense against a love so strong it threatened something within her.

The next morning she lay in bed beside him, listening to the early-morning sounds of Palma awakening. A nearby cock crowed, a dog's barking joining the noise. Church bells rang, then stopped abruptly. Noisy motorbikes zoomed down their street, and mothers called children for school. It was eight o'clock. She was leaving with Amy at one. She slipped out of bed, pulling the sheet over Santi's shoulders as he slept.

On the small balcony, she squinted against the sun. She could see the spiky cathedral towers rising out of the morning mist. When she turned, she saw the purple mountains looming, the hills around them dotted with *fincas* and pines. Down the street, the small café was noisily pulling up its shutters and she knew that in an hour or two old men would sit at the outside table, reading their newspapers, sipping *café con leche* and playing dominoes. She said good-bye to it all as the sun rose higher, yellow and warm, promising a hot day. Had she missed Manhattan? she asked herself. No, not at all. But she missed Santi already, a sick feeling in her stomach reminding her of their parting. He would visit New York, she reassured herself, in three weeks. He would meet her children and win their hearts. Her thoughts got a little hazy at this point. Mark's approval would be necessary, of course; she had decided that from the start; but he was bound to love Santi, too. As Santi tiptoed up behind her now, clasping her in his warm, sleepy arms, she thought, Who could not love him?

At Palma airport that afternoon, she found herself wanting to bawl like a baby. Only by hanging on to the fact that they would be together in three weeks' time could she control herself. She made herself laugh when Santi presented them with a huge *ensaimada* of the kind sold at the airport in cardboard cartons and carried home by all the tourists.

They shared the longest kiss she had ever tasted, her lips clinging to his as if seeking reassurance that everything would go according to their plans, their dreams. She could not help imagining plane crashes and car accidents destroying their love story.

"Okay now, lovebirds, you really do have to say goodbye!" Amy told them when their flight was called.

Santi's arms reluctantly let her go as Amy tugged her toward passport control. She turned to him to nuzzle her nose in his ear for the last time. He watched from behind the barrier as she left him.

"Three weeks!" she called to him. "Just three weeks, my darling!"

"Okay, now we really have to board the plane!" Amy pulled them apart for the last time. Marcella took one last look at him, and tears began to stream down her face. She gave a little wave and let Amy guide her to the carpeted passage leading to the plane.

Amy tossed her hand baggage into the luggage rack and arranged her white angora cardigan over her seat so she could nestle into it like a cat. Marcella mopped her wet face.

"We'll order champagne the moment they open the bar," Amy promised, squeezing by into her seat.

"Amy, you're incredible!" Marcella tried to laugh, buckling her belt. "There's nothing in life you believe can't be fixed up by drinking, eating, or sex."

"Well, you must admit, they blur the edges!" Amy said.

"I don't want my edges blurred," Marcella said. "I want to remember every moment of this trip, crystal clear. Even the misery of the return!"

She hardly heard Amy's chatter during the flight to Madrid, through their wait for the New York plane and their flight to Kennedy Airport. She was trying to picture Santi and what he was doing now, what he was eating in his little apartment, who he was seeing in town. Thank God she had taken dozens of photographs of him. He belonged to her now, and she resented anything that happened to him without her presence. She spent an hour of the flight writing him a long letter to mail the moment they arrived. It was the first love letter she had ever written, she realized, amazed. What would she show him in Manhattan? she wondered, addressing the envelope. Would they visit the tourist sights, like the Empire State Building? Or would they stay in the apartment all day, talking and making love? No, she thought, too awkward. With Mark in and out. She would have to book Santi into the hotel down the street so they would have their privacy.

"As I see it," Amy said, as if reading her thoughts, emptying a packet of peanuts into her mouth, "your only problem now is Mark!"

FOURTEEN

All eyes in the Carlyle Lounge were on the singer in the spotlight. Mark sat at a white piano in tuxedo, wing collar, and white tie, seeming older than his eighteen years, singing Gershwin songs in a melodious tenor that hypnotized the chic, hip audience. Marcella could hardly believe the transformation. Mark was a born performer. His chiseled face, straight nose, and full lips, his combed-back dark hair and poised bearing, suggested a mysterious new star. And the audience were congratulating themselves at being in on the debut of a show-business career that would "buzz" the industry, a star about to be born. The Gershwin songs he was interpreting in such a fresh way took on subtly neurotic overtones that Gershwin had surely never intended. The innocent emotions of the 1930s songs made the audience smile knowingly. They applauded wildly after each song, especially for "The Girl I Love," which everyone knew had been written as "The Man I Love." Mark's no-tricks delivery kept the emotion true.

No one was more spellbound than Marcella, who shared a prominent table with Sonia and whose face glowed with love for Santi, for Mark, for all mankind, on this special evening. The different emotions she felt passed transparently over her features, like rich layers of a watercolor, deepening her beauty. She had wanted to take Mark's performance in stride and dismiss it, but his artistry was forcing her to admire him. She watched and listened to the love songs with a particular passion in her gaze. Santi would be with her in eighteen days and she interpreted all the lyrics in that light.

"Where did he find that getup?" Sonia whispered. "Charivari?"

"Cole Ferrer lent him everything," Marcella murmured, "including his music. And *you* supplied the instant fans! Thank you so much, darling."

Sonia shrugged carelessly. She was dressed in a long, clinging black dress that somehow emphasized her youth although it was much too old for her. Her behavior was artificial and stylized, and Marcella felt awkward sitting with her after all that had happened. For the first time, she wondered whether Sonia's exaggerated behavior was the result of a few deep snorts of coke. She glanced at Sonia as she played self-consciously with a long cigarette holder. Why would Sonia be any different from the other fast movers in her glittery world?

She had come through on her promise to deliver up a generous handful of models, photographers, and journalists in various degrees of dress-up. Sprinkled throughout the cocktail lounge, they added the fashionable glitter essential to this kind of debut. The music folk predominated, however, and they stared at Marcella, trying to place her, intrigued by her glowing looks. Her Majorcan tan suited her. Santi had brought her body to life with his love. Pleasantly rounded, her full bosom and hips perfectly proportioned, she possessed a new sensual assurance. A man, a beautiful man, loved her, and that did more for her than any of Amy's beauty treatments. Her close-fitting Chanel dress was a deep red. Her jewels were small, adding just the right amount of richness to her ears, wrists, and neck. She kept her eyes on Mark, concentrating on every nuance of his performance. He reached the end of a bittersweet Cole Porter medley and her eyes glazed as if she were drifting into a dream.

The audience broke into loud applause and she shook

herself from her reverie to add to it, Mark standing to acknowledge the cheers. Sonia jumped to her feet and her friends in the audience followed her lead as if they were playing Simon says. Sonia held her hands above her head, and her friends followed suit. Soon everyone had been urged into a standing ovation.

Mark smiled the guileless, spectacular smile of a child. He deserved his success. Facing front, he was of a movie-star handsomeness, exaggerated by his eyes, which, under a spotlight, revealed their deep sapphire glow. He bowed deeply, thanking them, then made a slow-motion progress through the crowd. Hands stopped him to touch, shake his hand, or pat his back. Girls leaped up every few feet to embrace him, and a woman gushed, "Cole would be so proud! You're set to inherit his mantle!"

Sonia sat down with a sigh, shooting a triumphant glance at her mother. "I think we can safely say that Mark's been seduced away from the dreary classics," she announced.

"Oh, I see . . ." Marcella nodded. "*That's* why you've been so cooperative! You think it'll hurt me. But you're a little late, darling. Mark has given me his solemn promise that he'll go all out for the Italian scholarship with Gianni."

Sonia made a face. "Mark should play what he enjoys playing, that's all." She shrugged and turned the empty bottle of champagne upside down in its ice bucket, signaling for a waiter. "Let's have another of these," she said brightly.

Marcella looked across at her, smiling. "I'm too happy to be provoked by anything you say or do tonight, Sonia," she announced. "I've always wanted us to be friends. If you can't accept that, that's your problem!"

Sonia peered closely at her. "Don't tell me you're in love?"

Marcella laughed. "What makes you think that?"

Sonia groaned. "Because I know all the stupid signs. My makeup man falls in love once a day. *He* gets that look on his face, too. I have to laugh."

"You're only seventeen, darling," Marcella pointed out. She watched a beautiful blond drape her arms around Mark and kiss him hard on the mouth. Mark didn't seem to know her.

"Are we going to meet this guy, or are you ashamed of your children?" Sonia asked.

Marcella lit a cigarette. "His name is Santi Roca and he'll be here in three weeks' time. I'd love you to meet him if you can spare the time."

"Sure!" Sonia's eyes gleamed. "What does little Markie think about it?"

"I haven't told him yet." Marcella glanced away from Sonia's probing violet eyes. "I wanted to wait until after this, so . . ."

Sonia burst out laughing. "So he wouldn't throw a jealous screaming fit!" she cried.

"Sonia," Marcella said warningly. "You have this thing about Mark—" She stopped. Mark was at their table, his face a mixture of pride and weariness. His outfit was askew, his hair ruffled.

"I wasn't *too* lousy, was I?" he asked, laughing. He bent down to kiss his mother and she put an arm around him.

"You were absolutely wonderful, Mark. I fought it all the way, but I had to give in," she told him.

"Not bad at all, Markie-boy." Sonia pecked his cheek and flung her rope of pearls around her neck like a flapper girl. The waiter arrived with a fresh bottle of champagne and popped it noisily as Mark sat down.

"To your music and your talent, Mark!" Marcella held up her glass.

Sonia drank her glass down quickly and stood up. "I have to check out the downtown scene," she told them. "Too much Upper East Side air chokes me."

"Sonia." Mark stood to kiss her. "Thanks for bringing the entourage. I appreciate it."

She laughed. "Let's see what they write before we thank anyone. *Ciao!*" She pushed through the crowd, calling, "Francesca? Jason? Leonide?" gathering up people, their outlandish outfits proclaiming them as her group. The girls looked like vamps or ballerinas in net and sequins. The men wore brocade fezes or tied bandanas tightly around their heads.

"Who *are* they?" Marcella asked Mark.

He made a face, sipping his wine. "Journalists, hangers-on: a piss-elegant little clique who get their kicks deciding who's in and who's out. The problem is that lots of people actually believe them!" He drained his glass and poured more champagne.

A man with a lot of gold rings and flashing links appeared behind Mark and clapped him on the shoulder.

"Can we talk?" he honked, imitating Joan Rivers and winking at Marcella.

Mark looked over at his mother. "I have to spend a little time with Cole's friends, Mom," he told her. "Will you stay here or what?"

"Not if both children have deserted me," she said, gathering her jacket from the back of the chair. "I have Donald waiting outside. Just see me to the car, please."

Out on the sidewalk, as he kissed her good-night, she held him for a moment and told him, "I'm very very proud of you, darling."

She was up at ten the next morning while Mark was still sleeping, and went out to buy fresh croissants and the *Post*. Back in her kitchen, she read the Page Six gossip as she brewed coffee. They were in the first paragraph, headed "Million Dollar Babes."

> Marcella Balducci Winton, best-selling million-dollar author, is adept at turning out child prodigies. Not only is daughter Sonia a fave rave top model, but last night son Mark (18) wowed a tough Carlyle Lounge audience, standing in for his teacher Cole Ferrer. Jacinthe Music Academy pupil Mark sang Gershwin and Porter in a style that left the ladies breathless. Talent scouts for several record labels are vying for contracts, but Mark insists he will audition for a scholarship with Italy's top classical pianist, Franco Gianni. Mother Marcella, sitting with the head-turning Sonia, looked suitably proud.

When Mark hobbled into the kitchen, bleary-eyed and disheveled, a half hour later, she looked up at him.

"Who alerted the talent scouts?" she asked as he poured orange juice.

"Cole, I guess. . . ." He squinted at the newspaper she

held out. "I didn't get to bed until four! God—I think this is my first hangover!"

He plopped into a chair and she pushed a plate of croissants at him. "Cole's terribly ambitious for me," he told her, tearing a croissant apart.

"Don't even think about record contracts yet, Mark," she said. "You're not ready to be turned into some kind of half-baked pop star."

"It's too late," he confessed, sipping some coffee. "I agreed to do an album last night."

"Mark!" she cried. "Without asking me about it, first?" He shrugged lightly. "It's no big deal. Cole records for this label. They're kind of specialists. They just want some Broadway show tunes. I don't even go into a studio; we're going to use live recordings from my performances over the next two weeks."

"Damn it," she sighed. "I wish you'd reconsider, Mark."

"Listen, probably no one will ever see or hear it," he prophesied. "It's the kind of cult record that specialty music stores in the Village keep on their shelves, all covered in plastic and dust! And why is it so darned important that I stick to classics, anyway? Are you the keeper of the flame or something?"

Marcella pulled a chair up and sat across the table from him. "I've just always felt it is so much more of an accomplishment to be a great classical pianist, Mark," she explained. "So many people can play pop. How many musicians can do justice to Chopin, as you do? You want me to be proud of you, don't you?" Mark nodded.

"And your grandfather was so proud of music being in our family's blood," she went on. "He paid for your first piano lessons, you know. It's probably silly of me, but I love the thought of how happy he'd have been to know you played really well."

Mark stood and walked behind her, putting his hands on her shoulders. Bending down, he whispered, "What will I be if I agree?"

She twisted around to look up at him. "You'll always be the light of my life, darling. You know that."

He kissed her head, and sat down. She watched him dunk the croissant in his coffee.

Then she took a deep breath and made herself say the words she had tried so hard not to rehearse.

"Mark, while I was in Majorca I met a wonderful man," she began. "I wanted to tell you about him the moment your opening night was over. . . ."

He looked up from the croissant. "Yeah?" he asked. "I knew there was something different about you since you got back. I thought it was my music!"

She held his gaze. "His name is Santiago Roca," she told him. "Everyone calls him Santi. He's an art dealer in Barcelona, but he works in Majorca also and keeps two homes there. He's coming to New York in two and a half weeks. I think you'll like him a lot, Mark."

He smiled. "He sounds great!" he said, reaching across to squeeze her hand. A tiny nerve under one eye always flickered when he was upset and she watched it twitch now as he gazed distractedly around the room. She waited until he looked back at her.

"It was bound to happen one day, Mark," she said. "He's very important to me and—"

"I thought you'd only just met him," he broke in.

"That's right, I have," she agreed. "But I *know,* Mark. We both have that psychic thing, don't we? We're able to sum up people instantly. Well, with Santi I knew when I met him that he was going to be the man. *He* knew, too. Just about the first thing he said to me was that we'd be together for the rest of our lives!"

Mark gave a crooked smile. "That's some opening line!" he cracked. He got up from the table. "I'd better call Cole before some gossip gets to him and puts down my standing ovation!"

He bent down to her before he left the room to whisper in her ear. "You're starting to believe your own novels, Mom."

She frowned, hurt.

"I *do* believe in them!" she called after him. She believed more than ever now that she had started writing *Forever Begins Tonight,* her story of two women in Majorca, one of whom meets a man very much like Santi.

Santi called her every night before she went to sleep. It was eight a.m. in Barcelona. He could only afford three minutes, he said, so he called just to tell her he loved her.

His voice was a wonderful reassurance that he did really exist. Now that she was back in New York, it was only too easy to feel he had been a dream. However, New York felt very different to her now. Mark was out each evening, performing at the Carlyle, and she no longer had that urge to visit Members. Like a reformed alcoholic, she regarded her former vice with horror. The Marcella who had done that seemed like an entirely different woman. She liked the new Marcella so much better, the soft romantic Marcella who awaited the great love of her life to join her in her own city.

She went to two more of the performances Mark gave at the Carlyle and visited her mother, and suddenly Santi was arriving the next day. She had reserved a small suite for him at a hotel on her block, and she went to check the room and decorate it with bouquets of flowers on the day of his arrival. She glanced at her chaste bed before leaving the airport. Her need for privacy and her fear of upsetting Mark meant they would be making love in an anonymous hotel room, not in her own home. Perhaps she could smuggle Santi in here one day when Mark was out at school, she thought. Just so she could know that Santi had slept in her bed, had shared it with her. On an impulse, she grabbed a red rose from a vase in her living room before Donald drove her to Kennedy Airport.

When Santi strode out of customs, a broad smile on his face, they fell into each other's embrace and hugged fiercely. His sunny Majorcan smell transported her right back to their idyllic week on the island, and tears forced their way out of her tightly closed eyes. She felt sobs pushing up inside her and gulped to hold them back. Breaking away from him, she looked at him. She had wondered how he would look here, out of his element, among all the big glossy Americans. Now she saw that he more than held his own. He was a little exotic here, definitely European, more appealing than ever. Best of all, his eyes were overflowing with love for her.

"Oh, welcome to New York, darling! Welcome!" She handed him the rose, holding on to his arm. He carried a small suitcase and a round carton that contained a fresh *ensaimada* from Palma for her. When they reached the car, he pulled an impressed face.

"You rented this just for me?" he asked.

She laughed as Donald came for his suitcase and stowed it in the trunk, opening the doors for them.

"It's mine, Santi," she confessed, shamefaced, as they got in. "But it is my *only* extravagance!"

"I see . . ." he said, following her onto the backseat. "When you said you were an author, it did not make this much impression! In Spain, most writers are poor. I suppose you must sell many many books?"

"Millions!" she said, kissing him. "Aren't I lucky, Santi?" She held on to his hands tightly and he leaned over her, covering her face with little kisses.

"Now I am alive again," he told her. "Since you left, I was like a zombie. Nothing had any taste, nothing made me laugh, all I could think about was this moment!"

"And I've been the same!" she admitted.

"I have never been given a rose by a woman before," he said, placing it carefully on the window shelf behind him.

With him, New York looked entirely different as the car approached the city. The sun was going down rosy-red and the buildings' windows were lighting up. The city had never looked so poetic to Marcella.

"Look!" She pointed out the Manhattan skyline.

Santi stared. "Just like in the movies," he said. "Is it really so crazy and dangerous?"

"Not for us, darling," she whispered. "For us it's a honeymoon city, cozy and full of love."

He stared, fascinated, out of the windows, asking questions about each neighborhood as they passed through it, clutching her hand when they drove across the bridge into Manhattan.

At his hotel, they followed the bellboy with his suitcase like two bashful newlyweds. The moment the boy left, Santi pulled her down to the bed and embraced her.

"I love you," he told her. "I love you."

She gave herself up to the luxury of being held in his arms and allowed him to undress her, kissing each part of her body as it was revealed. When he stripped, his body was bronzed, fit, and hard. She felt absurdly Rubenesque next to him.

Once again, they melted into each other. He felt better than she had remembered; smooth, silky, holding on to her so tightly that they became one person. He made love to her hurriedly and she knew he had not had any form of sex since they'd parted. Neither had she. Once again, she relished everything he did to her, his mouth, his hands, and yet, just at that vital moment when she expected to be swept away by her pleasure, her concentration veered and she heard Santi's groans as he released all the love and desire he had saved. He was too overcome to notice her disappointment and was soon dozing lightly in her arms. She sat at the foot of the bed, watching him sleep, covering him with a blanket.

Later, she unpacked his clothes, hanging up his pants and jackets, placing his shaving things in the bathroom, loving everything of his that she touched because it belonged to him. He awoke a half hour later, refreshed, and she called down to room service for some coffee. Then she took him by the hand and they left the hotel and walked down Fifth Avenue past Tiffany's and Trump Tower and Rockefeller Center. He craned his head like a tourist and told her how beautiful he found New York, gazing with amazement at the well-dressed people and asking where all the muggers were.

"Oh darling!" She laughed. "You're so European. You'll love New York and I shall love showing it to you!"

And then it was eleven-thirty and he reminded her that for him it was five-thirty the following morning and he had not slept much the night before, either. She accompanied him back to his hotel room and watched him get into cream pajamas and slip into bed. Then she gently kissed him as he fell instantly asleep. She walked back to her apartment, smiling at all the doormen she knew. How wonderful it was to know that a few hundred yards away the man she had waited all her life to meet was sleeping, to know she would see him in the morning.

Santi called her at nine-thirty the next morning.

"I slept for almost twelve hours!" He laughed. "Now I want to have breakfast at Tiffany's with you!"

"Will you settle for the hotel coffee shop?" she asked. "I'll meet you there in half an hour."

She found him in a booth, hungrily eating toast and eggs and crispy bacon. He stood to kiss her as she joined him, ordering coffee only.

"This is so different from Majorcan food," he told her. "I like it very much."

She watched him eating, happy that he had such a good appetite. "Darling," she began. "Have you wondered why you're staying at a hotel and not at my home, where I'd much rather have you?"

He raised his eyebrows over the coffee cup. "Your children?" he guessed. "They would perhaps not like to see a foreigner sleeping in their mother's bed?"

She laughed. "Listen . . ." She picked up his hand and played with the fingers. "I told you how close Mark and I are, didn't I? It would take all day to explain how my husband took the children away from me once, and what that did to us. It would be a shock if he just found you sleeping in my bed. Do you understand, darling?"

"Yes, of course." He pressed her hand. "But surely he has met other men?"

She shook her head. "No."

"You have not invited a man into your home for all these years?" he asked, his eyebrows raised.

"No," she said simply.

"Perhaps you protected your son too much, Marcella?" he suggested. "And what about Sonia?" he asked.

"Sonia has her own life," she told him airily. "She's not a problem." She pulled him to his feet. "Now, find your camera, darling. We're going sightseeing."

Donald was waiting for them outside her apartment. She wanted to show Santi her city: the mixture of old and new; the corny things you "had" to do, like seeing the Empire State Building; and the unexpected places like the Cloisters and the lakeside restaurant in Central Park. She refused to think of anything but Santi's pleasure and impressions, dedicating herself to being his guide.

Santi met her children on his second night in New York and it was as awkward as she had dreaded. She had called Sonia several times to remind her about the evening, swallowing her pride because she wanted to show off both children to Santi. She would have to be a little vague about why Sonia was living on her own and about how little contact they had. It did not help that Santi's English was limited when it came to New York slang or that they were both exhausted from walking around the city. Mark was polite enough. He and Santi made small talk, waiting for Sonia.

Sonia breezed in an hour late, wearing a man's black bowler hat on her scraped-back hair and a transparent black net skirt like a petticoat over black hose and high heels. A heap of quasi-religious medallions and crosses fell from chains around the neck of her black silk blouse and two little black lace gloves with cut-off fingers completed her look. If she had not been tall, beautiful, and poised, she would have looked ridiculous, Marcella thought. As it was, she was disturbingly sexy and fashionable.

"Are you *on* something?" Marcella whispered as Sonia posed before the entry hall mirror, preening.

Sonia giggled. "A little wine and a little snuff, darling," she answered airily. "Where is he?"

"Sonia . . ." Marcella held her back. "You're insane to get into drugs, especially in your profession!"

"Are you kidding?" Sonia sniggered. "Anyway, tonight I was celebrating my second *Vogue* cover! I'm one step nearer my goal, Mother dear!"

Santi stood and smiled his radiant, guileless smile as they entered the room. If he was surprised at Sonia's appearance, he was too polite to show it, taking her hand in his as Marcella introduced them.

"My daughter, Sonia—Santi Roca," she said, as Santi kissed Sonia's hand. She stared at him, more taken aback by him than he was by her.

Marcella watched Mark, happy and relieved that he was pouring on all his charm for the occasion. Now Sonia followed suit.

"Welcome to New York," she said, smiling radiantly back at Santi. "What d'you think of Manhattan? Come on out and see the view!" She took his arm and pulled him out onto the tiny balcony overlooking Central Park.

Marcella handed Mark an ice bucket. "Fill this, will you, darling? And get the champagne out of the freezer before it explodes. I made a few things to nibble on—I'll get those. . . ."

She busied herself with the food and drinks and glasses, unable to make herself search Mark's face to see the verdict.

"I have seen your photograph everywhere!" Santi complimented Sonia. "In the airport, in the pharmacies—your mother has shown me some fashion magazines. You are very beautiful."

"Yeah, if they put all that gook on my face, I'm okay . . ." she allowed, coming back into the room with him. She had unbuttoned her silk blouse on the balcony to show a little silicone cleavage.

" 'Gook' means makeup," Marcella explained, setting a big platter of crackers and caviar on the piano.

"*Mountains* of it!" Sonia nodded, digging into the caviar. "It's like—where am *I*, under all that, y'*know*? So, what do you do in Spain? Something to do with art, Mother told me. . . ."

"I sell art," Santi said seriously. "Paintings. In Barcelona, people are just beginning to buy art by young painters. Previously—"

"I know Leo Castelli," Sonia broke in. "I'm saving up to buy a Warhol lithograph from him. Marilyn Monroe. It's supposed to be a good investment. Would I have heard of any of your artists?"

"They are not yet famous in America," Santi apologized.

Marcella watched them, holding herself back from protecting Santi against Sonia's sharp streetwise cynicism. When Mark returned with the champagne, he opened it with a pop and carefully filled four glasses. Marcella handed one to Sonia and one to Santi, waiting to toast. Sonia was babbling. "I believe in *now*!" she told Santi, her legs wide apart as she took a stance in the center of the room. "That's why I'm in a hurry to achieve as much as possible while I'm real young! Who knows when we'll get blown up or some nut on the street slashes my face? I have nightmares about seeing a *Post* headline, 'Headless Model Found,' and finding out it's *me*!"

Mark gave a shout of laughter. "You have nightmares about reading the *Post* and *not* seeing your name in it," he said.

Santi smiled, looking from one to the other, not quite understanding. Marcella stopped them.

"You're both talking nonsense and you can't expect Santi to understand. The *Post* is a gossipy newspaper," she explained to him. He nodded.

"And you, Mark?" Santi turned to him. "You live for your music?"

Mark shrugged. "Until I find something better to live for. . . ."

"Let's drink to that!" Sonia cried, holding up her goblet. She charged her glass so heavily against Santi's that it almost smashed. Then she swallowed the entire contents with a gasp and refilled her glass. Marcella drank quickly, too, nervous about this clash of personalities in her living room, wanting so much for them to get on well that it was all she could do to stop herself from placing her children's arms around her lover's neck. She felt uncomfortable. Santi would think she had raised two uncontrollable spoiled brats. She stared at the man she loved and then at her children. Two different forces in her life, tugging in two different directions. Santi was smiling his radiant smile, not quite following all the badinage and jokes hurled between Sonia and Mark. Can't you see what he is? she wanted to scream at them. Can't you see how good he is? Why don't you both just shut up and let Santi speak?

"I'm modeling for Bill Blass tomorrow and I have to be fitted tonight, so I can't stay," Sonia chattered.

"Would you like a little more champagne?" Santi offered.

"*Claro que sí!*" Sonia cried.

"Ah, you speak some Spanish?" Santi asked delightedly.

"I have a Puerto Rican cleaner." Sonia made a face. "It's all you can get. I know how to tell her to do the housework."

The canapés had all been nervously eaten.

"Help me make a few more," Marcella suggested to Sonia. In the kitchen she quickly spread more crackers with caviar, squeezing some lemon juice onto each one.

"Ask him a little about *his* life, Sonia," Marcella urged.

Sonia opened the fridge to peer into it. "I'm trying, Mother dear, but he doesn't exactly speaka da lingo, you know. Can't you go for an American or an Englishman next time?"

"There won't be a next time," Marcella said. "Try to speak *his* lingo. He understands everything if you speak clearly and cut out the slang."

"Listen!" Sonia swiped a stalk of celery from the fridge

and stuck it in her mouth. "*Don't* ask me to speak clearly *tonight*! After the kind of day *I've* had, you're lucky I showed up here at all!"

Marcella hurried back into the living room as Santi was requesting Mark to play the piano. She handed around canapés as Mark sulkily opened the piano. She could see he was torn between wanting to impress Santi and trying to appear indifferent. Sonia threw herself onto the couch, one leg over the arm, sipping champagne and crunching loudly on her celery. Mark rippled through some Gershwinesque chords. Santi gave Marcella a loving look and beckoned her over to him, leaning on the piano. She tried not to feel foolish when he took her hand and held it as Mark played. She leaned against him uncomfortably, telling herself that her love for this man was all that mattered, not the impression he made on her children.

Mark sang "Embraceable You" in his beautiful light tenor, squeezing every ounce of romance from the song. For a moment, he seemed to be encouraging their love and she glimpsed an impossible picture of them all as a new, united family, with both children happy that she had found a man who loved her. She watched Mark and saw that he was unable to resist this chance to display his enormous charm and talent, to make another conquest, even if it was of a man he did not want to like. When the song ended, she quickly poured herself another glass of champagne as Sonia and Santi applauded.

"Now I see why your mother was so proud of you when she described you to me," Santi said to Mark. "I love Gershwin very much."

Mark looked surprised. "Do they play much of it in Spain?" he asked.

"Oh, of course." Santi nodded. "We are behind America, it is true, but Gershwin has been around for sixty years!"

"Santi adores music," Marcella told him.

"What kind?" Mark asked, twiddling with some notes in the treble.

"Ravel is my favorite," Santi said. "Chopin, Debussy, Satie."

"Highbrow stuff, eh?" Mark rippled off a few bars of *Clair de Lune.* Marcella watched his charm struggling to be let out. If he would only let down his guard, she knew he and Santi could be great friends. They had music in common. And they had *her* in common. She smiled ruefully to herself: that was the trouble!

"Gotta go!" Sonia jumped to her feet and dashed around the room, kissing everyone. She threw her arms around Santi's neck. "Have a fabulous visit, Santi," she wished him. "I'm sure my dear mother will make the best guide! Mark? See ya around."

Marcella followed Sonia into the hall, watching her check her face and hat in the mirror. "Would you like to join us for dinner on Friday, Sonia?" she asked. "Amy will be with us and she'd love to see you."

"I can't," Sonia said. "I've bought a horse and I'm keeping it out on Long Island in a friend's field. I go there every weekend to ride and it's like the big love of my life!"

Marcella smiled. "So you *do* believe in love?" she asked.

Sonia shrugged, pulling her hat down onto her head. "If it's a horse, absolutely!" she agreed. She pressed the elevator button in the hall outside and pecked Marcella's cheek. "Thanks for the drinks!" The elevator arrived and she stepped in, turning to face her mother. "Good luck with your two men. *I* approve even if Mark won't." She tapped the ground-floor button. "These triangles can be *such* a bore, darling!" She grinned mischievously. "I'd say *yours* is pretty unique!" The sliding doors met, cutting off the expression on her face.

Mark left a few minutes later to have dinner with Cole. Alone with Santi at last, Marcella poured them each a stiff Scotch.

"We need this," she said, handing one to him. "Forgive them, darling?" She fell onto a sofa, kicking off her shoes. "I realized tonight what spoiled little brats they are!"

"Spoiled?" Santi frowned. "Brats?"

She swallowed some Scotch. "When you give children too much," she explained, "*love* them too much!"

"No . . ." He leaned over her, kissing her forehead. "They are wonderful children. Mark is a musical genius, and Sonia is so beautiful. You should be very proud of them both."

Marcella pulled a face.

He sat down next to her. "Of course they are worried if

a stranger is introduced. If we marry, *I* shall be their father. That is very important. Especially as their real father is alive and they must love him very much."

She closed her eyes, groaning inwardly. She had not yet told Santi that Harry was in jail. She had not wanted to heap too much on him at once. She caught his hand and held it. "You make everything sound so simple, darling."

He laughed. "Because it *is* simple, when two people love each other!"

They dined with Amy that night, using Amy's famous name to get a good table at a hot SoHo Thai brasserie. Like all New Yorkers, Marcella had a love-hate relationship with the city. She agreed that walking down Fifth Avenue at twilight was a great experience, as was seeing Manhattan from a boat at any time of the day. But that evening, in the noisy, chic restaurant crowded with exhibitionists, as rude waiters juggled expensive, tiny portions, she saw it all through Santi's eyes and it suddenly looked ridiculous. There were no restaurants like this in Palma. You could choose from dozens of portside places where delicious fresh fish was served beautifully without any chichi or fuss. She watched Santi deep in conversation with Amy and longed to be alone with him. When dinner finally ended, long after midnight, Amy's car and driver took them all back to Central Park South.

They made love in Santi's room and she lay in his arms, contented, glowing with the warmth of their love. Her pleasure had once again eluded her, but she was training herself not to care, to simply enjoy his caresses and relish whatever he did to her, as if sex did not have to lead to a climax. Hopefully, her body would sort it all out as she got used to this luxury of love and sex and time, learning to align them so she could enjoy the completeness.

"What are we going to do, Santi?" she asked, finally breaking their silence.

"Marry and live together forever," he whispered into her ear.

"How will our lives fit together?" she asked.

She felt his tiny shrug. "Our lives will find a way. As our bodies will find a way."

She allowed herself a few minutes more in his arms, then forced herself to sit up. It was nearly two a.m. "I'd better go, darling." She slithered out of bed and felt for her clothes.

"And why not spend the entire night with me?" Santi asked, switching on the light. He leaned on one elbow, watching her. "You think Mark does not know we make love together?"

She pulled on her dress. "I just have this feeling I must get him to accept us little by little," she explained. "If I suddenly stay out all night . . ." she trailed off.

Santi said nothing, but she could see he was hurt.

When she got back to her apartment, she saw the light still on under Mark's door. She went to bed, but then suddenly felt wide awake, so she got up and began correcting the latest edit of *Music of Love*.

Mark's soft knock at her door came twenty minutes later. "Come in," she called.

He peered around the door, entering the room slowly. He was in his robe.

"Mark . . ." she said warningly.

He took a step toward the bed, a pleading look in his eyes.

She made herself say the words. "What did you think of him?"

He sat down at the end of her bed, still holding her gaze.

"Be very careful what you say, Mark," she warned. "Remember, this is my life!"

He reached for her hand. For the first time in her life, she did not want him to touch her. He brushed her fingers against his lips. Then he threw himself onto the bed next to her and tried to hold her.

"No!" she cried. She could not allow this. Not while Santi's touch still lingered, while his smell still coated her skin.

"Don't do this to me," Mark said, muffled into her neck.

She sat up in the bed, straining away from him. "Don't *you* do this to *me*!" she cried. "Don't you dare try to make me feel guilty for loving a wonderful man like Santi! This is when you can prove you love me as much as you say you do! You'd be *happy* for me if you really loved me, Mark! He's the best thing that's happened to me since giving birth to you. *You've* had eighteen years of my undivided attention—"

"And now it's *his* turn?" Mark finished for her, his mouth set in a bitter twist.

"Yes, Mark," she agreed, nodding. "Now it's his turn."

He sat up and glowered at her. "But you're not some kind of . . . *thing* that gets divided up and ladled out to people, in *turns*! You're my mother and *you* made our world like this! *You* made it just us two together, and you have no right to just throw me out because you've found some guy who—"

"I'm not throwing you out!" She stroked the back of his neck and he lay his head in her lap. "We both knew one day I'd find someone or you'd find someone. . . ."

His blue eyes glistened as he looked up at her. "But I *haven't* found anyone, and I never will!"

"Don't be so silly," she soothed him. "You're only eighteen. Of course you'll find someone. There were dozens of beautiful girls at your opening night, throwing themselves at you!"

"That's just crap!" He sat up, placing his hands on her shoulders. As she stared into the dark blue eyes she could feel everything he was thinking, feel the force of him, the raw primal need of a child.

"Oh, God, Mark, what have I done to you?" she whispered, frightened. "What exactly do you want? That I never look at a man? Never fall in love?"

"I need you too much," he whispered through clenched teeth. "I'm not equipped to handle life. I only know my music. People affect me so much and I can't handle their demands on me! You're the only person who—"

"That's not good!" she stopped him. "A mother can't be the only person you trust or love. . . ."

"But you promised me I'd always be the light of your life!" he cried.

"You *will* be!" she assured him. "But that doesn't mean I don't need a man to love and take care of me."

"What's wrong with *my* loving you? *My* taking care of you?" he asked.

She stroked his forehead. "Mark, you don't understand. A son's love isn't a substitute for a husband's love. Women have needs, just like men. . . ."

"Amy has needs, but she finds ways to take care of them!" he challenged.

She looked at him nakedly. "I'm not Amy," she told him. "And this isn't something that mothers and sons should discuss, Mark. I could marry Santi next week if I chose, but because you and I are close, I wanted *you* to love him. Accept him as you would an elder brother or as a good friend. If you let Santi know you as I do, he'll love you, too."

"I don't *want* him to love me!" Mark cried. "I don't need his love. Just *yours*! All yours!" He jumped off the bed. "Oh, God!" he muttered, clapping his hand over his mouth, taking a few staggering steps toward her bathroom. Suddenly, he choked and bent double, vomiting. He lay down on the carpet, gasping.

"Mark!" Marcella ran to the bathroom for a towel and mopped up as he lay on his side groaning. She poured him a glass of water and he leaned on an elbow, sipping from it.

"I'm sorry," he kept saying. "I'm sorry."

She mopped his brow with a washcloth saturated in cologne, the refreshing smell soothing them both.

"I wanted to wish you well," he told her. "I wanted to be happy for you, but I just—" He made himself focus his eyes on her. "I don't think I can do it without you."

Her heart sank. She reached out for a cigarette and lit one. Soon, he fell asleep on the carpet and she stared out the window at the navy sky, at the few windows still alight around her.

She went to bed and slept from sheer exhaustion. At six in the morning, as the dawn showed in the sky, Mark stumbled into her bed. He grunted something and was soon breathing heavily at her side. She clung to the back of his body, reminding herself that this fully grown man had sprung from her, had once been small enough to hold in one hand.

The next day was their Statue of Liberty day. She camouflaged her lack of sleep with artful makeup, the way Amy had taught her for those early-morning TV talk shows.

On the ferry from Battery Park, she shook her mind free of her troubled thoughts and watched Santi enjoy the ride while he took dozens of photographs of her as the breeze ruffled her hair. She smiled for them, imagining how he would look at them before he slept in his Barcelona apartment after this trip. Everything would fall into place, she promised herself.

Later, when they walked down Wall Street, she tried not to remember the times she had visited Harry there; that other life seemed decades ago. Donald waited with the car in SoHo while they toured the art galleries. On the way back uptown, the car passed by Members, the black building deserted in the daylight. She shivered slightly, turning to smile at Santi, clinging to his arm. She would never need that dreadful place again.

In his hotel room she relaxed on the bed as he took a shower, her eyes wandering around the room, noting how he stored his things so neatly, the packets of exposed film piled by his guidebooks. As he sang in the shower, his deep happy voice tore at her heart and she knew that she would be crazy not to marry him, that no one like him would ever come into her life again. Suddenly he was with her on the bed, damp and clean smelling after his shower, holding her tightly.

"Love me?" she asked.

"What do you think?" he teased.

"I think you love me a lot," she said. "But not as much as I love you."

"How can you say that, Marcella?" he said, annoyed. "*I* was the one who said we would always be together, at the café, the first time I met you! You would not even have noticed me!"

She laughed, thrilled. "Let's always argue about who loves who the most," she proposed. They went on teasing each other, then making up and kissing. Finally she broke away from him.

"I've got to go home and freshen up, darling," she said. "Why don't you take a little siesta? We'll have a romantic dinner tonight. Anywhere. No reservations—we'll just walk in somewhere, okay?"

He smiled sleepily. "*All* our dinners are romantic!"

The apartment was empty when she got back, the mail piled on her writing desk where Mark always left it. There were messages from Amy and Scott, about books and promotions. She showered and changed. She was waiting for the elevator when Mark came up in it. She pulled him back into the apartment with her, making a sudden decision.

"Pour us both a drink, darling," she told him, hugging him.

He poured them wine, his face both frowning and curious. Pulling up a chair to face him, she took a sip of her wine. "I'm going to marry him, Mark," she said. "You're the first to know. I haven't even told Santi yet! And you are going to understand and be happy for us!"

"I see . . ." He drank his wine, his face suddenly blank. "What made you decide this?" he stammered slightly, lowering his gaze from her stare. "You *know* what it will do to me!"

"It's nothing to do with *you,* Mark," she told him. "The world doesn't revolve around you. I've been wrong to bring you up as if it did! This is about *my* life—mine and Santi's! It's two people's eternal happiness against your temporary unhappiness. It's simple mathematics!"

"But my feelings aren't mathematics!" he cried accusingly.

"You won't be so selfish," she said gently. "You'll let me love both of you!"

"And if I don't accept it?" He peered up at her.

She leaned to kiss him lightly, standing up. "You *must* be happy for us, Mark," she said, fluffing her hair in the mirror. "You don't want me to end up like Amy. I know she seems very glamorous and successful, but to me her life is sterile. I must go, darling. Santi's waiting for me."

She walked quickly to Santi's hotel, letting herself into his room with his key. He was sleeping so peacefully that she did not have the heart to wake him. She sat, watching him for a few minutes, feeling at peace with herself and the world. As if her real life was just now beginning—at thirty-seven! When the clock showed nine she woke Santi with a kiss. They walked through the midtown streets together, exploring bookstores where she pointed out her own books to him. In the Village, they ate a bistro meal in a French restaurant off Sixth Avenue, the small room bedecked in hundreds of fairy lights. On their way home, she stopped the cab at the Rainbow Room and hustled Santi up to the restaurant. The maitre d' knew her from several dinners she had shared with Volumes people.

"Just a bottle of champagne, Henri," she greeted him. They were served the champagne at a window seat near the bar where they could gaze at Manhattan sixty-five stories below.

"This is supposed to be the most romantic place in town," she told Santi as they clinked glasses. "I wanted to come here because I'm ready for the question you want to ask me, Santi!"

His eyes lit up. "You will marry me?" he asked, reaching for her.

"Yes, yes, my darling!" She clasped his hand. "I want to live with you and sleep with you and grow old with you!"

"And you will live in Barcelona with me—and Majorca?" he asked.

"Let's split the year!" she suggested. "Six months in Spain, six in New York?" She held up her glass again. "Here's to us!"

They drank the champagne and then embraced each other as the people around them discreetly looked the other way.

Walking home after midnight, dizzy with champagne and happiness, they clung to each other. The streets were almost deserted and Marcella had the impression that the city had been holding this moment for her, to reward her for all the years she had been lonely.

"I must find a ring," Santi was saying. "Something antique, yes? And I must call my parents and one or two friends. And I think tonight I deserve to share your bed with you!"

She glanced at him, squeezing his hand. "Do you think that's wise?"

"Yes! You can no longer hide me away now that I am to become your husband. Now we must lead our own life."

"Very well, but we'll have to lock the bedroom door," she told him. "Mark has a habit of walking in unannounced."

"And Sonia?" he questioned, "is she more permissive than Mark?"

She hesitated, then answered, "Sonia doesn't live with us. She has her own apartment."

Santi raised his eyebrows. "At seventeen?"

Marcella eyed him, shaking her head. "Yes, I know it sounds a little crazy, but you have to understand we're a slightly crazy family. If I told you the entire story, you'd think I was making it up, Santi. Sonia was taken from me by her father when she was twelve. She lived with him for two years. She never quite got over that. Of course I'd prefer her to live with us, but in America, children don't necessarily listen to their parents. Sonia needs to be independent."

"And she earns enough money to be independent?" he asked.

She nodded. "Modeling pays extremely well."

When they reached home she went ahead of Santi to peer into Mark's room. It was empty. For a moment she feared he might be sleeping in her bed, but her room was empty too.

She closed and locked her bedroom door. It was a dream come true to have the man she loved in her own bed. Why did this have to be such a forbidden luxury? They should have slept together here from the start. How hurt Santi must have felt, being shunted into a hotel, as if he were some visiting acquaintance.

"Forever begins tonight," she said as she got into bed next to him. This time there was no defense, no problem. They made love as if they had always shared this bed. Fulfillment was effortless, totally satisfying. Sex in Members' theater had been dangerously exciting, of course. This kind of happy, secure loving, this "forever" sex, was completely different. And it more than made up in sheer happiness what it lacked in excitement. She clung to Santi as he drifted into sleep, letting the rhythm of his heartbeat soothe her. She hoped she could fall asleep, but she found herself listening for Mark's return. Damn him! Ruining her first night in her own home with her future husband! She must have drifted off later because when she heard someone trying to open her door, her clock showed it was nearly two a.m.

"Mom?" Mark's voice whispered urgently.

She climbed out of bed, glancing at Santi sleeping

deeply. She unlocked the door and peered out. Mark stood there disheveled and unsteady.

"You're drunk," she said, shocked.

"Why'd you lock the door?" he asked.

"I—" She bit her lip. "Oh, this is ridiculous. Santi's here," she said.

"I want to sleep with you, Mom," he moaned.

"Don't be silly, Mark. Go to bed now." She kissed his forehead.

"Is he moving in?" he asked.

"We'll talk about it tomorrow. You woke me up. Go to bed!"

She locked the door and returned to her bed.

"What is it?" Santi asked, turning sleepily.

"Nothing." She kissed him. "Mark was drunk!"

Now she was quite unable to sleep. Furious with herself and with Mark, she lay wide awake. An hour passed. Her body was too exhausted to move, but her mind was alert, darting all over the place. The champagne they had drunk had made her so thirsty. Fifteen minutes later she gave up and got out of bed, pulling on her robe. On her way to the kitchen for some apple juice, she noticed Mark's room was dark and heard the sound of snoring coming from it. He never snores, she thought. On her way back, the noise was even louder. She pushed the door ajar and heard a strange rattling sound in his throat as he breathed. Perhaps he was getting a summer cold? She switched on his light and saw him lying facedown on the bed, fully dressed. She bent down to pull off his shoes, wondering whether she should undress him or simply throw a blanket over him.

She found a blanket from the linen closet in the hall and took it in to him. As she pulled it over him, she saw the empty bottle of sleeping pills and the scrawled note: "I couldn't face life without being your light. Your *only* light!"

She yanked him over onto his back, slapping his gray, drugged face. Her heart jumped with panic and she felt her body turn cold as she screamed, waking Santi. Babbling, she called for an ambulance. Then she called her doctor, leaving an urgent message with his service. She and Santi together held Mark upright, supporting him between them and forcing him to stumble around the apartment until the ambulance arrived.

The briskly efficient attendants carried Mark out of the building on a stretcher. They pumped his stomach in the ambulance as Marcella and Santi followed in a taxi. It seemed to take hours to get to the emergency ward of the hospital.

"If you let him die, I'll never believe in love again," Marcella prayed. "If you let him live . . ." She frowned, trying to think of the biggest sacrifice she could offer God. She glanced sideways at Santi's anguished face. "I'll give up my love," she offered. "Just don't let Mark die! Oh please don't let him die!"

She squeezed Santi's hand until he winced with pain. Whatever happened now, she would lose him. If Mark lived, she must honor her pact with God. If Mark died, then life would be over for her, too, because there would be nothing of her left, not for Santi, not for any man.

FIFTEEN

It was nearly five o'clock when her dear, tired old Doctor Greenburg, their doctor from Little Italy, to whom she had remained loyal, bustled into the brightly lit waiting room.

"He'll be all right, Marcella," he nodded.

She burst into tears and threw herself against his tweedy chest, hugging him. The doctor smiled over her shoulder at Santi, embarrassed.

"Oh." She broke away. "Doctor Greenburg, this is Santi Roca," she introduced them, dabbing her eyes.

"Let's get you home now." The doctor patted Marcella. "Mark will sleep through this afternoon."

He insisted on driving them home in his shabby car. On the way, he said, "It will have to be reported to the police, I'm afraid."

"Can't you say it was food poisoning?" Marcella's tear-stained face gleamed in the light of the street lamps.

"I'll do all I can," Doctor Greenburg promised. "But I am not going to break the law, my dear. Not even for my favorite patient."

At five-thirty, she was in bed with Santi, tiredness spinning her into its welcome blur.

She woke at ten, exhausted, Santi sleeping soundly next to her. She dressed quietly, leaving him a note to say she'd be back for lunch. After calling the hospital to check that Mark's condition was good, she found Donald waiting outside with the car. The first thing she had him do was drive to a newsstand and buy the *Post.* There were no headlines. Then they drove to the hospital. She was at Mark's side when he awoke, his eyes puffy, his expression confused.

She watched his face as the realization of all that had happened came to him. They exchanged a look filled with the import of what he had tried to do, and with their love for each other.

"What am I?" he said, squeezing her hand weakly.

She shook her head, horrified, staring at him. "How could you do that to me, Mark?" she asked.

"What am I?" he asked again.

"A spoiled child," she told him. "A monster." With a cry, she fell on his pillow, her face against the side of his cheek. Mark hugged her. How could she have gone on living if he had succeeded in killing himself? she wondered. You could never understand, she told Santi in her mind. Not unless the person you loved most in the world came from your own body.

After leaving Mark, she stopped at a market to buy something for lunch. When she got home, she found a note from Santi saying he was taking a walk in Central Park. She ran to the balcony to see if she could spot his trim figure among the trees. The phone rang and Mark told her he wanted to check himself out of the hospital and come home.

"The doctor's just seen me and he says I'm okay," he told her. "I'd rather recuperate in my own bed. . . ."

She sent Donald in the car to fetch him and felt torn between waiting at home for him or finding Santi. She could not bear the thought of seeing Mark and Santi together, staring accusingly or sorrowfully at each other. She hurriedly packed a picnic lunch and waited for Santi in the foyer downstairs. When he returned from his walk, she took his arm and guided him back into the park. At the Sheep Meadow, they spread a tablecloth on the grass and sat on either side of the picnic basket. After inquiring about Mark, Santi tried to distract her. He was full of plans for their future and spoke of possibly opening a branch of his gallery in Palma and building an addition to the Deya house so that Mark and Sonia could stay there. Marcella let him talk, not really listening. Her mental picture of Mark's face last night, gray and deathlike, kept interrupting her thoughts. She kept thinking of how she would be feeling today if Mark had succeeded in killing himself.

"Marcella?" Santi said. "You're not listening to me. Mark *is* all right, isn't he?"

"What?" She came to with a start. "Oh, darling, I'm sorry. I guess I'm still in a state of shock. Mark should be home by now and I should be with him. I was just thinking it might be quite a while before any of us comes to Majorca again."

He frowned. "But you said last night we would be spending half the year in Spain!"

She reached for his hand. "Mark needs me here," she told him. "I never realized before how dependent he is on me. He must be back in shape for the summer examinations. There'll be his audition for Gianni in Italy in the fall and . . ." She dropped her eyes from his questioning gaze. "I can't leave him now, Santi . . ." she mumbled. "So," Santi gave a wry smile, "I am not to expect your undivided attention?" he said. "These plans we have been making are just fantasies, yes?"

She pressed his hand. "Give me a little time, Santi. Mark needs me. Last night was a terrible shock. I hadn't realized how—"

"But you cannot think he truly intended to kill himself?" Santi asked.

She pulled her hand away and sat bolt upright. "He swallowed a whole bottle of my pills!" she cried. "If I hadn't gotten up for something to drink, he would have—" She stopped, her eyes filling with tears.

"Died?" Santi finished for her. "I don't think so. He was practically next door and he made a lot of noise when he came home. Why did he knock on your door?"

"He didn't know you were with me," she explained. "He was upset because *he* wanted to sleep with me—" She stopped, her hand to her mouth.

"Sleep with you?" Santi laughed. Then he suddenly became serious. "Is this normal?"

"Well, no, it's—" Marcella shook her head and let out a deep sigh. How could she begin to explain it all?

"So Mark is not normal?" Santi said. "He wishes to sleep with you. He pretends to kill himself—"

"It wasn't pretending!" Marcella cried. "He swallowed those pills!"

"Knowing he would be found," Santi said. "Making himself the center of a drama."

A small part of her froze off as she stared at him.

"You think you know Mark's motives better than I do?" she asked him. She stood up to brush off her skirt and took their paper plates to a garbage pail. When she returned, he had packed the uneaten food in the basket. He stood too, watching her guardedly.

Her love for him mixed with exasperation and just plain exhaustion. Turning to leave the park, she felt him catch her wrist.

"Wait," he told her. "I want to ask you some questions, Marcella. And you must give me honest answers!"

She took a deep breath, holding his gaze. "I'm so tired, Santi. Maybe this isn't the best time for an interrogation. We didn't get much sleep and—"

"I want to know one thing," he interrupted. "Do you think you will ever find another man who loves you as I do?"

She stared at his strained face, biting her lip. Finally she said, "If you love me, you'll wait for me."

"Of course I love you!" he exploded. "I would wait a lifetime for you, *if* that would change anything. But if you give in to this boy now, he will *never* let go, Marcella! And we are not children. I'm forty-two. I want my happiness with you *now,* during the best years! You cannot let a child —who you yourself admit is not normal—run our lives?"

She broke away to walk toward the park exit, Santi alongside her.

"I didn't say Mark wasn't normal," she told him. "He simply needs me more than most—" She stopped, looking up at him pleadingly. "Look, he's going to graduate at the end of this month. Then he'll try out for this Italian scholarship in Bologna. This is something we've been working toward for *years,* Santi! I can't just stand by and watch Mark lose his chance. I *have* to be there with him. I'm counting on it to break our closeness. I know he's too dependent on me, but that's *my* fault! A year of living on his own in Italy will put everything right. . . ."

He handed her a handkerchief. "He's so talented," she told him. "So highly strung. Some of his teachers think he's a genius. Naturally, genius demands its own—" She broke off, blotting her tears.

"If your son must be the most important person in your life, then . . ." Santi shrugged resignedly. "Perhaps our lives *are* too different?" He seemed about to say more, then fell silent as they walked out of the park.

He handed her the picnic basket as they neared his hotel.

"Aren't you coming up to the apartment?" she asked him.

"I want to think a little about us," Santi told her. "If there is a solution to this, I must find it. I will call you later."

She found Mark sitting up in bed. He gave her his dazzling smile as she came in holding the picnic basket.

"How do you feel now?" she asked, sitting on the edge of the bed.

"Much better. Almost fine!" He took her hand. "Forgive me, Mom. I'm sorry."

She leaned to feel his forehead. "Hungry?" she asked.

"Ravenous!" he laughed. "What do you have in there? I feel like the wicked wolf getting a visit from Little Red Riding Hood." He peered into the basket.

"They're just leftovers from a picnic, I'm afraid," she said. "But neither of us ate much. There's cole slaw, chicken legs, and some rolls. Don't drink the wine, Mark; I'll get you some apple juice."

She brought him a glass of juice and sat watching him eat. "Do you realize how incredibly selfish you're being?" she asked him.

He glanced up. "I realize *everything* I'm being. That's just why I thought it would be better for everyone if I was conveniently out of the way."

Her eyes filled with tears. "Were you out of your mind?" she asked.

"Probably," he agreed. "*And* pretty drunk."

"Really!" she said. "But not drunk enough to forget to leave me a note that would have made me feel guilty for the rest of my life?"

Tears ran down her face and Mark watched her, as if impressed. He pushed the food away and she held him for a moment, thinking of Santi, of the two men facing each other across her mind and heart. She truly felt she loved them equally, so what happened when an irresistible force met an immovable object? Some kind of explosion in which the onlooker—herself—got hurt?

She stood up. "I'm going to see Amy," she announced.

Amy was just back from promoting her new novel, *The Art of the One-Night Stand.* Sitting among her unpacked suitcases, she listened to all that had happened, her head at a slant, trying to remain impartial.

"My!" She shook her head when Marcella finished. "We *do* make life difficult for ourselves, don't we? Where's Santi now?"

"He says he's thinking up a solution," Marcella said. "He expects me to just walk out on Mark. If I don't choose him, I think his Spanish pride is going to force him back to Barcelona in a huff and he'll never see me again!"

"I don't blame the guy," Amy said. She shook her head at Marcella. "Don't be a fool, Marcella. I know I kid around a lot, but if I found a man like Santi, I'd hang on with my *teeth.* There just *aren't* any men like him anymore. He's like some gorgeous innocent man out of the nineteen-fifties!"

"And that's why his thinking is thirty years behind mine," Marcella said.

"Nevertheless, he's pure gold," Amy enthused, "and he's right about Mark. You *can't* let him blackmail you. It's selfish and wicked and . . . *immoral!*"

"You call Mark immoral?" Marcella cried.

Amy winced, but she held Marcella's angry stare. "I don't deserve that, Marcella," she said. "Not because of that old chestnut 'all I've done for you,' but because whatever I do with my life, I don't go around hurting other people. Mark is setting out to ruin your relationship with this man, and *that's* what's immoral!"

"I'm sorry, Amy," Marcella apologized. "But if Mark killed himself, how could I ever live with myself again?"

Amy pursed her lips. "I agree with Santi. I think it *was* just a cry for attention. You can't forswear love for the rest of your life because of an overpossessive little boy."

Marcella sat down suddenly, looking beaten. "Did I deserve this, Amy?" she asked her.

"Who said we got the children we deserve?" Amy cracked. "Look at Sonia!"

"Sonia had a messed-up childhood," Marcella pointed out. "But Mark had all my attention. I invested all my love in him and—"

"Made him one thousand percent dependent on you!" Amy finished. She stood and put her arm around Marcella. "Now I know why I write books instead of rearing kids— it's a hell of a lot easier. Come!" She urged Marcella into the living room and rummaged among a stack of magazines. "Scott sent this over this morning." She opened a paper and brandished it in Marcella's face. "It's next Sunday's Book Review. I'm number three!"

"Congratulations!" Marcella kissed her. "I'm happy for you, Amy. But I'd exchange all the sales of my books for just one hour in Santi's arms!"

"Okay! So you just answered your own question!" Amy grabbed Marcella's arms and gently shook her. "You know your priorities. Go for them!"

Marcella returned to her apartment and looked in on Mark. He was sleeping. Santi called her at dusk, just as the lights were going on in the neighboring buildings.

"I think I have the solution," he told her. "I'm coming over."

She refreshed her makeup and set out a bottle of chilled wine.

Santi arrived ten minutes later, holding a bouquet of red roses.

"Thank you, darling!" She took them and he held her in his arms tightly, kissing her. He followed her to the kitchen and hugged her from behind as she filled a vase with water and arranged the flowers.

In the living room, she poured their wine, handing him a glass. Santi's face glowed with triumph as he toasted her.

"Where is Mark? I would like to tell you this together," he said.

"He's still sleeping," she told him, pulling him down to the sofa next to her. "Tell me first!"

He took a sip of wine. "I walked around Manhattan," he told her, "asking for God's help."

"And did He help?" she asked.

"In a way, yes!" Santi nodded. "I walked so far. Down strange streets we did not visit together. I saw such poor people lying on the sidewalk begging for money or sleeping. Then I came back uptown and I saw such strange people—people dressed funny or walking funny. *I* don't know, *crazy* people! And then I realized that New York *is* crazy. It's difficult to think straight here! There is too much of everything—too much poorness, too much richness. If *I* feel crazy here after only a week, naturally your children must feel worse for having lived here all their lives. So I found the solution."

"What?" she gasped.

"You must all come to Majorca," he said, his eyes bright. "You *and* Mark and Sonia. There is room for you all. The children can stay in the apartment and you and I at Deya. You saw yourself how calm and beautiful Majorca is. In a few months Mark will accept everything and we will all be happy!" He was so triumphant that Marcella's heart turned over.

"We'll ask them of course, but . . ." She stopped, thinking. "I don't see how it could work. Sonia's modeling keeps her based here. Mark has an audition in Bologna next month. . . ."

"And you could write there!" Santi said, not listening. "You said yourself you could write there."

"I'll need some time with Mark here, first," she said. "Maybe find him a good therapist. Get him some help."

"What *I* propose is not help?" Santi frowned.

Marcella threw her arms around him and hugged him. "You're so good and kind and generous, darling!" She spoke into the warmth of his neck. "And you're absolutely right about New York being crazy. But we like it like that. We *thrive* on it! And Mark and Sonia would never want to leave it. I'm going to have a hard time getting Mark to go to Italy for a year!"

Santi looked at her as if seeing her for the first time. "I thought I knew you," he told her, "through and through—the very essence of you. But now I see you here and I don't know what to think!"

"Don't say that," she cried, grabbing his hand. "You *do* know me! I let you know me as no other man ever has. But you don't have children, Santi; you can't know what it feels like. They're my flesh and blood! You do your best for them, but there's no guarantee how they'll turn out. I loved Mark more than anyone has a right to be loved—for eighteen years! Of *course* he feels abandoned now that I've found you!"

Santi got up and paced the room. "There is a bigger difference between us than I could have guessed," he said. "I thought you shared my dream. To live in Majorca—what more could one ask? I tried to show you the simple, beautiful life of the island I love."

"Yes, my darling, you did show me!" she agreed. "And I shall never forget it. That gorgeous house in Deya! Rubbing oil on the figs! The dear little bent lady next door who was so happy for us . . ."

"Is that all it is for you?" he asked. "Some memories? A summer romance like the tourists have?"

She held his gaze. "You know it was much more than that. It's just that we need to—"

"*You* need!" Santi shouted. "*Mark* needs! We discuss your needs a lot, but what about *my* needs?" He turned her face so that she was looking at him.

"I'm sorry, Santi," she said helplessly. "I'd love to have introduced you to a perfect family—"

"I didn't expect that!" he said. "*I'm* not perfect, but you have not had time to notice all *my* faults. Spaniards—Majorcans—are a proud people. We will give you our love, our hearts, our *lives,* but we must keep our pride."

She stared at him. "I haven't taken your pride, Santi," she said softly.

"Then don't treat me like a fool," he said. "Just tell your son that we are getting married!"

She nodded numbly.

"This is not just pride—these are the fundamental questions of life, Marcella. Yours, Mark's, and mine," Santi continued. "And if you do not accept my offer, then I leave tomorrow."

He jumped to his feet and walked into the hall. She followed. "Forgive me for being so serious, Marcella," he asked. "My friends tell me I am sometimes a very funny man who makes them laugh. You would never guess that?" He smiled. "But I have fallen in love only twice in my lifetime. That's all." He made a formal little bow as he opened the front door.

"Where are you going, Santi?" she asked quietly. "Can't I come with you?"

"No," Santi said. "You stay with your son while he sleeps. And think over all I've said."

That night, she thought of nothing else. In bed later, unable to sleep, she tried to understand the puzzle her life had become. When she finally lost consciousness, she suffered anxious dreams. She awoke next morning with no solution, no answer. She showered and dressed, finding Mark fixing breakfast in the kitchen. She could not bring herself to tell him of Santi's offer because if he sneered or laughed at it she knew she would despise him. He would try to make Santi appear naive or stupid, and she would be unable to explain how earnest his offer was. Amy said Santi was pure gold—perhaps pure gold was too rich for crazy New Yorkers to appreciate?

"Breakfast?" Mark offered, displaying the eggs.

Marcella shook her head. "I'm meeting Santi. I have a suspicion he's leaving today."

"Oh?" Mark looked up from his eggs. "Did we scare him off?"

She gave him a look. "You may have," she told him. "You've got to understand that our . . . closeness is a bit hard for outsiders to understand." He reached out guiltily for her, but she turned and left the kitchen.

Santi was sipping coffee at his usual booth in the hotel coffee shop. He stood up as she came in. They embraced and he poured some coffee for her.

"Stay another week as you'd planned and we can talk some more," she suggested.

Santi shook his head. She hated seeing him in this obstinate mood. "We have a saying in Spanish that our actions speak louder than our words," he told her. "We could talk for ten years and it would just be saying the same things. So enough words, Marcella. Now we *act!* I have a business to take care of. I offered you everything I have—my love, my life. I have offered your children the same." He gave a shrug.

"I only know I love you," she told him.

"Then come with me to Barcelona this afternoon," he urged. "I cannot play these American games, Marcella. In Spain, children do not dare to interfere with their parents' lives."

"I can't just leave Mark," she said. "Not now."

"So Mark does come first?" he asked.

There was a silence and she thought how funny it was that it had taken them hours of thinking and talking to come to such a simple, final question. She looked fully into his questioning gaze: his dark eyes which showed his love for her and his proud, strong character. Everything depended on this moment.

"At this time, yes," she answered, seeing the love flicker in his eyes. "Mark's well-being comes first."

The fact that Santi was leaving her did not sink in until they were on the way to the airport with Donald driving and her stomach churning with anxiety. She tried to view the situation objectively, to understand that this was the only action his pride allowed him to take, but she still felt as if she were being abandoned.

"This is ridiculous," she murmured. "We love each other! We both agree on that. We shouldn't be separating."

He did not answer. He leaned forward to Donald as they neared the airport. "Just let me out at Iberia. You don't need to park." He turned to Marcella. "We will spare each other long good-byes. That just makes it worse."

They followed the signs to Iberia, and Donald obediently left the engine running when they stopped, fetching Santi's suitcase from the trunk. But Marcella couldn't bear the purring of the engine like a meter signaling their time running out. She leaned over the front seat and switched it off.

Santi turned to her. "Thank you for everything, Marcella." He kissed her and she could see he was making a great effort to control himself. His look seemed to be asking her forgiveness at not being able to accept something that went against his beliefs.

She sat stiffly as he left the car, took the bag from Donald, and thanked him for his services, shaking his hand warmly. He leaned in through the window to say, "I love you!" then turned and walked quickly through the entrance to the terminal.

Marcella watched the back of his figure in disbelief. Donald got into the car and started up the engine, but she threw open the door, jumped out, and followed Santi. She stood at the back of the line, watching him check in, seeing him thank the clerk as he took the boarding pass. She willed him to look up and see her. When he turned and met her eyes she saw the pain he too was in. She ran to him, taking his arm.

"This is ridiculous, Santi! We love each other! We found each other—we can't just let each other go!"

His face lit up. "You'll come with me to the ticket desk to find out if there is a spare seat?"

"No," she said. "No, I can't. But let's make a date we can look forward to. I'll come to Spain or you'll return here—"

He looked in her eyes and she stopped. Kissing her cheek lightly, he murmured, "Good-bye," almost absently and went to passport control. He lowered his head to pass through the metal detector. She stood among groups of embracing passengers, some of them crying, so that the tears coursing down her face did not seem out of place. As Santi reached the final barrier he gave her a funny little salute and vanished.

She turned to walk back to the car, the automatic airport doors hissing apart as she approached. How had it happened? This kind of love—so sure, so preordained—*couldn't* happen only to go wrong!

Outside, the air was smoggy, the gas fumes from revving cars and idling limousines making the area noxious. Donald opened the door for her. She stared blankly out of the windows as they drove toward the city.

"Home, Mrs. Winton?" Donald asked as they crossed the bridge. She glanced at his solicitous eyes in the rear-view mirror. He was really a most kind and discreet man, and in one way he knew her better than anyone. She could hear from his voice that he was trying, in his way, to console her.

When she couldn't answer, he said, "I'll take you home then," as if deciding for her. But she thought, No, not home! At that moment she never wanted to see her home again. She loathed everything about her life—her apartment, her writing, her son, her reflection in the mirror.

"Take me to Fifty-seventh and Eighth," she told Donald curtly. She had thought she would never return to the no-man's-land of darkness and shame, but she would not be able to get through the rest of that day without some kind of help, and this laughably poor substitute for love was the only antidote she knew.

"You can go home," she told Donald when he pulled up, forty minutes later. "I won't need you anymore tonight."

She stood at the back of the theater, not really understanding why she had come. There were a dozen reasons and yet there was no reason at all. It was better than going home. For a few moments, accustoming her eyes to the dark, the old life beckoned her back to its seductive, false comforts. Except for one thing: she hated the idea of sex. Yet her body needed some kind of touch, some reassurance. She shivered at how complicated she had become. Perhaps she needed to punish herself in some way, to see how low she could sink on the human scale of happiness, from the sublime joy she had recently known, all the way down to this. She looked around the dark theater. It was funny, but all she could feel in the tawdry, familiar setting was love! In the mood she was in, she felt that the men seated alone, turning their heads in her direction, were there to console her for her loss. It was as if they all knew everything and were waiting here to make it all right. She stumbled sideways, into the embrace of a tall, gray-haired man who hovered nearby as if they had had a rendezvous. She was so numb that for a moment she almost believed he was her father. He put his arms around her and she relaxed in her father's loving embrace which had always made her feel no harm could ever come to her. She inhaled his clean, cologned smell, tinged with the aroma of tobacco, so like the memory she held of her father. Only when he began to press urgently against her did she break away and run from the theater.

She crossed immediately to the other side of the street. It was a mild June evening, still light. But life had suddenly, completely changed. It was not at all as she had believed it to be—a series of faltering steps that led toward happiness. Instead, she saw it as a series of subterfuges, hiding out from what one most wanted. Because if you got that, there would be too high a price to pay. The price *she* had always paid. In her books she had said that love was the only meaningful part of life, the part that made the rest worthwhile. Now she realized love was even more important to her than she'd thought. It was so potent that it constituted a threat to one's security; she could become as dependent on Santi's love as Mark was on hers. *That* must be why she had scared Santi off, together with the very real threat to Mark's well-being. So . . . now that she knew love was a dead-end, perhaps she should give all her time and attention to her writing and her son? That was probably how it had been planned for her life to be. That was the sacrifice. Nobody got it all. And that is what she must keep telling herself.

She was still telling herself this when she entered the darkened apartment and, not switching on lights, felt her way straight to the drinks cart. Two, three, four shots of Scotch failed to dull the pain. If anything, the liquor made her hurt more. Santi! God, just thinking his name hurt!

No, Marcella, she told herself, you did not do the right thing. You did the wrong thing. But you hardly had a choice.

The handsome man wearing dark glasses on the evening flight to Barcelona had resisted the pretty cabin attendant's attempts at flirtation. Instead, he asked her for writing paper and an envelope. He nibbled the end of his pen for a long time before starting to write:

My dearest love, Marcella,

I am writing this on the plane after thinking of you for every second since we parted. I had to leave because I wanted to make as strong an objection as I could to the way your life is with your son, the power he has over you. Selfishly, I need you and I want you, but I feel I have a right to you.

I believe we were born to be together. Unselfishly (can we ever be that?) I truly believe it would be better for you to let go of Mark the way animals let go of their young ones, with love—and yet firmly.

I always thought my Spanish-Majorcan pride was a good thing, but now I see that too much pride could make me lose you. I am preparing to forget pride, because life without you would be so inferior to life with you. To keep my morale strong now, I must believe that in a few days' time, you will see I am right and be true to yourself, not to Mark's weakness. He must grow up in a realistic world where a mother does not place her son's happiness before her own, at least not if the mother is logical, normal, young and beautiful, and able to inspire the kind of love you have inspired in me.

I have always thought a man should not live on hope, but in these past hours I have realized that I cannot live without hope. I therefore await word from you. Until I hold you again in my arms, until my lips are pressed again to yours, where they should be, I wait, my darling. Forever, your Santi.

He read through the letter carefully and then sealed it. It was not exactly what he wished to say, but his English was limited and he was feeling as sad as he had ever felt in his life. He sighed and slipped the envelope into his pocket. Maybe, he suddenly thought, it is better not to send it at all? He would decide that in Barcelona.

She plunged into work, correcting final proofs for *Music of Love,* which Volumes was planning to rush out for late fall. She arranged her life so that she was alone as much as possible. If she couldn't be with Santi, she wanted no one. The lonelier she felt, the more compelled she was to write.

She wrote deep into the night, until dawn came and the noise of traffic once again filled the street outside. She felt she was writing her first real love story because now it was something that had happened to *her*. The story of two American women traveling to Majorca had to be written while the experience was still fresh in her mind. It had to be gotten down on paper while she remembered vividly the piney Palma air, the sounds of the street outside Santi's apartment, the subtle colors of the olive trees in Deya, the lovemaking. This time she would describe making love quite differently from the way she had in her previous books—it would be less sexual, more spiritual, more romantic. Each time she typed the title at the top of a page, *Forever Begins Tonight,* she would remember Santi's first utterance of the words and feel that stab of love mixed with pain.

Sharing her passions with a million readers was cathartic. This writing was a cry from her heart and soul. Her readers would understand what she was saying, she knew. At last she could let them know what a woman in love really experienced.

Mark was attuned enough to her feelings to sense that he should keep out of her way. Her late working hours meant that she slept until noon. The first thing she did when she got up was go to her desk and look through the mail that Mark brought up. If no letter from Santi appeared, she would make herself a promise not to write to him. But during each long night of work, usually toward three or four in the morning, she invariably broke her promise and indulged in the sheer pleasure of writing him a long, love-filled letter. She left these letters out for Mark to mail on his way to school, marked "Special Delivery." He did not like his role of mailman. When Marcella rose early one morning, meeting him just before he left the apartment, he blurted out "Why do you have to keep writing to that guy? I thought it was all over?" At that moment, she hated her son, and he must have felt it through her chilling look.

"You don't need to read the names on the envelopes," she told him coldly.

"You mark *his* 'Special Delivery,'" he pointed out. "Of course I see his name."

She held his gaze. "It saves me a trip to the Post Office, Mark," she said. "And I really think it's the least you can do for me. I mean, under the circumstances. Don't you?"

He came over to hug her. "I'm sorry," he said. "Of course I'll mail your letters."

She hugged him back, a little halfheartedly, reminding herself, "*I* made him selfish!" And maybe it was a gift. Maybe it was better to be selfish in a selfish world.

Santi had warned her of his pride, but his silence was killing her. Three weeks after his departure she dropped all her resolve and dialed the number of his Barcelona gallery. She was answered by a female voice who said, *"No está,"* when she asked for Señor Roca.

Now she avoided Amy, Nancy, and any women friends with whom she had sometimes lunched. She wanted to divide her life very clearly into "before Santi" and "after Santi," making the "after" part as different as she could.

"You don't have to come to Bologna with me," Mark told her flatly in July. "There's a group of us going to Gianni's auditions; it might be awkward if you came, too."

"But I thought I'd give you moral support, Mark," she protested. "I'd handle all the travel arrangements, make sure you had your music, your passport, money . . ."

"Cole Ferrer is coming with us, along with another teacher. They'll look after us," he assured her. "Anyway, we're not kids."

It hurt, but Marcella knew she must encourage his first stab at independence. "You're sure you'll be all right, Mark?" she asked.

"Don't worry!" he said. "We'll have a lot of fun."

"Forget about fun this time, Mark," she advised. "Just give the best damn performance you've ever given in your life!"

He was away for five nights. When he called to tell her that he'd been accepted by Signor Gianni as a pupil, she opened a bottle of champagne and toasted him over the phone.

"Congratulations, darling. I knew you'd do it!" she said warmly.

"I knew, too," Mark said matter-of-factly.

They said good-bye and she sat at the dark window of her living room. It was after midnight and she slowly sipped the wine. "To Mark!" she said aloud, raising her glass. He would make it. He would be a brilliant, successful musician. A concert pianist known throughout the world. It helped, she thought, drinking. It really did. It would make up for the feeling she now had that her life just didn't mean anything. You never get it all, she thought, feeling the wine relax her. "Not happy children, a successful career, *and* love. But now that Mark was taken care of for the next year . . .

Her thoughts were interrupted by the telephone's jangle and she answered carelessly, thinking it must be Mark again.

"Marcella?" Santi's voice, so close to her, was like an instant cessation of her dull ache, an easing of the pressure on her soul and heart.

"Santi?" she gasped. "Is that really you?"

"What time is it there?" he asked. "Did I wake you?"

"It's twelve-thirty, darling. How wonderful to hear from you! You can't know how I've missed you! How are you?"

"I am okay," he said. "And Mark?"

"He's fine, now, Santi," she told him. "He just called me five minutes ago from Bologna. He's been accepted by Gianni—that Italian maestro I told you about. He'll start a year of studies with him in September."

"You must be very happy, Marcella."

"I would be, darling, if I didn't miss you so much. Why did you wait so long to call?" she asked.

"I wanted to see if I could live without you, Marcella," he told her.

"And can you?" she asked breathlessly.

"I don't think so," he said.

"Oh darling, life is hell without you!" she confessed. "We belong together, you know, Santi?"

"I agree," he said. "And I have a new idea for us, perhaps a way for us to be together."

"What is it?" she smiled.

"I talked to various friends about this problem," he told her. "One friend in particular, who is a psychologist. He told me about suicide and how it is often a desperate cry for attention. Mark has never had the attention of his father, has he? I have thought so seriously. . . ." His voice faltered.

She said, "When did you ever do anything *not* seriously, Santi?"

"I never wanted children," he continued. "I felt this was not a world into which we should bring fresh lives. It was one of the reasons for my divorce, because my wife wanted a child. I refused that responsibility. Perhaps that is why I seem less understanding about Mark than I should be. A father would balance his life. He would be less dependent on you. So I took legal advice, and I am prepared to adopt Mark. As if he were my own son. What do you think?"

Marcella took an intake of breath; she had been holding it as he spoke. "Oh, Santi, it's so generous and sweet of you, but—" she began.

"After Italy, he can live with us in Majorca, if he chooses," he went on. "I could open a new branch of my gallery there. We would be a family."

She closed her eyes tightly, biting her lip. "Santi," she said. "It's such a wonderful offer and I know how much thought you've given it, but not having a father isn't Mark's problem. He has a father. His father is in prison."

"In prison?" Santi said. "For what?"

"He found a way to make money in the stock market that was illegal," she told him.

"I see," Santi said, and she could hear the disillusionment in his voice. "You did not tell me this."

"I wanted to spare you the grisly details," she sighed. "I did warn you that our family was a little crazy, didn't I?" She tried to laugh but there was silence at the other end of the line.

"Look, darling," she suggested. "Let me see Mark through this year in Italy and visit you as much as I can. After he's through with Italy, we'll—"

"No," Santi cut her off. "If we don't settle the question of Mark now, he will always come between us. I know it, Marcella."

"Let's solve any problems as they arrive, Santi," she proposed. "Meanwhile we'll spend time together. We love each other enough to withstand the problems, don't we, Santi?" She heard his long sigh as if his mouth were near her ear. It made him feel so near to her and she longed for his warm hand, his caress.

"Marcella, the kind of intense love you need—and give —brings its own problems," he said. "Maybe too many problems?"

"But what happened to our 'forever' love?" she cried.

"I haven't forgotten it," he assured her. "I never will. But you did ask me to marry you, Marcella. And my dream of love is as intense and all-consuming as yours. I need it to be equal!"

"It *is* equal, Santi!" she told him.

"Not if Mark continues to come before me. Not if he is getting more of your love than I am!" he pointed out.

"That's the same old argument, Santi!" she said. "You're as bad as Mark! Making me choose between you! I can't cut off one leg and one arm and half my heart! Mark will always be part of me. He's going to have a brilliant career and I want to be there, *always,* encouraging him. You don't know what a parent feels for a child—you've never had one!"

"That's what I propose to share with you," he said. "By adopting Mark."

"Mark would never accept!" she cried.

"Ask him!" Santi suggested.

"I don't need to ask him," she replied quickly. "I *know* what his reaction would be. He'd just laugh!"

"Laugh?" Santi echoed.

Oh God, Marcella thought, why did I use that word?

"Maybe I am tired of being laughed at, Marcella." Santi's voice turned ice-cold. "Maybe we should just say good-bye, *now.*"

"No! Wait! Don't sound so final!" she cried. "We'll see each other soon, won't we? You did get my letters?" But the line was buzzing and she realized he had hung up.

Santi walked down Las Ramblas, Barcelona's busiest street. It was not actually a street, more a walkway down the center of a wide boulevard, filled with stalls selling such items as flowers and magazines and caged birds. It was jammed with people at all hours of the day, but this afternoon Santi saw none of them. He was angry at having just had his adoption offer turned down out of hand. Yet he knew that within a few minutes the anger would seep away and that horrible lonely feeling would descend on him again, that sense of life being out of his control, which he had vowed he would never allow himself to feel again.

There was only one way to handle a feeling like this when it was caused entirely by a woman—and that was to cut it out of one's heart like a man. With work, with travel, with anything that would replace that precious emotion. He stood at a cross street waiting for the traffic to stop. Why did he have this unshakable conviction that Marcella was fated for him, that of all the women he had met or was likely to meet, only *she* had that special quality? It was so illogical; he must conquer it if he did not want to remain unhappy.

He was walking up Las Ramblas toward his parents' apartment. He had managed to delay this meeting with them for the three weeks since New York, for he knew he would be thoroughly grilled about his trip. He had not yet mentioned Marcella; he had pretended his visit was to explore a possible tie-up with a Manhattan gallery. Perhaps his mother would see through his fabrications and ask some of her famous, cutting questions? She longed for him to remarry, he knew. What could he tell her? That she had come very close to being the grandmother of two neurotic American teenagers?

He shrugged, crossing the street, regarding the parakeets and doves fluttering in their cramped quarters in a pet stall. Why did we make prisons for ourselves? How had Marcella and her son constructed such an exclusive, limited world for themselves? Would it not be better if he attempted to forget this adventure, or should he write all his feelings—as he longed to do—in one long, utterly honest letter to Marcella, thus leaving the door open for some hope? For right now, hope seemed as necessary to him as oxygen.

When Mark returned from Italy, they celebrated his success at Amy's Southampton retreat, where Amy, ignoring the fact that Marcella had become so reclusive, treated her kindly and tenderly. At her glamorous parties she defended

Marcella from "wolves" and married men, respecting her solitude. A famous writer said he had fallen in love with Marcella. They had spent a day on the beach and he had been her rapt neighbor at the dinner table, but she was quite oblivious to him as a man, even when Amy interceded on his behalf.

"I met the man who was born for me, Amy," she explained. "We had something too good for him to just forget about us. Our story isn't over yet, I *know* it isn't!"

She watched Mark playing the piano to amuse Amy's guests, marveling at the spell he cast. He had been offered recording contracts by people who had seen him perform at the Carlyle, but so far she had managed to persuade him not to sign, certain it would not do his classical career any good.

There was an unspoken understanding between them now that they were beholden, in some new binding way, to each other. She wrote a few more impassioned letters to Santi, trying to explain herself, assuring him of her "forever" love, whatever he thought of her and her crazy family. She had another person to worry about now; her mother had not been doing well lately, and on her visits to her, she clung to her mother's hand, willing her to get well. Although she hardly recognized this old, bedridden lady who barely glanced at her, it was her mother and she hated the thought of losing her.

They were at Amy's last dinner party of August, when some presentiment made her call the nursing home for the second time that day.

"We've been calling your number all afternoon," the nurse told her. "I'm afraid your mother passed away."

The gravediggers stared goggle-eyed at Sonia as they lowered her grandmother's coffin carefully into the earth. The grave alongside Aldo Balducci had been bought for Ida at the time of his death. The entire neighborhood had turned out for the funeral in the Little Italy churchyard, and everyone seemed to be staring at Sonia. Since she normally wore black anyway, she had had her entire wardrobe to choose from. She had come up with a miniskirt over long tights, a black sweater, a black felt hat pulled over her hair, and dark glasses. Marcella knew she was supposed to be honored that Sonia had even bothered to attend this family event. Normally, she almost never saw her, had followed her progress as a top model in the glossy pages of *Vogue* and *Bazaar* or had read snippets of news in the *New York Post*.

Marcella felt a numbed grief at losing her mother. Her visits to the home—weekly checks just to make sure Ida was well treated—had become a habit. Ida had died a little old shell of a lady, not knowing who anyone was. Even so, Marcella would miss her. She glanced at the faces in the crowd, getting little shocks when she recognized school friends. They looked so much older. Did she look old, too? Or was that what money had done for her—bought off age? Were they all as bored with their husbands as she had been, and so overeating and neglecting themselves in a kind of perverse revenge? She felt great empathy for them.

When Father Carmello said, "Let us pray," she closed her eyes and pictured her parents, but she found she was not praying for them. Oh God, she prayed, don't let Santi forget me! She felt he should be with her here, now, supporting her with his presence, his love.

Father Carmello gave a short address, mentioning that he had known the Balducci family since beginning work in that parish. When he ended, he invited the congregation of friends to join Marcella and her family for the traditional wine and cake, to be served in the church hall. Marcella walked between Sonia and Mark to the hall. Sonia was silent, withdrawn, as if she had posed for so many fashion photographs that she no longer knew how to act at real-life events, especially a formal, serious ceremony. Marcella hesitated when a woman held out one of her books, expecting her to sign it.

"I'm not sure this is the right place," she murmured.

"Oh, Marcella, don't you remember me?" The plump woman grinned into her face as if daring Marcella to recognize her.

"Sisi!" Marcella cried, embracing her. She had been one of the girls who had listened, hypnotized, to her first stories.

Sisi hugged her delightedly. "I always said you'd make

it, Marcella. I knew you'd be a successful writer one day! Now I want you to sign this very personally!"

"I bought your book as soon as it came out in paper-back, Marcella," another voice said.

"Andrea!" Marcella hugged her old friend.

Sonia was plucking at Marcella's arm. "I have a booking uptown," she muttered. She pecked Marcella's cheek and touched Mark's arm. "Don't be sad. Grandma's better off out of it."

Marcella watched her as she cut a quick swath through the crowd.

"I'll help her find a cab," Mark said, following her.

"Oh, your daughter is so beautiful!" one woman told her. "So beautiful! We saw her on television the other night. I said, 'I swear that's Sonia Winton,' but my husband said—"

"Yes. Thank you." Marcella made herself acknowledge their compliments. They meant well. They couldn't realize that the sight of Sonia set off a host of conflicting emotions.

"And your son is so handsome. Is he going to be a model, too?"

"No, he's studying the piano. I hope he'll become a concert pianist!"

"Oh Marcella, how wonderful! How proud you must be!"

"Yes. Thank you," she stammered. She clutched at Mark when he returned, wanting to tell him to enjoy his awkwardness with these decent people. She whispered, "This is probably the last time we'll belong here. For better or worse . . ."

She took some white roses from the reception area and wandered out to her mother's freshly covered grave. As she threw the flowers gently onto the dirt, the tears finally flowed.

When Father Carmello came to stand quietly by her side, she saw that the open frank face had begun to show lines, and there was an empty look in his expression, the look of self-denial.

"Thank you for saying such nice things about my parents, Father Carmello," she said. "I really appreciate it."

"I thought them fine people," he said simply. "Little

Italy's changing so. I miss the real old Italian families like yours, Marcella. I was so sorry to hear about your husband. Do you go to church? Have you confessed recently?"

"No," she said, lowering her eyes. He waited. This burial had released all the memories of her father's funeral. How bad she had felt that day, believing she was somehow to blame for his death. God, what a guilt trip she had been on! And now she was divorced, had met and perhaps lost the great love of her life, and was standing in the very same place, alongside the same priest who had married her. She closed her eyes and swayed dizzily. She touched Father Carmello's sleeve hesitantly and led the way into the empty church. He followed her. She walked toward the confessional booth. How much would she be able to tell him? Would she be able to put into words the visits to Members? The voices of the people at the reception in the hall next door echoed in the old building as Father Carmello took his usual place behind the grille. Inside the booth, the smell of musty wood overcame her as she fell to her knees. Her throat clogged with grief and memories and dust. She began to choke, taking great gasps of air and spluttering.

"I *can't.*" She coughed, and he came around to her side, gave her his hand, and helped her out as she tried to recover. "I can't!" she said again.

"That's all right, Marcella." He put his hand on her shoulder. "This isn't the right day, perhaps. But I'm here anytime you want me. Don't forget us, Marcella. And don't forget God."

"I won't," she vowed. "Thank you, Father."

She knew she would never return. What she had to confess was too much for the church. It would have to go, disguised somehow, into her books. Her readers would absolve her and understand. They would find nothing odd in her conviction that she was a good person. Nothing strange about her visits to Members for uncomplicated, necessary sex, after which she left as unsullied, as pure, as when she had entered. Nothing surprising in the fact that she was strangely proud of her life.

When she and Mark got into the Rolls, her friends and the assorted visitors clustered around the car, touching its shininess, waving good-bye. She told many people to come see her, knowing they never would, knowing that "uptown" was like another country to them. The car took them slowly out of Little Italy, perhaps for the last time.

In early September, Marcella accompanied Mark to Italy. First, they spent a week sight-seeing in Rome and Florence, experiencing the strange joy of discovering their heritage. She saw men in the Roman streets who reminded her so much of her father that she wanted to cry. In Bologna, she helped settle Mark into a top-floor room at the modest students' pensione he had chosen. Maestro Gianni gave a welcoming lunch for his new pupils and their families. Marcella adored Bologna and wanted to stay on, but her new book was due out soon and Mark had to be left to get on with his own life. She flew back to New York to get on with hers.

By October, Mark's "cult" album of show tunes was suddenly everywhere. She heard it played on FM radio and saw it in music-store windows on Broadway and in the Village. She had a hunch that Cole Ferrer had had a hand in promoting it, but she consoled herself with the thought that now that Mark was in Italy, he was far enough away from Cole's influence to follow the course she wanted for him. She had won *that* round!

When *Music of Love* was published late that fall, Marcella refused to do a publicity tour or any television interviews. "I'm not a performer," she advised Scott. "From now on, I only do signings." Scott was furious, but Volumes had so many advance orders for *Music* that it was an obvious success even before publication. As her agent, Amy was brought into battle, but she saw she could not change Marcella's mind.

"From now on, my books will have to sell on their own merit," Marcella told her. "I'm not going to be part of that circus. Scott can bitch all he likes."

For the first time, she got respectful reviews acknowledging her as a cut above the popular potboiler author. Critics commended the romantic sweep that took the reader through three decades of European concert halls and musicians' rivalries. Amy was treating her very carefully, never insisting that Marcella do anything against her will. A day before the official publication date, they toured the bookstores in Amy's car, checking out the displays for the book. There was a whole window for it in Waldenbooks on Fifth Avenue, and Doubleday's had arranged a giant stack to greet customers as they entered the store. Most other stores had ordered fifty to a hundred copies.

With the publication of *Music of Love,* Marcella reached the point in her career where she became a "brand name," when just the fact that her name was printed in large letters on the book's cover was enough to sell it. This was a testament to her talent, to the undeniable fact that a great many readers had loved her first two books enough to make them automatically want to read her third.

Scott called her three weeks after the book came out, his voice excited yet strangely awed. "Marcella," he asked, "are you sitting down? I have *The New York Times* Book Review for next Sunday in my hand; you came in at number one!"

"I don't believe it!" she gasped. "Scott . . . I just don't know what to say! Thank you for letting me know." She replaced the phone gently, amazed at the tears pouring down her face. She was not sure why she was crying. Her success? Or the fact that it had come at such a moment in her life? She stared out at Central Park. How ungrateful, how wicked of her not to be jumping with joy. There were writers all over the world who would kill to be in her place. And it didn't matter to her at all. She would exchange it all to be with Santi in his house in Deya, to wake up in the night feeling his lips pressed against the back of her neck, to turn over in the morning and find his dark eyes watching her with love. All she could see in the future was writing at her desk, dashing out to Members for a quick fix of sex, attending Mark's concerts as his fame grew, and feeling that empty hurt inside for Santi's arms, Santi's murmuring voice, Santi's lips. She nearly dialed his Barcelona number so many times, wrote numerous love letters that she tore up the next morning, planned trips to Spain and then canceled them an hour later. He had to want *her* as much as she wanted *him:* chasing him would cheapen their love. So she was very strict with herself and stuck to her rules—no calls and no more letters. But how was she going to find the will to continue with her life? She knew the answer would involve a radical change and even more work. She knew the answer would involve thinking of many other people besides herself. And she was ready to reach out to that new solution.

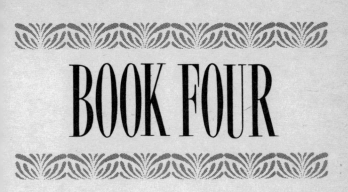

BOOK FOUR

BOOK FOUR

SIXTEEN

Manhattan, Spring 1990

Top models wear makeup only when paid to do so; the more successful the model, the more naked the off-duty face. Sonia thus sported only the merest brush of color on her fashionably full lips as she strode down Madison Avenue at her usual high speed. She glittered like a dark diamond, her straight black hair flowing from beneath a carelessly tied silk scarf, her short skirt showing off the flawless legs that were almost too elongated for real life. It was a brilliant April morning, the chill sunshine coating buildings, people, and cars with a hard-edged light. Passersby turned to stare as this gorgeous tall creature nimbly sidestepped them, as strange as a visitor from another planet, the planet of Beauty.

To accentuate her eyes, she usually wore purple or lavender or black. Today, it was black, a light cashmere cape draped across one shoulder, her glamour spreading an aura around her, dusting the lives of the people she passed with the glitter of a dream.

For a few minutes, she graced a chic Italian café with her presence, gulping down a perfect cappuccino, tossing a five-dollar bill to the handsome waiter who knew her face and called, *"Ciao, bella!"* after her as she ran off, winking back at him through the window. Now that she was eighteen it was clear that she had one of those magically constructed faces that become better defined, more exquisite, with each year. She would be beautiful at thirty, fifty, *eighty,* and knowing this gave her a throwaway confidence that is the mark of a great beauty.

By the time she reached Sixty-fourth Street, the coffee was working. Not calm at the best of times, when she drank coffee she felt almost crazy, her mind buzzing uncontrollably. She welcomed this rush of sensation, using it to plan the coming evening, to which she had looked forward for months and now half dreaded—because it was so important. She had told no one of her plans for that night. If anyone asked, she would be vague and mysterious. She had pulled strings for four months to get these seats and she was not about to jeopardize one moment of pleasure. A wicked gust of wind suddenly blew across Madison, blinding all those without wraparound sunglasses. A little girl rubbed her eyes, then pulled her hand out of her mother's to run to Sonia at a red light and ask, "Are you famous?"

Sonia shook her head and strode briskly away from her. She didn't like children because they saw through her. Men never did. They were too busy staring at her long, lean body or into the violet irises.

When she reached the studio, everyone crowded around to greet her, kissing and fussing. An assistant went for coffee, a *New York Post* was thrust into her lap, and Jason, the face designer, tied a large bib around her neck.

"No dark circles! No bags! Sonia, I love you!" he cried, setting out his colors.

"What are you wearing?" She sniffed the air.

Jason glanced down at himself. "Oh, Eau Sauvage," he remembered. "I like that extreme strength they do. That's me, darling, *très extreme*!"

"Reminds me of my brother," she closed her eyes again, "and it's weird because he's over from Italy and we're lunching today."

"This *is* the Mark Winton who has that album of show tunes out?" Jason drawled.

Sonia nodded.

"Lucky *you.*" Jason sighed. "I *love* his album. *So* romantic!" He began layering color on her eyelids. "The photos on the album don't give much away. Is he or isn't he?" He raised his eyebrows as she squinted at him in the mirror.

"Who cares?" Sonia groaned, closing her eyes.

"*I* do!" Jason cried. "Tell me and I'll sell the story to the *National Enquirer*!" he chuckled. "Oh, how about an overlay of Frosted Fuchsia? To bring out those gleaming little Liz Taylors?"

"Little Markie's sex life is a big secret," Sonia said. "Even from himself. My mother would have this heart attack if he ever came out of his little musical closet. They probably both like to think he just hasn't met the right girl!"

"That's what *my* mother thinks," Jason agreed, pressing a Q-tip loaded with pink powder to the corner of her eye. "Your mother writes those books, right? Romantic bestsellers?"

"Yeah . . ." Sonia muttered. "Everyone in my entire family is a fucking genius. Except for my poor dad. He's dying of cancer in a prison hospital." She opened one eye to look at Jason, adding, "At thirty-nine!"

Jason shook his head. "*God,* what a *bore* for him!" He took a step backward, squinting his eyes at her reflection. "Now that's what I call burnished!" he said. "You can't beat Chanel."

"She sent Mark to Italy," Sonia said as he began to work again on her. "I figured it must be because they have less AIDS in Italy than here!"

"*Really!*" Jason groaned. "They have less AIDS anywhere!"

"Anyway, Mark's managed to stay alive and well," she said. "But I'm not exactly one of his fans."

"Sibling rivalry?"

"No." She shook her head. "I just happen to hate goody-goody types, I can't stand a holier-than-thou attitude."

"Close your eyes," Jason instructed. "I'm gonna blow on your eyelids."

Only the cognoscenti of who was who in Manhattan would have recognized them, yet Sonia and Mark's arrival for lunch at the Italian restaurant in the east sixties caused a stir. They each had their cult following, and an intimate, expensive Italian restaurant in the east sixties was just the place to find a cult following or two. People whispered to each other. The fact that these two were here confirmed that this was *the* hot place. Their neighbors shot them curious glances and then relaxed in the knowledge that for the next hour at least they were safe.

Sonia had not dressed up, but her top-model appearance excused everything. That face and the long legs and the suitcase-sized shoulder bag more than made up for the black polo and the little black skirt under the cape.

Mark shepherded her to a table with care, as if afraid that she might suddenly explode in anger if the least little thing went wrong. He was slightly taller than she and shared the same coloring, the same intense eyes fringed with luxuriant dark lashes. The attractive young waiter who recited the *plats du jour* couldn't seem to decide which of the two he found more exciting. Sonia scanned the menu expertly, making a face.

"Well, it's *not* rack of lamb with goat's cheese lasagna," she decided, "*or* fettucine with sweetbreads . . ."

The waiter nodded, disappointed. "They're both very good," he said. "And our other special today is salmon marinated in walnut and dill vinaigrette, garnished with white parsley and blueberries."

They ordered salad "collages" and cappuccino.

"Why don't you answer my letters?" Mark asked. "I feel so out of touch with New York."

"I'm sure other people fill you in." Sonia took off her scarf, narrowing her eyes at him. "You said my letters read like obituary columns, remember? And I was only trying to bring you up to date on all the beautiful young men who had died. . . ."

"That's not exactly what I needed to know," Mark said. "I wanted to know what music was selling, which movies and shows were hits . . ."

"I guess I'm sensitive to criticism," she said. "It put me off writing."

"What are you so prickly about today?" he asked.

She took a sip of water. "Daddy has cancer, Mark. He's very sick."

"I'm sorry." Mark's face was strained. "That's terrible. Why didn't you tell me? Does Mom know?"

"No," she said. "They have no contact now. I'm the only one who visits him."

"Is he in pain?" Mark asked.

"Sometimes. He's—oh, what do you care? You haven't seen him in years, anyway."

"We were hardly what you'd call close," he said gently. "To put it mildly, we hated each other's guts."

"He hasn't been the best daddy in the world to me either," she admitted. "But I still do my fucking duty. I'm at that godawful prison hospital every Sunday."

"That's *your* conscience," Mark said. "Mine is clear if I *don't* see him."

"Go see him just once," she asked. "Just say hello."

"What about you visiting Mother?" he asked. "We could trade visits."

"I can't see her, Mark," she told him. "I blame her for it."

He flinched. "Oh? You mean 'loving Mother can be hazardous to your health'? You think she's cancer causing?"

Sonia nodded. "Yes, I do! The minute I knew Daddy was sick I did a lot of research. The medical feature writer for *Vogue* let me use her library. I read about the latest theories and so-called cures. Visualizing yourself well and stuff like that. I studied dozens of case histories. My own theory is that cancer is caused by unexpressed aggravation!" She stared meaningfully at him. "*Not* cigarettes, *not* saccharine, but unexpressed aggravation. And Mother gave him plenty of that!"

"Everyone gives everyone plenty of that. That's life, Sonia," he told her.

She made a gagging sound. "That's straight out of one of *her* books!" she mocked.

Ice water was replaced reverently before them by a very new, very careful busboy. Sonia beamed her thanks at him. She sat back as their enormous platters of salad were served and a peppermill brandished and ground.

"I guess 'family' was the wrong word for us," she grimaced when the waiter left. "You two were simply a mother and her cherished son. Dad and I had the bad luck to get in the way."

"Maybe." Mark shrugged. "There's certainly very little of Mother in *you*!"

"I didn't get her boobs, that's for sure," Sonia said, glancing down. "I had to buy these! I guess Mother's greatest legacy to me was overactive sex glands!"

Mark frowned. "Oh really? You think Mom likes getting trussed up in black leather and slapped around like you?"

"I don't know, Mark!" Sonia opened her eyes mock-innocently wide. "Maybe she's the fuckin' Virgin Mary? Do *you* have any idea what she does for sex?"

Mark stared at her incredulously. "I don't spend time wondering about other people's sex lives, Sonia. Especially my own mother's!"

"Or even your own?" she drawled.

Mark shrugged. "I'm a late developer," he said.

She nodded vaguely. "And your relationship with Cole Ferrer is strictly business and you're still a virgin? *Please,* Mark! Get real!"

He watched her carefully. "This is really funny," he said. "You think you know more about my sex life than I do?"

"Sex *is* one of the few subjects on which I'm expert," she told him. "Sex and makeup and horses!"

They ordered more coffee and she shook sweetener into hers.

"I hope you're being careful, anyway," Mark said as she sipped her coffee.

"Oh Mark, if you mean AIDS or condoms, forget it!" She rolled her eyes. "Cocksuckers have never attracted me, Brother dear. I like *real* men—another thing I got from my mother. Or would you rather not hear anything that drags little Mommy down off her pedestal?"

Mark felt his face flush. He had forgotten Sonia's knack for raising bile. "I love Mom very much," he told her simply. "Is that a crime? You love Dad, don't you?"

"Er . . . not in quite the same way," she sniggered. "Like, for example, sleeping with him is *not* one of my fantasies! You really ought to see a shrink soon if this state of mind continues, Mark!"

"You should think about seeing a shrink, too," he said. "People say you only enjoy sex if you get beaten up!"

"Yeah . . ." she nodded slowly, her eyes glazed. "And sometimes not even then. I did see a shrink once," she confided. "Not for the problems you think I have! I was worried that the only time I was really happy was when I was on a horse! I thought that was something to worry about. *Now* I think it's the only healthy thing about me—relating to animals better than to humans! I'm about to sign a big cosmetics contract any week now and it'll mean big, *big* bucks! I can buy a co-op, stable my own horse, really get my life together." She held up crossed fingers.

"Will you be happy then?" Mark asked.

"If I'm not, I'll find ways of cheering myself up," she laughed. "I'm going to cheer myself up tonight, actually. Tonight is going to be something special. You're the first person I've told that to, Mark. *See?* There must be *some* sisterly feeling left after all!"

"You're not into drugs?" he murmured.

She giggled. "Guys are more dangerous than drugs," she told him. "At least, the guys who turn *me* on."

"Be careful, Sonia," he begged. "Remember that time I had to rescue you?"

"Don't ever throw that up in my face!" she cried. "I don't need any criticism from a cocksucker who has the hots for his mother!" Her voice was loud and the entire restaurant fell silent. Mark did not even glance at the nearby tables. He kept his eyes on her face, and he felt his own face burning red.

"Take that back, Sonia," he said quietly.

Her eyes widened in mock surprise as she dabbed a napkin to her lips. "Every little boy dreams of screwing his mommy; haven't you read your Freud?" she taunted. "Are you gonna tell me you're not still sleeping in her bed?"

Mark stood up, reaching for his coat from the back of his chair. He threw some money on the table. "That should cover my share," he said. He made as if to go, but something in her stare kept him there. "You're insane, you know that?" he asked her. "You're certifiable. I don't even know why—"

"Yes?" Her violet eyes blazed with a fury that, curiously, he felt was not directed at him. "Tell Mother to stop my allowance!" She laughed. "I haven't had a cent from this family since I was fifteen! *You* spend the money she earns from her pitiful books! I'm sorry for the trees they cut down to print them on, to tell you the truth! I'm about to land a multimillion-dollar contract, so what can either of you do to me now?"

"I'm sorry for you, Sonia." He shook his head pityingly at her. He turned to leave but she grabbed his wrist, pulling him back.

"Wait, Mark!" She looked up at him, her beautiful long neck arched in a pose that many fashion photographers asked for. "Remember when Daddy used to call me his princess?" she whispered. "He really loved me then, didn't he?"

He shrugged. "I guess so. Why?"

Tears began to roll down Sonia's face. "I do go to see him every Sunday," she told him. "Like I said. I *try* to see him! But *he* won't see *me*!" She wiped the tears from her cheeks with a quick flip of her hand. "Even though he's dying, he refuses to see me." She gulped, twisting the napkin in her hands.

Mark looked down at her, fascinated. "Why?" he asked her.

She stared at her hands, then raised her eyes to his once more. They were the frightened, immature eyes of a child. She almost whispered. "You know the kind of scenes I get into. One of the guys I was involved with ended up in the same jail as Dad. He told Dad all about this crazy girl he'd been with before he realized Dad was my father! And now Dad won't see me. I'm the only person in the world who loves him and he won't see me!"

Sonia had shaken off her wretched mood by late afternoon. The only person who mattered would be Ray LeVar, she reassured herself. It was his voice that purred from the stereo as she took a long soak in the tub. At the same time, she listened in to the messages being left for her on the answering machine. Her agency confirmed a booking. A stylist called to say she'd found a diamond earring Sonia had mislaid. A guy she'd met at a weird club suggested they get together. None of this disturbed her train of thought. Only Ray mattered. Only Ray would matter. She would have to be very careful about what she wore. Couldn't look

too elegant tonight. To look too elegant could be dangerous. Dangerous! The very word made her heart beat faster.

She made up slowly after her bath, sitting on the edge of
the tub. When the phone rang at six o'clock, she let the
machine answer. It was her current beau, David LaSalle.

"Sonia?" His voice was crisp, urgent. "Pick up, baby. I
know you're there."

She slipped her mascara wand carefully into its snug
tube and applied a second black coat to her lashes.

"I know you're listening," his voice said.

She giggled to herself. "You stupid fuck," she said
aloud.

"When am I going to see you?" the voice asked.

She laughed. "That depends entirely on tonight," she
answered, although he could not hear her. "Maybe never
again!"

"Are you gonna pick up, Sonia?" David's voice sounded
more urgent. "Or do I have to come over there and break
down the door?"

"With your manicured hands?" she jeered. "Or will the
driver do it for you?"

"Please, baby." His voice became cajoling. "Didn't we
have fun the other night?"

She penciled in an eyebrow, tongue between her teeth.
The other night had netted photographs in the *Post*, *WWD*,
and the *Times*. "Now and then I have to do something
respectable with a rich society playboy," she said.

"I thought you liked me?" the voice said reasonably.

"Oh, *barf*!" Sonia cried at the machine. "David LaSalle,
a poor little rich boy. You fuck good—what d'you want—a
medal?" The funny thing about it was how they kept coming back for more. There seemed to be an unlimited number of masochists ready to apply. Last week, lying in bed
next to her, David had listened in with her to all the incom-
ing messages, jeered with her at the men calling her name,
some of them famous. He had believed she was letting him
into her world, flattered to be on the other side of all this
agony. He hadn't dreamed she was setting him up for this!
Now he could picture her doing the same thing with some
other guy beside her! The line went dead. He would call
back—that's what New York was all about. Sonia was an

expert at this game of sudden unavailability. In Manhattan it was a love potion.

She did her hair, bending down so that it tumbled forward over her face and she could fluff it up with the dryer. She was thinking about her father and how she had mailed him the first tear sheets of her modeling sessions, to show him how pretty she could look. Finally his terse note had come telling her to stop sending the photographs. She had continued to love him because it was her responsibility. If you were the only person in the world who loved someone, how could you possibly just stop? Oh Daddy, she thought. You could beat cancer! I could nurse you through any illness if you believed in my love!

The phone rang again: it was David.

"I'm sorry about before," his voice rang out. "I want to leave a real message now, Sonia. Maybe you really are out there working your pretty butt off. Anyway, I just wanted to tell you that leaving a message for you gives me a hard-on. Call me when you get in, baby. Let's get together later or just talk dirty, okay? I love you."

There was a long pause and she glanced at the machine. The ON button continued to glow red. Suddenly he was pleading again. "Pick up, baby, I know you're there. Be nice!"

"For Christ's *sake!*" She hurled her makeup mirror at the answering machine and it smashed against the black plastic, littering her bedside table with glittering shards of glass. The cleaning lady would get it. She stood at her open closet, completely forgetting David. Ray has to look at me and *know*! It has to be a subliminal signal. *You,* sexy black soul-singer; *me,* sexy New York model-girl. They would just look at each other and there would be an electric crackle! She reached for a short purple dress: her eyes would stand out like mauve headlamps! Sheer hose to make her legs look nonstop. Five-hundred-dollar glittery little Manolo Blahniks for her feet. Well shod. That expression always made her smile. Like a little filly! God! She ran a hand through her hair. She was like some ditzy teenager going to her idol's concert. No one would *believe* this! But what was the point of having New York at your feet if you didn't sometimes make use of it? She sat on the bed to smooth her hose, to slide each stockinged foot into its expensive shoe.

At eight o'clock, Sonia was sitting in the first row of Madison Square Garden's curved auditorium, on the aisle, her elegant legs stretched before her, the seat next to her empty because she had bought that, too. On it, she lay the long-stemmed red rose she had bought before leaving in a taxi for the concert. The stem was encased in a tiny phial of water, a transparent sheet protecting the flower. She would stand and hand it to him or, if he was out of reach, throw it at his feet.

She looked like a page torn from *Vogue*, her nails and jewelry glossy and perfect, her hair pulled tightly back showing off her exquisite face. The tinted glasses she wore as protection against her neighbors' stares added more mystery and made them stare even harder. She *must* be someone famous, she could see them thinking.

"Sure he likes white girls?" she had asked the man who helped her get the seats.

The man laughed. "He like any color girls!"

"And he *will* see me?"

"He'll see *you* all right!"

She fanned herself with the souvenir program, glancing at her watch. They certainly knew how to build up the suspense at these things. It was eight-twenty and the audience began to slow-clap and chant, "We want Ray! We want Ray!" Sonia wanted to chant, too. She glanced through the program. There was little in there that a LeVar fan did not already know. The brief biography confirmed that Ray had left Georgia at fifteen, determined to make it in the music industry, that after backup singing for some of the biggest stars in music, he had finally gotten a break and recorded his first solo album. It had become a cult hit and won a Grammy. His second album had made him a star. Overnight his cult following had turned mainstream. Now, at twenty-eight, he was at the peak of his popularity.

The lights dimmed and people yelled and whistled. Sonia's heart jumped, then beat faster. LeVar's entrance was beautifully done. A spotlight fell upon an exit door, which suddenly opened. A white towel draped around his neck, a floor-length white toweling robe covering him, LeVar burst into the auditorium like a boxer, marching through the crowd surrounded by bodyguards and security men and members of his band. The powerful spotlight followed his progress to the stage. The crowd went wild with screams and whoops, and Sonia's heart turned over at the sight of him. He was radiant, his honest, childlike smile beaming on everyone as he was escorted to the stage. The crowd's roaring turned to a full-throated screaming. The overamplified orchestra struck up a mesmerizing, throbbing beat with a bass so low and evident that it seemed to pass through every seat and up the spine of every spectator. Everyone immediately recognized the introduction to LeVar's biggest hit, "Battle of Love." When he reached the stage, Ray's guards thrust him up onto it and he threw off the white robe and ran to the center of the thrusting oval extending out into the orchestra stalls. His shimmering, pailletted jacket created an aura of light around him. His group of backup singers, two sexily gowned women and a tuxedoed man, swayed behind him in perfect unison.

The audience quieted as the introduction was stretched out, one or two female screams piercing the air as Ray peered around the hall, the mike at his mouth, establishing an immediate, intimate contact.

Finally, he drawled, "Are you gonna join me in the battle for love?" in his husky voice, and the audience responded with a loud *"Yeah!"* She watched him moving just above her. If she leaned forward and stretched out her hand, she would almost be able to touch his gleaming black patent-leather shoe. Her face lost its sulky pout and became animated, alight with anticipation.

"Are you gonna join me in the battle of love, I say?" he laughed.

"Yeah!"

She stared up at the face she knew so well. She had been in love with him since the first time she had heard his voice. And now he began to sing. The husky, deep voice throbbed through the bodies of his listeners and seemed to recognize, acknowledge, and soothe all their pain. On the third line of the song he began to move. No one moved like Ray LeVar. Michael Jackson did his double-jointed jerks and spins, James Brown had shuffled and fancy-footed, but Ray just sort of melted into a beat with the lower half of his body, giving sexy little jerks, as if guying the way his body moved against a woman's, pretending it was the music, the rhythm, that made him move, when everyone knew damned well it was sex.

He sang a back-to-back medley of his songs, the songs everyone had played for the last year, sighed to, made love to, suffered to. It was as emotional and charged as if he had read their minds and knew exactly what they had all been through. No one understood falling in love like Ray. No one else could make you feel the exact feelings a man went through during his courtship, his affair, his love. And no one could make you feel his suffering when the affair came to its end and his woman had left him. When he sang of this, every woman fell in love with his vulnerability and wanted to assure him that she would never let him down. His interpretation of the lyrics, his husky notes, his sighs, his growls, the little cries that punctuated his singing, touched his listeners' hearts and made him unique.

Sonia stared straight up at him through the two-hour, nonstop set, the auditorium heating up as entire rows of the audience got to their feet to dance, clap or sway to the beat. Sometimes she felt he was looking directly at her and she squirmed in her seat, keeping her eyes fixed on his. Sometimes he shook his head and a drop of sweat flashed like a diamond in the spotlight and fell on her.

The two hours went by so quickly, in an enchanted rush. At the end of his last song he leaped off the stage as the spotlight faded to a tiny circle of light on his face, the crowd roaring with disappointment that it was over. For a moment he was standing next to her. She grabbed the rose and jumped to her feet, pressing it into his hand, kissing his smooth, wet cheek. Suddenly, his other hand clasped hers and she was being pulled down the aisle with him, outrunning the people who stood and charged at them, threatening to engulf them. They reached the exit just in time, dodging the grabbing hands and arms, Sonia's hand still held tightly in his.

"Who is she, Ray?" someone asked.

A portable dressing room had been set up in the foyer for this moment. He turned to her in the sudden light as his dressers stripped off his clothes.

"Who are you, baby?" he asked. "I ain't never seen such a beautiful girl. I been watching you all through the show."

He showed no embarrassment as he was stripped down to his underpants, but she was aware of the powerful bronze body that three assistants rubbed dry with towels and then anointed with cologne.

"Sonia Winton," she told him. "I've been crazy about your singing ever since I first heard you."

"Yeah?" He peered at her curiously, smiling.

The cheering, screaming, and chanting from the audience inside had not abated. An assistant held the door ajar.

"Okay, Ray," a big man urged. "She's just a fan. You can go now, miss . . ." He tried to push her back into the auditorium.

"Hey, wait! No! No!" Ray protested, snatching Sonia back by the arm. "You cut that out, Lee. That ain't no way to treat a lady! And she *is* a lady!"

To her he said, "I been watching you while I sang. I never seen anyone concentrate that hard on the words before. You were lip-synchin' them with me, huh? Knew 'em all?"

"Of course!" She gave him her most intense look. He had allowed them to zip a black silk jumpsuit on him, emphasizing the strength and size of his body. A makeup girl patted his face with a puff, smoothed his hair with her hand. They were now stamping for an encore, chanting, *"Ray! Ray! Ray!"* in hoarse, staccato shouts. The makeup girl held up a mirror into which he briefly glanced, nodding.

"Sonia?" he frowned. "Is that what you said?" He took her hand gently as an assistant placed a clean white towel around his neck. "Sonia, will you join me in the battle for love?" he asked.

She parted her lips to say something, but for the first time in her life, words failed her. She just looked him straight in the eye, trying to convey to him all that lay in wait for him. Ignoring all the hands that plucked at him, he leaned toward her, planting his lips very gently over hers. She was amazed at how soft they were and felt the warm, mint-scented breath from his nostrils.

"You'll wait here until after my encore?" he asked her. "You won't just disappear?" His eyes were as open and naive as they had been onstage when he spoke to the audience. They looked questioningly now into hers, awaiting an answer.

She nodded. "I'll be here," she said. The scenario was going exactly as she had dreamed it would!

"Lee?" He beckoned to the large black man. "Take care of her." He held her rose as he ran back down the aisle toward the stage to sing his most famous hit, "Falling in Love with You." Sonia stood among his rapt entourage as they watched his spotlit figure through the open door to the auditorium. No man had ever made her feel like this! Oh God, it was all going to come true!

It was after two by the time they reached the Hotel Pierre. Only Ray's two personal bodyguards were with them as they took the elevator up to his suite. Each time they passed a mirror, she glanced at herself, as if to believe that this was really her, that this was actually happening. Ray was larger than life, more glamorous than anything she had ever experienced.

Backstage, after the concert, all had been popping corks, sweat, towels, kisses, cries and flashing cameras. Ray's hefty entourage had been unable to keep a phalanx of well-wishers from storming backstage to compliment Ray, to touch him, to say they had been there. Sonia was forced back into a corner of the hot dressing room, a plastic glass of champagne in her hand. Just as well, she decided. No point in advertising her crush on Ray before anything concrete had happened. A fashion photographer with a famous black model on his arm recognized her and leaned over to whisper in her ear. "I thought tramps didn't go to Harlem in ermine and pearls?"

"Fuck off!" Sonia hissed at him.

Then that huge guy, Lee, had taken her to one side and given her a kind of pep talk. At first, she had not understood one word of what he was trying to tell her.

"I just don't want you getting too surprised here, miss, you know, like . . . later on," he said with a strange mixture of familiarity and respect. "When Ray invites a lady to share his company for the evening she should be, like, prepared, y'know? He's a big guy. He's famous, and . . . well, it's just a lot better if you know what you're in for."

"But I'm a big girl, Lee." She sipped her champagne, looking at him over the glass. "What is it? Drugs? Whips? I can handle it."

Lee did not smile. This guy is all business, she thought.

"Listen, what's your name?" He bent his head a little closer. "Sonia? Listen, Sonia, you seem like a nice lady and you seem smart. Ray has gotten into spots of trouble in his life, you dig? Nothin' too heavy, you understand, but . . . well, trouble is trouble, right? When trouble happens you take care it don't happen again! Do you understand what I'm saying now?"

Sonia touched the huge gold crucifix that swung from a thick gold chain around Lee's neck. "I always wondered who bought these," she said. She really had no idea of what he was trying to tell her. A potential paternity suit, maybe? A quick blood test for AIDS?

"Why don't you get to the point?" she muttered. She allowed a waiter to refill her glass, catching Ray's glance in the mirror. He closed his eyes dreamily, then shook his head at her, as if he were dreaming. She laughed, her stomach jumping with excitement.

"Ray . . . killed a girl once," Lee murmured discreetly in her ear. "By accident, of course. He didn't mean to kill her, but, well, as you can tell from his music, he's a passionate man. He gets carried away by his emotions. He . . . didn't realize his own strength is the gist of it. He killed a girl."

"So?" Sonia shrugged, a strange chill of desire and fear creeping over her body. "What d'you expect *me* to do? Make a citizen's arrest?"

Lee shook his head. "You're a cool one," he said. "But I ain't done. I'm trying to explain to you that to get him off the hook, to make sure he was not incarcerated for years in jail, where he would have been totally unable to record, certain conditions had to be agreed to. Y'see? He can still have girls, sure, he wouldn't be Ray LeVar if he didn't have girls, but, well, to put it frankly, Sonia, when he makes love to a lady, he has to wear handcuffs."

"Handcuffs?"

"Yeah. Just to make sure it doesn't ever happen again," Lee said. "I mean, *ever*!"

In his suite, the behavior of his bodyguards underwent a subtle change. They changed from being pals of Ray to being quite deferential, almost like servants. In the living room, in which several vases of giant white lilies, roses, and orchids towered over everyone, one of the men walked to an antique chest of drawers and returned holding a pair of slender handcuffs. Sonia watched as Ray stood still, allowing the men to strip him down to his underpants. He was a hefty man, chiseled from black rock. His face had a fascinating smoothness, half lover, half panther ready to pounce. The combination of features—the wide straight nose with surprisingly delicate nostrils, the beautifully shaped full lips, a tuft of black beard under the lower lip—contrasted disturbingly with his slightly hooded eyes. The eyes could change from second to second; they could be menacing, almost Oriental, or they could suddenly open wide with an innocent, childlike expression. His chest muscles were delineated by two straight hard ridges of muscle. His hair was cut short, stylized, oiled and neat. His ears were small, his cheekbones high and round.

He looked across the room at Sonia, standing, legs apart, as the men silently, efficiently stripped him.

"Couldn't *I* do that?" Sonia asked.

One of the men glanced at her apologetically. "It's better if we do it, miss," he said. "Then we'll scram."

"Yeah . . ." Ray grinned. "Get outta my face, will you, you two? I wanna be alone with Sonia. Beautiful Sonia! We got a lot to say to each other."

He obediently placed his hands behind his back for them to click on the slender cuffs, like a criminal giving himself up to the police. He seemed quite unperturbed by what they did, although the men did not stop apologizing as they manacled him.

"Sorry to have to do this, Ray."

"Excuse me, Ray. . . . There you go!"

Ray smiled at her over their heads and she felt her insides revolve. She could see desire was already causing him to jut out against his briefs, so white against his dark belly. She saw very clearly the outline of his thick sex, pressed up against his stomach by the tight underwear.

"Okay." He faced the men. "Now *git!*"

"We through, Ray," one laughed. They looked over at Sonia. "He's all yours, miss."

She saw them to the door. One of them said, "Sorry to spoil the occasion, miss, but it's in your own interest."

She smiled graciously. "I know. Thank you."

She locked the door after them, sliding in the bolt of the chain and turning off the lights of the suite. She turned toward him knowing exactly where he was standing. As she walked, she unzipped her dress and let it fall off, stepping deftly out of it. She kicked off her shoes as she reached him. She pressed herself against him. His skin was unbelievably smooth. She thought of a dolphin, an otter. She could feel his heart beating.

"You know why they do this to me, Sonia?" he asked quietly. "Know why they lock me in cuffs?" His lips brushed her temple.

She nodded. "Lee told me." She pressed her mouth into the hollow of his neck.

"He did?" Ray groaned. "I guess he figures my ladies must be prewarned now. It scares off some people."

"Not me," she murmured. She tried to encircle his body with her arms and could only just manage it. It was like holding a giant, a myth, a fantasy. "Nothing scares me, Ray," she told him. "Especially not *you!*"

"Y'see, just one time, I got carried away," he said as if repeating a lesson. "And I killed this girl. This lovely, innocent girl . . ."

"No." She shook her head against him. "Don't talk about it now."

Suddenly Ray let out a choked moan and sank to his knees in front of her. "I'm so sorry, Sonia!" he cried, pressing his face into her belly.

She felt her desire for him swell to some mad emotion. "You didn't mean to kill her," she assured him. "It was an accident." My God, she thought, this was like being in some gangster movie! Was this really *her*?

"You think God knows that?" he asked humbly.

She made a face in the dark. "I'm sure He does," she said.

"Sonia?" He looked up at her and she could just see tears glistening in his eyes. "I pray to God every morning and every night to forgive me for what I did to that poor girl!"

He sobbed against her, his hardness pressing against her leg, his wet tears splashing upon her making her want him even more. She reminded herself that this man was the idol of thousands of women, but that was not what was so exciting. It was the menace and the contriteness, the emotion, the soul.

"Do you think God has forgiven me yet, Sonia?" he asked her.

"I wouldn't expect anything from that fucker," she said.

"Huh? What?" He didn't believe his ears.

"Yes, Ray," she sighed, holding his ears and pulling them gently. "Yes, I think He has. He's *totally* forgiven you! It's like it never happened!"

"Oh Sonia, oh baby!" he gasped. "If only I could believe that! Like it never happened! I'd never hurt you, baby!"

"Oh yeah? So how come they chain you up like a fuckin' mad dog?"

Ray chuckled. "That's the agreement. The agreement my manager made with the police."

She led him toward the bedroom.

"I'd never hurt *you,* baby," he said again.

She put her arms around his neck, hanging her weight off him. "I wouldn't mind if you did," she told him. "I might even like it if you felt like roughing me up a little!"

"Aw, now, baby," he protested, "don't say things like that to me."

She pressed herself against him, hard and close. "Why not? I'll say it!" she cried. "Whatever you did to me would feel great!" She put her hand down to feel his massive, heavy cock. "Anything! If you kissed me or if you spat on me! If you stamped on me! It would all feel wonderful to me, Ray!"

"Oh, baby . . ." he grinned. "Oh, you got me all excited now!" And just saying those words to him had excited her. It had degraded her a little.

"But I'm not into that no more." He sighed as she caressed his big body. "That's not what I'm about, Sonia. Ray LeVar is clean now, you hear me?"

"I hear you." She gave his cock a firm squeeze. "Whatever you say, Ray, whatever you want. I just want you to know how crazy I am for you. How I love your talent, your voice, your music. I want you to fuck me the way you sing your songs, Ray. Deep inside me. For hours!"

"Sonia!" he gasped. "I never heard a lady talk like that before. Oh, it makes me want you, baby. How I want you!"

Bending, he nuzzled her neck, her breasts, under her arms. His long hard tongue flickered over her body igniting new secret spots that suddenly yearned to be touched again. No man had ever licked under her arms. On an impulse she darted behind him, thrusting her head up under his joined hands so that they were pinioned together. Pressed against him like that, his arms imprisoning her, they hobbled into the bedroom and fell onto his bed.

"Fuck me for hours, Ray," she gasped. "Never stop fucking me!"

She did not believe in sleeping through an entire first night with a man. She felt it put her at a disadvantage—he might feel she was his property. So at four in the morning she asked to be taken home. Ray sleepily summoned the guards and kissed her good-bye. After his concert and their lovemaking, she could see he was really out of it. She was much too cool to ask when they'd meet again. She simply took it for granted that after the incredible sex they had had she would be hearing from him. She heard them spring open the locks on his cuffs as she prepared to leave, dark glasses covering her eyes, her hand fluffing her disheveled hair. At least he would sleep more comfortably without her, she thought.

She was whisked into a limousine that waited outside the Pierre twenty-four hours a day for just such emergencies. In the car, they tried to joke with her, asking for her telephone number and address.

"This *is* for Ray?" she asked warily.

She sat alone on the backseat. The guard who wasn't driving turned to wink at her.

"You kidding me?" he asked. "The last time one of Ray's men tried dating a fox Ray liked, he was taken out in the back somewhere and shot!"

Sonia's eyes widened. She scrawled her address and

number on a card and handed it to him. "Christ!" she said. "How many deaths has this guy been responsible for?"

The men laughed.

"He didn't kill him!" the driver threw back over his shoulder. "Just had the cat shot in the leg. I seen him recently—he still limping!"

They laughed about it all the way to her street.

She was up at eight-thirty the next morning for an icy shower that shocked her into consciousness. At nine, the doorbell buzzed.

"Me-ee!" Leonide singsonged into the video intercom, pulling a funny face. He staggered up the two flights of stairs, a willowy, tall, dark-haired boy with an aquiline nose. He wore tight black jeans, a black turtleneck, and a red bandana tied around his head. If there was a best friend in Sonia's life, Leonide was probably it. He had changed his name from Leonard years ago because he felt Leonide was "more balletic" and thus had more energy. Still in her shower robe, she let him in, pecking his stubbly cheek.

"For us!" He thrust two paper bags at her. She dived into one for warm croissants from a French bakery. The other contained two styrofoam cups of espresso, piping hot.

"Thanks, Leonide, but you shouldn't have," she told him, sipping the coffee. He laughed, kicking the door shut behind him, swinging the heavy makeup bag off his shoulder.

"I know how domesticated you are, darling, and I refuse point-blank to drink your coffee. Life's too short!"

She watched him collapse in a chair, shake a packet of saccharine into his cup, and stir it with a plastic stick. He stared wide-eyed at her.

"Where the fuck *were* you last night, Sonia?" he asked. "We looked for you in every downtown boite we stopped into. We even hit that weird one where they hang up people on the wall. Thought we might see *you* dangling up there!"

She glanced into the mirror behind him. No trace of last

night on her face. "I wasn't downtown," she said. "I was uptown."

"Oh?" he queried, his eyebrows shooting up high. "How far uptown? I mean, are we talking *above* Eighty-first Street?"

She smiled. "Would you believe Harlem, darling?"

"Oh, Sonia, *please,*" he grimaced, aiming his empty cup, stick, and bag into a wastepaper basket. He delved into his makeup bag and removed his little pots of color, unrolling velvet rolls of brushes and cotton-tipped wands. "Don't tell me you're going black on us now, darling."

She fell back into her one comfortable chair and he bit his lip, concentrating, as she presented her pale, unmade-up face to him like a blank canvas on which to work his magic. One of the top makeup men in New York, Leonide approached his work as an art form. Ever since doing some promotions in Tokyo, he had specialized in a Kabuki-like whiteface. He now brushed on his trademark white powder before digging in with pencils and brushes.

"I mean, okay, I've had my periods," he murmured, brushing dark gold shadow on her eyelids. "Sometimes I've sworn off white skin forever. I mean, *why*? When café au lait is *so* delicious? And I'm not talking *black*-black, Sonia: I'm talking Argentinian, Puerto Rican, half 'n' halfs. . . ."

She reached out to flick on the stereo, to shut him up. The last thing she needed to hear about on this important morning was Leonide's sex life.

"I was so naive when I came to this city." He shook his head fondly at himself, ignoring the Ray LeVar song. "The first time I—"

"Watch it!" she cried, as a cotton-tipped swab poked her eye. "All I need today is a red eye!"

"Excuse-moi," he apologized. "What is today, anyway? A shoot or what? Why are we in your home?"

She giggled. "It's all in aid of a lunch, darling," she told him. "Caresse is giving me the last inspection. Carmen and I have been summoned to meet little Mrs. Caresse herself. Probably in a solid-gold wheelchair. She *is* the richest woman in America!"

"Closely followed by *you*?" he asked. "Isn't this contract worth five million or something?"

"Eight!" she corrected.

He whistled. "You'd better go easy on all the F-words, darling. Isn't she a fucking Mormon or something?"

Sonia nodded. "A Mormon or a Jehovah's Witness, I forget which. Same difference. So I have to act virginal." She clasped her hands as if praying. "Think I can get away with it, Leonide?"

"Yes," he said. "I think you'll get it. My God, and you're only—what? Sixteen?"

"Eighteen," she corrected, "although right now I feel thirty!"

"What exactly took place last night?" he asked.

"Stop jabbering and concentrate on my face," she said. "There's a magnum of Moët et Chandon in this for you if I get the contract. That's *daily,* darling!" She closed her eyes as he worked, scenes from the previous night appearing to her as if she were in a private screening booth. As she remembered, she tried not to fidget, impatient to be with Ray again.

It had simply been the sexiest night of her life. If he didn't see her again, he was a fool. He had been on his back in the giant bed, the sheets pulled way down for action. She had straddled him, keeping on her bra and panties, sensing he would like that. His cuffed hands were pinned behind his back but he didn't seem to notice the discomfort. She played with herself for him, sliding her hands inside her panties, under her bra, and he had watched her, getting—she could see—harder and harder at the prospect of possessing her. Her throat had gone dry; she could hardly swallow. Lust makes you thirsty, she had thought. At first she'd imagined she would miss a man's hands stroking her. But he had more than made up for it with his tongue and lips, nibbling and licking any part of her that brushed up against his face. He tore off her silk bra with his teeth, her nipples popping out, upright against his moving tongue, and he sucked hard on them for one tantalizing moment before she pulled away. Then he begged her to crouch over him so he could tear her panties off with his teeth, telling her to spread her legs so he could explore her with his long tongue. As he licked, as he inserted the unbelievably strong muscular organ of his tongue between her legs, probing, she had screamed with delight. It was as if he had two sex organs, one to explore her, the other to flex rigidly in her hand as she held it, telling herself excitedly it would soon be inside her. His tongue probed her bud, flicking against it again and again, varying the pressure exquisitely, breathing cold breath, then hot, so that she was near to coming from his mouth alone. With each stroke he groaned, as if in the most delicious agony. She took these explorations for several minutes before realizing she must have him inside her. She bent lower over him, almost curling herself into a ball, inching down his powerful chest while adjusting his sex with one hand behind her so that it stood at exactly the right angle for her to slide back on. Hovering on the edge of her ecstasy, she pushed back onto the tip of his hard sex. She heard his gasp as she slid him all the way up in her, clenching herself to hold him tightly, testing the resilience of the shaft as she moved forward, backward, a satin cat, oiling him, gripping him, releasing then clenching him again with her well-worked, efficient muscles. He began to move his hips in earnest, up off the bed to match her, to answer her. *God,* he knew how to fuck! This was the real thing. She moistened her lips, bent down to his ear, and whispered, "Okay, now *fuck* me! *Fuck* me, Ray. *Fuck* me, you big black fabulous stud!" Oh, words! How men loved dirty talk!

She had judged him precisely. This had been exactly what he'd wanted to hear. He went wild, bucking and growling beneath her, sending that thick, fleshy tube up against her, inside her. His throaty growls of pleasure—the very same guttural yelps of joy he used to punctuate his songs—snapped something inside her. For one incredible moment, fantasy met reality, fused into a storm of erotic sensation in her body and brain. It built up until it overcame her and she pressed harder on him, trying to get as much of him as she could inside her. They turned full circle on the bed and he fell full-force atop her, piercing her, his sex straining up as she crossed her legs behind his back. His black man smell aroused her so much, the cleanness of him, the bigness of him. He opened his jaw wide, sucking each breast into his mouth. This last sensation as he bit gently on each nipple, nearly hurting, pushed her over the edge. The waves of pleasure began, almost knocking her unconscious with their force. Holding on to his wide shoulders, clasping her arms behind his neck, she came, gasping and crying from the intensity. When he came, two seconds later, she had never heard a man roar so loudly. He sounded like a bear caught in a trap, an animal surprised by pleasure. His whole body shuddered and she stroked the wonderfully soft fold at the back of his neck, calming him the way she would calm a horse after a ride.

Yes, she thought, snuggling contentedly against his satiny body, that was what he reminded her of. Some mythical creature, half man, half beast! It was the most erotic and dangerous fantasy she could imagine. She felt as if he belonged to her, his hands chained, his body submissive to her will. As he fell into a deep sleep, she stayed awake, her hand absently stroking his body, imagining him now as a horse, now as a lion, and—where the skin at the side of his ribs was so smooth—as a dolphin. Oh, if only his paws were free to stroke her! She felt over her lip with her tongue— he had sucked so hard on it that it felt quite swollen.

"And *what* happened to your mouth?" Leonide asked, standing to paint it.

She was jerked rudely from her reverie. "What is it, a bruise? Oh . . . *no!*" Leonide groaned. "Say you're not into that Beauty and the Beast bit again, Sonia, *please!* Is this another of your brutes? A *black* brute this time? Don't you ever go for sweet, gentle men?"

"Like you?" she retorted. "What can I tell you, darling? I don't get turned on by fags. Never did!"

Leonide sighed. "There *is* a whole gamut of sensibilities between fag and brute, you know," he said. "Who said you have to deal in extremes?"

She shrugged. "The brutes can be so gentle, Leonide," she told him. An expression that was almost beatific appeared on her face, as if she knew something he'd never know.

She glanced appraisingly at her reflection when he was finished. What he had done to her violet eyes and beautiful cheekbones! "Yes." She nodded to her reflection. "That's me, all right. That's the other Sonia . . ."

Leonide quickly repacked all his tools and bottles. "Talk about the three faces of Eve!" He shook his head. "Now you look as if butter wouldn't melt . . ."

He zipped her into a slinky black Donna Karan dress and they left the apartment together.

"Not a word about last night to anyone," she cautioned. "Or I'll get one of my brutes to strangle you with your own ponytail!"

"Will you please lighten up?" He opened the front door for her. The Caresse limousine was waiting. "God, you're positively paranoid, Sonia, I swear to God!"

She kissed him good-bye as the driver opened the back door for her.

"Sorry, Leonide, but my nerves are shot to hell," she apologized. "I want this contract and you know how super-proper the people at Caresse are? They even have a fucking morals clause in their contracts!"

"Yeah?" He put on his big dark glasses. "Then why the hell are they wasting time looking at *you*?"

"Shut-up!" She pushed him, giggling. "I can put on a very convincing lady act if I need to. I've had years of studying my mother, remember! She's been miss goody-goody for years as she makes zillions out of writing soft porno. If she can get away with it, so can I!"

In the Caresse boardroom, she submitted to the ritual of talking with the president, watching quietly as aides projected giant color close-ups of her lips, her eyes, her cheeks. They studied the huge screen, discussing her hair, her bone structure, her nostrils and teeth, as if she were an animal, as if she were not present. The head of Idols, Carmen Frantzen, now her personal manager, did all the talking for her. Sonia could do this, Sonia could do that. Sonia had been trained as an actress, as a dancer, as an athlete, as a sportswoman. Sonia only had to sit there and look beautiful or enigmatic or both. Richard Avedon was mentioned as the possible director of the new commercials that would launch the next Caresse Girl. Would Sonia have any objection to swinging on a flower-bedecked hammock from a helicopter fitted with a safety net, flying over Central Park? That is, *if* they could get permission from the city? Carmen assured them that Sonia was completely unafraid of heights.

Sonia watched with only half a mind on all this. The

other half was wondering when she would hear from Ray. If he called this evening, it would be a fantastic ploy to not be there or to just leave on the answering machine, but she was not sure she had the guts to do that. It wasn't possible that she had fallen in love, was it? Was this what it felt like? A kind of craving, as if for a cigarette or for a drink, but for a human being? A need to be touched by him, held by him. Hurt by him. She wanted him so badly that her body ached, and it was only twelve-thirty!

"What do *you* think, Sonia?"

Everyone around the board table was staring at her. The president looked expectant—he had addressed a question to her.

"I'm sorry?" She blinked, looking to Carmen for guidance.

"Mr. Bellamy was suggesting a shade lighter rinse in your hair," Carmen prompted, giving her a meaningful look. "Like a very dark russet, and maybe tying back your hair very simply with a ribbon."

"We don't want to scare off Middle America with too much of a high-fashion image," the president explained gently to Sonia.

Sonia nodded seriously, looking at the president. "I like that," she said thoughtfully. "I love simple things."

"Simple but good," someone said.

"The luxury of utter simplicity?" a writer suggested.

"When simplicity *spells* luxury?" the president tried.

A few people took notes during the short silence as they mulled these concepts, staring at the photograph on the screen.

"Can we go back one slide?" the president asked.

The screen clicked back to a slide of Sonia smiling, her hands in her hair.

She smiled over at the president of the firm, Jack R. Bellamy. A gray-haired man in his late sixties, he was credited with turning a middle-of-the-road cosmetics company into a multimillion-dollar enterprise by using Caresse Girls who appealed to the public. He caught her eye and smiled. If he thought he was going to fuck her, he had another think coming. Or maybe Caresse people didn't fuck around? Perhaps, she thought, that would be one of the perks of working for such a highly moral company?

"Lunch?" Carmen suggested, since they seemed to have reached a stalemate over Sonia's hair color. "We have a table at Le Cirque for one o'clock. Do you think we can all squeeze into one limo? Mr. Bellamy? Mrs. Caresse?" Mrs. Caresse, a frail little old lady, widow of the founder, had not yet uttered a word.

"Better yet, why don't we walk?" Jack Bellamy suggested—possibly, Sonia thought, to show he was still active. "It's a lovely day."

"It's a dynamite day," a hairdresser in the party agreed.

Sonia let Carmen fuss around Mrs. Caresse. The other assorted bigwigs of the company and its advertising agency fell into a line. Of course, the president chose Sonia as his walking partner.

The solemn little procession walked slowly up Madison Avenue, with Carmen considerately holding Mrs. Caresse's arm, looking back sharply at the dawdlers when they strayed too far behind. The busy shoppers on Madison followed them with stares and double takes as Sonia's flawlessly painted face passed. Carmen gave her an encouraging wink that clearly said the contract was as good as in the bag. Sonia forced herself to make witty small talk with the president. The only down thing was her groin and how it ached. The muscles had really been turned inside out last night! If that was what he was like with handcuffs, he must be quite incredible when—

"I've been a fan of yours for quite some time," the president told her. "Ever since your first *Vogue* cover—you remember? The one with your tongue stuck out so cheekily?"

"You liked that, did you?" she laughed. "I thought I was being very cute."

"I very much hope we can reach some kind of agreement today," he said. "I'd personally be very happy if you were to become the next Caresse Girl."

She flashed him a mysterious smile. She would personally be very happy, too.

"There is *one* thing I need to discuss with you in private, Sonia," he frowned slightly. "And this is probably about as private as we'll get." He touched her elbow hesitantly. They were at Fifty-ninth Street and the sun was shining brightly. She lowered her sunglasses over her violet eyes and stared at him expectantly.

"There's . . . well, it's a little embarrassing." He held her arm, guiding her down off the curb as they crossed the street. "But it's very much in the tradition of . . . the image of Caresse. We've always had this little . . . morals clause in the contract. It *is* rather personal and I'll come clean and admit that some girls have found it, frankly, a violation of what they call their human rights. I hope *you* aren't that political, Sonia. You certainly don't look it!"

She gave him one of her looks and for a moment he felt the icy shaft of her contempt. His expression changed, he seemed almost frightened of her. What is it, you dumb fuck? she wondered. She smiled sweetly.

"Do I have to wear a chastity belt or something?" she asked.

He laughed, relieved, a false laugh much louder than her joke was worth.

"Oh dear no, nothing as drastic as that, dear. It's—well, it simply states that our Caresse Girl cannot allow the slightest breath of scandal in her life. Of course, what you do in your own home is nobody's business but yours, but *if* you are to become our face, our spokeswoman so to speak, there cannot be even the slightest hint of—"

"But how exactly do you define 'scandal,' " she asked, her eyes wide, as if seriously interested. She was tempted to ask him if he had any idea how big, how thick, how juicy Ray LeVar's cock had been last night and whether he realized how good it had felt snug and tight up a little white girl's twat? A little white girl whose twat now ached and who might possibly be worth eight million by the end of that afternoon. She almost laughed aloud, but the eight million dollars stifled the giggles.

He took her arm confidingly, as if they were just two humble people dwarfed by the enormous problems of corporate image.

"We won't define scandal right now, Sonia," he murmured, guiding her into the canopy-hung entrance to Le Cirque, the others close behind. "This isn't exactly the right time or place." She let out a deep breath, smiling at him.

"But I think"—he pressed her arm a little tighter—"you know very well what I mean."

She stared into his gray, smiling, bland eyes, her smile fading. Could he possibly be hinting . . .

He bent toward her, still smiling. "There have been rumors. For eight million dollars I think we'd be entitled to expect you to clean up your act."

Halfway through lunch, Carmen was paged to the phone. Sonia toyed with her salade niçoise, bubbling with anger. She had ignored the president ever since his warning, while continuing to dazzle the promotion and advertising agency people. Carmen returned to the table with a little frown on her face. Sonia recognized it as a bad-news frown.

Outside, amid fond kisses and the arm of the president around her for a fatherly hug, they broke up, refusing all offers of lifts to their next appointment.

"We're going straight to my office, Sonia," Carmen said firmly, linking Sonia's arm as if afraid she would escape. The president and his entourage disappeared into a waiting limo. Evidently walking *to* the restaurant was about all he had energy for.

"Think we got it?" Sonia asked out of the side of her mouth as she waved them off.

"I'll tell you that in just one moment." Carmen let go of her arm to fumble in her purse for change and stopped at a newsstand, grabbing a *Post*. "But for the moment . . ." she continued, turning to Page Six, "I'm starting to think you're the most rebellious, perverted, and just plain *stupid* model I've ever handled!"

Sonia did a double take. "*Now* what have I done? I let the advertising wimp play kneesies all through lunch. I denied having vertigo for their fucking helicopter commercial. What else could I have done? Gone down on the president under the tablecloth?"

Carmen's eyes moved fast across a Page Six paragraph.

"That might not have been such a bad idea," she murmured. "Here!" She thrust the paper at Sonia. "Unless you do some very fast talking, I think we just lost our annuity."

Sonia pushed up her dark glasses and found the small photograph of herself. "Sonia Winton, rumored to be the next Caresse Girl," she read aloud, "was front-row center at the Ray LeVar gig at Madison Square Garden last night, rocking to the beat, evidently a fan. Carrying a single red rose, Sonia was escortless at the SRO concert." She handed back the paper to Carmen. "Fuck it!"

"You may well say that." Carmen folded the paper grimly. "Wait until her holiness Mrs. Caresse reads that! As she is probably doing right now. You'd better get a pretty good explanation ready!"

"Like—I adore his singing?" Sonia raised her eyebrows.

"A little better than that," Carmen advised as they walked down Madison toward the agency office.

Sonia suddenly stopped, facing her. "Listen. Jerry Hall has Mick Jagger, doesn't she? Christie Brinkley has Billy Joel. Why the fuck can't *I* have Ray?"

Carmen gave her a withering look, continuing her march. "Because Mick Jagger and Billy Joel aren't black, dear."

Sonia shook her head. "No, they just try to sing that way! God, what a fucked-up society! It's so hypocritical. For two cents I could tell them to—"

"Stuff their eight million dollars?" Carmen finished for her. "Eight *million*, Sonia? Don't bluff a bluffer, darling. You want it so bad you've already spent it! A SoHo loft? Or are you more into Central Park West? A duplex with a roof garden, maybe? Come *on*, Sonia!"

Sonia shrugged. "Well, why *shouldn't* I have a loft? Everyone else has one. What do I have to do to get their fucking approval, anyway? Become a fucking nun? This is worse than my fucking parents! Say I went to the wrong fucking theater. If they don't believe it, fuck 'em. They're not the only cosmetics firm."

Carmen shook her head warningly. "Oh, Sonia," she growled, "if you didn't have the world's most photogenic face, I swear I'd smash it in!"

In her stark black-and-white office, Carmen poured them both a stiff cognac. Sonia tossed hers back in a swallow.

"Okay." Carmen sighed, sipping her drink. "Do I really have to spell out, all over again, exactly what a contract with Caresse means? Contrary to your touching belief, there *are* no other firms. Not of that caliber. Estée Lauder is perfectly happy with Paulina, and Lancôme adores Isabella. There's only Caresse left, for God's sake, and may I remind you I've been grooming you for this ever since you stepped through that door?"

Sonia grabbed a cigarette, lit it, and took a furious puff.

"If they change their minds now, what am I gonna do, Carmen?" she burst out. "Kill myself? Becoming the Caresse Girl is not exactly my prime goal in life."

"Let me ask you something, then." Carmen sat on the edge of her desk, leaning back, eyes narrowed. "I've never tried to pry into your private life, but what *are* your goals, exactly? You *are* the most talked about model. Caresse would be really sticking out their necks if they use you. What do you really want out of life, Sonia? I assume it's not a husband and kids. Have you set yourself *any* goals?"

"Let's see now . . ." Sonia's violet eyes flickered coldly around the room. "I think right now my biggest goal is for you to shut the fuck up. You get a fucking commission from every fucking dollar I earn; you want my goals, too? My '*goals*'—as you put it—would make you pee in your pants. My goals would scare the shit out of you. Fuck it, Carmen, I don't even *have* any goals. Does that satisfy you?" She glared around the room furiously, as if she longed to smash it up. "Just send me the checks, deduct your fucking commission, and leave me the fuck alone!" she screamed.

Her words echoed in the bare, chic office. She stared sullenly down at her immaculate nails.

Carmen took a deep breath and looked heavenward.

"I'm so glad we know where we stand, Sonia," she said. "For a moment there, I almost thought we were on the same wavelength."

Sonia glanced at her and giggled. "God forbid!" she said.

Carmen put down her drink decisively, reached for the phone, and dialed a number, looking at Sonia.

"Mrs. Caresse, please," she said. "Carmen Frantzen."

She continued to stare at Sonia as she waited, the phone cradled to her ear. She covered the mouthpiece to whisper to Sonia, "She's making me hold."

Sonia collapsed into the Mies Van der Rohe chair and lit another cigarette.

"Mrs. Caresse?" Carmen finally said. "I *know*! *We're* absolutely bowled over by it, too. It's so utterly and totally unfair and *untrue*! Yes, well, you know what gossip columns need? *Gossip*! And that's exactly what *this* is, gossip pure and simple. Yes, she *was* there, as it happens, I'm not denying that, but she was supposed to be at a totally different concert and her driver got the theaters confused. She's so beautiful she creates a kind of frenzy around her whenever she appears in public. That should work very well for Caresse!"

"Oh, brother." Sonia sighed.

"This *won't* cast any shadow over today's wonderful meeting, I hope?" She winked at Sonia, making an "O" with her thumb and forefinger. "That's right, five o'clock was the time given, and I shall be right here, waiting to hear from you. I know in my heart you'll make the right decision, Mrs. Caresse, and you won't regret it. Sonia will be the jewel in Caresse's crown!"

She hung up and dialed a new number.

"Jack? Carmen. I just wanted you to know that I've spoken with Mrs. Caresse and cleared up those very ugly rumors that Ray LeVar's people seem to be spreading about Sonia. Would you believe her driver took her to the wrong theater? She was supposed to be at the opening of Michael Feinstein! And her date was—" She covered the receiver and hissed, "Who's that society guy you're seeing?"

Sonia shrugged.

Carmen took a giant step and grabbed Sonia's hair, wrenching her head back.

"David LaSalle," Sonia said through clenched teeth.

"David LaSalle, of the Boston horse-breeding La-Salles!" Carmen said. "I mean, really, you can't talk much more blue chip than that! I didn't want it to cast any kind of shadow over today's wonderful meeting. I'm a thousand percent sure you'll make the right decision and I'll be here at five to hear it. You saw Sonia today. You saw what she has to offer. She'll be the jewel in the Caresse crown, Jack. I've been running Idols for twenty years and we've never had anyone of her caliber."

She hung up, glancing at her watch. "We have an hour and a half to twiddle our thumbs, Sonia," she told her. "But it sounded all right to me. Keep your fingers tightly crossed. You may never have to model clothing again.

Which is just as well, because from what I hear and know
about you, I'll bet your body is covered in bruises right
now. That Ray LeVar hunk doesn't strike me as the delicate type."

Sonia giggled. "They want me for my face and hair,
no?"

"Mostly."

"So don't worry. I've gotta run, Carmen. I'm expecting a
call. Call me when you know, okay? Or leave a message."
She kissed Carmen on both cheeks. At the door she
turned. "Sorry I'm such a fucking bitch," she said.

Carmen shrugged. "Listen, Sonia. Your face is your fortune, right? No one said anything about your having to be
charming, too. Is he wonderful, Sonia? Dynamite?"

Sonia closed her eyes. "To *die* for!" she said.

She was in her tub sipping white wine when the call came.

"We're rich, baby!" Carmen screamed, and they both
whooped and yelled for a minute. "Call Mr. Bellamy and
thank him for this great honor, Sonia," Carmen advised.
"Like *now*!"

Jack Bellamy took the call personally.

"Just after lunch there *was* a hairy moment," he confessed, "but you're so beautiful, Sonia, we're going to give
you the benefit of the doubt this time. After all, as I kept
telling Mrs. Caresse, last night you didn't know you were
the Caresse Girl. But you must remember what we discussed today. We do expect a squeaky-clean image. Don't
let me down, dear. I'm talking to you from the lofty age of
a grandfather. Young girls the age of my granddaughters
purchase Caresse products all over America. We have to
set them a good example. You're too beautiful to throw all
this away, and we happen to think you'll do a fine job for
Caresse."

"I will, Mr. Bellamy," she breathed in her most grateful,
most suitably chastened voice. "Thank you all so much for
your confidence in me."

"No, thank *you* for giving Caresse a beautiful new leading lady, dear."

She hung up and immediately blew a loud Bronx cheer.
A cool eight fucking million *dollars*! She laughed aloud. No

need ever to work very hard again. No more backbreaking catalog shoots. No more rushed four-day locations on some dumb West Indies isle, wasting time while other models and stylists talked about their boring lives. Now she could devote herself to living life as *she* liked it! And if everything with Ray had to be hushed up, if she had to skulk around in a blond wig or something, it would be even more fun!

She wrapped herself in a toweling robe and poured herself some more wine. This was the very first time in her life she had waited for a man to call her, she realized. If he didn't call tonight, she would go crazy. The calls were already starting to come in; each time the phone rang she thought it was Ray. People called to congratulate her on the not-yet-official news. Page Six and *Women's Wear Daily* called her for quotes. She just listened in to all their messages. At seven-thirty she lit a joint. The front door buzzer went off as she inhaled her first puff. The video intercom showed a black face, and her heart leapt. Then she saw it was a delivery boy holding flowers.

It was an enormous bouquet of white lilacs, lilies, roses, and orchids. The boy watched soulfully as she tore open the tiny envelope: "Sonia—you're beautiful! Love, Ray."

She stared at the card, then at the youth, who stared back.

"That's *it*?" she asked him. "Two hundred bucks' worth of flowers and no follow-up?"

The youth shrugged, glancing at his watch. "I only deliver the stuff," he said. She gave him five dollars and showed him out. Then she kicked the flowers to the floor and stamped on them. If he thought she was only worth two hundred bucks a night, he—

There was another buzz from the front-door bell. This time the video showed Ray! There was no time to make up or dress or clear up the mess she'd made with the flowers. *Fuck it!* she whispered. She was naked under her robe. She peered down the stairway and saw him running up, his two henchmen hurrying behind him. Of course, she thought, to lock the cuffs. Her heart gave an excited lurch and she held out her arms to him. She realized that this strange mixture of happiness and pain was *love*—for the first time in her life.

SEVENTEEN

Manhattan, September 1990

"*Sacrifice.*" Marcella spoke quietly into a tiny tape recorder. "The autobiography of Marcella Balducci Winton. The book you've been begging me for, Scott."

She reclined on the backseat of her navy Rolls as it snaked its way across Manhattan on the humid September evening, the car's air-conditioned interior contrasting deliciously with the heat outside. Suddenly, swollen raindrops hit the roof and sidewalk with a sizzle, releasing that bittersweet smell of the previous summer. Marcella rolled down the window to breathe in the warm rainy air.

The rain lasted only one furious minute before stopping just as abruptly, leaving the road shiny black, as if oiled. Donald, her loyal, dignified driver, kept his distance from the other vehicles, a lone, stately carriage in a one-vehicle caravan.

"Take me past Doubleday's on Fifth, will you, Donald?" she called. He made a left turn onto Fifth Avenue, and there, stuck in traffic, she saw the display of her new book.

"Marcella Balducci Winton's fourth consecutive bestseller!" the banners trumpeted. Several huge pyramids of the book were stacked on the floor, the title facing outward, repeated over and over again as if to brainwash passersby. *Forever Begins Tonight.* "*You* gave me that title, Santi," she silently told him. "What happened to 'forever' for us?"

It had been over a year since she had watched him disappear into the airport and she had filled the time with work and trips and this book. The story of their love. Slightly changed, of course, because in her version they lived happily ever after. Critics agreed it was "the best Winton yet." As it should be, Marcella thought grimly. It contains all my love, my soul, my guts.

They passed a music store and she noticed Mark's album still on display, the one he had assured her would be confined to cult status. So much for cults, she thought wryly. The black-and-white cover photo showed Mark dressed as a glamorous nineteen-thirties-style entertainer. He was staying on another year in Italy, the result of a protracted battle between them. Somehow, she had persuaded him to sign on for a course in Italian Renaissance music. He had spent the previous summer in New York, filling in again for Cole Ferrer at the Carlyle Lounge, where he sang each night. The one advantage to losing Mark for another year was that he would also be a long way from Cole's influence. She believed that one more year in Italy would finally change Mark's ideas about playing modern music. The Italian Renaissance course also carried academic credits that could lead to a teaching degree.

"Teaching is about the *last* thing I want to do!" Mark had stormed, when she had first suggested it. "My show-tunes album did pretty well. The record company wants another live album."

She had begged him to get one more year of studies and a degree under his belt before returning to New York. "Then you'll be a free man!" she'd promised. "Concertgoers won't take you seriously if you keep putting out these albums," she said worriedly.

"Who wants to be taken seriously?" Mark wisecracked. But finally they had made a deal.

"If I stay on another year in Bologna, will you approve a second album?" Mark had asked one morning. Wearily, Marcella had agreed. And now she regretted giving in. Mark's second album would be out soon, promoted in record-store windows all over town. And her other child was even more famous.

Sonia was on television every night, tantalizing viewers with her pitches for Caresse. The commercials had caused a sensation: Sonia swinging from a helicopter over Central Park, leaning from the Eiffel Tower, swimming with dolphins, or laughing astride a galloping horse, Sonia whispering, "Caresse me!" in low, sexy tones as the camera zoomed in for a close-up and she stared provocatively into the lens. The sales of Caresse products were booming and "Caresse me" had become a national catch phrase.

Marcella was now almost as well known as the mother of Mark and Sonia Winton as for the amazing sales of her books. *Music of Love* had stayed on the best-seller list for months, outselling all her other books, and *Forever Begins Tonight* had entered the list at number one, where it currently resided. The extra fame of her two children was what made Scott want her life story, she guessed. He probably envisioned something along the lines of "How I Raised Two Child Prodigies," she thought wryly, but he would be knocked off his feet by what she was about to come up with. For she had decided that it would be meaningless to write about her life if she were not totally honest. The hundreds of letters she received each week were painfully honest, her readers pouring their hearts out to her as she had in her first letter to Amy. She understood how important confession was: this would be hers.

It had not been an easy decision, and even now she was not completely sure that the book should be published. But the problem with putting her love, soul, and guts into *Forever Begins Tonight* was that there was nothing left to write about. She felt empty. So when Scott suggested an autobiography, it became a new challenge.

"Who'd want to read about my life?" she had laughed.

"Doesn't everyone you meet ask you whether your books are based on you?" Scott had asked.

"Of course," she had answered.

"So do what no best-selling lady author has ever done!" he cried. "Write *your* life. Let them see the real Marcella. They'll gobble it up!"

"They'll gobble it up, all right," Amy agreed when they discussed it. "Then they'll chew you up and spit you out.

You'll lose all your mystery, Marcella. You can't possibly do it!"

Amy's disapproval had made her hesitate. And even now—now that she had decided to do it—she was dictating the book, almost afraid to see it in print, embarrassed even to let a secretary type it. She knew there was curiosity about her. The gossip columnists and other journalists had dubbed her "Garboesque" since she had stopped giving interviews a year ago. Now that her books sold on her name alone, there was no need to go through the humiliating horrors of a Johnny Carson interview or spend a sleepless night before doing an Oprah.

She had needed work to keep her mind off Santi. She had reached out for as many activities as she could cram into her time to keep her distracted and busy. But with Mark in Italy, she felt very much alone.

At first, she had thought that by helping others she could stop brooding over what was missing from her life. At a midtown school two evenings a week, she tutored an eight-year-old Dominican boy with reading difficulties, and then walked him home through Hell's Kitchen, tailed by Donald in the Rolls. She also regularly helped at a downtown center for the homeless, serving meals and talking to the people there. She backed up her voluntary work with generous contributions, always anonymous. These things helped her, but they could not satisfy her the way Santi had just by walking with her around the village of Valldemossa. As the car inched down Fifth Avenue, clogged by traffic and polluted with fumes, the idea of an enchanted little village high up in the mountains of Majorca appeared to be a dream, a vision from another century. Fourteen months, twenty-three days of not hearing from him! And, after pouring her heart into love letters to him, she had stopped too, afraid to call Barcelona again in case his voice answered, brusque and final. He had been too proud to accept her decision—it was as simple as that. He had not loved her enough to wait. No, that was not fair, she chided herself. He had loved her very much, she knew that. It was *because* he loved her so much that he had not written. He had chosen a dramatic, harsh way to show her how wrong her life was.

Now, staring at the display of her new novel, she wished

they could drive around the city all night. New York was now divided territory: the streets on which she had walked with Santi and those they had not seen together. She only valued "their" streets, of course.

She was glad she had not tried to call him again. This way she could allow herself to believe that one day she would look up—from a book signing or at a lunch table—to find Santi's eyes on hers, the intense expression of love in his gaze making him forget to smile.

They drove on, past Barnes and Noble, past Waldenbooks, past Rizzoli, all of them featuring her book, the black-and-white portrait of her hanging over it, like an icon, from two invisible wires. The author projected well. Self-assured yet vulnerable; beautiful but not intimidating. The pain in her gaze drew in the viewer, just as her writing drew in the reader. She looked like a woman with a story to tell, one who had paid her dues. Thank God, Donald did not mind working nights, because he provided a solution to those sad hours at dusk when it felt as if all Manhattan was preparing for a date. At this time she could not stop thinking of Santi: knowing that Donald was waiting downstairs was the incentive to get herself together and leave the apartment.

During their nocturnal jaunts around the city, Donald would stop at various places, allowing her to alight like a butterfly here and there, to glance in a window of clothing or books, or to stay safely locked in the backseat as Donald fetched her an espresso in a styrofoam cup, or tomorrow's newspaper. She would have him halt at Forty-second Street and Eighth Avenue so she could watch the flotsam and jetsam of New York, lit by the vivid neon of porno palaces. They said that this was the best thing about New York, the way you could go from high to low in a matter of minutes, of yards. It certainly kept her mind off Santi and about what she would be doing at the end of the evening, when Donald let her off near Members.

She was a coward, a cheat, and she wondered if she would really have the courage to tell her tape recorder and her readers what she did for sex. *Could* she be the author of a sexual autobiography such as no woman had ever written? Could she face being a notorious writer whose longings, addictions, and sacrifices, whose *guts,* sold for twenty bucks in a hardback edition and, a year later, as a five-buck paperback?

They had reached Fifth Avenue.

"Where to now, Mrs. Winton?" Donald inclined his head.

She rolled up the window to let the car get icy cool again. "Charivari," she called out. "Charivari will open for me."

Some heavy shopping would help. It usually did, for five minutes. And she needed clothes. Being lonely and beautifully dressed felt somehow less lonely than being lonely and scruffy.

Donald approached Fifty-seventh Street from Madison, rolling to a gentle stop in front of her favorite store. It was closed, but two assistants were dressing the windows—Sandy, the girl who usually helped her, and another girl. The girls pulled the expensive clothing onto the mannequins, impatient with the stiff limbs, like mothers dressing sleepy children for school. Marcella got out and strolled to the window, peering in. Sandy looked up and ran to the door, unlocking it and poking out her head.

"Hi, Mrs. Winton!" she beamed. "We're not really open. Is this, like, urgent?"

Marcella nodded. "Did you get in that new shipment of Yamamoto? I've been longing to—"

"Okay." Sandy held open the door and Marcella slipped in, feeling ridiculously privileged as she hurried up the steps to the room that boasted the two precious rails of Japanese clothes. She held up a huge linen shirt against herself.

"Something nice to sign books in," she told Sandy.

"Forever Begins Tonight?" Sandy cried. "I'm reading it right now! Got it yesterday. I love it. I don't want it ever to end!"

"Thank you, Sandy," she smiled. She studied the blouses. "My problem is, I can never decide. Do I go with black, white, navy, or plum?" she mused.

"Take 'em all!" Sandy laughed, as if she did not know that the combined price of the four shirts was more than she earned in two months.

"Okay, I will!" Marcella agreed. It was the kind of high having money could buy you. For five minutes.

At the black lucite cash desk, Sandy was writing up the bill when she suddenly jammed her pen in her mouth, staring up in awe at Marcella. "Your books . . ." She shook her head. "You always—like—*know* how people feel. I mean, it's exactly how *I* feel!"

"Why, thank you, Sandy. This is wonderful feedback," Marcella said, signing the receipt.

"I had my cards read last week," Sandy told her, holding the credit carbons high in the air and theatrically tearing them this way and that. She dropped the black confetti into a large ashtray. "This uncanny little guy who lives, like, around the corner here? It was scary! He seemed to know all about me. Told me I was going to meet someone famous. Maybe it was you."

The blouses were swept into a glossy black bag, tufts of white tissue wafting from the top like white flames.

"Enjoy!" Sandy instructed, handing it to her. The bag was remarkably light, considering it had cost over three thousand dollars.

"He foretold your future?" Marcella said. She could not see her own future at all clearly; maybe he could help her?

"Would you call him and ask if he could see me right now?" she asked Sandy on an impulse. "I'd *love* my cards read!"

Sandy flipped through her Filofax. "He's neat," she said. "He's into crystals and energy and rechanneling. Shit like that."

She watched Sandy dial. "Charles? It's Sandy! From Charivari? *Hi!* Listen, I have a customer here who needs some heavy-duty card reading. Can she come round, like, *now*?" She widened her eyes at Marcella as she nodded. "Great! Her name's Mrs. Winton. Be nice to her; she's special!"

She handed Marcella a printed card. "Here you go, and good luck!"

Sandy held open the door for her and locked it firmly behind her. The window had been finished by Sandy's assistant. It showed the backs of four female mannequins in a line, one man facing them. They all wore black. Donald placed the shopping bag in the trunk. When he got back into the car, his head turned slightly, awaiting her instructions. Her heart began to beat faster. Should she go there now? To where her body longed to go? This early in the evening? She glanced at her watch. As she did so she realized she was holding a small card. She peered at the embossed, art deco type. The fortune-teller!

"Sixty-fifth and Broadway," she read.

The word for the foyer was glitzy, the chandelier much too big for the little hall, the building brand-new, expensive, yet somehow a little sleazy and fake, as if it were a temporary set for a television series. A Puerto Rican doorman called up her name, then nodded her to an elevator carved from woodgrain Formica. She was hoisted to the fifteenth floor, accompanied by Muzak. She stepped out into a dim corridor.

"Hi!" a nasal voice greeted her. She turned to see a short young man at an open door, nodding and smiling. "You must be Mrs. Winton," he said. "My nine-fifteen meeting." He held out his hand. "Charles Palozzi," he said. He acted as if it were all very official, like a meeting with a famous surgeon or a noted attorney. "Please step inside!"

Marcella walked into his apartment. It was neat and tidy, with spotless parquet flooring. All the furniture was small scale, set close to the walls, as if to make the owner seem larger. He wore a black suit with a black polo shirt buttoned to the collar. He watched her as she glanced around the room. Obviously he had carefully considered each item, anxious to exhibit only good taste. The large television was turned off, and a tiny black metal café table with two matching chairs suggested a miniature Paris bistro. A long low black-leather sofa filled a wall. A portrait of Marlene Dietrich hung in an art deco frame. The coffee table was stacked with fashion magazines.

"I'm in the fashion industry," he told her. "Seventh Avenue. Heard of Giorgio Romano?"

Marcella shook her head. "I'm afraid not."

Charles shrugged. "Give him two years," he predicted. "Bigger than Armani."

Marcella nodded. "And you do this in the evenings?"

He frowned. "Tell cards? Right!" he cried. "Everyone loves the way I read their cards. It's turning into quite a thing for me. Can I ask you a question?" He said it as if it were one word, canIaskyouaquestion? He pointed at her shoes. "Are those real Chanels? I mean, you actually *bought* them at Chanel, right?"

She laughed. "Why, yes, I did."

"Oh *wow!*" He shook his head, blowing out a lungful of impressed breath. "They have to be, like, three seventy-five, four hundred, right? They're beautiful! I have a book on Chanel. She's my idol!"

Marcella smiled. "That's a good idol to have."

"Wanna sit down?" He looked up like a little boy anxious to please. "Mind if I remove my jacket?" He wriggled out of it, folding it carefully over the back of a chair. His powerful body was built up out of proportion to his small size. Huge biceps stretched the knit short sleeves of his Lacoste shirt. His neck was very thick. Marcella sat down. He placed a knotted kerchief on the sofa next to her, untying the knot to reveal a worn tarot pack.

"Hold the cards for a while." He handed them to her. "They'll pick up your vibes. You want something to drink while we're waiting?"

"Some Perrier if you have it, thank you," she said.

He ran to the alcove that hid the kitchen and peered into the fridge. "Club soda," he said. "Okay?"

He filled a large crystal glass and came back with it, handing it to her. "Yes, I do all the fashion people," he said, placing a square mat beneath her glass. "Calvin Klein, Ralph Lauren, Christian Lacroix. I read Andy Warhol's cards."

"Really?" She sipped her soda. "Did they foretell his death?"

He stared at her, eyes out of focus for a moment. *"Well,"* he shrugged, "she was always a sick woman!" He sat down abruptly next to her. "Soda okay?" he asked. "Listen, I usually charge two hundred to read the cards, but as you're a friend of Sandy, I said fifty. I could make a thousand a day easy, just reading the cards, but I love fashion too much to give it up. I love the models and the way they walk and do their hair . . ." He jumped up to give a parody of a haughty model strutting down an imaginary catwalk and Marcella laughed aloud. He struck another pose, hands on hips, throwing back his shoulders and head.

"Fashion!" he declared.

He sat down grinning at her and she covered her confusion by lighting a cigarette. This was an experience. She was glad she had come. Perhaps she could use him in one of her books—a colorful minor character? He drew up a small table, poured a Diet Pepsi into a tumbler and quickly downed it all.

"Cut with your left hand," he gasped. "Three times. Keep your wish in mind."

She watched him deal the cards, rapt in concentration. I won't believe anything he tells me, she consoled herself. After dealing, he stared at the cards for a moment. When he next spoke it was in a voice so different that it sent a chill through her. The ingratiating, would-be professional manner had disappeared, replaced by an expressionless monotone.

"Oh, your son is going to get real sick," he said, matter-of-factly, as if they had just been discussing Mark. "You could save him. He doesn't have to die."

Marcella sat up straight.

"You'll be widowed within three months," he said. "Are you close to someone called Sheila?"

"Sonia," she corrected. We nearly called her Sheila, she thought. Harry wanted to call her Sheila.

"Who is she?" Charles frowned.

"My daughter."

"She's very foolish!" he cried. "She's in very great danger if you don't warn her. She could die! You have a lot of money flowing in to you, but it doesn't make you happy. Your secret life poses a big threat to your health . . ."

"My secret life?" she echoed. No one had been told about that. He gazed steadily at her with his honest brown eyes. "You know what I mean," he said simply.

She tried to laugh. "Now you're getting scary," she said. Goose bumps broke out on her arms in the warm room.

"What does the name Sandy mean to you?" he asked.

"*Sandy*? The girl who told me about you?"

He shook his head impatiently. "This is a man."

"Santi?" she asked.

"Someone who loves you and you don't feel worthy. Why?"

Probably because of my secret life, she thought.

"He's a very fine person," Charles said. "You are, too.

You shouldn't be so ashamed of yourself. We all have these needs."

Marcella was at a loss for words. She remained silent.

"Your work," he continued. "Do you write or something?"

"Yes."

"For the movies, right?"

"Not exactly."

"What?" he asked.

"Books," she said. "Novels."

"One of them will be a movie," he assured her. "A big success. You'll go to California. There's a lot of travel for you. Europe. You love your son so much. You've made him the most important person in your life."

She fumbled in her purse for a much-needed cigarette. The crazy people of this world are able to pick up on my thoughts, she thought. He looked up at her, his brown eyes tired. "Any questions?"

"Yes." Marcella swallowed. "Will I be happy?"

He pored over the cards, his lips moving soundlessly, frowning. When he looked back up at her, his eyes were finally sympathetic.

"It's weird . . ." He laughed nervously. "It's . . . like . . . you have to suffer for your art."

At the door, she handed him fifty dollars.

"Do you usually tell clients their entire families are dying?" she asked.

He looked faintly surprised. "Is that what I said?" he asked.

Donald opened the door to the car. So what else is new? She tried to laugh herself out of this mood. A warm breeze blew down Broadway as people poured out of Lincoln Center into the coffee shops, restaurants, and bars. Her body shook from his predictions. He had got enough right to scare her. He had told her the truth as he'd seen it. Except for Mark. Mark couldn't be sick. He had sounded fine the last time they'd talked, just a few days ago.

"Where to now?" Donald asked. As she opened her mouth to reply, it crossed her mind that all this danger threatening each member of her family was because of her, but she brushed that thought aside. You decided on a no-guilt policy, remember? she reminded herself.

"Ma'am?" Donald asked.

"Take me to Broadway and Fifty-seventh," she said. As if she had not known that the evening must end there. It was the only place it could end if she was to sleep tonight. Her body craved for it to end there. There was a demolished block just before Broadway, and the sudden black space engulfed them. She glanced at her watch as Donald stopped the car on the corner. It was ten-thirty. Perfect.

"Be back here in an hour, will you, Donald?" she told him. She took the membership card from her purse and hid the purse in the door pocket. Donald gave her a reproving look as she climbed out. Of course, a woman shouldn't walk around here alone at night, but she could not possibly let him see where she intended to go. She waited until the car was out of sight before she began to walk west.

Over the years she had come to know this dowdy stretch of storefronts very well, the sad window displays engraved on her memory like a bad dream. She noted the ridiculous hot-dog handles on Nedick's plate-glass doors. On another block she peered in at a palmist, a sleepy gypsy who sat darning in the window of a storefront under a flickering pink neon sign and a life-sized plaster statue of the Virgin Mary. A police siren wailed piercingly close by and a young black man in a hooded sweatshirt suddenly approached her, his hand out for change. Marcella shook her head, clutching the membership card. A bag lady looked up from her perch in a doorway to say very distinctly, "*I'll* choose when I want to die!" Marcella walked quickly on. It was important to look as if you knew where you were going and were in a big hurry to get there.

As she neared Members, the black building almost invisible in the night, she saw the usual pitiful crowd hanging around outside, beggars hoping for crumbs. Her heart began to beat faster as she approached. She kept the card ready to slide in the slot before anyone peered too closely at her. She expertly clicked open the door and took the black escalator down one floor to the land of strange men's hands and silent pleasures, of gasps in the dark and that peculiar mixture of humiliation and ecstasy that made up her vice. She stopped at the mock box office, leaning against the black mirrored wall for a moment, eyes closed. She could never visit this place without begging for Santi's forgiveness. It's a trap, she told him. I can't escape. Only your love could have saved me.

The new Caresse Girl was launched with media exposure on a scale unknown in the history of American modeling. Sonia's portrait had been taken by the best photographers in the world, and the ten-page folio ran in every fashion magazine. The two-minute commercials came next, filmed at beauty spots in Europe and America. The way Sonia whispered the catch phrase "Caresse me!" had transformed her from fashion model to star. When people talked of the century's top models, they could peg Lauren Hutton to the seventies, Paulina to the eighties, and Sonia Winton to the nineties. At least, that is what everyone predicted and the gossip columns repeated.

One more day's work was required from Sonia for this season, a session that would unite all the previous Caresse Girls for one fabulous group portrait. It had taken months to arrange because some of the former girls had become rich or famous or now lived in Europe. Ginny Schatzberg, for example, had become La Comtesse de Rouche, and an earlier girl, Francine Harding, was now a mature soap opera queen. Finding a day and a place to fit everyone's schedule had nearly driven the organizers crazy.

"Avedon washed his hands of it," Carmen told Sonia, "so they got Alex Rose just in the nick of time. They're spending fifty thousand dollars just for a chartered plane to bring the countess from Paris."

The statistics and gossip were lost on Sonia because all she could think about now was Ray. If someone had planned to make a man irresistible to her, they could not have done better than to come up with Ray and then made Ray's and her schedules totally incompatible. Three weeks' intense work of filming the Caresse commercials, had heightened her need for him. When they could get together, their nights had gotten better and better. She was now adept at slipping between his pinioned arms and rubbing herself against his back, turning herself upside down to dive against his body and place her spherical breasts in his hands. She had driven Caresse's staff crazy by being at Ray's beck and call, ready to drop anything, rearrange any schedule, to accommodate his cross-country tour. She would fly to Portland, to Denver, to Houston, following the tour just for the night, flying back the next morning before Ray had even awakened. Standing backstage in the shadows, watching Ray bathed in spotlights as he sang all her favorite songs, the careful way his entourage now called her "Miss Sonia," the tearful partings and meetings—all this had put her life on a new level. Even the creepy *Enquirer* reporter they had to pay off to keep their romance quiet—fifteen thousand dollars each—had just made them laugh. Her elegant image from the Caresse commercials got left behind when she disguised herself for these trips. She wore blond wigs and tarty clothes to throw people off the scent. And when she couldn't get to see him, she would do anything to take her mind off him, even if it meant returning to her previous haunts—places she'd sworn she would never visit again, places where dangerous people lurked, people who had intrigued her before she knew Ray, before she knew love.

So far, not a night had passed when they were together, without Ray sobbing his terrible confession.

"I killed a girl! I killed a girl, Sonia," he wept, and she listened, mesmerized, assuring him, as was their ritual, that God had forgiven him his mistake, as if she spoke for God. After that particular power to forgive him had been exercised, they could get down to the real business at hand, and no one had ever made love to her like Ray. It just got better and better, until the wide-eyed adoration, the pathetic dependency on her forgiveness, the innocence and ferocity, the feel of his heavy, smooth body and the taste of his lips, the sound of his deep murmuring in her ears, took her over, became part of her so that she felt strangely empty without him. She had never needed a man before. The only creature she had ever been dependent on had been her horse, but now she had found a man for whom she could feel as much. By accident she had stumbled upon the exact cocktail of sex and love she had needed. And she had got under his skin, too. He said he loved her. She made him promise he wouldn't see other girls.

Like anything really good in her fashion-model existence, her relationship with Ray was addictive. Her body yearned for his weight, his heaviness, his powerful black sex that brought her to those crashing, limitless climaxes. Being in bed with Ray was like swimming with a shark, playing with a tamed but dangerous animal. And now that she lived, breathed, and dreamed of Ray, now that the Caresse contract was all sewn up, she had found, at last, a goal in life! How pleased Carmen would be to hear that she had one, even if it was not yet anything more than an idea gathering force in the depths of her mind. She had not put it into words, even to herself, but something in her knew what it was to be, and it thrilled her, awed her, kept her in a constant state of nervous excitement.

The very last thing she wanted to do that morning was pose with a bunch of former Caresse Girls, especially Francine Harding and the countess, both of whom were reputed to be prima donnas, hard to work with. She had been unable to see Ray for a whole week while he was working Las Vegas and she had suffered from their separation. Last night she had lost control and gone to a notorious S-and-M club in the East Village, getting home at four, not remembering much of what had happened.

"I hate these ex-Caresse Girl events!" Francine Harding was saying in the dressing room where seven of New York's former top models fussed before a mirror. "I hate high school reunions, too! I went to my first one, ten years after graduation. When I saw there was no one anywhere *near* as cute and hip and successful as me, I split!"

"Is *she* here yet?" Francesca, the stylist for the shot, came in to look around. "I thought not," she said. She glanced around at the women. The countess was being as nice as she could be—chatting to everyone and helping to keep Francine calm and cooperative. The other exes, who had found various degrees of success and happiness, from rich husbands to careers as actresses, to modeling for the new over-forty fashion magazines that had suddenly sprung up, like *Lear's* and *Mirabella,* sat around watching.

"She'll want to make an entrance," Francesca announced to the room. "And all I can say is: *let* her! Believe me, in all my years as a stylist—and I handled many of you when you worked for Caresse—I've never met anyone so downright ornery as this kid! She's gorgeous in the print shots and the commercials, I admit it. And everyone's saying 'Caresse me!' as if it's some new in-joke, but I'm telling you, she is a—"

Someone hushed her as the door swung open and Sonia crashed in. She was all in black, with dark shades covering her eyes.

Saying nothing, she glanced at the crowded dressing table and threw her bag onto a corner of it, looking around for a chair.

"Good morning, Sonia darling, had your coffee yet?" Francesca asked.

"No, get me a cup, will you, Francesca?" Sonia asked. She took out a brush and began brushing her hair.

"These are your ex-colleagues, all former Caresse Girls." Francesca introduced them. "And this is Sonia Winton, our current girl—as if you didn't know."

"How do you do?" said the countess, a stunningly beautiful woman of around forty-five. She approached Sonia, extending her hand. Sonia shook it dazedly. The others lined up to shake her hand too, as if she were visiting royalty.

"Did you really get eight million?" asked the countess as Sonia sat back in her chair, waiting for the coffee.

"Less agents' fees," Sonia nodded.

"You're a damn lucky girl," the countess told her. "You know what they paid me, when I was a Caresse Girl? Granted, it was ten years ago, but we didn't think in millions then, darling. I think I got a hundred and fifty thousand and all the Caresse makeup I could use. Unfortunately, I was allergic to it."

The other women laughed.

"But that didn't stop me from taking it by the caseload," she continued. "I'm still selling it to my friends. Colors they haven't produced since the seventies."

Francesca's assistant came in with coffee and danishes for everyone. In another room, Pablo, the makeup artist, and Christian, the hairstylist, worked on the models one by one. Sonia tried to doze as she waited her turn.

"Sonia!" Francesca breezed into the dressing room. "Lucky you. You get the Blass! *Quel* glamour!"

The others stared enviously at the skinny black silk

crepe dress Francesca carried so lightly over her arm, as if it were spun glass. Sonia gave it one disdainful glance.

"Forget it, it's backless."

"So?" Francesca cried.

"So I don't do backless today," Sonia stated.

Francesca shook her head. "You don't understand, Sonia: Alex says it's the shape around which the rest of the group will be based, and *you* have to wear it! You'll be the *centerpiece,* Sonia . . ."

"I don't *care* if I'm the fucking centerpiece, I don't do backless today," Sonia said firmly. "Find me something else."

The room fell silent, all watching.

"We don't *have* anything else," Francesca said helplessly. "It's been so difficult arranging everyone's schedules so they could be here for this shot, you think I had time to find backup dresses, too?"

The countess said, "Let her wear my dress. I'll wear the backless."

"That's not the point, Ginny," Francesca explained. "Your dress is a pouffy Lacroix—it's not Sonia at all. And Alex wants her in black for the—"

"Tell Alex to go fuck himself," Sonia said.

Francesca sat on an empty chair next to Sonia. "Will you give me a break, please, Sonia?" she begged. "We're booked to start shooting at ten sharp and it's already nine-thirty and only half of you are made up! I can't take this much *stress*! Everything about this project has been difficult, please don't *you* start!"

Sonia fixed her with a calm look. "I'm only saying I can't do backless. Not that I won't! I *can't!*"

Francesca sighed. "What is it? You broke out on your back or something? Whatever it is we can fix it with makeup."

Sonia shook her head. "Not this time."

Francesca ran a professional eye over Sonia's black tee shirt and tights. She closed in for the kill, bending a little nearer. "Listen," she murmured. "I'm sure whatever it is you have, we can . . ." She reached out as she was speaking and grabbed the back of Sonia's tee shirt. "*Show* me!" she cried. "At least let me see if we can fix it! I bet it's nothing at all." With a quick movement, she pulled the cotton shirt up over Sonia's shoulders. There were gasps and a scream as Sonia's naked back was suddenly revealed in the glare of the mirror's spotlights. Sonia screamed too, a humiliated, furious cry as the other models clustered around to gaze at the bruising, the weals, the open scars of a beating, done, by the looks of it, with a leather strap.

Sonia coolly pulled the tee shirt down over her shoulders, searching the floor for her shoes. "What can I tell you, girls?" She looked up at their horrified faces through her hair. "My man gets a little carried away sometimes. And, Francesca? I'll make damn sure *you* never work on one of my sittings again."

She reached out and clawed Francesca's face. Then, grabbing her black raincoat and big carryall, she left the stunned room. The models burst into a storm of excited chatter.

"Oh, Francesca! Get her some witch hazel, somebody!"

"Pour her a drink!"

"Oh, sit down, honey—someone call for a doctor. Maybe she should get a rabies shot?"

Several solicitous hands dabbed at Francesca's bleeding face with lotions.

"Did you see her back? God, did *she* get beaten up! What sort of girl would allow a guy to *do* that to her?"

"They say she's going with Ray LeVar. He killed a girl once."

"Oh my God, poor Sonia!"

"Oh, don't be sorry for *her*! She's getting eight million dollars!"

"Yeah, the poor little rich girl!"

"She's a bitch. Nobody likes her. She doesn't have a friend in this business."

"She doesn't have a friend, *period*."

The countess strolled to the window and looked out. "I'm sorry for her," she said. "Even *with* the eight million."

Sonia strode furiously down Madison Avenue. It was cold and windy and she pulled the collar of her raincoat up and huddled into it. Now everyone would know, and there might be a blind item about her if one of those bitches sold it to Page Six. Damn it to hell, she thought. Meanwhile she had a free morning, a big treat when all her hours were usually accounted for. She would get into trouble for messing up their big reunion picture, but who cared? The whole point about working for Caresse was that she would not have to work alongside other bitches.

"Their inflexibility is to blame!" she yelled at Carmen over a pay phone on the street. "Have you ever heard of not having a backup dress ready?"

Carmen sighed. "I'll try to fix it. But don't slap any more stylists, okay, Sonia? It doesn't exactly enhance your image in the industry, and Caresse wants everyone to adore you."

"I need something nice to do," Sonia said. "I'm going to buy some clothes. Can I charge them to Idols? You can take the money out of my next check."

"You do that," Carmen said soothingly. "Have fun."

Like most models, Sonia hardly bothered about her own clothes. She had taken a delight in dressing down for her nights out, wearing anything that came to hand, as long as it was black. But Ray liked brighter clothes, flashier styles, and she enjoyed dressing up for him. On the rare occasions when they could go out together, in some hick town near where he was performing, where an entire restaurant could be closed just to serve them, she had put on something glittery or sparkly, and he had loved it. Now, she ran through Givenchy, Sonia Rykiel, and Valentino, finding a sequined sweater, a pailletted blouse, violet leather pants, a fluffy fuchsia coat. By two, she was starving and stopped to refuel at Ambreuse, an expensive Italian restaurant. Pasta and espresso and she was off again. By five she had charged over forty thousand dollars and was starting to enjoy shopping.

Her last stop was Charivari, her presence there causing some flutters among the hip sales staff. As she browsed the racks of black pants, she heard a familiar voice.

"Sandy?" it called out. "You'd better show me a large size. I've been indulging my sweet tooth!"

Sonia frowned, approaching the mirrored changing cubicle. "Mother?" she called.

"Sonia?" Marcella opened the door an inch and peered out, wearing an ecru-colored slip. "Darling! What a lovely surprise." She poked her head out and they kissed. "Are you free for a drink?"

Donald drove them the few blocks to the Pierre. They were about to get out of the car when Sonia shook her head. "Do you mind if I change my mind?" she asked. "I suddenly don't feel I can walk into one more bar with everyone gawking at me. Can we go to your apartment?"

Marcella looked at her. "Of course!"

She redirected Donald and within fifteen minutes they were sitting in Marcella's living room overlooking the park. The October evening was getting dark and Sonia stared out at the trees as Marcella prepared glasses and bowls of nuts and olives.

"This is such a treat." Marcella placed the bowls on the table. "My famous daughter visiting me. Everyone mentions your commercials to me. Remember my old teacher Nancy Warner?"

"No." Sonia shook her head. She regarded her pile of shopping bags with a giggle, rummaging in them to pull out a glittery sleeve or a flash of color.

"Changing my image," she announced to Marcella. "Just blew fifty grand on these duds."

"I thought models got them free," Marcella said.

Sonia shrugged. "No one ever gave *me* anything," she said. "You better pour me a straight vodka on the rocks, Mother dear, I've had a lousy day."

She took the drink Marcella handed her and toasted Marcella's glass, gulping down some vodka. Kicking off her shoes she tucked her long legs beneath her on the couch. "Still seeing that gorgeous Spanish guy?" she asked.

Marcella swallowed. "No," she said casually. "I don't see him anymore." She pushed some bowls of nuts and chips toward Sonia.

Sonia reached out for a chip, looking up at her. "Still going to that place?" she asked.

"Which place?" Marcella frowned. She knew exactly what Sonia meant, but as usual, she hadn't been ready for her.

"*You* know. . . ." Sonia took a second gulp of vodka, closing her eyes tightly as she swallowed, as if it were medicine.

"I don't go there anymore," Marcella said. She went to

the kitchen for more ice, pouring herself a glass of wine from the chilled bottle. When she came back to the living room, Sonia was asleep. Marcella placed her drink gently on the table, looking down at the beautiful face. In her sleep the frown and sulky expression left Sonia and she looked angelic and sweet. In spite of all the problems and hurts, Marcella could not help feel a kind of pride that this beautiful creature had come from her. She eased Sonia's legs up onto the couch, careful not to disturb her sound sleep.

Marcella glanced at her watch. She was due at the homeless shelter. She left a note for Sonia, inviting her to stay until she got back at nine.

Marcella caught a taxi to the shelter, where she helped serve dinner. Afterward, she found another taxi, expecting to return to an empty apartment. But Sonia was asleep just as she'd left her. When Marcella entered the living room, Sonia sat up dazedly.

"What time is it?" she asked, glancing at the dark windows.

"You've been asleep about two hours. You must be terribly tired," Marcella said.

"Yeah . . ." Sonia brushed a hand over her hair, sitting up. "They don't hand you eight million bucks just like that. They make sure you sweat blood for it. And I thought being the Caresse Girl would be a joke! They wanted Christmas commercials in Iceland, skiing commercials in Denver, winter cruise commercials. Christ, I hardly got *Sundays* off! There was so much money and overtime and technicians and equipment! If I fluffed my one line we had to start all over again. . . ."

Marcella watched her delve into her huge soft leather bag on the floor for a cigarette. She lit one and leaned back.

"Where do you live?" she asked Sonia, sitting at the end of the sofa. "That's a funny question to ask my own daughter."

"No . . ." Sonia pulled out a small pad and wrote down an address. "I'm in the same place. Remember? *You* signed the lease! But I just bought this loft on Eighth Avenue. It'll be incredible if it ever gets finished. Two floors, an indoor swimming pool, everything . . ." She yawned.

"I went to see a clairvoyant a couple of weeks ago, Sonia," Marcella told her. "Someone in the fashion business. I couldn't take him too seriously because he was such a funny little guy—"

"Charles Palozzi?" Sonia said.

"Yes! Do you know him?"

"I've seen him a couple of times."

"He seemed to think that everyone around me—you, Mark, even your father, was in danger."

"Well, he was right about Dad," Sonia said grimly.

"What do you mean?"

"Didn't you know?" Sonia stubbed out her cigarette. "Didn't Mark tell you? We talked about it over our last lunch. Daddy has cancer. He's pretty sick."

"But that's terrible," Marcella cried. "I'm so sorry, Sonia."

"He hasn't wanted to see me since his trial," Sonia said. "He can't forgive me for improving my boobs and changing my nose. Among other things."

"He always loved you so much," Marcella said. She watched a tear coursing down Sonia's cheek. "And you still love him, obviously."

Sonia smudged the tear away with a finger. "I'm the only person who does," she said.

Marcella frowned, thinking. "I'm terribly sorry about him, but now I'm just as worried about you and Mark. That clairvoyant—"

Sonia laughed. "Oh, he's been telling me I won't make it to twenty-one since I first saw him." She shrugged. "That doesn't bother me one bit."

Marcella leaned forward. "Why doesn't it bother you? What do you really want out of life, Sonia?"

Sonia wrinkled up her nose. "Why does everyone ask me that dumb question?"

"Because nothing ever seems to be quite enough for you," Marcella said carefully. "And if you're only eighteen now, what will you be like in ten years' time?"

"Dead!" Sonia giggled. "If Charles is right. Floating around in some other galaxy."

"Don't you ever want to fall in love?" Marcella asked her.

Sonia burst out laughing. "That's straight out of one of

your books," she said. "And I'm in love right now, as it happens, for the first time ever!"

"But that's wonderful, darling," Marcella cried. "Who is he? Can I meet him?"

Sonia made a face. "Caresse wants me virginal and pure. I signed a morals clause, would you believe? One breath of scandal and I lose the eight million!"

"But why should being in love be a scandal?" Marcella questioned.

Sonia raised her eyebrows, smiling. "Take a guess!"

"He's married?" Marcella tried.

Sonia's eyes twinkled. "Something like that. You know me, always wanting something I can't get."

"No, I don't know you," Marcella said. "You've never let me get to know you. Why not tell me about this man if he's so important to you?"

Sonia shook her head, her dark hair swinging. "You'll hear about it sooner or later, I'm sure." She dismissed the subject. "How about visiting Daddy?" she suddenly asked.

"Do you think he'd want to see me?" Marcella asked.

"Why not?"

"I'd . . . have to think about it awhile," Marcella said.

"Well, don't think about it too long. It might be too late!" Sonia said sharply. "So . . . let's see now, who else is in danger? Mark? I guess that's why you packed him off to Italy, huh? Guys are dropping like flies from AIDS here."

Marcella stared at her. "What does AIDS have to do with it? Mark doesn't take drugs. . . ."

"Er—there *are* other ways to catch it." Sonia raised her eyebrows. "I figured you sent him there to escape AIDS or Cole Ferrer or both?"

Marcella felt a chill of fear go through her.

"Mark's in Italy because he won a scholarship," she said carefully. "With Gianni. Surely you know that? He's staying on another year, working for a degree."

"So you're not scared that absence will make the heart grow fonder?" Sonia asked, collecting her things. She slipped on her shoes. The vitality had returned to her face now and she stretched her lithe body luxuriously.

"Are you trying to hint that Mark and—" Marcella trailed off.

"Mark and Cole Ferrer, *yes!*" Sonia nodded. "Oh, why is Mother always the last to know?"

Marcella swallowed. She had tried to get too close to Sonia, and like an unfriendly cat, Sonia was striking back.

"Why are you looking at me like that?" Sonia asked. "You write a lot about sex and you go to that sex pit at Members. Can't you stand to think of your son and that prissy queen?"

Marcella glanced down at the drink in her hands. She had an almost irresistible desire to hurl its contents into Sonia's grinning face. With a great effort of will, she stood up, her expression controlled. "You'd better go now, Sonia," she said. "Before we both say some unforgivable things."

Sonia shrugged and gathered up her bags. On the way to the door she stopped. "You will visit Daddy?" she asked.

Marcella bit her lip. "I don't think so," she said. "I don't see what good it would do."

Sonia rang for the elevator and disappeared into it without another word.

Marcella came back into the apartment feeling disturbed. She took a stiff Scotch and paced the living room. It was after ten, a little early for Members, and Donald was not working tonight and so would be unable to collect her. She would have to brave the streets alone.

"Mark?" Marcella picked up the phone three weeks later to hear Sonia's voice. "Mark, he's dead!"

"Sonia?" Marcella said. "Is that you?"

"He's dead, Mark, and he wouldn't even see me on his deathbed!" she slurred.

"Sonia!" Marcella cried. "Mark's in Italy. Who's dead? Your father?"

"Who are *you*?" Sonia drawled.

Marcella heard the smash of glass behind Sonia's voice. "Where are you, Sonia?" she asked urgently. "Are you at home? Do you want me to come over?"

"Yeah . . ." Sonia said slowly. "Come over. I wanna party! I can't find the fuckin' bathroom. I smashed everything in the place! Bring some friends!"

Marcella ran to find the piece of paper with Sonia's address on it.

Out on the street, the doorman quickly hailed her a cab and she was whisked to the East Side address. Pressing Sonia's bell had about as much effect as she thought it would. She tried the super.

"I'm Marcella Winton, Sonia's mother," she explained to the small man in an undershirt who came to the door. "She isn't answering the door and I'm a little worried. Do you have a passkey?"

He led the way up the two flights of stairs, a resigned expression on his face, as if he had often done this.

Outside Sonia's door he asked, "You sure she's in there?"

Marcella nodded. "Yes. She just called me."

He unlocked the door, but as he pushed it open a chain stopped it.

"Shit!" he said. "I'll have to go down for some tools. If I can saw through one link, it'll save a lot of damage."

She called Sonia's name several times after he'd gone, pressing her mouth to the gap and shouting. Just as the super reappeared holding a small saw, Sonia's face wavered in the doorway.

"Unchain the door," Marcella instructed.

Sonia's face was white, her hair disheveled, her eyes unfocused. She slowly undid the chain, watched by Marcella and the super.

"Thank you so much," Marcella said to the man, handing him a ten-dollar bill. She followed Sonia inside the almost empty apartment, the staggeringly strong waves of perfume and liquor hitting her immediately. In the living room, which boasted only a long couch and a coffee table, she saw that Sonia had smashed every bottle she owned, rainbows of oil, perfume, alcohol, and wine mixing on the walls and floors. A white cat picked its way delicately among the shards of glass.

"He's dead!" Sonia said tonelessly from her bedroom. Marcella walked in to find her sitting on the edge of the bed, staring at a blank wall. "I don't know why I even called you. I thought you might want to be at his funeral. Mark sure as hell won't come back for it."

"Of course I'll come with you." Marcella put an arm

around Sonia. She suddenly remembered the trauma of losing her father, and pity came instinctively to her. Then she felt a cold chill of fear. The clairvoyant had predicted she would be a widow within weeks, and the prediction had come true.

As she stared at Sonia, trying to remember all that the strange little man had told her, the phone began to ring. It rang three times and Sonia showed no signs of moving.

"Do you want me to get it?" Marcella asked, but it stopped ringing as the answering machine leaped into service. After the beep came, they heard the breathing of a man with his mouth too close to the receiver.

"It's me, Sonia," a deep voice said. "I bet you're surprised I got your private number, huh? I told you I had contacts. I know you're there because I can see the light on in your room. I'm gonna get my revenge for what you did to me the other night, Sonia. No one fucks with me and gets away with it. Remember what I did to your back? Well, now I'm gonna do it to your face. You'll like that, little Miss Caresse-me!"

Marcella's eyes widened and she looked at Sonia. Sonia just stared at the wall.

"I know you're there, Sonia," the voice jeered.

"Sonia, for God's sake turn it off," Marcella cried.

"I'm gonna beat you up just the way you like it, Sonia!" the voice continued. "I'm comin' over now. Get ready, here I come!"

He hung up and the machine clicked as the tape spun and got ready for the next call.

Marcella looked fearfully around the wrecked apartment, pulling Sonia to her feet. "You're coming with me," she told her. "Get some clothes and pack an overnight case! We'll go to my apartment."

But Sonia tottered into the living room as if she hadn't heard her. Marcella peered into the bathroom to see if she could grab a toothbrush at least, but everything in there was smashed, too, the bath a litter of glass and perfumed, colored liquids slowly draining away.

Somehow she got Sonia into a taxi and back to her apartment. Sonia allowed herself to be pushed around like a zombie. Marcella got her to Mark's room and led her to the bed. Sonia lay on it, staring at the ceiling.

Marcella bent over her, trying to sniff her breath. "Have you taken anything?" she asked her.

Sonia stared at her. "I'll just sleep," she said. "Just sleep."

Marcella got very little sleep that night. She kept waking to check that Sonia's breathing was regular.

In the morning, she found Sonia in the kitchen drinking black coffee. She was pale, her hair a mess, hardly recognizable as the glamorous Caresse girl.

"I guess I should thank you for saving my life or something?" she muttered when Marcella came in. "Except that I'm not sure I wanted it saved. . . ."

Marcella put her arms around her. "Don't say that, darling. If not for me, what about the man you said you loved?"

"He's in Europe, but I'm calling him this morning, soon as the time is right," Sonia said. "First, I wanna make plans for the funeral."

"Where do you want it?" Marcella asked.

"I thought of Frank Campbell's on Madison, but then all the fashion people would hear about it and it would end up as a freak show," Sonia said. "The prison suggested some godforsaken little cemetery in New Jersey. Let's do it there."

It pelted rain on the day of the funeral. Only Amy, Sonia, and Marcella stood at the plain grave in the New Jersey cemetery. Sonia wore a long black raincoat that reached the ground. Her face was white, stripped of makeup, her eyes red and swollen. She carried a bouquet of white roses and a black umbrella, a black felt hat pulled down over her hair.

Marcella and Amy both wore black, Amy's coat lined in fur, a huge black golfing umbrella held aloft over them by Marcella. As Harry's coffin was lowered into the grave, Sonia sobbed loudly. Her sobbing had the wracked, hopeless sound of someone who could never be consoled. It was even more pathetic because it was the only sobbing heard; Marcella was dry-eyed, no emotions surfacing to mourn Harry.

Both women tried not to watch the intensely personal

sight of a young woman grieving for her father, but Sonia's face was haunting and their eyes were drawn to her. The ghost of the sexy girl who whispered, "Caresse me!" on television could just be seen, like a superimposition, a double exposure. Marcella brooded on her own worries; the clairvoyant had seen something, and one third of it had already come true. She really should visit him again.

Amy gave her arm a faint squeeze when the brief service was over. Sonia walked a few steps toward the chaplain to thank him, then stood before the open grave, slowly tossing each white rose down onto the coffin as the rain drummed down on their umbrellas.

Sonia turned to them, her face cold, her expression glazed. She could have been thirteen or sixty at that moment, her purple eyes like amethyst marbles. Amy took her in her arms and kissed her. Marcella did the same. Sonia was as stiff as a wooden doll.

"He wouldn't let me come to see him when he was dying," she told them, with a mirthless little laugh. "What a hard man. He never forgave me for . . . well, for being what I am!"

She turned away from them to lead the way across the bleak yard to the car. Donald leapt forward to take the umbrella. The chaplain was a few paces behind them. Marcella turned to thank him, shaking his hand. Sonia did not get into the car, but stood looking back, as if unable to believe that this was all, that she would never see her father again.

Suddenly there was a screech of brakes as a huge stretch limo with smoked windows pulled up alongside their car.

"Who is this?" Amy swung around to stare at the car as the back window began to buzz down.

For one moment, Marcella thought it might be Mark, come to surprise them, but as they stared at the descending window, Ray LeVar's big face leaned out.

"Sonia?" he called out, and she looked up with a little smile on her face. "Oh baby, am I too late?"

"Ray!" Sonia cried, running over to the car. "I thought you were in Europe?"

"I canceled the tour," he said proudly. "I canceled the tour when I heard your daddy died! Am I too late?"

"It's all over, Ray," she nodded. "Can I bum a lift back to town with you?"

Marcella and Amy stood, watching as the back door of the limo swung open.

"Mother, Amy, this is Ray LeVar," Sonia introduced them. She was too exhausted to smile. Ray stuck his hand out into the rain, leaning out of the car, one foot on the gravel. He wore a glossy black leather coat, its Russian collar fastened up to his neck. He was absurdly glamorous in this bleak setting. They all shook hands politely.

"Well, I'm real pleased to meet Sonia's mother," Ray said, beaming at Marcella. "And I'm sorry it has to be on such a sad occasion as this. I'm *real* sorry, Mrs. Winton!"

Sonia climbed onto the backseat next to him. "Thanks for coming," she said, waving to Amy and Marcella. She seemed pale and fragile. The door shut on Ray's polite wave, and the window slid up as the car rolled away.

Silently, Amy and Marcella climbed into the Rolls, settling back on the seat, pulling the throw over their knees. Donald started the engine and they drove off, some distance behind Ray's limo. *"Well!"* Amy finally breathed. Marcella closed her eyes.

"Now I see why she hides him away . . ." Amy said. "Shocked?" she asked.

"That he's black?" Marcella asked. "No. If she was truly happy I wouldn't care if her lover was green. It's the idea that *she* thinks she's living dangerously that shocks me."

"Maybe she really loves him?" Amy suggested. "He is kind of divine!"

"Yes. He seemed like a very sweet man." Marcella sighed. "I hope he knows what he's getting into with Sonia."

Sonia leaned her head against Ray's shoulder on the backseat of the limo, taking a long deep drag on her cigarette. "I can't believe you cut short the tour just for me," she said in wonder. "That's the sweetest thing anyone's ever done for me, Ray."

"She seemed like a real nice lady, your mother," he said. "I mean—a *lady!*"

She snorted. "That's how much you know!"

"And the other lady with her?" he asked.

"That's her agent, Amy Jagger. She's a writer too. She's okay. But don't let my ma fool you. She had her fake-lady, fake-solemn look on her face all through the service. Like she was trying not to shit in her panties. She'd have preferred it if my dad had died years ago. . . ."

"Shh, Sonia," he hushed her, hugging her with one arm. "Don't speak that way, baby. You don't know how weird that is, your beautiful mouth opening up and all these words full of hate comin' out. You gotta learn to love your neighbor, Sonia. Didn't your momma ever teach you that?"

Sonia giggled. "My neighbor's one thing. Just don't ask me to love my mother, 'cause I *can't*! She killed him!"

"My poor little fatherless chile." He moved his arm to encircle her. "So pale, so sad." He stroked her cheek. "*I'm* your family now, huh, Sonia? Big Ray's your family and he's gonna take care of you. You like that, baby?"

She snuggled close to him, closing her eyes. "Oh yes," she murmured. "Take care of me, Ray. *Please* take care of me!"

They drove along in silence for a while and he hummed a tune to her.

"Listen, Sonia." He gave his low rumbly laugh that reverberated right through her. He hummed a few bars of "White Christmas." "Name that tune, baby!" he urged her. "Know what I mean?"

Sonia frowned, her eyes still closed. "White Christmas?" she guessed sleepily.

"Right!" he agreed. "Know what that means? You and me could be sharin' a *real* white Christmas together this year! With snow and everythin'!"

"Where?" she muttered.

"London, England, Europe!" Ray said proudly. "I'll be there for two weeks, end of December. You'll come with me, Sonia, yeah?"

"Oh, Ray, you know I want to," she sighed. "They have so many fuckin' commercials lined up for me to shoot, I don't know if we'll be finished by then. They're getting Harvey Kistler to direct, Ray. Know who he is? He's the finest director in the world!"

"He couldn't make you look more beautiful than you do right now, Sonia," he told her.

"Oh yeah?" she answered. "My father's funeral isn't exactly my finest moment, you know. I don't have any makeup on or anything!"

His bearlike arm squeezed her. "I like you like this. This way, only *I* know you're beautiful! Now don't tell me those people won't give you a few days off at Christmas. Christmas is a holiday for everyone Sonia! Boy, you shoulda seen how the LeVars celebrated Christmas in Georgia! You just tell 'em you going to meet Ray in London!"

She took his big hand and wrapped her hand in it. "Are you kidding?" she sighed. "It was hard enough getting away to Vegas that time!"

"You're not goin' to let Ray spend his Christmas all alone, are you, Sonia?" he asked mournfully. "With all those pretty little British chicks just achin' to keep me company? All my concerts are sold out!"

She gave him a look. "I'll be there," she assured him. "I'll get the time somehow. I'll tell them I must spend the holidays with my family."

"That's right!" he laughed. "*I'm* your family now, Sonia. Don't you forget it." He was soon asleep, his big body lolling next to hers every time the car swerved. She watched the dreary freeway speed by, her mind working feverishly. Whatever happened, she was going to give Ray the best Christmas present he'd ever had. If it killed her.

EIGHTEEN

"Wanna spend Christmas with me in Bermuda?" Amy asked Marcella in November. "I'm going with Jo Anne Brindley, my other client. We'd love to have you with us. . . . White, clean beaches. Transparent sea. The best lobster you ever tasted, and a few bronzed millionaires floating offshore in their white, white yachts! What do you say?"

Marcella groaned silently. It would simply be a replay of the Majorcan trip. Without Santi.

"I don't think so, Amy, thank you," she said. "Mark's coming home for Christmas and we're going to spend it together."

"He could come too," Amy said hopefully. "Well, call me if you change your mind."

How did it get this way? Marcella wondered, hanging up. Dictating her life story, she was discovering many intriguing questions and answers. The answers to how she had ended up like this, successful and lonely, were all to be found in the honest confessions she made to the little tape recorder.

She had refused to face what Sonia had hinted about

Mark and Cole Ferrer. It was easier to pretend that Cole
Ferrer did not exist. But then she got a telephone call from
him.

"I'd like to invite you for lunch," he said. "Next week
sometime, before Mark gets back."

Marcella tried to wriggle out of it. "That's very sweet of
you, Cole, but I'm working on a new book and I don't like
to break up my day by lunching out," she told him. "Why
don't you come up here for a drink when Mark is back?"

"This is *about* Mark," Cole said seriously. "We'll be better on neutral territory."

The words sounded a warning within her. Neutral territory was where enemies met. Why did Cole think she was
his enemy?

"Very well," she agreed. "What about Monday?"

She had never seen anyone so correctly dressed as Cole
Ferrer when she picked him up in her Rolls that day, down
to his opal tiepin and fresh carnation boutonniere.

"You must be as bored with Le Cirque as I am," he said,
directing Donald to an even more exclusive restaurant, hidden in a town house in the upper sixties. "I took the liberty
of making a reservation," he told her as they pulled up.

He was completely at his ease with her, she noticed, his
confidence that of someone who held all the aces. Writing
her autobiography left her feeling vulnerable and raw. She
took a deep breath as she stepped out of the car; she really
did not feel up to verbal sparring with this man.

Aux Truffes was as grand as a medieval pageant. Nothing on the tables was not bound in linen napkins or tied up
with flowers or herbs. Bundles of exotic grasses were
strewn nonchalantly on the tiled floors and handfuls of pet-
als scattered on the tables.

They were shown to one of the best tables. Seated opposite Cole, she studied the long face, the heavy-lidded eyes,
the thick mouth, wondering what there was about him to
inspire Mark's loyalty.

"Kir royale?" he asked. He also ordered a bottle of
Pouilly Fumé, specifying the year. "Their caviar blinis are
to die for," he suggested. Marcella nodded. She had
dressed carefully, against the critical scrutiny he now gave

her, but she found she did not value his obvious approval of her suede boots, black cashmere dress, and fur-lined jacket.

"You look fabulous!" he complimented her.

She said nothing, waiting.

"When is your new book coming out?" he asked.

"It's out," she informed him.

"Oh? I must get it!" he said. Their drinks arrived and he raised his glass. "Here's to a very happy holiday season," he proposed. She watched him drink without joining him.

"You must be terribly proud of Sonia," he said. "She's everywhere. Those commercials are divine."

"I don't see very much of her," Marcella confessed. "We haven't been close since her father took her from me when she was twelve."

"Oh dear!" Cole raised his eyebrows. "You've had quite a life!"

Bread and dishes of olives were placed on the table for them. She waited. Finally, Cole appeared to be ready to get down to business. He sat up a little straighter.

"I was in Bologna last week, Mrs. Winton," he began.

She looked at him. "Really? Mark didn't tell me." She stilled the leap of hurt inside her. "How was he?" she asked.

"Well . . ." He dabbed at his mouth with a napkin. "I think he's heard enough about the Italian Renaissance to last him several lifetimes. . . . I know you speak to him every few days, but, well . . . he tells *me* things he doesn't dare bring up with you." He replaced his glass carefully and leaned toward her. "I want you to stop giving him such a hard time."

"*What?*" she interrupted. Now she needed a drink. She took a big gulp of her cocktail. "He's studying with the world's most respected pianist. Millions of students would give—"

"Let's not kid each other, Mrs. Winton," Cole broke in, leveling a look at her. "Mark Winton and Gianni, however respected, are on two completely different wavelengths musically. Evidently the maestro overheard Mark playing some Gershwin the other day and had a fit! He simply doesn't recognize that music has advanced much since eighteen seventy-five!"

Marcella smiled. "Mark knows what a purist he is. He should have been more careful."

"The point is that Mark only comes alive when he plays Gershwin!" Cole said urgently, fixing her with his cold stare. "He never expected to get chosen for Bologna, but he was a good sport and he was willing to try. He did his year there and somehow you talked him into another. Well, now he's had enough. He's discovered his forte. He discovers it each year, actually, playing at the Carlyle, but he tried to go along with your wishes. Now he knows he is going to be the best interpreter of Gershwin, syncopation, and jazz this country has ever had. He wants to leave the course now because he's had an offer to tour the country next spring. It'll sell thousands more albums for him and—"

"No!" Marcella cried, smashing her hand on the table, making the crockery jump and their chic neighbors glance up. "Don't start stirring things up now! Mark promised to complete this course. He's honor-bound to—"

"To be true to his own talent and taste, surely?" Cole finished for her. "And I'm afraid all Renaissance and no boogie makes Mark a dull boy."

Their blinis arrived and she leaned back as the waiter served them.

"Mark will tell you all this himself when he arrives next week," Cole told her. "I just wanted to clear the way for him. He's a little frightened of your . . . will."

"What business is that of yours?" Marcella snapped. She glanced at the blinis, unable to take one bite. "And where do *you* fit into all this?"

"I shall become his manager," Cole said.

She stared at him. "So it's all been arranged?" she asked. "Between Mark and you?"

He frowned at her for a moment, as if puzzled. Then, as if he had decided to come clean, his face cleared. "Look, Mrs. Winton," he began. "We're two intelligent adults, are we not? I could talk for hours on how devoted I am to the music Mark plays or to his incredible talent and star quality, and it would all be true. But this is nineteen ninety now, right? And there's no need to . . . well, to fuck around, as they say. The honest to goodness truth is: I love Mark!"

Her fork dropped with a clatter to her plate as she stared at his assured expression.

He smiled. "You cannot know what a relief it is to tell you," he said.

Suddenly, to Marcella's anger and embarrassment, she burst into tears. Cole quickly proffered a large white handkerchief, which she took, recoiling at its heavy scent of patchouli, dabbing at her eyes.

"This is the most terrible moment of my life," she told him. She tried to mop the tears but they would not stop. It was as if all her life had led up to this stupid moment; sitting in a pretentious restaurant with a hateful man telling her he loved her son. She had begged her father for Mark's music lessons, bought him a piano, urged him through all his exams, given up Santi, got him accepted in Italy, and now this tall, mocking man stood in their way.

She handed back the handkerchief, swallowing hard. "I don't usually cry in public," she told him. "It's just that the whole point of my life up to now has been to—" She stopped. Perhaps it was not a good idea to appeal to Cole Ferrer's sympathy. She swallowed and began again. "Is this your tactful way of telling me my son is . . . homosexual?" she asked. It was, she congratulated herself, no mean feat just to get that word out.

Cole gave a weary shrug. "I don't think Mark is ready to actually label himself as anything just yet. Nor, to my deep regret, to love anyone." He took another sip of the wine and laughed. "Isn't this quite absurd and fantastic? So Victorian! I almost feel as if I'm requesting Mark's hand!"

"No . . ." She forced down some champagne. "You want to take over his life. To ruin his life with your 'love.' If you really loved him, you'd want him to lead a normal, fulfilled life."

"Mark's only twenty," Cole pointed out. "He has plenty of time to find out about himself. I didn't have a sexual experience until I was twenty-five."

She glanced up with a flash of anger. "Your sex life is the last thing I'm interested in!"

"Pity . . ." Cole smiled. "*I* think it's fascinating, but you're quite right, we aren't here to discuss that. And I respect Mark far too much to force him into any mold. If he were free of you, we could find out together exactly what he wants from life."

"Hasn't he told you?"

"Mark is strangely inarticulate when it comes to what he wants," he told her. "I'm afraid you've somewhat robbed him of his free will. Quite unknowingly, of course." He looked with concern at her untouched plate. "Don't you care for the blinis? They'll change them if you wish."

"I've lost my appetite," she said.

Cole ate hungrily. "The hothouse atmosphere of your apartment stifles him," he told her. "It's airless, unhealthy. Let him go, Mrs. Winton. Even baby birds have to leave their nests *one* day. The mother usually gives them a little push. It's the only way they learn to fly. . . ."

"You think Mark will learn to fly from *you*?" she asked, trying to show her contempt for him through her eyes. Something must have got through because Cole flinched. He finished his blinis as she watched, wishing they'd choke him.

"He'll be the best jazz pianist of this era, black *or* white!" he promised. "There are two record companies panting to sign him on long contracts, prepared to go to a million! Mark would be financially independent; nothing makes a person grow up quicker than that!"

"You're wrong on that, as it happens," she pointed out. "Sonia's been independent of me for years and she's still extremely immature for her age."

He spread his hands. "Be that as it may, I'm only trying to make all this a little easier on you and Mark."

"Out of the goodness of your heart?" she questioned.

"And because I'd welcome the challenge of producing a great entertainer—a subtle interpreter of Gershwin, Porter, and Kern."

"And *I* love the way Mark plays Chopin, Bach, and Debussy!" she said.

Cole frowned at her. "You're in love with the idea of Mark striding out onto that Carnegie Hall concert platform in white tie and tails, applauded by an adoring audience. He can *have* all that, and more!"

Marcella made herself sit up straight. "I don't think we have anything to discuss," she told Cole. "Mark must be the one to decide how he lives, and of course I'll be talking with him about everything when he gets here. If he chooses your . . . ideas, I guess I'll be forced to accept it."

He raised his eyebrows. "You're really terribly conventional, then? In spite of your books?"

She nodded. "I suppose I am." She got to her feet, telling him, "No, please don't get up. Finish your lunch. I need some air. Excuse me."

She walked quickly to the doors, which a waiter held open for her. Cole half stood, looking after her, the napkin curling from his lap like a white cat.

When Mark called to let her know his arrival time at JFK, she controlled her voice, although the anger had been building up in her since the lunch with Cole. Above all else, she was furious that she had been placed in the position of sitting opposite Cole Ferrer while he told her he loved her son. Mark should have protected her from that.

"I'll be there," she told him. "Have a safe flight."

She could not find the heart to decorate the apartment properly. She just placed a few branches of fresh holly and mistletoe around the room and filled glass bowls with silver balls, stacking the wrapped gifts for Mark and Sonia and Amy and Donald and his family under a tiny pine tree.

Christmas always had a mixed effect on her—one side of her loving every aspect of it, the other side missing her parents, wishing she had a huge family to celebrate the holidays with. This year, she was feeling the negative aspects. She had invited Sonia to be with them, leaving a message that Sonia had not returned. Mark chose the day before Christmas to arrive. Donald drove her out to the airport only to learn there that the flight was an hour late. She sat in the bar sipping a martini, trying to make herself feel like smiling.

Mark looked drained, exhausted, as he carried his large overnight bag through customs. He threw the bag down and held out his arms to her, and in spite of herself, she hugged him to her.

"Darling, you look so pale. Has the maestro overworked you?"

"I think I overworked myself!" he laughed. "I guess I need a break. How are you?"

"Oh, fine. . . ." She walked to the car waiting outside for them. The first thing she said to him as they settled in the backseat of the Rolls, car rugs over their laps, was: "I had lunch with Cole Ferrer last week."

His eyes bulged with surprise and she felt a pang of relief. At least it hadn't been his idea.

"How did it go?" he asked. "Did you run out of things to discuss?"

"I ran out of patience, I'm afraid, Mark," she said, looking at him. "Mark, how could you have placed me in that position?" she asked, closing the sliding glass doors between Donald and them. "I always thought we'd be able to communicate without intermediaries. I also could have done without a man telling me he's in love with my son!"

Mark laughed out loud. "Is that what he said? But that's ridiculous! Cole could never love anybody but himself. And his lush of a mother, perhaps. It's grotesque!"

"Do you love him, Mark?" she asked, looking him in the eyes.

He stared at her. "I don't think in those terms," he said. "I mean, I love you, as my mother, but there's no one else in my life I *love.* I respect Cole tremendously. I'm fond of him, as I would be of a close friend."

"He wants to turn you into a miniature version of himself," Marcella said. "That's what scares and sickens me."

"I see. . . ." Mark cupped his chin in his hand, staring out the window. "So he scares and sickens you?"

"I didn't say that," Marcella cried. "But what *do* you find so admirable and attractive about him?"

"He believes in my talent," Mark said softly. "He helps me become more . . . myself. He shows me there is more to the world than just you and I. . . ."

"Oh, thank you!" Marcella said sarcastically. "When I was with Santi didn't I tell you that the world didn't revolve around you! *You* were the one that said you couldn't live without me!"

"I know." Mark closed his eyes. "I know . . . but I'm growing up now, Mom. I'm changing. I hope I'm maturing in some way. . . ."

"I had such plans for you, darling," she told him. "A great classical music career lies ahead of you. Why do you fight me all the way? Do you realize what an honor it is to be chosen by Gianni? How many students would—"

"Gershwin means a lot more to me than Chopin," Mark said, seeking her eyes. "What can I tell you?"

She sat back on the seat, lighting a cigarette. The Manhattan skyline came into view, sparkling in the dusk.

"You and I have closed out the world, Mom," he told her. "Just the two of us, always just the two of us . . ."

"That's Cole talking, not you." Marcella turned on him. "The Mark I knew *loved* our life together! You don't need Cole Ferrer, Mark! You worked so hard for years to get to this position, how can you possibly give it all up? A couple of albums of old songs, a couple of concert tours, and you'll be yesterday's news! A classical career lasts a lifetime—"

"But nobody asked me what *I* wanted," Mark said quietly. He stared at her with his intense blue eyes. "I just did as *you* wanted. Now *my* taste is coming out and I see I *do* prefer jazz. It's much more exciting to play than to pound out the same old classics over and over again. With jazz, music is an adventure. I *need* to be able to improvise."

"Finish your year," she said. "Then if you feel the same way in a year's time—"

"No!" Mark shouted. His blue eyes shattered as she stared into them. "I've never said no to you before. I've been your baby for twenty years. Now I have to *grow*. I do not like playing Chopin, Mom. Do you understand? I like playing and singing Gershwin and the other songwriters. . . ."

She flinched with the hurt of his talking to her like this, hugging herself as if he had punched her in the stomach.

He looked across at her helplessly. "Ma, life doesn't always go the way you picture it. God, you should be the first to realize that. Look at us—how have we all grown up? Sonia's a sickie. I hope to God I'm not one too, but if I am, it's *your* fault. From the moment I could talk you were always there, giving me so much love, making me need you so much. Now I'm emotionally paralyzed! I don't know what I really want. There's a beautiful girl in Bologna who is in love with me. I'd like to be in love, too, but I can't give anything back! Do you know what that feels like?"

He looked up at her desperately and she cringed inside. "I still need you," he said quietly. "I may not be able to go through with all I plan to do, but I have to try! Donald!"

He opened the glass partition and Donald turned. "Stop here, please!"

They had reached Fifth Avenue in the seventies. Mark opened the door of the car.

"Wait, Mark!" She grabbed his sleeve. "You're making me sound such a monster when all I wanted was the very best for you!"

"I know," he cried. "That's why this is so hard!" He grabbed his overnight bag from the floor, standing on the sidewalk as he unzipped it, pulling out a wrapped gift.

"Here—" He thrust it at her. "This is for you. Merry Christmas!" He slammed the door and patted the car for Donald to start up.

Marcella lowered the window as they cruised down Fifth Avenue, matching Mark's long, determined strides.

"But where are you going?" she called. "I have Christmas all ready at home for us. I didn't go with Amy to Bermuda so we could spend—"

"I'm spending Christmas with Cole this year, okay?" He glanced sideways at her. "Is that okay? Am I *allowed*?"

Marcella flinched as if he had hit her. She raised the window, tears running down her face. The car picked up speed, losing Mark in the crowd of Fifth Avenue strollers.

After a tactful pause, Donald asked, "You want to go home, Mrs. Winton?"

"No," she muttered, mopping her eyes. "No." She looked at her watch. It was five o'clock. She couldn't go home. She took a deep breath, trying to think. "Take me to the corner of Seventh Avenue and Fifty-seventh Street, and come back to that corner in an hour," she instructed. She walked quickly to Members. In the dark she held out for a young man, one almost as young as Mark. As if the theater sensed her need, the glow from the screen showed a clean-cut, preppie type taking the seat next to her after glancing along her row. She leaned back comfortably, available. It was a novelty to hold a soft head in her hands, to stroke the back of a young, male neck. The faltering hands that touched her so warily were more exciting to her that day than the assured grip of a mature man.

His hand was gently moving between her legs when he whispered in her ear. "What are you doing for Christmas?"

Marcella smiled grimly to herself. "Nothing much," she

answered. Sometimes, during these dark meetings, men liked to talk. Perhaps to foster the illusion that this was a relationship and not just two strangers touching in the dark.

"Wanna spend Christmas Day with me?" he whispered, his hand on the back of her neck, gently caressing it.

"What would we do?" she asked, going along with the game. He took her hand and placed it in his lap. To her surprise, he was limp.

"I'd fuck you all day," he said. "You'd love that, wouldn't you?"

Marcella didn't answer. She let her hand fall from his lap and looked to each side to see where she could move away from him.

"Wouldn't you like that?" he insisted, his hand tightening on the back of her neck. "I'd call up a few friends to come over and we'd gang-bang you."

She felt a prickle of fear as he suddenly clamped her neck in his hand. She had always promised herself that if anything strange happened to her in this place, she would leave and never return. Surely it would not happen to her today of all days? She gathered her coat from the seat next to her and made as if to get up and push by him.

"I have to go," she whispered.

"Wait!" His hand moved up to grab her hair. "Don't you *want* us to gang-bang you on Christmas Day?"

"Let me go." She tried to move her head, but he gave her hair a vicious tug and pulled her head down to the back of the seat.

"Tell me, you prissy little bitch!" he hissed. "Tell me how much you'd like to be gang-banged."

She tried to keep calm, to notice how many people there were in the theater. Not many. If she screamed, would they call the police and would it get into the papers? She could not afford that kind of publicity.

"Tell me!" he urged.

"Okay." She tried to keep her voice calm. "I'd love to be gang-banged by you and your friends; now please let me go, I have an appointment!"

"Oh, you have an appointment?" he mocked. He gave her hair another tug backward, her neck so taut that she could hardly swallow. She gasped, her eyes swiveling frantically around her. Again, he jerked her head back fiercely, and tears of pain ran down her face as she felt her hair tearing out at the roots. Her hand flew to his lap and she touched him there.

"That's right, make it hard for me!" he instructed, leaning back in his seat, closing his eyes.

"Why don't you take it out?" she whispered. "It'll feel a lot better if it's in my hand. . . ."

He unzipped his pants, letting go of her for a moment, and she made a fist with her hand and punched him in the groin with all her might. He doubled over in pain and Marcella made a dash for the exit. She ran along the mirrored, curved corridor to the foyer and into the elevator, pushing the button marked LOBBY over and over, terrified he'd be right behind her. The doors slid closed as she thanked God. Out on the street, she pulled on her coat against an icy wind, her face still flushed with panic. She gingerly felt over her sore head as she walked, a handful of her hair coming loose. She stopped at a garbage basket, holding on to its cold metal edge to steady herself, and threw the hair into it, leaning over, fighting nausea. Well, now it had finally happened, she thought. The end of an era in her life, a real sign that her run of luck at the movie club was over. Time to cut out this unhealthy part of her life and begin to live like a decent woman. As she straightened up, she suddenly felt him behind her, his voice at her ear, his tight grip on her arm.

"That was a mean trick, punching me in the balls," he said. "We're gonna make you real sorry you did that!"

"Please!" she sobbed, stumbling over a curb and making them both nearly fall. He savagely jerked her upright. A woman passed by them, oblivious, and Marcella cried out, "Excuse me!" as he pulled her quickly away. This could not be happening to her—not in broad daylight. Not with all these people around her? As he propelled her alongside him she told him, "I'll scream if you don't let me go," her voice trembling.

He laughed. "I figure you have more to lose if they find out what you let me do to you in that theater. You let me touch your pussy and you were *loving* it. You wanted it, and boy, are *you* gonna get it!"

They stumbled on together up to Fifty-seventh Street,

passing a bum, a child, an old lady, no one who could possibly help her.

"I've got some money," she told him. "I'll pay you to just leave me alone!" She tore her arm from his grip and for a moment broke free, but before she could run away, he caught her and clasped her arm again.

"Oh, you'll beg," he said. "I'll like it when you beg. When we're all taking turns, you'll beg for more!"

"You little worm!" she couldn't stop herself saying. "Is this how you get your kicks? Bullying women?"

"You'll see how I get my kicks." He laughed. "Tonight, with the boys and you. Now walk *faster*—" He gave her a shove with his knee. "You can walk a lot faster than that, you prissy whore!"

She twisted her ankle, falling against him, clinging to him as she half knelt on the cold sidewalk.

"I can't!" she sobbed.

"Mrs. Winton!" She heard Donald's voice as if it were an angel calling from heaven. The navy Rolls was standing on the corner, Donald staring at her from the open window.

"Donald!" she screamed across the traffic noise, feeling the boy's grip on her tighten. "Help me!"

Donald got out of the car. Six feet three inches of imposing bulk. Never had she been so grateful for having employed him. The boy let go, taking a swing at her. She fell onto the sidewalk as he ran off down the street. Donald bounded over at the first clearing in the traffic, bending over her.

"You all right, Mrs. Winton? You want me to go after him?" he asked.

"No, let him go. Just take me home," she gasped.

He half carried her to the backseat of the car, putting her legs up on the seat for her. "You want we should go to the police, Mrs. Winton?" His anxious face, full of sympathy and indignation, hovered over her.

"No," she said. "No, just take me home. . . ."

He got into the front seat and started the car. "What did he do? Just grab you in the street?" he asked.

"Yes . . ." she answered.

"Did he get anything?"

"No. No, Donald. Thank God you were here. . . ."

"I thought it was strange, that guy and you. Thought I hadn't seen him before. What did he do?" he asked again. "Just grab you?"

"Yes," she said wearily. "He was trying to mug me, I guess."

"You shouldn't walk around alone like that, Mrs. Winton. Not a lady like you."

"I know. I was stupid. I won't go that far west again," she promised him.

By the time they arrived home she had pulled herself together. "Come up, please, Donald," she told him. "I want to give you some presents for your family."

"That's real nice of you, Mrs. Winton. Are you sure you're all right?" he asked.

"I just need a drink." She made herself laugh. "It's not every day I get mugged!"

"Oh boy." He stood back for her to enter the elevator. "This sure wasn't your day, Mrs. Winton." Then, realizing he had said a little too much and overstepped his own behavior code, he gave her a sorry headshake, his kind face creased in sympathy.

They let themselves into the empty apartment she had decorated so halfheartedly, as if she had known that Mark would not be there to share it with her. She stared at the pile of gifts she had wrapped for him.

Shakily, she poured a large Scotch for herself. She turned to Donald, waiting near the doorway. "Would you like to toast in the holiday with me, Donald?" she asked him.

Donald twisted his cap in his large hands. "That's real nice of you, Mrs. Winton, but I don't drink. Stevie Wonder, he sang that song 'Don't Drink and Drive,' you know?"

"No, you're quite right." She poured a soda for him. "But at least let's toast the New Year!"

She handed him his glass and he embarrassedly clinked it against hers. "To your family's health!" she said.

After Donald drank, he proposed, "To *your* family's health, Mrs. Winton," and they drank again.

Donald cleared his throat. "If you're spending the holiday alone, you're very welcome to spend it with me and my family, ma'am."

She touched his arm, handing him the two Bloomingdale's shopping bags crammed with gifts for his wife and children. "That's so sweet of you, Donald, but I'd better stay here. Mark may decide to come home and I want to be here if he does."

Donald looked at her with such doubt-filled eyes that she felt compelled to add something. "He's at that rebellious age," she tried to explain. "I'm sure he didn't mean most of what he said."

Donald gave an infinitesimal shrug, as if he had heard nothing of their argument. "Now you have a real nice holiday, Mrs. Winton," he wished her. "And if you change your mind, you got my phone number. I'd come and get you in the car. My wife would be real pleased."

She shook hands warmly with him. "Thank you so much, Donald. For everything. Don't forget your card!" She handed him an envelope, which had five hundred dollars tucked into a Christmas card.

"Bye," he said, closing the front door softly behind him.

She played her telephone messages. One was from Sonia, saying she was flying to London for Christmas and couldn't join the family on the twenty-fifth.

She walked into the living room to collapse on the sofa. She felt too sad to cry. Santi, she thought. It's Christmas Eve and I'm all alone. Left at home while everyone's at the party. You loved me, I know you loved me. What happened?

She drank herself into a stupor, the tensions and the violence of the day slowly unwinding until she was a limp, sleeping rag doll curled up on the living room floor.

The telephone awoke her at ten o'clock on Christmas morning. It was Amy, sounding bright and lively from Bermuda, wishing her a happy Christmas. They chatted for a few minutes, then she hung up and lay flat on her back, stiff from her night on the floor. It's Christmas morning, she told herself. One of the quietest days of the year. I have over ten million dollars and I'm all alone. The joke's on me.

She called her two ex-teachers, Nancy Warner and Miss Woolfe, to wish them a merry Christmas; then she called Scott MacEvoy to wish him and his family a good holiday.

Two family friends in Little Italy came next; she caught up on their news and assured them everything was fine with her. When she hung up, the apartment was very quiet and she was very lonely. She had believed a writer's solitude was important and she had nurtured no new friendships. Men had been too tricky, and women's lunches had not appealed to her. Worse than loneliness, she could not get Santi out of her mind, wondering what he was doing on this day, how he was spending it, whether he was in Deya or Barcelona; memories of the house in Deya swept over her —rubbing oil on the figs, watching Santi build a fire, being held in his arms, the smell and the feel of him. Could he walk around his garden or visit Valldemossa without thinking of her?

Christmas Day stretched emptily before her, but she decided not to feel sorry for herself. She still had her gift— her gift to communicate. She had received an advance copy of next Sunday's *New York Times* Book Review, and *Forever Begins Tonight* was at number one for the twelfth week in a row. It was being given as a Christmas gift to thousands of women, and that thought alone cheered her because it was such a compliment. On an impulse, she fetched a copy of the book and inscribed it lovingly to Santi. She wrapped it in the most beautiful paper she had, handmade Japanese textured paper with bits of colored fabric woven into it, tying it with thick satin ribbon. She put it in a padded envelope and addressed it to his Barcelona gallery. Maybe if he read the happy ending she had added to their love story, he would be inspired to contact her.

Next she opened Mark's Christmas gift. It was an exquisite antique purse in needlepoint that he must have spent hours hunting down in Bologna for her. She smiled ironically at the enclosed card that read, "With love, Mark." Evidently, that love did not even extend to his calling her on Christmas Day.

By noon, after a warm shower and some breakfast, there was nothing left to do but write. She would use her gift for communication to communicate with herself!

She sat down at her desk and found her journal—a diary she sometimes kept. She wrote what was in her mind. She let it all pour out, heading the first page "Time to Take Stock." She wrote what a successful thirty-eight-year-old woman alone on Christmas Day was thinking. She wrote of her resentment at the ingratitude of a son for whom she had sacrificed the man she loved. Of her hatred of Cole Ferrer; of her bewilderment at her daughter; of her feelings at the death of a man who had once been her husband. She wrote of sex in the Members theater and yesterday's disturbing incident. She wrote her thoughts about Santi and how she felt their story was not yet over, that she would see him again someday. Sharing her life with a man was her last goal, now that her books were so successful, but Santi had taught her the Spanish saying: "You can't look for love, love finds you." Love had found her once, then lost her. What should she do now? Be patient enough for it to find her again? If only she could put herself back into that philosophical frame of mind, that blessed state she had been in when she had first glimpsed Santi in Palma Cathedral. But you couldn't just thrust yourself into a state of mind, she answered herself, it had to take you over. In her own simple words she was trying to work out her system of survival, a way that a woman like herself could look forward to each day without being dependent on a son, a man, or a habit—whether alcoholic, medical, or sexual. She became so engrossed in her writing that she forgot about feeling sorry for herself. And that was as it should be. That was why she had become a writer in the first place. Work was the only answer, she realized. And continuing to help others as much as she possibly could. Most of all, she wanted her books to inspire her readers to live their lives to the fullest, the way she had been inspired by Amy's sagas. And she wanted to add a further dimension she could only describe as spiritual.

She was not the wisest woman in New York or the best writer, not by a long shot. All she had to offer her readers was a certain view of life, a unique consciousness through which her experiences had filtered, a range of emotions that, today, she felt she had plumbed to the depths. And all she wanted to do now was use that experience, mine those feelings, warn other women to grab happiness when it came. No sacrifices.

She stopped writing at three-thirty to carve the turkey she had cooked. She preferred sandwiches to a real meal, anyway, she told herself. The fresh cranberries from

Zabar's lay in their cellophane wrap in the refrigerator, unused. She sat in her neat kitchen overlooking Central Park, eating her Christmas sandwich, feeling strangely near happiness. She popped open a bottle of champagne and poured herself a glass. Perhaps she should be feeling ashamed of her life, but she felt oddly proud. I haven't hurt anyone, she thought. That in itself is an accomplishment. But then she remembered Santi's face as he had left her eighteen months ago. It was not true: she *had* hurt someone. Hurt him so much he had never written to her.

She poured more champagne. If there was truly to be a fresh start to her life she would need to see somebody: that strange little seer on Broadway who, months ago on that hot September night, had warned her of the dangers faced by her family.

It was a crazy idea, she realized, but just the right zany thing to do on Christmas afternoon, after the Christmas sandwich! She would try to find the seer's building, buzz him and see whether he was home. If he was out or busy, she would just turn around and come back. If he was free for a reading, she could use an update on what fate had in store. She was just a little tipsy as she pulled on her black mink coat and set out.

Christmas Day had spread its peculiar hush over Manhattan. It was no good pretending this was a day like any other. The people on the street looked different, there was little traffic, and the streets seemed tinted a cold, metallic gray. She huddled into her mink coat as she crossed Columbus Circle. Some homeless men were huddled around a fire burning in a garbage can. They called out "Merry Christmas!" to her and waved, and her worried face creased into a smile. They seemed to be enjoying the day a whole lot more than she. She went over to them and handed each one a five-dollar bill. "God bless you!" one of them said, and the words suddenly sounded strange to her on this dark day.

Would she recognize the glitzy building? She remembered there had been an enormous chandelier, too big for the lobby. Up Broadway she walked, opposite Lincoln Center, past the only coffee shop open, filled with people. She found the building, pretentiously called Lincoln Dwellings, and spoke to the doorman, describing a small young man with overdeveloped muscles and wavy black hair who lived on a high floor and told people's fortunes. She felt ridiculous.

"You don't remember his name?" the man asked her, frowning.

"Something very Italian like Balducci, Ricconi, Grissini." She laughed.

"Palozzi? Charles Palozzi?" he asked.

"That's him," Marcella cried. It was like being a detective.

"Fifteen-A," the doorman said. "Want me to announce you?"

"I think you'd better," Marcella said.

"Who shall I say?" he asked, dialing a number.

"Tell him Mrs. Winton."

She glanced at her watch. It was five-thirty and it was starting to get dark.

"Hi, Charles? A Mrs. Winton to see you." He frowned and handed the phone to her. "Wants to speak to you."

She took the receiver. "Charles? I'm so sorry to bother you today. You probably don't remember me, but you read my cards a few weeks ago. I wore Chanel shoes, remember?"

"Oh, *I* know who you are!" the nasal voice buzzed in her ear, sounding wonderfully familiar, as if he were her last friend in New York. "We're just cooking the turkey. Wanna come up?"

"You're sure I'm not disturbing anything?"

"Nah, everybody's welcome on Christmas! Fifteen-A. Come on up!"

In the elevator she wondered who would be with him. Probably another overmuscular young man, she thought. It would be the strangest Christmas she had ever spent, but better than staying home alone. Besides, she did need her cards read.

Charles was dressed in a close-fitting black tuxedo with a black bow tie. His two helpers were his sisters, both enormous ladies in their thirties, whom he solemnly introduced. Rosella and Andrea. While they basted the turkey and took snacks from bowls of cheese, nuts, and olives, their two husbands were seated quietly talking in the living room.

"I'm sure they both just got out of jail!" Charles whispered, beckoning Marcella into the corridor as he hung up her coat. He kept convulsing with laughter, his hand to his mouth. "My sisters wrote to them when they advertised for pen pals in *The Village Voice*! Come in and take a good look at them," he giggled. "You'll *die*!"

Marcella was introduced to two Cuban men in the living room. They seemed pretty harmless as they shook hands and said hello. Although Charles was in a tuxedo and the two sisters in tentlike, floaty chiffon dresses, the men were dressed in sweaters and jeans, as if they hadn't realized it was Christmas.

Charles opened the fridge and brandished a magnum of Moët et Chandon at her. "See this?" he asked Marcella. "A hundred and twenty bucks a bottle! Nothing but the best for my family!" He came near her to whisper, "*You'll* appreciate it, anyway!"

"What a beautiful fur coat," Rosella said from the hall, stroking Marcella's coat where it hung against the wall. "Sit down, join us, there's enough food for everyone!"

"Yeah, and if there isn't, it won't hurt *you* to eat a little less," Charles shouted.

Rosella, about two hundred and fifty pounds, screamed, "Big mouth!" and gave her brother an affectionate shove.

"Rosella drives a taxi," Charles told Marcella proudly.

"Only at nights!" Rosella cried from the kitchen. "Daytimes I work for City Hall."

For some reason, Marcella felt she had been expected here. Charles opened the oven door to inspect the turkey.

"Is it ready?" he asked. Over his shoulder he said, "It's like open house here on holidays. Ralph and Ricky Lauren, Calvin and Kelly, Christian Lacroix and *his* wife—they all said they might pass by, so I have plenty of food!"

That was the last thing anyone said before they began serving and eating the food, heaping paper plates with enormous helpings of turkey, coleslaw, sweet potatoes, cranberry sauce, and gravy. The husbands said nothing; everyone ate very seriously, chewing the turkey, reaching for salt and pepper. Charles played the perfect host, opening the magnum and refilling glass after glass of champagne, telling bits of fashion gossip that the sisters and their husbands did not seem to appreciate.

No sooner had the second helpings disappeared than there was a terrific commotion as the two fat women crammed themselves into the tiny kitchen, washing up every article that had been used and replacing them all in Charles's pristine cupboards. The husbands turned on a football game on the television and sat belching and picking their teeth. The dinner had taken about fifteen minutes.

"This is the first real family Christmas I've given in my own home," Charles told her proudly as the sisters worked. He glanced at the husbands, who looked as if they were about to fall asleep, and rolled his eyes.

"Charles, I hate to ask you on a holiday, but could you read my cards again?" Marcella asked him. "You were so uncannily right the last time. I'd love to know what you see today."

"You want a reading?" His face brightened. "Sure. It'll have to be in the bedroom, though." He shot his sisters a look. "Ex-convicts spoil the vibes."

She followed him into a large empty room in which there was nothing but a pile of fashion magazines and a black futon.

He got a pack of tarot cards and made her hold them, sitting on the bed.

"My fee's gone up." He squinted up at her worriedly. "I'm gonna have to charge you, like, two hundred," he said. "It being a holiday and all. Cash."

She nodded. "That's all right."

He watched her, his tongue playing with the gap in his front teeth. "Like the tux?" He got up from the bed and twirled for her. "Bet you those two in there have never seen a Giorgio Romano tuxedo before. Twelve hundred, retail."

She tried to look impressed. "It fits you perfectly," she said.

He shrugged, sitting down. "They had to alter it for me. That makes it custom, right?"

"Absolutely," she said.

He took the cards from her and she watched as he carefully dealt them out onto the black bed.

"What kind of children do you have?" he asked. He had done that thing with his voice again. Changed it, made it toneless. It was too real to be an act, she thought, much too real. Either he was the greatest actor in the world or there was really something psychic about him. She stared at him, her body turning cold.

"They . . . I . . ." She couldn't think how to answer.

"I see them in such weird situations," he said. "Who is Sheila?"

"Sonia," she corrected him.

"That's right, Sonia. Why do I always want to call her Sheila?"

Because that's what Harry had wanted to call her.

"She's really asking for trouble," he said. "She's playing a game like Russian roulette, but it's not that. It's not with a gun, but it's steel, metal, and it's just as dangerous!"

"What about my son?" Marcella cried.

"He's in trouble, too." Charles frowned but his eyes were not really looking at her or at the cards. He was staring at the blank wall alongside the bed as if watching a movie. "He doesn't have to die. You could save him!"

"No!" Marcella leaned over to place her hands on his broad shoulders, the shoulders that were much too wide for his height. She shook him. "*Why* are you saying this? You said that before! Stop scaring me! What do you *really* see?"

He lowered his head, studying the cards. When he looked up at her again he wore his usual unconcerned expression, his tongue poking at the gap in his teeth.

"Something wrong?" he asked. "You shouldn't touch me when I'm reading. I forgot to tell you that."

"These things you're telling me!" Marcella blurted. "Are you sure?"

He shrugged. "I don't know, but you better believe whatever I say because I'm always right. People come back to me. *You* came back to me!"

"What else do you see?" she asked wearily.

He glanced sharply at her. "Listen, I don't mind reading the cards for you, but don't touch me, okay?" he warned.

"I'm sorry," she said.

He studied the cards again and after a few minutes his

voice changed. "It's very hot where your son is," he muttered. "God, he's hot! He's not well!"

She nodded. He had looked sick yesterday. She would swallow her pride and call him at Cole's. Just to make sure he was okay.

Charles tidied up the cards as if his job were over.

"You seem to see both my children in great danger," she told him.

"Oh yeah?" He raised his eyebrows and tried to look concerned. "Well, the cards change every day. Almost every hour. If you came back tomorrow it could all be different."

She shivered, delving into her purse for the two hundred dollars.

He apologized as he took the bills. "I'm sorry to charge so much, but it being Christmas Day and all, and having to neglect my guests . . ."

"That's all right," she said, getting up. As they walked along the narrow corridor back to the living room he giggled, whispering, "What do you think of my sisters? Think they chose the right men? I kept beggin' Rosella to go on a diet, so she could meet a better class of man. Am I right?"

Marcella frowned, trying to think of a tactful thing to say. "They seemed very nice," she tried. "I must get back now. I shouldn't have just barged in on you like this."

"Rosella!" Charles shouted. "Get Mrs. Winton's coat!"

"My daughter says she's seen you sometimes," Marcella suddenly remembered.

"Oh yeah? Who's your daughter?" he asked, as Rosella came out to the little hallway, stroking the fur coat.

"Sonia," Marcella said. "Sonia Winton."

"Sonia's your daughter?" His eyes bugged. "The Caresse Girl? I *love* her!" He did a little jump of joy. "She said she was up here? I don't remember her. She must've looked different. Sometimes people don't tell me their real names—like, testing me out, y'know?"

She nodded.

"Marcella! Where'd you *find* a coat like this?" Rosella helped her into it. "It's *so* beautiful. Must've cost an arm and a leg, huh?"

"I'll get you one for next Christmas," Charles promised her.

"Thank you so much for a wonderful meal." Marcella headed for the door, Rosella alongside her, still stroking the coat. "Say good-bye to everyone for me, will you?" Marcella said.

As Charles opened the door, Rosella took her in her arms and embraced her, as if they were old friends.

"Have a happy holiday," she wished Marcella. "And if you ever get tired of that coat, tell Charles to let me know, okay?"

Charles had to stand on tiptoe to kiss her cheek. She felt absurdly like clinging to him and begging him to take back his prophecies.

It was dark as she walked back across Columbus Circle. The men she had given money to had disappeared, leaving a garbage can full of smoldering embers. There was only one message on her answering machine: It was from Cole Ferrer, requesting Mark to call him. A stir of worry nudged her. She wrote down Cole's number from the recording. Wasn't Mark with him? Where else would he be? She quickly dialed the number.

"I'm dreaming of a White Christmas . . ." Cole's voice sang out over his answering machine. Marcella grimaced at the sound of it. "I'm out decking the halls with boughs of holly," the message continued. "If you'd like to leave your greeting, I'll get back to you."

"Cole," she said. "This is Marcella Winton. I'm a little worried about Mark because he isn't staying here, and the message you left for him obviously means he isn't with you. Please call me as soon as possible."

She hung up and poured herself a large Scotch. There was nothing to do but wait.

Sonia lay across three Concorde seats, all hers. She had gotten away by pleading exhaustion, which was not so far from the truth! And Leonide had used his famous Kabuki whiteface, mixed with a little green, to make her look sickly. Now, stripped of makeup, shrouded in a purple scarf and dark glasses, she sipped champagne, leafed through a pile of magazines, and sang along with the advance copy of Ray's new tape playing through her earphones. She already knew every note of each song. The album, to be released in the new year, displayed Ray's voice at a new peak. It had been recorded with great care and taste, a blues-tinged album that she was sure would sell more than his other two albums combined. And as she listened to Ray's sexy voice groaning in her ear, she could not help wriggling with delight at the thought that in five hours she would be in London and in his arms.

The plane was full, but she stretched luxuriantly across the whole row. What was the point of having money if you didn't blow it? She patted her purse, stuffed with hundred-dollar bills to buy Ray the best Christmas present he had ever had.

She was met at Heathrow by Ray's driver.

"Where's Ray?" she asked as he loaded her luggage into the Bentley.

"Still sleeping, Miss Sonia." He laughed. "It's eight in the morning here."

She sat back as they drove through the sleepy, gray suburbs, making herself remember how exhausted he must be after his concerts. Too bad, because she had splashed ice water on her face and eyes in the plane and then made up carefully just in case Ray had stayed up all night to meet her.

"How's the tour going?" she asked as the car headed smoothly for the center of London.

"Sellin' out each night, Miss Sonia!" the driver said. "You ain't never seen scenes like we gettin' at Wembley. All those little English people, s'posed to be so meek and mild? They go crazy when Ray starts singin'!"

It was nine-thirty when she checked in under the name of Susan Windsor, to match the initials on her luggage, at the Montcalm, a luxurious hotel near Marble Arch, where rock stars could stay in privacy and comfort. She had her own suite and was shown to it. She unpacked a few dresses, then walked along the corridor to Ray's suite, knocking softly on the door.

"Hi, Miss Sonia!" Elmer opened the door to her, speaking softly. "You have a good flight?"

Elmer and George, Ray's favorite aides, were playing cards in the small anteroom. George looked up and waved. Sonia indicated Ray's room with a jerk of her head. "Can I go in?"

Elmer shook his head. "He still sleepin', Miss Sonia. Is there anything we can get you?"

She shook her head impatiently. "Look, you guys, how about giving me a break?" she pleaded. "Let me slip in there with him so I can wake him up. . . ."

Elmer exchanged a stern look with George.

"I don't see as how we can do that, Miss Sonia," George said, politely. "Ray, he fast asleep and he don't have his cuffs on. Ray don't like it if you wake him before he ready. He got to bed real late last night."

"Can't we forget the fucking cuffs for *one time*!" Sonia cried. "I fly all the fucking way from New York and I can't even—"

"Shh!" Elmer hushed her, pulling up a chair for her. "He wake up in an hour or two," he assured her, patting the seat. "He be real happy to see you. Been looking forward to you coming all week, Miss Sonia. Let me order up some breakfast for you? What you like? Orange juice? Eggs and bacon?"

"I don't *want* anything to eat or drink," she said firmly. "I just want to be with *Ray*!"

"Okay, you take it easy now, Miss Sonia," Elmer soothed her. "You lie down and rest awhile. The minute Ray wakes up I'll tell him you're here."

"I've *been* resting on the plane!" she said. She walked out, tight-lipped. Elmer ran alongside her, trying to soothe her. Out in the corridor she grabbed hold of his arm.

"In my room for a moment," she said urgently.

Elmer looked back worriedly at Ray's suite, following her as she unlocked the door.

"Sit down," she ordered when he entered her room. She closed the door behind him. "Okay." She stood before him, her legs apart. "How much?" she asked.

Elmer's eyes flickered. "What you askin' about, Miss Sonia?" he said faintly.

"The *key*!" she cried. "The key to the fucking cuffs! How much for it?"

He laughed nervously, shaking his head. "Oh, no sir! No *sir*! That more than my job is worth!"

"Okay," she said. "How much *is* your fucking job worth?"

Elmer pulled a face, raising his eyebrows. "Lessee . . .

forty? fifty thousand a year? Somethin' like that. Yeah, Ray's real good to the people around him, he—"

"I'll give you fifty thousand," she said simply, opening her purse. "I have it right here in cash. No one needs to know. Fifty thousand bucks for a fucking stupid little key, Elmer!"

"Whooee!" Elmer suddenly whooped, hitting his knee. His face creased into a big smile. "I knew Ray had something, but fifty grand just to have his arms around you? Whooee!"

"What do you say?" she asked patiently. "Want me to go in there and talk to George?"

Elmer laughed. "Uh-uh! George, he more scared than me! I couldn't do this to you, Miss Sonia. Shit, I *like* you too much!"

"That's very nice, but so what?" she said.

He shook his head. "Me and Ray's been friends from way back. Knew the dude in Georgia, see? I love Ray, but that man, he need some kind of restrainin', as you'd say. Y'see, I was with him the night he killed that gal. He didn't mean to kill her all right, I swear to that. Swear to God on that."

"Okay, but he'd never harm me," she told him. "I can handle him."

Elmer rolled his eyes doubtfully.

"We're in love, goddammit!" Sonia cried. "Those cuffs hurt! Look!" She pulled up her black sweater to show him her bruised ribs. "This is from *weeks* ago!"

Elmer glanced away. "He do more than bruise you, you take those cuffs off him," he muttered. "That man, he get carried away by love, I'm telling you! That's why the ladies go so crazy about him—because they *know* he get carried away!"

"Okay, look Elmer . . ." She touched his arm pleadingly. "Haven't *you* ever wanted something real bad? I mean, what am I asking for, the moon? I just want one *normal* night with Ray. Like two normal people in love, is that such a lot to ask?"

Elmer thought, his eyes moving. "That's what they tell me, Miss Sonia," he said finally, shrugging. "Me and George. They tell us: don't you ever leave him alone with no girl without those cuffs. It's worth your job. Or maybe worse, Miss Sonia. Those guys in charge, they like the Mafia! You do somethin' against instructions like that, they *kill* you! I ain't kidding. You realize what kind of bread Ray brings in? How many albums he sells? In the States, ten million maybe? That's retail seventy, eighty million bucks. Worldwide, you make that a hundred and fifty, two hundred million bucks. People do a lot of weird stuff for two hundred million bucks, Miss Sonia."

Sonia leaned against the wall wearily. "What if you just *lend* me the key, Elmer? That way you can leave him wearing the cuffs and if anything gets found out, it won't be your fault. Lend me the key for an hour and I'll get a copy made. Come on, Elmer, that's got to be worth ten thousand, no? That'll buy a helluva lot of coke!"

"Oh, I don't use that stuff, Miss Sonia," he laughed uneasily. "I like the healthy life."

"Look . . ." She took wads of hundred-dollar bills from her purse. "I'm going to count it out. It's all fresh, new money. This is one thousand. Two, three, four . . . C'mon, Elmer, count it with me!"

"Oh *man*!" Elmer slapped his knee again, looking the other way, shaking his head sorrowfully as if this were not really happening.

Cole called back at midnight.

"Mrs. Winton? Sounds like our boy has gone AWOL?"

She was too worried to even register her disgust at hearing him call Mark "our boy."

"We had an argument on the way home from the airport," she told him. "He got out of the car before we arrived home. He said he'd be spending Christmas with you."

Cole cleared his throat. "Yes. Well, I'm afraid our first Christmas together lasted all of two hours. He didn't seem at all well to me and I suggested he go straight to bed. He was determined to tell me about some girl in Bologna with whom he imagines he's involved. Mark can be quite difficult at times. I told him that he had chosen a rather cruel time to give me this news. He knows how I feel about him and I—"

"I don't want to hear about your stupid quarrel!" Marcella cried out. "Where *is* he?"

There was a short silence and Cole said testily, "I was *coming* to that." He took a breath. "What this is about is Mark trying to assert himself, I think. With you, then with me. He's finally discovering his own will. I suppose it's a healthy sign? Anyway, he just walked out, leaving me a charming gift but . . . well, that was the last I heard. I called to wish you both a happy—"

"Do you have *any* idea where he could be?" she interrupted.

"Naturally I assumed he was with you," Cole said. "I suppose he might have turned about, in a fit of pique, having argued with both of us, and gone back to Italy."

The panic and fear leaped up in her now. "Cole, listen," she said. She had to confide in someone. "You'll think I'm crazy, perhaps, but I've just seen a clairvoyant who told me that both my children are in great danger. Sonia's on a plane to London, so there's nothing I can do about that. I've called Pan Am and they say the flight is on schedule. I'm terrified there's a bomb in it: the clairvoyant saw death connected with steel! And he said Mark was somewhere very hot. He said I could save him!"

"I don't think you're crazy at all," Cole said calmly. "I have great faith myself in soothsayers, prophets, and seers. I suggest you call Mark's pensione in Bologna. And please let me know what they say."

Wembley Stadium was ugly, a huge concrete sports arena in the middle of an anonymous suburban neighborhood, several miles from London's center. The audience, made up of enthusiastic young fans, mostly white, with a sprinkling of West Indians, were fairly subdued until Ray came through the arena to the stage, throwing off his white toweling robe to reveal the sparkling, diamond-studded jacket, jumping up to the round stage to gyrate alongside four backup singers. Then the crowd roared and whistled, as noisily as any American audience.

It was Ray's best concert yet, and certainly his biggest. Afterward, Sonia snuggled up to him on the backseat of the enormous limousine as it slowly nudged its way through the crowds thronging the grounds, buying souvenir tee shirts and commemorative programs.

"God what a night!" She held on to his strong arm as he peered out the tinted windows, grinning happily.

"They just love me here, Sonia!" he cried.

"Of course, Ray! They love you everywhere!" She kissed him.

"You liked the show? You really liked the show?" He lay back against the seat. "These English folk need love and emotion, too. They seem controlled and cool, but deep down inside they need it just like everyone else."

By the time they reached his suite it was nearly one a.m.

"They said a Christmas concert wouldn't work." Ray smiled, throwing off his coat and jacket. "They said everyone would stay home. But I knew! I *knew,* Sonia! There are thousands of people who don't spend Christmas with their families: I knew they would come to see Ray!"

She picked up the phone and ordered a light supper and champagne. Elmer and George retired to the corner of the room, playing cards and pretending they weren't there. When the champagne arrived, she took a couple of glasses over to them.

"Merry Christmas, you guys," she said, giving them the wine. She winked at Elmer. "We have some sandwiches and hamburgers. Take what you want. . . ."

She arranged a plate of food for Ray and picked morsels from it as he ate, sipping her champagne and refilling his glass.

"How'd all those commercials go?" he asked her.

"More or less okay. . . ." She pulled her cashmere sweater off one shoulder and mimicked the commercial for him. " 'Don't kiss me! Caresse me!' That's the new line I get to say for next year's spots. I had to say it about four thousand times before they liked the delivery."

"Ha!" Ray laughed. "Don't kiss me, Caresse me! That's cute! Do *I* get to kiss you, too?" He leaned over to her and his soft lips enveloped hers. She broke away, breathless.

"You get to kiss me at any time and do anything you want to do to me, baby," she whispered in his ear. She glanced over at the guards, sitting in the shadows, pretending not to hear. She hated their presence at intimate moments like these.

"Oh boy . . ." Ray slid his hand up under her sweater,

grazing her breast. "I get to caress the Caresse Girl! I get to do anything I want!"

"Better believe it, lover," she whispered.

He nuzzled her ear. His huge body was wrapped in a velour warm-up suit and she could see the outline of his aroused sex through the baggy pants. "Thank you for comin' all this way to spend Christmas with me, Sonia," he whispered. "It means a lot to me, baby. It's like bein' with family."

"What about your family, Ray?" she asked. "Don't you usually spend the holidays with them?"

He glanced up at her sadly, replacing the champagne glass. He turned to his guards. "They got that coffee in this hotel?" he asked. "That coffee I like with the whipped cream and the whiskey?"

"Irish coffee, Ray," Elmer said softly. "That stuff called Irish coffee."

Ray turned to Sonia. "Want one, baby? Make you sleep good."

"No, thanks, I don't need it. I'm still jet-lagged, remember."

"Okay, order me up one!" Ray called, "and get a couple for yourselves, too. Well . . ." He sighed, putting an arm around her. "Let me see now, we was talkin' about my family. The LeVars. Sonia, you ain't never *seen* a Christmas like the LeVars used to have! My daddy, my mam, my grandma, and us four brothers—Marlon, DeWitt, Grover, and me. Yeah, we had some fine holidays. . . ."

Sonia stared at him. "Where are they now?" she asked. "You're talking about them as if they were all dead!"

Ray shrugged. "Far as I'm concerned they may as well be, Sonia. See, after that . . . that accident, with that girl, y'know? My family didn't want to . . . how should I say it, *receive* me! Understand? I was not welcome in my family anymore."

She patted his cheek. "You poor baby."

"So," he sighed, "you the only family with me this Christmas, Sonia. The beautiful Sonia!"

She watched the two guards when they opened the door for the waiter. He made a big thing about pouring the coffee, adding the whiskey and sugar, then dripping the heavy cream over a spoon so it formed a layer on top. She saw Elmer give him a ten-dollar tip before seeing him out. They all sipped the coffee with much smacking of lips, Ray saying it tasted better than the Irish coffee they'd had in Vegas, or was it Denver?

He went to the bedroom to change into his black silk pajamas. It was after three when he came out, his hands behind his back to be cuffed. Sonia looked on as the men flipped on his cuffs, saying good-night to her and to Ray, and finally leaving.

As soon as the door closed, she was on him, slithering out of her clothes, pressing her mouth against his ear, his lips, feeling him to see if he was aroused. He was rock hard.

"Oh Sonia," he groaned, twisting his head as he kissed all over her. "Oh baby!"

"I can't stand it," she sighed. "Wanting to touch you all the time and those two always watching, listening . . ."

"Okay . . ." He pressed his lips to her temple, soothing her. "We got all night together now. Tomorrow morning, too. Just us two. But that ain't enough for me, either, baby."

"What do you mean?" She broke away to look at him.

He looked at her sadly and soulfully. "I wanna marry you, Sonia."

"Whooo!" she yelped, laughing, pinching him here and there over his body. "There goes my Caresse contract!"

"Un-uh!" He reared away from her, very serious. His big dark eyes stared into hers. "A big firm like Caresse gotta be very careful, you understand?" he said. "They can't tear up no contract on account of you marryin' a nigger!"

"Don't use that word, Ray," she cried, clinging to his arm. "I *hate* it!"

"It's true, though, ain't it?" he asked. "Racial discrimination is against the law." He looked quite pleased with himself for having figured this all out, and she felt a sudden pang of pity and love for him.

"My morals clause," she said, hugging him close. "I signed this contract that says the least little breath of scandal—"

"That's just what I'm *saying,* Sonia," he explained patiently. "Ain't nothin' scandalous about a girl *marrying* the man she loves, is there? They couldn't fire you just for the fact that you marryin' a black man, could they?"

"I don't know . . ." She frowned. "We'd have to look into it. I'll call Carmen in the morning. . . ."

"You do want to marry me, don't you, Sonia?" He frowned. "You do love me as much as I love you?"

"More!" she said. "Much more!" She kissed his ear, glimpsing herself for one crazy moment as Mrs. Sonia LeVar of Las Vegas, living in some sparkly castle on the edge of a desert, sunning herself by a palm-lined turquoise pool, hosting lavish dinner parties for show-business legends. Bringing a touch of fashion to the vulgar world of entertainment might almost be a fascinating challenge. She pulled the tiny package from her pocket and presented it to him on her palm.

"Merry Christmas, Ray darling." She kissed him. "I'd like to think that this is the best Christmas present anyone ever gave anyone!"

He frowned, taking it from her. "Oh, baby! I haven't had time to look in one store for you. What you gonna think of me?"

"It doesn't matter." She put her hand on the back of his thick neck. "I have you! And that's all I want." She stroked his neck, gripped his muscular arms, and let him nuzzle his nose against her face. She dropped the present into his cuffed hands.

"Well!" he laughed. "They say the best gifts come in little packages!" He turned the packet this way and that, weighing it in his palm.

She took his cock in her hand and gave it a meaningful squeeze. "Don't you believe it, Ray. You disprove the rule!" she laughed.

"You wrapped it so prettily, Sonia," he said, pulling off the paper with his big fingers. "I hate to tear it. It's goin' in my scrapbook, naturally! With the date an' everything!"

She giggled. "You romantic fool!"

"What is it? A *key*?" He frowned, feeling it. She held it up. "What's it to?" he asked. "Don't tell me you bought me an English car, Sonia?" He shook his head at her. "You know how many cars I got?"

"Oh, Ray . . ." she pouted. "It's not for some dumb

car. It's much more exciting than that. I'll give you three
guesses and then I'm using it!"

He looked up at her, suddenly serious, his eyes wide. In
the intimate lighting of the suite, they looked hooded, almost oriental. "Not the cuffs, baby?" he moaned.

Sonia nodded, excited. "So we can spend the night together like two normal human beings. So you can make
love to me the way you want!"

"No . . ." He shook his head, a pained expression on
his face. "No, Sonia. You know what happened the last
time I made love how I wanted. It ain't right! They said
from that day onward I always gotta wear the cuffs when
I'm alone with a lady. Always!"

"Well, fuck 'em," Sonia said simply. "Rules are made to
be broken, right?" She darted behind him and fitted the
key into the lock. The cuffs' action was smooth, strong;
they sprang open effortlessly. Ray looked down at his
hands, rubbing his wrists.

"You shouldn't have done that, Sonia," he said, glancing
up at her. "It ain't right!"

She slid onto his lap. "Don't be silly. Don't be such a big
softie. Hold me, Ray. Hold me!"

He tentatively put his arms around her. "It ain't right,"
he muttered again.

"Oh baby, it feels right to me . . ." she groaned. "It
feels very right to me! Now let's take it real slow and easy,
Ray baby. I want this to be the best night of our
lives. . . ." She pulled him to his feet and he padded after
her into the bedroom.

Marcella called the pensione in Bologna all through the
night. Different people spoke to her. Finally, a night porter
told her he had seen Mark return and that he was in his
room but not answering his phone.

"Could you go up there and see if he's all right?" she
pleaded. "I'm worried that he's sick. Please go up and
speak to him. I'll call back in fifteen minutes."

"He is on the top floor, *signora*," the porter groaned.
"The elevator is not working. . . ."

"I'm his mother!" Marcella said. "I'm very worried.
Please!"

She watched the clock for the next fifteen minutes. If the little clairvoyant had said nothing, she would have imagined Mark sulking up in his room, not wanting to speak to anyone after his. New York tantrum. But the words, "He doesn't have to die. You could save him!" rang in her ears.

She called back to speak again to the porter.

"Did you see him?" she asked. "Did he speak to you?"

"No, I think he sleeps."

"Okay. Thank you. I'll call again tomorrow," she said.

"Yes, *signora*," the man said wearily.

She called Cole to report.

"The main thing is that he's safe somewhere," Cole said.

"But the clairvoyant?" Marcella said. "And Mark did not look well. I felt he was coming down with something, didn't you?"

Cole sighed. "I don't know what to think!" he said. "Maybe he's just sleeping off a tremendous jet lag or a huge hangover."

"Yes. Maybe," Marcella agreed doubtfully. "I'll call again tomorrow. If he still doesn't answer, I'll fly to Bologna. It's a long way to go to settle an argument, but after seeing that clairvoyant, I can't rest."

"I'd come with you, but my engagement at the Carlyle starts tomorrow," Cole said. "It's the holidays and I don't dare let them down. . . ."

She said good-bye, thankful he wasn't free to make the trip. Sitting next to Cole on a long transatlantic flight would have been more than she could bear.

It took her hours to get to sleep that night, until she finally used a sleeping pill. What a Christmas! she thought. "He doesn't have to die, you could save him!" The tiny seer of Broadway. The two huge sisters—one a taxi driver. The jailbird husbands. As Marcella slowly lost consciousness the images of the day took form, dreamlike, in scenarios only slightly more weird than life itself.

"I found the Lord when I was fifteen, Sonia," Ray told her.

They were in bed, naked, and he was holding her in his arms. Like two normal people, she thought happily.

"Yes, ma'am," Ray nodded in the dark. "I found the Lord! Amen!" Sonia opened her eyes wide. She was never quite sure how to respond to this. Religion had never been her scene. In fact, anything religious reminded her uncomfortably of her father and the way he had assured her that God would never approve of her since she had fooled around with the body He had given her.

Ray had been a very tender lover, but she was a little disappointed. Far from increasing the excitement of their sex, his new unhandcuffed freedom had diminished it. He had not been carried away. Although the passion had mounted and she had loved everything he had done to her with his unshackled, perfectly good two hands, it had not gotten out of control.

"Each time I make love to you, it feels better," he told her as she relaxed in his arms.

Playing with sharks, mounting the black horse, my own tame wild creature, she liked to think.

"Religion is very important to you, right?" she asked, letting her hand fall gently in his lap, feeling his sex still semihard, as if he were remembering the delight they had both experienced fifteen minutes ago. She glanced over at the clock. It was four-thirty in the morning. As usual, sex with Ray made her want more.

"Don't you believe in our Lord, Sonia?" he asked. "Doesn't He comfort and guide you?"

"Well . . ." She bit her lip. "Not exactly."

She reached out to switch on the small bedside lamp. The peach-colored shade illuminated Ray's body and face, making him look as if he were carved out of dark gold. She leaned over him, staring into his face. Calmed, tired, he was totally serious, she realized, his face as naive as a child's and as trusting. She reached out for a sip of champagne.

"Tell me, Ray," she asked, replacing the glass. "Did you believe in the Lord while you were killing that girl?" she asked. She was a little surprised at herself, but she had not been able to stop the words spilling from her mouth.

Ray flinched as if she'd struck him. Then he made himself smile, slowly. "How many times have I told you, baby?" he asked humbly. "I been asking God to forgive me ever since then. I speak with Him every night to ask forgiveness."

"Yeah?" Her heart began to flutter with fear and desire —two emotions she liked mixing together. "And what does He say?" She had meant to sound sarcastic, but Ray thought her question over very carefully. He closed his eyes for a few seconds, then opened them, staring directly into her gaze. He took her hand and placed it over his heart.

"He say, 'Ray, you didn't *mean* to kill that girl. It was an accident.' That's what He say. He say, 'You didn't want to kill her—you were lovin' her.' "

"Yes, loving her to death!" Sonia laughed.

Ray suddenly grabbed her head and yanked it roughly back. "And that's *enough*!" he yelled into her ear, almost deafening her. In the sudden silence his voice echoed painfully in her head. The jolt of fear that shot through her was better than any drug, any drink. Her eyes bulged as he held her neck in a viselike grip, giving her a taste of his immense strength.

He released her, covering his face with his hand.

"Oh, Sonia, I'm so sorry." He groaned. "I'm sorry I shouted, baby." He caressed her shoulder, leaning his forehead against hers for a moment. "Forgive me, baby? I love you so much. But don't try to get me mad. I *know* you tryin' to get me mad. You can't understand me, Sonia. You see, what I felt about that poor girl was . . . well, it's a lot like how I feel for you. Sex and all. She liked excitement, too. Like you. It's so good, sometimes you get carried away. That's all that happened. It's like when a boxer kills an opponent, y'know? Happens sometimes, when they don't know their own strength. I didn't hurt you just then, did I, baby?"

She shook her head. "No, you gentle giant. You didn't hurt me."

She half sat up to kiss his lips. He growled as she nibbled on his thick soft lower lip, moving his body so that his sex was rubbing against her, erect again.

"But it's interesting," she said, breaking away. "You see no contradiction between what you did and believing in God. As long as you believe in God, it's okay, right?"

"That's right, Sonia." He began to make love to her again, his big hands enjoying the novelty of roaming over her body, nobody watching, nothing harnessing his desire. He caressed her rib cage, brushed across her breasts, touched her between her legs.

"Did you believe in God at that very moment you were killing her, you fucking hypocrite?" she asked.

Again, the words had just come unbidden out of her mouth, surprising and frightening her. She felt his body tense and she suddenly realized what she had been arranging over the last weeks, knew why that key had been so important to her.

"I *told* you, Sonia," he said slowly, his face hovering over hers. "I been asking God's forgiveness ever since. You got no right to call me a hypocrite, baby. Please don't do that!"

"You're a murderer, Ray," she told him. As she said that she reached down for his cock. It had never been so hard. "That's why you turn me on."

He held her tightly in his arms, frowning, as if fascinated with what she had to say. Then he thrust his mouth close to her head. "You'll never speak about that girl again, you hear?" he whispered urgently. "Never!" His embrace was like iron; she was unable to put up the slightest resistance to his grip, to the vise of his arms.

"I've paid my dues," he told her. "I gave a lot of money to the girl's family, and whenever we're in Georgia I visit that poor girl's grave. I've paid my dues, Sonia!"

He sat astride her, his sex aloft.

"Why is this getting you so excited, Ray?" she asked, looking at him. "Am I tuning in to where you really live? Where you really come alive?"

He glanced down at himself, shamed. "You know what makes me want you, baby," he said. "You *know* what it is, right? But why you have to talk like that to Ray, huh? You know Ray loves you, baby. . . ."

She spread her legs, arching her back.

"Get inside me again," she urged. "I want you there. I only feel complete when you're in me. . . ."

She threw back her head as he entered her. The feeling was unbelievably wonderful.

"We've never felt this good!" she gasped.

"I know it," he murmured, flexing himself inside her.

"We'll make a deal, Ray," she proposed. "I won't mention that girl again if you don't mention that fucker God to me, okay? Because *if* He exists, which I and several hundred million other people like me doubt very much. He must be one screwed-up sick fucker who I wouldn't *want* to come to me, ever!"

Ray looked down at her in admiration, almost in awe, as he began to move his pelvis. "Man . . . God could strike you down *dead* for saying that, Sonia," he groaned wonderingly, shaking his head. "I gotta admire your guts just for *sayin'* it!"

"It doesn't take any guts," she told him. "What you don't believe in can't harm you. . . ." She began to answer his body with thrusts of her own. "You know this is going to be our best time ever, don't you, Ray?"

His eyes were closed, his pelvis rotating slowly. "Ooh, yes," he groaned. "Yes, I know it. . . ."

He was so high up inside her she felt herself filled with him. They moved against each other, her buttocks lifting from the mattress to stay pressed to him.

"Fuck religion!" she told him. "Fuck God! Fuck *me*, Ray!" She could feel the coiled, reserved strength held back in him, could feel him trying to stay gentle with her, trying to spare her, his hardness comfortingly deep inside her.

"Oh, baby, this is as close to God as *I'll* ever get," she sighed to him. Ray fell on top of her, encircling her slim body with his arms. The contrast between her delicate, thin limbs and his muscular, thick body was much more evident now that he could hold her in his arms. Her fragility excited him and he lingered wonderingly over her wrists, her ankles, and her neck, moving faster inside her, starting to pant. The bed began to creak violently as he speeded up, and when she opened her eyes she saw his face twisted into a distorted expression, half pain, half desire, the very two feelings *she* craved! He squeezed her torso between his two strong arms, holding her in place, tight, tight. She could hear his teeth grinding, hear his breathing become wild, see the muscles in his cheeks and temple clench. And then suddenly she had no breath. No breath, no breath! she gasped, her eyes bulging, but no fear either, she realized, amazed.

"I can't stop myself now," he grunted over her. "You sure Ray ain't hurtin' you, Sonia?"

She answered him with her body, staying with him as he reared and lunged.

"Oh, Sonia," he whimpered, leaning his forehead down to hers, the sweat from his face dripping onto her. "Maybe you better put the cuffs back on me, huh? I scared I may love you too hard, now . . ."

She shook her head vigorously and he seemed to go a little crazy at that, bucking and grinding until the bed bounced with their rhythm, spraying her with his sweat and spittle. He squeezed harder and she blacked out for a moment. And suddenly she was not lying on a hotel bed in London under Ray's heavy body—she was riding Red! She was cantering along the freeway to La Jolla, feeling Red's sweat and the sea-spray on her face as they rode. She was the fourteen-year-old Sonia riding with that exhilarating mixture of fear and joy, to freedom, to freedom! The riding rhythm became their loving rhythm now, they were identical! She remembered that look on her child's face, that pure emotion of joy—before anything really bad had happened to her. Ray was squeezing the last breaths out of her now. Before she had become so soon, so early, a woman. She had ridden that beautiful animal, its powerful body, its muscles and limbs moving in perfect coordination with hers. A man can be as beautiful as a horse, Laurie had said, and her daddy had called her princess. *His* princess! She had only been perfectly happy when riding a horse. She could still just hear Ray's grunts as he moved faster, beside himself, embracing her so strongly, stronger than he knew. She felt a strange satisfaction; she had accomplished everything she had ever desired.

The last breaths of life were being squeezed out of her now, Ray's face grotesque, his eyes rolling, his lips stretched in a grimace. She understood that he no longer knew what he was doing and she forgave him. She took all the blame. Just before she died, the words "God forgive me," formed mentally, breathed soundlessly from her lips. Then she heard a crack which she knew was her spine breaking. She felt no pain; he had numbed her. She was dead now, although Ray continued to work inside her, oblivious, not stopping until he had achieved his wildest pleasure yet, a burst of fulfillment marked by a long drawn-out cry, his arms still holding her tightly, tightly, not knowing what he'd done. He slept instantly, as if unconscious, his grip loosening gradually until the lifeless body finally fell from his arms.

The shrill jangle of the phone cut into Marcella's confused dream. She reached out, asleep, for the receiver, to stop the terrible noise. As she woke, the premonition that this call was about Sonia came unbidden to her mind.

She listened to the news a strange voice was telling her. "No!" she screamed. "No!" And then her emotions shut off. It was too big, too horrible to be immediately comprehended. There would be years in which to digest it. She made herself listen to the news as if it were about someone she did not know. Sonia was dead. Yes, I see, she said. Murdered. Yes, I understand, she said calmly. By Ray LeVar, a black pop singer. Yes, I met him. At Harry's funeral. He gave himself up to the London police this morning, confessing to a previous murder. They had been trying to find her number for hours, because of course as Sonia's mother they thought she should be among the first to know. I appreciate that, she automatically thanked the voice. She's just trying to shock everybody, she had told Amy. It would be in that day's papers. MODEL KILLED BY BLACK POP STAR. BLACK POP IDOL KILLS CARESSE GIRL. MODEL MURDER! They would have the best possible raw material to make up into their juiciest headlines. The kind that really stopped you in your tracks as you walked past the newsstand. Her head was whirling. You saw these headlines in the *News,* or in the *Post,* HEADLESS BODY FOUND. MADMAN KILLS WIFE, SON AND SELF. Sometimes they almost made you smile with their crudeness. You never, ever thought they could be about someone you knew. Your own family. Your daughter. The daughter you never really knew but who always seemed to have this bitter rage inside her. Against herself!

After hanging up the phone, Marcella hid under the blankets. Then, through the numbness that her mind sought to contain her grief, to maintain her sanity, a new thought sounded, like a new note in a musical refrain, a green shoot pushing its way up through the dirt. That clairvoyant had been right about Harry *and* Sonia: what about Mark? He doesn't have to die, he had told her twice. *You* could save him, he'd said. What was she waiting for?

She got out of bed and dressed and packed a suitcase like a woman walking in her sleep. It was five-thirty in the morning on the day after Christmas. She would just go down to the street and get the doorman to find her a cab. Drive straight to JFK. Await the first flight to Italy. Pisa, perhaps. Then a long cab ride to Bologna. Go to Italy, she thought, sliding her case into the elevator. Go straight to Italy. She locked the front door. Do not pass Go. Do not collect two hundred dollars. She had lost one child, she was damned if she was going to lose both.

BOOK FIVE

NINETEEN

Marcella pushed against the locked glass doors of Mark's pensione in Bologna, ready to tear them down with her bare hands. It was nearly two a.m. and she was sobbing with exhaustion from the nightmare trip. The flight to Pisa had seemed endless, and during it she had been haunted by grotesque images of Sonia being murdered, Sonia dying, Sonia dead in some hotel room in London. Somehow, knowing her murderer was that gentle giant she had met at the cemetery made it worse, more of a mystery. Marcella could not imagine what had gone on, although she somehow knew that it must have been Sonia's own fault. But not wanting to imagine it—indeed, closing her mind to the tragedy—had not stopped her subconscious from providing lurid dreams as she slept fitfully in the plane. Losing a child in this way was like having part of you cut off. The grief made her ill, unable to read or eat, as she urged the plane to reach its destination faster, faster! The long ride by taxi from Pisa to Bologna took another ninety minutes, speeding along surrealistically empty freeways lit by blinding modernistic lamps. By the time the taxi pulled up at the modest little pensione, she had imagined breaking down the door to Mark's room and finding every possible scene awaiting her—from Mark on a blood-soaked bed to Mark swinging inert from a noose. Only the tiny clairvoyant's words, "You could save him, he doesn't have to die," gave her hope.

Breathless, she pounded on the pensione doors, peering through them to see, infuriatingly, the night porter slumped over a newspaper, fast asleep in an armchair. Glancing back helplessly at the taxi driver, who was counting the fistful of lire she had thrust into his hand as he had slung her suitcase onto the pavement, she gestured at the locked doors. Pocketing the money, the driver helped out with some hefty pounding of his own, finally succeeding in waking the old porter.

It took a large tip to get him to believe she was Mark's mother and wanted to be shown to Mark's room. Even then, he insisted on examining her passport and comparing their names, getting her to sign a police form, before finally bending to lift her heavy case with a grunt. Heaving and wheezing, breathing garlic fumes and wine in her face, he ushered her into the tiny elevator.

"Presto!" she urged. *"Pronto! Per favore!* Do you know my son? I'm afraid he's sick. . . ."

He shrugged, fumbling with his huge bunch of keys as the ancient elevator creaked its way to the top floor. By the time it stopped, some inches short of the floor, Marcella felt ready to faint.

She waited, leaning against the wall outside Mark's room as several keys were tried. Finally the door swung open. She gasped at the fetid air that rushed out to greet them. The windows were tightly shut, the odor of breath and body filling the small room. The only light came from a bedside lamp, its shade a sickly chartreuse, casting a greenish pallor over everything.

Mark lay naked across his bed like a recently excavated Greek statue, his body the same bronze color and seemingly as lifeless. Marcella stood frozen in the doorway, staring. Was she too late? She entered the room, her purse falling to the floor as she stared down at him. The old man dragged in her suitcase behind her, mumbling. Marcella saw that Mark was breathing. A quick search for pills or a syringe revealed nothing.

"Il grippe . . ." the old man muttered, setting down her suitcase with a grunt and peering over her shoulder at Mark. "There is a wave of influenza sweeping Italy. People have died from it, *signora*." He crossed himself, held one hand over his mouth, and left the room. Marcella locked the door behind him.

First she covered Mark with a blanket and flung the windows wide open. It was cold outside, but she had to air the room. Sweat ran in rivulets down the front and back of her body. She took off her suit and laid it over a chair, sitting in her slip on the edge of the bed, watching her son. You can save him, the little clairvoyant had said. She closed the windows and ran water into a basin, soaking a towel. She emptied half a bottle of cologne over the towel, wrapping it around Mark's forehead. He mumbled incoherently, his eyes opening wide for a moment, staring at her in his sleep.

"I'm here, darling," she said softly. "It's all right. I'm here." She removed her shoes and panty hose and climbed into the narrow bed alongside him, holding him in her arms. His breath was sour and she averted her head.

Mark went from fever hot to icy cold in her arms. Sometimes the breath rattled in his throat and he let out a delirious moan. She snuggled under the blanket to hold him when he was cold, letting him go when his body burned. Each hour, she sponged his body, soaked a clean washcloth and squeezed a few drops of cold water between his parched lips. By pushing him to the edge of the mattress she managed to change the sheets on the soiled bed, replacing the sweat-soaked pillow with a fresh one from the closet. As she bathed him, she examined his body for unusual marks. There was nothing. She dissolved two aspirin in water and forced them down him. She whispered comforting words in his ear, hoping he would sense her presence.

There was no thought of sleep for herself, although she was near to exhaustion. She used all her energy to will him well. She attempted to absorb his fever into her own body, mopping his brow, turning the cool towel to place the fresh side against his forehead, massaging cologne into his chest, back, and shoulders. Mark groaned and stirred, muttering incomprehensible words, his breathing slowly becoming more regular.

Now, as she held her surviving child, she could allow herself to feel some of the pain for the loss of her daughter. Lying alongside Mark's body, exhausted, she relived the births of both children, remembering all the hope and love she had had for them when they were babies. She held Mark in her arms, nurturing him, rebearing him. A million sensations and thoughts swirled around her brain, her ideas of sex and love and motherhood crystallizing until the only theme that retained any importance for her was this son in her arms regaining his health. And once he did, she would have to let go, because she could no longer control and guide him or let him control her. She saw everything so clearly now. How her mistakes had not really been mistakes but simply part of her life, a life that had swept along without much regard for what was right or wrong. Human life was only slightly more civilized than what went on among the animals of the jungle, anyway, with only the fittest surviving. She held on to her son through these long moments that would change her life and his forever. Finally, she was unable to fight sleep any longer, and mother and child slept together in a deep primal closeness.

She slept until ten o'clock, waking with a start as wintry sunshine poured into the room. Mark was sleeping more peacefully, his face relaxed, his breathing more regular. She felt that he had passed the danger point. She washed at his little basin, dressed, straightened the bed, and went downstairs to a nearby café for a cappuccino and toast.

The concierge at the pensione's desk during the daytime hours was a lady, and Marcella spoke to her about Mark, in her halting Italian, asking for a doctor to visit him as soon as possible. She registered at the pensione as a guest, saying she would continue to stay in Mark's room.

The doctor was there within the hour, a white-bearded, serious man who woke Mark gently in order to examine him.

Mark greeted them casually, as if it were no surprise to him that his mother had suddenly materialized in his small room, but she could see from his glazed eyes that he was not completely conscious. The doctor spoke a little English and prescribed antibiotics and sleep, urging Marcella to let Mark drink as much as he could.

Mark fell asleep as soon as the doctor left, and she went downstairs to buy bottles of mineral water, fruit, Mark's antibiotics, and some newspapers.

Back in Mark's room she opened the window a few inches and lit a cigarette, sitting on a straight-backed chair, reading the papers. The British papers contained no mention of Sonia, but there was a small paragraph on the front page of the *International Herald-Tribune* detailing Ray LeVar's arrest. She read it reluctantly, not willing to look again into that chasm of pain she had closed off for the moment while she dealt with Mark. The article mentioned that the police were holding Sonia's body for examination. She let the paper fall from her hands and stared out at the terra-cotta roofs of Bologna and the silvery sky. How would she be able to face making arrangements for a funeral? Should she have Sonia's body flown back to America, or should she go to London and have a quiet cremation there, hopefully away from the inquiring press, since Sonia was relatively unknown in Britain? These were questions she was quite unable to answer at the moment. She would wait until she got back to New York and could speak to her lawyer and to Amy, for much-needed advice. Meanwhile, this small room on the top of a students' pensione could provide a welcome refuge from the world, from ringing telephones and curious faces.

She woke Mark every two hours so he could drink some water, supporting him to the bathroom and settling him back in bed, making sure he took the antibiotics. He was not ready to talk yet and sank back into sleep the moment he lay down.

At four, she took a long warm soak in his tub, and after making sure he was comfortable she walked outside in the winding streets and grand plaza of the town. Bologna was a majestic city that at any other time she would have enjoyed exploring.

In the evening she started to clear the untidy room, sweeping up clothes, socks, and shoes and replacing them in the heavy old wardrobe and the mahogany chest of drawers. She felt curious about the life he had been leading here. There were no signs of the girl he had claimed was in love with him, no photo of her near his bedside, nor any of herself or of Cole. The room was ascetically devoid of decorations beyond what she had supplied when he had moved in, the pile of music scores on the floor the only sign that its occupant was a musician.

She tidied the papers and music, glancing back at Mark's sleeping face as she worked, seeing him as a separate person now, no longer an extension of herself and her hopes. The pain of knowing he had drifted away from her, had goals and tastes different from those they had formed together, was no longer so deep or so desperate. It was his life, and she saw how powerless she was to control it, how powerless anyone was to control another's life and have a peaceful coexistence. When Mark awoke, they would forge a new relationship. He would no longer be at the emotional center of her life. She was free, but strangely empty and sad, as if now she was of no use to any other human being. Her feelings were slowly rearranging themselves, like the aftershocks following an earthquake. The death of Sonia gave her a primal jolt each time she allowed herself to think of it.

She neatly folded Mark's sweaters and tried to replace them in the drawer, but the drawer would not close. She began to empty it of the bunched-up clothing and found some packets of envelopes in the unmistakably bright blue stationery she used. Mark must have carefully kept the letters she'd written him, she thought, smiling. But then she read the top envelope of one of the packets and saw that it was not addressed to Mark. Staring at it, her heart stopped for a moment as she read the name of Santiago Roca and the Barcelona address. The envelope bore no stamps: it had not been mailed.

She rocked back onto her heels on the threadbare carpet, stunned, quickly untying the package, trying to make herself believe this. She shuffled through the letters. None of the envelopes had been stamped or mailed. They had each been neatly slit open, the letters read and replaced.

"Oh my God!" she cried aloud, turning to Mark as he lay peacefully sleeping. Could I really have brought up such a monster? She stared at the prostrate body of her son. *Could* you have done that to me? Each day, when I left out a letter to be mailed to Santi on your way to school? Each day when I ran to look so hopefully at the mail you brought me?

A sudden thought struck her and in a frenzy she tossed the remaining clothes from the drawer. She looked carefully through some papers nestling under Mark's socks, almost knowing what she would see. Sure enough, there was a thick white envelope with those impossibly important-looking Spanish stamps stuck all along one edge, addressed to her from Santi. She gave a little cry, pressing the envelope to her heart. Could you have loved me that possessively? she asked the sleeping Mark. And is what you felt for me even worthy of the word "love"?

She looked closely at the envelope. It had been mailed in the first week of September, while Mark had still been in New York, just in time for him to intercept it. She smiled wryly to herself. How many times had she been tempted to use undelivered letters as part of a story, rejecting the device as too old-fashioned? In today's world people wouldn't wait for letters, she had thought. They would pick up the phone and call. Unless they were proud half-Majorcan, half-Spanish men like Santi! She remembered telling Amy that Santi was out of the nineteen-fifties. Of course! When declarations of love had to be written! So that they could be treasured, kept, reread many times. Assuming this was a declaration of love! Tremblingly, she opened it, standing near the window so it would catch the filtered light of Bologna.

My darling Marcella,

So I shall be the one to write even though you are the writer? Not one word from you! And I am writing only this one letter, which comes from the depth of my heart. If this is not answered, I shall understand and not force myself into your life. I know you think I am old-fashioned, but I am not of the school that believes the male must pursue and pursue the female until he wears her down with his insistence. For me, romance is fifty-fifty, and that is what I thought we had. In fact I know we had it—until New York.

You gave my life meaning, Marcella. The meaning I tried to get from God in the cathedral that morning. Ideally, humans are supposed to be self-sufficient, and before you my life was busy and successful, I had my friends and family, my group of artists to sell, my gallery, my house in Deya, yet there was an empty core because I had no one to love and to love me. As you gave my life meaning when we were together, so it has lost its meaning again since losing you. But have I really lost you, after finding you so beautifully on my magic isle?

This last long year since New York has left me without much interest in my work; my gallery and several artists' livelihoods will suffer if I do not pull myself together. The problem is I don't want to pull myself together—for what? The mixture, same as before? I needed you, Marcella! I needed a soul mate, a lover, a friend, and a partner. You were all those things to me, my darling—here in Majorca and then in New York—until I saw you with your son and the way you looked at him. As if—forgive me—he was the man in your life and not me; that openly adoring look without criticism that no mother should ever give her son after he reaches the age of eight! His suicide attempt forced the problem into the open very quickly. But maybe it was better to deal with this problem right away, before we became even more entangled?

You said Mark would laugh at my offer to adopt him, and that was another reason for my anger. Who is Mark to laugh at someone offering to take on such responsibility? In America you use psychologists and doctors where here we send a boy out to earn his living. Well, perhaps Italy will accomplish Mark's independence as you hoped.

So. If I do not want to return to my old life, what shall I do? I need to put some distance between myself and my problems. I want to think about things other than myself, such as human behavior which puzzles me. Important things. The sky, perhaps, or evolution, seas, volcanoes. I cannot claim to understand life. I could not have been more sure of anyone than I was of you, and yet look at us now! Yet, remembering the days and nights we shared in Majorca and New York, I cannot believe we are destined to again be strangers. Do I understand so little of what it means to be a parent,

Marcella? I realize your children are important, but are they more important than yourself? Important enough to make you sacrifice the happiness we could share?

Forgive me that this letter is so long and written so poorly in spurts and jumps. It has taken me over a week to write! To cut a long story short: I have decided to leave my gallery and Barcelona for a while. I will place the gallery in the hands of a very capable assistant, who will be overjoyed at the opportunity to run it his way. He cannot make more nonsense out of it than I have since returning from New York!

I shall go to my house in Deya and plan my new life from there. Majorca has always been good for me when I am unhappy and confused. (Look what happened last time!)

This time I am not so much confused as tired and, above all, missing you. My soul got very used to yours during our short time together. Now it is lonely.

I will always love you, Marcella. Unwillingly, I find that I do wait for you. Indeed, I must wait for you, however hopeless that might be. I need the belief that one day we'll find each other again and that you will be free then to be mine. I write my Deya address here in case you decide to write.

I said that a man must not live in hope, remember? But now I know I shall never see the mailman cycling up my road without foolishly hoping he carries a letter from you.

Forever, my darling. Santi.

She sat holding the letter until it grew dark, not turning on the light, letting Mark sleep on oblivious to her anger, to the tears pouring down her cheeks. She thought of shaking Mark awake and confronting him, then of running away to someplace where no one knew her and she could hide for the rest of her life, as Santi was doing. But she saw it all too clearly to remain angry for long. Whatever your child did to you was your own fault—hadn't she always said that? And when Mark was very young and she had poured all that love and attention onto him, more than a child could possibly withstand, she had known she was doing something wrong and she had known the results would prove that. Without meaning to, she had made Mark this way. It was the old story of "the sins of the fathers," except that this time it was the sins of the mother.

"Can I have some water?" Mark suddenly asked, making her jump.

She looked up to see him watching her. She got to her feet and poured him a glass, sitting on the bed, supporting him as he drank thirstily.

"How long have I been asleep?" he asked, handing back the glass. He still had a dazed look in his eyes as he stared at her.

"A day or two," she said, settling him down. "You've been sick, but you're going to be all right. How do you feel?"

"Tired," he said, falling back on his pillow. "Very tired." Just before he fell asleep again he mumbled, "When did you get here?" But he was snoring before she could answer.

She felt the relief of knowing he'd be well. Then she picked up the letters she'd written to Santi and placed them in her suitcase. She was about to plunge into a morass of pain and regret, to revel in her misery and martyrdom, when a new thought struck her. And suddenly, she found herself neatly folding all her clothes and packing them. *Who said it was too late?* a new voice prompted. *Who said it was all over?* She glanced again at the date Santi had written. September the fifth. Now it was only December. He was probably still in his idyllic house in Deya, meditating on volcanoes or whatever he thought he was doing. She must find him, show him all these loving letters he had never received, and tell him he was absolutely right about children not having the right to steal your happiness!

All the love she had for Santi came flooding over her now that she was free, now that her love no longer belonged half to Mark. Mark was out of danger now. She would tell the concierge to send the doctor tomorrow. She had done as much as a mother could or should ever do for a son. Now it was up to Mark, and he had the talent and the strength to make it.

She quickly dressed, made up, wrote a long, careful letter to Mark, telling him about Sonia, his sickness, and how she had discovered her letters to Santi. She told him she was going to deliver her letters to Santi personally. She left his pills by the bed with a note on how often to take them.

She checked around the room to make sure she had her passport, her money, her case. And now it's time for *my* life, she thought, staring down at him. And I pray to God that you have not destroyed it or Santi's life! Santi *must* still be there waiting—oh *please* let him be waiting, because now she could accept and return his love. Now she could love him as no woman had ever loved a man. Now she would teach him the meaning of the title *Forever Begins Tonight*, maybe this very night!

She bent over Mark to brush his forehead with her lips. His face was as handsome as ever, if pale.

"Good-bye, my selfish son," she told him. "Good-bye, the light of my life! The light that has shown me so clearly what my new life must be!"

She carried her suitcase out of the room, softly closing his door behind her.

She slept through the flight to Madrid. In Madrid she changed planes for Palma. She wanted to call Santi, but she did not have his Deya number, or the energy or vocabulary to request it from Spanish information. She reread his loving letter. If she found him, perhaps he would accompany her back to New York and take charge of the arrangements for Sonia's funeral. They could discuss all that after they had renewed their vows of love to each other.

The two-hour wait in Madrid allowed her to put through a call to Amy in New York, but she only got her answering machine. "Amy, I'm in Spain," she stammered. "I guess you heard the terrible news about Sonia. Then Mark was sick and—" she frowned, grasping for words. "About Sonia's funeral—I'll be in touch. The London police are holding her body for a postmortem. It's all so horrible I—" She broke off again, trying to control her voice. "I'm in Madrid en route for Majorca," she said. "I'm going to find Santi."

The plane touched down in Palma at ten that night, and she took a taxi directly to the Son Vida. As much as she longed to see Santi, she was too tired to go to him in her

present state. She needed a good night's sleep and a decent
bath and a change of clothes.

When she checked into the hotel she tried, with the
hotel's operator, to find Santi's number in Deya, but there
was no such listing. Since he was so eager to escape the
outside world, perhaps he did not even possess a telephone? She tried to picture Santi—her beautiful vibrant
Santi, as a recluse. Then she pictured his smile of delight
when he saw her, his face lighting up, his arms clinging to
her, never to let her go. And forever *would* begin tomorrow
night, a little late but just as he had prophesied. But first
she must sleep! In her room she fell onto the bed and slept
for twelve straight hours. At noon she awoke and took a
hot shower, ordering a pot of coffee and a sandwich to be
sent up.

After eating she found the courage to call London to
find out about Sonia. She finally reached the detective handling the case, who told her they had to keep the body for
another week.

"Oh, thank goodness!" she said.

"Ma'am?" the detective asked, and she could picture
the bland British face frowning at the crazy American lady
who did not seem to care about her murdered daughter.

"No, I know that sounds terrible, but I'm in such a state
of shock, I don't know that I could handle all the funeral
arrangements now," she explained. "Maybe in a week, I'll
feel more able to. . . ." She trailed off.

"I quite understand, Mrs. Winton. And I'm very sorry."

She hung up and took a deep breath, swallowing down
the hysteria that threatened to erupt. She stood in front of
the window, looking out at the Majorcan mountains, making herself breathe deeply of the pure, soft air. There is
nothing you can do for Sonia, she told herself. She's dead
and the body is just a shell. Her spirit is free and it is
floating around somewhere. Maybe even watching me.
Hopefully approving. Now, Santi comes first.

She had the hotel valet steam and press her suit. It was
three in the afternoon before she was ready. She stepped
out of the hotel and spoke to the taxi driver who waited at
the head of a line of taxis on the gravel driveway.

"Deya?" she asked, raising her eyebrows.

He nodded, a wizened little man with a black beret

perched on his head and a newspaper in his lap. She got into the backseat and he drove off, down the hill, the way Santi had driven on their excursions together. Her heart was beating fast. She had made up and arranged her hair carefully. The red Chanel outfit suited her, and the sling-back high heels elongated her legs. She wanted to be at her most beautiful for the only man she had ever loved. All her letters were in her quilted purse, so that she could present him immediately with the evidence of her love, explaining away the apparent betrayal that had separated them for so long.

The taxi drove slowly down the mountain, skirting Palma, through the pine trees, climbing the terraced orchards. The sun was out and the island was as beautiful in the winter light as it had been in late spring. Although the air was mild, the sun shining through the window dazzled her. It took nearly forty-five minutes to get to Deya, and once there she had to begin from the little restaurant they had eaten in, retracing their steps up the steep curving road behind the village that led to his house with its surrounding garden.

The taxi sputtered and wheezed up in first gear, the driver grumbling at the road. Don't expect him to be sunning himself on his terrace in December, she warned herself. He might not even be there. Yet she felt Santi's presence; it was unimaginable to her that he was not somewhere near.

The house looked very closed as they approached it, the shutters tightly locked, but there was someone bent over the plants in the front garden, trimming bits of trees and bushes. That person stood as the noise of the taxi's engine penetrated the trees. It was Santi's neighbor, the little old bent lady.

"*Señora!*" Marcella called, winding down the window. "Hello!" The woman peered suspiciously at her, walking toward the car. Then she suddenly broke into her toothless smile and cackled. "The American!" she cried. "How well you look! What are you doing here?"

Marcella could just understand her rapid Spanish.

"I've come to see Santi!" she told her. "Santiago Roca!" Her heart beat so fast she could hardly say his name. "Is he here?"

The old lady frowned, making even more lines in a face already crisscrossed with wrinkles. Her little eyes darted about. Marcella tried not to scream. Who would ever have thought her fate could rest so squarely upon the narrow shoulders of this kindly little witch? she thought. But it did!

"The priest is in the monastery," the old lady said simply, as if reciting a nursery rhyme.

"No, no . . ." Marcella laughed. "Not the priest, señora. Señor *Roca*! Santiago Roca! *Santi!* The man who lives here, in this house! Where is he?"

"In the monastery," the woman nodded, pointing. "In the hermitage. *There!*" She pointed a gnarled finger to the hills facing them, their outlines a little hazy in the distance.

Marcella shook her head, looking exasperatedly at the driver. The woman approached the car and put her hand on the edge of the window. "You can visit him." She nodded. "They are allowed visitors!"

Marcella sighed. It was impossible. Everyone on this island was a little nutty, a little eccentric, if not downright insane. Yet the woman's wizened face was not stupid as she watched Marcella with her sharp little eyes.

"Santi? Yes?" she asked. She nodded. "Santi Roca. There!" She pointed. "In the hermitage!"

Marcella suddenly remembered his letter. A distance from his problems, he had written. From human behavior which puzzles me. He meant *me,* she thought. But is it possible that he could have become a monk? A priest? "That is where you will find me if you leave me," he had told her once as they'd passed the monastery, the very monastery that the bent little lady was now indicating. But that had been a joke, surely. She had met him in a cathedral. Had religion been more important to him than he had wanted her to know?

"Santi is there?" she asked the lady. "In the hermitage?"

The old lady nodded. "Yes. Since October."

"How long does it take to drive there?" she asked the driver. The woman chatted quickly with the driver.

"Fifteen minutes." He showed her his watch.

"Let's go!" Marcella urged.

She waved good-bye to the woman, wanting to give her something but knowing money would be insulting.

Faster! she urged the driver, without uttering a word. *Faster!* What the hell was Santi doing in a monastery? Staying there as a guest? Feeding the poor? Fear attacked the pit of her stomach. What if all this chasing came to nothing? Could she picture herself climbing aboard a plane and flying back to Manhattan without him? No, she answered herself, *no!*

She wound down the window as they climbed the hill. The air was chilly up here, but she needed to smell the pines and the earth, hear the bells clanking from around the sheep's necks. The sound drifted over to them from hundreds of yards away, across valleys and fields, filtered through trees. The light was a mixture of silver and gold. The stunted olive trees with their twisted gray trunks, the leafless almond trees—everything appeared so dead in winter, but the tall cypress trees all seemed to be pointing the way to Santi.

"That's it." The driver pointed up to a forbidding place nestled high in the hills. She leaned out of the window to see it, an ancient stone building with no sign of life. What on earth would the love of her life be doing in there? Praying, or fasting, or taking a vow of silence? Surely the bent little lady had got it all wrong and she would find Santi back in his gallery in Barcelona and they would laugh together at the idea of his becoming a monk.

The entrance to the hermitage was down a long narrow lane, built up on either side by twelve-foot-high stone walls. The walls towered over visitors, as if cutting them down to size. Only a simple iron cross on a corner parapet announced that this was a religious retreat.

She felt a coldness steal over her as the taxi crawled up the graveled drive. Then a spurt of anger. *Was* this a spiritual place where intelligent men devoted their lives to God, or a place where disillusioned people hid from the world? However hard she tried, she could not picture Santi here. The man who had pulled her down New York side streets to discovery, to adventure, could not live shut off from the world he found so fascinating.

She told the taxi driver to wait, having no idea how long she would be. As she crossed the stone-flagged patio, undecorated and bleak, she wondered where the joy was. A life lived for God should be joyful, surely, she thought. If

Santi was incarcerated here she must get him out and make him happy again. She reached the door and took a deep breath before ringing the rusty iron bell.

It was no simple matter to see Santi, once she had established that he was indeed there. She was told she would have to talk to the father who ruled this little roost. Everything inside the room where she was bidden to wait was made of cold, ungiving stone. It was spotless, but to her it was inhuman. A narrow window cut into the wall showed just how thick the walls of the old building were and let in a beautiful view of the sea beneath them. The walls were so deep, so solid, that real life seemed centuries away. Marcella saw the undeniable appeal of burying oneself here. Santi could not have chosen a more suitable place for getting away from it all, from all the messiness of human emotions.

Luckily for her the father spoke some English and seemed to respond to this unusual visit from a beautiful, elegant woman. He was in his early sixties, with gray curly hair and beard and amused dark eyes. His face had an ascetic quality—the very opposite of sensual—that reminded her of Father Carmello. He wore a brown robe.

She felt she should appear to be on a spiritual mission and cursed herself for dressing up in her Chanel suit. She should have looked more simple, but how could she have guessed she would be ending up in a monastery?

After hearing her out, the father said, "Santiago came here voluntarily. I cannot force him to see anyone if he does not want to. I will ask him. You will wait here, please."

She waited in the uncomfortable room, the air so much colder and damper inside than outside. She longed for a cigarette, but she knew that would be disrespectful. Her dry lips desperately craved lipstick, but she did not move to put any on. What was taking him so long? Was it possible that he would refuse to see her? Would he be in a robe like the father who had just spoken to her? She might burst out laughing if he was! To imprison yourself in such a quiet place must take amazing discipline, she thought. Or an incurable wound. Then, when Santi appeared in the doorway, she knew that she had inflicted that incurable wound.

He stood there watching her, their eyes meeting with a

shock, as if no time had passed since their good-bye at Kennedy Airport. He was slightly thinner, and the glow in his eyes seemed dulled. But when he returned her searching gaze, she saw the dark eyes shine, saw a spark within them that could be rekindled. His skin was paler and he wore jeans and a navy sweater, managing to invest even that humdrum outfit with a casual elegance.

She parted her lips to speak and felt herself burst out crying. "Santi, *Sonia's* dead!"

She ran toward him to throw herself in his arms, but he held her back, his face distraught, his hands on her elbows steadying her.

"This is terrible! What happened?"

"She was murdered!" Marcella cried. "In London. Somebody killed her! Oh Santi, I—"

She broke down and he handed her a large white handkerchief, still steadying her with a firm hand as he waited for her to gain control.

"Is this why you came here?" he asked her gently. "To tell me that?"

"No." She fumbled in her purse for the package of letters, placing them on the dark wooden table. "My letters were never mailed to you," she cried. "I wrote you over twenty letters to tell you—" She stopped. It sounded too worldly to say, "how much I love you," in this austere place. She showed him his letter. "And I didn't read this letter until yesterday!" she said.

"Why not?"

"Mark hid them all," she told him. "You thought I hadn't replied, and I thought you'd never written, and all the time . . ." Her voice trailed away and stopped because he was not following the scenario she had written in her head for them. In that scene, when Santi heard that Mark had hidden her letters, he threw his arms around her and said, "So now we can take up where we left off, my darling!" But now, in real life, Santi said, "Does that really change anything? Some letters? It was a love that was not destined to be, after all."

"What do you mean, some letters?" she cried, picking up the blue envelopes and brandishing them. "Look at these! You can read them! We'll read them together! Because every word I wrote then I mean *now*!"

He shook his head. "I could not go through all that again, Marcella. I am too strong now to submit myself to all that."

"Strong?" she laughed, her voice catching in her throat. "Hiding away in this godforsaken place? Don't tell me you believe in all this?"

He smiled the smallest of smiles. "I do not believe in anything at all now," he told her.

"Not even in our 'forever' love?" she cried. "Have you forgotten that?"

He shook his head. "My problem is that I cannot forget. But there are other reasons for living: they do wonderful work here. With poor people, children of gypsies, young kids on drugs. The old. It is useful work, and I pretend to be more devout than I am, so I am allowed to stay. I find it calming."

"But this isn't *life,* Santi!" she said. "It's hiding from life. And you're not here because you really want to be. You're here because of *me!*"

He looked up to say "Yes," quietly, and she saw the naked love in his eyes. She glanced down at his brown, lean hand and reached for it, taking it in hers, feeling the warmth, pressing the long fingers.

"Please read my letters," she pleaded. "I've made terrible mistakes with my children, but I've been punished. Surely you can love me again?"

He gently withdrew his hand. "I never stopped loving you, Marcella," he said in a low voice. And he looked into her eyes like the old Santi. "That is terrible about Sonia. Terrible! I shall pray for her . . ."

"But you don't believe in anything!" she cried.

He nodded. "A prayer can simply be a strong statement," he told her, "a thought against all the evil in the world."

"We were meant to be together, Santi," she sobbed. "This isn't the place for you. You belong with me. Let's go to Deya together. Now! I was at your house this morning and I saw the old lady . . ."

Santi looked at her with such a regretful, melting look that she nearly forgot her dignity. She longed to cover his face with her kisses.

"I lived in Deya for months before I decided to come

here," he told her. "Something inside me died at not hearing from you. Everything disgusted me. This was the only way I could give my life some meaning again. Maybe I lost the side of me you loved?"

Tears streamed down her face as she listened. It was too cruel to be this close and yet not be held in his arms. She would not break the spell by applying a handkerchief to her wet face. As long as they were still talking together, something might still happen, something could be saved.

"I never felt complete without you," she said. "I tried channeling my love into my books. I tried sex with men whose names I didn't even know! I've done the most disgusting, low—"

"Now you are just talking nonsense, Marcella," he stopped her. "You are trying to shock me and . . ." He made a dismissive gesture. A veil descended over his face and she realized she would hurt herself even more now if she opened her heart further to him. If she wanted there to be anything left of her spirit and personality, she must stop now. She was not getting through to this man, who may as well have been sitting frozen or behind an impenetrable glass wall, this man whom she loved more than she would ever love any other man on earth.

"So I've really lost you?" she asked him. "I've sacrificed us all for nothing, Santi? Ruined our lives?"

"Ruined?" he repeated. "No. But the only way we can continue our lives with some dignity is for you to leave now, Marcella."

She wiped her face with a handkerchief and took a faltering step away from him. "Is that what you *really* want, Santi?" she whispered.

He nodded. A tic in his cheek showed her the effort he was making.

"No." She shook her head. "You don't want this! You can't!"

His face looked pleading, supplicating. "Please, Marcella," he begged.

She picked up his letter to her, leaving the ones she had written him. Santi watched her, almost approvingly. She took the deepest breath she had ever taken, her chest hurting, her face turned away from his. Let him at least admire her for not getting on her knees and begging, for not completely humiliating herself. He stood aside. She took a long look at his lean face, his eyes, trying to extract as much strength from the sight of him as she could. Then with all the remaining power she had in her, she made herself leave the stone room, walk out of the building, take the long walk across the patio, leave the hermitage without glancing back.

Her body obeyed her furious will to keep walking, although she had no idea where she was going. She left the building unseeingly, her feelings not yet caught up with her, to be postponed for as long as possible to some future time.

She did not see the taxi waiting for her at the end of the walled-in drive or the driver asleep over his newspaper. Even if she had, she would not have got into the car. She would just walk, moving ahead blindly until something blocked her or something destroyed her. She climbed over a low stone wall in which wind-smoothed stones fitted together without cement. She stumbled down the side of the monastery gardens, a large sloping farmland on which fruit trees bore figs, almonds, and oranges. Her legs carried her down this slope as it grew steeper and she tripped over the bulbous roots and scratchy undergrowth. She was not thinking, merely existing in a blurred landscape of pain where trees with twisted, sharp branches tore at her clothes and flesh. She tripped, she fell down the hillside, she scrambled to her feet and continued the descent. The olive trees seemed to know something she didn't; the secrets of life, perhaps? How else had they become this ugly? Knotted, blackened, and twisted, they had been on this island for several hundred years and seemed to mock her with their grotesque fairy-tale shapes, as if they had witnessed far more pain than she could ever imagine. As if the pain of one puny human being counted as nothing. So many people must have stumbled past them, tended to them, picked their fruit, kicked their barks in impatience, pissed against them, made forbidden love under them. She was just another in the long line of women doomed to be disappointed in life and love, and the trees knew this and laughed at it. The hill became so steep now that she could not control her speed. She continued to stumble, to lose a shoe, to fall. She didn't care.

For the first time in her life she hated herself. For losing, for having borne a daughter destined to be killed and a
son who meddled selfishly in her life and in the life of the
man she loved. For not knowing how to accept—how to
grab—the love and happiness that Santi had offered. For
letting herself take the transient sexual thrills, the hesitant
touches of that whole army of anonymous lovers in the
dark. For degrading love.

When she finally lost her footing at the edge of the ditch
and plunged headfirst into it, falling until she hit the bed of
branches at the bottom, she almost welcomed the fact that
her punishment, self-sought or sent by God, had finally
arrived. She lay panting, hurting from the fall. She was
about to burst into tears when she suddenly found herself
laughing hysterically. It was just too ridiculous to think that
the crazed odyssey of the last week—one that had taken
her from Manhattan to Bologna to Majorca—could end up
here, in a godforsaken ditch. She laughed and laughed until
she was exhausted. Then she began to shout out for help.
She had battled too many challenges in the last years to
give up now. One dumb ditch was not going to stop her!
She must stop feeling so sorry for herself, take control of
her life again, even if it was to be a life without Santi.

"Help!" she called out. *"Help* me!"

Santi stood in his bare room listening to the rain, playing
with the packet of blue envelopes. If he held them to his
face, he could smell Marcella's fragrance. The scent
brought into his room all the world he had tried to banish,
along with the needs, the desires, the belonging to that life
out there. All the longings he had believed buried stirred
inside him again and he cursed them. He stared at the
envelopes, knowing he must not allow himself to read
them, but knowing that he would. How could he possibly
resist? The answer to that was simple. He could find a large
brown envelope in the library, address it to Marcella, and
mail them all back to her.

The rain pounded fiercely against the small windowpane
of his room and he knew he would have to read the letters,
if only to put a stop to this new dissatisfied feeling. He
would scour them for the false phrase, the lie, and congrat-

ulate himself that he had not fallen victim to the curse of love once again. He laughed at himself as he reached for the envelopes. Why don't you face the truth? he asked himself. You're as in love with her as you've ever been. Even more so. He cursed the stubborn pride that did not allow him to change more quickly, to react as his real urges wanted him to. He always needed so much time to think things over, to study his choices.

He sat down on his narrow bed and read her letters greedily, one after the other, consuming her words of love, the passions she had written simply, so that he would easily understand them, the notepaper stained with her tears, and now with his.

When he was finished, he rinsed his face in the icy cold water from the earthenware jug on his basin and rubbed himself dry with a rough towel.

Night fell as he tried to find the truthful solution. He had two choices: to remain here, secluded, or to run after Marcella, find her, stay with her for the rest of his life, as all her letters urged. Which would be the honest, truthful choice? He knew which one he wanted to choose, but could he go back on his fierce vow of pride to forget her?

An urgent knock on his door, unusual for the restrained life of the hermitage, interrupted his thoughts.

He opened the door. "Yes?" he asked.

A monk told him, "A taxi driver at the door is asking about your visitor. I told him she had left a long time ago, but he doesn't believe me. Will you speak to him?"

Santi frowned, sweeping the blue letters into a drawer, following the monk down the stone corridor to the entrance.

The driver was adamant that he had not seen the American lady leave. He admitted to sleeping for some time in his car, but could not understand why she had not awakened him for the long trip back to town. A search of the monastery grounds failed to find her. Santi took the driver to the nearest village and made a call to the Son Vida to ask if a Mrs. Winton was registered there. Yes, she was registered, but she was not in her room. They paged the public rooms for her, but she was not there either.

"What can we do?" the father asked Santi when he got back.

"I will wait until midnight tonight," Santi told him. "If she has not returned to her hotel by then, we must call the police. She left here very distraught. She may have wandered away or gotten lost. . . ."

The father patted his arm. "We can all help to look for her," he said. "We have torches and we are all strong. She is a very beautiful woman."

Santi looked into the understanding eyes of the father and nodded in agreement.

Her mood of defiant courage lasted all of two hours.

During the night, a thunderstorm drenched her. Her attempts to climb out of the ditch had all failed, leaving her, she was certain, with a broken leg. At dawn, she awoke to rain trickling into her ears. Her limbs were swollen and sore and her leg ached horribly. The red earth had turned to mud, caking her hair and her clothes. It suddenly struck her then that she might very well not survive this, and this realization brought the first real chill of fear. She closed her eyes, trying to rest, as the rain slowly eased. Dawn streaked gold in the gray sky and birds flew above her. The day passed slowly as she drifted in and out of consciousness. What would they think of her? Would they think her stupid? brave? a victim? Maybe she would never be discovered—the ditch filling with mud and branches, completely covering her body. She would be buried naturally, organically—that at least was a comfort.

Another night came and the pain in her leg got worse. She slept through the following dawn into the afternoon. By then, her strength was completely gone. Look for me, she prayed. Look for me, Santi! Read my letters and call my hotel and find out I'm missing! If you love me, you'll know where to find me! You said you never stopped loving me! Electric spasms of pain shot through her leg, making her cry out. She had wet herself, wept until no more tears would come, stopped pretending to be brave. She was so tired and so cold that she did not even want to survive this. She knew she could, if she made one of her almighty efforts of will, but the energy was no longer there. She had been through more than anyone could be expected to survive. Now her punishment would not be death after all, but a continuation of life. And she could no longer face life without Santi as part of it. She forgave Mark, a fact that filled her heart with joy, but now she was deathly afraid because the blackness of the unknown ahead was infinite and terrifying. She could only hope that with God's help . . . she broke off the thought. What right did she have to expect that? Her thoughts trailed away. She no longer had the energy to even think. She simply lay there quietly, taking in nothing more than the distant clanking of sheep's bells, a tinkling and tolling that got louder and louder until it changed to a metallic clanging that drowned out everything else. There were bells ringing in her ears now, and great dizzy-making whistles, high-pitched whines like screaming. Was this how you died? she found herself wondering. Oh God, was this how she was to be taken from this earth? So alone, without even Santi's hand to hold? And then she saw the ghosts of her father and her mother standing in the ditch beside her and she smiled.

TWENTY

Manhattan, February 1991

"So you're just going to sit here and mope?" Cole Ferrer asked. He stood by the doorway, peering in at Mark's darkened room. It was eleven in the morning, the usual time of Cole's daily visit.

"Mark?" he called. "Did you hear what I said?"

Mark stirred and looked up. He was curled on the neatly made up bed, wearing jeans and a tee shirt.

"Mark," Cole said gently, "lying in a dark room for weeks on end isn't going to accomplish anything, you know."

Mark returned his gaze to the curtained window.

"Isn't it time to stop playing Judy Garland in *A Star Is Born*?" Cole smiled.

"*Cole!*" Mark's shout startled him. "When *you* lose your entire family in the space of a few months, when *you* have to bury your murdered sister because your mother is missing, presumed dead, tell me you'll go straight to the Carlyle Lounge and sit down at the piano to play 'Swonderful'!"

"Maybe I would, baby," Cole said, sitting gingerly at the foot of Mark's bed. "Sometimes work is the best escape."

"Well, I'm not ready to escape yet."

"And I don't buy that losing-a-whole-family bit," Cole continued. "You never visited your father. You said yourself that Sonia was a flake, and who said you've lost your mother? I bet she's sitting in the sun right now writing her next novel!"

"No." Mark leaned back against the headboard. "She would never do that to me. Not even as a punishment."

"A punishment?" Cole pounced on the word. "A punishment for what? For leaving her alone at Christmas?"

Mark glanced at him. "Yes. Tell me again why she came all the way to Bologna. How did she know I was sick?"

"You *looked* sick," Cole said. "And you weren't answering your phone. She visited this clairvoyant or psychic on Christmas Day. He or she told her that both her children were in danger. That's when she called me. Naturally, the moment she heard that awful news about your sister, she grabbed the next plane to come to you!"

"And you've no idea who this psychic was?" Mark asked. "He might have something to tell me about her. They sometimes help the police with crimes."

"She didn't mention his name," Cole said. "Or her name. I don't even know what sex the person is."

"We could place an ad in *The Village Voice*," Mark suggested.

"And get every crank in the state claiming to know something?" Cole said wearily.

"But it could lead to something!" Mark insisted.

"Save it until you're really desperate," Cole advised.

Mark sat up on the bed, hugging himself. "Don't you think I'm desperate now?" he asked.

"If you're so desperate, why aren't you in Majorca, looking for her?" Cole asked him.

Mark turned to him with an agonized expression. "I know I should be there," he said. "But I can't bring myself to go. I'm . . . paralyzed! The idea of picking over hillsides and mountains, poking about in leaves or grass for a sign of my mother's shoes, or suddenly finding her leg or her arm sticking out of some bush just—" He broke off. "I just couldn't do it, Cole! I *couldn't*!"

"So instead you lie around on your bed, expecting some miracle?" Cole jeered.

"Right!" Mark shouted. "That's all I can do, Cole! Any objections?"

Cole expelled a long sigh, shaking his head sorrowfully. He sat gingerly at the foot of the bed, facing Mark. "Is there anything at all I can do, Mark?" he asked gently.

Mark shook his head. "I'm on the phone twenty times a day to the police, to the American consuls in Barcelona and Palma, to anyone I can think of who might be able to help. I can't get to Santi, the guy she went to see, or maybe he just won't return my calls. I've left a hundred messages for him. They told me he's helping the police search the countryside. He's probably mad at me because he thinks I should be there with him. And he's right, Cole! I know I should be! It's just that I can't—" He broke off, burying his face in his hands, sobbing. Cole stood and leaned over him, his hand out to touch Mark's shoulder. He thought better of it and stuffed his hand into his pocket.

"Would it help if I went over there with you?" he offered. "We could search together."

Mark shook his head, wiping his eyes with the back of his hand. "I just can't do it, Cole. I'm not a man right now, I'm a quivering jelly. Sonia's murder and now this. . . ." He shook his head again. "It's all I can do to sit and wait here. I take my little walk each morning, then I come back and wait. I just can't do anything else."

"Okay." Cole patted his shoulder. "I'll be back tomorrow, same time, same place, same channel," he said. "If you need me tonight, you know where to get me. But *please*, Mark, make a little effort. Don't just slide down into this nothingness. Try to stay in the land of the living, will you?"

"Yeah." Mark nodded absently. "Thanks, Cole. See ya." He watched Cole struggle into his thick black overcoat.

"Ciao!" Cole winked and Mark heard the front door close.

He got off his bed and wandered into Marcella's bedroom. The hint of the fragrance she used hung tantalizingly in the air, as if she had just left the room. He slid open the doors of her closets and softly touched the blouses and dresses hanging silently, as if they might tell him something. He performed this ritual each morning before leaving the apartment. He looked at her shoes and sweaters and underwear, all neatly stacked on the shelves. She had left his room in Bologna neat, too, as neat and tidy as only a mother can leave a son's room. Apart from the cleaning and the letter she had left him, he had no recollection of her visit. That had been the most disturbing thing of all— to wake up the next morning, over his grippe, to feel her presence so strongly, and yet have no memory of her being there. He found out that she had stayed two days, summoned a doctor, and asked the concierges to keep an eye on him after she left. Even when she knew he had betrayed her trust, she had been concerned for his well-being, and *that* was tearing him apart.

The moment he'd gotten over his flu, he had rushed to London to claim Sonia's body, flying back with it to New York for the funeral. The service at a midtown funeral parlor had turned into a circus; fashion models, fashion freaks and groupies, press and photographers, none of whom had been close friends of Sonia's, had removed any last shreds of respect or reverence that Sonia's short life might have warranted. By some bizarre coincidence, Ray LeVar had been extradited back to the United States on the same day as the funeral, doubling the sensational press coverage. As a result of that nightmarish day and his mother's disappearance, Mark had withdrawn into a zombielike existence.

Almost worse than Marcella's disappearance was the knowledge that she had found the letters he'd hidden. That was the shameful part he was unable to confess to anyone. Telling it would make him appear partly responsible, somehow, for her disappearance. It would take away any right he had to sympathy from Cole and Amy, and from all Marcella's readers who had written to Volumes with prayers for her safe return. If anyone knew of his interference with his mother's life, he would be condemned as a sneaky little worm, which was how he now saw himself. He had gone from being the golden boy with everything to a sneaky little worm. This sudden plunge in his shaky self-esteem could be handled only by sleep-walking through life, at least until something happened, some end to this awful not-knowing.

He closed her closet door carefully and left the bedroom, feeling as dissatisfied and guilty as usual. He turned on the answering machine for the inevitable hopeful wishes, crank calls, and other messages that flowed in daily.

He took the elevator down, making himself think of practical matters like going to the bank, calling the garage where the Rolls was serviced, getting the apartment cleaned. He was going to be a very rich young man, for he stood to inherit every penny of his mother's royalties, although the thought of that made him physically sick. There was also a new problem: Caresse Cosmetics was suing Sonia's estate to get its three-million-dollar first payment returned. It was a nasty aftermath of her unpopularity in the industry, and Caresse threatened a long drawn-out battle.

Scott had called him half apologetically to tell him that Volumes was reprinting Marcella's first three novels in response to the sudden huge demand. Because of all the publicity, sales had grotesquely picked up on her books, thrusting *Forever Begins Tonight* back onto the best-seller list. The mysterious disappearance of a bestselling author, the mother of a murdered model, had whetted the public's appetite, making Marcella's books sell out everywhere. Reprinting was imminent: it was business as usual. Mark left the apartment building and turned right. He passed the hansom cabs on Central Park South, noting that in the cold weather the smell of the horses did not travel very far. Then there was the bitter, burnt smell of pretzels drifting from the little stand in its usual place on the corner of Fifth Avenue and Fifty-seventh Street. He wandered past Tiffany's, noting the Japanese girls photographing each other in front of the store's entrance, sipping coffee from cardboard cups, emulating Audrey Hepburn in *Breakfast at Tiffany's*.

For a few seconds he watched as a cripple laboriously wrote out his begging sign. Another panhandler, skinny and dirty, had just hung his sign around his neck: "Dying of Aids. This city has turned down my request for welfare. Help me die a dignified death." Mark handed him ten dollars, for which he was not thanked. During his short walk, he had already handed out two subway tokens and some loose change, and been asked for "two million dollars for a condo," by a laughing man who had decided that humor was the best approach. Mark had inherited his mother's gift of observation and her sensitivity to people, and he was able to put himself in their place immediately. That was the problem. Every time he put himself in his mother's place as she discovered the letters he had hidden, a wave of shame swept over him. And the feeling kept recurring—he couldn't wipe out the painful memory. Over and over again he imagined how she must have felt, how she must have looked at him as he slept off his grippe, the expression on her face.

Abruptly he turned and retraced his steps purposefully back to the apartment.

As usual the apartment seemed strangely quiet as he let himself in, the day's mail in one hand. Without the familiar quiet tapping of Marcella's typewriter, it felt like a month of permanent Sundays had settled over the place. She had never worked on Sundays, and they had laughed about that, saying her brain refused to function on a day of rest. He played back his answering-machine messages.

"Are you okay, Mark? Need anything?" Amy's husky voice buzzed from the machine. "I'm home all day. Call me."

"Mark?" the next message said. "This is Scott. Call me when you can."

He dialed the Volumes number immediately.

"Did you get any news?" he asked Scott as soon as he got through. One of Scott's theories was that Marcella might have been kidnapped, and he had gotten everyone to half expect a ransom note.

"No. Nothing," Scott said. "How are *you* doing? Bearing up? We have another sack full of mail for Marcella. Do you want me to send it over or should we keep it here for the moment?"

"Keep it there," Mark said listlessly. "One of these days I'll go through it. Is that what you called me about?"

"No, I wanted to ask you if you knew anything about an autobiography your mother was working on," Scott said. "It would have been pretty complete by now—she started it months ago. Maybe it's in her office, or she might have had it with her and was working on it when she came to see you."

Mark shrugged. "Does it matter? There are so many

papers in her office. I guess I'll go through them when . . . if . . ." He trailed off.

"Right! Fine!" Scott sounded a little ashamed of himself and Mark suddenly realized he was sniffing out another Marcella Balducci Winton book to publish while the interest in Marcella ran high. "I just thought I should mention it to you," Scott said. "Obviously a large part of it would be about you and your sister. I had suggested she tell what it was like being a mother to two famous children."

"I see," Mark said.

"She was dictating it," Scott said. "On tape."

"Oh. Thanks for telling me about it," Mark said. "Bye, Scott."

"Mark? If there's anything we can do . . ." Scott began.

"Sure. Thanks. Bye." Mark hung up quickly.

He found the cassettes neatly piled to one side of her desk, untitled but numbered. All he had to do was pop them one by one into his Walkman or the stereo system in his bedroom. He preferred the Walkman, which gave him the uncanny experience of hearing his missing mother's voice talking from inside his head.

"Sacrifice," her voice began. "The autobiography of Marcella Balducci Winton. The book you've been begging me for, Scott."

By two o'clock the next morning he had played the last tape. After that he looked at the writing she had done on Christmas Day, detailing her state of mind. He now knew everything he could possibly learn about the woman who was his mother—about his childhood, his father, the way he had been raised. And much more about the sexual life of his mother than he had wanted to know.

He went to the kitchen to pour himself a glass of wine, his mind suddenly crystal clear. It was as if he had spent an entire day with his mother, listening to her pouring out the doubts, hopes, fears, and goals of her life. The sexual revelations were shocking, he supposed, but he could not judge, could not relate to them because he had never been torn in two by the urges she so graphically described. At twenty he had never had sex with anyone! A late developer.

He walked thoughtfully into the living room. Had she actually intended to publish this stuff? Branding him as the overloved son of a woman who was addicted to strangers' hands pawing her body, as if she belonged to any bum on the street, anyone who felt like giving her a cheap thrill. He knew he should be outraged and disappointed, and yet somehow he admired her. At least she had had the passion and spunk to go out and get what she needed. He understood her so well now, understood how she had made him so important to her life, so dependent on her. Because she had been dependent on *him*! And with this new understanding of their lives, he found some compassion for himself, felt less ashamed and more understanding of why he had hidden her letters. It had been a cowardly, despicable betrayal, but it had been done so he could survive. It had been the last gasp of a drowning man.

He sat down at the piano. His hands hovered over the keys. He had not played since returning from Bologna. His fingers felt stiff and unmusical. Playing was the last thing he felt like doing, but he forced himself through the entire *Suite Bergamesque* by Debussy, his mother's favorite piece, remembering how honored he'd feel when she would ask him to play for her after her bath; the way he would glance at her lovely profile as she closed her eyes, listening.

His grief surged up in him.

"Please . . ." he whispered, tears running down his face as he reached the last note. *"Please . . ."*

Who was he begging? he wondered. Some power? The gods, plural? If you wanted something badly enough you could make it happen, she used to tell him. You concentrated and thought and it was like an irresistible force. It was like that silly Astaire song, "Something's Gotta Give," that Cole sang for encores at the Carlyle.

She had made him believe *he* had that special power. He had used it for passing auditions, for getting through concerts, for singing at the Carlyle. Now he had to summon all his magic to get the gods to act for him, to make something happen, to make something "give"!

If this miracle happened, if she turned up now, he would set her free from his selfish needs and finally change from a child into a man, a man she could be proud of.

He knelt by the piano stool and tried to pray. He felt

ridiculous at first, but slowly he gathered his strength and put everything he had into it. He had been kneeling for half an hour, his legs going numb, when he imagined he heard the phone ring. Then he realized it *was* ringing. He got stiffly to his feet and stumbled toward it, lifting the receiver. It was three in the morning.

"Yes?" he asked.

There was some crackling and static. Then he heard a man's voice. "Listen carefully, Mark," it said. "This is Santi. You must say nothing to your friends, nothing to the police, to anybody, do you understand? Your mother is alive."

Mark sat tensely on the plane to Madrid that afternoon, staring unseeingly at a magazine, reliving the conversation.

"Can I speak to her?" he had asked Santi.

"I'm afraid that is not possible," he had replied. "She is not well. We need you here. I had to keep her hidden away, guarding her privacy. You will understand why when you get here."

His stomach churned with excitement and foreboding. He had told no one where he was headed, only leaving messages for Cole and Amy saying he would be out of town for a few days.

He changed planes in Madrid, first calling the number in Palma that Santi had given him. Flights had never seemed so long. When the plane finally taxied to a stop at the Palma airport Mark was the first down the stairway. He ran through passport control and customs clutching only a large overnight bag. At the barriers he searched the crowd, recognizing Santi immediately. As he ran toward Santi, expecting to embrace him, Santi let fly a fist to his jaw and Mark fell to the ground.

Mark wrapped some ice cubes in a napkin and applied them to his aching chin. Over lunch at a small Catalan restaurant in town, the two men sat glaring at each other.

"And I owe you another one," Santi told him sternly. "That blow was for not mailing your mother's letters to me. The next one will be for not delivering my letter to her!"

Mark glanced up at him. "So you're a real macho guy?" he jeered.

"No," Santi said quietly, shaking his head. "But I have been longing to hit you since I first saw you, Mark. Your face was so empty of reality and experience of life. Now you can begin to grow up. But part of growing up is realizing the terrible damage you have done to two people's lives. Do you understand?"

"Yes," Mark replied, lowering his eyes. He patted his chin. "I've realized a lot of things in the last few months. But please, tell me how my mother is. Does she know I'm here?"

Santi gave him a hard look. "She knows nothing at all. And you will find out, all in good time. You made me wait more than a year to hear from your mother, so I suppose you can wait one more hour, no?"

Mark chafed under Santi's treatment. "That's not fair!" he burst out. "You've got me all the way here and now you're—"

"I made you come all the way because I need you," Santi said firmly. "Not because I wanted the pleasure of your company. If I did not need you I would perhaps never have seen you again, Mark. So you are lucky I let you see your mother at all! You would have kept her from me for the rest of my life if she had not discovered the letters, no?"

Mark said nothing. He gave a great sigh and added fresh ice cubes to his napkin.

"I'm not hungry," he said when the waiter handed them menus. "It's eight in the morning, New York time, and they gave us three meals on the plane. Why can't we go straight to her?"

Santi smiled sadly. "She is in a hospital where the visiting hours are at four. Eat something, Mark. You will need your strength." He ordered soup for them and wine.

"Does anyone know she's been found?" Mark asked.

Santi nodded. "Of course. The police have been informed. But I kept away all newspaper people. It has been a full-time job guarding her privacy, but you will see why I did it when we visit her."

"But what *happened* to her, for God's sake?" Mark cried. "Did she have an accident?"

"An accident, yes." Santi nodded. "And for the past eight weeks I have been totally responsible for her. I wanted to nurse her back to health myself, Mark."

"But why wasn't I told she was alive, at least?" Mark asked him.

Santi stared at him with intense eyes. "Because you had done enough damage to her and to me! I wanted to kill you, Mark. So I thought it was better to ignore you!" Santi took a gulp of wine, sitting back as their soup was served.

Mark studied him. "Listen, Santi," he began. "You have every reason to hate me, but I've lived with losing my entire family within a few weeks. Father, sister, mother! Did you know Sonia had been murdered?"

Santi nodded. "It was the last thing your mother told me before . . . her accident. I am very sorry, Mark."

"Okay, but I lived with that for eight weeks!" Mark said. "And I've regretted what I did every moment of every day."

Santi took a few spoonfuls of soup, indicating that Mark should eat his.

"For God's sake, tell me what's wrong with her!" Mark cried.

Santi nodded. He lay down his spoon. "I will start at the beginning," he said. "For more than a year I had been trying to forget your mother. I told myself to wipe this woman from my mind. That is not easy when you love someone so much. Have *you* ever loved someone like that?" he asked.

Mark shook his head.

"I thought not," Santi said. He took a few more spoonfuls of soup, and by now Mark knew enough to stay silent and wait for Santi to continue.

"I gave up my art gallery," Santi said, "and finally retreated to a hermitage—a kind of monastery run by monks who allow people to stay and work with them if they choose. I am not very religious, but I wanted to do useful work and retreat from the world for a while. Your mother interrupted this retreat last December, suddenly appearing at the hermitage with all her letters in her hand. It was like a vision! But I was not ready for it. I had tried so hard *not* to love her. I am too stubborn to change in one moment like that! Even though she gave me the letters you had not mailed and explained the story, I was too proud. You understand?" Mark nodded, his eyes staring at Santi's tortured expression. Santi took another gulp of wine.

"I told her it would be better if she left. That it would not be possible to begin over again. Your mother has her pride, too. She was very upset—more upset than I realized. She ran out of the hermitage. It is up in the hills, far from anywhere. She must have been too upset to know what she was doing because she just *ran* down a hillside, along paths only animals used. She ran such a long way that we did not even start looking in the area where she was until two days had passed, during which there had been much rain. We found her in a ditch. She had pneumonia and a broken leg. Cuts and many bruises. But all that is nothing compared to her mental state when we found her. Mark . . ." Santi's eyes filled with tears as he put his hand on Mark's arm. "She does not know who she is! She has not said a word since we found her!"

Mark watched as the tears flowed down Santi's cheeks, matting his long black lashes. He had never seen a man cry so unself-consciously, without shame. He leaned across the table to touch Santi's shoulder. He had hated him all through lunch, but now, seeing him so torn up over his mother's condition, his heart went out to him.

Finally, Santi wiped his face and stared at him in anguish. "I can never forgive myself!"

Mark shook his head. "No," he said in a low voice. "I'm the one to blame. If I had mailed the letters in the first place, this would never have happened."

Santi shook his head, burying his face in a large white handkerchief and blowing his nose. He wiped his eyes, glancing around at the other diners.

"We will not argue about who is most to blame," he said, replacing his handkerchief. "For eight weeks she has had good care in a special place where they understand these things. Her leg is healed. Physically, she is well. I thought that by talking constantly to her I could bring Marcella back. But now I need you! She loves you so much I am putting all my hopes into thinking that if she sees you perhaps the sight of you will jog her memory. Perhaps you can wake her from this sleep she is in."

Mark jumped to his feet, brushing the napkin off his lap.

"Of course she'll know me! I swear she will. Let's go immediately!"

Santi drove them in his little orange car up into the mountains, past Deya, past Valldemossa. It was early March and the almond trees were just starting to bloom, their beauty lost on Mark. As was the beauty of the dark green cypresses, the gnarled olive trees, the bleating of the new white lambs, the smell of the sea and the pine-laden air. The landscape was dreamlike, he could see that, but it was a dream that could so easily turn to a nightmare if his face, his voice, did not have the desired effect on his mother.

The head nurse at the hospital spoke excellent English and chattered away to Mark, pleased to get the chance to show off. She led him and Santi into a large room full of old women with slack-jawed faces, vacant expressions, and confused stares, all wearing faded old dresses and gray smocks.

"What kind of place *is* this?" Mark asked, looking around him.

"It's for women who are physically well," the nurse replied cheerfully, "but a little confused up here." She indicated her head. "We try to make a real home for them because some of them are not sure where they are. Now where is Marcella? Sometimes she walks about . . ." The large room led to a sunny anteroom facing a small courtyard filled with potted plants. A woman sat straight-backed and aloof in a tall chair, her back to them.

"She seems quite calm today," the nurse told him, ushering him through. "We always dress her nicely. She has such lovely clothes and we like her to wear them, so she can feel as normal as possible. She has her hair done every week. Do you have any candy for her? She loves that! Marcella, look who's here!" she cried. "Marcella, your son has come to see you."

Mark heard nothing the nurse said. His eyes were on the woman who sat in a violet silk dress. He was waiting for her to turn to them. He took a few steps into the room, staring at her profile, willing her to look at him. He felt Santi's hand on his arm, gently restraining him.

"Very slow now, Mark," Santi warned. "This will be a shock for you. And perhaps for her too."

Mark broke away from Santi's hand and moved toward his mother. "Mom?" he said.

Some curious women had followed the men into the anteroom and were watching Mark's face intently for his reaction. He placed himself in front of this woman who was his mother so that she could not help but see him. Her makeup had been applied well, her hair casually ruffled. Although her clothes were immaculate, something about her posture was wrong. It was as if she had been placed in a position and was obediently holding it for an unseen artist painting her portrait. Now and then her arms bent at the elbows and her hands came up in a gesture of exasperation or impatience. When she finally looked into his eyes he saw what had happened to her face. It was as if a very clever caricaturist had superimposed all her features onto some unearthly being, some doll. Her eyes did not recognize him and held no expression. Her face was so familiar and yet so different that he could not say exactly what was wrong with it.

"Hi, Mom!" he said. He looked her full in the eyes. Her eyes did not avoid his. Her uncomprehending stare was neither friendly nor hostile. It failed to convey anything.

"Oh my God," Mark cried. He turned away from her with a sob, running to the door that gave onto the interior patio. He wrenched at the handle, but it was locked. "Get me out of here!" he cried, turning to Santi. "I've got to get out!"

Santi signaled to the nurse for the key and she slipped it into the lock, opening the door. Mark hurled himself into the courtyard, running quickly over to a well there and leaning on its edge, looking down the deep, dark shaft to the water twenty feet below. Leafy green ferns grew down there, hidden from light, and his tears fell on them.

After a few moments Santi followed him, leaning next to him, his arm around his shoulders. Santi's eyes filled with tears. Mark turned to him and the two men held each other.

"I tried to convince myself that she was improving,"

Santi whispered. "Somehow it did not seem so bad until I saw *you* looking at her. Mark, I'm afraid we've lost her. . . ."

They had each loved her so much, and each understood the grief the other felt at that moment.

"You were my last hope, Mark," Santi said.

Mark broke away, making himself enter the sun porch to confront his mother again. He fell to his knees beside her. "Mom?" he said. "It's *Mark*! You know me, don't you?"

Marcella gazed at the young man beside her, even seeming a little interested in the scene. Mark put his head in her lap, sobbing.

Santi pulled at his shoulders. "Come now, Mark." He tugged at him. "A man must have his pride. This isn't fair to her."

"*Fuck* your pride!" Mark cried, looking up at him with red, tormented eyes. "This is my *mother*. She's everything to me!"

Santi nodded. "For me, too, she is everything, but what good does this do?"

"But she must know me, Santi! She *must!*" Mark cried. "What am I?" he asked Marcella. "What am I, Mother?" He looked up at Santi. "She always said I was the light of her life!"

He reached for her hand and she allowed him to hold it, giving him a sly smile as though expecting him to have something in his hand for her. It was a look he had seen in the eyes of dogs and beggars, and it was utterly alien to his mother. He opened his hand to show her there was nothing in it and she snatched away her fingers.

"Keep some candy for her," a passing nurse told him kindly. "Have a piece of sugar in your pocket next time. She'll like that!"

Mark turned his agonized face to her. "She's not an animal. I can't feed my own mother cubes of sugar. What am I, Mother? What am I?" He shouted the words into her blank face as she recoiled.

Santi pulled him away. "Don't do that to her, Mark. Please!"

Mark's mouth twisted. "I'm going to keep asking her until she answers," he said stubbornly. "Some part of her brain must know me. I'll work with her night and day until I reach her. I can do it, Santi. We'll get a piano and I'll play her favorite pieces. You'll see how that will work! If I can just focus her mind on what's happened to her, I know she'll fight. That's the sort of woman my mother was!"

"I know very well the sort of woman she was," Santi said quietly, turning away. He could not watch Mark with her anymore. It was too grim and disappointing. He had wanted so much to believe that Mark was the magic key to reclaiming Marcella's sanity, but now he feared she had gone too far from them.

He glanced back at her to find her eyes warily on Mark, as if trying to make sense of his words. Santi leaned against a wall.

"Who am I? Who am I?" echoed in the room until the words finally became meaningless.

"I don't want her given any sedatives," Mark instructed the nurse.

"Yes, that is all very well to say, but she is very difficult to manage without them," she told him. "She fights us sometimes because she knows something is wrong."

"Put her in a private room. I don't care how much it costs," Mark ordered. "Her mind should be clear and open. She needs all her clarity and energy to break through. I'm renting a piano, nurse. I've read that sometimes music can revive a person in a coma—music they love!"

"But your mother is not in a coma," the nurse argued. "What makes you think you know better than the doctor? He took an X ray of the brain and—"

"Please!" Mark put his hand on her arm, flashing one of his charming smiles. "I'm her *son*. I can *feel* what she needs! You want her to get better, don't you? You'll love her when you see her as she really is—she's the most wonderful person you can imagine!"

The nurse melted. "I'll do what I can. Of course, I want your mother well!"

Mark hugged her and gave her a quick kiss on the cheek. "Then that's what we're *all* working for!"

The piano arrived a few days later, carted in on the backs of two alarmingly elderly men. It was put in Marcella's room. She looked at the piano as she had looked at Mark, as she looked at the food they placed before her. It was just another object, though larger than most.

When Mark began to play, Santi had to admit that she seemed calmer, interested, her eyes losing some of their vacant stare, her arms forgetting to make their jerky movements. But Mark's fantasy of her recognizing him at the very first notes of her favorite Debussy suite remained a fantasy. Instead, she would sit for hours listening to the music he played, showing no reaction. However, it was reported to them that the music floating through the home calmed many of the other more restless patients. Mark visited his mother every day to play.

By dusk each evening, he was exhausted. Santi showed him some of the island, invited him to his house in Deya and his apartment in Palma, but Mark could not be away from Marcella long before he would think of some other piece to play for her or some key word to repeat to her that might trigger a reaction in her memory.

He stayed at a small hotel near the hospital. Santi drove him to restaurants in Palma or Deya where they dined on simple Catalan fare. Sometimes, Mark requested Chinese food. From the international phone boxes, he called Amy and Cole, reporting on his progress. He allowed Amy to release only the news that Marcella Balducci Winton had been found, suffering from exposure, and was slowly recovering in a Majorcan nursing home. A flood of get-well cards were forwarded from the Volumes offices, accompanied by letters from Scott informing Marcella of the astonishing, steady sales of her books.

"How long are you planning on staying there?" Cole asked him plaintively each time he called.

"Until she gets well," Mark told him firmly.

Sometimes he was sorry he had pledged himself to such a tough schedule. Sometimes he hated the creature who had been his mother, wanting to shake her personality back into her, to force her to return to the mother he knew.

When the warmer days of May arrived, Mark began to feel that the only thing showing any progress was his piano playing. Certainly there had been no discernible difference in Marcella's behavior, however much they willed it. The other thing that had improved was the relationship between the two men, as Mark slowly began to feel a grudging admiration for Santi. Because Santi was the only soul Mark knew in Majorca, and because they spent their evenings together after dinner, talking of art and music and travel, they had almost been forced into liking one another. There were enough traces of Marcella in Mark for Santi to overcome his resentment, but above all they were both dedicated to getting Marcella well, and that gave them a lot in common.

"Were you ever tempted to actually become a monk?" Mark asked Santi one night after dinner in Santi's town apartment.

Santi smiled, sipping Palo, the Majorcan aperitif that Mark had also acquired a taste for. "I don't think so, Mark," he said. "I like the other temptations of life too much. . . ."

"I know what you mean," Mark lied.

Santi usually dropped him off at his hotel early, or Mark would take a taxi, spending the later hours of the night writing long rambling letters to his friends in Italy and New York. The temptations of life were *not* something he understood, however sophisticated his facade. Relationships were mysterious, unknown things to him. His desires, so deeply hidden, were still waiting for him to grow up and acknowledge them.

He had started trying to bring back his mother's memory with the vague idea that it would take a few weeks, perhaps a few months. By the end of May, after working with her nearly every day for three months, he and Santi had a meeting with the doctor in charge of the clinic, and they reluctantly came to the conclusion that there was no marked change in Marcella. The music calmed her, but that could be accomplished with a stereo system. Mark went to Palma to buy one that very afternoon, along with a collection of tapes of her favorite composers.

He returned to the hospital by taxi, holding the machine and the tapes. Santi was sitting with Marcella, talking to her, her face the usual blank.

"I'm giving up," Mark announced, setting the bulky package down on the bed. "While I was buying this I realized she didn't really need me here—the tapes will have the same effect."

Santi looked at him, his eyes sad and understanding.

"It's stupid to pretend there's any change in her!" Mark insisted, as if to convince himself. "The doctor said she could continue to live like this, perfectly healthy, for years and years. If that's the case, I can't continue playing the piano for her day after day."

Santi turned his attention back to Marcella. "You must do as you think right," he said quietly.

Mark set up the speakers and slid in a cassette. The strains of Ravel's *Daphnis et Chloé* flooded gently into the room. Marcella smiled slightly.

"You see?" Santi cried. "You see how the music makes her smile?"

Mark nodded. "That's what I mean. A tape is as good as I am!"

That night they dined together in the little Catalan restaurant at Deya where Santi had first eaten with Marcella two years ago.

"You want to just leave her here?" Santi asked him as their soup was served. "You did not think of taking her back to New York, to her own familiar surroundings?"

"Yes." Mark sighed. "I thought of that. I'll do it one day. Perhaps in the fall. Meanwhile, she's being very well looked after here and . . ."

The two men exchanged glances.

"Well, she's *not* my mother anymore!" Mark burst out defensively. "The spirit, her personality, her soul, have all left her body. We're fooling ourselves, Santi. She's just a shell."

"No . . ." Santi's voice was thoughtful and low. "Her eyes change when you play the piano, I would swear it!"

"So what?" Mark said. "Dogs' ears prick up at sounds we can't even hear—what does that prove? It doesn't mean anything!"

After dinner they walked slowly up and down Deya's main street. Santi was very quiet.

"You just don't understand, Santi." Mark pulled at his arm to swing him around, facing him. "I love her so much that this is killing me! I'm starting to hate her because of that dumb look on her face. It's not how I want to remember my mother!"

"You think I want to remember her like this?" Santi asked urgently. "But I will continue to take care of her. It will be a privilege for me. She was the most wonderful person I ever met. Because of her I found out so much about . . . oh, life and love, many things . . ."

Mark sat down on a little stone bench, his chin in his hands. "I need a break from shouting, 'What am I?' a thousand times a day, Santi," he groaned. "I promise I'll come back. I'm not abandoning her."

"When will you go, Mark?" he asked.

"In a few days, I guess. I promise I'll be back."

Santi shook his head slowly, smiling. "You don't need to keep promising me, Mark," he said. "I cannot bear to admit defeat, so I shall stay. I have a little land near my house I can sell. Maybe I can begin work with a friend of mine who has a gallery in Palma. That way I shall be close to your mother and see her every day, or almost every day. Keep my eye on her."

Mark nodded. "Maybe we'll just have to accept it," he suggested. "Be happy that she isn't in pain, that she isn't conscious of what's happening."

They said good-night warily, as if unconvinced by their own arguments.

Mark made his travel arrangements the next day, trying not to feel excited about getting back to the streets of Manhattan again—good old dirty Manhattan with its screaming sirens, panhandlers, and crazies—*life!*

For a day or two they discussed moving Marcella to an apartment with a private nurse, but they decided it was better for her to be among other people, less isolated.

On his last day, Mark sat holding her hand, meeting her strange stare.

"I'm leaving you tomorrow, Mom," he told her. "I'm going away. Maybe I'll never come back. Because I can't take *seeing* you this way! I thought I could help you, but this is destroying me. Please try to understand. If I thought it was doing me any good I'd play the piano for you until doomsday!"

He sat down at the keyboard and played Gershwin for the first time. He turned around to her after he finished and saw her eyes suddenly moving, darting about, her lips mumbling wordlessly, as if annoyed at the change from Chopin.

Deliberately he played the worst kind of honky-tonk jazz he could dredge up. She turned her head from side to side.

"What am I, Mother?" he shouted at her. "What am I?"

He broke for lunch with Santi at a nearby bistro, then returned to her room at three.

"I'm leaving tomorrow," he told her again as her blank face regarded his. "I'm never coming back here again unless you tell me what I am. What am I?"

She stared at him. Was it his imagination or did she seem to be struggling with a thought? Was he so used to her condition that the tiniest flicker in her eyes registered such an impact on him? He sat at her feet, taking her hands in his. "Tomorrow I'm leaving you and I'm never coming back." He played only Gershwin and honky-tonk all afternoon for her, twisting to see her expression after each piece, wondering if there truly was a new reaction.

Santi came to collect him at seven as dusk was descending over the island. Mark was sitting with Marcella's hand in his, wishing that there was some comforting pressure coming back from her.

"So you are really saying good-bye?" Santi asked.

Mark nodded, looking up at him. "For my own sanity now," he said. "Maybe when I'm back in New York I'll find the energy to come back here and work more with her. I don't know. . . ." He stood up.

"Try once more," Santi whispered urgently, touching him. "For the last time, try with all your might. I have not lost faith."

Mark bent to take Marcella's hands. "I'm leaving you now," he shouted at her. "I'm not coming back, not ever! I'm going to New York tomorrow unless you tell me what I am. What am I?"

Santi looked away from the expression on Marcella's

face. Her eyes darted around the room. Her mouth was half open as if searching for a word. She seemed to be trying to understand.

Mark dropped her hands and went to the piano. "Help me wheel this out!" he suggested. "Maybe if she sees me taking it away it will upset her. I'm sure she loved the music." He opened the door and the two men began to guide the upright piano out of the room, pushing and panting with its weight.

Marcella suddenly got to her feet, watching them, frowning as if in protest.

Santi's eyes widened. "She wants to keep the piano!" he cried. "Oh Mark, she understands!"

"Keep *moving*!" Mark shouted. "Don't stop. We're leaving you, Mom! We're never coming back! There'll be no more music. I'm going forever unless you tell me what I am! What *am* I? What *am* I?"

Slowly, she felt herself becoming aware that she was standing. Then it felt as if she were waking on her feet from an intense nightmare. A nightmare so long it had plunged months of her life into blackness. She stared at the two men heaving a large black object out of her sight through a gap in the wall. She had been asleep with her eyes open for many days. She had been asleep during the last hours, too, yet something within her was sorry at their action. The sounds from this black box had been soothing. She seemed now to hear, as if hours after the words had been spoken, the threats that one of the men had been making all afternoon. Going. Never coming back. Why should that matter to her? She would miss the sounds that came from this black box when the man placed his hand on the black and white slats. The sounds like . . . she frowned . . . *music*! From a . . . *piano*! It had a name. Everything had a name, a *word*! She had forgotten how to speak! How to use her voice. The younger man bore a startling resemblance to someone she loved—her son! The other man was also someone she could not look at without feeling an echo, a memory, as if he had been someone very important in her life.

They were leaving her now, depriving her of the presence she had become used to. She felt a kind of anger, a confused excitement, mount in her until her voice, an attribute she had completely forgotten she had, gurgled up in her throat and made her want to scream aloud so they would hear her and stop what they were doing. He was her son and she suddenly understood what he had been shouting. He was leaving her forever if she did not answer his question. His question had been, "What am I?"

She panicked for a moment, shaking her befuddled head. What was the answer? And where was she? She stared helplessly around the bare room, which she did not recognize at all. Perhaps if she simply stood still and did not move, those swirling thoughts in her head would clear and the words would push themselves into her brain. She waited. Of course! He often used to ask her that question, and she must somehow answer, "The light of my life!" If she could form the words, if she could remember how to say them, she could stop him from leaving.

Mark and Santi were in the corridor leaning against the piano when they heard the sounds Marcella managed to utter. Standing in the doorway looking after them, she sounded the five syllables that only her son and her lover could have known to be communication and that only Mark knew meant "The light of my life." They ran back to her room. She was suddenly in a state of extreme agitation as all the blocked channels started to function again. She was wringing her hands, pacing restlessly to and fro. As she looked from Mark to Santi and back again to Mark, they saw her expression had changed. However fearful, however hidden beneath layers of confusion, she was finally human again, finally Marcella! She closed her eyes tightly, shaking her head, swallowing hard, her hands clenched into fists at her sides. When she opened her eyes she was looking straight at them, raising her arms. With a sob and a shout, both men ran to her, holding her tightly. She was moaning, trying to talk. They heard her choking breath as she began to sob a mixture of grief and relief.

This was the moment, Mark thought, wriggling out of his mother's embrace. He ran to the door of the room and they did not notice him leave. Glancing back he saw Santi embracing his mother tightly, tears streaming through his closed eyes. He closed the door quietly on them and took a few steps down the corridor. Opening the door to the patio, he stumbled out, making for the well. He held on to the cool stone edge looking down into the water far below, biting his knuckles to keep himself from sobbing, his body wracked with emotion. The bright leafy green ferns growing so deep in the darkness of the well had often given him a kind of comfort, as if demonstrating that there was always hope, that even in a dark, dank place something beautiful could always grow.

He looked ahead to all the months of hard work, the willpower they would all need to bring back the Marcella they loved. This time he would not interfere with the love she deserved and that he now understood better. He suddenly saw his own life stretching limitlessly ahead of him as an adventure in which he played the central role. A late developer, but he *would* develop. The choices were wide and he would have to choose a way, he knew, but now it did not seem quite so terrifying. He had become, painfully, finally, a man, an adult.

Mark took a deep breath and wiped his eyes. The sky darkened and he glanced up at it. An enormous flock of starlings swooped and circled high in the purple Majorcan sky, their thousands of dots forming into ever-changing shapes, split-second silhouettes that quickly became a glove, a profile, a bottle. The precision was astounding, as if they had rehearsed their patterns in a disciplined drill. It was one of the many everyday miracles to be witnessed if you only looked around, testifying to there being *someone, something* responsible, surely, for the destiny of every creature on this earth. Including his mother. Including himself. He was not yet able to believe in just one God, but he whispered "Thank you" to the starlings, to the ghosts of Chopin or Gershwin, to whomever was listening.

Marcella clung fast to Santi. Both for her balance and her sanity. It was the strangest, dizziest sensation to feel senses stirring, awakening, to feel her personality, herself, slowly begin to inhabit her body again.

She could smell Santi's familiar scent, feel the strength

of him as he held her so tightly, as if assuring her with his grip that the love flowing through him was all for her.

"Forever," he promised in her ear, and she smiled at the beautiful word and tried to repeat it. She broke away to look into his glowing eyes that stared deep into her soul, showing her that their love was as strong as it had been since that first night, that first look.

"Forever," he said again as they embraced. She knew exactly what the word meant but she could not quite pronounce it. Words were her tools, and now she would have to learn to use them again. To say them. To write them. To make them express all she wanted to tell. Words were frightening and wonderful and, out of them all, the best was *their* word: forever!

ABOUT THE AUTHOR

After attending London's Saint Martin's School of Art, Harold Carlton worked as an illustrator for *Elle* magazine in Paris, and for *The New York Times* and *Mademoiselle* in New York. In the late 1960s, he criss-crossed America twice on a Greyhound bus, writing of his experiences for the *London Sunday Times*. He published four novels under the pen name of Simon Cooper. *Labels* (Bantam, 1988) and *Sacrifice* are the first novels to appear under his own name.

When not writing, Mr. Carlton travels and has explored Morocco, Bali, India, New Zealand, and Australia, as well as much of Europe. Pastimes include talking, reading, and seeing films. Harold Carlton was born in London, has lived in New York and California, and now lives in Majorca.